A MOST EXCELLENT ADVENTURE • SERIES
REMEMBRANCES OF TIMES GONE BY

Book One
Tales From the Village
When We Were Kids and the World Was New.

Book Two
Gone fer a Sojer
We Were Soldiers Then, and Young!

Written and Edited by
Richard L. Salmon
Kansas City, Missouri
Leathers Publishing Company
Leawood, KS
1998

ISBN 1-890622-50-8

DEDICATION

To the sons, daughters, grandkids and other descendants of my era—all the girls and boys—I dedicate this collection of remembrances of a long gone and different world. That world we lived in was, in many ways, not nearly so pleasant as our world today. But in other ways it was so much better, but better or worse—it was one that we will not know again.

I particularly dedicate these remembrances—with all my love and devotion to my — mother whose good humor got us through many dark days, to my beloved and patient wife Daisy, dear son Rick, cherished son Jeff, adored daughter Karen, favorite Granddaughter Chantelle, esteemed Grandson Keith, treasured Grandson Brian, precious Grandson Alex and—hopefully—generations yet to come. Thanks to you and to all my old friends, not least, the good people of Pilot Grove for helping to make my life "A Most Excellent Adventure"!

KIDHOOD

We charged in like young barbarians, where angels feared to tread.
The forests were dark and frightening but before us the monsters fled.

Our dogs and cats were brothers, our bikes were rocket ships.
Buck Rogers to the stars, the moon but morning trips.

We swung on our Tarzan swing and slashed with Zorro's blade.
We were Roy Rogers on Trigger, we were the evil Slade.

We looked upon the future and saw a distant land.
Our folks would live forever and time was shifting sand.

We filled life with living, grins, scabbed knees, and noise.
Now my mirror sees an old man, but this book's for girls and boys.

—Sonny Salmon

Dick Salmon at Citibank Conference Las Palmas, Mallorca 1985.

ABOUT THE AUTHOR

I was born in Pilot Grove—in the same house on Fourth Street where my mother, my sister and brother were born. I lived there until I "Went fer a Sojer" in 1945. But, I haven't lived there since and quite a number of people would be justified in asking—"Sonny who...?" So here is a brief bio-sketch.

I worked the telegrapher job ('swing shift' 4PM to midnight) in Pilot Grove during my senior year in High School. I graduated in May 1945 and worked as the 'graveyard shift' (midnight to 8AM) Katy telegrapher-clerk at St. Charles, Missouri.

In June 1945 I volunteered for the Army and served in the Pacific including the first post-war atom bomb tests in the Marshall Islands. When, years later, some of the army participants in those nuclear tests claimed the tests were the cause of all their medical problems, I thought the radiation exposure fifty years ago was what caused my flat feet, nearsightedness, hearing loss, fat middle and forgetfulness, that is, if not for the Bikini atom bomb tests, I would still be a lad of 18*.

In 1947, returning to the US for discharge, but not being very happy with the civilian jobs on offer, I re-enlisted intending to be a 'lifer', a career soldier. I had—as an ancient song proclaims—'gone fer a sojer'.

Thus began the life of a gypsy: When I returned from the Korea War in December 1951, Daisy and I were married at *Colorado Springs, Colorado* in May 1952. I was a First Sergeant at *Fort Carson* and we were settling in nicely in Colorado Springs, but soon were transferred to *Fort Bliss* near *El Paso, Texas* where our first child—Conrad Richard "Rick"—was born. After air defense artillery missile training (Nike) we moved to the *Chicago* Air Defense Region and lived in *North Chicago.*

We found that family life doesn't play well in the Army, so I got out to use my GI Bill in 1954-1957. We lived in *Boonville, Missouri* and welcomed a second son, Jeffrey, while collecting a BSEE at the University of Missouri-Columbia. We went to *Winston-Salem, North Carolina* in 1957 to work for Western Electric's Defense Division. In North Carolina we learned to speak a foreign language— 'southron'—and completed our family with a daughter—Karen Denise—in 1958.

In 1963 we moved to *Princeton, New Jersey* to work at Western Electric's Princeton Research Lab concurrent with a Master's Degree program at Lehigh University.

During this two year period, Rick collected a bum knee from football, Jeff collected a scar on his face from a rock fight and kids at Ben Franklin Elementary School gathered around kindergartener Karen to listen to her Carolina ('Southron') accent.

"Hey Karen, say hot dog."

Karen: "Hot dawwwg."

After graduation in 1965 I was assigned to Western Electric's Lee's Summit Plant and lived in *Kansas City.* In 1969, after eleven years with Ma Bell, I took a job with Midwest Research Institute.

After leaving active Army duty in 1954, I had remained in the US Army Reserve and my vacations for the next 16 years were spent at Army Reserve summer camps in Wisconsin, New Jersey, Mississippi and Illinois. In 1970 I graduated from the U.S. Army's Command and

---

* *I am being facetious here—truth is, if not for the atomic bomb, I'd probably have been a participant in the planned 1946 invasion of Japan and might not have been here today! Hooray for Harry Truman!*

General Staff College at Fort Leavenworth, Kansas. My military career had come full circle—my active Reserve career ended where my Regular Army career began in 1945.

In 1976 I took a job with Citicorp in *New York City* and we moved to *Hartsdale, NY.* Hartsdale is one of the bedroom communities for New York City commuters. The next year we moved to *Antwerp, Belgium* where I managed Citicorp's European Planning Research Office. We transferred to *London, England* in 1979 and lived there for eight years. The picture on page iii was taken during this period. We returned to *New York* in 1987.

We retired in 1988 and moved to *Laguna Niguel, California* near our daughter Karen and her family, but Daisy got homesick for Missouri and we returned to *Kansas City* in 1991.

In 46 years of marriage, we've moved 37 times. For Daisy, all the romance and adventure seems to have gone out of it and our 1991 move may have been our last. At any rate, you can see why I failed to keep in touch with all the folks of Pilot Grove.

ACKNOWLEDGMENTS

As you might imagine, I have many folks to thank for the loan of photos and memorabilia as well as the sharing of stories of the "olden days". I had discussed my thoughts with **A.J. Wolfe** as he was planning the very successful 1997 PGHS Reunion and he loaned me some valuable material including his own bio-sketch (which I found good but excessively modest). He also gave me the run of the old "Calaboose Museum." **Les Chamberlin** let me rummage through his souvenirs. The very first to respond to my request for input following the June 1997 PGHS 75th Anniversary Reunion was **Irene Felten**. Irene (Gerke) Felten was PGHS Class of 1943. She loaned me the contents of several scrapbooks. **Ralph Esser,** Mom's Fourth Street neighbor of many years, surprised me with an extremely well kept and well preserved scrapbook. He was the source of the Pilot Grove High School Starette excerpts in the "Merchant Princes" chapter. **"Winky" Friedrich** of Pleasant Green House let me copy a Mexican War era letter written by her Great-great Uncle Conkright. Also, I should recognize the work, long ago, of Mrs. Mitzel and her crew who did a county cemetery census. Her work provided some of the vital statistics in this book.

I particularly appreciate the little tales that **Wally Burger, his sister Marjorie (Burger) Schmidt and Janie (Brownfield) Goehner** gave me—some good stories along with the loan of piles of photos. **Jack Schmidt (Marjorie's beloved) found Goethe's "Der Erlen König" in English for me. See page 162. Doris (Quinlan) Koonse** let me look through her scrapbook and copy much of it. She was the source of the 1937 "Letters to Santa." **Charlotte (Heinrich) Savee** helped tremendously with material on the Heinrich's store of old. **Martha Sandy**, younger daughter of Dr. Charles Sandy, let me copy her scrapbook material. **Mrs. Pauline McCreery** sent me photos of her family and reminded me of some of the village tales**. Norbert Zeller** let me use a treasure trove of photos he had taken while while attending PGHS. **George "Babe" Heim** not only helped me remember details of old events, he contributed a few stories which I had forgotten. A lots of thanks to **Emil Bock** for identifying folks on old photos. Emil's memory is quite amazing.

Photo credits: Generally I have credited each photo in the caption. In some cases you may see "your" photo credited to someone else. This may not be an error. I received some duplicate material. I credited an item to the first one to send it.

I also received photos from **Ruth (Hays) Wood, LaVahn (Klenklen) Brown, LeVern Klenklen, Charley Brownfield, Marie Jeffress** (Homer's widow), and many others. All these folks cited herein helped immensely, but if there are any errors, misstatements or misunderstandings of fact—those errors are mine alone.

Contents

Contents (cont'd)

Contents (cont'd)

Contents (cont'd)

Contents (cont'd)

Contents (cont'd)

Contents (cont'd)

Contents (cont'd)

Contents (cont'd)

Contents (cont'd)

Contents (cont'd)

FOREWORD

The majority of the tales in this book are set in the 1930s and 1940s—two of the most stressful and turbulent decades in the history of this country. Those folks who lived through these anxious times—the eyewitnesses to history—never thought of themselves as a part of history happening. Their thoughts were of—the corn crop, the family Sunday dinner, the St. Louis Cardinals or Pilot Grove's chance against those ace hoopsters from Prairie Home. It has only been in light of hindsight that we realize those were very different times and worth remembering—a time of bad news and good music. I hope I have captured some of the essence and personal histories of those days long gone by.

This book is not a history of Pilot Grove. Nor is it "all about Pilot Grove". I reckon for every tale set out here, a dozen more have gone untold, but those that are told—though blurred by time—are focussed by the heart. The head forgets but the heart remembers—the sounds, the sights, the feelings even the aromas.

It is also not a novel. There is no development of characters, there is very little plot and most of the little tales are self-contained. You can start reading anywhere and skip around. An extensive Table of Contents and a Names Index will help you browse.

For a more formal history of the region, I recommend the 1973 Pilot Grove Centennial Book (Les Chamberlin may still have a few copies) and/or Ann Betteridge's excellent "Discover Cooper County". In one of two departures from the 1930s and 1940s time frame (Appendix A, "The Burnhams"), I used material from the Centennial book as an aid to showing Pilot Grove life and times at the outset of the Civil War as seen through the eyes of some of my ancestors. Appendix B, "Cpl. Henry Kendrick" (the other departure from the 30s and 40s) is based on the official account (Illinois State Archives) of my Grandfather's four years of Civil War. Grandpa Kendrick was the Pilot Grove town marshal, drayman, lamplighter, etc. for several decades of the late 1800s.

I debated, then included Book Two "Gone fer a Sojer." This will be a bonus for you—"buy one, get one free." It's a bonus for you but it was my life for nine years! You may find it interesting.

In Memory of our Schoolmate

Norbert G. Zeller - Pilot Grove High School, Class of 1941.

NORBERT G. ZELLER

Norbert G. Zeller, 75, Kansas City, MO, passed away May 28, 1998, at St. Joseph Health Center. Mass of Christian Burial will be 9 a.m. Saturday, May 30, at St. Matthews Apostle Church; interment at Mount Olivet Cemetery. Friends may call 6-8 p.m. Friday at Muehlebach Funeral Home, with a prayer service at 7 p.m. Memorial contributions may be made to Little Sisters of the Poor Nursing Home.

Mr. Zeller was born in Pilot Grove, MO. He was an engineer coordinator for Wilcox Electric Company, retiring in 1975 after 31 years. He was a Navy veteran and a member of St. Matthews Apostle Church. He was a volunteer for Little Sisters of the Poor. Survivors include his wife, Geneva L. Zeller, of the home; sons, Bruce A. Zeller, Lee's Summitt, MO and Edward M. Zeller, Blackwater, MO; daughters, Miss Georgia A. Zeller and Mrs. Donna M. Brown, both of Kansas City, MO; brothers, Kenneth Zeller, North Kansas City, MO, and Charles Zeller, Independence, MO; and six grandchildren. (Arrangements: Muehlebach Funeral Home)

It was with deep sorrow and regret that we learned of the passing of our old friend and schoolmate, Norbert George Zeller. Schoolmates knew him as Norb. Later, he used George. He was very enthusiastic about this book and its attempt to capture the spirit, the joys and the sorrows of our years growing up in Pilot Grove. He contributed a number of photos and memories which we will always cherish. Vaya con Dios, Norb.

BOOK ONE

Tales from the Village

When we were kids and the world was new.*

*Like you, I have always tacitly assumed the history of the world and all mankind started when I was born and will end when I shuffle off the stage.

HIZZONER...

Mayor A.J. Wolfe as a 19 year old Corporal, 22 Amphibian Truck Battalion, USMC. See p. 5. In the summer of 1941, hard-won PGHS diploma in hand, he joined the USMC to see the world and cruise exotic south Pacific islands.

The islands he cruised were Guadalcanal, Tarawa and Eniwetok where he collected souvenir scrap metal from the 4th Imperial Japanese Marines. A.J. and his lovely and gracious wife, the former Betty Schlotzhauer, are semi-retired after a long career in the restaurant and food service business.

A.J. poses below at the 1991, 50th reunion of his class. Classmates are identified on p. 143.

Emil Bock and wife Catherine. Emil, cited on p.24, was the longest serving Postmaster in the history of Pilot Grove. Emil's bright mind and memory was key in identifying folks in old photos.

Ex-mayor Leslie Chamberlin near the end of his 1969-1975 term. Leslie is most proud of the 1973 Pilot Grove Centennial and the souvenir book produced during his tenure.

Les graduated PGHS in 1940 and started to college in Kansas City but "my friends and neighbors extended me an invitation I couldn't refuse and I spend several years as ground crew in the 8th Air Force in England and Europe." See p.8.

Les tells a tale (p. 10) of a terrifying incident in a British Lancaster bomber when he hitched a ride from France to England for R&R—after the war had ended.

VILLAGE FOLKS

I acknowledge all who helped with this book but I only have pictures of these 'Associate Editors'.

Ralph and Mildred Esser. Ralph kept a beautifully preserved scrapbook of his high school days much of it appears in Ch. 7, beginning on p. 48.

Clemus and Irene (Gerke) Felten. Irene was first to respond with her 50 year old scrapbooks. I see why she excels in all she does. More on her on p. 136 and elsewhere.

Kenny and Doris (Quinlan) Koonse. Doris was the source of the Letters to Santa Claus (p. 51)—plus much more.

Wilbur and Alice Quinlan. Wilbur is full of good stories (for example, "Pilot Grove Vice" p. 19). I used some but had to leave it to him to write his own book someday.

VILLAGE LIFE

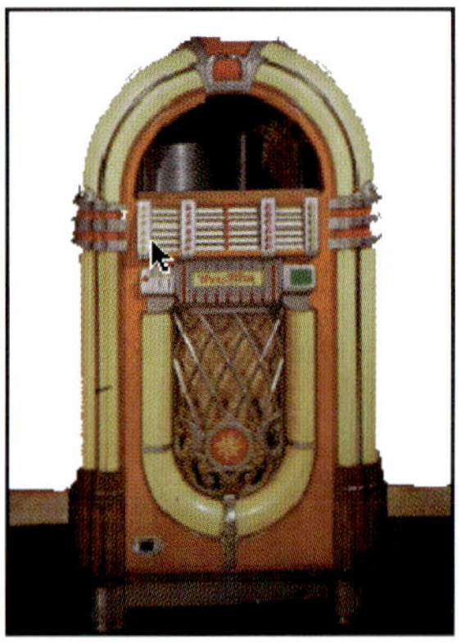

The jukebox at Chouteau was a nickel a play—6 for a quarter. Bring your own Griesedieck! See p. 82.

On Saturday nights Bob and Bill Egender set up an outdoor movie and we were treated to 'shoot 'em ups' for a dime. Popcorn by Raymond Bader. See p. 100.

Jim Sousley only knew 2-3 guitar chords, but he was very good—and free. See p. 34.

In 1936, Dad bought one of these new-fangled contraptions for $5. See p. 68.

After Dad's death in 1940, 'Widder Salmon' tried various ruses to keep the wolf from the door. One was selling cosmetics. See p. 65.

VILLAGE PLACES

St. Joseph Parochial School—Pilot Grove. In the 1930s and 40s, Benedictine nuns from the Ft. Smith, Arkansas Convent taught here.

Sadly, most small midwest towns lack enduring landmarks—buildings that become places in the heart.

Of the five shown here, only three remain standing and only one of them survives from my era.

Comedy and Tragedy.

Pilot Grove Public School. The history of the world and mankind began when I started to school here in September 1933. I'm kidding! This building was built in 1922 and razed years ago.

The old **Pilot Grove High School** was the scene of many a comedy and tragedy—not all of them on the stage.

George "Babe" Heim, shown here (summer of 1947) testing the front door was one of the "Personnae Dramatis" in many of these—"Charley's Aunt", "Antics of Andrew", "For Pete's Sake" and others. I also have it on good authority that Babe was a star in other dramas—off the stage.

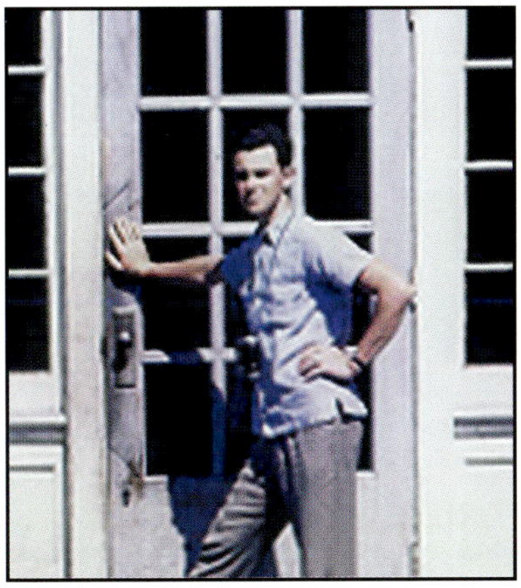

St. John Parish Church, a beautiful landmark in Clear Creek—has a place in many hearts.

The Methodist Episcopal Church (South) stood at the corner of Third and Roe. Most of my ancestors celebrated their rites of passage here—my father and mother were married here, my grandmother, my grandfather, two aunts and my father were buried from here. I was duly christened and baptized here.

When I was six, Frances Brownfield (later Rybak) was my Sunday School teacher and it was here I learned a lesson out of Matthew XXII, 21. See p. 46.

In the 1940s, the Methodists finally got over their Civil War snit with the Yankees and dropped "(South)" from the name.

St. Joseph Parish Church Pilot Grove. For decades parishioners had to make do in the basement. The grinding economics of the depression era delayed completion of this elegant, mission-style church. .

This 1988 photo shows a beautiful building well worth waiting for.

WORKIN' ON THE RAILROAD

The Katy's John Scullin and his Irish track laying crew advanced the railhead to Pilot Grove in 1873 (from Parsons via Sedalia). Sam Roe laid out lots in his cornfields and incorporated the town. Great Grandfather Burnham built the house at 110 E. Fourth St where I was born.

For 70 years the Katy was Pilot Grove's link to the world. The railroad also provided jobs—my father and uncle worked for the Katy all their lives and, but for World War II, I might have also. Technology laid the Katy low. The mighty Mikado 2-8-2 locomotives were beautiful, monstrous beasts but inefficient. While I worked for the Katy 1943-1945, the coal burners gave way to oil and finally—the end of steam came in about 1948-49. The romantic old steam engines with their lonesome whistles were replaced by diesel as shown below left. See Ch. 8—"The Katy Years" p. 161.

Katy depot Pilot Grove about 1949.

Mrs. Pauline McCreery (Right) with daughter Merline Sharp and son Beuford. Pauline was my 1944 Katy Telegrapher-Clerk mentor. See p. 169.

Telegraph key

In 1939, C.A. Coley, Scoutmaster of Wolf Patrol, Boy Scout Troop 76 taught me, among other things, Morse Code. This got me the Katy job in 1944 and then into the Signal Corp when the Army was begging for Infantry.

A section of the beautiful Katy Trail along the Missouri River beneath the Rocheport bluffs. In the summer of 1943, I worked on the Katy roadbed applying fine Missouri chatts which compact as hard as clay pan. It also wears well as a trail bed and when you bike the Katy trail Boonville to Sedalia, enjoy the roadbed I helped lay down over 50 years ago. See p. 169.

FIGHTER PILOT

Sopwith Camel. This British WWI fighter was used by some Yanks. The Lafayette Escadrille flew the SPAD.

The Red Baron's Fokker Tr.1 triplane is decorated for Jagdstaffel 1—Richthofen's "Flying Circus".

After being enchanted by the model airplanes flown by Ridge and Lane Harlan at the school grounds, I called on my boyhood mentor, neighbor Wallace "Chappie" Chapman, to teach me to build such airplanes. One was the Sopwith Camel (above left), but my first was the Red Baron's Fokker triplane (above right). The Red Baron was German Ace Baron Manfred von Richthofen who is now mostly honored on frozen pizzas but enjoys an occasional scrap with Snoopy, see below.

In 1949, I debarked from the Katy Flyer at the San Antonio station (below left) and began my Aviation Cadet training at Randolph Field. I hoped to update my aircraft from the old Spads and Nieuports to something like the F-15 Strike Eagle (below center). Sadly—like Snoopy—I was shot down. See Ch. 14 "Cadets" p. 231.

Katy Station, San Antonio, Texas—summer 1949. It was somewhat busier when I arrived here for Aviation Cadet training.

F-15 "Strike Eagle"—my ultimate objective.

I wonder if **Freiherr (Baron) Manfred von Richthofen** would enjoy the delicious Pizza that is marketed in his name.

Snoopy, flying a Sopwith Camel which looks a lot like a dog house, has another losing dogfight with the Red Baron.

GONE FER A SOJER

Military Regalia Collection

Left—I began collecting the "bright and colorful bits of metal and cloth" that now evoke nostalgic memories. The first were this Army Service Forces patch, Signal Corps collar device and WWII Victory Medal. I was awarded the exclusive Victory Medal in September 1945. Only 12 million others got this award. I wore many of these insignia. Most of the rest were worn by folks from Pilot Grove.

1st Marine Parachute Regiment. Kenny Koonse and Jack Heim.

First Marine Division — A.J. Wolfe

First Marine Fighter Wing. My unit (Avn Engrs) supported this Wing in North Korea—1950.

13th Armored Division. smashed Hitler in Europe. Henry Twenter

Second Infantry Division. My pal and mentor, Wally Chapman, wore this when he died in the France's Bocage country.

Right—Bronze Star for Valor. Awarded posthumously to PGHS teammate Pfc. David Brunjes—Saipan, 1944.

Left—Purple Heart. Kenny Koonse, A.J. Wolfe, Wilbur Twenter, et al.

Fifth Air Force. My brother and I wore this patch in Korea 1950-1951.

34th Inf 'Red Bull' Division. Ivan Ninemire got dysentery. Carl Waller got captured—at Kasserine pass.

Eighth Air Force. Heavy bombers and support units in Europe. Leslie Chamberlin.

Twentieth Air Force. B-29s on Okinawa supported Korea operations. I wore this patch in 1949-1950.

Below—Korea Campaign Medal w/5 battle stars, National Defense Medal and UN Korea Medal for my service Sep 1950 to Nov 1951.

Above—V Corps, Ft. Bragg, NC.

Right—82d Airborne Div also Ft. Bragg.

Below—Air Defense Artillery School, Ft. Bliss, TX 1953.

Above—Parachutists Wings—82d Sig Co, 82 A/B Div. Other alumni—Art Schuster Jr., Earl "Cooter" Davis Jr.

Above—5th Army Ft. Carson, CO.

Left—US Army-Pacific Ft. Shafter, HI.

Below—Ryukyus Cmd (Okinawa)

4th Signal Bn—epaulet device.

Air Defense Artillery collar device.

86th AD Arty Bn—epaulet device.

ANCESTORS

I have included two Appendices on some of my maternal ancestors—the Burnhams and the Kendricks. They were residents of the village many years ago—Great Grandpa Burnham was an area farmer. Grandpa Kendrick was Town Marshal, Lamplighter, Drayman, Dogcatcher and—what do you need done? More importantly…they have some interesting stories to tell. See Appendices A and B beginning p. 315.

Hiram Matthew Burnham 1822-1895, and his wife Madama Lafayette (Beatty) Burnham 1834-1882. (1870s photo) Married in 1851, Hiram was born in Warwickshire, England and immigrated to New York with his family in 1826. Madama was born and grew up in Saline County, Missouri. The Burnham farm was just off the Santa Fe trail 4-5 miles southwest of Boonville and a mile north of the 135 I-70 exit (Kuecklehan's station). The Jones Chapel cemetery was deeded by Hiram and lies at the southeast corner of the old farm. A poignant and tragic story of Hiram's younger sister Mary Morgan is told in letters beginning on p. 323.

Cape Ann, Massachusetts. The first of the Burnhams to come to the new world were cast ashore here—shipwecked—in 1635. Three brothers, John, Thomas, and Robert, sons of Robert and his wife Mary (Andrews) Burnham, of Norwich, Norfolk County, England, came to America early in 1635 in the ship Angel Gabriel, in charge of their maternal uncle, Capt. Andrews, master of the ship. They were wrecked on the coast of Massachusetts about 30 miles from Boston.

This picturesque Warwickshire village would have been similar to Hiram Burnham's English birthplace.

Hiram volunteered (5th Missouri Infantry) to go fight the Mexicans in 1846, but Taylor's victory at Buena Vista(above) cancelled need for the Missourians. See letter, p. 321 from a soldier not so fortunate.

Left—This tintype of my maternal Grandfather, **John Henry Kendrick**, was taken in Sep 1861. He was 16 when he volunteered for the 50th Illinois Infantry Regiment at Alton, Illinois. He was severely wounded in Georgia Oct 1864. His story is told in a letter from a Chattanooga hospital, p. 337.

Right—John Henry was too young for a musket. He became a musician—a drummer—he couldn't play the fife. After Shiloh, he elected to take the Sharps musket and bayonet because he couldn't bear the musicians' duties with the dead and wounded.

Backward, Turn Backward O Time in Thy Flight,
Make Me a Child Again, Just for this Night!
—Elizabeth Akers Allen

"Don't be a-lookin' back, somepin' might be a-gainin' on ya!" —*Satchel Paige.*

LOOKING BACK

THE WORLD HAS TURNED OVER MANY TIMES since I took leave of Pilot Grove, and my hopes and dreams have long since vanished, but I still remember the schoolmates, the friends, the folks and the times of my old hometown. More than 50 years of hindsight contribute much to the nostalgia, happiness, sadness, triumph and tragedy that I feel as I assemble those remembrances.

Often, as I labored over old photos trying to coax out a bit more of the story they have to tell, a magical moment occurs and those faces suddenly come alive. Their eyes sparkle as they smile from across the span of a half century. I catch a glint of the eyes as they look bravely into the future. Occasionally a cold hand touches my heart for I have an awesome advantage over these forever-seventeen young folk—I know things they do not know. They are looking forward—I am looking back. The cold hand reminds me that fate will not treat all of them kindly.

> Bright eyes burning like fire.
> Bright eyes how could you close and fail?
> How could the light that burned so brightly
> suddenly turn so pale?
> 'Bright Eyes' from Watership Down.

But, of course, the Good Lord compensates. I get a warm glow from the faces of those whom I know are to be treated to a happy fate. There are many such.

Thomas Mann said, "You can't go home again!" I understood what he meant when I left home a month after my 1945 graduation (See graduation picture, Fig. 1-1.) from Pilot Grove High School (See Fig. 1-2.) and 'looked back' only infrequently. Things were never the same. Some old friends were no longer around and most disturbingly; those that were had gotten older, accumulated wrinkles, wives, worries and wee ones. Also, most alarmingly, they were...well, *older.*

They got older but as for *me*, I've always seen myself as that 17 year old stripling lad—dressed out in the gold and black of the PGHS Tigers—old number 10—nimbly dribbling the basketball, penetrating defenses of the dreaded adversary as I race down the court. Within range and with 2 seconds to go—I launch the tournament winning shot (a high, arching ball, then—SWISH! No backboard, no rim, nothing but net). The crowd goes wild! YEEEE HAAA!

All this while keeping one eye on those gorgeous gals in the bleachers—Doris, Patty, Alice, Irene, Bonnie, Judy, Rebekah, Margie, Dorothy, Winnie and all the others.

Of course, this scene never occurred—but the vivid pictures of the fantasy live on in my mind.

Fig. 1-1. Richard L. "Sonny" Salmon graduated from PGHS on 18th May 1945 and went to the Army 3 weeks later.

Fig. 1-2. I took this photo of Pilot Grove High School upon my return from Hawaii in 1947. This 1922 vintage "Old Main" building was demolished in the 1980s.

VILLAGE LIFE

I know some people whose preferred view of Pilot Grove was in the rear view mirror...through a cloud of dust.

Do not count me among them. Despite the desolation of the Great Depression, the terrible droughts, the death of my father and later the wartime separations, losses and deprivations that we all suffered, my memories are of an idyllic boy's life. Some of this was due to my family (they mostly just left me alone), some to schoolmates, but some also must be credited to the village folk.

Many of these bit players in my life are gone now. The players change but the play goes on. I've seen very little change in the spirit of small town folk, their view of life and the common values they hold—friendship, integrity, helpfulness, openness, generosity and compassion for a neighbor who is going through a bad patch.

This book is *not* a history of Pilot Grove. It is *about* Pilot Grove, some of its people and events as seen through the eyes of a child, a boy, a youth and a young man who was born and grew up there, and called it home long, long ago.

WHY I WROTE THIS BOOK

Several reasons—

- **My warranty is running out**.

> *Threescore Years And Ten*
>
> The days of our [life] are
> threescore years and ten…
> so soon passeth it away,
> and we are gone.
> —*Psalms xc.9*

Psalm xc.9 sounds to me like my warranty has expired. I've long wanted to leave my kids and grandkids a remembrance of my life and times. Psalm xc.9 tells me I'd better do it now!

But, there were other motives:

- **Consideration for my Audience**. It is a rare individual indeed who will suffer the endlessly retelling of Grandpa's tiresome old "war stories". Committing them to paper spares those who've 'done heard it' while making them available to those who haven't.

- **Historical Record**. I would have loved to have had diaries, journals or old letters from, my Greatgrandpa Burnham who went off to fight the "Messicans" in 1846, or Grandpa Kendrick who was desperately wounded in the Civil War, or Grandpa Salmons who was a homesteading pioneer in Montana. I suspect 100 years from now some of my descendants may have similar wishes. Thus, by self-appointment, I became the family griot.[1]

- **Preservation**. In making a backup copy for my computer hard disk one day I had a whimsical thought: how do I backup my main memory—that one lodged between my ears. These stories are somewhat of a 'backup' memory of personal remembrances.

- **Mental Exercise**. Believe me, trying to recall minute details of events of half century ago challenges the old gray cells. It is good exercise for those faculties that we often neglect—our minds.

- **A Tribute**. To recognize those 'Heroines with Hearing Aids and Warriors with Walking Sticks'—those children of depression and war that share my era: the lean 30s and the mean 40s. Thousands of these folks who grew up in small towns could (and often, have) written such stories.

- **Remembrance**. Folks of this era of high-tech direct marketing, inhabit uncounted databases. We sometimes forget that those whose existence predated computers leave a much less exhaustive record of their lives. We owe them more than a gravestone epitaph.

PRESERVING MEMORIES

In July and August 1997, I requested photos and other Pilot Grove memorabilia and received enough to assemble a representative sample of village life and times—particularly of school life. There is probably a lot more out there, maybe some folk were reluctant to release it to me and the US Mail. I don't blame them, after all, looks are deceiving. What looks to the casual observer like a box of trash is actually a priceless collection—little pieces of someone's life. I respected that and treated all loaned material with great care.

I had similarly assembled photos, letters, stories, etc. in an earlier book about my paternal ancestors and relatives. Since my father was a 'stay behind' when his family moved to Montana early in the century, I had no source of information about the Montana branch of the family.

Unfortunately a precious hoard of such material was lost. My father's younger sister—Hulda Lee (Salmons) Weber—had followed a lifelong hobby of collecting family photos, letters, diaries, oral accounts, etc. When she died (in Columbus, MT in the 1980s), her grandson drove up from Idaho Falls to close out her estate and among other things, moved her collection of family memorabilia to the back garden where he struck a match to it.

So there are two lessons: even if you are not going to formally assemble your remembrances, at least mark up the photos with names, places and dates so someone else can do so later. (When Mom went into Katy Manor at age 95, she gave me a large box of old photos—not one had a name, date or place attached to it and for the most part I haven't the faintest clue as to who they are and they now escape her memory as well.)

Secondly, don't assume that that collection of old photos, souvenirs and other mementos is trash. Some day, someone will find them priceless.

[1] Griot - A human repository for the oral history of a people. See Alex Haley's "Roots". In "Roots" the griot was the reservoir for the history of the Mandinka tribe.

CRYPTOLOGY AND REMEMBRANCE

Two millennia before the birth of Christ—in Luxor and the Valley of the Kings along the narrow blue ribbon of the Nile, Egyptian High Priests began attempts at immortalizing the venerated dead entombed there. In prehistoric Egypt there was already a well developed culture of the afterlife complete with a complex mythology sanctified in stone carved hieroglyphics. Mausoleums and sarcophagi were hieroglyphically engraved to catalogue the honors, accomplishments and events accrued to the life of the eminence entombed therein.

Later generations of rulers, concerned that succeeding generations would weary of these boring recitations, began instructing tomb carvers to make puzzles out of the inscriptions. This was an attempt to intrigue the readers and pique their interest. They did this with secret writings and codes. They desperately wanted to be remembered!

The ploy failed. If the message is boring, how does it help to make it more difficult to read? But, in one of those "unintended consequences" of which life is filled—although the original objective of this secret writing was not achieved—the art and science of *cryptology* was born.

Now those of you who've spent sleepless nights, worrying why the study of secret codes is called "Cryptology" (literally, the study of secret writings on crypts) finally have your answer.

Although no one goes to such lengths as the ancient Egyptians, most of us would also like to be remembered. We know that a time will inevitably come when there will be no further *living* memories of our life. The funny stories, the accomplishments, the little tragedies and triumphs that make up a life story will fade. It is important to the continuity and integrity of a family line, to the generations to come, to a community to have some memory of people and deeds which went before. Most recognize this fact and it seems to have renewed an interest in family and community histories.

Since making puzzles out of a life story seems not to work, I have taken a different tack—don't make it puzzling, make it interesting! One of the techniques I have used is to interweave actual historical events as background for the details of life stories being documented. Thus, with the fixed points of well remembered contemporary happenings and specific personal events as anchor points, an exquisite life-story tapestry can be completed by the addition of meticulous details, which, while occasionally fictional in some trivial detail, nevertheless accurately portray the sense of the times and are totally in agreement with the anchor points of fact. I make extensive use of this technique with no apologies. As Robert Browning said:

"Art is the lie that helps us know the truth."

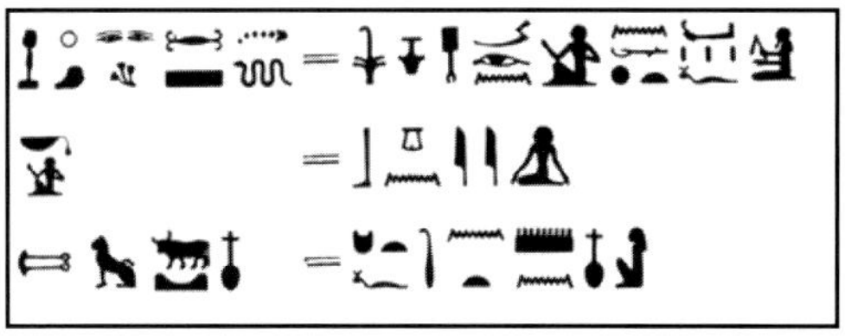

Fig. 1-3. Example of Egyptian secret writing. Hieroglyphic encipherments of proper names and titles at left, plain equivalents at right. From "The Codebreakers" by David Kahn.

FACTS, FACTOIDS, FICTION AND FACTION

Napoleon said, "History is a set of lies generally agreed to." But the essence of these *personal* stories is true. I freely admit that I have used some simple literary techniques to make the telling more interesting[2]. For example, some precise details: the phases of the moon, the hours of sunrise and sunset, etc. that I occasionally use to achieve that 'exquisite detail' that Tom Clancy does so well, are not from memory. They are true, correct and accurate but they result from use of an ephemeris[3] for the dates in question. My memory of those times is good, but not so good as to recall, for example, phases of the moon. Thus, these passages are certainly not fiction but may be termed "faction".

I also have had the advantage of the passage of time and numerous retelling of some of these stories. True life, even loudly exaggerated, has deficiencies in organization and plot line and a muddiness of symbolic content. It's hard to draw even the most common wisdom from the messy events of daily existence until they've been told over and over, polished and improved upon a few dozen times.

Some of the factoids, fiction and faction arises with the photos and drawings. Some of the originals were in frightful shape. I digitally enhanced some of them. My Scots ancestors had a saying—"*Ye cannae make a silk purse of a sow's ear.*" I tried anyway—with modest success.

For example, I rebuilt the old Pilot Grove Methodist Church (demolished long ago) from a photo on page 52 of the Pilot Grove Centennial Book plus my own memory.

Similarly, I reconstructed a tintype of my grandfather taken on the eve of his great adventure—the Civil War. A thumb print on the lower right quadrant of this tintype (over 135 years old) had, over the decades, badly eroded part of the photo.

I reconstituted the picture. The entire process caused him no pain whatsoever and he now has two arms as God intended. I know he would be pleased to have his left arm back! You can see the restored version in Appendix B.

[2] Shakespeare says, "An honest tale best speeds being plainly told." - Richard III

[3] Ephemeris - A reference book giving positions of celestial bodies for dates and hours of the day at various latitudes and longitudes.

Fig. 1-4. Logo of the Missouri-Kansas-Texas Railroad. Dad and Uncle Shelby worked for the 'Katy' all their lives. I started as a 15 year old 'Gandy Dancer' in 1943 while in High School. I was a full time Telegrapher my Senior year, but WWII saved me from the Katy!

Fig. 1-5. Katy Telegrapher 2d shift 1944-1945. Morse code was a Boy Scout craft.

Fig. 1-6. "Pop" Tracy's Cafe—Headquarters for the village teenage hangers-on in the 1940s, A.J. and Bettie Wolfe ran the Cafe 1952-1964. Photo - A.J. Wolfe.

SUMMARY

Chapter 2 is a salute to some of Pilot Grove's mayors and other town notables. Some of this is from E.J. Melton's 1937 "History of Cooper County", some is from my personal memories and the recall of friends.

Chapters 3 and 4 contain little vignettes, thumbnail bio-sketches of some village folk and what they got up to from time to time. A taste of village life in general including some memories of the war years 1941-1945.

Chapter 5 chronicles some of the village pastimes and entertainments—Toby Shows, the movin' 'pitchers', the town ball team, etc.

Chapters 6 is about school days, "School Chums", "Teachers" as well as the stuff that the students got up to in the 1930's and 40s—the class plays, the basketball tournaments, even some 'unsanctioned' activities.

Chapter 7 is a salute to and memories of some of the village merchants—Heinrich's, Warnhoffs, Mellor's.

Chapter 8 contains stories of the Katy railroad and my first "real" job.

Chapter 9 chronicles school and other memories of the Spring of 1945, graduation and my final good-bye to Pilot Grove. It completes Book One — Tales From the Village.

Book Two "Gone fer a Sojer", is a bonus. It chronicles my adventures in the US Army from 1945 to 1954—from a recruit in signal training at Camp Crowder, MO to the Pacific Islands, the wild Kansas Plains, to the "All American" Division at Ft. Bragg, NC, then to Okinawa, through the Korea War, to Camp Carson, CO for a wedding amidst a battalion of mule artillery, Ft. Bliss, Texas and the deserts of New Mexico. Final episode is played out at a Nike Air Defense installation in Chicago where I hung up my spurs and went for a "college boy" at Missouri University.

Two Appendices include a few stories and a little information on my (maternal) Burnham and Kendrick ancestors.

Fig. 1-7. Methodist Church at Third and Roe-razed in the 1970s Photo - Charlotte (Heinrich) Savee.

Fig. 2-1. Cpl. A.J. Wolfe 22d Amphibian Tractor Bn. 1942

"These then are your mayors. With the sword of justice they rule prudently. No petitioner who go to them in dignity and honor will be denied."

—William Dunbar

OVERVIEW

A PUZZLE I HAVE WRESTLED WITH HAS BEEN the attraction of the office of Mayor in Pilot Grove. I'm ready to be enlightened on this but it seems to me to be a lot of hard work, complex dealings with state and federal regulations and bureaucrats as well as mundane paperwork for very little reward and an occasional condemnation by a disgruntled citizen.

Pilot Grove has been served in this office by some very dedicated and public spirited men over the years. To me, this says more about these men than the office.

In recent years these included:

Dr. Charles Sandy 1931-1935
Charles T. Babbitt 1935-1943
Leslie Chamberlin 1969-1975
Barney Wessing 1975-1989
A.J. Wolfe 1989-present

In this chapter, I write about the four that I knew — A.J. Wolfe, Leslie Chamberlin, C.T. Babbitt and Dr. Charles Sandy.

A.J. WOLFE 1989 - PRESENT

A.J. Wolfe had a bit part in the story of Babe Heim's eating his pickup windshield one Four Roses befogged Saturday night in the fall of 1945. ("No Anesthesia Required" in Chapter 4).

But, A.J. is da Mayor and as such is deserving of more! In view of this and his service to the civic betterment of my old hometown, I asked him for a biographical sketch.

PROLOGUE

A.J. wrote, "I was born Oct. 17, 1923 in Pleasant Green, MO, the only son of Lee and Mary Eckerle Wolfe. In 1929 we moved to Blackwater for my first seven years of school. In 1936 we moved back to the Pilot Grove area. I graduated from the 8th grade at East Oakland — a one room school with one teacher and eight grades. This was the most fun I had at school.

"In the fall of 1937 I started to high school at Pilot Grove, MO, part of a class of 44 kids from the other County schools, St. Joseph and St. John's. I was very docile at that time, but life in the big city soon fixed that.

"After four years of uneventful school routine, I was able to graduate, with a lot of help from Dixie June Salmon and Deloris Zeller. I was not the Albert Einstein of the class.

"I then joined the US Marine Corps on June 6th, 1941 just 17 years old and out to see the world. If anybody knew about the Marine Corps back before Pearl Harbor they knew what a surprise this lad was in for.

"On December 7th 1941 the Japanese put the kibosh on my plans to see the world and have a good time. We began training seven days a week at least 18 hours a day. In April 1942 I was aboard ship heading for the South Pacific. We island hopped all the way to Guadalcanal where the first U.S. offensive land action of World War II took place on Aug. 7, 1942. What a shock! But we hung in there and headed back toward the Central Pacific by way of Tarawa, the Makin Island raid then on to the Marshall Islands.

"In February 1944 on Eniwetok Atoll [in the Marshall Islands] the war came to an abrupt end for me. I was hit by a mortar burst. After a stint aboard a hospital ship and then a base hospital in New Caledonia, I was evacuated to the States in June 1944. After some 26 months in the Pacific, then about ten months hospital stay in the Portsmouth, VA Naval Hospital — I was discharged July 13th 1945 with a medical discharge. Pilot Grove never looked so good.

MARINES BLOODED AT TARAWA

A.J. has glossed over his Marine Corps activities in the Pacific. Let me add some details plus a sketch of one such activity which many have forgotten, or in the case of younger folks, never known.

A.J. was assigned to the 22d Amphibious Tractor Battalion. Amphibious tractors (Amtracs) were very lightly ar-

Fig. 2-2. The 2d Marines paid a blood price for Tarawa. November 1943.

mored personnel carriers launched from troop transports and capable of 'swimming' through the surf to land a load of about 15 Marines onto a hostile beach.

To make such an operation understandable to the folks of the 1990s, think of a big fun park —Disney World, say. At this fun park the paddle boats are combined with the shooting gallery. As the paddle boaters paddle like mad for the shore, the gallery shooters shoot at them — with large caliber weapons!

MOTHER OF ALL STORM LANDINGS

The 22d participated in the landing at Guadalcanal, which A.J. mentioned above as the first U.S. offensive action of the war, but Tarawa Atoll was the 'mother of all Storm Landings'.

The term 'Storm Landing' comes from a 1943 communication of Col. Saburo Hayashi, Imperial Japanese Army — "The tactics of the Americans call for hurling enormous firepower at us and then making forced landings frontally. "Storm Landings" are common practice."

Col. Joseph Alexander who wrote the definitive book on WWII amphibious warfare ("Storm Landings", Naval Institute Press, 1997), defines 'Storm Landings' as — 'risky, long range, large-scale, self-sustaining assaults executed against strong opposition and within the protective umbrella of fast carrier task forces.'

At Tarawa major lessons were learned in this new game of storm landings. The way the game is *supposed* to be played is like this: the Naval Task Force cruises within range of the proposed landing site with 20-30 ships ranging from destroyers to battleships. The Fire Support element unloads 10,000 tons of high explosives on the island. Carrier aircraft join the fun with 500 lb bombs, napalm and strafing.

After 2-3 days of these preparatory bombardments, the Marine Amtracs go churning in. The marines land, mop up, have coffee and cigarettes and take a day off for beach volleyball and swimming — then on to the next assignment. The admiral commanding the fire support for the Tarawa operation bragged that he would "Obliterate the island!"

That's the way it was *supposed* to go!

THE WAY IT REALLY WENT

Col. Alexander described how it *really* went at Tarawa: "The Marines struggling to seize Betio Island [Betio Island is the main island of Tarawa Atoll] would need every possible advantage to gain the edge. The twin gambles of attacking through the lagoon and using jury rigged LVTs as assault craft had paid off — but then the wheels came off. The vaunted "obliteration of Betio" by preliminary bombardment had proven so ineffective that a battery of four Japanese dual purpose (antiaircraft, anti-boat) 75mm guns in open revetments along Red Beach remained untouched.

"These guns, firing horizontally and point-blank, exacted a fearsome toll among the LVTs shuttling reinforcements from those units in boats stalled by the exposed reef. The battery maintained this deadly fire until an improvised storming party of Marines snuffed them out one by one with grenades and bayonets. The Japanese fought like banshees.

"Rear Admiral Shibasaki the Japanese Atoll commander had identified every yard of the island with a firing grid. Howitzer crews plotted their targets using pre-positioned aiming stakes; machine gunners maintained assigned fields of fire along the barbed wire and tetrahedrons; riflemen kept their cover and concealment. The attacking Marines fought with their own ferocity, but any man who lifted his head above the seawall attracted bullets from a dozen sources, most of them dangerously close at hand.

"...ISSUE IN DOUBT"

"Here was the classic vulnerability of an opposed amphibious assault. The initial assault force, ashore but hard hit, held on virtually by its fingernails. (One radio message from the beach to the seaborne command headquarters included "...issue in doubt.") Behind them, stalled by the reef and receiving heavy fire, hovered the reinforcements critically needed for momentum, acceleration, and support. The tide was inexplicably weird. Even a neap tide should have risen enough by now to permit boat passage over the reef-but low water prevailed for nearly thirty hours.[1] The Marines' alternate plan:

[1] Forty-four years later, physicist Donald W. Olson would discover that D-Day at Tarawa occurred on one of only two days in 1943 when the moon's apogee coincided with a neap tide, resulting in a tidal range of only a few inches rather than several feet.

use empty LVTs to shuttle fresh troops in from the reef— came a cropper as Japanese gunners found the weak spots on the thinly armored vehicles. Machine guns drilled them full of holes; howitzers and mortars dropped high explosives squarely into their open hatches; high-velocity guns blew them apart and set them ablaze.

"Julian Smith's (2d Marine commander) attempts during the next twenty-four hours to land three sequential infantry battalions by wading from the jumbled reef provided a shooting gallery for Japanese gunners, cost hundreds of casualties, and scattered the survivors—disorganized and often weaponless—along a mile and a half of ghastly beach. By the end of the second day the 22d Amphibian Tractor Bn had lost its intrepid commander, Major Drewes, half of its amtracs and men.

The island was finally secured four days later with the following "butcher's bill":

FINAL BOX SCORE

JAPANESE	
Killed	4690
Taken prisoner	17
Escaped	0
AMERICAN	
Killed	1026
Wounded	2296

Though the Marines suffered only half casualties of the Japanese, it was enough to bring Admiral Nimitz bushels of letters of reproach from widows and mothers of those who died there. Admiral "Obliterate The Island" never again made such brash statements.

A.J. continued on to the Makin Island raid then the Marshall Islands where, as he relates — "...the war for me came to an abrupt end at Eniwetok."

EPILOGUE

A.J. concludes his bio-sketch — "In 1949 I married Bettie Marie Schlotzhauer. That's the same 48 years later.

After a career of managing food service operations at several public institutions as well as operating their own restaurants, A.J. and Bettie have settled down to an active retirement in Pilot Grove. A.J. and Bettie (Bettie Marie Schlotzhauer Wolfe) have, in their retirement, given enormously of themselves, taking on community projects such is the old jail restoration and town museum. Bettie, showing me the old clock that once hung in Pop Tracy's Cafe, said,"I just love this old stuff."

A.J. was voted Mayor of Pilot Grove and took office in 1989. While we were working together on the PGHS 75th Anniversary Reunion, he told me that he was on his ninth year. I said, "I had the idea that every two years interested parties met over coffee at Paula's to nominate the next mayor. Straws were drawn and the *loser* had to take the job! You must be awfully unlucky."

Fig 2-3. Bettie and A.J. Wolfe show off their redecorated Pilot Grove Cafe — 1954. Source: PG Calaboose Museum.

Fig. 2-4. Easter Special - 1954. You should have invested in T-Bone steaks!

Fig. 2-5. "Da Mayor" A.J. Wolfe on the re-election campaign trail. Photo source: Pilot Grove Calaboose Museum.

[The 75th anniversary of Pilot Grove High School was celebrated at the school on June 29th 1997. More than 700 people attended. At the Reunion, Mayor A.J. Wolfe spoke. His speech was worthy of preservation—here it is.]

WE ARE SURVIVORS!

Consider the changes we have witnessed! We were born before television. Before penicillin, before polio shots frozen foods, Xerox, plastic, contact lens, Frisbees and the Pill. We were before radar, credit cards, split atoms, laser beams and ball-point pens. Before pantyhose, dishwashers, clothes dryers, electric blankets, air conditioners, drip-dry clothes and before man walked on the moon.

We got married first and then lived together. How quaint can you be? In our time, closets were for clothes not for "coming out of", bunnies were small rabbits. And rabbits were not Volkswagens, designer jeans were scheming girls named Jean and having a meaningful relationship meant getting along with our cousins.

We, thought fast food was what you ate during Lent and outer space was parking in lovers lane. We were before house husbands. Gay rights. Computer dating. Dual careers and commuter marriages. We were before day-care centers, group therapy and nursing homes. We never heard of FM radio, tape decks, electronic typewriters, artificial hearts, word processors, yogurt and guys wearing earrings. For us, time sharing meant togetherness not computers or condominiums.

A chip meant a piece of wood. Hardware meant hardware and software wasn't even a word.

Back then "made in Japan" meant junk and the term 'making out' referred to how you did on your exam. Pizzas, McDonalds and instant coffees were unheard of. We hit the scene where there were 5 and 10 cent stores, where you bought things for five and ten cents. Decks and Heinrich's drug store sold ice cream cones for a nickel or a dime. For one nickel you could ride a bus, make a phone call, buy a coke at a local cafe, buy enough stamps to mail one letter and two postcards. You could buy a new Chevy coupe for $600, but who could afford one? A pity too, because gas was 9 cents a gallon!

In our day, grass was mowed, coke was a cold drink and pot was something you cooked in. Rock music was a Grandma's lullaby and aids were helpers in the principal's office. We were certainly not before the differences between the sexes was discovered, but we were surely before the sex change. We made do with what we had and we were the last generation that was so dumb as to think you needed a husband to have a baby. Buckle up went from keeping your feet dry to getting a ticket.

No wonder we are so confused and there is such a generation gap today!

But, we survived! What better reason to celebrate?

LESLIE CHAMBERLAIN 1969-1975

Les says, "Sonny asked me to tell a few things about my life and times as well as my terms as Mayor of Pilot Grove. Well, one of the town's achievements of which I am most proud came during my second term of office, It was the Pilot Grove Centennial Celebration. The amount of cooperation and hard work that the various committees did was reminiscent of the war years feeling—we're all in this together!" I am thankful that our success will be memorialized for years in the centennial book .

This book was researched, written and edited by volunteers who were rightly very pleased with their accomplishment. There were numerous, community-wide contributions to this book and it has been widely used as a model for similar projects. We never thought we would sell 1,000 copies of the book but since the additional cost was quite minimal, the printer talked us in to buying 2,000. We sold over 1,000—made a small profit—and still have a few left.

"I love Cooper County. Except for a few years my family lived in Louisiana when I was in grade school and some years that I spent in Europe at the request of Uncle Sam, I have lived here all my life. I was born here — near Boonville — in 1922 but soon moved to Pilot Grove. We lived in a little farmhouse west of the town cemetery. My early memories are of the winter snows that brought the town kids and their sleds to our hill for a Olympic class, downhill toboggan course. I graduated from PGHS in 1940. I think our class was the first to use the new auditorium and stage built a short time before. This is now the "old" auditorium.

"Sonny reminded me of his Halloween disaster in 1937.

BATTLE OF BRITAIN

Since one of the climactic events of WWII was played out only a few miles from Les' Hounslow Base, it may be worth a mention here. During WWII, Hounslow was near the Fighter Command at Uxbridge from where the "Battle of Britain" was directed. Winston Churchill describes a visit to Uxbridge in his book "Their Finest Hour" — "I arrived at the fighter control center on Sunday afternoon September 15, 1940 at the beginning of the largest attack the Germans ever mounted on London. From the balcony, I watched the WRENS shuffle their markers about on the giant mapboard table that represented southern England airspace. The readiness status of each Spitfire and Hurricane squadron was noted by a colored light under the squadron designations around the walls of the room. Green—ready and available; Yellow—committed; and Red—in the air.

"The flights of German bombers were arriving over the channel at a rate that was threatening the capacity of Fighter Command. The Luftwaffe did not have the heavy bombers like the British Lancasters or the American Flying Fortresses. Their war strategy was to produce greater numbers of smaller, faster, attack bombers called "schnell bombers". These were the Junkers JU-88s, Messerschmitt ME-110s and Heinkel HE-111s. They had thousands of them and most were sent against England that day.

"At 2:00 PM, I noted that all the Readiness lights were red! Every single RAF fighter aircraft that could fly was in the air! The WRENS were still showing new incoming Luftwaffe flights crossing the Channel. I thought: '...if the Luftwaffe can keep it up, we're done for! All fighter squadrons would have to return for refuelling and would be caught on the ground, defenseless.'"

Of course, they could not keep it up and that day marked the turning point of what the Brits call the "Battle of Britain".

Fig. 2-6. Leslie Chamberlin, Vice President of Senior Class PGHS 1940 - Source: Senior Class Photo.

Fig. 2-7. Former Mayor Leslie Chamberlin during his last term of office. Source: Pilot Grove Calaboose Museum.

He fell or jumped off my pickup when a gang of us were driving around the old berg. He fractured his skull and I thought for a while my butt was in deep doo-doo. Deep trouble because I was not yet 16 years old and did not have a drivers license. Anyway, all agreed that it wasn't my fault and I continued to drive Dad's old pickup, but occasionally had Jake Brownfield the City Marshal on my case.

"I started to college in Kansas City in 1940 but my "friends and neighbors" extended me an invitation I couldn't refuse and I reported to Fort Leavenworth, KS on December 9th, 1942 and became a proud member of the U.S. Army Air

Corp. I ultimately found myself in England as a ground crewman in the Eighth Air Force at an airfield near the town of Hounslow just to the west of London near the present day Heathrow, England's premier international airport.

"After the D-Day invasion, our Wing moved onto the continent and by the spring of 1945 we were in Germany. I have never seen such devastation. There were hardly a brick left standing. We led an austere life, no beer, no girls, no nothing!

"That was one of the reasons everyone was eager to get back to England when things lightened up in late spring and short furloughs were permitted. There were other reasons: We just wanted to hear folks talking English—although, admittedly, some of the younger guys had about as hard a time understanding the Brits as the Germans. They used to say about England and America: '...two nations, separated by a common language!'

"I lucked out in April. The war was still on but everyone knew that it was only a matter of days. Skytrains of heavy bombers went over every day and there was less and less to bomb. I got a week leave in London with 3 days to get there and 3 days to get back. Sounds like a lot but I had to go to Paris to hitch a plane, there was absolutely zero civilian transport available across the channel. Some trains were running in Germany and France, I took one down part of the way but also had to hitchhike on truck convoys.

"There was virtually no civilian traffic but military traffic was horrendous. There were giant truck convoys carrying supplies to the units in central and southern France. That didn't mean that it was easy to get a ride but I finally managed to get to Le Bourget Field northwest of Paris. The Air Corp sergeant managing leave transport said that all spaces were booked for U.S. transports flying to England that day but the Limeys might have something.

"The RAF flight operations office was on the other side of the field. We wangled a lift on a jeep and lined up for space. We were in luck. A burly Cockney sergeant said (I had been around London for over a year and was somewhat familiar with the Cockneys, so I translated), "There is a Lancaster bomber not totally loaded and you Yanks can leave in a couple of hours if you want." He looked at us carefully as though he expected us to turn him down. I later learned why.

"Just before dusk we clambered aboard the Lancaster. It began dawning on us why the Cockney Sergeant thought we might refuse the ride. Forget about seatbelts, the old Lancaster didn't even *seats*. The plane was crammed with passengers (British and American servicemen) fitted into every nook — in the bomb bays, in gun turrets and just sitting on the floor. There seemed to be an awful lot of soldiers, but I suppose with no bombs this was an easy load. We got as comfortable as we could, jammed up against the bulkheads and fuselage. When we got airborne, the wind began whistling through a thousand holes in the skin.

"The Lancaster had been designed in the 30s and many of them had been flying combat operations for more than five years. The Brits had taken the night shift in bombing raids. They couldn't hit anything so they didn't try, they just carpet bombed everything close to the target. The Yanks, with a little better bombing sights, took the day shift. The Brits bombed counties and the Yanks bombed cities. One consequence of the night bombing was that, flying low to get visual sights on their targets, the Lancaster took enormous amounts of flak. This particular old veteran had been stitched with machinegun fire, perforated with ack-ack and only minimally patched up. Some of its patches had patches! Hundreds of holes, large and small, were the source of the whistling breezes we were feeling. The cabin was not pressurized so we flew low and in the weather.

"As we finally cleared the English Channel and headed up the Thames Estuary, we could see the lights of the towns of England. It was a good feeling. All of a sudden one of the Brit transients who had been jammed into the forward gunners nacelle thus had a good view, cried out: "Lor' love a duck! Its London! The first time I've seen lights on in London in five years!"

"About the same time, a foot square piece of fuselage skin came off and in the resulting slipstream, something tore loose behind the flight deck and rattled right by me and out the hole. I thought the old crate was breaking up and began composing an appropriate prayer. A moment later the pilot came back and said he had hung up his blouse behind his seat and that was what had exited the flak hole. The brass buttons had made all the scary racket. We landed near London with no further heart-stoppers and I was happy to get "home" (I had been assigned here for over a year, the people spoke English and were kind to the "Yanks". It was sorta like home. Even the warm beer was familiar.)

"We were still in Germany in May when the war ended. It was a time of terrific celebration. The aircrews particularly sighed with relief. It's a little know fact that 8th and 9th Air Force air crews suffered a higher ratio of casualties than did the ground armies. The vaunted "Flying Fortress" was no such thing. As soon as the Messerschmitts learned how to do it, they could attack the 'Forts' almost with impunity. Sixty "Forts" were shot down in one day with 600 crewmen lost over Schweinfurt. They remained extremely vulnerable until the F-51s with wing tanks began long range escort duty. Herman Goering said, 'When I saw F-51s over Berlin, I knew the war was lost!' "

"In May, June and July everybody was sitting around wondering when we were going home. It was kinda like several giant corporations downsizing. Suddenly the 8th and 9th Air Force, a million man corporation transporting high explosive munitions to Germany on an around-the-clock schedule, no longer had a job. We were all very happy but wondered, 'What now?'

"The war in Europe was over but unfortunately, the war in the Pacific was not. The Japanese had demonstrated at Okinawa that they weren't saying Uncle. Some Pilot Grove boys were killed and wounded there. Loyd McCreery took some shrapnel in his chest. Cleo Ratje was killed by a kamikaze just after Easter. The Japanese had sent their most powerful battleship, the "Yamada", (its main battery had nine 18" guns) to blast its way through the sea defenses of Okinawa and devastate the U.S. forces there. It required a full U.S. Navy Task Force (58) but it was sunk two days out of Honshu.

"At Okinawa, the U.S. Navy suffered more casualties than all previous battles combined from the Revolution onward. U.S. forces suffered a total of over 49,000 casualties and ultimately killed over 110,000 Japanese. This did not give evidence that the Japanese were thinking of quitting.

"This was the reason that many of the guys in the Air Force in Europe were relegated to the infantry. I, along with a lot of other guys, got shipped back to England for infantry training. We would, barring some miracle, be formed into infantry divisions and participate in the invasion of the home islands of Japan, presumably in the fall of 1946. Based on the Japanese defense of Okinawa, Truman's war planners estimated we would suffer a million casualties.

"The miracle came—Truman's decision to drop the atomic bombs. It saved me (and a lot of other guys). The war in the Pacific ended and we all came home to live happily ever after. Well...more or less.

"After the war I went to auctioneer school in Decatur, IN. My dad had been an auctioneer all his life and as a child I had often tagged along. I loved the action at auction sales and have done some auctioneering most of my life.

"I've done a lot of things—I had old Fred Oerly's ice house and drayage business, then a farm supply business, I dealt a little real estate and worked with the Quinlan agency a while.

"I served a couple of terms as the Cooper County Assessor. I worked for the State Tax Commission and also the Department of Revenue.

"I have one child, Cheryl Christine (Chamberlin) Banks from my first marriage to Merline McCreery and one son Don Roy from my second marriage (to Margaret Beck (Shipman). Don put a tour in the Marines and is now attending the University of Missouri at St. Louis.

"That about sums it up—I guess you could say I've been a jack of all trades and master of none. I can't complain—I've been blessed with a wonderful wife. I have some great kids. All in all, I've had a good, full and happy life.

Fig. 2-8. Charles Thomas "Chuck" Babbitt at about age 30 - 1920.

CHARLES THOMAS BABBITT

C.T. "Chuck" Babbitt was mayor of Pilot Grove from 1935 to 1943. In the write-up below which was excerpted from E.J. Melton's History of Cooper County, the writer extols the many virtues of this remarkable man. I am proud to say that I was distant kin. My mother and he were second cousins, thus I was his second cousin, once removed. Speaking of that kinship, I suppose it now high time I 'fess up.

Now it can be told—when Chuck was collaborating with O.B. Franz in a poultry processing business in Pilot Grove around 1940-1944, I worked for him during the holiday season. I was a freshman and sophomore and—because I was a cousin, I didn't have to work my way up from the bottom in that enterprise. I started right out as a turkey plucker at the handsome rate of 6¢ per turkey. By working from 5PM until midnight, I often made over $2 a night! However, after the 1942 season, I mentally accessed my list of potential careers and scratched ~~turkey plucker!~~

FROM COOPER COUNTY HISTORY P. 553-554

[Author's note: I have edited the article heavily but it still comes off a bit excessive. But, give the gentleman his due. He did contribute to the job market, the price of turkeys and his product graced the table of many Missourians on Thanksgiving Day and Christmas of those years.]

CHARLES THOMAS BABBITT, Pilot Grove poultry plant operator and proprietor of a rapidly expanding baby chick hatchery, has overcome handicaps that would have defeated the ordinary mortal.

Born August 1, 1890, two miles south of Pilot Grove, he was an orphan when two years old; his parents, William and Amanda Oswald Babbitt, natives of Cooper County but of Scotch-Irish and Dutch descent, died about nine months apart. Mr. and Mrs. J.L. Painter, of near Bell Air, took Charles to rear.

[See the 'Mary Morgan' story in Appendix A - The Burnhams. My great-grandfather's baby sister was Mary Morgan (Burnham) Babbitt. Mary Morgan died in childbirth on New Year's Eve 1861. Her newborn was also named Mary Morgan. Mary Morgan Babbitt married James Lewis Painter and is the aunt who took C.T. to rear. Mary and James Painter were also the grandparents of Robert L. "Bob" Painter who partnered with Earl Hays in the 'Hays and Painter' funeral and furniture business a number of years in Pilot Grove. Bob was my third cousin and I could have exercised kinship privilege in those days and gotten a 10% discount on my funeral, but didn't need it.]

When Charles Babbitt was in the fifth grade at Bell Air district school, an accident to his left eye constantly threatened blindness. His education was seriously interrupted.

In 1911 be entered Central Business College in Sedalia and purely by observation in 12 months completed the course and was graduated. His progress was responsible for introduction of touch typing at the College.

Mr. Babbitt then entered the state institution for the blind in St. Louis. He completed a nine months' course, paying his expenses by learning to make brooms which he sold from house to house. In school he mastered Braille and other subjects.

He returned to Cooper County, farming until 1914 when he went to Kansas City, learned piano tuning and followed it until 1917. He returned to the farm, then became the distributing representative for an oil company.

On April 21, 1919, Charles Thomas Babbitt married Miss Rose Lee Eckerle, of Pleasant Green. She was a daughter of Andrew and Margaret Glenn Eckerle.

After representing the oil company two years in Pleasant Green, Mr. Babbitt continued the same work for one year in Pilot Grove where he and Mrs. Babbitt established their home.

Mr. Babbitt then opened a poultry buying station at Pilot Grove for Swift & Company on a commission basis. He continued on that basis for eight years. Then on March 1, 1933, became an independent operator.

As buying agent for Swift, Mr. Babbitt purchased each month about 5,000 pounds of poultry and approximately 100 cases of eggs. During 1936 he handled more than a million pounds of poultry and many months exceeded 400 cases of eggs, increases of more than four-fold, this when drought and other adverse conditions had reduced poultry production.

During November and December, 1936, Mr. Babbitt purchased more than one hundred thousand dollars of turkeys, a tidy total for a season when that regal American bird sold at a very low level. Mr. Babbitt closed the Thanksgiving turkey market at 14-1/2 cents while over Missouri the prevailing price was 12 cents except in territory that he affected. And he closed the Christmas turkey market at 16 cents, while other Missouri buyers were paying 13 cents except in the area again affected by the stimulated market in Pilot Grove.

Through the 1936 turkey season, Mr. Babbitt paid an average of 15 percent above the prevailing Missouri market, or a total premium of $15,000 to farmers. He employed up to 47 pickers. Pilot Grove merchants' trade increased and the community has progressed more than most its size.

In 1936 Mr. Babbitt established a hatchery with 18,000 capacity at his plant. Operating from the first state and international baby chick regulations, he found a ready local market with people who long had dealt with him. In 1937, he increased the capacity to, 53,000, and the first batch came off February 16.

Mr. and Mrs. Babbitt have five children: Charles William, "Billy", born October 2, 1920, and now a sophomore in Pilot Grove High School; Mary Margaret, born February 19, 1923, a freshman; James Lloyd, August 31, 1925, now in the sixth grade; Martha Mae, October 27, 1932; and Homer Lee, September 21, 1934. Before Homer Lee was two and one-half years old he knew half the ABC's from playing with blocks. At that age he also sang lustily, "Jesus Loves Me".

Mr. Babbitt's only brother, Leslie, married a sister of Mrs. C. T. Babbitt. Mr. C. T. Babbitt has two sisters, Mrs. Leslie Haley and Mrs. Fred Stuber, both of Pilot Grove.

[Author's note: The late Mrs. Lesley Haley was the mother of Marshall Ray, Kathryn and Dorothy Haley.]

Mrs. C. T. Babbitt's five brothers are: Fred Eckerle, who married Annie Diel; John Eckerle, who married Della Shepard, now deceased; Henry Eckerle, who married Velma Woolery; William Eckerle, who is single and lives on the home place; and Robert Eckerle, who married Miss Grace Polley. Mrs. C. T. Babbitt's two sisters are Mrs. Lee Wolfe and Mrs. Leslie Babbitt.

Charles Thomas Babbitt has built solidly in Pilot Grove. Liberal prices to the producer and small margins for himself, coupled with good management and boundless energy, have brought volume and expansion. A modern cold storage plant and an indoor loading dock are features of his business. His plant superintendent, Roy Mowery, has been with Mr. Babbitt for 12 years.

In civic and commercial life, religion and education, Mr. Babbitt gives liberally in time, energy and means, for richer, fuller life to individual and community. The boy threatened with blindness, who educated himself under great handicaps, has prospered and provided rewards for the efforts of scores of his fellow townsmen and for hundreds of farmers. Cooper County is richer for the achievements of Charles T. Babbitt and for the example that he and his family sets.

Fig. 2-9. Charles Sandy, age 17, Linn, Kansas. Photo - Martha Sandy.

Fig. 2-10. The Sandy family in Kansas City, a few years before relocating to Pilot Grove. Martha, Meriel, Mattie May and Dr. Charles. Photo - Martha Sandy.

DR. CHARLES SANDY MD

Dr. Charles Sandy was voted Mayor of Pilot Grove for his first two year term in 1933. The Depression had set in and village finances were extremely meager thus the duties of the Mayor during his tenure tended to be mostly ceremonial. That not much happened in the upper echelons of village administration is attested by Dr. Sandy's younger daughter Martha. When, in 1998, I asked her about her father's mayoral duties, she was shocked. "I didn't know he was Mayor!"

She sat across the meal table from him three times a day, each evening she listened to the news with him...and she didn't even know he was Mayor. Clearly the office of the Mayor was not a beehive of activity in 1933.

Our family doctor had been Dr. William S. Barnes (also a subject in this chapter). Dr. Barnes had delivered my sister, me and my brother in that order. But the good Doctor had passed on to his reward in 1933 and we thereafter mostly saw Dr. Sandy for any bumps, or maladies that rated a $1 office call. I mention under "The Medicine Cabinet" how my dad was so concerned when I fractured my skull one Halloween night, that he popped for a $2 house call.

Charles Sandy was born in 1873 near Linn, Washington County, Kansas. He was the son of English immigrants who had trekked from Southend-on-Sea, England to the wilds of Kansas at the close of the Civil War. He was a good student and in the milieu of growth that the nation was then undergoing, he could have his choice of occupations, but he seemed to have had a hard time making up his mind.

He received a teaching certificate from Washington Institute but quickly determined that he really didn't want to be a teacher. He worked in several clerical and retail jobs but settled on the Rock Island Railroad. He became a locomotive engineer running out of Horton, Kansas to Atchison.

At the turn of the century, this job not longer challenged him so he enrolled at University Medical School in Kansas City. He graduated with his MD in 1909 and started his internship at Kansas City Emergency Hospital where he met the young nurse Mattie May who was to become his wife.

He practiced medicine in Kansas City for some years until—as daughter Martha says, "He took a notion he wanted to be a country doctor." The family moved to Calhoun in 1929 which, Martha says, was a disaster. The next year, learning that Doctor Ziegler of Boonville wanted to quit his Pilot Grove coverage, Dr. Sandy moved there. He practiced in Pilot Grove for 18 years except for a few years during the war when he commuted to Kansas City to act as Medical Director at the Pratt and Whitney Defense Plant. "Commuted" means that he spent weekends in Pilot Grove. Doris Quinlan (later Koonse) commuted with him in 1944 when she worked at an insurance company near Union Station.

In 1951, age 78, Dr. Sandy semiretired and moved to Prairie Village (Kansas City Metro area) and opened a small practice in Grandview. In 1959 he was honored by the Missouri State Medical Association for his 50 years of practice.

Fig. 2-11. Martha tends her bird house at the family home—Fourth and Teller in Pilot Grove.

Fig. 2-12. Dr. Charles Sandy 1960. He passed away February 21, 1963.

I visited with Martha Sandy at her lovely lakeside home north of Kansas City in the winter of 1998. She showed me the bricks she had Leslie Chamberlin truck up to her for a patio some years ago. They were from the old Pilot Grove Presbyterian Church which had been razed. She graciously permitted me to copy memorabilia from the doctor's life.

Martha herself has led an interesting life. She graduated from Pilot Grove High School in 1933, ran a little craft shop in Pilot Grove for a while before returning to her Kansas City birthplace. She was working at TWA (which stood for Transcontinental Western Airlines in those days) when she enlisted in the Marines—BAMs she called them. Please don't ask me to explain that.

Discharged in 1945, she returned to Kansas City and took a job with Hallmark Cards in the Creative Department where she worked until her retirement.

I asked her if the Sandys were Scots. "No," she answered, "My Sandy grandparents immigrated from England."

BEDSIDE MANNER

I thought they were Scots because of the name and because of the dour disposition of the doctor. He had a 'no nonsense, fix it and get on with it' type personality. Indeed, he was rather typical of the medical practitioners of his era.

In the 1930s, the term "Bedside Manner" had not yet been invented and the 'touchy, feely' epoch was not to arrive for several decades. There were two reasons for this brusque manner of many doctors. First, it was generally accepted by their patients that life entails a certain amount of pain and suffering and one might just as well accept it. Whining had not yet been brought to the state of high art that it enjoys today.

Secondly, there was—compared with today—a limit to what even the very best doctors could do. Sew up cuts, swab abrasions, set broken bones, perform a few surgeries and announce with confidence "He'll be OK."

People died from medical problems that would be easily treatable today. In the 1930s, miracle medicines and operations were still in the dreams of the research scientists.

Janie Brownfield Goehner relates an illustrative story. "When I was six or seven, I had permission to spent the day playing dollhouse with Patty Schilb. I began feeling bad early on and walked home. When I voluntarily gave up a day of playing, mother knew I was in trouble. I had a high fever and terribly sore throat. Dr. Sandy was out of town so she called Dr. Boley.

Dr. Boley took but a moment to diagnose scarlet fever and by law had to quarantine the house. Within two days, Dad had it, as did Charley and Dutchie. Poor mother was run ragged tending to four patients. To make it worse, the disease had a strange psychological effect—food cravings. I craved doughnuts. I whined and complained so much that mother spend several hours in the kitchen making up a batch. When she produced them, the very sight of them made me sick and I couldn't eat any! Dad had a similar experience with ice cream. I was very sick, but Dad lost nearly 50 pounds and nearly died with scarlet fever!

Hulda Heinrich was the wife of the local pharmacist, J.D. Heinrich Jr., who now owned the Drug Store. Hulda called Mom and told her of an article she had read of a class of miracle drugs—the sulfas[2].

When Dr. Sandy made his next house call, Mom, in desperation, told him of her conversation with Hulda. The doctor was offended and stormed out of the house slamming the door, "Perhaps you should just consult with Hulda Heinrich!"

But, the next day, Dr. Sandy drove the 200 mile round trip to Kansas City and obtained a course of sulfa and brought it to the house. It was new to him and he insisted that Mom sign a waiver before he gave her the medicine. But the sulfa drug worked! We were all well within 2-3 days."

Marjorie (Burger) Schmidt reports that: "Mrs. Sandy, an RN, was invited to speak to the PGHS Freshman girls on the subject of, ahem, "The Birds and the Bees".

"Marjorie concludes: Had it not been for that excellent seminar, I might have been puzzled to this very day!"

[2]Sulfa drugs, or sulfonamides, were the first systemic drugs effectively used to combat bacterial infections in humans. Since the advent of antibiotics, however, their use in therapy has become quite limited. Sulfa drugs are still used, for example, against streptococcal infections (Scarlet Fever is a streptococcal infection), urinary-tract infections, and ulcerative colitis. Drug side effects include reactions in the kidney, liver, skin, and bone marrow.

During WWII Sulfanilamide was included in army first aid packets as a topical treatment for gunshot and shrapnel wounds.

Mr. W.E. Deck, President
Citizens' Bank
Pilot Grove, Mo.

Pilot Grove, Mo. 11-14-29

Dear Mr. Deck,

Some time ago I received a communication through the mail stating my rent would be $10.00 a month and the bank would furnish the heat and light. The writer of that letter never consulted me at any time as to whether I wanted any light or heat or anything else.

I have always used as much light and heat as I needed and paid for it however little or much it might be. I do not propose to have anyone tell me how much light or heat I need nor how much I shall pay for [it]. If I care to go without light or have my room cold that is my business an no affair of the bank.

It has always been the rule in this building to furnish our own heat and light so we could pay for whatever we wanted to use and no more. To force some other plan on us is arbitrary, unfair and unjust.

I have always tried to be as saving on light and fuel as possible because it was in my interest to do so. If I have to pay a higher flat rate you may be assured no such savings will be attempted.

It takes two or more to make a bargain or a legal contract but I was never consulted about this move at all. This seems to be a one sided affair with a request to 'sign here' or get out.

Under the circumstances as I see it, this is just a polite or otherwise way of telling me to get out as you want the room.

Yours truly,

/s/ Chas. Sandy

[Author's Note: I have excerpted from E.J. Melton's 1937 "History of Cooper County" his articles on—Dr. Barnes, Dr. Schilb and G.B. Harlan.]

DR. WILLIAM SILAS BARNES SERVED NOBLY

One of Cooper County's most popular physicians was the late lamented William Silas Barnes, of Pilot Grove. He embodied all the fine qualities of the country doctor. His life of service is a monument to a memory.

He was born July 4, 1871 at the home of his parents, Hannibal Tabler Barnes and Elizabeth Frances Pemberton Barnes, on a farm near Marshall, Saline County, Missouri. He died in Cooper County, May 29, 1933, after practicing medicine for one-third of a century in Pilot Grove. He was one of four children. His three sisters are residents of Pilot Grove. They are Mrs. De Etta Marr, Mrs. H. N. Simmons and Mrs. J. W. Richey.

The Barnes family originated in Germany. Theodore (Teter) Barnes immigrated to the colonies before the American revolution, where he enlisted for service in the third company first battalion of the Cumberland county militia in 1781.

Theodore Barnes married Mary Sciester of Washington County, Maryland. He had five sons and two daughters.

The late lamented Dr. W. S. Barnes of Pilot Grove was descended through the son Michael, born in 1781, in Berkeley County, Virginia, and married Phoebe Tablier, who was a descendant of Lord Ridgely. The line of descent of the subject of this sketch was through their son, William Easterday Barnes who was married to Eliza Tabler of Frederick County, Maryland, Jun 3, 1841.

The following autumn William Easterday Barnes and his wife emigrated to Missouri. They proceeded to the Arrow Rock Tavern where they spent the winter. The tavern was then kept by the mother of George Caleb Bingham, noted artist. In the spring they located near Marshall on the farm where he died at the age of 89.

One of their six children was a son, Hannibal Tabler Barnes, who was born on April 2, 1844 at the family home near Marshall, and enlisted as a Confederate soldier at the beginning of the Civil War when he was 17 years old. He fought in the First Battle of Boonville, June 7, 1861, and in the battles of the Little Blue, Big Blue, Westport, Mill Creek, Newtonia, First Battle of Lexington, and at Fayetteville, Arkansas.

Veteran of four years of war, Hannibal Tabler Barnes, age 21, entered the St. Louis Medical College from which he was graduated in 1867. (This college now is part of Washington University, where he is listed as an alumnus.) Later he was a surgeon at the Confederate home in Higginsville. He practiced many years in Pilot Grove. He died on august 15, 1928.

He and Elizabeth Frances Pemberton, a daughter of Richard Pemberton and Sarah Durrett of Saline County, were married, September 2, 1867. She died may 20, 1904.

Their only son, William Silas Barnes, was educated in Pilot Grove Collegiate Institute. Early evincing a liking for medicine, the youth's interest caused his father to remark, "Silas has the most profound inclination toward drugs of anyone I ever knew." William Silas Barnes entered Beaumont Medical College in St. Louis which later was consolidated with the St. Louis Medical School to become a part of St. Louis University.

After graduation he returned to his home town and began practicing with his father in Pilot Grove. Known as a studious, serious-minded boy, he was immediately recognized as a conscientious physician and a surgeon of more than average ability. Starting when roads often were difficult to travel even on horseback, he was to serve his home community for one-third of a century. On a basis of mileage traveled, he stood at the top among Cooper County practitioners.

On April 20, 1918, William Silas Barnes married Miss Mary Elizabeth Tutt, a daughter of Charles Philip Tutt of Bunceton and Mary Lavinia Grantham of Mexico, Missouri. Mary Elizabeth Tutt was one of seven children, five of whom are living.

Mrs. Barnes is the fourth generation of Tutts in Missouri.

Of the union of W.S. Barnes and Mary Elizabeth Tutt were born two children: William Tutt Barnes, called Billy, and Elizabeth Virginia Barnes, called Betty.

Dr. Barnes did much charity practice. The snowstorm never was too bad, the blizzard too rough, or the temperature too low for him to go long distances when emergency called.

Likewise, there were nights of driving rain when roads became quagmires or there was sleet or frozen muck where the horse sank knee-deep with every step. But whether the weather was fair or foul and the roads dusty or muddy, Dr. Barnes made his calls.

He was fond of fine horses and for many years maintained several in his stables, including race and saddle stock. Freeman Mack, colored, drove for Dr. Barnes for many years and cared for the stables. Later, a son, Billy Mack, now of Boonville, succeeded his father. Billy Mack visited Dr. Barnes during his last illness at St. Joseph hospital, in Boonville, recalling events and personalities associated with their days of horse racing.

He was a devoted lover of dogs. One or more of his pets was always at his heels, and for years his two pet Boston Bulls were his riding companions when he made trips in the car. Always on his desk in a prominent place was the "Eulogy on the Dog", by Senator George Graham Vest.

In its obituary of Dr. Barnes, the Boonville advertiser said of him in part:

"Dr. Barnes was always a personal friend to the common people. With him work was a duty. He depended upon himself, was independent as a man may be. He lived a use-

DR. WILLIAM T. BARNES, SURGEON

Fig. 2- 13. Dr. William Tutt Barnes (Westminster Class of 1941) is the son of Dr. W.S. Barnes and Mary Tutt Barnes, and a third generation doctor. He served as the director of the Cardiovascular and Thoracic Surgery Department at Geisinger Medical Center in Danville, Pennsylvania, between 1965 and 1975. He is currently engaged in private practice surgery with the firm of Barnes, Hendricks and Associates in State College, Pennsylvania. Dr. Barnes earned an A.B. degree from Westminster in 1941. He also holds M.S. (1943) and M.D. (1946) degrees from Northwestern University.

ful life and, with his arms filled with gathered sheaves, he passed from this life to the great life beyond.

To him to do right was not simply a duty, it was a pleasure. Doctor Barnes was an absolutely honest man. Honesty is the oak around which all other virtues cling. He knew that a promise could not be made often enough or emphatic enough to take the place of a good deed. He followed the splendid truth that 'the higher obligations among men are not set down in writing signed and sealed but reside in honor'. Dr. Barnes was never known to consciously do wrong. He never took an advantage: he never worked in the dark: he stood out boldly for what he believed was the best interest of the public. He knew his many friends, and bravely did his work and spoke his thoughts. His hands were always stretched to the unfortunate.

"His life was full of kind deeds, especially to the poor. He filled homes with sunshine. No one can estimate the good accomplished by this gifted man where he practiced his profession. And were every one to whom he did some loving service to bring a flower to his grave he would be now sleeping beneath a wilderness of blossoms."

William Silas Barnes was of strong convictions and outspoken, always a loyal friend. Position or rank meant nothing to him. He looked beyond artificialities to the individual himself. He won many admirers and true friends who recognized in the stalwart country doctor a painstaking practitioner, a solid citizen and a gentleman, kind and generous to the core.

Fig. 2-14. Three generations of Schilbs: Enslie Jr., Enslie III, and Enslie Sr. Alaska, 1970s. Photo-E.I. Schilb Jr.

DR. E. I. SCHILB'S CAREER OF SERVICE

OF GREAT PROFESSIONAL ABILITY, HE ALSO GIVES UNSELFISHLY OF HIS TIME TO CIVIC AFFAIRS, AND HAVING SERVED AS MAYOR OF PILOT GROVE AND IS NOW A MEMBER OF THE BOARD OF EDUCATION.

The world usually recognizes ability. The people of Pilot Grove are proud that many former residents in distant cities return regularly to the home town for dental work.

Dr. Enslie Irvin Schilb of Pilot Grove is kept very busy in his modern office. He is seldom available except by appointment. He keeps up with developments in professional periodicals and he maintains up-to-date equipment.

Dr. Schilb has served his community in many ways. He has been mayor of Pilot Grove and now is a member of the board of education.

Enslie Irvin Schilb was born April 1, 1893, on a farm near Otterville. He is one of three children of Francis Schilb, now deceased, and Sophie Spieler Schilb.

Dr. Schilb's mother, who now resides in his home, was born six miles east of Boonville in 1866. She is a daughter of the late Mr. and Mrs. Ernest Spieler.

Enslie Irvin Schilb attended the Pilot Grove public schools and was graduated from the Pilot Grove Academy. He entered the dental school at St. Louis University in 1912 and was graduated in June, 1915.

Immediately thereafter he began practicing his profession in his home town. In January, 1918, at Jefferson Barracks he enlisted in the army as a private in the dental detachment. The following June was called to service at Camp Pike, Arkansas, and later was promoted to first lieutenant, which commission be held when be was discharged December 21, 1918 and returned to Pilot Grove to reopened his office.

He married Mrs. Kathryn May Scott of Pilot Grove December 17. 1919. She is a daughter of W. A. Scott and Birdie Lee Scott of Pilot Grove and is an attractive, talented young woman. Of this union were born two children: Enslie Irwin

Jr., born January 31, 1925, and Patricia Lee, born May 19, 1928. Both children were born at St. Joseph's Hospital.

Son and daughter show much promise in music. Enslie Irwin, Jr., is advanced on the clarinet and piano. He plays the clarinet in the Pilot Grove Band and Orchestra. Patricia Lee plays the violin and piano.

Dr. Schilb is active in the Presbyterian Church and in Masonic bodies, being identified with both the Chapter and the Commandery. He has been a member of Leonard Thoma Post Number 52, of the American Legion, for many years. He is very active in the Parent Teachers Association having contributed much to its success and is also a member of the Central Missouri State and American Dental Associations and Psi Omega, dental Fraternity.

He also finds time to play solo cornet in the Pilot Grove Band and in the Pilot Grove Orchestra. Those organizations, directed by Mr. William Deck of Pilot Grove, have been outstanding for a decade.

Dr. Schilb, although still a young man, has attained a high degree of professional success. As a civic leader he has helped to maintain Pilot Grove thriving and progressive, second in importance in Cooper County only to Boonville.

His professional skill has accumulated for him a wide acquaintance and a reputation of the highest ethical standing. He is modest, conservative and substantial.

PERSONAL REMEMBRANCES

The foregoing bio-sketch appeared in E.J. Melton's 1937 "History of Cooper County". I have edited some of the genealogical information, otherwise it is as originally printed. On his term as Mayor—Patty doesn't remember the year. Following are some personal remembrances.

Although I had had a cavity or two filled earlier, my real challenge to Dr. Schilb was an accident which broke my two front teeth leaving an inverted Vee gap. He did a double root canal and capped this with two gold crowns. A few weeks later Mr. Shier, the Vo-Ag teacher and basketball coach drove me into the unprotected north wall of the gym when I went in for a layup shot. The crowns splintered. They were replaced. Two weeks later in another basketball game Shier's elbow came into violent contact with my teeth again and the crowns gave way. Mr. Shier may have been what the Italians call a "Boccigalupe".

After the third accident, there wasn't much left to work with and Dr. Schilb had to put full gold crowns over both teeth. I had had them for about 15 years when they just wore out and I got implants.

Janie Brownfield Goehner told me of her visit to the dentist. "I was about seven years old on my first visit to the dentist. I was in the chair, apprehensive but not really knowing what to expect. Everything seemed to be going OK. What gave me a start was Dr. Schilb going into his waiting room and speaking to my mother.—'Mary I think you'd better come in here and hold Janie's hand. I've broken off a needle in her gum and she may get a little upset.'"

[Author's note: Hard to conceive now, but needles were reused by all health practitioners. They were resharpened, autoclaved where 600° steam sterilized them and kept ready for next use.]

"Surviving this trauma," Janie continues, "I had an appointment a week later to complete the work. Mother was busy and asked me to walk down to the Dr. Schilb's office."

"Dr. Schilb worked with me for a while then—in frustration—called mother. 'Mary, can you come down here and pick up Janie?'

"'Mom said, 'Are you finished already?'"

" 'No! I just can't get her to open her mouth!' "

My old friend, Vern Klenklen, explains why he held Dr. Schilb in high esteem. The alternative was old Doc Jones.

Vern woke up one morning with his jaw swollen and painful. Papa George checked him out and said, "Looks to me like that wisdom tooth is coming in wrong, Son. I'll stop by Dr. Schilb today and ask about it."

Vern said, "What he was really doing was getting a bid on a tooth extraction. Dr. Schilb quoted one dollar. Since Doc Jones only charged 50¢, he was the low bidder.

I went into Doc Jones office that afternoon. Even his equipment scared me. He had the most antiquated dental equipment in the state. His drill must have been World War I surplus. It was powered by bicycle pedal contraption that spun up a heavy flywheel and which was turn geared up 100 to 1 to drive his drills. I prayed that he wouldn't have to use any of that stuff on me. Of course, he didn't.

I was shaking so badly I had trouble getting into his chair. He fixed my bib and immediately picks up his forceps.

I said, 'Ain't you suppose to give me a shot or somepin?'

'Naw,' he says, 'You're a big boy now, Bernie...er, Vernie. You wouldn't want to be treated like a baby now would you?'

He applied the extractors, but broke off the tooth and had to pry out the individual shards one at a time. He had alcoholic tremors so badly I'm not sure he even pulled the right tooth. It felt like he had ripped out my jaw.

So, I learned *why* he was the low bidder—no anesthesia!

Fortunately, the issue never came up again, but I don't think I could have faced the old doc again regardless of those terrific savings."

EPILOGUE

Enslie went off to a military V12 program after graduating from PGHS 1943. After college and Kansas City Dental School, he entered the U.S. Army Air Force (later the U.S. Air Force) where he served for 30 years.

He is retired now and lives with wife Peggy in Tampa, Florida. They have 3 children and 4 grandchildren.

Patricia Lee "Patty" graduated from Lindenwood College in St. Charles in 1950 and married Thomas Hurster the following year. They had 5 children and 11 grandchildren. Tom was killed in a aircraft accident in 1994.

Patty now lives in St. Louis and manages a metal fabication firm—Bohm and Dawson, Inc.

GEORGE B. HARLAN SERVES IN MANY FIELDS

HE IS HONORED BY PUBLISHERS AND STATE POLITICAL LEADERS, AND HOLDS KEY POSITIONS IN HIS COMMUNITY, WHERE HE HAS OWNED AND EDITED THE PILOT GROVE RECORD FOR TWO DECADES.

When the Republicans of Cooper County wanted a strong man as a candidate for representative in the legislature they nominated George Bascom Harlan, a World War I veteran and editor of the Pilot Grove Record for the past 21 years. He was one of three Republicans in Cooper County elected in 1934.

In the House of Representatives he immediately was recognized as a leader of the minority party. He wrote a weekly news letter to about half of the Republican papers of Missouri, interpreting news of the session from the Republican viewpoint. These won instant favor and were widely read.

George B. Harlan had a state-wide reputation before he entered the legislature, having held many positions of honor and trust. His accounts of the session and his timely comments added to his prestige.

When Jess W. Barrett was practically drafted by the republicans to run for Governor of Missouri in 1936, he asked Mr. Harlan to be his out-state campaign manager.

Mr. Barrett had been Attorney General of Missouri, Commander of the Missouri Department of The American legion, and President of the Missouri Bar Association. Besides serving in numerous other capacities. He proved a popular candidate and his campaign was well presented by Mr. Harlan.

General Barrett won the Republican nomination by a top heavy majority. He carried every county and every precinct in the state. It was a personal tribute to the candidate and reflected much credit on Mr. Harlan as out-state manager.

In November, 1936, the Missouri Press Association at its regular annual session, at Hotel Statler, St. Louis, elected Mr. Harlan vice president, in which position he now serves.

George B. Harlan was born June 27, 1889, on a farm north of McGirk, Moniteau County, Missouri. He was one of a family of seven children, having three brothers and three sisters.

G. B. Harlan was educated in the public schools of Moniteau County and entered the newspaper business in 1910 when he bought the Central Missouri Leader at Centertown in Cole County. He sold it in 1915, and purchased the Pilot Grove Record, which he has owned and edited ever since.

He married Miss Dale Latimer of Cole County in May, 1916. She is a daughter of Dr. M. A. Latimer, who died in 1929.

G.B Harlan died in 1952. His wife Dale died in 1970. They are buried in the Pilot Grove Cemetery.

Fig. 2-15. George B. Harlan was an outstanding State legislator, an administrator and served a term as sheriff of Cooper County, but he is mostly remembered as owner-editor of the Pilot Grove Record and later the Cooper County Record.

PILOT GROVE VICE

G.B. Harlan was Cooper County sheriff in the summer of 1945. By that time I had "gone fer a sojer" and was playing war games in the wilds of the Missouri Ozarks at Camp Crowder, MO. This story of Sheriff Harlan smashing a Pilot Grove vice ring was told to me some time later.

Bud Paxton's Barber Shop was located on the west side of Roe between lst and 2d Streets and was beginning to be called the "Paxton-Quinlan Barber Shop" since Wilbur had returned from his wartime seafaring days, graduated cum laude from barber college and bought into the tonsorial enterprise. Wilbur, in the years to come, would achieve greatness as the town and regional raconteur and teller of tall tales, but right now he was concerned.

Behind the barber shop there was a jumble of old sheds and open spaces that in this pleasant summer of long dry days was the venue of a "rolling crap game". Men came and men left but there always seemed to be a number of fellows talking to and rattling dice and exchanging money. Not a little liquor was being consumed and the dice games were sometimes quite boisterous.

Now these fellows, all townsfolk and well known to Wilbur, were not out-and-out desperadoes, but none of them had been lifelong altar boys either if you catch my drift. They all eyed Wilbur when he came out the back door of the barber shop for some task. Wilbur always pretended not to notice them and made such trips sparingly. He was concerned that they might think he was spying on them.

For several weeks these crap games went on desultorily, One hot afternoon, as was his wont, Wilbur took advantage of a lull in business to go next door to the Tip-Top Cafe for a cold Coke. All of the "Altar Boys" were there nursing Falstaffs. There had been a buzz of conversation, but his entrance dropped a chill curtain of silence over the entire cafe. He spoke to one or two and they sullenly turned their back on him, muttering to one another.

"Oh boy! Something has happened here and maybe I'd better watch my back!" he thought.

Bud could not guess what had happened, so after shutting up shop that night, Wilbur stopped in the Tip-Top again. He looked around warily but none of the crap shooters was in evidence.

The proprietor, Dick Schuster was alone in the cafe. Wilbur asked, "Dick, you saw how those guys treated me this afternoon. What's their beef? Do you have any idea?"

Dick grinned, "Do you honestly not know?"

"No, I don't know. They've been a pain in my butt for weeks shooting craps outside my back door, but I didn't say anything to them."

"Hmm, you really don't know what happened do you? Well, *you* didn't say anything to *them*, but someone *did* say something to the law! They thought it was you. To be truthful, I did too."

The truth will always out and it did in this case as well. The *real* rat-fink was a crap-shooter's wife. She was getting a little disturbed that the old man was coming home week after week with an exceedingly slim pay packet. She had a little telephone chat with Mr. Harlan.

G.B. was an impressive man, 56 years old and over six feet tall. He weighed in at over 200 pounds. He was not at all a man given to physical violence but he gave the impression that he could hold his own if need be. Thus, when he made a trip to Pilot Grove and confronted these gamblers, they listened carefully as he explained the error of their ways and instructed them on the path of righteousness They all earnestly agreed to take that path in lieu of a trip to the County jail and the court of Judge Roy Williams. But they were all in a black mood over being ratted on.

As G.B. took the occasion to visit with some of the Pilot Grove folks to renew acquaintances (sheriffs are elected, you know), he came across my little brother Bob. "You're Bob Salmon, aren't you?"

"Yessir, Mr. Harlan."

"How old are you, young man?"

Bob, sweating a bit, wonders where this is leading. "I'm sixteen."

"Don't you think that's a little young to be in the bootlegging business? Look, Bobby, I know you been making that home-brew raisin jack and selling it to them crapshooters back of the barbershop. I've just had a little talk with them and they agreed to cease and desist and avoid going to jail. I'm asking you to do the same thing! "

"Yessir, Mr. Harlan, sir."

DA COUNCILMAN

Wallace W. Burger was born January 4, 1895 the son of John William and Mattie (Martin) Burger. He died December 22, 1951 and is buried in the Pilot Grove Cemetery.

I've never asked, but the name may derive from the Scottish "burgher", meaning the inhabitant of a borough, a citizen. Scottish usage however, had connotation of a *civic minded citizen, a responsible member of the community*. In this sense, the name was accurate.

The Burgers were: Wallace Walker Burger, his wife Mary (McCutcheon) Burger, son Wallace M. (not Junior) and daughters Marjorie and Mary Louise. Wally, as Wallace (the younger) is still called, graduated with my sister, Dixie, in 1941. Marjorie was class of 1944 and Mary Louise was class of 1949. When I was growing up, they lived on the north side of College Street two doors west of Harris. Wally and his sisters now live in the Johnson County section of the Kansas City Metropolitan area. Mrs. Burger also lives in Johnson County and celebrated her 100th birthday in November of 1995.

My memory of Mr. Burger was of a bluff, hearty man—a giant man full of optimism and good cheer. He was a community leader and was instrumental in getting the waterworks and sewers in Pilot Grove in 1935-36. As a town councilman, he also got the streets of Pilot Grove paved and that dusty street in front of our house that turned to a rutted bog in the spring rains was permanently fixed.

He worked with Tony Seltsam and other directors of the Citizens' Bank in 1932 when a bank holiday was imposed after the financial crash of 1929. With depositors reassured, the panic that permanently closed many banks was averted.

I mention him in the Bert Wells -Red Horst story. Though Mr. Burger had no responsibility in that matter, he was a councilman at the time and assumed responsibility for cooling off some hot heads and preventing further blood shed.

The memory that most sticks in my mind was his role as Santa Claus. He had both the girth and the personality for it, so he played Santa to the town's little ragamuffins (including me) for many years until he finally talked Homer Chamberlin (Les' father) into playing the role and gave up this prestigious and highly rewarding job. In the Advent Season, Santa Claus awarded each of the town's little urchins a one-pound cello-pak of Christmas candy, some mixed nuts for shelling and a big orange. The town merchants contributed the candy, fruit and nuts. Mr. Burger organized a bag stuffing party in his basement (Marjorie, Mary Louise, Janie Brownfield, Dorothy and Marion McCutcheon often helped) and produced a mound of kiddy treats.

After the town water system was installed, a fire truck was acquired and played a key role in the annual Santa's visit as well as other town festivals.

Fig. 2-16. Wallace Burger (the elder), holding baby Lou, examines some cattle he has just unloaded at the Katy pens. This is the facility described under "Sheep Drive" below. Photo - Marjorie Burger Schmidt.

Mr. Burger was a W.W.I veteran and a member of Pilot Grove's Chapter of the American Legion. He often made the annual Armistice Day speech. In the olden days, Veteran's Day, November 11th, was called Armistice Day and commemorated the end of World War I—The "Great War". The American Legion prepared the program and the speeches were often delivered from the Fred Oerly truck scales platform, see Fig. 2-18 next page.

I remember how, one year, he used a little aid to start one speech. As the chattering locals were milling about, he cleared his throat. No one paid attention. He then burst into his speech and—on cue—someone on the ramp at Zeller's Elevator (building in background of Fig. 2-18) about 40 feet away, fired off a volley of 12 gage shotgun shells as fast as he could work the pump. "Kablooey, Kablooey, Kablooey, Kablooey!"

"...and at this very hour on this day in 1918, all that hullabaloo ceased!" That got the crowd's attention. He then went on to present a rousing address, while some nervously looked over their shoulders.

He loved the cool shade of the Chouteau Springs spa and made use of the small swimming pool. He and Roy Williams, a friend from Boonville and also a 6 ft 3 in 250 lb. giant used to "Cannonball" into one end of the pool and create a tidal wave that inundated the ladies at the other end. He never missed a band concert there. He never played an instrument himself but sparked the development of a town band.

While on active duty at the Great Lakes Naval Training Station, John Philip Sousa (if you born after 1940, you never heard of John Philip Sousa, so see side-bar next page.) had occasion to visit the installation and present an exhilarating band concert. Mr. Burger never forgot it. In later years (1930s and 1940s) he could always be found on the front row as Bill Deck conducted the band at Saturday night concerts in the town square. His usual request: "Stars and Stripes Forever", his favorite march.

Many of my cohorts of the 1940s era remember Wally's McCutcheon cousins; Charles, Kenneth, Dorothy May and Marion. Those two pretty girls broke hearts when the family moved. Well...maybe the boys did too. Perhaps it was the McCutcheon genes that gave Wally such pretty sisters.

I asked Wally for Pilot Grove stories from his youth—here's one.

THE GREAT SHEEP DRIVE

"There was, in years gone by, a small stockyard or—more accurately—animal pens, adjacent to the Katy Railroad's commercial sidetrack in Pilot Grove. The pens were just off First Street northwest of the lumberyard. There was a watering tank and an unloading ramp. This was the reception point for 100 head of Merino sheep that dad had shipped up from Texas—Texas yearlings," Wally remembers the highlight of his summer of 1935 when as a lad of 12 he was engaged as a sheep drover.

"We only needed to move them out to the farm. There were 3-4 of us. I think I offered Janie Brownfield, Wilma Quinlan and some other little kids a quarter to help and we did not anticipate any big chore. We had no dogs. I don't suppose there was a trained sheep dog in the entire state. No one would have known how to work them anyway.

"We worked the sheep out of the pens and then drove them west on First Street. A few straggled when we crossed Roe and we were concerned that some of them might get on the track and be hit by a train. But there wasn't much traffic on the Katy anyway and we got them herded in and moved on to the calaboose corner and then up onto College Street.

"It was on College, just beyond my home, that the great sheep drive of 1935 began to come apart. There were a number of large homes with expansive front lawns along College. The sheep, which had been cooped up in the rail cars for several days, saw these lawns and gardens as manna from heaven and immediately spread out to help themselves to the lush, rich, green grass, succulent flowers and vegetables!

" 'Hey, man—I ain't never seen nothin' like this in Texas!' may have been their thinking.

"They were uncontrollable. I saw several of them go munching down a row of petunias like a hedge trimmer. As I tried to herd them back onto the street, Mrs. Simmons came out her front door screaming and wailing, 'My lovely petunias—gone, all gone!'

Mrs. Simmons was the sister of Dr. William Barnes and the wife of the local hardware store owner, Harv Simmons. She was clearly not finding the sight of sheep devouring her petunias amusing.

"By dint of brute force, threats, screams and thumping on them with sticks, we finally got them under control and back enroute, but my ears were burning with all the fulmina-

Fig. 2-17. "Would you please leave off eating those flowers?"

Fig. 2-18. Armistice Day. The Oerly Truck scales was the speaker's platform. Sound effects were from the Zeller elevator (in rear). Photo - Burger.

tions and insults the ladies were hurling at us.

"The telephone rang on into the night that night and dad had to exercise all his powers of diplomacy to soothe and mollify the good ladies. The next day I went around with him and while he expressed his apologies and empathized with the victims, I tried to salvage some of the flower beds.

"As for me, on my mental list of potential careers, I struck off ~~sheep drover!"~~

BULL VALLEY[2]

In the Spring of 1938, Ralph Warnhoff was a graduating Senior at PGHS and had been deputized by his older brother, Walter Jr. "Beau" to draw a map that would permit him to navigate the Byzantine route to Barney Twenter's place in Clear Creek.

Barney Twenter was the proud papa of six of the most handsome kids in the county—Mildred, the oldest; Esther, whom Ralph had dated; Viola Mae (graduated with my sister in 1941 and dated Wally Burger for a time.); Earl; Bessie Jean and Doris. See pictures of two of them next page. Quite a number of young swains had mastered map and compass to find their way out to the Twenters. So many young hopefuls had mastered the route that Wally and Ralph called it "Bull Valley".

But Beau was nervous. "After Clear Creek I get lost. I don't want to take chances. You guys," he pointed to Wally and Ralph, " have been out there often enough—you should be able to draw me a map from memory!"

"OK. OK!" says Ralph. "Your date is Saturday. We'll have you a map ready by then."

Saturday morning and Ralph shows up at Wally's doorstep. Marjorie hears them arguing in the basement work room. "You turn right there at that windmill and then go north..."

"No, no, no! You turn *before* the windmill and..."

Wally, "Look, here's what we had better do..." He ex-

[2] There is no such place as "Bull Valley". "Bull Valley" was a jokey name applied to the Barney Wessing farm of the 1930s era. Barney's son Earl, and later his grandson, operated this farm.

JOHN PHILIP SOUSA

America's greatest composer of MARCH music was John Philip Sousa, b. Washington, D.C., Nov. 6, 1854, d. Mar. 6, 1932. The popularity of his 136 marches--headed by "The Stars and Stripes Forever" (1896)--gained him the title the March King, but he also composed 15 operettas, 70 songs, 27 fantasies, and more than 300 arrangements, and wrote 132 articles and 7 books, including his autobiography, Marching Along (1928), and 3 novels.

At the age of 13, Sousa enlisted as an apprentice in the U.S. Marine Band. He left the Marines when he was 18 years of age and played violin in theater and symphonic orchestras, also gaining valuable experience as a conductor. He reenlisted in the Marine Band in 1880--this time as leader--and began composing; his first hit march was "The Gladiator" (1886), and his "Washington Post March" (1889) became a ballroom rage associated with a new dance, the two-step.

He left the Marines in 1892 to form his own band, which quickly became the most successful in the nation; tours through Europe in 1900, 1901, 1903, and 1905 and a global circuit in 1910-11 brought him worldwide celebrity. With the U.S. entry into World War I, Sousa again enlisted, this time to lead the Navy Band, and he continued an active musical life until his retirement in 1931.

Fig. 2-19. Wally and Ralph marked the course for Beau to find "Bull Valley."

Fig. 2-20. Earl (PGHS 1944) and Bessie Jean Twenter (1947). Earl married Trudy Seifner and now, after 40+ years of farming, is semiretired. They have 6 children and 6 grandchildren. Jean, as she preferred to be called, married Kenny Bock. Tragically she lost her battle with cancer in 1990. She is sadly missed by her family and friends as well as all those who knew her during her PGHS tenure 1943-1947.

plains his plan in detail. The boys then retire to the barn and begin hammering and painting.

When Beau shows up for his map, they explain to him and he reluctantly agrees. As he proceeds to the Wesley Chapel corner he sees the first sign: "Right to Bull Valley". Then "5 miles to Bull Valley" then at each turning "Left (or Right) to Bull Valley".

Finally, "Bull Valley 1/2 mile ahead" and he looks at his watch—5 minutes early—sighs relief and turns into the driveway glimpsing Mildred peeking from behind the curtain.

"RATHER HAVE MY PUP"

Wally had been carefully briefed about the imminent arrival of his little sister, Marjorie. His mother was well aware of the danger of damaging his tender little ego by ending his reign as "only child".

"Wally," his father reassured him, "You'll have a new little playmate—someone who will always be here for you." Wally was noncommittal.

After the blessed event and when the household had settled back to its regular routine, Wally was ushered into the presence of his new, tiny, pink sister. He looked at her carefully as she wriggled in her crib and gooed at him.

"See, Wally, a little playmate all your own!" His parents eyed him anxiously.

Wally was thoughtful. He looked up at them, "Dad...Mom—I'd really rather have my pup!"

NICKEL A KISS

Wally has lunch sack in hand and is ready to walk across town to school. He is in Miss Madge Goode's second grade.

"Could I have a nickel, Mom?"

His mother knew that a small candy concession was operated out of superintendent Lockridge's office. One could get a giant Baby Ruth, Snickers or Mars bar for 5¢. Some kids came in from the country at an early hour and their long day sometimes meant they sort of ran out of fuel before they ran out of day.

"Well, yes, Wally—but I've talked with your father about you taking these nickels to school and he wonders if all those sweets are good for you."

Wally was puzzled. "I'm not buying candy, mother."

"Well, then, what are you doing with this money?"

"I give a nickel to Charlotte Heinrich and she gives me a kiss!"

"What! She gives you a kiss? Do other boys...Wally should you be doing this? Is this wise to spend your money for..."

[Author's comment: Was Wally getting his money's worth? What do you think? Charlotte is pictured **below**. Since she was 14 in this picture you must morph her back 6 years to imagine her at age 8. I think Wally got value for money.]

Fig. 2-21. 1936 PGHS Freshman Charlotte Heinrich 14.

Fig. 2-22. Wally Burger up on Sandy and Ralph Warnhoff on a pantomime mule, ca 1931. The "Bull Valley" adventure occurred about 10 years later.

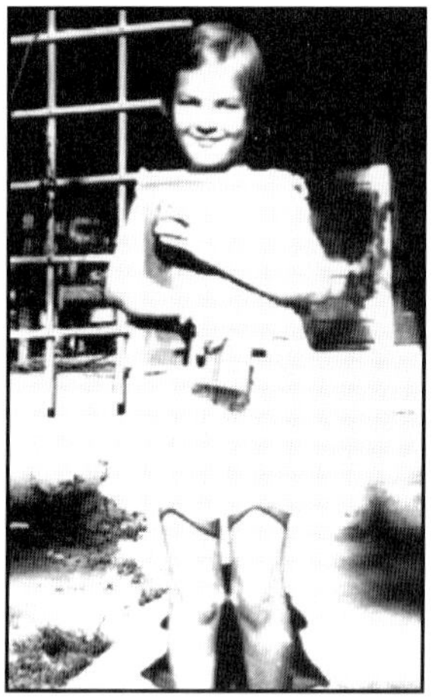

Figs. 2-23 & 2-24. Marjorie Burger. Left-First day at school, Sep 1932. Right-PGHS Graduation, May 1944. Marjorie is married to Jack Schmidt and lives in Overland Park, KS.

Fig. 2-25. Mary Louise Burger about 1941.

Fig. 2-26 Emil Bock and his wife Catherine - about 1940. Emil was Pilot Grove's longest serving Postmaster 1951-1973.

DA POSTMASTER

I visited with Mr. Bock in April of 1998 because he seemed to be the only one in town who could consistently identify folks in old photographs. I was amazed when he carefully studied my old photo and said, "That is so-and-so, this is his older brother and this is so-and-so." He not only scored high on his eyesight (I could hardly make out details of some the people), he has a superb memory. Some of these photos were decades old. Emil will celebrate his 93rd birthday in July 1998. He and Mrs. Bock still live in the comfortable house on Harris Street they moved into in 1938.

The Bocks spent some of their early married life operating a grocery store in Keytesville, MO before moving to Pilot Grove. Mr. Bock owned and operated a Standard Station for a number of years prior to selling out to Wayne Roach and taking the Pilot Grove Postmaster's job.

In addition to his long years of service with the U.S. Post Office, Emil was a founding member and served 25 years as a volunteer fireman.

They have seven children—Jim, Dorothy, Maurice, Gerald, Barbara, Margie, Bernice, and Judy.

Fig. 2-27. Mayor Barney J. Wessing has his headquarters all decked out for the holiday. The license plates says 1977.

B. J. Wessing
Fire Chief 47 years
Very Active Community Leader

BARNEY WESSING

MAYOR 1975-1989

Barney Wessing, after a half century service to the town and community, is now no longer in good health and is enjoying—as best he can—a well deserved retirement.

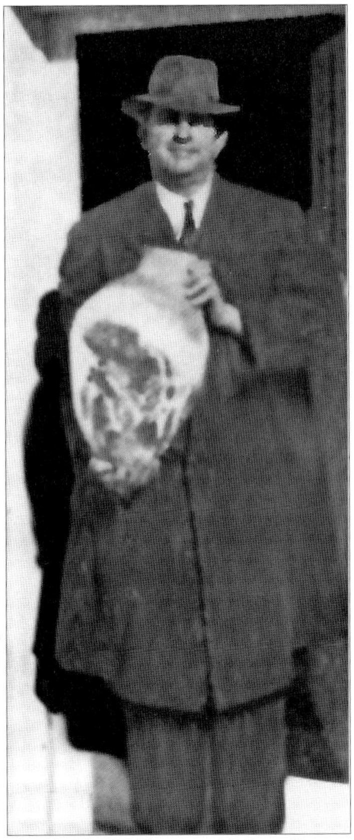

Fig. 2-28. Wallace and Mary Burger cured hundreds of award winning hams in the 30s.

DA BANKER

Fig. 2-29. Edgar Schupp was "Cashier" at the Citizens' Bank longer than any other cashier. Photo taken May 10th, 1985 for a Boonville newspaper article.

"Longin' fer da ole home town and da ole folks at home!"

—Steven Foster

OVERVIEW

At the end of each year, Time Magazine chooses a "Person of the Year" who is featured on their cover. This cover choice always initiates a fire storm of criticism—who was chosen, who was not chosen and why. The basis of the criticism is the erroneous assumption that that person is being honored. The Times says, "These people are important newsmakers and that alone is the basis for their selection.

I anticipate similar criticism, so let me be plain. These people herein are folks that *I remember*. There is no particular significance in their inclusion or in the order of their inclusion here. It is very unlikely that being mentioned in these pages will be a ticket to fame or fortune—nor will failure to be mentioned condemn anyone to the life of a pariah.

THE CHAPMANS

Eugene Wallace 'Chappie' Chapman, mentioned as my teacher and mentor in "Model Aeroplanes' in Chapter 5, lived with his mother Mame, across Fourth street from the Salmons. He had two older brothers Earl and Ernest that had gone off to seek their fortunes long before my time. Earl, the oldest, became a Superintendent of Schools at Chillicothe, MO. Earnest 'Peanuts' made a career in the Navy and was a survivor of the Japanese attack on Pearl Harbor.

Fig. 3-1. Wallace "Chappie" Chapman, 22 years old, November 1942. He wears the 2d Infantry Division "Indian Head" shoulder patch, PFC stripes and the French Fourragere (awarded the Second Division in WWI).

Fig. 3-2. Chappie's shoulder patch insignia— 2d Infantry Division.

Mame's husband Emery, had abandoned his undertaking business and his family when Wallace was 6-7 years old, and, it was whispered, gone to live in sin with a woman named Brown in Kansas City. Abandonment was the 'poor man's divorce' in those days.

Mame was a squat, red-faced imitation of one of Charles Dicken's harridan fishwives. She had a sharp tongue and a ear out for scandal and gossip. She once showed Mom how she kept her flashlight and clock beside her bed so she could note the time that the various kids on the street got home.

St. Joseph's Catholic Church was just off Fourth Street and about two blocks southwest of her home. Inevitably newlyweds and their wedding party departed the church to careen down our street, making a happy din of honking horns and clattering tin cans. Mame carefully noted the names and dates of these weddings. Then she would carefully count off 270 days and mark an "X" on the objective date for the new bride.

I overheard Mom and Mame talking about the war one day in 1942. Mame says, "God forbid they should ever come over here with their fighting. But I guess we'll be OK."

Mom asks, "How can you say we'll be OK?"

Well," Mame answers, "The nearest battlefield is at Boonville[1]. That's 12 miles away!"

[1] Captain Nathan Lyons, a Regular Army officer, led a small Union force in a successful attack on Confederates at Boonville in June 1861. There is a monument near the Lyric Theater commemorating this battle. Incidently this battle, which was fought on what is now the town golf course, caught Hiram Burnham (my great grandfather) in Boonville on a shopping trip. Hiram didn't get home for two days.

Fig. 3-3. Army Medics tend seriously wounded in the Normandy Bocage country. Chappie could have been one of these.

Fig. 3-4. In 1903, my mother started to school in this school building (demolished in the 1930s) north of the Katy depot. Mom was a schoolmate and lifelong friend of Sarah Morris who later married Hardy Coleman.

CHAPPIE

Chappie was 7 years older than me and was like a big brother. In addition to the Fokker Triplane mentioned in Chapter 5. He also taught me to build stern-wheeler paddle boats out of shingles, bean-shooters out of tree forks, slingshots from old leather shoe tongues and inner-tube bands.

We made kites by ironing waxed bread wrappers over a frame made of lathe strips and string. We made rubber band rifles out of an old board and a tacked-on clothes pin. We often took an old inner tube down to Kempf's 'Tin Shop' and when no one was looking, used their tin cutting guillotine to cut 200-300 rubber band 'bullets'. I know that I was often somewhat of a pest, but he was mostly patient and I cherished our pal-ship. I vividly remember that winter day in 1941 that marked the beginning of the end of our comradeship. It was an unseasonably pleasant Sunday afternoon in December. Chappie and I were in the street practicing passes with my football when his mother called him. I heard her say "...Pearl Harbor...Japs...". I ran home to find Mom grimly staring at the Crosley. It was December 7th, 1941. I was 14, Chappie was 21. He was off to war within the year.

He came home on leave (See Fig. 3-1. Dixie took this picture in his back yard.) One night at the movies (Casino theater in Boonville) he met a lovely young woman—Elizabeth Mary Hellinger. On his next leave they were married. After an short honeymoon he returned to his unit and shipped out for England to await the invasion. His bride kissed him good-bye never to see him again and I lost my mentor. There would be no more wind-up Fokker Triplanes, SPADs or anything else.

CHAPPIE COMES HOME

The sad closure of the Wallace Chapman story occurred on the 3rd of July 1944 in the "Bocage Country" —the hedgerows of Normandy. PFC Chapman, 33rd Infantry Regiment, 2d Infantry Division was struck by German shrapnel and severely wounded. Fig. 3-3. illustrates medics caring for wounded in Normandy. Chappie could have been one of these casualties.

He died two days later. His remains were repatriated as a part of a 1948 project to 'bring the boys home'. These 'boys' were in coffins. Chappie now lies beside his mother in the Pilot Grove Cemetery.

THE COLEMANS

The Colemans were descendants of some of the founders of Cooper County and the city of Pilot Grove. On February 20th, 1827 Enoch Moss received a land patent on some land roughly situated where the Herman Ries farm now lies. In 1838 he sold this land to Dr. Sam and Sarah Coleman[2]. A cemetery, long since closed, is located on this land and some of the Colemans were buried there. It was a grove of tall, somewhat scraggly trees on this land and adjacent to the Katy tracks that may have given Pilot Grove its name. Elementary school teachers pointed this out to us in the 1930s and I had taken it as settled fact. It appears that it may not be[3]. Several other theories exist. I will not quibble. I am simply going to assign THE Pilot Grove to the Coleman land.

Morris, the older son, must have graduated PGHS in 1936 or so. Morris never knew me, but I admired him for his personal drive.

He had an unrelenting ambition to go to college. I'm sure that his family would help, but Morris took an arduous and dangerous job at the McDowell Quarry, one of the few going concerns in the county. He had an outgoing and positive personality along with dogged deter-

[2] Pilot Grove Centennial Book, page 5.
[3] ibid

Fig. 3-5. Suzanne Coleman, class of '41 spring 1941.

Fig. 3-6. Barbara Coleman Class of '46 - spring 1945.

Fig. 3-7. Carole Coleman Class of '48 - spring 1945.

mination and was greatly respected by the Pilot Grovans who knew his story.

Morris graduated college right into World War II. He was trained as a Naval Aviator and was good enough to become a flight instructor at Naval Air Station Miramar near San Diego. Miramar is now the home of the Navy's "Top Gun" (carrier fighter pilot) school.

He set up his younger sister Suzanne for tragedy when he brought a college chum home to meet her. They married, but. Lt. Ritchie was killed in a B-25 crash in the Philippines and Suzanne became an early W.W.II Gold Star winner. Morris' younger brother Bill graduated in 1938. He, along with a lot of the older guys, used to go out to the Horseshoe Bend swimming hole.

Bill greatly peeved me one summer when he returned to town and allegedly told a story of having saved me from drowning. I was peeved because it wasn't true and such a story could, and nearly did, get me grounded. But mostly I was puzzled. I could swim better than most and could remember no incident that could have been construed as 'saving Sonny Salmon from drowning'. My take was that he had grabbed someone floundering in the creek, jerked them out and had mistaken him for me. Or ... maybe he was just B.S.ing with some of the hangers-on at Schweitzer's filling station and someone made a bigger story out of it than he intended. At any rate, Bill soon was off to do his war service and all was soon forgotten about the 'drowning' incident.

Of the three Coleman girls, Suzanne was the oldest and graduated with my sister Dixie in 1941. Because she was an exalted senior when I was still in Junior High, I only knew her from afar. But, it is said, "even a dog may *look upon* a queen". She was a classic beauty and I rated her as 'very sophisticated older woman'. She was 18.

Carole was possibly the prettiest of the girls, a real cutie with a pert, turned up nose. But the guys of my class usually exhibited the same disdain for the 'children' of Junior High that the older girls held for us when we were there. Never mind that these rosebuds were becoming full bloomed roses.

Barbara was nearer my age—class of 1946. If Wheaties had wanted a photo of an 'All American Girl' for their cereal boxes, they could not have done better than Barbara. Oozing vitality, she had beautiful strawberry blonde hair, a pixiesque twinkle in her soft brown eyes, a stunning smile (at least it stunned me) and a light golden complexion with just enough freckles to make a guy want to kiss her. The thing I most remember about her was her boundless energy. It is probably a good thing that girls basketball rules were so restrictive in those days, she would have really run all over the opposition—she tended to do so anyway.

I was self-conscious and embarrassed when I was around her. My heart was usually doing a tintinnabulation like clog dancers on a hardwood floor. I was afraid she would see my shirt front thumping. Sadly, shy Sonny never got up the courage to ask her for a date.

Fifty years later, while rummaging through old school artifacts to find the exact composition of the 1944 PGHS boys championship basketball team, I found a souvenir program. Many people had autographed this December 1944 CCAA Tournament Program (held at Pilot Grove). One autograph was— "Barbara Coleman—Hi there Sonnie! What's cookin' good lookin'."

Being older and wiser I now see evidence of an enchanting coquette to which the old Sonny was boorishly insensitive. Well, anyway, if 1944 ever rolls around again ...

Fig. 3-8. Grace Quinlan (at right) was the first resident of the newly opened Katy Manor. Shown here later with a fellow resident and the Administrator.

THE QUINLANS

A family that I admired for their 'grace in adversity', was the Quinlans. I remember that Friday the sixth of January 1933. Dad came home from work and told us that Raymond Quinlan had drowned in a boating accident on the Lamine. Mr. Quinlan was 36 and left seven children.

I was a contemporary at PGHS with Doris. Marjorie was older and graduated in 1940. I knew Jerry in Boonville when I returned to Missouri and was attending MU Columbia. He was a meat-cutter (at A&P?) where I occasionally stopped for chit-chat while grocery shopping.

Jerry had an extra helping of the Quinlan personality—energetic, ambitious, outgoing, an extremely likable fellow. I was happy to know some years later he got into a profession where he could use those attributes—real estate.

Not long after Wilbur got into the barbering profession, he established himself as the Studs Terkel-like[4] oral historian of the Pilot Grove metropolitan area. I have said before that this work is *not* a history of Pilot Grove. If I had Wilbur's knowledge and story-telling ability, maybe it *could* be.

There must be something about the barbering profession that creates story tellers. My barber and old friend Vern Klenklen is also an excellent raconteur.

When I went to my father's funeral in April 1940, I was twelve years old, about the same age as Wilbur when he lost his father. At the funeral, some well-intentioned matron patted me on the back and said, "Now you're the man of the family, Sonny. You'll have to fill your Daddy's shoes." I pondered on this.

[4] Studs Terkel created a new literary genre with his tape-recorded, first hand witnesses to history. cf "Division Street", "The Good War", "Talking to Myself" and others. These were stories about and by little people told in their own words.

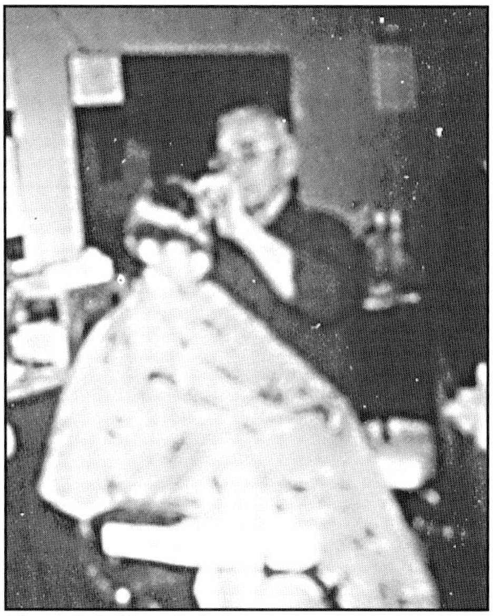

Fig. 3-9. Wilbur Quinlan works his magic on one of Pilot Grove's little inheritors.

We returned home. I found a pair of my Daddy's one pair of 'Sunday-go-to-meetin'" shoes. They were black, had a nice shine and were rather long with a blunt toe.

I sat on my little stool, took off my right shoe and inserted my foot into Dad's shoe. It was far too big! To my great disappointment I could not fill it!

I wonder if Wilbur felt like this. I remember him delivering groceries on a weird looking bicycle. It had a regular 26" wheel in back but a tiny, 12 inch wheel in front with a huge wire basket over it. He peddled around town delivering for Heinrich's. He must have been 12-13 at the time.

I had hoped, in these reminiscences, to include some of the stories that Wilbur tells so well. The logistics proved too difficult—Wilbur has enough to do without spending the necessary time with me. I still pray that he will some day put down on paper for us all the stories from his amazing memory of the people and events of our old hometown.

Wilma was much younger than me and other than noting that she was a very pretty girl like her older sisters, I have little recollection of her from High School. Doris, however, I remember well. She does

[5] You may not find this in your dictionary—*boadaceous* is derived from *Boadicea* who was the legendary queen of the Iceni tribe in Britain. She led a brave but failed revolt against the Romans in 67AD. Her exquisitely proportioned body is now cast in bronze driving a three horse chariot at the north end of the Westminster Bridge in London. She is a model of feminine beauty, therefore, I suppose"boadaceous" means Boadicea-like.

Fig. 3-10. LEFT Doris Quinlan, graduation photo, 1944. RIGHT Jerry, Doris and Wilbur Quinlan in the limousine about 1940..

Fig. 3-11. Bernard "Bud" Kempf (Driving), Roy Lammers Jr., LaVahn "Bonnie" Klenklen (left) and Doris Quinlan. Ca. 1944.

Fig. 3-12. Wilbur Quinlan and nephew Randy Koonse, 1973. Wilbur got first prize for this lovely beard.

not know this but she helped me solve a mystery that had greatly puzzled me when I was about 14 years old. The mystery was: what in the world did the guys see in watching *girls* basketball?

When the boys finished their game, they showered and changed quickly not to miss any of the girls' game.

Then the PGHS girls team took the floor in royal blue shorts and white satin blouses. Doris led the team out and I understood. I'll have to search for a word to describe them—how about *boadaceous*[5]? What beautiful young women! There were a lot of pretty girls on the team that year as in other years. It's just that I have that image of Doris registered in my memory cells.

Anyway, now I knew why girls' basketball was so popular among my friends of the rougher gender.

Doris Quinlan and Bonnie Klenklen (Vern's twin sister) were among the group that sat on the curb in front of Pop Tracy's Cafe on warm summer nights in 1943. We entertained ourselves by telling stories. I had a repertoire of 'Cherman' jokes which I told with an atrocious German accent. Doris and Bonnie, full of graciousness and good humor considered the jokes good enough for a laugh. See Fig. 3-11. for some of that crew.

In the summer of 1995 Bob was giving me a busman's tour of Pilot Grove—I marveled at all the new street signs and I learned some street names that I had never known. We happened by Doris and her husband Kenneth. They had just completed their new home on College Street and offered a tour. We accepted and were treated to a delightful exhibition of their dream home.

I came away with two unrelated impressions—the expanse of porch (verandah?) on three sides of the house. A beautiful touch but very unusual and I wondered at the inspiration. Then I conjured up a 1930s memory of walking barefoot in the southwestern quadrant of town—down the street past the Quinlan home where the street gave out to a narrow track and proceeded to join College Street at the corner of Uncle Shelby's lot.

By the way, wandering around aimlessly was one of the blessings of growing up in a little town during the depression. Preadolescent kids like myself rambled around town like stray dogs without a thought of danger. There was no danger! The greatest danger in a place like Pilot Grove during our passage through the 1930s was the risk of being bored to death!

I rambled by the old Quinlan homeplace—it was a large, two-story, frame house of a battleship bluish gray hue and had an expansive front porch. Soooo, the porches

[5] Derived from *Boadicea*, queen of the Iceni tribe in Britain. She led a brave but vain revolt against the Romans in 67AD. Her exquisitely proportioned body, cast in bronze, drives a three horse chariot at the north end of London's Westminster Bridge. She is a model of feminine beauty, hence "boadaceous" =Boadicea-like.

Fig. 3-13. Kenny was a lifelong member of the Marine Parachute Regiment Association.

Fig. 3-14. Kenny won the Purple Heart on Iwo Jima.

Fig. 3-15. Marine Memorial in Arlington - Raising the flag on Suribachi.

are a manifestation of nostalgic childhood memories?

The other thing that stuck in my memory was Doris herself. I would presume that she had suffered at least an average amount of travail, distress and tribulation that we are all heir to—if so, she bore it well! She was the same happy, smiling, mirthful, gracious and beautiful woman I remember from a half century ago.

DORIS AND KENNY

After graduation and some further training, Doris took a job with an insurance company in Kansas City, "...near the Union Station," she said. She usually went home on the weekends and for a time commuted with Doctor Sandy who was the Medical Director at the Pratt and Whitney defense plant.

At the end of the war, when the boys were flooding home with victory smiles on their faces, she met Kenneth Koonse, a discharged Marine. They were married in 1946. I've heard rumored that Doris' mother hand crafted a wedding gown from Kenny's parachute. By the time their Golden Wedding Anniversary rolled around they had five children and four grandchildren. Sadly, Kenneth passed away in 1997.

I tell a little bit of Kenny's story below. Here's why: I sometimes have nightmares as I reminisce about the 30s and 40s. I cherish my memories of the 1930s Great Depression and 1940s Great War—eating stones and spitting bullets—but I would hardly care to relive that era.

The nightmare is that our grandchildren or great-grandchildren do it all again. Paraphrasing the philosopher George Santyana, "Those who forget their history are doomed to relive it." To help inoculate them, I have

Continued on page 33.

Fig. 3-16. The Doris Quinlan - Kenny Koonse wedding party 1946. L-R Bernard Eichelberger (Best Man), Wilma Quinlan, Doris, Kenny, Wilbur Quinlan.

Fig. 3-17. Tournament Champs—The Pilot Grove Tigers, who won the CCAA Tournament are (L-R) Roger Quesenberry, ALAN KOONSE, Harold Lammers, Kenny Meisenheimer and Dave Wendleton. February 1967. Basketball aces run in the family!

Fig. 3-18. C.A. Coley drives Pilot Grove's firetruck as W.W. Burger (at left, hanging on the side) introduces Santa Claus (a.k.a. Homer Chamberlin, Les' Dad). Christmas season 1936 or 1937. Photo - Wally Burger.

Fig. 3-19. Jo Ellen Coley 1942 Graduation photo. Yearbook annotation: "She speaks and acts just like she thinks."

THE COLEYS

The Coley family lived across Fourth Street from us from the mid-1930s to the early 1940s. Jo Ellen was a gifted pianist and maybe won some kind of award—explaining the crown in photo right.

Jo Ellen's father, C.A. Coley was a telephone lineman in Pilot Grove and was my Scoutmaster (Wolf Patrol, Troop 76 in 1939). He was a WWI veteran and enlisted in the Navy's Sea Bees (Construction Battalions) after Pearl Harbor. He served in the Pacific.

He returned to his lineman trade after the war. Sadly, in a tragic accident, he tangled with a high voltage line and was killed several years later.

My brother Bob some months ago told me he had seen Jo Ellen in Pilot Grove. He said she was just as pretty as we remembered her in high school.

Sadly, Jo Ellen passed away in June 1998 and now lies beside her beloved "Gene' in St. Joseph Cemetery.

LEFT—Neil Coley was a playmate. He once built a telegraph set from junk wire, batteries, a 10-penny nail and a board. Neil would have graduated with my brother Bob in 1947 but the family moved away sometime after 1942. The pictures at left are from the 1942 "Tiger" Yearbook. Photo at right is from Marjorie Burger Schmidt.

Fig. 3-20. Neil Coley, 8th grader in 1942.

Fig. 3-21. Jo Ellen Coley 1937.

Fig. 3-22. Santa visits Pilot Grove's little crumb crunchers - December 16th, 1933.

included a few stories in these reminiscences about real Pilot Grove people which may teach better than dry history books. Kenny Koonse was one of those real people.

Kenny volunteered and trained in 1943 for the Marine Parachute Regiment. Through the war in the Pacific, he was fortunate (or unfortunate, depending upon whom you ask) that the Marine parachutists were not used much. He transferred to the 5th Marine Division and participated in the landings on Tinian and Saipan.

On 19 February 1945, the Fifth Marine Amphibious Corp (3rd, 4th and (Kenny's) 5th Marine Division) launched an amphibious assault on Iwo Jima; Iwo Jima, located 750 mi south of Tokyo, has an area of 8 sq mi and a maximum elevation, Mount Suribachi, of 546 ft.

The Japanese had three airfields on Iwo Jima from which they bombed U.S. bases in the Mariannas. More important was the need for emergency airfields by B-29 bombers as they returned from bombing runs on Japan.

Total Marine casualties at Iwo Jima were 24,891 (including Kenny, who won a Purple Heart there). This included 6,821 dead. The Japanese forces, numbering around 21,000, were almost totally annihilated. The total bag of Japanese prisoners was taken off the island by one small landing craft. It was a bloody price, but by the end of the Pacific war, 2,251 B-29 bombers carrying 24,761 crewmen had made emergency landings on Iwo Jima.

The American flag being raised on Suribachi was the basis for the famous sculpture in Arlington, Va. The U.S. Navy controlled Iwo Jima until its return to Japan in 1968.

SEMPER FI!

THE TWENTERS

In early December 1933 the dreary weather with gloomy skies and chilling damp was only partially offset by the warmth of the Christmas season. Even as depressed as times were, all the kids knew there would be a few things under the tree and when we went back to school we could compare 'I gots me' items with schoolmates. "I gots me a BB gun." "I gots me a cowboy suit!" "I gots me a scooter!" "I gots me a set of Tinkertoys!"

On Saturday morning 16th of December, the town fathers sponsored a Santa Claus visit in a ceremony at the Oerly Coal, Ice House and Truck Scales facility. Santa and his helpers—Councilman Wallace Burger, officiating—passed out a bag of treats to each of the town kids. This bag contained about one pound of hard candy, filberts, almonds, walnuts, pecans plus one orange and attracted a long and appreciative line of the town's little inheritors.

But an event during this particular Holiday Season cast a pall over the warm glow of anticipation that we all felt. On December 23rd a terrible traffic accident took the life of two town fathers and breadwinners. Dan Twenter and Frank Schuster were killed outright when their truck was broadsided by an oncoming Graham Paige Coupe as they were making a left turn from the westbound lane of US40 highway onto Route M, the westernmost Pilot Grove access road. It was late afternoon on a gloomy winter day and visibility was poor. Dan was 38 years old. Frank was 53.

Mrs. Twenter was now left, at Christmas time, pregnant (Mary Helen was born in the new year) and with a house full of boys and young men. Ralphie was about 3 years old, Wilbur was a bit older than me. Henry Twenter was about Dixie's age. (I mention Wilbur later in a Christmas 1944 story.) Leonard was the eldest son.

The tragedy was bad enough but occurring in the Christmas season made it seem far worse.

Neighbors and relatives rallied and there were profuse expressions of sorrow, condolences and grief. There were gifts and food packets galore. I went with Mom to deliver a basket of foodstuffs and several popcorn balls that Dixie, Bob and I had helped make for the holiday. Something strange transpired at that visit.

I helped lug the basket to the Twenter's home which was just two doors east of our place. Being invited in, we set it on the kitchen floor. Mom expressed our condolences at her loss and Mrs. Twenter thanked us for our consideration. She and the older boys were very courteous and gracious. But there was an indefinable coolness. I thought so at the time and Mom confirmed it when we returned home and she was giving Dad an account.

He said, "Well, the family has just loss their father.

Mrs. Twenter has lost a husband. You wouldn't expect them to be in a party mood!" We let it go at that.

Seven years later the Salmon family went through a similar experience. Dad died in the Katy hospital in Parsons, Kansas in April of 1940. In the aftermath I came to better empathized with the Twenters' feelings. As neighbor after neighbor came by our place to give their condolences for the lost of our father and breadwinner, we were grateful for the concern and greatly appreciated the food. There was, however, a niggling feeling of bitterness and suspicion that we were being considered objects of charity. I subconsciously resented it, and though I was only 12 years old I recognized instinctively that the ultimate humiliation of a man is to have his family responsibilities taken on by outsiders.

I realize that this shame is almost totally unknown today. But in those days self-reliant people rejected charity except as an absolute last resort. That was our feelings and I suspect it was the feelings of the Twenters also. As their subsequent lives played out, they demonstrated that their feelings of self-reliance were justified.

THE TWENTERS - EPILOGUE

Mary Twenter and her family offer an admirable example of successfully coping with disaster which is thought to be a universal American trait but is not.

Mary's sons immediately set to work to pick up the slack. Leonard, at 17 the eldest, had been helping his grandfather on the family farmstead. He remained there and contributed to the family as he could. He farmed that land until his death in 1995.

Henry, then 14, began working for Barney Wessing in the Ice and Coal business that Barney had purchased from Fred Oerly. He worked there until he was drafted in WWII and served in Patton's Third Army—13th Armored Division in Northern France and Germany. Henry didn't tell me this but he may owe his survival to a change in U.S tactics at about the time that his armored division entered Germany. See side-bar right.

Henry returned to B.J. Wessing for a few years after the war then began farming out on the old Mile Corner Road. His son now runs the farm. He took his job as a rural letter carrier in 1960 then retired to a pleasant home in Pilot Grove after over 30 years service.

Wilbur recovered from his harrowing encounter with Sepp Diedrick's 6th Panzer Army (See "The Secty of War regrets..." Ch. 8.) and returned to Pilot Grove to marry and start a family. He worked in a furniture business in Springfield for a number of years. He retired in 1994, built a home in Pilot Grove but sadly, only lived six months to enjoy it.

NEW TACTICS AFTER THE BULGE

As American battle units began moving into Germany following the recovery from the Battle of the Bulge, fanatical resistance, particularly from German SS Divisions, slowed progress.

A small group of Germans could fire a Panzerfaust or an 88 anti-tank round and the entire American column had to stop while infantry were sent forward to take the town, building by building. This often took 3-4 days and cost casualties.

At Bitburg in the western edge of Germany's Eifel Forest, this tactic was revised. Patton did not like his armored columns stopping for *anything* and he certainly couldn't permit 2-3 anti-tank gunners halting the march of his mighty Third Army.

At Bitburg, the German SS Division—Totenkopf (Death's Head)—prepared to defend the town "to the death". Totenkopf was made up of 14-16 year old fanatical Hitler Jungen (Hitler Youth).

Patton's leading tank column was fired upon at their entrance to the old town. But, this time—rather than deploying infantry to hazard their way through the town—a report went up the chain of command and the tactic changed.

Unfortunately for Totenkopf, in recent weeks the logistic trains had caught up. Ammunition was abundant. Orders came down to Bitburg—pull back one mile and fire marking shells on the town.

In minutes, division artillery (36 105mm and 18 155mm howitzers), Corps artillery (about 150 guns of various caliber), Army artillery (about 200 very large caliber guns) plus 15-20 fighter-bombers of the 9th Air Force—began unloading on Bitburg. In three hours, nothing was left standing. The Third Army resumed its march.

Armband, SS Division "Totenkopf".

Little Ralphie, was 3 when Mom, Bob and I carried a token of our condolences to the widow and her boys in the sad Christmas period. Ralph has done very well in the lumber business. He has owned and operated what was originally the C.J. Harris Lumber Company since the 1970s. He is married and lives in Pilot Grove.

Mary Helen, the baby of the family, never knew her father. She was born several months after his accident. She worked a while at Deck's Drug Store during and after her tenure at Pilot Grove High School.

She married Vernon Knedgen and lives in Clear Creek with her family.

Fig. 3-23. Shoulder patch of Henry Twenter's 13th Armored Division of Patton's Third Army. The three colors—yellow, red and blue—represent the cavalry, artillery and infantry respectively.

Fig. 3-23. Born too soon. Jim Sousley might have been on the Grand Ole Opry in a later era.

SAFETY NET

I have said elsewhere that in the 1930s there was no "safety net" for families that had catastrophes befall them. This is not entirely correct. Henry Twenter told me of a government (State?) sponsored "Sewing Room" that operated in Pilot Grove in the early 1930's. Mrs. Mary Barnes (Dr. W.S. Barnes' wife) supervised this facility for a time.

Presumably it was no longer in operation in 1940 when my mother was widowed. She certainly would have been there as she was a very good seamstress and made all my shirts until I was in high school.

Of course, the Roosevelt administration initiated a program to assist families with dependent children (AFDC) and late in the decade a program to distribute commodity surpluses was of some value although this was mostly a scheme to unload excess farm products.

THE SOUSLEYS

Tom Sousley moved into Pilot Grove with his three nearly-grown kids in the mid 1930s. Old Tom had suffered the grievous loss of his wife and newborn at childbirth in their hometown of Versailles. I supposed he just wanted a change of scenery because there was no more work in Pilot Grove than in the Versailles-Eldon area.

They lived in a modest house directly behind the Chapmans. I knew their place well because my best pal, Homer Jeffress, had lived there with his family until the year before. The Jeffresses had moved because the evil and much maligned landlord 'Mr. Snake' (his name was Schnecht which was close enough to 'snake' to let their hostility make the substitution) had the temerity to demand his monthly rent. The Jeffresses had been abandoned by the father when their fifth child—pretty little Ruthie—was born. There were no 'safety nets' in the 1930s.

Tom Sousley's little family consisted of Jim, May and Marjorie. When years later I heard a quote attributed to Dorothy Parker—"You can never be too rich or too thin" I thought of Marjorie. She was never in any danger of being too rich but she may have been right at the edge of "too thin". She was a very pretty girl but slender to a fault, a child of the 'hungry 30s'. She was born 40 years too soon. Later, in the 70s and 80s, she could have made a fortune as a 'waif' fashion model. However, in the 1930s starvation was not yet a fashion statement.

Fortunately for Tom, his older daughter May gave incontestable evidence that he was not starving his kids. May was very well developed with curves in all the right places.

Although Jim was much older than me and I could not say that he was within my circle of chums, he was much admired by us all. Here's why: In the summer of 1937 Jim, lacking any gainful employment opportunities in or near Pilot Grove, did what thousands of others did. He caught a west bound freight and 'rode the rails' to seek his fortune. He found work in Colorado and spent the summer there working on a ranch.

He returned in the fall with three new assets—a white, ten-gallon cowboy hat very much like Ken Maynard wore in the movies that Bob and Bill Egender brought to Pilot Grove; a five dollar Fender guitar (try finding a $5 Fender guitar today!) and a modest repertoire of country and western songs.

In the warm evenings of September we would hang out down town, spending our nickels at Pop Tracy's Cafe for Smoozies and Fudgicles, then watch for Jim and his guitar. He often took up venue in front of Heinrich's store.

He could sing all the old favorites: Red River Valley, Red Wing, Birmingham Jail, etc. He had learned and perfected 2-3 chords. He used these same chords on all his songs. Steadying himself with one foot behind him on the trunk of one of the large maples[6] that grew on Main Street, he would adjust his Stetson and commence the concert. He always drew a crowd, not so much because he was a terrific musician but because amusements and diversions in Pilot Grove were very scarce. ...And, he wasn't bad. Besides, what've ya got better to do?

I've heard 'buskers'[7] in the London underground who were not nearly so good and they made $50-100 a day! Jim didn't get a dime!

Jim's sister May ultimately married a guy who did very well at Armco Steel and is now sharing his retirement in Independence. With her good looks I knew she would do okay. Her younger sister Marjorie married Raymond Bader and raised a bunch of good-looking kids.

In the fall of 1941, 18 months after Dad's death, Slim Wassmann salvaged 100-200 ties and stacked them in our back garden. Old Tom was one of a log sawing crew that worked them up for the 'Widder' Salmon's firewood. In that project Tom suffered a painful and distressing wound.

Slim, possibly propelled by a misplaced sense of guilt—upon Dad's death, Slim got his job—organized this firewood cutting project. The railroad characteristically discarded old cross-ties as waste and was very happy to have anyone drag them off the right-of-way. He enlisted Louie Walje, one of his section hands, Tom Sousley and Herbie Shoen.

Herb had an old Model T Ford truck with everything back of the cab stripped off and a home made sawmill rigged. The giant saw blade was driven by a power take-off.

Herb was now in legitimate pursuits. Just before the country changed its mind on Prohibition, Herb had been 'detained at the Governor's pleasure' for a year and a day down at Jeff City for a crime that no longer existed—he had seized the entrepreneurial opportunity to provision a thirsty community with a much needed commodity—corn whiskey. Herb was of the stock that made this country great. A year in the slammer never diminished the esteem in which he was held.

Slim admonished me sternly to stay away from the cutting operation. I was 14. I wanted to be treated as an adult but Slim would not have it. In fact, if the OSHA of today were to inspect such a facility—unguarded blade, no power control or shut off—it would have been shut down and the proprietors sent to prison. It was a disaster waiting to happen!

As Louie and Tom fed a cross-tie into the saw the screaming blade would often hit an imbedded rock. They hit old pieces of spikes that had broken off in the tie. They broke teeth off the saw blade. They used an unbalanced blade that wobbled alarmingly. With 120 pounds of deadweight cross-tie it was an arduous and hazardous job skidding the ties through the blade.

Of course, the inevitable happened. Working over uneven ground, Tom lost his footing as he approached the blade with his end of the tie. He stumbled, lurching into the blade. The teeth went through the thin fabric of his overalls and bit deeply into his thigh.

Herb got the saw shut down. They got an improvised tourniquet on the leg and sent me up the street for Dr. Sandy. Dr. Sandy then lived at the 4th Street corner opposite the school. Slim and Louie made a 'fireman's carry' with their hands and, lifting Tom bodily, carried him home to await the doctor. Thanks be, the wound was not so deep as it appeared to be, based on the bleeding. No tendons were cut and Tom made a full recovery and lived a long and full life—into his 90s. I suspect, however, he declined further sawmill opportunities.

THE BADERS

The patriarch of the Bader family was 'Johnny Pete'. He was well into years when I knew him. His first wife and the mother of his kids was already deceased. Johnny Pete had one bad eye—destroyed by accident, cataracts or disease—I never knew. This 'cotton-eye' along with his rugged and ruddy face scared hell out of the kids and he was not much bothered by Halloween Trick or Treaters.

Johnny Pete had several children: Otto, Orville, Raymond and Chester. (I describe Chester's tragedy elsewhere) I don't know if there were others.

Otto, called 'Tootle' by his friends, lived with his family two doors west of our old home place on Fourth Street. I can remember the older girls. They were real cute but younger than me, just children when I was in High School. Otto was married to one of the Scheidt girls and it was his wife's brother, 'Heinie' Scheidt that figured in another tragedy for the Bader family.

In 1936, Otto owned a 2-1/2 ton truck and made a living in the transport business. He was dealing with some matter at the C.J. Harris Lumber Company one summer afternoon. As he finished and mounted his truck to return home, Heinie came running out of the lumber yard and yelled to Otto to wait up for him. Otto didn't hear and started off. Heinie jumped for the running board, lost his footing and fell into the path of the rear duals. The wheels passed over his head. Heinie never regained con-

[6] Elwood Gerke cut down these trees around 1970 and nearly got lynched by some of the town preservationists.

[7] Buskers - Street musicians.

sciousness and died 2-3 days later.

Orville and Raymond ran an auto repair business for a number of years in an ancient, ramshackle barn of a building that had been one of Pilot Grove's livery stables in the last century. This old livery stable was owned in the 1920s by Bruce Davis whose son Ellis helped run it. It stood on the south side of Second Street near C.J. Harris Lumber Yard.

A story, probably apocryphal, was told of a Livery Stable transaction that the younger Davis had with an old German farmer—Mr. Fogelpohl[8].

You should understand that long before I had heard of the stereotypical tightness of Scotsmen, I knew of the frugality of the Germans. Mr. Fogelpohl was no exception and on that day was determined to get the best possible rate for boarding his old nag for a week. He finally negotiated Mr. Davis down to one dollar for the week. But before Davis could shake on the deal Fogelpohl added, "Mr. Davis, mit dot rate I must haff all der manure...for mein roses."

Mr. Davis replied, "Mr. Fogelpohl, at one dollar for the week there isn't going to be any manure!"

Orville Bader had had some sort of accident when he was younger which affected his gait. It may have affected his pelvic bones. If you've ever driven behind a pickup with a badly sprung frame you'll get the idea. He waddled a little. Someone said that an auto had fallen on him. Someone else said he had ruptured himself by lifting a Model A Ford. He also had a speech impediment which I had also attributed to the accident though on more careful thought it probably was not.

Orville was in Pop Tracy's Cafe every morning for his coffee break and always ordered the same thing—"cup of coffee and a piece of apple pie." Only he pronounced it "Opple" pie. Seizing upon this small idiosyncrasy we street urchins nicknamed him "Opples".

Raymond worked with him for many years but also kept a weather eye out for other entrepreneurial opportunities. Raymond had a withered leg, a congenital defect, and had to get around on crutches, thus his horizons were limited. Again, the social safety net had not yet been invented.

When Bob and 'Bill' Egender began bringing their 'movin' pitcher show' to town, Raymond bought an ancient popcorn machine and sold freshly popped, hot buttered popcorn in the movie house. The winter venue for the movies was the old garage next to the Standard station on First Street. Bob and Bill never failed to extract a

Fig. 3-24. Raymond Bader's "Dime Bag" was not so fancy as this. He used a brown paper sack.

pile of dimes from all the kids and not a few adults.

Bill's real name was Wilhelmina. She and Bob were in their late 20s or early 30s and were a handsome couple, but they, like everyone else, had to work very hard to scratch out a living. They had an old Ford panel truck in which they hauled around an equally ancient film projector. They made a circuit of the little towns in central Missouri and once a week brought a couple of hours of amusement to mirth-starved people.

I particularly remember one bitter December night when I braved the piercing winter winds to see the weekly 'pitcher show'. Bob 'n Bill had taken note of the faithful attendance and had bumped up admission to 15¢. I had a quarter. At the intermission—they only had one projector and had to turn on the lights to change the reel after the cartoon and the Tarzan serial—I clutched my 10¢ change in my hot little hand and rushed back to Raymond's popcorn concession.

Raymond had found an antique popcorn machine, cleaned it up and demonstrated his mechanical wizardry by overhauled the mechanism. He was dealing out bags of popcorn at 10¢ the bag—the original 'dime bag'.

Raymond says, "Hello there Sonny, how many?"

"Just one sir."

"You want butter on that?" He was waving a metal syrup dispenser with flip top lid.

I was suspicious, "What's that?"

"Popcorn butter, Sonny. Now do you want some or not? No extra cost."

That was all the reassurance I needed, "Pour it on." He upended the dispenser and glug-glugged about a half cup of flavored cooking oil onto my popcorn.

[8] Fogelpohl Hill is named for this family.

As I ate my way about half way through the bag I could see this was solid grease. It was dripping through the bag and the popcorn didn't taste all that good any more. I thought of sharing the rest of it with my pal Homer Jeffress, but I fought off that charitable feeling. I spent my last dime on this and I'm gonna eat it all! That night I had my first episode of a middle age affliction—a world class case of heartburn.

Homer and his little sister Barbara attempted to break the Bader monopoly in popcorn by bringing their own. They would present themselves to the ticket seller equipped with a half-peck grocery bag of popcorn and a quart mason jar of Koolaid. Popcorn was cheap, but it was mostly sold 'on the cob'. Shelling popcorn was not a job for sissies. Those little round kernels were affixed to the cob with some kind of celestial glue and if you shelled more than an ear or two you would wear a blister on the heal of your palm. But the challenge to Mr. Bader failed and soon Homer and Barbara were coughing up their dimes like all the rest of us.

A final note on this Bader family vignette: The name Bader, I believe, is of English origin. In England, it is pronounced as though it were spelled Badder e.g., when we were kids, you were bad, but I was even badder.

One January while we lived in England, the Queen, in her New Years honors list, awarded Douglas Bader a knighthood. He is now to be addressed as 'Sir Douglas'.

Bader was a Squadron Leader and a hero of the RAF in the 1940-1941 Battle of Britain. Early in the war he had destroyed half a dozen German Messerschmitts. In 1942 he was shot down over England and lost both legs in the crash. After a long recuperation and rehabilitation, he demanded and was eventually permitted to fly his Spitfire again—with two wooden legs! This says something about the desperation of the Brits during the 'Battle of Britain'.

After a number of additional victories he was again shot down, this time over Germany. As this legless ace fighter pilot was taken into the POW Stalag, his captors joked with him, "We got your bottom half two years ago. Now we have your top half."

Are the Pilot Grove Baders kin to him? You never know. If I were them, I'd say, "Yep, fifth cousin three times removed on Dad's side, don't you know?"

PISTOL WILSON—HOW HE GOT HIS NAME

In the 30s and early 40s before all the boys went off to war, a traditional annual Pilot Grove 'turkey shoot' was held in Ries' field about where the telephone warehouse now stands. Entrants paid a dollar or so, brought their own guns and participated in several events. The main event was shotgun trials but there was also a pistol competition.

Wesley Wilson entered the pistol event and won it by a wide margin. He had an old .22 caliber 7-shot revolver that seemed to be charmed that day. Nearly every shot rang the bell. He collected his turkey and went home. At the end of the day one of the judges was looking at the bell next to Wesley's firing position. "Hey Joe, come look at this!" The bell on the target post next to Wesley's was dented on the side. This could not be! The bells were hung at the back of a 4 x 4 post at the exit of a 1 inch hole bored through the post front to back. The objective was to put a bullet through the 1 inch hole and ring the bell. At 20 paces and especially with the old klunker pistols that were being used—this was very, very difficult. This was why everyone was so surprised at Wesley's outstanding marksmanship.

"Marksman hell, he just shot at the bell on the next post. He had a 5 inch target instead of the 1 inch he was supposed to shoot at. The wonder was not that he rang the bell so often. The wonder was that he ever missed! Well, too late now. Next year we have to do these pistol targets a little differently."

So Wesley was spared the ignominy of losing his turkey. No one wanted to confront him, but from that day ever forward he was known by the nickname, "Pistol".

OLE FOGELPOHL'S HORSEWHUPPIN'

The old Fogelpohl place stood just off what is now Route M, 3-4 miles northwest of Pilot Grove. Nearly all the family had died or moved by my time so I never knew them except by reputation. The story of Ole Man Fogelpohl and the livery stable may not be true but it was characteristic of the storied tightfistedness of the old gentleman.

The old man came to town one day on a business errand. It was after Prohibition was lifted because he deemed himself having worked hard enough to wet his whistle with a nickel beer at Chet Oster's. Chet Oster was one of the first to get back into the saloon business after the Volstead Act had caused him to hibernate for 14 years. Chet's place was next door to what is now Paula's "Taste of Home" on east First Street.

Ole Foggie's being in Chet Oster's was not out of character since he would drink one beer and then graze the free lunch counter like a starving wolf. Chet Oster never made any profit off ole Foggie.

Someone offered to buy Foggie a beer. He fumbled his Waterbury out of his overall breast pocket, consulted it and "...allowed as how" he might indeed have time for another beer, "...you being so kind as to stand me for it." Then someone else came in and in one of those series of coincidences that happen once in a lifetime, Fogelpohl drank free beers all afternoon. Then, greased by a dozen mugs of Griesedieck Brothers' finest he slipped into a previously unknown mood of generosity, bonhomie and openhandedness (truly *terra incognito* for Foggie).

Carried away with this rare spirit, he whips out his wallet, plonks it on the bar and waves to the assembled clientele, announcing, "Der trinks ist on me!" Oster, who knew Fogelpohl well, blinked in disbelief. The wholesale stampede to the bar left ole Foggie with a beer tab in excess of $5 which Oster was careful to collect before poor old Foggie got back to planet earth.

That was Friday night. On Saturday, Mr. Felten, Foggie's neighbor, wanting to borrow a tool, walks over to Fogelpohl's place and pounds on the front door. With no answer he goes around to the barn and hears the old man yelling. Thinking something amiss, Felten hurries to the barn to be confronted with an incredible sight.

The old man had dropped his overalls and with a horsewhip was flailing himself hard enough to flay the skin right off his rump while bellowing, "Fogelpohl, you going to do that again?" ...and then answering himself, "Nein, nein, nein!"

THE ECCENTRIC MR. TODD

I do not mean to accuse the Germans as the sole repository of frugality in the village. Everyone was frugal. Some of the Germans just took it to comedic lengths. But there was comedy among others too.

Billy and Jack Todd lived with their parents on the family farm just off the Cottonwood School Road. Their father ranked very high and possibly surpassed the Germans on parsimony. One summer day during the Depression Mr. Todd appears in Warnhoff Mercantile with his giant, battery powered, tabletop radio under his arm. Harry approached, "Need a battery for that Mr. Todd?"

Harry was a bit puzzled. Warnhoffs sold the batteries for these old clunkers, but since they all took exactly the same battery, there would have been no reason to lug the 20 pound monster to town.

"Nope," says the taciturn Mr. Todd.

Harry persists, "Well we don't repair those things you know. If you'd like to leave it, there's a guy who comes in from Boonville Wednesdays and takes them back for repair. He's quite reasonable and he usually gets it back the next week."

"Nope," answers Mr. Todd, "She plays fine!" Harry stares at him with furrowed brow.

Finally Todd explains, "I brought it to town with me

Fig. 3-25. "Them batt'ries is too expensive to be a-listenin' to soap operas!"

to keep the old lady from playing it!"

Harry's jaw dropped.

" I've told her and told her that she's got to quit listening to them damned soap operas and running them batteries down. The last time we bought one from Sears Roebuck they had bumped their prices up to 89¢. I'll tell you one damned thing, I ain't paying them kinds of prices for the old lady to listen to them dumb soap operas! I came home unexpectedly one day last month and caught her listening to them, so I just told her, 'That's it, from now on when I leave this house, the radio goes with me!'"

CHILDREN OF THE VILLAGE

"Each child of the village is reared by *all* the village."

I thought of this adage when, on the campus of the University of Missouri in 1954, I ran into Maurice Shier my PGHS science teacher. He was in the company of two colleagues whom he introduced. Then he put his arm on my shoulder and told them, "Here is an example of how young, fatherless boys can still make it in a small village [he was alluding also to Homer Jeffress]."

"At Pilot Grove we were able to give them a good basic education that prepared them for this." He waved his arm indicating the imposing university setting.

He was partly right. We were raised by the village. My mother went to work in Boonville after Dixie graduated and left the nest in 1941. Bob and I were 'home alone' but doing okay with the oversight of teachers and many kindly neighbors.

Mr. Shier was not totally correct. I was in Fort Bliss, Texas in the fall of 1953 when I made the decision to quit the military career and go to MU for an engineering degree. In order not to be surprised on qualifications at the last moment, I determined to preregister at the university and have my high school credits checked out. If I were deficient, I needed to know about it now, not next year.

Well, I *was* deficient. Fortunately I had plenty of time to take correspondence course through USAFI[9]. I took algebra, plane and solid geometry, trigonometry, inorganic chemistry and physics. At Summer Enrollment 1954 came around I was up to the mark. Sorry, Mr. Shier but your lauded PGHS curriculum was quite weak in science. These courses were never offered.

I would have to include Mr. Shier as one of my 'village counselors' although he was primarily a 'Vo-Ag' teacher and—being a 'townie' —that was not one of my subjects. But, I had mixed feelings about him. He was a good teacher and a very moral and upstanding role model. But, fact is, he knocked my front teeth out not once but twice (accidently, of course) and I viewed him as a klutz. The accidents occurred in basketball games and his only fault was in being a big, ungainly mass of muscle that couldn't get stopped when he raced after me as I scrambled down the court for a lay-up shot.

My shot was a slam dunk but so was my mouth when he collided with me and drove my face into the tile wall. Dr. Schilb's beautiful gold handiwork had no more been set in until in another basketball game Mr. Shier's elbow pushed it from my upper incisors into my tonsils.

If my comments on the my lack of science courses at PGHS seem like complaining, I don't mean to. I feel very fortunate to have had the opportunities that I had. In fact, in looking back over fifty years or so, I must conclude that apparently I am a member of an extremely exclusive club. I've never had much to complain about. I've never considered myself to be a victim of anything or anyone. I've never been seriously discriminated against. Those in authority over me in military and civilian life have acted honorably and fairly. Does that make me unique in America or what?

VILLAGE IDIOT

In Pilot Grove 'Village Idiot' was not an official office but was tacitly awarded on merit. No fanfare, no revelry, just an unspoken agreement that the subject was fully qualified.

The vocation of Village Idiot has a long and honorable tradition dating from the Middle Ages when kings, dukes and lords aspired to have within their employ the most entertaining, comical and amusing jesters available. Contests were held among the village idiots and winning could assure a long and prosperous sinecure on the comedy stage down at the local castle. Folks were clearly much less discriminating in their entertainment in those days.

In the period of my adolescence and youth I would nominate Raymond "Highway Robbery" Raines as Pilot Grove's "Village Idiot".

Slab-faced Raymond was in his early 30s with shirt size 44, hat size 5 and the IQ of a fence post. He was about six feet tall and weighed in at about 190 pounds. He had a black, craggy brow and pepper and salt hair—prematurely gray. But his watery blue eyes gave him away. Gazing deeply into them, one was inevitably struck—there was no one at home in there.

Kids of my age often followed him around taunting him with the epithet "Highway Robbery". But, Raymond had a fierce protector in his mother, "Sukie" Raines who did not see her son in such lights. Ma Raines had a tongue like a rapier and a vocabulary that would stun a longshoreman. When she was around, she would come charging at us lashing out with her sharp tongue and rich vocabulary to drive off his tormentors like a pack of hyenas.

Aside from being the butt of jokes, mockery and childish pranks, Raymond served a useful purpose. When the 15-16 year old village youths needed a bottle of 45¢ Bardenheier Muscatel wine to lubricate some teenage festivity—we could count on Raymond to purchase it for us. We would watch him carefully as he went into Ikey Schweitzer's liquor store on 1st Street and transacted the deal with the clerk who could easily observe the underage conspirators dancing around outside. After all, "Bidness is bidness!"

When Raymond came out with the jug the entire retinue scurried off to a darkened doorway where he was paid off. His 'fee' was the first slug out of the bottle. We stood watching him, holding our breath as he upended the bottle and attempted to set this 'fee' as high as possible without drowning. The remaining 2/3 - 3/4 of the bottle then got passed around the 4-5 co-conspirators. Two rounds usually finished it off. We then considered ourselves sufficiently lubricated for whatever frolic was at hand.

Raymond's academic life had ended early and he entered the job market. When he wasn't wandering after the fairies he hung out down town looking for work and—not too surprisingly—often found it. It was wartime, many casual jobs just needed a strong back. A brain was superfluous.

I remember seeing him one winter afternoon in '44 sitting on the stoop of Olsen's Feed Store soaking up the meager warmth of the sun. He was watching for the Griesedieck Beer delivery truck.

[9] USAFI - United States Armed Forces Institute, an Armed Forces correspondence secondary school accredited by virtually all US colleges.

Throughout the depression of the '30s and the war of the '40s, beer was one commodity that never saw interruption in demand though supply sometimes was a bit of a problem. Raymond was a welcomed relief for a beer truck driver. He was tireless in rolling in the dollies stacked high with cases of long-neckers. The many beer and soda drivers serving Pilot Grove would reward him with a few bucks and that was his pin money.

Raymond had one habit that was peculiar even for Village Idiots. When he had swilled down his Falstaff longnecker, he would peer into it raptly, like a scientist scrutinizing a test tube. With one eye squinted shut and the other at the mouth of the bottle he then held it to the light of the front windows and gazed with meticulous intensity. With his grizzled beard, unkempt hair and disheveled clothing he looked like a pirate with telescope sizing up the horizon.

In the winter of 1948 when I was on Christmas home leave from Ft. Bragg, I braved a biting north wind that was turning cheeks rosy to drop into the Tip-Top Cafe. The storm, now blowing itself out, had deposited 2-3 inches of snow, the first of the season, beautiful, but with the accompanying fierce northern gale, it brought portents of a wintry Christmas. Wintry blasts be damned! I was now 21 years old and was going celebrate my majority by knocking back a few Falstaffs.

The Owner-Proprietor-Bartender of the Tip Top was then Dick Schuster who cheerfully removed the crown of a Falstaff longnecker and slid it down to me. "Here's yer catnip, Sonny," says he.

The place was empty except for Raymond and I. Raymond was also having a beer at the bar. He finished it, wiped his mouth with his sleeve, let off a great sigh, burped then went through his spyglass routine. I asked him what he saw. "Nothin' nothin'," he answered. I don't know whether he was embarrassed at being caught doing something stupid or whether he literally meant he was looking for another sip of beer and found 'nothing'.

I was reminded of a story I once read of Lord Admiral Nelson just before the sea battle of Trafalgar. Admiral Nelson also claimed to see 'nothing'.

In 1805, in the tenth year of the Napoleonic Wars, Nelson had cornered the French and Spanish fleet off Cape Trafalgar (SW coast of Spain) and was preparing to administer the coup de grace. Just as he signaled for maneuvers that would destroy the combined enemy fleet, his quartermaster brought him an order just received from the chain of semaphore-signaling picket ships.

This order, if carried out, would permit the enemy to escape his trap. Nelson said, "Give me the glass, I can't believe this!" The quartermaster handed him the telescope. Nelson brings it up to his *blind* eye[10], scrutinizes the horizon for a few seconds and declares, "I see no such signal. Carry on with the order to engage!"

Alas for Raymond, by the mid-20th century, the golden days of court jesters, buffoons, harlequins, jokers, comics and village idiots—with free meals, warm places by the fire and the esteem of the court—had faded into history.

THE BEUMERS

It was a pleasant Saturday afternoon in the summer of 1935. My 'main man' Homer (Jeff) Jeffress and I were getting up an informal game of cops and robbers, cowboys and Indians or war. I had this brand new, repeating, rubber-band rifle and Jeff had his homemade model—a whittled down 1 x 4 board fitted with a clothes pin.

These weapons had a range of about 8 feet and, at point-blank, could deliver a very satisfying sting.

"Ammunition" for these rifles was made from old inner tubes which had been sliced into thin rings down at Kempf's tin shop. When no one was watching, we would sneak in to the sheet metal cutting 'guillotine' and slice up an inner tube before anyone knew we were there.

Fred Beumer was the Katy station agent at Pilot Grove and lived directly across the street from us, one door west of my pal and mentor Wallace "Chappie" Chapman. Mr. Beumer was a veteran of the "Great War" (in 1935, World War sequels had not yet been numbered.) It may have been his experience that set the tone on violent games in the Beumer household.

The Beumer household was composed of: Fred, his wife, daughters Aletha and Maxine who were in high school and little Freddie. Aletha and Maxine, being 'older women' i.e., teenagers—were completely out of my league, but I remember what attractive young women they were. I saw them in their high school athletic togs once and—wow! Of course, they were never a consideration for cowboys and Indians, but Freddie was!

So, Freddie—then 4-6 years old was invited to join the small street gang of ragamuffins (Jeff and I) and we were off to a romp around the Beumer front lawn, "Bang, bang, you're dead!"— "No, I'm not! You missed me by a mile!" This went on for a few minutes.

Then, Mrs. Beumer appeared on the front porch to size up the situation. "Freddie, stop the play and come here!" We followed him to the porch steps, puzzled as to what we may have done wrong.

[10] Nelson had already lost one leg and one eye in the wars with the French. Although the battle of Trafalgar was the greatest sea victory in the history of the English Navy, it was not without cost. As Nelson signalled his fleet "England expect every man will do his duty..." and sailed into the battle, a French sniper in the fighting top of a French man of war fired at him. He was hit and died a few hours later.

"Freddie, you must never point a gun at another person. Don't even pretend that you are killing someone! Now you boys can pretend that you are hunting. See those birds in the trees? Pretend you are shooting them!"

We were puzzled more than anything. What had all those hundreds of movies taught us? Gary Cooper in "Farewell to Arms", Wallace Beery in "The Big House", Tom Mix in "Destry Rides Again" etc. As P.J. O'Rourke says, "War and killing is the ultimate male juvenile fantasy. What was more fun than knocking down buildings and killing foreigners?"

Fig. 3-26. Katy Dispaatcher 'Mac' McCreery, 1943. 'Mac' passed on in 1974 and was buried in Liberty.

"We continued our shooting games, now firing our impotent rubber bands at the blackbirds who watched us suspiciously. They showed their disdain by splattering the sidewalk with mementos of their visit to the mulberry tree in Mame Chapman's backyard.

It didn't work and Jeff and I drifted away to other amusements. Freddie did not again join us in our lethal games.

The old earth has made many circuits since those ancient days and I have thought on this lesson a time or two. What would the world have been like if all the world's mothers had taken the same view on violence as Mrs. Beumer. I have no impression that the Beumers were of any specific pacifist group, but Freddie's mother must have been terribly chagrined at the unpleasantness to come a few years later in 1939-1945. The only saving grace was that Freddie would have been too young to participate.

THE MCCREERYS

I have told some tales of the McCreerys—Mac, Pauline, Beuford, especially Loyd who was a mentor to an informal "Young Ruffians Gang" of which I was a member in good (?) standing—Merline and Bobby. These paragraphs will simply serve as an epilogue.

Most of the family spent all or a good portion of their lives in railroading and, of course, that is how I came to share so many memories with them. Mac had worked in Pilot Grove in the 1920s and both Beuford and Loyd were born there. He was Katy Station Agent in 1943 when he

Fig. 3-27. Pauline McCreery's Merline and Beuford. Her 89th birthday party - 1996.

was promoted to Dispatcher. But after the war and with all railroads cutting back and the Katy cutting to the bone, Mac took a job in Kansas City in a "Railway Communications School" teaching some returning veterans the thing he knew—railway dispatching, train orders and the management of rail traffic.

In 1947 when I returned from service in the Pacific, I visited the school. Students sat at their work stations around a enormously long conference table. A model railway layout guided Lionel freight trains around the table. Mac sat in an elevated tower and issued orders to the various way stations to control the simulated railway traffic. It was hokey. Even as naive as I was, I could see this "school" was designed mostly to cash in on the new GI Bill. Most of the students realized that too but what the heck, it beats working! I suppose Mac thought, "It's a living —why should I worry about it?"

Loyd (1st Marine Division) was seriously wounded on Okinawa, but he was patched up at Tripler General in Hawaii and returned to his division in time for a half year in China. At least no one was shooting at him. He was mustered out in 1946, tried to reenlist but was rejected because of his injuries. (Pieces of Japanese shrapnel worked out of his chest for the rest of his life.) He enlisted in the Army and served in the 25th 'Tropic Lightning' Division in Korea plus several years in California, but quit short of his pension. Loyd passed on in 1987 and now lies beside his father in Liberty Cemetery.

Beuford had returned from his service in the U.S. Army Air Force, married his high school sweetheart Marjorie Talley and worked as a trainman out of Kansas City. He lived in Overland Park, Kansas until his retire-

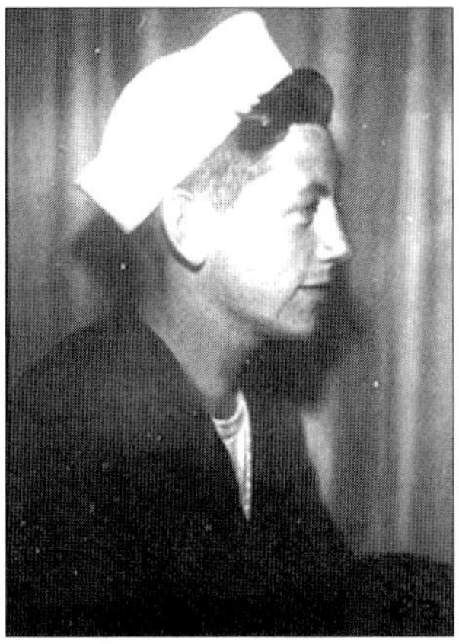

Fig. 3-28. Loyd McCreery. Left as a USMS Fireman 1943. At right he has recovered from wounds on Okinawa and returned to 1st Marines then in China - late 1945.

Fig. 3-29. "Aunt Isabel" Quinlan worked at the Pilot Grove Post Office in 1925. Note the "Kroger" store on the right. I think this was George Day's. In the vacant lot to the right of the grocery store, a croquet court was installed in the mid-1930s.

ment when he returned to Pilot Grove. He died in 1996. Marjorie still lives in Pilot Grove near the Katy Manor.

As I have winnowed the stacks of memorabilia—play bills, recitals, commencements, etc. from ancient days, I have often come upon Merline McCreery's name. She was a singer of much promise and added her grace to many a school function. I regret that by the time her musical talents began maturing, I had left the scene and 'Gone fer a Sojer'.

She married Cecil Sharp and now lives and works as an allergy specialist Nurse Practitioner in Liberty.

Bobby told me, "Just out of high school, dad asked me if I'd like to work on the Boonville Bridge. This is a sweet job, you just raise the bridge for a riverboat every week or so and read a lot of comic books. But, I told him no, it would drive me nuts. I went to California to join Loyd and enlisted in the Army. I had intended to make a career of it but as the years passed, circumstances changed and I got out. Mom and Dad bought an Excelsior Springs liquor store from Paul Willenbring. After Dad died, I came back to be closer to the family.

"I ran a bar in St. Joseph for a while but after my wife died, Mom said come on down here and save some money by sharing my house."

Bobby solved a mystery for me. He had been one of the informal Pilot Grove Flying Club that came to grief in the winter of 46-47. Bob Burnett crash landed with Smokey Zeller and "Chief" Lewis aboard. Bobby, fortunately was not with them that day. I had personally never seen the plane and was curious as to what it was since it had a enormous cowling over what was obviously a giant radial engine—very different from the more common Piper Cubs and Wacos. Bobby said, "It was a Stearman—very easy to fly."

Then I recognized it. It was a later model of the Stearman PT-13 used in the early war years as a Primary Trainer. I have never been in one. When I was in Cadets, we used the AT-6 North American "Texan".

Pauline (I have a hard time calling her Mrs. McCreery) asked if I had seen her greeting card. She had sent Mom a congratulations card for her 100th birthday. I asked her, "How did you know she had a 100th birthday?"

"It was in the Katy Manor newsletter."

"Why do you get the Katy Manor newsletter?"

"Well, Sonny, I've kept in touch with folks in Pilot Grove and with the Katy Manor. *I thought that when I get old, I might be interested in going there*!"

Pauline was 91 years old in 1998.

THE OLD PHILOSOPHERS

It may be interesting to read the words held dear by some of my contemporaries. Ralph Esser's favorite poem may reflect the thoughts of others in Pilot Grove—

DOWN ON THE FARM

Down on the farm, about half-past four
I slip on my pants and slip out the door.
Out in the yard I run like the dickens
To milk all the cows and feed all the chickens;
Clean out the barnyard, curry Maggy and Jiggs,
Separate the cream, and slop all the pigs.

Hustle two hours, then eat like a Turk,
But heck, then I'm ready for a full day's work.
Then I grease the wagon and put on the rack,
Throw a jug of water in the old grain sack,
Hitch up the mules, and slip down the lane,
Must get the hay in..... looks like rain.

Look over yonder .... sure as I am born
Cows on the rampage, hogs in the corn.

Back with the mules, then for recompense
Maggy gets astraddle the barb wire fence.
Joints all aching, muscles in a jerk....
Whoop! Fit as a fiddle, for a full day's work.
Work all summer till winter is nigh,

Then figure at the bank and heave a big sigh.
Worked all year, didn't make a thing,
Less cash now than I had last spring.
Some folks say there ain't no hell.
Shucks! They never farmed .... how can they tell?

When spring rolls around I take another chance.
As the fuzz grows longer on my old gray pants.
Give my gallusses a hitch, belt another jerk.
By gosh! I am ready for a full year's work.

William Childress, in his years of Pilot Grove residence, contributed much to local lore and amusement. Here are some of my favorites—tombstone epitaphs. (From his "Gas Tank Tour of the Ozarks".)

"Old cemeteries are apt to be anywhere and if you like to take headstone rubbings, go for it! You may discover some headstone verse which crops up like:"

Here lies my wife
Thank God she's quiet
Through all my life
Her tongue ran riot!

My husbin likt the forrest
And did chase wimmen threw it
Bragt like he wuz bull of the woods
But seltum wuz up tew it.

You ain't old when yer hair turns gray
You ain't even old when yer teeth decay
But, Bud yer gettin' old and ya better go to sleep
When yer mind makes dates yer body cain't keep.

Marjorie Burger Schmidt clips her church bulletin as well as the Kansas City Star for little golden nuggets—

GOLDEN RULES FOR EASIER LIVING

1. If you open it, close it.
2. If you turn it on, turn it off.
3. If you unlock it, lock it up.
4. If you break it, admit it.
5. If you can't fix it, call in someone who can.
6. If you borrow it, return it.
7. If you value it, take care of it.
8. If you make a mess, clean it up.
9. If you move it, put it back.
10. If it belongs to someone else and you want to use it, get permission.

FROM THE KANSAS CITY STAR

"As a soon-to-be octogenarian, I am appalled by some of the changes in American culture since World War II.

For instance:

•What used to be called modesty is now called a sexual hang-up.

•What used to be called Christian discipline is now called unhealthy repression.

•What used to be called disgusting is now called adult.

•What used to be called moral responsibility is now called being "freed up".

•What used to be called chastity is now called neurotic inhibition.

•What used to be called self-indulgence is now called self fulfillment.

•What used to be called living in sin is now called a meaningful relationship.

•What used to be called perversion is now called an alternate life style.

•What used to be called depravity is now called a creative self-expression.

•What used to be called ethical anarchy is now called the theology of liberation.

•Are we really better off than we were?"

DON'T QUIT

When things go wrong as they sometimes will,
When the road you're traveling seems all uphill,
When the funds are low and the debts are high,
And you want to smile but you have to sigh,

When care is pressing you down a bit,
Rest if you must, but don't you quit.
Life is queer with its twists and turns
As every one of us sometime learns

And many a failure turns about
When he might have won if he'd stuck it out
Don't give up though the pace seems slow...
You may succeed with another blow.

Success is failure turned inside out...
The silver tint of clouds of doubt.
You can never tell how close you are
It may be near when it seems so far;
So stick to the fight when you are hardest hit,
It's when things seem worst that you must not quit.

Fig. 3-30. At the dedication, Sunday, October 30, 1932, of the marker at the grave of the pioneer mother, Hannah Cole, in Briscoe Cemetery. Many descendants of the Courageous Hannah Cole appear in this photo by Rehmeier. The restoration of the pioneer Briscoe Cemetery and the erection of the bronze tablet on a granite boulder were achievements of the Pilot Grove Chapter DAR, Mrs. Charles a. Stites, Chairman of Historic Sites, ably assisted by Mrs. Marshall Rust and Mr. C.J. Harris. From "History Of Cooper County Missouri" by E.J. Melton - 1937. Courtesy Wally Burger. Lower right corner Charlotte Heinrich, Enslie Schilb and Beulah Brownfield. Lower left corner-Wally Burger. Top left-WW Burger holding Mary Louise. Man in white hat at left is Gump Stoecklein.

LIKE A PATCHWORK QUILT

Life isn't given us all of a piece;
It's more like a patchwork quilt...
Each hour and minute a patch to fit in
To the pattern that's being built.

With some patches gay and some patches dark
And some that seem ever so dull...
But if we were given to set some apart,
We'd hardly know which to cull.

For it takes the dark patches to set off the light
And the dull to show up the gay...
And, somehow that pattern just wouldn't be right
If we took any part away.

No, life isn't given us all of a piece
But in patches of hours to use
That each can work out his pattern of life
To whatever design he might choose.

—Helen Laurie Marshall

"GRANDMA'S RECEET

Grandma's laundry lesson to her son's new bride—some years ago.

1. Bild fire in back yard to heet kettle of rain water.
2. Set tubs so smoke won't blow in eyes if wind is pert.
3. Shave one hole cake lie soap in biling water.
4. Sort things, make 3 piles. 1 pile white, 1 pile cullord, 1 pile britches and rags.
5. Stir flour in cold water to smooth, then thin down with bilin water.
6. Rub dirty spots on board scrub hard, then bile. Rub cullord, don't bile, just rench in starch.
7. Take white things out of kettle with broomstick handle, then rench, bleu and starch.
8. Spread tee towels on grass.
9. Hang old rags on fence.
10. Pore rench water in flower bed.
11. Scrub porch with hot soapy water.
12. Turn tubs up side down.
13. Go put on clean dress, smooth hair with side combs, brew cup of tee, set and rest and rock a spell and count yer blessings.

Thanks to Henry Twenter

"In my time, the follies of the town crept slowly among us,
but now they travel faster than a stagecoach.
—Goldsmith

OVERVIEW

THIS CHAPTER PRESENTS SOME TALES ABOUT life in Pilot Grove in my childhood and youth. They are not a comprehensive accounting of those years nor intended to be. The only objective is to preserve a sense of the times and people who now mostly just clutter up my musty, dusty old attic of memories.

SUNDAY SCHOOL LESSON

It was Sunday morning 22nd of May 1932—the Lord's day, and it was one of which He could be justly proud. It was a beautiful morning with all the spirea and wisteria blooming frantically in front of the old red brick Methodist Episcopal Church (South) at Third and Roe. The terrible drought that would afflict all the Midwest that year (and start the "Okies" exodus to California) had not as yet manifested itself. However, later in the year this drought and the dry heat it brought was thought to have initiated the slow but inevitable and ultimately, fatal, deterioration of the building. Some faults were beginning to show along mortar lines—subsidence cracks and gaps.

This church was built in 1886 to serve a congregation which had not yet come to terms with the late row between the Union and the Confederacy. That separation, signaled by the notation 'South', i.e., Methodist Church (*South*) lasted for over 100 years. Speak of holding a grudge!

Many of my ancestors celebrated the rites of passage at this old church—baptisms, christenings, weddings and funerals. My Kendrick grandparents, my aunt Allie and my father were buried from this church. Dad and Mom were married at the parsonage in the spring of 1914 and I have a ornate certificate testifying to my baptism here on the 4th day of September in the Year Of Our Lord 1927 and signed by Reverend Samuel Price Cayton.

But on this day the old place looked magnificent. In the deep shade of the majestic elms the grass, freshly trimmed by Frank Moore, was lush and green. Frank Moore was the old 'colored' man who performed the duties of a church sexton. The trees were budded or leafed out and all was right with the world. I had my face polished and hair well slicked down. I wore my white Buster Brown shirt, short navy blue wool shorts, badly scuffed shoes ineffectively treated by daubing on a little Dyanshine. My dark socks were appropriate but steadfastly refused to stay up over my calves.

I would start to Miss Madge Goode's first grade in the fall, thus I had not yet achieved the discipline to sit still for an hour or so and had to be bribed. Mom gave me two nickels with careful instructions: "Now, Sonny—one nickel is for the collection plate and with the other you can go down to Pop Tracy's or Deck's and get yourself an ice cream cone afterward." I would have an escort for the two blocks from church to the drug store. Pop was open on Sunday and Bill Deck opened the drugstore for a few hours on Sunday morning to push a little ice cream to the churchgoers, otherwise the commercial district was shut up tighter than a drum. I do not remember who my escort was but it was not my sister Dixie, 3 years older. She was too wise to take me under escort. I was then, as now, a Royal Pain In The Butt and she would have demurred the honor.

Fig. 4-1. The Methodist Episcopal Church (South) stood at the corner of Third and Roe Streets for nearly 100 years. Frances Brownfield was my Sunday School teacher but should not be held responsible for any of my personal flaws.

Mounting the front steps I looked up at the tall mournful looking man who was the official greeter. I saw three inches of shirt sleeve beyond his coat and an equal flash of white socks under his trouser cuffs as he graciously opened the door wide for me. Dad called these 'high water pants'. As he said, "A fella only needs one suit. Get yourself a good one for your wedding and if you take good care of it and keep it in good repair, they can use it to 'lay you out' for your funeral. Do it right and one is enough."

I suspect that for a few, this final use of that good suit (the funeral) might be hastened by continuously cramming the body of a 200 lb middle-aged man into a suit tailored for a 140 lb youth. Our greeter this day with coat sleeves only making it halfway past his elbow looked like such a person. He may have been a candidate for apoplexy. Diagnosis: a size 20 neck in a size 14 collar.

The great, heavy door—a modest imitation of the ancient cathedrals of Mediaeval Europe—swung open and I entered the vestibule and sanctuary. At age 6 the scent of altar flowers, polished pews, musty hymnals, the sight of the stately pipe organ and the beautiful stained glass said to me: "You Are In the Presence of God!"

After Sunday School, I bounced into Mom's busy kitchen slurping a vanilla ice cream cone. She wiped her floury hands on her apron and looked at me suspiciously, "Did you remember to give in your nickel to Miss Brownfield's collection?"

I looked at her and began to get an impression she was not going to like my answer. "Not exactly, Mom."

"WHAAAT!" she let out a screech like a cat with his tail caught under the rocker. "I gave you two nickels and I see you have your ice cream cone. How did this happened?"

"Well, Mom I lost my Sunday School nickel! I whined. "It was an accident. I had my ice cream nickel in this pocket (indicating the left) and my Sunday School nickel in the other. When the collection was tooken up, the Sunday School nickel just wasn't there!"

She stood there arms akimbo and explained in some detail the flaws in my logic.

Thus my lesson was—paraphrasing Matthew XXII, 21— "Render therefore to the ice cream man his nickel but *first* render unto God the nickel that is God's."

Miss Brownfield our Sunday School teacher later became Mrs. Frances (Brownfield) Rybak.

JOY

In the early 1970s I had the honor of being a staff member at Midwest Research Institute (MRI) at 425 Volker Boulevard in Kansas City. MRI's main building sits on the south bank of Brush Creek and faces the south facade of the Nelson Art Gallery across the vast green expanse of the Theis Mall. But that is not important to the story. What is important is the proximity of MRI to J.C. Nichol's famous Country Club Plaza.

With a full hour lunch break, zipping over to the Plaza for that 'just remembered' birthday or anniversary gift or a Hallmark card was very convenient and that's what took me there on a sunny, but cool, pre-Christmas day.

Completing my errand, I was strolling back to the Institute soaking up the sun against the chill days to come. I was distracted with the pre-Christmas window displays at Woolf Bros (Gentlemen's Clothing) when I felt a light touch on my shoulder. I wheeled to face an attractive young matron. Her garb said "Johnson County gentry". She smiled. I panicked. Here, obviously, is someone who knows me and I haven't a clue as to who she is! What we have here, Mr. Salmon, is a practical test of your innate ability to dissemble, fake and feign familiarity while desperately searching for some hint of her identity.

Fig. 4-2. Beethoven Statue - Munster Platz - Bonn, Germany.

"What was that song you were whistling?" she asked. I was surprised—I didn't realize I was whistling anything.

"Oh...uh...that's Beethoven's Ninth Symphony. You may know it as "Joy". It's a favorite of our pastor, Ted Nissen. He often programs it in the Advent Season."

I still was not sure whether I should know her and the Ted Nissen ploy was to draw her out should she know me from the Colonial Presbyterian Church. Colonial is at 95th and Wornall in Kansas City but many of the parishioners are from Johnson County.

"Oh. Beethoven, huh? He was one of those old guys wasn't he?" Here she betrayed herself—with a comment like that—she obviously was not of the Johnson County gentry—I'm home free.

"Yeah, he was a classic composer if that's what you mean and yes he'll be about 200 years old his next birthday but his stuff has aged very well."

"Okay. Pretty tune. Thanks. Good day."

"Good day, ma'am." I resumed my trek back to the office, but the encounter stirred some latent memories up in the dusty attic of the long-ago. As I walked, pieces of the jigsaw puzzle turned into a mosaic of another November day upon which I had heard "Joy" for the first time.

That November of 1934 was not one of any great joy. Winter had set in early that year and a foot or so of snow had accumulated. Initially, everyone greeted the beautiful snow. Kids grabbed their sleds and headed for schoolhouse hill. Grownups welcomed the transformation of the drab reality of the muddy, rutted streets—the piles of refuse in the alleyways awaiting spring pick up and the stark, black trees naked of foliage but then, with the first snow, all covered and decorated with a whipped cream topping.

But now a month had gone by since that snow and it was mottled with ashes, coal dust and a lot of disgusting stuff best not identified. The town dogs had capped off all the drifts with sprinklings of yellow ice filigree and the townscape was uncommonly gloomy.

There was much to be gloomy about. We hadn't seen the sun for nearly three weeks and spirits were sinking along with the thermometer. We were in the third consecutive year of what would be the nation's worst depression. Hitler had come to power in Europe and was making threatening noises. The Japs had taken over in Manchuria and were running amok in China. But mostly, we were concerned about the 25% unemployment rate at home and were seeing visible evidence that this was not just one of those meaningless government statistics. People were hurting. Dad had a job but...who knows? Roosevelt had been in office two years and we were watching and listening for anything that he could do for relief—praying for a savior.

One of the first things that Roosevelt did was repeal Prohibition. This brought great joy to some "...Happy Days are Here Again. I can get myself a beer again..." But those who put great hope and faith in drowning their troubles in the products of Joseph Schlitz, Augie Busch and the Griesedieck Brothers found that these troubles were Olympic gold medal swimmers and totally invulnerable to drowning. Many of Chet Oster patrons found that after half dozen tall mugs of this remedy, they had a sore head, a painfully full bladder and were 90¢ poorer into the bargain.

On this particular November Sunday afternoon, I wandered into the parlor and into the company of the rest of the family. I began grudgingly picking up my toys as I had been instructed to do several times. Weather had kept us under house arrest for too long. I was well bundled up to walk to school. It was only a half block away. But, it was too bitterly cold to go out to play. It was particularly cold that Sunday and the icy north wind sucked heat right through the window panes. The teakettle steam condensed on the panes and froze into beautiful but icy crystalline patterns.

We had a giant wood-burning stove that was fed railroad tie chunks every hour or so. It was hot—red hot in places—but the other side of the room showed breath. Mom came in from outside and stood by the stove to thaw out. The stove was so hot her bare legs turned mottled and blotchy[1].

"Heap on the wood—the wind is chill.
But let it whistle as it will.
We'll keep our Christmas merry still."
—Scott

Dad sat in his rocking chair directly in front of the Crosley. This radio was our connection to the rest of the world but mostly a source of bad news. The daily 6PM news was a ritual for him. The nearest radio stations were in Kansas City. There were a number of "clear channel" stations throughout the country that broadcast with such power they could be heard nearly nationwide but only at night. The evening news came from WDAF, the NBC station in Kansas City and the stentorian voices of Lowell Thomas, H.V. Kaltenborn, John Cameron Swayze, et al.

But today was Sunday and NBC was featuring a Christmas Music Program "...directly from New York City we bring you Walter Damrosch and the New York Philharmonic Orchestra..."

The social code of practice as well as the finer points of machismo carefully delineated what was "boy stuff" and what was "girl stuff" among radio programs. The news, "Jack Armstrong", baseball games, hog markets were "boy stuff". Mushy drama, soap operas and high brow music was "girl stuff". Thus, since the radio is not going to be turned off, one must carefully effect to ignore those programs that were not of the proper gender.

The old man was intensely reading the Sunday Kansas City Star, carefully oblivious to Mr. Damrosch's music. He noisily flipped the pages to demonstrate his total disinterest in the music program. Actually, no one else was paying much attention either.

Then"...blah, blah, blah...Beethoven...blah, blah, blah" and the first notes of Beethoven's Ninth Symphony filled our dreary little parlor. I was so struck with the beauty of the music that I stopped rattling toys into my toy box. Mom, sitting near the natural light to repair a trouser leg, froze in mid-stitch. Dad stopped turning pages and was careful not to rustle the paper. Not to give himself away he continued to stare at the paper but he didn't move a muscle.

The glissando of shimmering, silvery notes seemed to fill the air like a beautiful new snow and when the French horn arpeggio cut in—goose bumps rose on my arms. Each of us pretended not to take notice but strained to capture and savor every note.

When it ended, I heard a small sigh from Mom. She smiled and asked Dad, "What was that?"

"What was what? You mean the radio? I don't know, I wasn't paying it no mind", he lied. He leaned over to dial in the Crosley better (maybe they'll play it again).

Absolutely nothing changed in our situation that cold November afternoon. The wind still rattled the window panes. The sun still appeared as a weak, watery, pale yellow blotch low in the western sky. The snow was still as unsightly as goose feathers scattered on the town dump. But at least at one address in Pilot Grove, spirits were lighter and happy talk soon turned to Christmas and plans for the family feast. A near-terminal case of the blue funks had been alleviated in one little corner of the world by Herr Ludwig Beethoven's wondrously elegant "Joy".

[1] The Scots called this condition "Tartan Leg". Remedy: Step back from the fire.

CELEBRATE GOLDEN ANNIVERSARY

Fig. 4-3. L-R. John & Carl Schweitzer, Dee Brownfield, Mrs. John Schweitzer, Mary Scheidt, Mrs. Norman Schweitzer, Louis Lechner, Norman Schweitzer, John Schweitzer, Jake Schweitzer, Mrs. C.L Schweitzer, Mr. C.L Schweitzer, Robert Schweitzer, Mrs. Dee Brownfield, Joe Schweitzer, Martha Schweitzer Rentel.

PILOT GROVE NOVEMBER 6, 1949

Mr. and Mrs. C.L. Schweitzer, Pilot Grove celebrated their 50th wedding anniversary Sunday at the home of their daughter and son-in-law, Mr. and Mrs. Dee Brownfield, one mile west of Pilot Grove. The color scheme of the living and dining room was carried out with gold colored paper, lighted candles, wedding bell, and large baskets of yellow mums, chrysanthemums and ferns, gifts of friends.

Two dedications were made over the radio "When Your Hair Has Turned To Silver," sung by Pat Dunn, and "Memory Waltz" was played in their honor.

A turkey dinner was served at noon. In the afternoon a three tier wedding cake was cut by Mr. and Mrs. Schweitzer and served with punch.

Mr. and Mrs. Schweitzer had the pleasure of the presence of their children and grandchildren with the exception of one son, Harold, of Honolulu, Hawaii, who was unable to attend.

The couple has eight children, Joe, Mary, Jake, Norman, John, Harold, Robert and Martha, and 17 grandchildren. Those present were Mr. and Mrs. J.G. Schweitzer and twin sons John and Carl of Windsor, Jake of Kansas City, Mr. and Mrs. Norman Schweitzer and daughter Norma Jean of San Diego, Calif., Robert of Sioux Falls, S.D., Mr. and Mrs. John Schweitzer and daughters Carol and Kathy, and sons, Jack and David, Mr. and Mrs. Norbert Rentel and daughter, Betty, and son, Buddy, and Mr. and Mrs. Dee Brownfield and daughter, Janie, Kansas City, and sons, Charles and Owen of Pilot Grove, Mrs. Schweitzer's brother, Louis Leckner of Clarksburg, and Mrs. Schweitzer's, sister, Mrs. Mary Dick of Pilot Grove.

50 YEARS ON

Charley and Bertha sat beaming
Their generations gathered in.
Said Charley, "It's 50 years! Sound your cheers!
And let all the fun begin."

Then brash little Janie piped up,
"Please Grandpa, if I may be so bold.
How'd you propose? Why was it you she chose?
That's a story I've not been told."

Old Charley blushed and took Bertie's hand,
And smiled into her deep blue eyes.
Said he, "Honor and love and help from above,
And it came to pass this wise—"

We were returning from a lovely day at the river,
It was mid-June in '99, the day of the longest sun.
Friends all together—we relished the weather,
Rowing and picnicking—all great summer fun.

I was handing her down from my carriage
When a capricious and naughty breeze
Whirled around, caught her long gown
And pinned it to her knees.

And in doing, uncovered her petite ankle
Naked there and plain for me to see
I averted my eyes and gazed at the skies
Too late, too late! All censuring eyes on me.

Well, I had planned to ask for her hand
I prayed in due course she'd be my bride.
But now it'd be wrong for a courtship long
It was a matter of a lady's honor and pride.

So what could I do but marry her
I was the agent of her disgrace
We published the banns and joined our hands
And I kissed my bride's lovely face!

—Sonny Salmon

THE PILOT GROVE STAR

Pilot Grove's "official paper of record" for over twenty years was G.B. Harlan's "Pilot Grove Weekly Record". (See the Chapter "Hizzoner D'Mayor and Other Notables" for additional information on Mr. Harlan.) In 1937, Mr. Harlan sold the printing plant and moved his paper to Boonville where it became the "Cooper County Record".

Mr. R.K. Jones bought the plant and moved his family to Pilot Grove. His family was his wife, daughter Juanita (PGHS 1942) and son R.K. Jr. "Bobby" (PGHS 1943). The Pilot Grove Star's first issue—Volume 1, Number 1—came out on December 16, 1937. It was heavy on ads congratulating Mr. Jones and welcoming him to the community. It was extremely light on news. Example: Otto Stoecklein and his brother assisted Earl Hays in moving a piano into the residence of Mr. and Mrs. W.W. Burger.

Fig. 4-4. Juanita Jones 1942. "She lives to the full every minute—gets all the fun and joy that's in it!"

Fig. 4-5. Bobby Jones, a PGHS Junior in 1942.

The real treasure was the letters to Santa which Jones coordinated with the schools and printed in this maiden issue. They are reproduced in their entirety in the following pages. The only difference in this reproduction is that I have put names in boldface and added the approximate age of the l'il darlings.

I am grateful for the packrat instincts of Doris Quinlan Koonse for this rich find. God Bless all packrats! Our histories would be poorer without them.

In the late 30s, I visited Mr. Jones facility—approximately where Meisenheimer's Funeral Chapel is now. Having nothing as a standard of judgement, I was completely baffled by the giant press and the Mergenthaler machine. In 60 years of 20/20 hindsight, what I saw there was a collection of ancient and archaic equipment that would even then have been ripe for the Smithsonian Institute.

In retrospect, I have great admiration for the hard work that Jones did. He was the owner, publisher, editor, reporter, typist, typesetter, pressman and distributor of a weekly newspaper as well as special publications, handbills, etc. He worked extremely hard for what must have been a very modest profit on the enterprise. He escaped when the Great Depression was terminated by World War II. I think he took the family to California. I do hope that he found a more lucrative business there.

At last sighting, Juanita (Jones) Spencer lived in Petaluma, California where she and her husband grow orchids and Bobby lived in Carson City, NV.

BELOW Fig 4-6. This looks like a Gutenberg Press Model 1. The Pilot Grove Star used a newer one, possibly Model 2. (...Just kidding!)

The Pilot Grove Star

THE ONLY NEWSPAPER DEVOTED SOLELY TO THE INTEREST OF PILOT GROVE AND COMMUNITY

Volume 1 | Pilot Grove, Mo. December 16, 1937 | Number 1

SANTA TO VISIT HERE SATURDAY

Many Plan to Participate in Community Christmas Program. Again Santa Claus has promised to attend the annual Christmas program here, sponsored by the business firms at the community Christmas program here Saturday afternoon at 2 p.m.

For several years Pilot Grove has entertained these youngsters with a fine Christmas, program, passing out large bags of candy and fruit following Santa's appearance from the far North. This paper received a wire from the jolly old fellow a few days ago saying, "Dear Mr. Editor, please use columns of The Star to inform the good boys and girls of your town that I will be seeing them there next Saturday." Signed-Santa.

Well we'll be looking for him won't we. You bet we will.

Now boys and girls we know you all like to have a good time, and we never saw the color of a youngster's eyes who didn't like a big sack of candy. We'll be here early next Saturday and be sure to bring mother and father with you. They will want to do their Christmas shopping with the genial merchants who helped to make this afternoon a big one.

Don't forget the date and time and be on hand early. We'll be looking for you.

LETTERS TO SANTA CLAUS

Pilot Grove, Mo.
December 14, 1937

Dear Santa,

I am trying to be very good. Won't you please bring me something nice?

Yours,

Mary Louise Burger [6]

P.S. Please bring daddy the new Pilot Grove Star for Christmas

---

Dear Santa,

I want a sled, a freight train, a drum, a set of blocks and a tractor. My little brother Jack is home with mother. He wants a train and some candy. I can thank you when you come to see me.

Junior Lammers ()

Dear Santa,

How are you. I am just fine. I want two Shirley Temple dolls, one five inches tall and another five inches tall with real hair and a play house nine inches tall. Two doll buggies, two pianos, two chairs for dolls, a table, a blackboard and a box of chalk. Mother wants a big blanket and my daddy a new tie. I want some candy and two oranges. Mother wants a new pair of stockings and clothes and I want that too. You see Martha is my little sister, four years old and we like to have our own play things. Hope you can find two of each.—C.O.D.

Viola Mae ~~Brunjes~~

Dear Santa,

Can't you afford to bring me a new coat and cap, also a drum, a bicycle, some candy and oranges? James and Jeannette, my little twin brother and sister are in the first grade. They could not come to school because it was too slick. Please bring them some clothes to wear. Hope you think of mother, daddy, grandmother and all.

I am your grateful little friend,

Betty Salmon (8)

Dear Santa,

I want a freight train and cars, an airplane that will fly, a tractor, a football, some candy and oranges.

From Leonard Joseph Zeller (8)

Dear Santa,

I would like to have a good football, a drum, a gun and a pair of overshoes. I like candy too.

Jr Stoecklein (10)

Dear Santa,

I will be waiting for you Christmas to bring me a pair of boots, a horn, a bicycle but no candy nor anything else.

Bernard Kempf (6)

Dear Santa,

We are all well. How are you? I hope you will be here this year. We will all be glad to see you. Wish you would bring me a sled, bicycle and a pair of stockings. Please do not forget teacher, Sister Mercedes and Reverend Father Richard. Merry Christmas to you Santa Claus. Now I will have to close this letter.

Your little friend,

Mary Salmon (9)

Dear Santa,

With Christmas so near, I am trying to be a good girl. I am almost eleven years old and I study my lessons every evening. Please bring me a pair of gloves and some ice skates. Bring mother, daddy and my brothers and sister something too. Don't forget Father Richard, Father Gabriel, my teacher, Sister Mercedes and the other Sisters.

Your little friend,

Lou Ellen Zeller 11)

Dear Santa,

I wish you would come down and pay the children of St. Joseph school a visit, and also come to the little play we a re having December 23. Please bring the little children something. I wish you would bring me a sled and a pair of boot socks. We are having icy weather. We are studying very hard. Don't forget Father Richard and father Gabriel, also the good Sisters. I wish you a Merry Christmas and a Happy New Year.

You friend,

Roy Day (10)

Dear Santa,

How are you Santa? I want a blackboard and chalk, a sled, a Shirley Temple doll and buggy. Don't forget Father Richard and Sister Mercedes. I must close now. Merry Christmas.

With love,

Rosemary Schuster (9)

Dear Santa,

How are you? I am ten years old and in the fifth grade. I am trying to be a good girl. Do not forget Sister Mercedes and fill up her stocking. I am trying very hard in school. Please bring me a pair of stockings, a pair of shoes and a rain cape. Don't forget Father Richard, my parents and all the poor children. A Merry Christmas and Happy New Year.

With lots of love,

Joanne Salmon (10)

Dear Santa,

I am a big boy and like to play ball with the second grade boys. Will you bring me a baseball, hat and glove, a rosary, a tractor, some candy and oranges? Don't forget mother and daddy.

Clarence Lammers (7)

Dear Santa,

I have tried to be good to my mother and father. Now I will tell you what I want for Christmas. I want you to bring me a color book, a pair of shoes, a new coat, a cap, a Shirley Temple doll and a pair of skates. Joe Ed wants a wagon too. Both of us want some oranges, nuts and candy. A Merry Christmas to you.

Your friend,

Winifred Reynolds (8)

Dear Santa,

I have been a very good girl. I am in the fourth grade. I want a doll that wets its pants and goes to sleep, a doll bathinet so I can give my doll a bath, and please don't forget some fruit and candy. Don't forget my mother, daddy and brother, Enslie. Yours forever,

Patty Schilb (9)

PS Please bring my daddy some hair tonic and a comb and brush.

Dear Santa,

I've been very good. I hope you will come to see me Christmas. My stockings will be on the mantle. I want a snowsuit more than anything, a pair of ice skates some books, a dress, a sled and I also want a sister too. I talk in school but that don't count. Merry Christmas.

Your friend,

Mildred Schlotzhauer (9)

Dear Santa,

I want a dog for Christmas, also a train. Please bring them to me.

Your friend,

Neil Coley (9)

Dear Santa,

I haven't been as good as I should have been but I am going to try to be better. I want a bicycle, a Shirley Temple doll, a pair of ice skates and some books.

Your friend,

Betty Jo Woolery (10)

Dear Santa,

I have been a pretty good boy. I was in only a few fights since last Christmas. I hope to be a better boy by next Christmas. What I want is a new watch, a rifle, a few books, a couple of boxes of rifle shells and a new drum for Christmas. If you bring anything else, it will be satisfactory.

Your friend,

Charles Brownfield (10)

PS Please bring my dad a new bird dog and an old goat with two little kids. Chas

Dear Santa,

I have been trying to be a good little girl so you will come see me Christmas night. I want a snowsuit for Christmas and I hope you will bring me one. If I can't have a snowsuit, I would like to have a bicycle. If I get one of them I will be satisfied.

Your friend,

Bonnie Jean Kirby (10)

Dear Santa,

I have been a good little girl but not as good as I should have been. I want you to bring me a sled with red runners a dresser set with comb, brush and mirror, a snowsuit and a wrist watch. If I get all this I will be satisfied.

Your friend

Marjorie Ellen Babbitt (10)

Dear Santa,

I think I have been a pretty good girl this year, so I hope you will bring me what I want. I would like to have a snowsuit, a sled some nuts, candy and oranges, so don't forget these. I would like to have a bicycle too. But if you bring the other things I will be satisfied. I hope you won't forget the other little girls and boys.

Your friend,

Catherine Davis (11)

Dear Santa,

I have been a very good little girl ever since last December. I want a pair of ear muffs, a wrist watch, ice skates and a pair of boots. I will be quite satisfied if I get all these.

Your friend

Dorothy McCutcheon (11)

Dear Santa,

I heard you was coming to Pilot Grove Saturday. All of the children in room one will welcome you here. I shall be glad to receive anything you bring me for Christmas.

Your friend,

Chas. Lee Schlotzhauer (9)

Dear Santa,

How are you? I am just fine. I study hard in school every day. I am ten years old and in the sixth grade. Will you please bring me for Christmas, a pair of gloves, a pocketbook, some handkerchiefs and something to play with. Do not forget Father Richard and Father Gabriel and my teacher, Sister Mercedes. I don't know what they want but fill their stockings. Do not forget the poor children. I will close. Merry Christmas and a Happy New Year. With lots of love,

Your friend,

Ethel Gerke

Dear Santa,

How are you? I am eleven years old and in the sixth grade. Do not forget my teacher, Sister Mercedes and fill up her stocking. I don't know what they want but fill their stockings. Please bring Father Richard and Father Gabriel something nice. Please bring me a wrist watch, scrap book, and cross and chain. Bring something for the poor children too. Also remember my mother, brothers and sisters, hoping to see you soon. A very Merry Christmas.

Loads of love,

Doris Quinlan (11)

Dear Santa,

How are you? I am trying hard to study my lessons. I milk the cow every morning and night so would you please bring me a watch. Fill my teacher's stocking full and please bring me some nuts, candy and oranges. Will say goodby.

From your friend,

Earl Quinlan (9)

Dear Santa,

How are you? I have been working very hard at my studies. I am glad that Christmas is coming soon. If you will please bring me a g men set, boxing gloves, ice skates and a baseball glove, I was playing today and fell down and bloodied my nose but it did not bleed long. Dear Santa will you bring your reindeers this Christmas. It is only ten more days til Christmas. I hope you will not bring me any switches. I am trying to be a good boy. With lots of love,

Your friend,

Leonard Meyer (10)

Dear Santa,

How are you? I am trying to be good at school and at home. I am eleven years old and am in the sixth grade. Remember my good parents and don't forget my teacher, Sister Mercedes and Father Richard and Father Gabriel. Please bring me a bicycle, a pair of ice skates. I hope you get here all right in your sled. I wish you a Merry Christmas and a Happy New Year.

Your friend,

LeVern Klenklen (11)

Dear Santa,

How are you? I am just fine. We have a new baby girl at our

The Pilot Grove Star

THE ONLY NEWSPAPER DEVOTED SOLELY TO THE INTEREST OF PILOT GROVE AND COMMUNITY

Volume 1 Pilot Grove, Mo. December 16, 1937 Number 1

LETTERS TO SANTA CLAUS (CONTINUED)

house. Will you please bring her a rubber ball? I have been studying my lessons very hard. Will you please bring me a pair of ice skates, a cannon and a cowboy suit? Don't forget my little brother who has an earache. He will not be able to write to you. Don't forget Father Richard and Father Gabriel and all the Sisters.

With love,

Bobby Twenter (9)

Dear Santa,

Now that Christmas is close, I am trying to be a good boy. I study my lessons every evening. Please bring me a bicycle and a wagon. Mother, daddy, Father Richard, Father Gabriel and my teacher, Sister Mercedes.

Your little pal,

Kenneth Zeller

Dear Santa,

How are you? Please bring me a pair of ice skates, a sled, a bicycle, a par of gloves, cookies and a story book to read. But don't forget the other children at home, and mother and daddy.

Your little friend,

Albert Imhoff (10)

Dear Santa,

How are you getting along? I am trying to be a good boy. Our lessons are very hard. Will you please bring me a ball, car, gloves and a truck? I hope you will bring Reverend Father Richard and Father Gabriel something nice too. I wish you a Merry Christmas and Happy New Year.

Your friend,

John Imhoff (11)

Dear Santa,

How are you? I am just fine. I am working very hard at school. I am eleven years old and in the eighth grade. Please bring me a bicycle, sled and a pair of ice skates. Do not forget my teacher, Sister Mercedes and Reverend Father Richard and Father Gabriel. I don't know what they want, but bring them something nice. Don't forget my dear parents and the poor. I hope I will see you soon. A Merry Christmas and a Happy New Year.

With lots of love, your friend,

LaVahn Klenklen (11)

Dear Santa,

How are you? I am just fine. I just want you to bring me a few things—a bicycle and a toy telephone. Be sure and don't forget Father Richard and Sister Mercedes, my father and mother too. I am nine years old and I am trying to e a good giver. We had lots of ice and sleet and every time I took a step I fell down. I must close now. Merry Christmas.

With lots of love,

Rebekah Meyer (10)

Dear Santa,

I heard you was coming to Pilot Grove. All of the boys and girls are going to see you. I hope you don't forget me. I am trying to be good. I hope you are well dear Santa. We have a Christmas tree in the school room. Please bring me a wagon.

Yours,

Bob Salmon (8)

Dear Santa,

I will see you at Pilot Grove Saturday afternoon. I will be glad to see yu and hope you will bring me something nice. I am trying to be good.

Your friend,

Billy Stevens (9)

Dear Santa,

I want you to come to see me and I want you to bring me something nice for Christmas. When you come please bring some candy with you.

Your friend,

Moseley Turley (9)

Dear Santa,

It will only be a few days until you will be coming to see us on Christmas eve, and you will also be coming Saturday. I am trying to be good.

Yours truly,

Virginia Boley

PS Please bring papa a big base fiddle and bring mama a billy goat and a few sheep.

Dear Santa,

How are you getting along? I am allright. It is so icy outside that you can bring your reindeers and sled. I want a sled and a cowboy suit. Please don't forget my daddy and my Aunt Mary and Aunt Annie, my grandparents, and my teacher, Sister Mercedes and Rev. Father Richard. I am getting tired of writing. I wish you a Merry Christmas and a Happy New Year.

Yours truly,

Edward Klenklen (11)

Dear Santa,

How are you? I am trying to be good since it is close to Christmas. If you please, I would like to have an autograph book, a story book, and a ring. Don't forget our teacher, Sister Mercedes and Rev. Father Richard and his assistant, Father Gabriel. I wish you would also remember my good parents. It is icy outside and fine to skate on. It is getting late so I must end, wishing you a "Merry Christmas and a Happy New Year".

With all my love, your little friend,

Mary Margaret Muessig (11)

Dear Santa,

How are you? I am working hard at school when are you coming to visit us? I hope you will come soon. Will you please bring me a stove, a cabinet and a stocking cap? We have ice on the pond. We have fun skating on the ice. I am in the fourth grade and nine years old. Please don't forget Father Richard Sister Mercedes, daddy and Aunt Mary. I wish you a Merry Christmas and a Happy New Year.

Your little friend,

Anna Klenklen (9)

Dear Santa,

It is so icy I would like to have a pair of ice skates, a sled, a pair of stockings, gloves, a hat and scarf. Bring daddy and mother something and don't forget Sister Mercedes and Rev. Father Richard. Merry Christmas and a Happy New Year.

Good bye, with love,

Marceline Brunjes (9)

Dear Santa,

I am in the fourth grade and go to the St. Joseph school. This year we have tried to be very good. Will you please bring me a pair of house slippers? Don't forget mother and daddy. Are you going to bring your reindeers this year? Please don't forget Father Richard and Father Gabriel. Please give my teacher, Sister Mercedes something useful too. Merry Christmas, Santa and a Happy New Year.

Lots of love, your little friend

Marjorie Hoff (10)

Dear Santa,

How are you getting along? I am just fine. I hope you will get here allright with your sled. I try to study very hard. I am trying to be good in school. Please bring me a ball, ball glove and bat.

Good bye. I wish you a Merry Christmas, Santa and a Happy New Year,

Kenneth Kempf (11)

Dear Santa,

I have been a good boy this year, at least I think I have. I get in a fight once in a while but I get in the wood. What are you going to bring me for Christmas? I'd like to have a rifle, bicycle, pair of boots and boot pants, a pair of ice skates and a sled. I hope you bring these.

Your friend,

Richard Salmon (10)

Dear Santa,

I have been rather good. I want a new dress, a case to carry my **** , bedroom slippers and a game of some kind. Don't forget my mother, father, brother and sister. I know you have many orders close to Christmas. I wish you could come to our Christmas program December 24. We are putting up our tree today at school. We have put up ours at home. Don't forget all my friends and relatives.

Your loving friend,

Marjorie Burger (11)

PS Please bring our tramp kitty something too.

*Word missing.

Dear Santa,

I have been trying to be a good little boy since last December. I have been trying to be good because there are a lot of things I want for Christmas. They are a bicycle, skates, football, basketball, watch, some books and a wagon. I hope you have been satisfied by my behavior. If not, I will try to do better. I hope you will bring me the things I want.

Your friend,

David Schlotzhauer (11)

Dear Santa,

With Christmas so near, I am trying to be as good as I can, but I am not good just at Christmas but am supposed to be all the time. Well, how are you? Hope you are OK. I am. Will you please fill Sister Mercedes stockings, and Rev. Father Richard's too? Of course I don't know what he wants but bring him something nice. Will you please bring me a dress, a purse and a fountain pen? Please don't forget my dear parents. I guess I better close my letter but before I do I must say a Merry Christmas to you and all your friends.

With lots of love,

Alice Marie Zeller (10)

Dear Santa,

I am a little curly headed boy in the first grade. I want a sled, a football, a streamline train and some candy. Hope you can read [my] letter. I tried so hard to write this nice. If you bring me these things you and I will be the best of friends.

Your anxious little boy,

David Donald Mellor (12)

Dear Santa,

I would like to have a big doll, a sled, a handkerchief and a color book. I wont ask for too much so the other boys and girls can have something. I wish you a Merry Christmas.

Your little friend,

Dorothy Louise Stoecklein

Dear Santa,

A Merry Christmas to you. Will you come to my house? I will be at Aunt Kate's house. I want a doll and a set of twin dishes and Martha Jane wants a doll and baking set.

Your grateful friend,

Mary Ann Schuster (7)

Dear Santa,

Please bring me a car, a new scooter, a football, a handball and a glove. Will be Happy if you can bring me these

Joseph Schuster

Dear Santa,

Please, I want a car and twenty pencils, a clock, a bicycle, some candy, oranges and peanuts. I will be glad for these.

Robert Imhoff (8)

Dear Santa,

I need a handkerchief, a pair of gloves, a purse and something nice to play with. Don't forget to bring some candy, oranges and peanuts, too. Many thanks to you

Martha Mae Gerke (7)

Dear Santa,

A Merry Christmas to you. I want a box of watercolors, a box of candy, some oranges and apples. Have a nice Christmas and lots of joy in the New Year.

Maxine Kempf

Dear Santa,

I would like for you to please bring me a doll with hair, a pair of gloves, a dog, pair of roller skates, a cap, doll buggy, some candy, oranges and apples. Have a nice Christmas yourself, Santa, and a bright New Year.

Ever yours,

Mary Lee Neckerman (8)

Dear Santa,

Daddy thinks I am a good boy. I want a coaster wagon, sled, truck with lights, bicycle and just lots of candy. It will tickle me to get all these things. I like you Santa so please don't forget what I want.

Junior Imhoff

Dear Santa,

Can you bring me a truck, also some oranges and candy?

Your grateful little boy,

Teddy Kempf

Dear Santa,

I have longed to have a pretty doll. Will you bring me some peanuts and candy also?

Your little friend,

Martha Lena Kempf

Dear Santa,

Have you a drum, gun, ball, horn, some candy and oranges for your little friend?

J.E. Schoen (12)

Dear Santa,

I want a watch, doll, pocketbook, handkerchief, horn, cap, coat, some candy and oranges. I want to thank you for all the things you will give me. Be sure not to forget my friend, Mary Lee Neckerman.

Clarabell Imhoff (8)

"I gots me a 'lectric train!"

Fig. 4-7. Fr. Gabriel, St. Joseph Parish, is mentioned in many 1937 letters to Santa. Santa's response is not recorded.

THE VILLAGE SMITHY

Under the spreading Chestnut tree
The Village Smithy stands;
The smith—a mighty man is he
With large and sinewy hands.
—Longfellow

In the 1930s, Pilot Grove's village blacksmith did not stand under a chestnut tree, spreading or otherwise. Bob Zahringer plied his ancient trade in a small, rather dilapidated brick shed off Second Street not far from the back door of today's "Paula's Taste of Home".

Zahringer[2] was not a precise fit to the stereotypical image of Tennyson's blacksmith. Yes, he wore the traditional great black leather apron but the resemblance ended there. If he had bulging biceps, I never saw them. His face was round with flabby jowls and a fish-belly complexion. He wore glasses that looked like Coke bottle bottoms. He was about the size of my dad—6 feet or so and weighed in at about 220 pounds. I would judge him to have been in his early-40s. He was never without his beat up old brown felt hat, so grease stained and battered it was impossible to imagine what it had looked like new.

With his coal fired forge, he heated iron and then formed it on his massive anvil by brute force and a 5 pound hammer. It suited the tight-fisted farmers of the community to repair machinery with an old cast off piece of scrap iron that Bob Zahringer could pound miraculously into the required shape—and at a fraction of the cost of new.

These repair tasks made up most of his work, but he was also a skilled farrier—shoeing horses "while you wait" as well as crafting new shoes for the work horses of the day. I'm sure his clients appreciated his latest fashions in equine hoofwear.

From our perspective at the century's end—it is surprising how much the horse still dominated farming in the 1930s. They were draft animals, supplying muscle power to do the farm work. They were also the principal mode of transportation for many rural folk.

Warnhoff's Mercantile, Mom's store of choice, got much trade from these farm families who commuted to town via horse and buggy (or team and wagon). Harry Warnhoff commissioned a long hitching rack behind the store. It was approximately where the do-it-yourself car wash is today.

The creosoted railroad ties were implanted and a 2-inch gas pipe fitted through bore holes to provide 25-30 feet of hitching space. They even had a little dedication ceremony when it was completed and the fact that quite a number of folks joined the celebration says something about the level of entertainment available in the town. We were easily amused during the Great Depression.

Fig. 4-8. The smith's shop was in a dilapidated brick shed behind Chet Oster's Bar and Grill.

Much of Warnhoff's trade in those days was pure barter. I suppose many of those farm folk went for months without the sight of paper money. They brought in full flitches of bacon, country cured ham, home-churned butter, backyard rendered lard and homemade cottage cheese.

Today, using selective memory, many old heads wax nostalgic about those days of yore. My memory may be better because, to be honest, when I passed the counter piled high with of this greasy, greenish tinged stuff near the back door, it nearly turned my stomach.

Mom did use a lot of the bacon. It still had the rind of course, and might have been called "Streak of Lean" except there was no streak and no lean!

A by-product of Warnhoff's hitching rail was the fertilizer (horse manure) that was there for the taking. So much horse and mule dung accrued that—despite the little old ladies modestly harvesting buckets of rose fertilizer—"...nothing finer for roses", said Harry Warnhoff—it had to be shoveled onto a wagon and hauled off several times a year. Most of these horses and mules were clients of the "Village Smithy" at one time or another.

I often watched Mr. Zahringer at work when Dad, several times a year, took him picks to be sharpened. It struck me strange that this section crew of 4 men had to

[2] This is the correct spelling of his name. I had always thought his name was "Zanger"—that's what everyone called him.

Fig. 4-9."Gaddyup Dan and shut up about your shoes apinchin'!"

have the blacksmith sharpen their tools, but in retrospect it was very plain—Bob Zahringer charged one dollar for sharpening 25-30 picks. He had a large, electrically powered grinding wheel and could do it in one-tenth of the time of the section hands using their hand grinder.

This electric grinder plus a naked electric light bulb hanging over the work area, was the only concession to 20th century technology in Zahringer's shop. His forge used a forced draft fan which was driven from a weighted flywheel cranked up by hand. You cranked up the heavy flywheel and its momentum would drive the fan for 3-5 minutes, enough to bring a horseshoe to white heat.

More importantly, the tool sharpening job was an opportunity to throw a little business (pronounced "bidness" in Pilot Grove) to local tradesmen. Dad, acting for the Katy Railroad, had little occasion to purchase services for his operation. When he did, he made sure it went where it did the most good.

Bob appreciated the business and I often saw Dad and him disappear for a moment into a back room to come out wiping their mouths on their sleeves. I peeped in one time and confirmed my suspicions—Bob had a pint of "Pine Mill" stashed in the rafters. I noted this and when I could drift away, I took a look through his trash barrel.

"Pine Mill" was one of the first whiskies to return to the shelves after the long dry spell of Prohibition. During these early post-Prohibition days, the government went nuts trying to answer the demands of the frustrated Prohibitionists that had been in the saddle so long. The blue-noses were sore losers. One of the demands was that legally produced whiskey should not give bootleggers a ready-made source for bottles. That is, they were afraid the empty bottles would be used for packaging moonshine.

Like it so often does, the government passed the problem off to the industry which addressed it in various ways. Pine Mill, a Kentucky sour mash distillery, utilized an innovative scheme. Their bottles had a silver quarter embedded into the base of the bottle. This 25¢ was added to the retail price—pushing the cost of a pint from 50¢ to 75¢, but the customer got an 'instant refund' of 25¢ by breaking the bottle. The incentive to smash the bottle never failed—well, hardly ever.

My colleagues and I found that often when a party got going real good, everybody got happy and forgot about the instant refund. (Not all liquor bottlers used this innovation.) They inadvertently threw the bottles into the trash. I used to carry a railroad spike which was real handy in retrieving silver quarters. I found 2-3 a month. We were doing something for the government, we were reducing the trash and we made a little money — real entrepreneurs.

Unfortunately, I never struck silver at Zahringer's shop. His name should have told me it was a forlorn hope. Any of the local German population would have had a stroke if they found they had thrown a quarter away!

I was with Dad one Saturday in the fall of 1935 when the railroad tools were being sharpened. Mr. Zahringer, sweating profusely, was trying to finish off some horse shoes so he could get to the railroad work. The Katy paid cash-on-barrelhead, no barter, thus it was business much to be desired.

He pulled one of the horseshoes out of the forge and tempered the iron by quenching it in a vat of water. The sizzling steel went from white hot to red and then began cooling down to 200-300° F. as he tonged it onto the anvil to await final forming.

He looked up the street and grimaced. I followed his gaze to a dandified dud coming down Second Street. The approaching fellow was certainly no local. He wore a short brimmed felt Trilby hat which made him stand out like a diamond in a pig's snout. Nobody other that city dudes wore a hat like that. He also wore a suit.

Here in the village, suits would be worn by a gent on two occasions—his wedding and his funeral—usually the same suit. This city slicker even wore gray spats and had 'salesman' written all over him. It was clear that he was headed in our direction and Zahringer was muttering under his breath… "Damned drummer! I really don't have time to listen to this…"

As the salesman entered the shop, Zahringer continued his work, not even acknowledging his presence. A loud "Ahem" failed to gained him attention. Now somewhat at a loss the salesman sees the horseshoe on the anvil and picks it up. It was still at 200° or so. Of course, he immediately dropped it on the cement floor. At the loud ring, Zahringer wheeled around. Seeing what had happened, he smiled, "You sure dropped that in a hurry, didn't you?"

The salesman went red with embarrassment. He drew himself up to look down his nose at the sweaty, grinning blacksmith. "Sir, I am a hardware expert. It doesn't take me long to look at a horseshoe! Now I'd ..." At this Zahringer let out a guffaw and slapped his knee. Dad laughed uproariously and I giggled.

Now totally flustered and humiliated, the salesman, attempting to salvage a small amount of dignity, did an about-face. He stormed back to his hotel, his face as red as his burnt hand. The village smithy never saw him again.

Dad said, "I think that fellow will be a little shy of coming in here again, Bob."

Bob laughed and said, "Well Dick, you know the old saying, 'Once burnt, twice shy'!"

COOKS, COOKERY AND COOKBOOKS

MY MOTHER, THE GOURMET COOK (...NOT!)

The widely held myth that females are somehow born with an instinctive ability to cook is given the lie by the example of my mother. She could not cook. Julia Child never consulted with Mom on matters of haute cuisine.

But let's be fair. She had obstacles. She was thirteen when her mother was crippled by a stroke. The facilities available to her were always primitive. Her older sisters had long since married and flown the nest. How was she to learn?

Mom had three cookbooks. One was the "White House Cookbook" published during the tenure of Warren G. Harding. This was a gift from a well-meaning if completely imbecilic friend. I thumbed through that cookbook once and pictured Mom — "...Oh my goodness! We should have gotten far more truffles for this dinner party! And Dick, go by Warnhoff's and get me some itsy-bitsy spoons for this caviar. By the way is this Beluga? I told Walter specifically that we must have Beluga caviar!" Get real!

The second cookbook was a 1934 gift from L.E. Brightwell of the Metropolitan Insurance Company when he achieved the unachievable—he sold my Dad a life insurance policy.

The third was a 1929 edition of "Any One Can Bake" compiled by the Royal Baking Powder Company.

They give away their secret opinion of the intellect of the Great American Bourgeoisie when they explain: "In a book so modest in size, we have deemed it best to try to do one thing well and so have confined ourselves to some the delightful dishes produced by baking."

Dear Royal Baking Powder Company: "Did the fact that you are selling baking powder have nothing to do with your selections?"

Years after my childhood days, Mom gave these books to me as keepsakes. They were still in pristine condition. There were no pencilled notes, no dog-eared pages, no coffee stains. I am led to believe she hadn't much consulted them.

Mom had two methods of food preparation: fry it in deep fat (bacon drippings) or boil it for half a day. I don't criticize—this is the way everyone cooked in the 1930s. The meat was tough. At least the cuts that we could afford were. Boiling for half a day made it somewhat less of a hazard to the teeth and gave a fighting chance to the digestive system.

Cooking oil was cheap because it was a by-product of the 'streak-o-lean' bacon that everyone used. One pound of bacon would produce 3 oz. of rind, 12 oz. of grease and 1 oz. of edible bacon. Bacon was always sold by the slab complete with rind. During our years in London, I nostalgically noted most London butchers still sell it like this. If you asked, they would cut off the rind all the while looking at you strangely.

Baking and roasting was Mom's forte. She was pretty good at a holiday spread. Baked chicken was her specialty. She baked it like turkey — with her special dressing and gravy. The gravy was always lumpy[3] but the dressing was good. She used a lot of sage plus oysters and hard-boiled eggs. It was quite good and I favor sagey dressing to this day — usually using so much that I'm up once or twice at night for water.

Best of all though was her twice weekly, home-baked bread. It was delicious and my mouth still waters when I remember the fragrant aroma that permeated the whole house when she was taking the hot pans of bread or rolls out of the oven.

PLAT DU JOUR CIRCA 1934

It was a hot and dusty summer day and we loved it because, barefoot, we could feel the warm powder of desiccated caliche clay being molded by our feet. Tossing this finely pulverized dust in the air, we could mimic an Apache war dance—what fun!

I looked at the sun now standing near its zenith and casting short shadows. "Junior," I said, "I'm gonna have to get on home now. Mom is expected me to show up for somepin' to eat."

"Junior" was Homer Etson Jeffress Junior my main man and first grade classmate. We were on summer vacation from Miss Madge Goode's elementary grades, Pilot Grove Public School. Junior was my main man because he had had a run at first grade in the 1932-33 session and had been held back. I caught up with him in 1933, but he was the veteran. He had been there in the trenches. He was a store of knowledge about this new experience—school.

"Don't go, Sonny!" he begged. "Look, I'll ask Mom if you can eat with us. Just stay." He returned after some whining to his mother, "Mom says it's OK. She's gonna start somepin' right now."

Willa Jeffress, Homer's mother, had been abandoned by her husband, a sometime house painter. Junior was very

[3] I have always thought that the food giants — Hormel, Swift, General Foods, et al — were missing a bet. They could assure the authenticity of 'home made gravy' if they would sell canned "gravy lumps".

proud of his father and often told me how his daddy "...makes $5 a day when he's working." Five bucks a day was a good wage in the 1930s. Homer Sr. had one problem — he didn't work very much. $5 per day times zero days equals...well, lemme see here.

The past spring he had executed a "poor man's divorce" — he just walked away.

So Willa Jeffress was, on this day, in no more postion to entertain Homer's friends to lunch than to attend King Edward VIII's Coronation. Nevertheless she made do. Here was the luncheon menu:

> **Weenies** - gently simmered in pure well water for 20 minutes. These exquisite epicurean delights are quite dear (15¢ per pound), so — one per guest, please.
>
> **Biscuits** - hot from the oven and made from scratch with country lard and sifted flour (i.e., all weevils removed). Again, one per guest, please.
>
> **Gravy** - for topping off the biscuits. Made from the 'weenie water' and delightfully seasoned with exotic spices (Morton's salt and Watkins pepper).
>
> **Grape Koolaid** - Freshly made from 2 gallons of cool well water, one entire package of Koolaid and one heaping teaspoonful of sugar. In a clear glass this 'nectar of the gods' exhibits a slightly bluish tinge attesting to its authentic grape origin.
>
> Sorry, no ice.
>
> [Today we might call this "Tincture of Grape" and sell it for a buck a bottle.]

This menu, I think you will agree, represents a luncheon fit for a king —well, anyway, we thought so!

FURRY FELLOWS OF THE FIELD AND FEATHERED FLYING FRIENDS

The children who endured the Great Depression —the "hungry years"—have views on Mother Nature's little creatures of the field, forest and sky at some variance from their modern counterparts. Today, little Johnny might squeal with delight at the sight of a bunny rabbit.

"Can we get us a pet rabbit, Mommy? If we had a rabbit, I'd feed it and take care of it! Can we Momma?" He had a vision of the little critter happily playing in his cage.

The 1930s vision would be—a nice plump rabbit, roasted to a turn and gracing the platter with a garnish of new potatoes, carrots and pearl onions alongside.

In Pilot Grove there were a number of youths, older than me who got their spending money as semiprofessional hunters. Indeed, it was during such a hunting trip that Chester Bader came to grief. (See Murder, Mayhem and Misdeeds). Rabbits, dressed ready for the pot brought a dime apiece or 2 for 15¢. Add a few garden vegetables and you have a fine meal for 3-4 people.

The people of the "Chute" were particularly found of rabbit and squirrel. They were also even more bereft of ready cash than the average Pilot Grovan, so the opportunity to feed the family for the day for 15¢ was gladly received. This was the basis for the scandal of the year.

It came to pass in this way. Two of the town's "Great White Hunters"[4] were desperately in need of a little money but the hunting that day had been especially fruitless. After a day of tramping the fields and woods in the biting cold of early November, they came up empty.

Glumly returning home, dispirited, cold and broke, they contemplated their plight. "Should we go out tomorrow? The weather is supposed to be a little warmer and maybe we can get a squirrel or two," says one.

"Look", says the other, "I only got ..." He searched his pockets, "...three .22 short cartridges. With the four you got, that's seven shots. That ain't hardly worth going out for. We'd have to hit something damned neart ever shot! I ain't got a dime much less 20¢ fer a box of cartridges! We got to get some money somehow."

As they sat on the stoop contemplating their troubles, an enormous black and white cat jumped up on the stoop and, purring, came to rub against them. "This your cat?"

"Naw, he just hangs around the neighborhood. Just look at that sucker—big and fat. I wonder where he eats? Looks like that fat possum we sold over in the Chute last month. Got a quarter for that dude as I remember!"

The thought struck them simultaneously. "Why not, it's an easy quarter? Nobody'll miss old Tom."

"OK, but we got to bury the pelt, I don't want no trouble with the neighbors. And we gotta cut the tail off, else this guy ain't gonna pass for no 'possum." The deed was quickly done and the Big Bookkeeper in the sky duly added "Caticide" to the long list of transgressions these two villains had already accrued.

There was, as expected, a ready market for such a plump, juicy "possum". The pot was made ready in the Simpson household. A few potatoes and onions were added and the family would be well fed one more day.

Of course, any wise ass that pulls off a coup like this cannot keep his mouth shut about it. A few weeks later the scandal broke and all the town knew. Surprisingly, there were

[4] I do not remember who these guys were and would not mention them if I did for reasons that are quite evident. The story, however, is true and may be corroborated by some of the village old heads who remember it.

no repercussions from an outraged cat owner. Maybe no one claimed ownership.

But, the fresh killed game market in the Chute *did* change:

"HEREAFTER FELLOWS, LEAVE THE TAIL ON ANY GAME YOU WANNA SELL ME!"

Contrast this response with the reverberations that would be likely today. C.W. Gusewelle writes in the Kansas City Star. He is a hunter. Tongue in cheek, he once wrote, "...while I enjoy hunting and relish the flavor of wild game, I rarely eat spotted owl unless whooping crane is unavailable."

He says he received excoriations from as far away as Massachusetts. Fanatical animal lovers (animal rights wackos?) expressed devout prayers that he would die of some protracted, agonizing and loathesome disease.

The problem with such people is that they think anyone who disagrees with them is the devil incarnate. With them, passion has become dementia. After all, he was not talking about eating the family Tomcat which might be regarded by some, justifiably, as akin to cannibalism.

Speaking of cannibalism let's go on to cookbooks.

COOKBOOKS

Goodwife Daisy is an avid collector of cookbooks. At last count she had in excess of 400 of them. The word 'excess' is used advisedly here. I tease her that with the distilled culinary wisdom of the ages at our fingertips, our table seems, quite often to be graced with chili and crackers. But then, I *like* chili and crackers.

She has volumes of Escoffier, Paul Prudhomme, Daniel Beard, Robert Carrier, Madhur Jaffrey, all the ethnics— Greek, Italian, French, Cajun, Chinese, Portuguese, Thai et al. She even has the 1950 edition of TM 10-412, "United States Army Recipes" about which more later. But one culinary opus she does *not* have is "Alfurd Packer - His Cookbook." I found a copy in Truckee once, but she demurred.

All along the spine of the Sierra Nevadas in northeast California, tucked away in the passes and mountain meadows, there are small mountain villages which survive mostly by serving the tourist trade in the summer and (I suppose) taking in one another's washing in the off-season. The clear and cool mountain air, the stately Sequoias, the beautiful pines of the high sierras form an irresistible magnet for the unwary flat-landers.

Unbelievably useless junk "...awaits your shopping pleasure — wonderful selections handcrafted in the mountains by native artisans" (actually imported from Taiwan).

Truckee, California is one such village. It is just off Interstate 80 west of Reno, Nevada and near Lake Tahoe. I was browsing in one of the numerous 'tourist traps' there one summer morning when I came across the cookbook section. Every one of these places, nationwide, has a collection of the local cookery, usually pulled together by a local church or community group as a fund raiser. They all look alike with black comb binders, pasteboard covers and inexpertly typed and xeroxed pages. They are cheap, but quite often have some very good recipes. Daisy has dozen or more such books.

I was thumbing through the pages of "Alfurd Packer — His Cookbook". It was pretty tame stuff for the most part. But, there *were* a few very appetizing recipes. Then something struck me!

Daisy saw me standing there holding this book and staring into space as I searched memory cells for the story of Alfurd Packer. (Alfurd is the way he spelled his name.) "What are you puzzling about?" So I told her, remembering more and more as I told the story of Alfurd Packer.

George Donner, an Illinois farmer, was elected leader of an immigrant party headed for California in 1846. For weeks they had toiled and plodded across the nearly trackless wastelands of Kansas, Colorado and Utah on the Oregon Trail. At Salt Lake City they left the Oregon Trail and struck out southwest for California on the newly-opened Hastings Cutoff south of the Great Salt Lake. This was before the Great Gold Rush of '49 and there was much controversy and little information about the best track through the Sierras. One thing that was known for sure— "...you don't want to get caught in the mountains in the snow season".

But they did! They ended up stranded in the Sierra Nevada at the outset of the worst winter ever recorded there.

Alfurd Packer was a member of the party. Alfurd was a dark, giant, hulking and taciturn man, a loner —and a butcher by trade. When the snows came early and trapped them in what is now called the Donner Pass, he saved them. That is, he saved *some* of them. Forty-six survived out of 87. But at a horrible price!

By the time the starving survivors straggled into Sutter's Fort, The Donner Party had written one of the darkest chapters in American history, a tale of humans reduced to the most desperate circumstances including, famously, cannibalism.

I would speculate that some local printer with a grotesque sense of humor jokingly named the cookbook for Alfurd Packer. I'll bet the ladies' club didn't catch on. I just know the tourists didn't. These Donner Pass events had happened a century and a half ago, though just a few miles from where we stood.

"So", I said, waggling Alfurd's Cookbook at Daisy, "You want this one? It's got all Alfurd's favorite recipes."

"No, thank you very much," she answered and that is why her cookbook collection shall forever remain incomplete.

CHICKEN SHADOW SOUP

The month of May is full of holidays and celebrations in our family. In addition to the standard, national holidays—Mothers' Day and Memorial Day, we have some personal holidays. My birthday which coincides with Cinco de Mayo[5] is doubly celebrated with a copious flow of Dos Equus, Corona and an occasional shot of tequila.

Daisy and I commemorate Armed Forces Day (third Saturday of May) as our anniversary. Of course the first day of May is Mayday, a holiday that should have completely lost its panache when the Communist world collapsed, but didn't because most European countries had co-opted it as "Spring Bank Holiday".

With all this it was not surprising when I got a jingle from older son Rick one May. "We're having a little cook-out. Why don't you and Mom come on out?"

I pretended to require careful study of this invitation, "What's on the menu?"

"Well, for one thing there's *Chicken Shadow Soup*." We both laughed. I have always been amazed at how he remembers trivial things from his childhood.

I told a story years ago about "Chicken Shadow Soup". It came from a 1930s cartoon. Popeye's pal, Wimpy—normally given to hamburgers—had a big iron soup pot in the backyard with a nice fire alight. On a perch well above the fire is a chicken. Popeye asks, "Whatcha cookin',Wimpy?"

Wimpy answers, "Chicken Shadow Soup".

You had to have been there in the 1930s to catch the full effect. It was a fact that foodstuff was stretched and stretched again to fill more and more hungry mouths— "Chicken Shadow Soup" was the ultimate.

Homer Jeffress and I peeped into his mother's soup pot one time to check out the delicious aroma being given off. The aroma mainly was from a couple of onions. There were also two or three carrots and a tiny bird. Mr. Olson called these "Fryers" and sold them live and on the hoof for about 15¢.

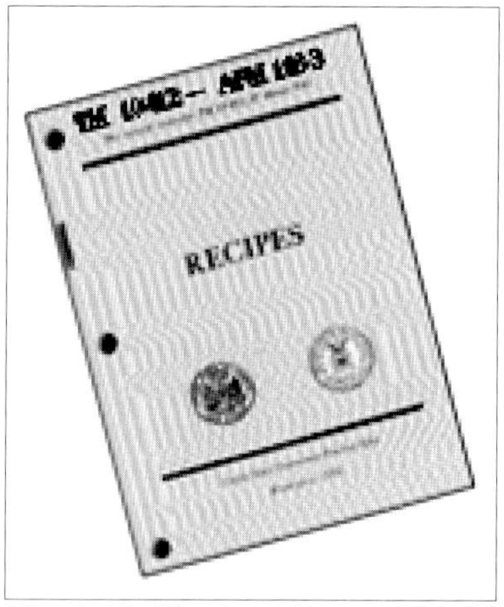

Fig. 4-10. The Army's answer to 10 million complaints about Army chow.

So Willa would feed the family chicken one day then chicken soup the next two days (adding water as required). And all for about 15¢. This chicken soup came close to qualifying as "Chicken Shadow Soup".

If Campbell Soup were to offer this soup today, they would include a statement on the can:

"NO CHICKENS WERE HARMED IN THE MAKING OF THIS CHICKEN SOUP".

"FIRST, SKIN ONE MULE..."

TM 10-412 is the official US Army cookbook. Daisy's collection would not be complete without it. Once, when I worked at Midwest Research Institute, we had an Army project. My boss at that time, Walter Benson, Colonel US Army retired, admonished us about proper research methodology. The lesson on how *not* to do it came from the US Army Quartermaster General (QM).

Their research plan was easy, straightforward and—dead wrong. They would do an analysis of all the meals that had been served throughout the war. This data would be easily manipulated by the new IBM data processors. Large databases would have high statistical validity, etc.

The results "proved" that one of the men's favorites was beans. They had eaten beans several times each week. Stew also must have been a favorite. They had it quite often, etc. What's wrong with this research plan?

Ans. The troops never had an opportunity to express any preference. They ate what was on offer! They ate beans because they were served beans. The same with stew. The QM rejected the research, restudied the problem and TM

WIZARD OF ID KC Star 5.Jun.1998
WELL... I'LL BE...
HEY, WAITER, THERE'S A PIECE OF CHICKEN IN MY CHICKEN SOUP
THE CHEF HAS BEEN LOOKING FOR THAT!
SWOOSH

Sir Rodney orders the Chicken Shadow Soup.

[5] Cinco de Mayo is one of those holidays that was mostly invented by merchants and food vendors to pry loose pocket change. It celebrates an obscure military victory over Emperor Maximilian. It is much celebrated in Mexican-American communities but most in Mexico never heard of it! Sort of like Santa Claus in Japan.

10-412 was one of the results.

As I was telling this story, Daisy asked if I could get a copy for her collection. "Of course I can", I said, and I did.

Weeks later and after seeing no evidence of a good old US Army messhall chow, I asked her if she ever made use of her TM 10-412. "No, it's not very helpful", she answered, "Impossible to scale down the ingredients."

Here is an example:

RECIPE FOR CHICKEN SOUP

INGREDIENTS	AMOUNT
First, prepare the stock:	
Chicken, bony parts	30 pounds
Water	8 gallons
Carrots, diced	2 pounds
Onions, diced	1 pound
Celery, diced	1 pound
Salt	5 oz.
Pepper	1 teaspoon
Then the soup	
Chicken stock	7-1/2 gallons
Carrots, diced	2 pounds
Onions, chopped	2 pounds
Celery, diced	1 pound
Rice	1-1/2 pounds
Salt	1 oz.
Pepper	1 teaspoon
Chicken, cooked, chopped	2 pounds
Butter or chicken fat	1 pound
Flour, sifted	1 pound

Possibly an earlier version of TM 10-412 (See Fig. 4-10.) would have started the recipe for stew with the instruction: 'FIRST, SKIN ONE MULE.'

DENVER BISCUITS

After tempting you with chicken soup, I feel I must give you a *real* recipe. Here is one from Mary Burger. Marjorie says, "Mother's biscuits were of such renown, menus for civic events were often warped around to include them. When I came home from school and entered a kitchen that looked like a light skiff of snow had fallen, I knew that Denver Biscuits would be on someone's menu tonight."

(Prepare dough day before baking). Scald and let cool:

1 qt. milk.

Mix with: 1 cup sugar

1 cup mashed potatoes

1 cake yeast add flour

Add enough flour to make a soft batter. Cover with damp cloth and let rise 2 hours.

Combine and add to first mixture:

1 cup lard
1 Tablespoon salt
2 teaspoons baking powder
1 teaspoon soda
Approx. 8 cups flour

Cover again with damp cloth. Let rise once, punch down, then refrigerate overnight.

On the second day, punch down, let rise; punch down again, let rise.

Roll out about 1/4 to 3/8 inch thick on floured surface.

Butter dough, fold over, butter top, cut out.

Place biscuits, just touching, in greased cake pans. Let rise once. Bake 12 minutes at 400°.

LIGHT — FLUFFY — DELICIOUS!

FOOD, FITNESS AND FANATICS

Before we leave the topic of food, I have a favorite lecture (actually, more of a rant) that I need to get off my chest. A visiting "Yank' captured the gist when I heard her on BBC in London. She said, "Americans have the notion that death is an option and if you only eat the right things and exercise dutifully, you don't really have to die!"

I have mentally catalogued all the foods that the "Center for Science in the Public Interest" has put on the proscribed list. They don't think anyone remembers this stuff and that they can go on pulling our chain indefinitely maintaining a continuous level of panic over all the things that are sure to kill us. I fooled them—I remember. For example:

Bacon is full of nitrates and nitrites that are sure to cause cancer. Cranberries are covered with pesticides and are sure to kill you. Saccharine, when fed to laboratory animals caused cancer in the kidneys (although to get an equivalent dose, humans would have to consume 50 gallons of soft drinks per day for 20 years). The ripening chemical applied to apples—Alar—*might* make little children sick. (But of a *certainty*, destroyed a number of Washington apple firms.) Hamburgers cooked over an open flame (backyard barbecue) drip fat into the coals and generate a number of carcinogens that will surely kill you. Customers must be advised of any pesticide or herbicide that is used on crops and must be clearly revealed to customers at the supermarket (State of California).

Net, net, if you read these notices carefully, you will find that everything sold in that store stands a better than even chance of killing you outright or, at best, giving you cancer.

IF IT TASTES GOOD—SPIT IT OUT!

I have a philosophy on fitness, eating and exercise—moderation in all things. Forget the fitness fanatics. Andrew Wile, MD seems to agree in his best seller, "Spontaneous Healing" (Fawcett Columbine, $11.95 at Barnes and Noble.)

He says if you exercise iron discipline and give up all the things that make life worth living, good food, wine in moderation and moderate exercise—you might add two weeks to your expected life span.

I would add that those two weeks will be spent in a nursing home being diapered by people whom you would not have invited to your home.

His T-Shirt message captures it all:

EAT RIGHT

EXERCISE

DIE ANYWAY!

I will freely admit that I possess all the muscle tone of an over-ripe banana, but the idea that one may cheat death by jogging, stair-stepping or jumping rope is a forlorn hope. In support of this, I give you the story of Jim Fixx.

Jim Fixx, the irritating, self-appointed national fitness nuisance and professional nagger, dropped dead—while jogging. On this event I have only this to say, "Of the manifold attributes of God, we must not forget—a sense of humor".

I have a friend who consistently demurs invitations to join in fitness frolics. He says, "I get all the exercise I need acting as pallbearer for my fitness-freak friends."

THAT DARNED CHOLESTROL!

There is an English fellow—Dr. Jonathan Miller—who, in addition to being a practicing cardiologist, is a producer and narrator of some extremely good health and medical science shows designed for a general audience. In the 1980s when we watched BBC a lot, he had a show "The Body In Question". I never missed it but when it started, goodwife Daisy took her book back to the bedroom for a reading period. Here's why—

On his second show, Dr. Miller's topic was cholestrol, arterial plaque and associated subjects. He illustrated his lecture with an autopsy which he perform right there before our eyes. After a quick opening stroke with an electric saw, he applied thoracic retractors then reached in to lift this lady's heart (the 89 year old woman was dead, in case you had not so surmised). Grasping a crown artery, he snipped off an inch or so. It looked like a piece of red rubber garden hose but with a special lining.

"Now look at this," he says, as he motions the camera in for a close up which must of sent the queasy among his audience directly to the bathroom. He pointed out the thick yellowish arterial lining. It looked like pure chicken fat.

"This is cholestrol! This lady did not follow good dietary habits and this is the result!"

It struck me then that at least half the population of the earth on that day would have loved to have such arteries at age 89. Try scaring people in Pilot Grove in the 1930s with the dire consequences of too much fried chicken, too many hamburgers and french fries, too many juicy steaks! "Wow," they would have said, "Where do I sign up?"

My final appeal to sanity involves my mother. She never has been a fountainhead of knowledge on nutrition and dietary do's and don'ts—didn't care really. For the last 50 years she has been a living example of all the eating taboos. She lives on cookies, Twinkies, M&Ms—in short—junk food. I'm sure it will all come home to roost one day and kill her just like the Center for Science in the Public Interest threatens, but in the meantime she laughed in the face of the horrible fate that awaits her as she ate ice cream and cake at her recent 100th birthday!

Quod erat demonstrandum and thus endeth the lecture.

THE CHRISTMAS TREE

In early April of 1995 my (then) 10 year old grandson Brian called to request my presence at a Fourth Grade 'Grandparents' Day' at Olathe Middle School. I acquiesced and began rehearsing my oooh's and aaah's for the presumed student 'Show and Tell'.

On the eve of 'Grandparents' Day' he called again to confirm the invitation. He casually mentioned in passing that the *grandparents would do the Show and Tell'*. We were to bringing artifacts from our schooldays and youth, i.e., the Stone Age, and explain these odds and ends. One lady brought an ancient flat-iron—the type that is heated on the kitchen stove—and challenged the 'l'il rascals' to guess its purpose. My son Rick, Brian's father, answered that it was used to hold a door open since that's what we had used in the years that he was growing up.

Rick alerted me that there would be numerous recitations of 'walking ten miles to one room schoolhouses and ten miles back, through snow drifts 6 feet deep and uphill both ways. In the event this turned out to be accurate.

We spoke in turn and I desperately searched my memory for something to say about walking to school. I was determined that Brian's grandfather not let him down. Although my topic was the Korea War (the only topic on which I had any artifacts to hand), I startled all by telling the truth about walking to school.

Sure, I walked to school. It was only about 100 yards. I didn't get up until about 8 o'clock. I washed my face, dressed and had my standard bowl of Quaker Puffed Rice fortified with milk and lots of sugar. Alone, Puffed Rice has all the consistency, taste and nutritional value of polystyrene packing peanuts.

"Why then did I always eat Quaker Puffed Rice?" someone asked. Ah, it was the boxtops you see. Send in boxtops and a dime and get: a Dick Tracy secret decoder ring, or a secret signaling device (whistle), or a police badge (I had Chief, Captain, Lieutenant, Sergeant and 2 Patrolman badges). Guess who got to be Chief in our Cops and Robbers games?)

I began my walk to school (actually I ran) at the school 'warning bell'. The 'warning bell' was an ancient harvesters dinner bell mounted on the roof at the southeast corner of the old main (1922) school building. A long rope enabled Bob Chastain the building custodian to ring it from the ground. This rope also enabled the local juvenile delinquents to sneak up to the school at night and ring the bell then run like fury. Bob soon learned to pull the bell rope into a second story window and thus put a stop to this scandalous and criminal behavior.

At any rate, to Brian's relief, my war stories offset my lack of martyrdom in the 'walking to school' contest and he saved face. However, the incident did bring to mind other stories that I told *my* kids when *they* were growing up, the ones that always start out: "We were so poor that we ..."

For example, "We were so poor that we had to use *real* grass in our Easter baskets!" or "We were so poor that we used a *real* tree for Christmas!" I remember harvesting one such tree. It was Christmas time 1935.

For several evenings before we set up the tree, there were animated after-supper discussions on decorating it. Dad dragged out the old lights and we went through the annual ritual of trying to find the one bad bulb which put the kibosh on the entire string. Connections were in series so if one bulb failed, none of them worked. This series electrical design saved about 1/10 of one cent in the manufacture of a Christmas tree light string therefore was obligatory. We made a game of it and, as always, after 10-12 kid-hours of labor, the light string was put right.

Dixie was then in Junior High and one of the ideas that she picked up in 'Arts and Craps' (as we called it) was the use of popcorn strings. It's ever so simple—you pop some popcorn (we bought it in ears and shelled it ourselves) then, using a needle and a very long piece of thread, string the kernels together. If you wanted to get real fancy some of the popcorn could be dyed pretty colors. You must use (non-poisonous) food coloring since inevitably some nitwit would have to eat some.

At any rate the string is left to the birds after the tree is taken down and we would not want to poison our little feathered friends. Never mind that they might hang themselves or choke to death on the thread.

Dick Tracy badges. Only 3 boxtops!

Finally came the day when the decorations were ready and it was time to get a tree. I had heard Mom and Dad talking earlier in the week—"...Harry Dedrick... some nice trees... Friday night..."

Harry Dedrick's brother George was discharged from his WWI service in the U.S. Navy and returned to the family farm in 1919. This modest farm lies south of Pilot Grove on Bellair Road. Harry was married to a very distant relation of Mom's (George never married and lived out a hermit life in a converted schoolbus back of the main house.)

Apparently, on the slender basis of Mom's relationship with Harry Dedrick, Dad had gotten permission to harvest a Christmas tree from his farm.

Friday evening arrived and Bob and I watched Dad as he slipped into his mackinaw and four-buckle overshoes against the December chill and the light snow that crunched underfoot.

"Can I go? Can I go? Can I go?" we demanded in unison."

"Of course! I was wanting you to help" he answered as we climbed aboard our old black '29 Chevy.

As we turned eastward on Bellair Road, I could see the sun just beginning to set behind us. Low streaks of stratus clouds were beautifully tinted red, pink and purple by the dying sun. Dad saw me looking, "Red sky at night - sailor's delight! We'll have a clear day tomorrow - colder than Billy-be-damned but clear."

Bob and I had on our imitation leather aviator's helmets with ear flaps in place. Woolen, green plaid mackinaws covered us to our knees and collars were turned up against the icy north wind. Brown cotton gloves guarded our fingers.

We passed the Dedrick home and stopped near a copse of cedars. Dad surveyed the trees a moment then opened his door. Bob and I did likewise. "No, no!" he said, "The light ain't too good but I don't see none a them trees that look worth draggin' home! I'm gonna take a closer look. You kids stay here."

He returned in a few minutes shaking his head. "I

Fig. 4-11. Thelma Fredrick, Mattie Jo Heim and Virginia Theobald - 1940.

wouldn't have none a them trees", he muttered, "Now, I don't know what to do. Mom and Dixie are expecting to decorate a tree tonight and we don't want to disappoint them. Let's go on out this road and look some more. It's getting dark but I brought a lantern."

We passed Fred Theobald's home[6] (Fred Jr. was a classmate). The Theobalds were—Fred Sr., his wife, daughter Virginia (PGHS Class of 1941), Fred Jr. (Class of 1945) and little sister Joanne 2-3 years younger.

The Theobald family pet was a red, 50 pound Chow named Terry, meaner than a junkyard dog. Terry had a mane like a lion which made him virtually invulnerable in a dogfight. He got into a brawl with my mutt Tex every time they got close to one another. Worse, he mopped up the ground with poor old Tex until Tex simply learned that discretion was the better part of valor. When Terry came in sight, Tex would remember some item that required his immediate attention back home and would depart with alacrity.

Homer Jeffress usually had a 'mongrel of the week' which also was regularly beaten up by Terry. A year after the Theobalds (and Terrible Terry) moved to the area Terry was found dead in the ditch, a hit and run victim. Neither my nor Homer's tear ducts were overworked at his passing.

Mrs. Theobald had been previously married to a fellow named Bullard (Bullock? Ballard?) and had two sons then grown and off to college. I met one of them when he visited his mother in the early part of the war—1941-1942. He was a 2d Lieutenant in the Signal Corps. It was this son that was the instrument of disaster for the family in a postwar year. He had gotten his private flying license and took up his mother and his young half-sister Joanne for a sightseeing flight. They crashed and all were burned to death.

Fred Theobald Sr. was the unusual character in the family. Although I doubt that he was much of a religious person, he definitely had a powerful Puritan streak. Old Fred always had a lurking suspicion that somewhere, someone was having a good time and it was his bounden duty to put a stop to it. He even looked the part of one of the Old Testament prophets—all hell fire and damnation.

The old man was a tall, lean, reddish blonde haired man with weather-beaten face and the gnarled, leathery hands of a long time farmer. He was continuous harassing Fred Jr. on some minor point or another. He could have been a model for the step-father in the movie "A Boy's Life" who beat his stepson for tossing away a mustard jar that still had 2-3 molecules of mustard left in it.

Thus, when Homer and I went out to the Theobald place on the weekend, Fred Jr. was always busy. If he finished a chore (often with our help), the old man quickly found him another one. I think he often made up tasks for Fred Jr. possibly to discourage our visits.

It was getting darker now but just beyond the Theobald house we could see a large stand of cedar on the south side of the road. Dad opened the trunk to remove and light a kerosene lantern. We jumped the ditch and encountered a 'hog' fence. The regular grid of the fence came up 3 feet off the ground and was topped by 3 strands of barbed wire. Dad held the bottom strand, Bob and I climbed through. Dad vaulted at the fence post.

We blundered into a small stand of firs and he said, "OK, you guys take the lantern and pick out a good one." We milled around in the flickering light, finally selecting a six-footer. We laid to with a hatchet but after a several ineffectual whacks had to hand it over to Dad.

At the fall of the tree a dog barked nearby. It sounded like that 'hound from hell'—Terry. A door slammed and a porch light came on at the Theobald place. "What do we do now, Dad?" I asked.

"You and Bob grab the tree and drag it - trunk first. We're getting out of here fast! This place is posted." He doused the lantern returning us to darkness. As we made our undignified exit, I could barely make out the signs, "POSTED", "KEEP OUT", "NO HUNTING".

Old Fred was anything but hospitable, so, in panic, we stumbled, tumbled and rolled out of the woods. Approaching a small gully, I hit a patch of snow and did an imitation of an Olympic Grand Slalom on my nose.

I saw Dad hung up on the wire but Bob and I zipped through quickly. I did, however, snag my mackinaw on the barbed wire and left a piece of forensic evidence. Dad joined

[6] In 1995 Marshall Ray Haley's widow lived in this house.

us as we dragged the tree into the back seat of the car. (Days later, it would later take Mom an hour to get the pine resin off the seat.)

When we were safely around the corner, Dad turned on the lights and barreled it at 20-30 mph out to Highway 5 and followed a circuitous route back home where we made our triumphal entry, dragging the tree into the living room to its appointed place. Home were the hunters, home from the hill. We had bested nature, man and beast to captured our prize Christmas tree! That's how we felt.

Reality was somewhat different. Dad stood there sheepishly hiding a dangling overshoe buckle. Bob had lost both his gloves. I had a patch missing from the back of my Mackinaw (bought for school last September), my nose was missing some skin, my face was smeared with snowy muck and Dad held his hand obscuring the drying blood from a brush with the barb wire. The tree was a scraggly, unsymmetrical piece of trash. Even *we* could see this in the light.

Mom said, "You know we could have got a tree from Warnhoff's. They're shipped in from somewhere out west."

Dad bridled, "And just what do them trees cost? Knowing Harry Warnhoff, I take it they're not giving them away?"

"Well, they run from 25¢ to a dollar."

"But Mom," I said, "This tree didn't cost nothing!"

Mom sighed, "Yes, right, we can't beat that."

The popcorn strings were put on. The lights were strung. The paper links that Bob and I colored with Crayolas (Dixie supervising) were pasted together in chains and strung. When we put up the star, we stood back and declared it beautiful.

For subsequent Christmases we had to make do with Warnhoff's trees, there were no further 'liberated' Christmas trees. But that winter, the smell of pine resin lingered in the back seat for weeks. Every time we piled into the car we got a nostalgic whiff of Christmas. It was magic!

TRY THIS HERE HAIR DRESSING, SONNY

A year after his death the pitiable amount of life insurance that Dad had been coerced into buying ran out. Mom began casting about for means to foil the wolf at the door. She was an excellent seamstress and thought this skill might sustain the family. She tried making colorful, dressy, organdy aprons. They were very well done and sold like hot cakes, particularly around Christmas. The only drawback and the factor that brought the enterprise to a halt was that Mom sold the aprons for 25¢. The raw material cost about 20¢ leaving 5¢ profit per apron for 1-2 hours of labor.

She got into the home sales of cosmetics as women in these circumstances often do. Her line was pretty cheap which suited her potential customers very well. This enterprise soon ended also because, like the aprons, the bottom line yield was about 5¢ to 10¢ per hour. But before she packed it in, I tried out one of her formulations.

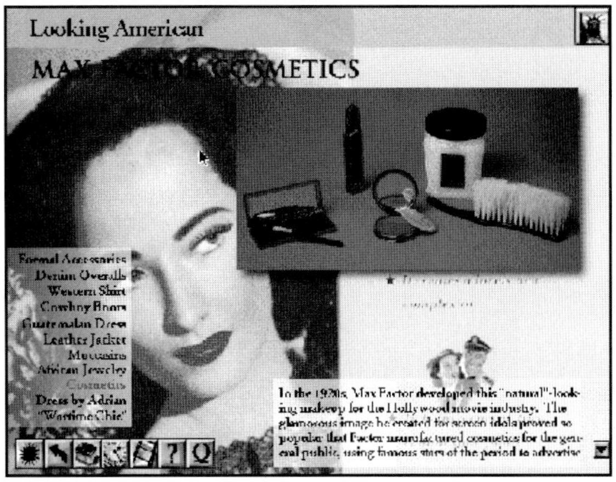

Fig. 4-12. Before the days of Mary Kay's pink Cadillacs, the financially strapped widder Salmon tried selling cheap cosmetics.

A problem I have had all my life is wavy, semi-curly hair which, like a long-haired dachshund or golden retriever, looks great if you spend most of your time combing and brushing it. Otherwise you find people crossing to the other side of the street when you approach.

One day Mom pulls out this bottle and proffers it, "You're always trying new hair tonic Sonny. Take a look at this."

"Dr. Rachenfrasch's Hair Dressing—Holds hair in place beautifully while giving hair and scalp a luxurious and therapeutic treatment. Maintains scalp exfoliation process with an exclusive pro-vitamin formula. Penetrates individual hair strands to give them a rich, deep luster. Holds hair in place even on breezy days."

Following the American tradition— "if some is good, more is better and too much is just right" —I sluiced about a half bottle on my hair and combed it in. I never paid any further attention to it, letting it do its stuff while I got on with my life.

I was 14, in the 9th grade and had moved up to the cavernous 'study hall' — home of the big kids — Senior High. The badly misnamed 'Study Hall' was crammed with desks with book stowage for each student in grades 9 through 12, maybe 100-120 kids. It was home base when we were not in a subject classroom. As you might guess, although we were supposed to be studying, it was mostly bedlam. The designation "Study Hall" badly missed the mark.

One afternoon in early fall, Homer Jeffress, Babe Heim and I were in the new (1937) gym—now the old gym— for basketball tryouts and practice. The boys used one end, the girls the other. Although this trio of rogues would be the

CONTINUED ON PAGE 69

PGHS FEEDER SCHOOLS

The improved road county network and improved bus funding enabled school consolidation to be essentially completed by the early 1940s.

Fig. 4-13. St. Joseph Parochial School, 4th and Harris Streets, Pilot Grove. In the 1930s and 40s, the teachers were Benedictine nuns from the Ft. Smith (Arkansas) Convent. St. Joseph uses lay teachers now. Photo 1988 from Mary (Salmon) Ninemire.

Fig. 4-15. 1938 Ford School Bus. Clemus Felten says, "Herman Reuter made this bus by putting a chassis on the back of a pickup truck. Benches were fastened to the floor for seating. When the weather was bad, and the roads were slick, he would stop at the bottom of Wessing Hill and put on the chains, taking them off when we got to the top. Sometimes we would walk up the hill or even help push the bus up. I rode this bus along with other students who lived west of Pilot Grove in 1938." Photo - Irene Felten.

Fig. 4-14. St. Martin's School, students of the school year 1935-36. 8th Grade: Rosaline Schuster, Georgia Widel, John Martin, Ralph Esser, 7th Grade: Frances Martin, Mildred Hoff, Isabel Schuster, 6th Grade: Bill McKinzie, Edna Martin, 5th Grade: Mary Bell Lammers, Kenneth Horst, 4th Grade: Estil Oswald, Emil Martin, Harold Lang, 3rd Grade: Edith Lang, Lawrence Gramlich, Earlene Wesselman, Mary M. Oswald, 2nd Grade: Suzanne Wesselman, Joan Widel, Raymond Lang, Raymond Martin, Wilbur Lammers, Lee Edward Roth, 1st Grade: Jeanne Oswald, Dorothy Bonen, Charles Lammers. Photo - Ralph Esser.

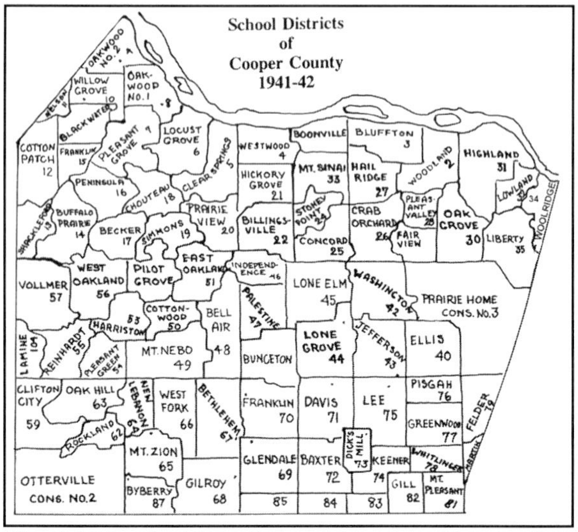

Fig. 4-16. By the 1940s, improved roads and bus funding led to consolidation of rural public schools into 6 consolidated districts. When the St. Martin's School closed, the only remaining parochial schools left in the county were: Sts. Peter and Paul in Boonville, St. Joseph in Pilot Grove and Zion Lutheran in Lone Elm. From Betteridge, "Discover Cooper County."

PILOT GROVE AREA PAROCHIAL SCHOOL STUDENTS - 1937

ST JOSEPH SCHOOL

Teachers at St. Joseph's School at Pilot Grove are: Sister M. Augusta, seventh and eighth grades; Sister M. Mercedes, fourth, fifth and sixth grades; Sister M. Constance, first, second and third grades.

The 100 pupils attending the 1936-37 term, by grades are:

Eighth Grade-Charles Klenklen, Norbert Zeller, Frank Imhoff, Gerald Lammers, Christopher Straub, Leo Day, Wilbert Twenter, William Cullen, Ernabelle Mellor, Dolores Zeller, Ruth Nelson, Mildred Lang.

Seventh Grade-Sylvia Kempf, Clara Salmon, Mildred Kempf, Ann Fahrendorf, Geraldine Klenklen, Edna Stoecklein, Dorothy Klenklen, Gertrude Kraus, Herbert Meyer, Jr., Vincent Cuttler, Ferdinand Meyer, Harold Kempf, Richard Smith.

Sixth Grade-James Lorenz, Junior Mellor, Glenn Neckerman, Charles Zeller, Jerome Kempf, Catherine Day, Florence Salmon, Dorothy Gramlich, Irene Gerke, Irma Vonderahe, Mary Helen Imhoff, Raymond Meyer.

Fifth Grade-Kenneth Kempf, LeVern Klenklen, Edward Klenklen, Joe Cullen, Frances Vollmer, Roy Day, Earl Quinlan, Johnny Imhoff, Joan Gramlich, Geraldine Lang, LaVahn Klenklen, Doris Quinlan, Lou Ellen Zeller, Mary Margaret Muessig, Esther Gerke, Corene Kempf, Imogene Kempf.

Fourth Grade-Donald Bonen, Estil Young, Roy Stoecklein, Ray Stoecklein, Leonard Meyer, Betty Joe Meyer, Joanne Salmon, Catherine Cuttler, Rebecca Meyer, Alice Marie Zeller.

Third Grade-Albert Imhoff, Thomas Kraus, Bobby Twenter, Kenneth Zeller, Marceline Day, Mary Louise Gerling, Marjorie Hoff, Anna Marie Klenklen, Rosemary Schuster, Mary Salmon, Gertrude Vollmer.

Second Grade-Anthony Arth, Leonard Gerke, Francis Gramlich, Robert Imhoff, L. J. Zeller, Clarabelle Imhoff, Thelma Lammers, Mary Lee Neckerman, Winifred Reynolds, Norma Lee Twenter.

First Grade-Bobby Gramlich, James Hoff, Eugene Hess, Robert Lang, Clarence Lammers, Roy Lammers, Jr., Ralph Twenter, Donald Twenter, Rosemary Arth, Martha Mae Gerke, Wilma Quinlan, Betty Salmon, Dorothy Stoecklein, Mary Ann Schuster, Deloris Kempf.

ST MARTIN'S SCHOOL

The Sisters teaching St. Martin's School at Martinsville, southwest of Boonville and northeast of Pilot Grove, are: Sister M. Alphonsa and Sister M. Ottilia. They are of the St. Francis Sisterhood, at Nevada, Missouri.

The school is conducted in an imposing modern brick building, entirely adequate

PILOT GROVE AREA PAROCHIAL SCHOOL STUDENTS - 1937 (CONT'D)

from every standpoint. Pupils are:

First grade-Roy Eichelberger, Lena Gramlich, Lawrence Lang, William Lang, Jr., Florence Martin, Wilbur Schuster, Augustine Schrader, Edward Schrader, Leonard McKenzie.

Second grade-Dorothy Bonen, Charles Lammers, Dorothy Jeanne Oswald.

Third grade-Donald Esser, Raymond Lang, Raymond Martin, Mary Schrader, Alberta Schrader, Suzanne Wesselman, Joan Widel.

Fourth grade-Lawrence Gramlich, Edward Lang, Edith Lang, Earl McKinzie, Mary Margaret Oswald, Lee Edward Roth, Earlene Wesselman.

Fifth grade-Harold Lang, Emil Martin, Estel Oswald, Jr.

Sixth grade-Bernard Eichelberger, Kenneth Horst.

Seventh grade-Edna Martin, William McKinzie, Jr.

Eighth grade-Isabel Schuster, Mildred Diel, Mildred Hoff, Gertrude Lammers and Frances Martin.

ST. JOHN'S SCHOOL, CLEAR CREEK:

Teachers-First through fourth grades, Sister Mary Consuella; fifth through eighth grade- Sister Mary Cecilia.

Children who attended from September, 1935, to May, 1936:

Graduates-Edgar Schibi, Virgil Kempf and Loretta Twenter.

Seventh Grade-Kenneth Young, Silas Wessing, Adolph Gramlich, Ralph Felten, Delphinus Kraus, Virginia Rentel, Viola Mae Twenter, Veloris Twenter, Agnes Marie Bauer and Pauline Kraus.

Sixth Grade-Agnes Marie Kempf, Lavina Kempf, Gerald Larm, Gilbert Twenter and John Earl Young.

Fifth Grade-Loretta Kempf, Dorothy Wessing, Roger Twenter, Wilfred Gerke, William Twenter and Alfred Twenter.

Fourth Grade-Ethel Kraus, Elmer Twenter, Henry Wessing, Earl Twenter, Albin Bauer, Walter Wessing, Norbert Kempf and Earl Francis Kammerich.

Third Grade-Elizabeth Kraus, Earline Felten, Dorothy Kempf, Julius Twenter, Vernon Knedgen, Homer Twenter, Harold Kempf and Elwood Gerke.

Second Grade-Edna Mae Wessing, Betty Lou Young, Lyle Felten, Clyde Twenter and Harold Bauer.

First Grade-Alice Marie Twenter, Bessie Jean Twenter, Therisa Kraus and Edwin Kammerich.

From E.J. Melton's "History Of Cooper County" 1937

powerhouse front three on the Tigers' team of 1944, we were, on *this* day, miserable freshmen and would be happy to just get a place on the bench. We didn't get to scrimmage much.

Basketball can be boring if you're not playing and since we had relatively recently become aware of the 'other' 50% of the global population — girls — we three wandered down to the girls' end to look over the talent offerings of the 1941 intake — female type. Rural and parochial schools only offered eight grades so there was a concentration of new kids in the high school freshman levy each year which, of course, included a lot of new girls.

While we were commenting behind our hands on the wide variance of physical maturity of the girls (if you catch my drift, nudge, nudge, wink, wink), Homer pointed out Dorothy Prewitt. She not only showed super talent at basketball, she was also—how shall I put this? Well ...she was a beautifully figured young lady. Dorothy had an older sister Gladys who was on the girls' first team. She also had a younger sister but the family moved away before we knew her very well, i.e., I don't remember her name.

After all our admiring comments on Dorothy (among others), I was pleasantly surprised to find that in the 14th rearrangement of seating in as many days, Dorothy wound up sitting beside me.

We exchanged a few pleasantries and friendly banter over the weeks and Dorothy had often given me the eye though she, possibly as shy as I was, never made an overtly flirtatious move. On my bad hair day, she did!

I noticed her out of the corner of my eye. She was looking at my hair. As I turned toward her she said, "Gee, Sonny, I love your beautiful wavy hair. Most girls would give anything to have hair like that!" I went all smiley inside. Then she reached over and touched it!

She snatched her hand back like she had stuck it in a cow flop, "Eeeyew. Whatta you got on your hair?"

I slapped my head. Nobody ever told me to comb my hair out after it set and what I had was hair that would deflect a .50 caliber, high velocity, armor piercing bullet. I thought, "Total humiliation! And by this beautiful, bewitching buxom, belle whom I so wanted to impress!"

MOM'S $5 WASHING MACHINE

My earliest memory of the family laundry was Mom doing the wash using two No 3 washtubs and a scrub board. After Bob was born this made five laundry customers for her to serve. I'm sure she redoubled her complaints to Dad. Finally, in the spring of 1936 he announced that he had found a good deal on an electric washing machine and the seller would deliver it on the following Saturday.

We expected something like Christmas, Thanksgiving and birthdays combined. A new washing machine, wow!

Fig. 4-17. This Maytag was ahead of its day when new, but that was in 1915 and this is 1936!

We were mightily disappointed. For $5 what you get is a 1915 model contraption composed of: a wooden tub shaped externally like the top half of a whiskey barrel which, in an earlier life, it might have been. Internally this barrel had a wooden, corrugated surface mimicking the old fashion scrub board; a 1 horsepower electric motor connected via a belt to an ancient reciprocating mechanism which activated a gyrator. This gyrator looked for all the world like an upturned three legged milking stool affixed to the reciprocating drive. A hard surfaced roller wringer broke all the buttons that survived the torture of the milk stool thrashing.

Two weeks of operation showed up another problem—the belt wouldn't stay on the flywheel. Supporting my view of Dad as an 'unhandyman' was his attempt to fix this by pouring molasses on the wheel. "That'll make her stick! Nothing's stickier than molasses!"

Of course it did not and obviously under dire threat he broke down and bought a *brand new* Maytag. This washer lasted over 30 years so he got his money's worth.

THE CCC CAMP

In the mid-1930s, my Uncle Shelby's 'old home place' stood directly across College Street from several hundred acres of vacant ground (part of the Dr. Barnes estate). This land, in 1937, became the site for a CCC camp which was active in the late 1930s. Since few people today have any knowledge of this Roosevelt 'New Deal' program—it might be of interest to include it as a part of Pilot Grove's history.

Fig. 4-18. LEFT Clara and Ivan. This 'wedding' picture had to wait 3 years for Ivan to return from Italy in 1944.

Fig. 4-19. 34th Infantry 'Red Bull' Division—Ivan's unit.

Fig. 4-20. Pilot Grove CCC Camp, June 4, 1942. View from College St. near present Senior Housing.

The CCC was the catalyst for my cousin Clara Salmon meeting and marrying one of the 'CCC Boys'—Ivan Ninemire—I will use their story for illustration. This story is typical and thus tends to answer the question, "What ever happened to all a them there CCC Boys?"

The CCC (Civilian Conservation Corps) was established in 1933 as a New Deal program to combat youth unemployment the during the depression. *Unmarried* young men were enlisted to work on environmental and resource-development projects such as soil conservation, flood control, and protection of forests and wildlife. Enrollees were provided with food, lodging, and other necessities, and were given a monthly salary of $30 of which $21 was sent to their families and $9 became their 'walking around money'.

While the primary objective of the CCC was improvement of land resources and I report elsewhere of a typical conference of the CCC and the FFA to this end—the big impact for many in Pilot Grove was social. The proximity of such a large collection of unattached, handsome young males quickened the heart of many a fair maiden.

The CCC cadre were Regular Army officers and strict military discipline was imposed. The Pilot Grove camp commandant in 1938 was Lieutenant W.W. Brodus. His Executive Officer was Lieutenant C.R. Cross who lived across the street from us in the house now occupied by Mr. and Mrs. Ralph Esser. A lieutenant got about $100 per month then. This salary was augmented by "rations and quarters" and other allowances, thus they did very well indeed.

The town kids, me included, used to hang out at the camp a lot. They had movies once a week—out-of-doors in the summer and in the "Rec Hall" in winter. In addition to the movies, the 'Rec Hall' contained a nine-pin alley. In a town where the main excitement was watching trains go by, the movies were packed. They passed around a collection cup and we chipped in a dime—a bargain.

We town ragamuffins often were invited for evening meals and it was there that I got my first taste of military discipline. Rough, wooden trestle tables were set with standard U.S. Army bomb-proof unbreakable crockery. At mealtime the men came in and took their places at table. When all were in place, the camp adjutant called "ATTENSHUN!" The messhall became dead silent and the camp chaplain began a prayer. After the "Amen" the commander commanded "SEATS" and the meal began.

Food was served family style, the KPs brought giant bowls of potatoes, beans, rice, platters of meat and baskets of fresh baked bread to the tables. I had never seen such bounty! Remember—we're talking about the hungry 30s! The CCC cuisine, like my later experience with the Army, would never be mistaken for the Ritz-Carlton but it was wholesome, it was in great quantities, and it was welcomed.

WWII TERMINATES THE CCC

In 1935, 2,600 CCC camps had an enrollment of 500,000. The CCC was abolished in 1942. By then, CCC khaki was being traded for U.S. Army khaki and—of course—Navy blue. Looming war lent urgency. There were a number of romantic stories that came out of the Pilot Grove CCC camp. Clara and Ivan's was one of the happy ones.

I knew several of the CCC guys and became one of the camp mascots. One of the CCC fellows I met was Ivan Ninemire. I may have known him before Cousin Clara did.

Martha Schweitzer (later Rentel)—Charley Brownfield's young aunt—was not to be so lucky. In 1942 her fiance made his transition from one uniform to another and went off to war in the Pacific. Short months later Martha got a letter from his parents enclosing a telegram from Major General Ulio, the Adjutant General, which began: "The Secretary of War regrets..." Martha's fiance had been killed in action. She walked around like a lost puppy for days.

CAUGHT IN THE DRAFT

In September of 1940 America had begun remedying a profoundly inadequate national defense capability. In that month the National Guard was 'Federalized' and called to active duty 'for one year' and even though the country was not at war, a conscription act was passed and, as in World War I, there was a lottery for those to be called up first.

Ivan Ninemire "won" the lottery and was selected on the second number drawn. He got his notice the first week of November to report for induction. Clara and Ivan were married on the 8th of November and kissed good-bye on the following Thursday.

Ivan shipped out of Camp Kilmer, New Jersey, the Port of Embarkation for Europe and North Africa in the fall of 1942 with the 125th Field Artillery, 34th Division. They were headed for North Africa and the first offensive operations for American troops.

A DATE WITH THE AFRIKA KORPS

Those who are W.W.II history buffs know that when these green troops landed in North Africa (Operation Torch[7]), they came up against the best of the German army—Field Marshal Rommel's Afrika Corp. Yet, with help from the British, they were able to send Rommel packing.

I joined the Army in the summer of 1945 and was assigned to Camp Crowder, Missouri for Signal Corps training. There, I met the Afrika Korp—all prisoners of war.

These Afrika Korpsmen wore standard issue GI fatigue uniforms (with a stenciled, "P" on the seat and knees of the pants and the back of the jacket). But, clinging to a little pride, they all wore their tattered and faded sand colored Afrika Korps forage caps. The Afrika Korps at Camp Crowder did all the KP and crappy details so we 'school boys' could do our lessons. I was in training as a "Radio Intercept Operator - Japanese". Japan was still in the war.

Ivan also met the Afrika Korps—two years earlier and collected two battle stars during his North Africa service. One was for the Battle of Kasserine Pass where the 34th Division was badly mauled and several thousands taken prisoner.[8] Fortunately, Ivan was not one of the Africa casualties but later nearly died with dysentery in Italy. He survived to enjoy a long career with the VA.

So now at least you know 'what happened to *one* of the CCC Boys'. I found the story interesting, not because it is unique but because it is an good example of the times: The 1930s and 1940s—paraphrasing Dickens—"...were the best of times. They were the worst of times." The nation's worst economic depression in history segued into the most horrific war the world has ever known. These world events were the backdrop for many human stories epitomized by Clara and Ivan, young people caught up in world events while trying to make a life for themselves.

[7] Kenny Kempf's older brother, William, was lost when a German U-Boat sank an American troop ship in North African waters. Oddly, the first Pilot Grove casualty was his cousin Carl Kempf who was bitten by poisonous snakes in his foxhole in North Africa.

[8] One of those prisoners was from Pilot Grove—Carl Waller. After Kasserine Pass, Carl spend the rest of the war on a German potato farm. When I asked him about fearing the Germans, he said, "Hell no! It was the American bombers that nearly killed me 8-9 times."

MY INTRODUCTION TO WORK IN THE VILLAGE

PAPER BOY

I may have been the first in my paternal lineage to wear a tie to work. It was Monday, 19th of August 1957 when I reported to the Western Electric Company, Defense Activities Division, Winston-Salem, North Carolina. I had completed my BS in Electronic Engineering at Missouri University, Columbia and hired on as a "Field Engineer - Nike Air Defense Missile Systems". I wore my powder blue Botany 500 wedding suit and...a tie!

This exalted status, however, did not come easily nor early. My rise to such illustrious heights was not meteoric. But, I had determined at about age 10 that the 10¢ allowance I got at Dad's semi-monthly paydays would not keep me in the life style to which I would like to become accustomed so I made myself available for other undertakings. One of these was delivering the Kansas City Star.

Lon Judy was the contract carrier for Pilot Grove and areas west. In the winter of 1938, I would roll out of my warm, cuddly bed at 4 AM and shiver my way up to his place on Second Street. I helped him roll and rubber band the papers then bagged my allocation (I had about a quarter of the town). I had a gen-yew-wine newspaper boy's over-the-shoulder canvas bag. Loaded, it weighed about 20 pounds. I slung it over my shoulder and mounting my ancient bike then slipped and slid on the packed snow and ice to make my tour around the southeastern quadrant of the town duly banging front doors with magnificently aimed newspaper missiles. I never broke a window. I usually completed my rounds by 5AM or so. I returned home and went back to bed!

One morning that winter Lon asked me to ride with him and help fold and throw papers on his rural route. This route was quite long, extending through Clifton City and on to Beaman, maybe a hundred miles. There were innumerable side trips we had to make. His subscribers were scattered all over western Cooper County with some in eastern Pettis County.

Lon was a big man then well into his 40s maybe 50s. He had an old black 1937 Chevy with the passenger side window broken out and replaced with a piece of plywood. It was quite cold so all windows had to be kept closed—except, of course, when he sailed a paper down a driveway at which time the interior temperature dropped 50 degrees and I shuddered in the icy blasts. Lon was pressed, like all family heads, in those days to make a living so he worked very hard and saved his pennies. He was an honest and good man but he had one habit that brought me to near catastrophe. He smoked an evil, old corncob pipe. Worse, he bought the absolute cheapest of tobaccos. I suspect that it may have been that foul, home-grown "long green".

By the time we got to Beaman that early winter morning I had to ask him to stop the car. I barely cleared the door when I tossed my cookies. When I got back in, he had holstered his pipe. We drove for a while with his window down to clear the green fog. He did not light up again.

THE DAIRY TRADE

I delivered milk for Tony Seltsam one summer. The Seltsams lived on the south side of Fourth Street, second house from the southeast corner of Fourth and Roe next door to Mike Meyer (Jake Meyer's brother).

This delivery job was easier than the newspapers because there were only 12-14 customers, all in our end of town. But the carrier was much heavier—try schlepping two metal carriers each with 8-quarts of milk. Two carriers times 8 qts per carrier x 32 oz per qt = 32 lbs. It was heavy lifting, but the work was soon done.

It was during my employment in the dairy trade that I learned of Tony Seltsam's "Doggie Surprise". See below.

In a period when Mr. H. A. "Tony" Seltsam was one of Pilot Grove's leading entrepreneurs—officer of the town's principal bank (Citizen's), managing partner of a local elevator, silent partner in several other enterprises and landlord of over a dozen rental properties, he also operated a small dairy. He was a beehive of enterprise. His daughter, Carmadale contributed an extensive biography to Pilot Grove's 1973 Centennial book describing some of her father's Pilot Grove accomplishments. I refer you to this publication for more engaging detail.

His tenants, more often than not, were strangers to the dollar and paid rent on a hit or miss basis. Tony demanded his money on the nail and quite often evicted hapless families. Today they would be called 'homeless' but in those days they somehow managed to find other lodgings. My old pal Homer Jeffress Jr. and his family had several clashes with Mr. Seltsam so Homer bore him no love.

He pastured a dozen or so Jersey cows on several hundred acres he owned bordering the public school grounds on the west and the Schuster place on the east. His milking parlor was in a barn complex across the alley and southeast of the current Ralph Esser home. Fred Beumer, the Katy agent lived in that house during the period of Seltsam's dairy.

His milking parlor was surprisingly modern for Pilot Grove in the 1930s. It was fully equipped with electric milking machines at each feeding stanchion for the Jersey herd Mr. Seltsam maintained.

My first personal contact with Mr. Seltsam came when he found it necessary to explain to Homer Jeffress and me that the windmill at the southwest corner of his cow pasture didn't really need all the attention that we were paying it.

This windmill was just across the street from Homer's place and just begged for an investigation by fascinated and inquisitive pre-teen boys. It had a ladder to the top from which you could see forever if you didn't get knocked off the ladder by a sudden shift in the wind! It had rather complex mechanical linkages to engage and disengage a clutch at the wind-driven power head via which the pump could be turned off and on.

One day Homer and I mastered the mechanical intricacy and started the pump which filled and then overflowed the giant watering tank. We noted this overflow several hours later when we saw the cows staring vacantly at the new stream of water in the tiny branch which had not seen water for weeks. We probably wasted enough water in that drought summer of 1937 to supply the entire town.

Tony Seltsam was not pleased. However, his reaction was no more than some sharp explanations, admonitions and a word or two to Mrs. Jeffress.

The dairy had a small clientele, mostly on Third and Fourth Street in the east end of town. I was offered a handsome stipend (about 25¢ per week) to make a few evening deliveries. I carried two, eight-bottle metal carriers as far as the Steigers on Third Street with a few stops in between. The "Doggie Surprise" incident occurred one night after my tour of duty.

TONY'S DOGGIE SURPRISE

Mrs. Seltsam had a little female dog, probably a terrier mix as I remember. It was during the early summer weeks that this lady dog came into season and subtly signaled—in those seductive ways that females have—her availability for connubial cavorting. That is, she might be open to callers of the gentlemen dog persuasion.

Of course the Seltsams had other thoughts on this subject and carefully kept her indoors safe from the innumerable stray mutts, all of whom were decidedly unsuitable.

At the rear of the Seltsam home was a screened-in back porch. A screen door exited to a wooden stairway leading 8-10 feet down to the back yard. As Fifi's season progressed, the males became more emboldened and climbed the stairs to this screen door. There, finding themselves cut off from their love did the only thing they could do. They marked their territory by hiking their hind legs to the screen door, warning off competitors.

After a few nights of these unrequited doggie romance capers, Mr. Seltsam was fed up. He rigged up a electric fence apparatus to the back screen door and grounded it to a piece of sheet metal tacked onto the top step. He told me about it when I reported for my dairy route the next day.

"I heard one of those mangy curs snuffling around the back steps just after dark. I turned on the battery and when I heard the buzzing of the transformer, I knew that it was sending 10,000 volt pulses to the screen door. I tiptoed into the kitchen so's not to scare him off. I wanted the word to get out to Pilot Grove dogdom that ole Tony's is a place you want to give a wide berth.

I was peeping around the door frame when he got to the top step and stepped onto the grounding sheet. That's half a circuit, I thought. Then he sniffed all the other dog calling cards, identifying each in turn I suppose.

[Dogs have 100,000 times the acuity of smell as humans. Their noses take in masses of information. I imagine the thoughts of Fido, snuffling the door frame: "There's old Rover, a bit redolent of chicken entrails. He's been up there at Babbitt's Poultry House again. Here's Spot. He's showing definite signs of end-stage renal disease! He's too old for this puppy making business anyway. I'll have to speak to him. Now this here is someone new: light essence of dead fish, bouquet of potato peelings...Potato peelings? That poor boob is really down on his luck!"]

Then he lifts his leg to cancel all these earlier—but totally illegitimate—territorial claims.

Now, I know that doggie wee is an excellent conductor of electricity. This rich golden stream of calcium and potassium ions, unmetabolized bits of bone, undigested road-kill, dead possum lipids, fatty acids and miscellaneous detritus from garbage cans has the electrical conductivity of copper wire.

His stream wouldn't even have hit the screen before 10,000 volts would pop a blue arc and at the speed of lightning the electrical charge would traverse the golden arch in reverse seeking its source. It would have really rung his bells.

Tony continued, "He yelped, jumped backwards and tumbled down the steps but hit the ground with all four feet spinning and throwing dirt. He disappeared around the house with his tail between his legs. I don't know about the others but I seriously doubt that Fifi will have the honor of his further amorous pursuit."

Now, for the animal lovers: I must reassure you that the surprise and affront to dignity were the most serious effects of Fido's being zapped in the crotch by an electric fence. A charge of 5-10,000 volts sounds quite lethal but it actually is not. The mechanisms use a high voltage but at very low amperage. In reality, the shock is much like the electrostatic zap you get in winter when you shuffle your rubber-soled shoes across a very dry wool carpet then touch a metal doorknob. *Tony had just made creative use of a non-lethal dissuasion device.*

THE POULTRY BUSINESS

During the war years, Chuck Babbitt collaborated with a St. Louis poultry wholesaler, the O.B Frantz company, to slaughter and dress turkeys for the Thanksgiving and Christmas season. During that time, many of us high school kids worked after school. We got 6¢ for each turkey we plucked. When the scalders were doing their job right, we could work 5PM to midnight and make $3-4. Big bucks, but I can smell those hot, dripping wet turkeys yet! Yuck!

But, I had made a foray into the poultry business before Babbitt-Franz. When I was ten, Homer Jeffress and I were engaged by a professional caponizer doing Theobald's roosters. Our job was to run those suckers down then hold them while the 'surgeon' did his dastardly deed.

Fig. 4-21. Fido: "I don't call 10,000 volts to the crotch a joke!"

Converting young roosters to capons was not a career that I would recommend. To this day I can smell the burning flesh as the caponizer made strategic incisions, reached in and pulled out special rooster parts to be burnt off with an electric wire clamp. Pheww! But...at 10¢ an hour we made our spending money. Deck's soda fountain here we come!

SUPERB ST. LOUIS SUMMER SOJOURN

My work in a St. Louis defense plant in the summer of 1944 was an introduction to one more career opportunity that I did not much care for (scratch ~~factory worker~~) although I greatly enjoyed the overall experience. Here then follows a true account of the key events plus the strange, sweet secret of that superb summer sojourn in St. Louis.

Until Christmas of 1943 I had tacitly assumed that I would return to the Katy Extra Gang for the summer of '44. The Extra Gang was then working near Clifton City. It was hard, dirty work with the occasional gut-busting and skin blistering task of unloading creosoted cross-ties from a moving train. But, it was steady and, for a teenager, the pay wasn't bad — 48¢ per hour for a 10 hour day, 6 day week.

EMERSON ELECTRIC

However, sister Dixie came home for Christmas (1943) and suggested I try St. Louis for the summer. She was working at Emerson Electric's Florissant Plant as a turret lathe operator and pulling down big bucks. Most of the normally all-male work force were off to war. Draft-proof female workers were in great demand. Dixie was a trained machine operator and commanded excellent wages.

While I was quite enthusiastic about going to St. Louis, that would be a leap into an unknown world for me, what's more I needed more incentive than just a *possibility* of a job. This move, even though only for the summer, gave me some trepidation. So I boarded the old Katy Bluebonnet to St. Louis one weekend in early spring to get the feel of the place, look at the help wanted ads and consider the living arrangements.

Dixie lived with cousin Florence at 1019 Hamilton Avenue just south of Wellston but within St. Louis proper. They had a third floor walk-up, one bedroom flat with a living room, dining room, kitchen, bath and sun room. The sun room was used as the extra bedroom. The apartment was just steps from a stop on the Hodiamont line, thus very well tied into the metropolitan public transportation network. It was a very nice apartment and with the wartime housing shortage of those times they were quite lucky to have it.

Thus being duly impressed, I committed to come down for the summer and try to find work at Emerson Electric. Florence had already planned to move out and I'd pick up her sun room, as well as an appropriate share of the apartment overhead. It was the last day of school, Friday afternoon 18th of May 1944 and I had just cleaned out my desk at PGHS, stored my school junk in my bedroom and packed up 'bag and baggage' expecting to catch the old Katy Bluebonnet to St. Louis. I had all my wardrobe in a small, cheap suitcase and a box of my favorite pulp fiction— The Lone Eagle, Ellery Queen Detective Mysteries, etc.—in a cardboard Campbell's Soup box.

Since the Bluebonnet didn't get in until midnight, I had time to say so long to all the crowd at Pop's Cafe. Babe Heim and his girl friend, Bonnie Kirby were having a coke with Elizabeth McCraw the Home Ec teacher when I popped in and they hailed me back to their booth.

It turns out that Bonnie was also to leave that night, taking a train to Tennessee to join her parents. Her father was in construction work, travelling and living all over the country and—in order to provide some semblance of a stable life—Bonnie lived with her grandparents, Pops and Mrs. Tracy during the school year and joined her parents over school vacation.

It took but a moment for Elizabeth to come up with the offer to drive both of us to St. Louis—me to join Dixie for the summer, Bonnie to catch a train on to Tennessee. Since I thought Elizabeth was sooooo cuuuuute, I jumped at the opportunity to spend an evening with her albeit while driving to St. Louis.

Elizabeth had a 1941 black Chevrolet coupe. It was a comfortable car but, in 1944, the road to St. Louis—US40—was two lane broken pavement with steep hills, sharp curves and went through the main street of every podunk town in eastern Missouri. In short it was agonizingly slow and difficult 250 mile drive. We departed at 5PM and darkness descended upon us long before we reached St. Louis.

The difficulty we had in driving at night in a totally unfamiliar city albeit to a well known landmark began to give me the willies about finding 1019 Hamilton Boulevard—my destination. Elizabeth was driving and I tried to help but I didn't know St. Louis in daylight much less night. I could see Elizabeth's knuckles whitening. She was getting more and more unnerved.

We finally found the Market Street Station and dropped off Bonnie with a profusion of good-byes, "be sure to write", "be good", "be careful driving, blah, blah, blah". Now the tough part started—getting to 1019 Hamilton—and it is already 10PM! We asked directions but we were so far off our target, they didn't help much. Once we got so far afield as Natural Bridge Road. We saw a sign saying we were approaching the Eads Bridge to Illinois. Everyone was in a tense mood when we finally found my pad on Hamilton. My thoughts of having all up for a drink (of Dixie's liquor) went aglimmering. I didn't offer.

Babe told me later that he drove all the way home while Elizabeth slept in the back seat. He push the Chevy as hard as he could and pulled up to his faithful old Dodge pickup at about 4AM. He turned the Chevy over to Elizabeth and hightailed it for the farm.

It was getting light when he pulled into the circle drive in front of his house. He went to his room, changed into work clothes and continued out the back door to join his dad who was just getting the old tractor fired up to plow some corn.

Unaware of all these tribulations I was settling into my new digs. It took me about 15 minutes to become ensconced and relaxed with a cold beer. Being 17 years old and out on my own I felt I had reached adulthood and was entitled to all the privileges and perqs appertaining thereto.

I perused the St. Louis Post Dispatch, Sunday edition and boiled job hunting down to Emerson Electric downtown because the commute would be easier—the Hodiamont street car line went right by both our apartment and the factory. I visited them first thing Monday and after a 'hear thunder and see lightning' physical exam I was on the payroll at 1820 Washington Avenue!

This plant made fractional horsepower electric motors that were used primarily in aircraft gun turrets. Picture the top and ball turrets on the B-17s. The turrets were rotated and the guns elevated by electrical motors from Emerson Electric. The wages were not the Katy's miserly 48¢ per hour — I would start at 86¢ per hour plus piecework bonus! After a few weeks training and familiarization, I began taking home about $56 per week. Since you will not be much impressed with this payroll magnanimity, I will use the BMP (Big Mac Parity) factor to convert it to equivalent, late-1990's bucks: My $56 paycheck could buy me $56 ÷ 20¢ per Big Mac = 280 Big Macs. Today, 280 Big Macs would cost about 280 X $2.50 per Big Mac = $420. That is, my take home pay was about $420 weekly in today's dollars.

STEAMY ST. LOUIS SUMMER

At the end of June the summer weather in St. Louis was living up to its terrible reputation. Though Mr. Carrier had invented air conditioning many years before, it simply had never caught on much. I don't remember ever being in one home or business that was air conditioned. The heat and humidity combine to a jungle stickiness in the St. Louis convergence of the Missouri and Mississippi Rivers. The apartment was on the third floor and when we were at home we kept all the windows open to catch any faint breeze that might blow by. Of course anyone who knows Missouri weather knows that all windows must be closed when you are away.

Murphy's Law — the law defining the perversity of nature — asserts that one hour after you leave home with the windows open there will be a toad-strangling rain accompanied by high winds which will flood your quarters, drenching everything you own.

The entire week of June 25th was composed of these hot, humid, sticky days. Rain threatened but never came. There was no relief. I slept on a roll-away cot in the sun room clad in shorts only — straining to catch a hint of a fresh breeze. I was laying there napping on Friday afternoon 30th June as Dixie busied herself before leaving for her swing shift job. I sat up quizzically when she packed a small bag. She saw me watching her and explained, "Leonard (fiance) and I are going to take an extra day off Monday the 3rd and make a long weekend. We're catching the bus after work tonight and going down to visit his folks in Carbondale [Illinois]."

"OK, I'll see if I can manage on my own." This was a facetious statement since I had always totally fended for myself. Indeed, because of our work shifts we rarely even saw one another.

I was feeling delighted that I would have the apartment completely to myself for four days. No need to creep around silently to avoid infringing on Dixie's sleep. I'd also have the bathroom to myself. I had a weekly pass on the Hodiamont streetcar line which would cut costs on any urban exploration I would like to do. I'd go to the movies. I'd get the latest issue of Ellery Queen's Mystery Magazine to which I had become addicted. I was looking forward to a carefree if sultry weekend. Then the telephone rang.

SURPRISE VISITOR

It was Elizabeth McCraw. "Hi, Sonny," she said. "I had to drive to St. Louis for some business and thought I would give you a call. Are you settling in OK? How do you like your job? We sure miss you back in PG."

"Look," I said, "If you have time, I'd love to see you. Where are you now?"

Elizabeth, a native of Mountain Home, Missouri, was a PGHS teacher. Her first job out of college was teaching Home Economics at Pilot Grove. She was a 22-23 year old, five foot four inch, petite blonde with beautiful baby blue eyes. Elizabeth was closer in age to the students than to the other teachers thus she and I along with Babe Heim and Bonnie Kirby often hung out together.

MY FIRST HARLEY

My problem with serious high school dating was my lack of wheels. I semi-solved that in August 1944 at the end of my St. Louis sojourn.

As the mucky, stifling days of that St. Louis summer ticked off slowly, I began considering my return to school in the fall. I had not blown my wages. In point of fact I was saving as much as possible. By mid-August I had $210 salted away. This money gave me the confidence to go motorcycle shopping. I felt that a proper automobile was so far above my finances that I wouldn't even consider one. No autos had been manufactured in the US since 1942, thus used cars were extremely pricey — and often of questionable quality.

This motorcycle passion was driven by my being forever wheel-less. This was the one abiding problem I had in the social whirl in Pilot Grove. Wheel-lessness restricted one's choice to local girls for dates. This might be OK — there were some pretty neat chicks in the old berg — but then one must then ask: 'Then what?' Choice of date venues was restricted to Deck's soda fountain or Pop Tracy's Cafe. There was not even a movie house in town!

One Saturday in mid-August I used my Hodiamont pass to whip down to Delmar Boulevard. The Delmar Indian Cycle shop had a sales floor covered with brand new Indian motorcycles. They had a few old klunker, used Indian bikes, but the real emphasis was on the new bikes. The new ones were US Army surplus and in the appropriate olive drab livery, US Army decals and the white stars of military field equipment.

A salesman caught my scent like a vulture and came on with a $100 smile and a hearty handshake. "Son, if you're looking for a super deal on a brand spankin' new bike, you've come to exactly the right place! What are you interested in?"

"How much you asking for these Army bikes?" I asked.

"We are having a special sale on these bikes this week. I reckon we'll be sold out by the end of the month." He went on with a 10 minute, rambling, 24 karat line of pure bull extolling the features of these "specials". He covered all the features, all that is, except the price. I became suspicious.

"How come the Army is selling these things? There was still a war going on the last time I checked." I asked.

He finally answered all my questions. "We're willing to let you have this brand new, military spec motorcycle for only $700. The Army declared them surplus because they're shaft drive bikes and — while shaft drive bikes are superior[9] to chain drive for highway and street running — they don't meet Army needs in off-road service. But, hell, you ain't gonna run this thing off-road anyways, are you?"

If the shaft-drive puzzle wasn't enough to dissuade me, the price certainly did. I was not so naive to assume that I would be able to buy something with my $200 and have money left over, but $700 was quite beyond my dreams.

I hoofed it to the Harley Cycle shop less than a block away. They didn't have any Olive Drab Army surplus motorcycles but did have quite a selection of 2-10 year old Harleys. All had been reconditioned, repainted and most looked pretty good. I found a 1937 74 OHV for $375 and cut a deal with the salesman. I paid 200 bucks cash on barrelhead and they agreed to hold it for me. I committed to paying at least $35 per month until it was paid out. I did this without the slightest idea of how in hell I would come about this $35. I wanted that bike so badly, I made myself a hostage to fortune.

The fall term at PGHS would start on the day after Labor Day, Tuesday 5th September, when I would begin my senior year. I had given in my notice at Emerson Electric weeks before. They would mail me my final paycheck. At work on Friday, 1st of September I said my good-byes to the guys at work. After coming off shift at 530PM (I was back on the day shift) I began assembling my gear, packing my suitcase and Campbell Soup carton and preparing to depart.

FAREWELL TO ST. LOUIS

I had a farewell beer in the Maplewood apartment with Dixie and Leonard and at 1000PM started my Hodiamont Line trip to the Market Street Union Station. At 1130PM the Katy Flyer pulled out of the station with me glued to the window gazing at the quay paralleling the river front.

It was a delightful and evocative scene that went gliding by. Antique cast iron Victorian street lamps illuminated the cobbled carriageway. No moon but a bright starry sky added a muted glow to city lights. Wisps of river fog wafted shoreward by a gentle summer breeze made it magic.

I remember seeing, in this setting, a soldier and his girl friend standing under one of the lamps in a passionate embrace near the Admiral excursion boat landing. I thought, "Just like a scene outa the movies! Poster: 'The Last Farewell — lovers, parting on the morrow, snatch final moments together.'" From someone's portable radio came the haunting strains of Norma McRae singing "I'll Be Seeing You":

> "I'll be seeing you—in all the old familiar places
> That this heart of mine embraces..."

Since that night the words of that song have always evoked the bittersweet memories, of separation, of love, longing and loss of that river quay scene. As the words and music touch the ears they also touch the heart for they accurately captured a common emotion of the times.

As I pondered the events of the summer, the lights of St. Louis faded behind us and the Katy Flyer click-clacked westward through Baden Yards and into St. Charles — homeward bound ending my strange but sweet, superb but sultry, summer sojourn in St. Louis - anno Domini 1944.

MURDER, MAYHEM AND MISDEEDS

HAM BURGLARS

Dad, as I have mentioned elsewhere, was never able to get the farming life out of his blood. In the fall of 1934, he and his brother Shelby fenced off our garden plot, built a farrowing house and brought home a pregnant sow. In the spring she duly presented us with a small litter.

Bob, who wouldn't start to school until the fall, seemed to get a kick out of irritating the sow by throwing pebbles and sticks at her. Becoming more bold one morning, he climbed over the fence and approached the farrowing house, raining rocks on the roof. Suddenly, thinking her piglets were in danger, the old sow came charging out of the house and attacked him. She was one browned off mama pig. She hit him with 200 pounds of enraged pig meat and knocked him on his butt. Before he could get up she had grabbed at his neck, luckily only collecting a mouthful of shirt collar. She was dragging him and shaking him when finally his screams brought Mom out with a broom to beat the old sow off. Bob has treated mama pigs with greater respect to this day.

Dixie and I, with a little help from Bob fed the piglets and generally cared for them through the summer months. These pigs were nothing but a disaster for us. We had fed them for months on end with little evidence they were adding any bacon. They didn't seem to be growing at all. Dad had thought they could be fattened on household table scraps. That was a laugh. With Mom in charge of the household there just wasn't going to be any scraps! We had to give up that strategy by January and start buying feed. I lugged it home from the feed store in my little red Radio

[9] This was a flat-out lie. I don't think any shaft-drive motorcycle has ever been successful.

Flyer.

In the fullness of time (and I expect after much complaining about the smell from the neighbors) these pigs fattened up and were butchered. I can remember that crisp November day. Fresh, hot and crisp cracklings from the lard rendering process were passed around the butchering crew. The latest batch of home brew was brought up from the cellar to wash them down. Lard was rendered. Sausage was ground, mixed and stuffed into chitterling casings. Hams, shoulders and flitches of bacon were treated with smoke, salted and laid down in the smoke house to cure. The scene could have been one painted by Pieter Brueghel the Younger of 16th century Flanders. Not much changed about butchering between the 16th century and the 1930s.

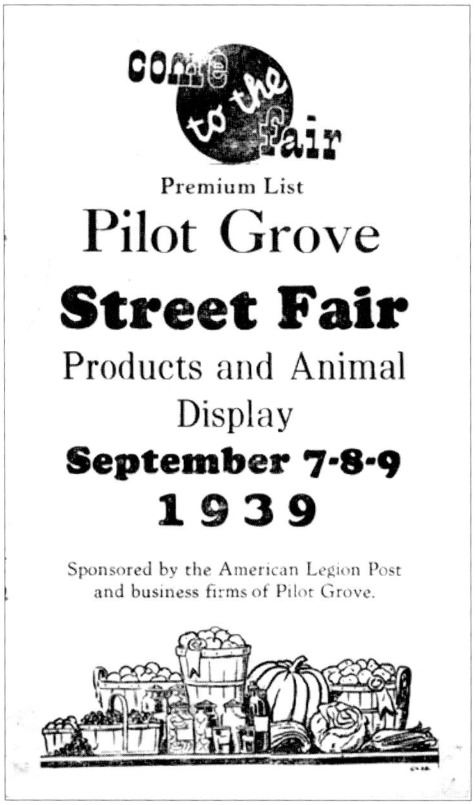

Fig. 4-22. Bert Wells was the Security Officer for the 1939 Pilot Grove Street Fair.

A few weeks after the big pig slaughter Mom comes running into the house screaming. We all ran out to see the smokehouse door standing wide open. Six hams and six pork shoulders were missing. To this very day, my beloved goodwife Daisy cringes to think of this dastardly crime.

'JUSTIFIABLE HOMICIDE'

Bert Wells, lived with his wife in a white frame house with green shutters and trim one door from the northeast corner of 4th and Roe (next door to old lady Figgins). At the time of the incident—summer of 1939—Bert must have been in his early 60s. He was a bit shorter than average with thinning gray hair. He was, like everybody else in the country, frantically trying to claw a living out of a depression racked land. He had taken a job as security officer for the Town Fair. That is what brought him on collision course with one of the town's tragedies at the street fair in September 1939.

CIATED PRESS SERVICE

SHOT FATAL TO LEONARD HORST OF PILOT GROVE

Funeral Services To Be Held Tomorrow Morning — Inquest Set for Wednesday At 9 A. M.

Fig. 4-23. Boonville Daily News clip Sep 11, 1939 - The killing of "Red" Horst.

It occurred on the sidewalk in front of Lammer's Cafe. It was a pleasant summer Saturday evening September 9, 1939 that he and 'Red' Horst had their fatal confrontation. 'Red' Horst was the youngest of the extended Horst family that lived on the southwest corner of 4th and Roe. The Horsts were good solid people. In 1937 Dad had bought a car—a gray '36 Chevy two-door —from Ham Horst, Red's older brother, who worked for Prigmore Chevrolet in Boonville. I remember him from that day. Like all the Horst boys he was very tall, well built and quite a handsome dude. His brother Red much favored him. Red was 24. He was unmarried and, it must be admitted, somewhat given to excessive celebration on Saturday night with accompanying adult beverages. Red was no different from the other young men of the town. They liked their beer and occasionally 'got a snoot full' as Mom would put it. Red possibly was more boisterous than his cohorts and was sometimes engaged in fisticuffs John L. Sullivan style—bare knuckles. Red was about 200 pounds and 6 feet tall.

To be fair to Bert, he was trying to peacefully rope in Red and get him to go home. Red would have none of it.

Bert, at 5 ft 6 and 150 pounds, was no match for Red. When Red knocked him down and, sitting on his chest, proceeded to pound him with his fists—Bert managed to unlimber his little .22 caliber, nickel-plated Saturday night special. He fired one shot which struck Red in the lower abdomen and traveled upward to pierce the tip of his heart. The round was a 'long rifle' which has more power and does more damage than a regular round. Red died within minutes.

But for the timely intervention of Wallace Burger, the killing may not have stopped there. Some of Red's friends, possibly with a bit too much Dutch courage under their belts, vowed to kill Bert and might have done so had not Wallace Burger, a town councilman in those days intercepted them in Pop Tracy's Cafe and calmed them down. He persuaded them that the town had enough trouble for one night and talked them into going home and sleep on it.

In any event, feelings ran so high against Bert in Pilot Grove that a change of venue was requested and he was tried somewhere in southeast Missouri. He was acquitted—justifiable homicide.

BILLY JOE PIATT SHORTENS SOME FINGERS.

Fig. 4-24 Billy Joe Piatt - 1945.

Billy Joe Piatt was a true albino. He had white hair, no skin coloration whatsoever and pinkish eyes. His unaided vision was probably measured at 5000/20. What you could see at a mile he could see at 20 feet. In an attempt to partially correct this deficiency he wore glasses that looked like the bottom of coke bottles. He had to have his nose on the page to read a book. He was born to a working family—thankful that they had bread on the table much less the wealth to address Billy Joe's problems.

The sad thing about all this was that Billy Joe was an excellent student, very intelligent and quite ambitious as well. He was enrolled in Vocational Agriculture in whose wood working shop I led him to disaster.

We were sophomores in the fall of 1942 and in one of the many scrap metal drives I had 'liberated' an old broken cavalry saber. The hilt was gone and the blade was covered with rust but I used a sledge hammer to break off a 12 inch piece of the high-carbon steel. I had drilled holes in the shank and 'rescuing' a small piece of a walnut board, crudely carved out two halves of a handle. I was going to make a small dagger. I showed these parts to him and explained how I was having trouble shaping the handle.

He said, "Come on, Sonny. We can use the electric planer on this. I'll show you how to do it."

All the power equipment in the shop scared hell out of me. Furthermore, I hadn't the least clue how any of the stuff worked so I tagged along as an 'observer'. Billy Joe powered up the planer and as it screamed into life I stepped back a pace. He made one pass holding the thin, one inch by 1/4 inch piece of wood on its edge. With his poor eyesight he had to hold his head inches from the screaming blade. I just couldn't look.

On the second pass the workpiece slipped and Billy Joe's hand went into the blades. His index, middle and ring fingers were shortened by one knuckle. Blood spattered all over the shop as I shut off the main power and yelled for Mr. Shier the Vo Ag teacher. For years whenever I saw Billy Joe at class reunions I surreptitiously glanced at poor Billy Joe's mutilated fingers and felt guilty.

However, in the years following graduation my contribution to Billy Joe Piatt's tribulations faded into insignificance compared with the grief his wife gave him. I met her at our 1965 reunion. She was a little, overdone trollop, a Tammy Faye Baker look-alike. She looked the type you see lurking under the street lamp in the seamier precincts of town.

She was much younger than Billy Joe and her marriage to him illustrated (in my opinion) an uncomplimentary, avaricious and mercenary nature. When she tired of him, or got a better offer, she discarded him like a squeezed lemon. He turned to the bottle and was found dead on the kitchen floor in the winter of 1968. He was dead of acute alcoholism and—I would guess—a broken heart.

HUNTING ACCIDENT.

In the 1930s country and village menfolk often reverted to their primordial role of hunters. Apparently there is some primeval instinct in male genes that drives some men to seek the wily rabbit in any era. In those times it was sometimes crucial to put a little meat on the table as well as a few dimes in the pocket. A cleanly dressed, plump rabbit would fetch 10-15¢. It therefore was not unusual for Warnie Wilson and Chester Bader to go off hunting rabbits as they did one Saturday just before Halloween 1937. Chester was 17, Warnie was about the same age.

To cross a fence, Chester crawled through and held the top strand of barb wire for Warnie. Warnie leaned his 12 gauge shotgun against the flimsy fence and crawled through. The shotgun falls, fires and sends a charge of #4 chilled shot into the side of Chester's head. The range was about 18 inches. The miracle was that Chester lived for 3 days although he never regained consciousness. Warnie gave up rabbit hunting.

The other notable thing about poor Chester's accident—he never went to the hospital. It would have been useless of course but can you imagine an accident like that today? Screaming sirens, ambulance rushing to the Emergency Room. But not in 1937, poor Chester, was just brought home and laid on his bed to die!

THE PILOT GROVE AIR FORCE

While I was enjoying my Hawaiian tour, all expenses to the account of the United States Army (Winter 1946-1947), some of my schoolmates were sampling the delights of flying. Bob Burnett, who had worked as a telegrapher-clerk on the Katy—the same career that Vern Klenklen and I had fleetingly followed—acquired a Stearman three-seater. It was the model that the Army Air Force used for primary flight training until after WWII—a radial engine PT-13.

In winter of that year Bob, L.J. "Smokey" Zeller and Marvin Perry "Chief" Lewis went for a flight that ended disastrously. See Fig. 4-26. An emergency landing ended the flight with the aircraft nose down in a wheat field.

When I was discharged at Ft. Sheridan, Illinois and returned to Pilot Grove I was fully briefed on the great air disaster.

WILBUR ROTHGEB'S FLYING MACHINE

Which makes my acceptance of an invitation, in the spring of 1947, for a county tour in Wilb Rothgeb's plane a

Fig. 4-25. - **BEFORE** Junior Gochenour (nearer camera) and Bobbie McCreery prepare for a strafing run on Fredrick's chicken house - fall 1946.

Fig. 4-26. **AFTER** Bob Burnett's flying career cracks up - January 1947. Bob and passenger Smoky Zeller suffered minor injuries, Marvin "Chief" Lewis was more seriously hurt.

little hard to understand.

Rothgeb was primarily in the hog hauling business in those days. He had a conventional stake bed truck suitable for double decking for hogs. He also had a semi-trailer truck with 2-3 times the capacity. It was this or a similar semi that he cleaned the pig poop out of and transported the village school kids to Highway 40 in 1937. We were excused from school that day and watched the 35th Infantry Division move trucks, tanks, artillery and men in convoy from Indiana to Colorado. Some of the soldiers tossed their addresses to the girls and, I'm sure, several mail romances ensued. Like I've said, Pilot Grove didn't hold much excitement in the 30s.

I was in a career hiatus in the spring of 1947. Bob (my brother) had told me about Wilb's plane and suggested we go look at it.

Wilb lived at the end of the Hall Street in the northwestern quadrant of Pilot Grove. It's the street where Curry Brownfield (the patriarch of the Brownfield clan) lived. Floyd Branstetter left his home on this street to go to his death in Italy in 1944.

Wilb was outgoing, enthusiastic and flattered by our interest in his little Piper Cub tandem two-seater. He said, "Hell, Sonny, climb in there and I'll take you for an air tour of Greater Metropolitan Pilot Grove."

He put me in the front seat which was a mistake. He hopped in the back, latched the door and immediately wheeled about for takeoff across the cow pasture. With the door closed and him leaning forward to yell something at me over the engine noise, I got the full blast of beer breath. As my peril dawned on me, we were off the ground over the Katy tracks and doing a climbing left bank to come back over downtown. It certainly was too late to change my mind! Apparently, Wilb had spent Saturday morning sampling the fruits of the brewers' art at the Tip-Top Cafe!

I thought about the two drunk GI "Ruptured Ducks" that picked me up in their Model A as I was hitch-hiking from Camp Crowder in the fall of 1945. On that trip we ultimately ended up in a ditch near the Wesley Chapel. But we were not flying and crashed softly. I thought of the Burnett crash and Bob wasn't even drinking.

I must say I did not much enjoy the narrated aerial tour of central Cooper County. When we landed the third and final time (the first two landings were followed by a 20 foot bounces back into the air) I dismounted with all due thanks to God. I did not kiss the ground as the Pope is now wont to do. This symbolic act was not yet de rigeur so, I went down to the Tip-Top and hoist a few celebratory Falstaffs!

MAKE DEPOSIT HERE

In the 1930s, the celebration of Halloween night was right up there with Christmas and the Fourth of July. The "Trick or Treat" ploy of buying off the little rascals had not yet been thought up. It was all Trick and no Treat. The favorite target of the l'il rascals were the outhouses that most townfolks used. The goblins kept score and there was rivalry among the town gangs. "We got 17 so far. How many you got?" If my memory serves, a record was set on Halloween night 1936 when the score went up to 30 some. The "jewel in the crown" of these pranks came in the mid-30s when old man Stanfield's one horse shay was installed on the roof of his machine shed behind his home in the southwest quadrant of town. This feat would never have been possible without Dudlow Rapp. Dudlow was the son of Fred Rapp sometime town constable and brother of Margie Rapp.

Dudlow was in his teens but he was built like the proverbial brick outhouse, 6 ft tall and over 200 pounds of solid muscle. Wally Burger said, "Whichever Halloween team had Dudlow would be a winner!"

In 1936 the water and sewer works came to town and the numbers of outhouses and therefore the number of outhouse tippings began falling precipitously. Within a few years the whole outhouse moving phenomenon began fading into antiquity. Something you could tell the grandkids

Fig. 4-27. The day after Halloween night 1982. The sign says "Make Deposit Here". Apparently there are still goblins of my era still around!

about while being interrupted by the little monsters coming to the door to be bought off. *This is what I thought.* But, apparently there are still a few of those intrepid souls (in moving an outhouse in the dark of night with unsure footing, you've got to be an intrepid soul) dealing in spookery of the disappearing outhouse. See Fig. 4-27.

NO ANESTHETIC NECESSARY

Babe[10] Heim and A.J. Wolfe were off to the Clear Creek dance. It was a pleasantly mild Saturday night in the fall of 1945. The big war was over, most of the young men were back home again and the country was getting back to normal. There was a joyous mood everywhere, and what better way to celebrate this night than a dance. These dances were held nearly every Saturday night and were great fun for Babe and A.J.

Clear Creek was (and is) an area lying 8-10 miles west-northwest of Pilot Grove comprising farms with rich, alluvial soil and prosperous farmers. Clear Creek has also long been an area with a very high ratio of good looking, unattached young women, therefore of profound interest to good looking unattached young men. Clear Creek was a bride market of sorts.

Babe Heim, my good pal in high school and the Tigers' ace hoop shooter (jersey number 4) was one of these young men. Babe was often the team high point man and he carried this basketball winning attribute over to his social relations with the fairer sex. He was a 'dab hand' with the ladies. He was not yet 17 years old but had been skipped ahead in his rural elementary school and had graduated with me in May 1945.

I had volunteered for the U.S. Army just after graduation and was at that time learning the trade of "Radio Operator, Intercept — Japanese" despite the fact that there were no further "Japanese Radio Operators" to intercept. I got up to the old homeplace several times during that fall and though I missed the exciting events of that particular weekend, I was briefed at my next weekend pass. Babe's scars were still fresh and pink.

Babe had teamed up again with A.J. Wolfe to exploit some exceptionally productive girl hunting. A.J., a Marine veteran of Tarawa and the Pacific War, had been discharged with a disability some months before and was sorting out his life and future. He probably felt that the slant-eyed little bastard (Jap mortar -gunner) who had loaded his backside with shrapnel probably did him a favor. It was the end of the war for A.J. and carrying a little scrap iron in his back didn't slow him down much in jitterbugging with the dollies.

The refreshments for these festivities followed a set pattern, Babe informed me. "What you do is—you get yourself a pint of some good hooch—and by the fall of '45 it was getting easier to get good likker—and a bottle of Coke or Seven-Up. I personally preferred Seven-Up. Take a slug of the Seven-Up then top the bottle off with the Three Feathers, Four Roses or whatever your choice of embalming fluid might be. You can take Seven-Up into the dance hall. They really didn't like you openly brandishing a whiskey bottle although everyone knew what was up."

Babe continued to brief me on that eventful evening, "The moon was in its last quarter that night but still threw enough light for mixing our drinks in A.J.'s old jalopy. I had, as usual, parked my old Dodge pickup in front of Pop Tracy's Cafe and then on to the dance with A.J. He knew the road better than I and if, perchance, I were to exceed my limit on the Four Roses, it would be better if he drove back to town."

"As it turned out, that's precisely what happened. I got carried away with a beautiful doll—Bessie Jean Twenter. I danced with her a number of times and—wow, what a gal! But, I had made too many trips to the car for refreshment and at about midnight, I noticed that the dancehall badly needed stabilizing. It would spin one way then the other. Also, the floor would rush up at me and I had to put out a foot to push it back.

"A.J. may have noticed this. He came over, 'Babe,' he

[10] In 1928, the year of Babe's birth, the baseball immortal Babe Ruth hit his 60th home run and was as big a hero as Lindbergh. The Babe's real name was George Herman. So what greater tribute to a new son than to name him for the national idol.

says, 'I think we better be getting home. It's after midnight and your ole man is going to be wondering about you.' Either A.J. had had fewer drinks or he was better at holding his liquor or his car knew the way home on its own—without incident he motored back to town and deposited me at Pop's Cafe. He eyed me closely as I boarded the old Dodge.

"'Ya reckon yer gonna be OK, Babe?' he was concerned. I assured him I was OK.

"I whipped onto Second Street, set a southwesterly course and headed for the barn like a hungry horse. I remembered to carefully negotiate the half-left turn onto College on the other side of Chuck Babbitt's place. Although the trees and shrubbery illuminated by the streetlights seemed to be dancing a Polka, I figured I was OK—I could keep 'er in the road.

"Just at the southwest edge of town past the tract where the old CCC camp had been, the road takes another leftward bend of about 30° and simultaneously, the macadam surface gives way to dusty gravel. I had slowed a bit and was starting into this turn when I met a car. This jerk was going hell for leather, in the middle of the gravel road, throwing up dust and gravel and he had his headlights on full bright. He never dimmed them and I was blinded. I felt a crunch as the old Dodge dropped off into a deep ditch on the right side. Then everything went black.

"When I came to, I put my gloved hands up to my face. My gloves were wet! The Four Roses is now beginning to clear and I could see the blood. I had gone through the windshield face first. My face and neck felt like it had gone through a meat grinder. I was still in shock when Hap Eckerle came along in a school bus and saw my plight.

"The next thing I remember was lying on the examination table in the offices of the Doctors Eggleston. [Dr. C.P. Eggleston and his wife, Bernice, both D.O.s, had a family practice in Pilot Grove for a number of years.] Mrs. Eggleston was removing the remaining shards of glass from my face and clinking them into an emetic pan. Dr. Eggleston was preparing the stitches. The final count was 47.

"Their dialogue seeped through the haze: '...anesthetic? ...don't know...lost lots of blood...' The doctor leaned over me and spreading my eyelids, assessed the pupils. (He also got a good sniff of my breath—30% Four Roses, 70% Seven-Up). 'Naw,' he says, 'Don't need no anesthetic for this one—he's already had one, self-administered!'

"So now I know what a football feels like when it is being stitched together. But the doc was right, I felt very little pain.

"As he finished his fancy stitchery I looked at the wall clock above his head: 4AM! My old man will really give me hell! Then dropping my gaze I see my old man! He's standing there at the foot of the table looking at me. I expected some harsh words but he looked at my pile of bloody clothing on the chair and said, 'When you're ready Babe,

Fig. 4-28. Babe Heim, summer of 1947.

I'll be waiting for you down stairs.' I guess he figured I had had enough punishment for my damfoolishment."

Fifty years on, the scars are almost totally gone except for a small one on his upper lip. Babe may not think of these scars in this way but his ancient, aristocratic Prussian ancestors would have been very proud of them as an honorable badge of courage—saber dueling you know.

THE MEDICINE CHEST - HEALTH CARE IN THE 1930S

THE PHYSIC

Dad, like most of his contemporaries, believed that one needed 'a physic' several times a year like an auto tune-up. He kept Epsom salts in the medicine chest for this but the premier 'physic' was Chouteau water. Ex-Lax and Feenamint were available then, but in his eyes, "...a bunch of sissy stuff only good for playing practical jokes."...which he occasionally did: "Here Boots, have a piece of this here chocolate candy." "Boots" Gramlich was a next door neighbor in the early 1930s. He is (was?) Corene (Kempf) Ware's uncle.

'Chouteau water' came from a pretty, little, arboreal resort folded away in the hills near Martinsville, four or five miles northeast of Pilot Grove just off the Boonville road—now Hwy 135. This resort—Chouteau Springs—was built around some foul-smelling but natural and ostensibly health-giving sulfur springs that had been discovered in the 1800s and named for Pierre Chouteau, [1789-1865, b. St. Louis] one of the richest, most powerful people in the West in his day. Chouteau may have had some financial interest in Chouteau Springs. It was originally platted as a major town. See Ann Betteridge's "Discover Cooper County"—Cooper County Historical Society.

There was an admission fee of 10¢ for official access

Fig. 4-29. "Nickel a tune, 6 plays fer a quarter...and a good time was had by all."

to the springs. Of course, there were other attractions at Chouteau—God forbid they should demand that extortionate fee for mere access to the waters. There was a small swimming pool, a dance pavilion as well as picnicking facilities. The dance pavilion featured a jukebox where you could dance to the ditty of your choice (78 rpm records) for one nickel (6 for a quarter). The pavilion dated from the turn of the century—*la fin de siecle*—as Pierre would have said. It was of heavy timber construction with a overhanging shingle roof. The quaint architecture reminded me of a Japanese resort.

This pavilion had a bit of panache and years after I accompanied Dad on his replenishment trips, goodwife Daisy and I enjoyed dates there. For example, one Saturday night in the summer of 1947 I procured[11] a bottle of champagne and Virgil Eckerle, Bonnie Kirby, Daisy Corbin and I rolled into Chouteau Springs in Eckerle's little red Ford convertible. We all got blitzed on champagne out of paper cups and—as Sarah Coleman was wont to say in her Pilot Grove Items (Cooper County Record) —"... a good time was had by all."

The magnificent elms and the shade they offered in the pre-air-conditioned world of 1930-1940s was a great attraction on hot summer nights and weekends. Some people did come however for the medicinal(?) bathing and imbibing of the mystical waters. As pre-teens, Homer Jeffress and I used to observe an old gandy—of advanced age, maybe 40. He came down from Kansas City, it was said, to rent a log-cabin lodge by the week, bathe in the mineral water and generally hang out. We were convinced he was one of Tom Pendergast's 'enforcers' laying low for a while after a 'contract hit' for Tom.

The springs gushed forth hundreds of gallons per hour and could not be contained within the park. The spillover ran into a small creek—Chouteau Creek[12]—and out of the park and beyond the jurisdiction of the toll takers. So, Dad, when he was resupplying his inventory of the curative waters, often bypassed the park, went down stream and dipped up a couple of gallon jugs (1-2 months supply) of the enchanted elixir.

[11] I was not of the age to be buying liquor so I 'procured' it by secret means.

[12] I70 passes over Chouteau Creek about 3 miles west of the I35 junction.

So Chouteau water and Epsom salts served as Dad's physic. When I was four years old Dr. Boley had to anesthetize my left big toe with a blast of liquid carbon dioxide[13] and excise an ingrown toenail. Sixty years later I had to have it done again. (I wondered if I still had a warranty on Dr. Boley's first operation.)

He told Mom to have me soak my foot in Epsom salts twice daily. I had never heard of Epsom salts being used to this purpose. I thought at the time that would be something like soaking my foot in Ex-Lax!

UNGENTINE AND SLOAN'S LINIMENT

Sore muscles, bursitis, arthritis, Charley horses, pleurisy and other ailments of indeterminate origin undiagnosed except that they involved a muscle—were treated with Unguentine. I can remember Mom slavering it on Dad's bare back like mayonnaise on a sandwich. It smelled to high heaven. I was careful never to use it before going to school. It followed the rule for evaluating medicines and home remedies—"...it ain't agonna do you no good unless it burns like hell, tastes like hell or stinks like hell!"

Sloan's Liniment was the other cure-all for the achy breaky back and shoulder muscles that 'real men' incurred. (In 1996, perusing a display of medical antiques in the doctor's office, I saw a Sloan's Liniment bottle. The "active ingredient" was listed as "capsicum". Being a fan of Tex-Mex cuisine, I recognized "Capsicum" as the chemical that puts the "Hot" in Red Hot Chili Peppers.)

Sloan's was purveyed by the Watkins man who never failed to make it by our place about once a month. Dad often laid on the bed and had Mom pour it on his back, that is until one evening when she got a bit too generous with the dosage. The surplus gushed down the natural channel of his back to saturate a 'no-go zone'. Here the 'counter-irritant' provided a level of therapy far in excess of the formulators' designed intent. Dad exploded off the bed and, holding his 'long handle' underwear at his waist, raced for the wash basin and towels. It was ever so much fun! I, however immediately moderated my giggles when he gave me a black look of disapproval. Thereafter he did the liniment himself.

Mom invariably patronized the Watkins man with extensive orders. Part of this was because he really did have some items that were not readily available at Heinrich's or Warnhoff's. Partly it was because the Watkins man was a traveling entertainer, full of racy stories and gossip.

[13] CO_2 was often used as an anesthetic in those days. Carbon dioxide was kept in a glass container under several atmospheres of pressure to keep it liquified and sprayed on the appropriate area to numb it by 'freezing'.

One of his nostrums was a home-remedy for coughs. Watkins provided a little bottle of some God-awful smelling (and tasting) pine tar derivative which was to be mixed—1 part in 5—with Karo white corn syrup. This made a quart or so of 'cough syrup'. The Karo masked the taste enough that you could gag it down. It was the treatment for coughs for the first 15 years of my life.

CAMPHO-PHENIQUE VS THE CHIGGERS - CHIGGERS WIN

Campho-Phenique was another wonder drug of the day when it came to dealing with the summertime scourge of the chigger. Many evenings I came in from play to get my feet and legs deluged with Campho-Phenique. Summer playmates gave the smell a wide berth but I didn't care. However, I did discover an anatomical no-go zone even for the miracles of Campho-Phenique. I once had a terrible itch right in my crotch. Following the American dictum that 'If *some* is good, *more* is better and *too much* is just right!" I splashed a goodly amount of Campho-Phenique on the offending area.

I can report to you that, for this purpose, Campho-Phenique—in doctor-speak—"is not indicated".

CURE-CHROME AND EYE-DINE

When we were little kids the multitude of scratches, contusions and abrasions to which little ruffians are subjected were fixed with mercurochrome or iodine. Iodine was the little bottle with the death's head on it and burned like hell. Mom always gave us that, "It won't do you any good unless it hurts." Aunt Pearl was easier and could be conned into using mercurochrome. Larger wounds were treated, usually with Cloverine or Watkins salve then wrapped with a clean rag held in place by adhesive tape. Pearl called it 'easy tape.'

HIT WITH NAPALM? TRY ZINC OXIDE!

There were so many creosote burns among railroad workers caused by handling cross-ties that the Katy issued big one-pound canisters of zinc oxide. We always had a can or two of it on hand although I didn't use it much until 1943. Four or five times during that particular summer I helped unload new cross-ties dripping with creosote. I have often thought that if an OSHA inspector, as they operate today, would have observed us unloading these cross-ties from a gondola on a moving train, they would have had a heart attack! We stood on the creosote slick bottom of the gondola. Slipping and sliding around as the work train lurched down the track, we hefted a 150 pound creosote-soaked cross-tie over our heads to rest it on the edge of the car then pushed it out. I learned then why we always had so much zinc oxide around the house. It was one of the few medicines in our chest that really was of value.

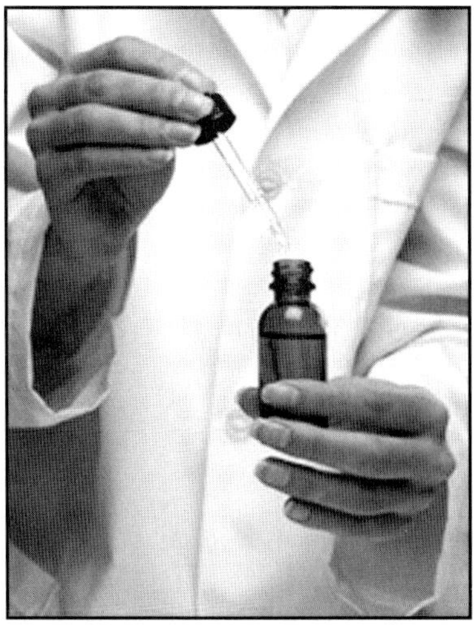

Fig. 4-30. Try this Campho-Phenique on them chiggers, Sonny.

SONNY'S HEAD COLLIDES WITH SIDEWALK - HEAD WINS.

On Halloween night 1937, I fell off Leslie Chamberlin's pickup and fractured my skull. This was felt to be of sufficient importance to warrant the extra dollar for a house call by Doctor Sandy.

On Sunday night October 31, 1937 a gang of kids were milling around Pop Tracy's Cafe when under-aged and unlicensed Leslie Chamberlin came by in his dad's old pickup truck. "Hop in" he said, "and we'll go see what the hob-goblins are up to in the old town tonight."

Some got in the cab with him. Most—including me—just jumped on the running board. The truck had stock racks so we could stand on the running boards and cling to the racks. At the corner of Harris and Third streets my hat blew off. This was an old bum's hat that I had added to my Halloween costume. As it blew off, like a dunce, (remember, I was just 10 years old) I whirled and tried to catch it. I fell onto the sidewalk, landed on my head and was knocked cold as a mackerel. I laid there for about two hours until Elon "Slim" Wassmann found me hemorrhaging from my nose and right ear. He identified me and carried me home.

I woke up several hours later lying on my cot with old Doc Sandy asking me how many fingers he was holding up. "Two," I answered. He put some mercurochrome on my skull at the point of its collision with the concrete sidewalk, and told Mom, "He'll be Okay." That was the extent of my medical treatment. For a week the left side of my face was paralyzed and I pulled clotted blood out of my right ear and my nose. But—old Doc Sandy was right—I was indeed "okay". Two weeks later the incident was nothing but a bad memory.

Frankly I was glad that I didn't go to the hospital. The 'Hospital' was St. Joseph's in Boonville. St. Joseph's was regarded the same as all hospitals—a place you go to die. I can remember the many times when some neighbor lady came to tell Mom the news of a mutual acquaintance. In low voices one would say, "They took her to the hospital you know!" They would both nod knowingly and mentally plan a pie for the wake. "We gotta a lotta extra rhubarb this year. I always thought rhubarb was real nice for a wake. Helps keep you regular, too."

"Come for the funeral, stay for the pie."

[From Cooper County Record, Nov. 5, 1937]

SUFFERS SEVERE INJURY

Young Boy Falls From Side Of a Moving Truck to Pavement

"Sonny" Salmon, ten year old son of Mr. and Mrs. Richard Salmon of Pilot Grove has been confined to his home this week recovering from injuries he received in a fall from a truck Saturday evening. With a party of other boys he was riding on the side of a truck when his hat blew off. In his haste to get his hat he jumped from the moving truck and struck his head on the concrete crossing at the junction of Third and Harris streets. Without knowing what had happened the truck and its occupants moved on leaving the boy on the street where he was later found by Elon Wassman, who took him to the home of his parents where he received immediate medical attention. He is recovering rapidly.

STRUCK BY LIGHTNING

Mamie Chapman's home was graced by rails made of galvanized steel piping. These rails were installed parallel to the front sidewalk and continued to the front steps. I never understood their purpose. They may have served as a hitching rack in bygone years. At any rate the rails were worn slick with kids playing 'skin the cat'.

One muggy summer afternoon in 1935, several of the neighborhood kids were playing on these rails when a bolt of lightning literally exploded right in our midst. All the neighbors heard the crash and some saw the bolt coming. I went flying butt over teacup, rolling out into the grass. I was stunned as were one or two others. We were deafened for a moment but there seemed to be no other damage. Since that day I have never had any fear of lightning—lightning never strikes the same place twice, you know!

The only effects I ever had—and I'm not sure this was

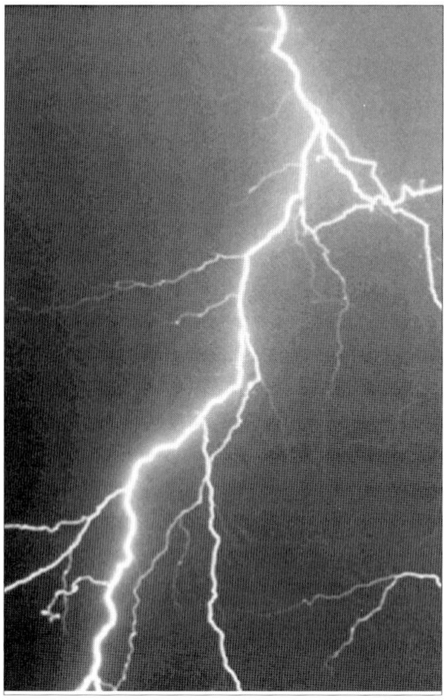

Fig. 4-31. Ball lightning struck the ground in the midst of the Fourth Street kids gang.

the lightning—was some terrible nightmares over a period of several months. These nightmares were something like Hieronymous Bosch's "Les Jardins des Delice." But all this might just have been the pickled pigs feet. (Or schweine hachse mit sauerkraut!)

DIXIE AND GANGRENE

In the summer of 1936 Dixie was a member of a Methodist Youth Group. This church group was very popular with the teenagers of the town. The Baptists had a similar group which met on alternate weeks. Some kids joined both. For young people who had little opportunity to even get so far away as Sedalia, the Youth Groups were a Godsend. Always key to the success of such church activities were the ministers. The Methodist Minister at the time was Reverend Bottoms. He didn't impress with his looks but was a dynamic and effective leader.

Rev. Bottoms had an old '26 or '27 Chevy—a four door sedan. It was a nice car in its day but woefully in need of repair in 1936. The Youth Group was composed of 12 - 14 kids. The good Reverend's only transportation was this family auto. So for an outing in Bunceton one day he piles them all in the 6-passenger car. Or rather, in and *on*, his car. Dixie was riding the running board when a lurch brought her knee into disastrous contact with a jagged, rusted out part of the rear fender. She suffered a severe, deep 4-5 inch gash on her leg and knee.

Rev. Bottoms rushed her home. She was helped onto her bed and Dr. Sandy—who lived 4 doors up the street—was summoned. He came and removed the rag which was stanching the blood. Rev. Bottoms was hovering in the background feeling guilty since he was responsible for the kids. When the ragged, bloody wound began bleeding again—KER-THUMP! Reverend Bottoms passed out cold as a mackerel and fell in the middle of the floor. There then followed a reenactment of a Chinese fire drill as he was attended to. In the end Dr. Sandy spent more time with him than he did with Dixie. Dixie's wound got treated with hydrogen-peroxide and two stitches. "Clean up with the peroxide, pour on the mercurochrome, wrap a clean rag around it. She'll be OK!"

She was not, however, 'OK'. The wound got infected. Two weeks later the suppurating wound turned green and smelled to high heaven. With Dr. Sandy out of town, Mom took her to Dr. Boley. Dr. Boley was the new doctor in town and not yet totally accepted by the old heads.

Boley removed the old stitches, did a standard debridement, sprinkled on sulfa powder and re-stitched the nearly gangrenous leg. Two weeks of daily ultra violet lamp treatment[13]—a standard bactericide in those days—and she healed up nicely. Of course, she carries souvenir scars to this day.

So the medicine chest contained: Epsom salts, iodine, mercurochrome, hydrogen peroxide, zinc oxide, Campo-Phenique, Unguentine, Sloan's Liniment and, of course, aspirin—in our case Sendols.

RACISM IN MIDDLE AMERICA

300% AMERICAN!

During the presidential election of 1940 there was a joke making the rounds that revealed more than intended about the level of bigotry in the country in those days. The election issues were heavily influenced by the gathering war clouds. Patriotism was to the fore.

Candidate 1: "Vote for me! I'm a 100% American. I hate the Japs, the Germans and the Italians."

Candidate 2: "Vote for me! I'm 200% American. I hate the Japs, the Germans, the Italians—and Jews, Negroes, Catholics and Episcopalians!"

Candidate 3: "Vote for me! I'm 300% American. I hate *everybody*!"

The America of my youth was not a model of virtue, tolerance and equality among ethnic and religious groups. Pilot Grove did not escape this blight.

Fig. 4-32. Dr. Charles A. Sandy in retirement, Prairie Village, KS 1960. Photo - Martha Sandy.

In the summer of 1935 an Indiana organizer visited town to recruit for the Ku Klux Klan. I was 8 years old and went with my dad to hear the speeches. To their credit, the Methodist Church refused the KKK request to use the church building. To their shame, they did permit the 'rally' to be held on church grounds. I was there and saw the 'crowd'. It was not exactly a tidal wave of support. There were about 10-12 men and when it came to decision time, none stepped forward. I'd like to attribute that to a higher morality but I suspect it had more to do with the $10 initiation fee.

As an eight year old child I hadn't a clue what the KKK was and had no interest one way or another other than it seemed to be something exciting going on in an otherwise dull town.

In later years of course, movements like this scared the hell out of me. He who is convinced that God would want him to do some atrocious thing if only He knew all facts in the case, speaks of a scary arrogance. From the Crusades and Torquemada's Spanish Inquisition down to the murderous car bombs in Beirut it has been evident that anyone that is convinced that God is on his side is dangerous.

I was sure at the time (December 1950) that some fanatic mullah, demented shaman or deranged priest (whatever China has for holy men) had issued such a Holy Fatwa to the Chinese Third Route Army to kill me personally (a la Salman Rushdie) in the name of some strange god or religious fervor—"...Sonny Salmon is to be terminated for the Good of Mankind and the Betterment of Socialist Peoples Everywhere." So it seemed at the time.

The KKK failed in Pilot Grove. Nevertheless the incident contributed to a cool Protestant-Catholic tension. It surfaced at the Bert Wells-Red Horst incident. Protestants tended to view the incident as 'justifiable homicide' which in the end was also what the jury concluded. Some Catholics tended to view it as an excess use of force so blatant as to constitute murder. It was an understandable position and with some merit.

When one dispassionately examines the tension of those days, particularly from a perspective of a half century, it surpasses belief! In reality, the village in those days

[13] It is interesting to note that this 'ultraviolet light as bactericide' was used in the spring of 1942 on Corregidor. US and Philipine forces had been driven back to the island fortress after suffering many wounded. They were surrounded by the Japanese and medical supplies ran out, so, in lieu of antibiotics the medics surgically opened wounds and uncovering them, placed the patients on cots in the sun. This was a crude form of ultraviolet light radiation. Pictures of this were in Life magazine.

was like most of the rest of the country—suffering a massive case of cognitive dissonance. I think such attitudes today would be very puzzling.

Insofar as racial prejudice is concerned, the village solved its "Negro problem" like Texas solved its "Indian problem"—it was exported! There are no Indian reservations in Texas.

I am being facetious here because there were and are black folks in the Pilot Grove community. But when W.W.II began, so much industrial work opened up that even black people got good jobs. They emigrated in droves to the cities of the industrial north, Chicago, Detroit and of course St. Louis, seeking and mostly finding, a better life.

THE WAR YEARS

For a generation Pilot Grove was disconnected from the external world by a debilitating economic depression. Prior to 1941, life was little different from the last century. The 1941 advent of World War II brought wrenching change to my sleepy little hometown. The draft brought a cold breath on the necks of young men 17 to 34 years old and severe shortages of gasoline, tires and new cars would shortly affect everyone's mobility. Sugar, meat and even clothing and shoes were rationed by 1943.

But the changes were not all bad. Farmers would find ready markets for their products for the first time in half a generation. Their problem now flipflopped—far from producing a market depressing surplus, now they could not produce enough. The manpower demands of the armed services as well as war production made jobs plentiful. As a matter of fact, serious labor shortages soon surfaced and the war effort demanded that women join the work force.

ROSIE THE RIVETER

My sister, Dixie, graduated from PGHS in 1941. Cousins Clara and Florence attended in 1939 and 1940 but finished elsewhere. Whenever I think of my sister Dixie, our cousins and their war production service—I think of Rosie the Riveter.

By summer of 1942—about the time that this terrific trio was in training at Fulton, MO—the pre-war estimatesof the enormous manpower requirements for the war began proving true. Volunteers and draftees were pouring into the Armed Forces by the millions. Factories were undermanned. A critical advantage that the US had—war materiel production—would be crippled without an answer to a question: Who's gonna make the guns and bullets?"

THE ANSWER OF COURSE WAS: The women—

Fig. 4-33. The war caused farm prices to soar. Soon Pilot Grove farmers were getting re-acquainted with money while they did their bit for the war effort. This is an excerpt from a 1941 newspaper article.

Start of a Purebred Hereford Herd—John Gerke started a purebred Hereford herd and today has four registered cows, a registered bull and four registered calves. shown above with the herd are, from left to right, John Gerke, M.W. Shier, Pilot Grove Vocational Agriculture Teacher; who has worked with the Gerke youths in high school, and the Gerke's sons, Norman, Wilfred and Elwood.Clipping from September 1941 Boonville paper courtesy Irene (Gerke) Felten.

'Rosie the Riveter'and her sisters. The spirit of these women was captured in a song of the early war years—"Rosie the Riveter". Rosie came to symbolize all the brave women who went off to the cities and the factories to do the job when the men went off to war. In one of the biggest social upheavals in the nation's history, women began moving into jobs that had previously been 'men-only'. The war could not have been won without them but they were on an unmarked trail.

NEW JEANS

Florence tells the story of the NYA[15] war production training program in Fulton: "Clara, Dixie and I were in this NYA training together. When we finished, several of us were offered machine operator jobs with AB Chance in Centralia, MO. When we reported to the Chance plant the personnel lady looked at us and said, 'You can't wear those clothes!'

"Since we had dressed the best we could to give a good first impression, I didn't understand her objection.

"The personnel supervisor continued, 'Your clothing is too nice to work on the factory floor. The machine shop is particularly dirty and greasy and your lovely slacks will be ruined in a day!'

'Well, OK,' I asked, 'What do you suggest we do?'

'Go down to Wilkins Mercantile and get yourselves some dungarees and sweatshirts. They're not very lady-

Fig. 4-34. AB Chance's "Rosie the Riveters" 1943. Florence Salmon, Pinkie Gates, Dixie Salmon.

Fig. 4-35. War Production poster - 1943.

like but they'll do you better on them dirty machines.'

"So," continues Florence, "That afternoon we walked downtown to Wilkins to get fitted out in dungarees."

"In Wilkins this old gandy hustles up to us rubbing his hands and inquires as to our needs.

"Dungarees," I said. He looked puzzled.

"Blue jeans. Overalls. Work pants." explains Dixie.

"'Why, we don't have nothing like that for ladies!' he explains, eyeing us like we had just dropped in from Mars.

"Then we're just gonna have to look in the *men's* department, aren't we?' I says to him. That's what we did.

"He was very anxious to help after we told him about our jobs at AB Chance. In the Men's Department he shows a counter or two of blue jeans. He had this yellow tape measure around his neck which he pulled off and started toward me. 'I'm gonna hafta get yer measurements, Miss.'

"He dropped to his knees and carefully set the end of the tape at my cuff. Holding it carefully between right thumb and forefinger, he grabs the other end with his left hand and traces the seam to its uppermost termination. Then, suddenly realizing where he had his left hand, he dropped the tape like it was a rattlesnake and scrambles to his feet.

'Awful sorry, Miss, I got no experience at measuring ladies. Maybe what you should do is just take several pairs a these here jeans in the tryin'-on room' he jerked his thumb at a draped room a few feet away, and find out what size fits you best.'

'The sizes is on the labels in the waist band, but you'd probably ought to get yerself a size larger, case they shrink when you wash 'em.'

We did get a size larger and it was a good thing but not because of shrinkage. As soon as we started getting regular paychecks we began eating a little better and moved up to a bigger size. We were eating higher up the food chain.

"NO JOB FER A LADY!"

"A factory job operating heavy machinery was a frightening change in life style for most of us who grew up in small towns. Not everyone was up to such a change. Of the girls in my class, only Dixie and I survived to go on to Emerson Electric's Florissant Plant near St. Louis."

Florence and Dixie are wearing their hard won jeans in Fig, 4-34. Jeans were not yet fully accepted by post-Victorian morality. At the beginning of the war many people were aghast at women wearing men's clothing these "shameless hussies wearing men's clothing." By the end of the war this Victorian social ethic was dead forever.

"Kirche, Kinder, und Kuche"

In honoring the women who left home and hearth to work in the war plants, the psycho-social frictions are

[15] NYA - The National Youth Administration was a part of Roosevelt's New Deal. It was to provide youngsters with part-time employment opportunities.

Fig. 4-36. Dixie and Florence Salmon, cousins and roommates at Centralia and later St. Louis, 1943.

always glossed over. In western nations at that time the proper tradition had always been that men were the breadwinners and women were to stay at home making pies and babies. The German version was "Kirche, Kinder, und Kuche" (Church, Children, and Kitchen.)

Rosie the Riveter was not always welcomed with open arms by fellow employees of the masculine gender. Dixie tells an illustrative story:

"JUST A GIRL!"

"At Emerson Electric's Florissant Plant we were making fractional horsepower motors which powered the gun turrets in medium and heavy bombers—the B-17 Flying Fortress, B-26, etc. I operated a lathe. With a few weeks of experience I could do the job better than anyone in the section, so when the company began upgrading some of the machinery, I was assigned a brand new, state-of-the-art turret lathe—all the bells and whistles.

"Noting this, an older man had a fit and complained bitterly to the boss.

Boss: 'You don't think she can handle the job?'

Worker: 'No, its not that. She's the best lathe operator in the Section!'

Boss: 'Well then what *is* it?'

Worker: 'Do I have to draw a picture? She's just a girl—a teenage girl!'

"Fortunately, the Boss was a fair man so the disgruntled worker got no satisfaction, but there was little love lost between us thereafter."

The war years were not all work and no play. In fact, another major social upheaval was the churning of population. There was also a new upward *economic* mobility—people who previously had had only nodding acquaintance with a dollar bill were suddenly flush. In addition there was a tremendous geographic mobility—farm and village to the major cities. City life was heady stuff and old heads worried "once they been to the city, how ya gonna keep 'em down on the farm?"

SHOE FACTORY

Irene Gerke was one of those "Rosie the Riveters". She graduated PGHS in 1943 directly into the war years. She was looking for a part to play in the national effort when her mother had an accident and Irene was usurped into a nursing role for several months. Following her mother's recovery, she took a job at the shoe factory in Boonville where she worked until she married Clemus Felten in 1949.

I greatly appreciate help from Irene who contributed much material for this book including most of the ration stamps and related paraphernalia.

My mother also worked in that Boonville shoe factory from 1942 until 1959 when she retired. Sister Dixie had gone to work in St. Louis but Bob and I were still in high school while she acted as both Mom and family breadwinner. It was not an easy job and I can empathize with those who worked there.

WAR RATIONING

Of the Federal bureaucracies that proliferated in the first months of the war, the OPA (Office of Price Administration) was in charge of fixing prices. Econ 101 teaches us that when prices are held below market value, shortages soon follow. Since price is no longer a viable allocation device, to ensure fairness, rationing must be imposed.

Janie (Brownfield) Goehner told me a "now it can be told" story about her 1945 Junior class raising funds to fete us Seniors. It involves sugar rationing.

D-DAY FOR DIVINITY

Janie remembers the fund raising efforts of her Junior class of 1945: "One day in early April of that year, Miss Lida Harris passed the word and class officers assembled in her classroom after school. We shoved the student desks around to form a semi-circle and listened as she reminded us of the Junior-Senior Banquet. She said, 'You know that the expense of the banquet is to be borne by the Juniors, so we have to come up with some ideas on getting some money.'

"Many ideas of varying practicality were tossed out but in the end, the winner seemed to be raffling off a box of home made Divinity candy. Of course, this option ran headlong into the rationing of sugar. In the spring of 1945, the country was subjected to rationing of gasoline, clothing, shoes, meat and sugar. But my classmates were quite inventive. The solution was to ask volunteers for 2-3 ounce quotas each and thus assemble enough for a deluxe box of candy.

"The plan was announced and little brown bags of sugar began accruing on Miss Harris' desk—anything

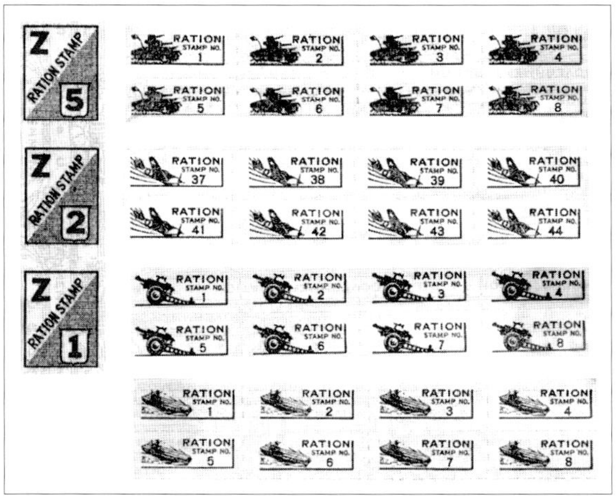

Fig. 4-37. War ration stamps 1942. From Irene Felten.

Fig. 4-38. The price card includes the ration points required for a cut of red meat - 1943.

from a tablespoonful to a half cup of C & H's finest granulated sugar.

"At our next planning meeting, I volunteered to make the Divinity. I didn't know much about it, but my mother was a whiz at candymaking and I would help. When I took the sugar home that day and told Mom that she (and I) were going to make Divinity for a raffle later that month, she was able to hide the terrific elation and enthusiasm I was sure she would feel. She reminded me, 'Janie, you know the weather must be just right for Divinity. A bit too much humidity and the candy will be spoiled. So far this month we have had nothing but rain and humid days.'

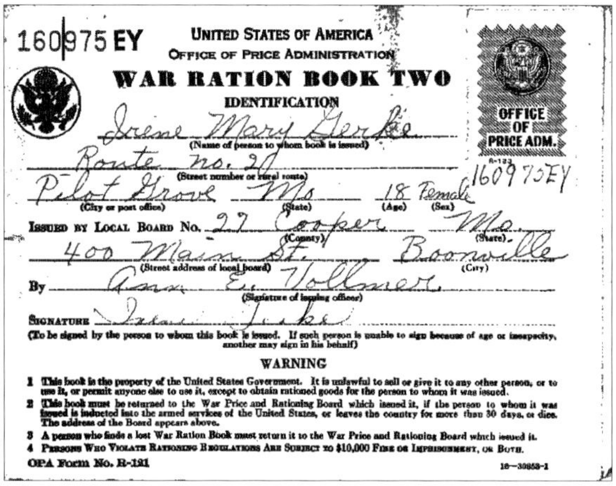

160975 EY

UNITED STATES OF AMERICA
OFFICE OF PRICE ADMINISTRATION
WAR RATION BOOK TWO
IDENTIFICATION

OFFICE OF PRICE ADM.

Irene Mary Gerke
(Name of person to whom book is issued)
Route no. 2
(Street number or rural route)
Pilot Grove (City or post office) Mo (State) 18 (Age) Female (Sex)
R-123 160975EY
ISSUED BY LOCAL BOARD NO. 27 Cooper (County) Mo. (State)
400 Main St. (Street address of local board) Boonville (City)
By Ann E. Vollmer (Signature of issuing officer)
SIGNATURE Irene Gerke
(To be signed by the person to whom this book is issued. If such person is unable to sign because of age or incapacity, another may sign in his behalf)

WARNING

1 This book is the property of the United States Government. It is unlawful to sell or give it to any other person, or to use it, or permit anyone else to use it, except to obtain rationed goods for the person to whom it was issued.
2 This book must be returned to the War Price and Rationing Board which issued it, if the person to whom it was issued is inducted into the armed services of the United States, or leaves the country for more than 30 days, or dies. The address of the Board appears above.
3 A person who finds a lost War Ration Book must return it to the War Price and Rationing Board which issued it.
4 PERSONS WHO VIOLATE RATIONING REGULATIONS ARE SUBJECT TO $10,000 FINE OR IMPRISONMENT, OR BOTH.

OPA Form No. R-121 16—30853-1

Fig. 4-39. Ration Book 1942. From Irene Felten.

"The banquet would be on Saturday evening, May 5th in the gymnasium. We planned to sell 100 chances on the Divinity at 25¢ each which would go along way toward paying our expenses. Now if we could just get that candy made... but the days went by swiftly and—no Divinity. 'The weather is just too damp!' Mom told me.

"An "All School Assemble" was posted for Friday afternoon, April 27th. This would give us our primary market for selling chances, although the committee had been selling a few each week since we came up with the plan. We would sell the remainder of the chances, then hold the drawing and award the Divinity candy prize at the Assembly. It would be very nice if we had the candy by that date!

"The featured attraction of that Assembly was a "Mock Graduation" where some of the Juniors portrayed the Seniors as well as some members of the administration and faculty. Mother made me a special outfit which was a caricature of Miss Harris' favorite purple ensemble.

But my great concern during that week of April 23rd was getting the Divinity made! I nagged mother on the weekend before the Assembly but she said, 'Janie, you know what the weather has been like. We will not get another shot if we mess up this batch. The forecast shows clearing at the end of the week. We'll just have to wait and see.'

"Thursday was the last day to make the candy or face disaster. That day started just like the rest of the week, but we had to commit. I stayed home to help Mom. With great reservation, we started cooking, but as the minutes flew by, the clouds thinned and by ten o'clock the sun was shining brightly and it turned to a warm, dry day.

[Author's Note: Something similar happened ten months before on June 5, 1944, when General Eisenhower had to gamble on the D-Day commitment based on a weather forecast. Both D-Day and Divinity Day were momentous decisions that came right in the end.]

"The Divinity turned out superb! The chances were all sold and my mother and I heaved a sigh of relief.

Fig. 4-40. Captain Eddie Rickenbacker with his SPAD 1918. Rickenbacker was America's number 1 ace with 26 confirmed "kills". Note "Hat in the Ring" logo on fuselage. Though members of this squadron were all Americans, they flew French airplanes. SPAD is an acronym for "Societe Par Aeronautiques et ses Derivees." (Corporation for aircraft and their derivatives.)

EPILOGUE - DREAMS AND REALITY

So—this is the way it was—life in the village when I was growing up. We dealt with reality as best we could while dreaming our dreams and playing out our fantasies. Every little boy has fantasies of an exciting life as: an airline pilot, cowboy, dump truck driver, soldier, sailor, or whatever is perceived as the most exciting life in his era.

I suppose little girls had these fantasies also but when I was growing up I knew of none that dreamed of being a locomotive engineer. Many wanted to be teachers.

In my era firemen, policemen and locomotive engineers were a big part of the mix. But all these dreams were fleeting, changing from year to year, even day to day and eventually settling on something more realistic like "I'm gonna be like my Daddy."

For me the fantasy was locomotive engineer until I was about 11 when I began reading pulp fiction including "The Lone Eagle." These multi-colored, glossy and brightly covered magazines offset the drab pulp paper interior of my pulp fiction. Artists conceptions—mostly fanciful—rendered some action scene from the stories inside. "The Lone Eagle" was one such pulp fiction magazine.

"The Lone Eagle" stories were based (extremely loosely) on the exploits of the Lafayette Escadrille, a collection of American college boys who went to France in 1915-1916 to fly and fight for France and just generally have a jolly time. They thought themselves immortal. *"The bells of hell go ting-a-ling-a-ling, for you but not for me!"*

This fantasy, which is described in the exquisite words of John Magee (see sidebar, below), was a driving force for thousands of adolescents of my era, so I don't apologize for it.

Thus, at age 11 my fantasy was to join that exclusive band. Like so many others, I never realized my boyhood dream, but it was not from lack of trying. I tell about "Cadets" in these tales (Chapter 14).

HIGH FLIGHT

By John Gillespie Magee, Jr*

Oh, I have slipped the surly bonds of earth
And danced the skies on laughter-silvered wings;
Sunward I've climbed, and joined the tumbling mirth
Of sun-split clouds—and done a hundred things
You have not dreamed of—*wheeled* and *soared* and
swung High in the sunlit silence.

I've chased the shouting wind along, and flung
My eager craft through footless halls of air.

Up, up the long, delirious burning blue
I've topped the windswept heights with easy grace

Where never lark,
or even eagle flew.

And, while with silent, lifting mind I've trod
The high untrespassed sanctity of space,
Put out my hand, and *touched* the face of God.

*Gillespie was a WWII RCAF Spitfire pilot who died in the air over Europe in 1941.

LESSON LEARNED: Failure of their dreams might be God's way of protecting little children and fools from their own folly.

A little work, a little play — to keep us going—and,
so good-day!
A little warmth, a little light of love's bestowing—and,
so good night!
A little fun, to match the sorrow of a day's growing—
and, so good-morrow!
A little trust that when we die we reap our sowing! and
so—good-bye!

—*du Maurier*

OVERVIEW

DURING THE DAYS OF MY YOUTH THE COUNTRY was either slowly recovering from deep depression or preparing for and fighting a world war. Times were turbulent and changing. The only constant was that my age group was usually totally bereft of jingling money much less paper. Thus, our pastimes were restricted to those that were free or very inexpensive. An example was swimming—we swam in the creeks, Chouteau cost 25¢ counting the park admission and the Boonville Kiwanis pool also cost a quarter—much too dear except special occasions!

SWIMMIN' HOLE

The road that heads out of Pilot Grove to the east—now Hwy 135—used to make a sharp bend, a ninety degree angle, at the 'mile corner'. In a long ago upgrading of the geometrics of this road, this torturous (and dangerous) 90° turn had been greatly relieved by a higher radius, banked curve so that even Estil Young with a skin full of Budweiser could negotiate it. (This corner had, in times gone by, given Estil much grief.)

The corner was called the 'mile corner' because the C.J. Harris Lumber Company, a homegrown Pilot Grove corporation, a forerunner of Home Depot, Builders' Square, Home Quarters, et al, had stuck up mileage signs along the roads leading into the town. One of them stood at that corner—"Pilot Grove 1 mile". The sign was composed of white 1" x 4" boards on a steel fencing rod and presented an image like an overdone Cross of Lorraine.

The lesser road continuing due east (now named "Mile Corner Road") was, in the early 1930s, lightly graveled and single lane. At about the 2-1/2 mile point (there was no marker) the road bends sharply to the right and continues south to the bridge over Petite Saline Creek.

The Kempf farm was located on the east at the bend. This area is characterized by a flat expanse of rich creek bottom land with Petite Saline Creek flowing in a gentle curve toward the northeast at the base of a rather steep bluff. The main road crosses an old (ca 1914) truss and span bridge and then climbs the hill. The old Roberts farmstead sat on the top of the bluff on the right of the road, the Les Babbitt farmstead on the left. At the Kempf farm you leave the gravel road and take a dirt track straight east for about 800 yards to a heavy copse of

Fig. 5-1. "This way to Horseshoe Bend Sonny."

alder and sycamore. A few more yards through the rustling willows and you find Petite Saline Creek rounding a bend (Horseshoe Bend) and running into the 'riffles', a span of shallow, gravel bottomed creek bed. The water ran cool and clear in the dense shade of the tall trees—picturesque and inviting. Fifty yards upstream and around that bend was the old swimming hole!

Horseshoe Bend was a serendipitous product of Roosevelt's depression recovery efforts. A major objective of his first term was to 'get the farmers out of the mud' with a network of "FM"—'Farm to Market'[1] roads.

In pursuit of this objective, the WPA took on Mile Corner Road and for several summers in the 1930's as we walked out to Horseshoe Bend we saw dump trucks dumping gravel, tractor and horse drawn graders and dozens of pick and shovel operators improving this roadbed. The source of the gravel was Petite Saline Creek. FDR was also making us a swimming hole!

TARZAN SWING

Before the swing story, I have to tell you more about Loyd McCreery. It was 1942 and Loyd was about 17 when we built the swing. Loyd was the second of four children of E.M. (Mac) and Pauline McCreery. The McCreerys lived across the street and two doors to the west of our place on Fourth Street. They had come to town in the late 1930s when Mac took Fred Beumer's job as the Katy station agent. (A promotion moved the Beumers to Paolo, KS.

Loyd, the second son, like his brothers and sister, had the physical attributes of his mother. She was, at 30 something, quite an attractive lady with light complexion, bright blue eyes and the curly black hair of the Irish. Loyd had a lightly freckled complexion and a mischievous smile. He was tall, almost willowy slender.

Loyd had been put together with a touch of perfection—except for his head which had a few crossed wires. Loyd was, well… different. If you looked closely into his twinkling blue eyes you might see peeking out at you a Leprechaun—descen-

[1] The lower tier of state roads in Texas still use this "Farm to Market" designation — FM4055, FM6302, etc.

Fig. 5-2. 1933 Bathing Beauties on the Petite Saline Creek complete with 'Peeping Tom'. Photo—Ruth (Hays) Wood.

Fig. 5-4. The Bicycle Rover Girls. Marjorie Burger and Delores Zeller 1939. Photo taken *before* biking to Chouteau and back on a sunny July afternoon.

Fig. 5-3. Carol Rae Schlotzhauer and Babe Heim at Kiwanis pool, Boonville.

Fig. 5-5. Kiwanis Club swimming pool, Boonville - 1937. Photo - "History of Cooper County" courtesy Wally Burger.

dant through eight or ten generations of genes from ancient Ireland. Further careful observation of Loyd's actions would also lead you to surmise that this Leprechaun was probably fiddling with the controls.

But in the summer of '42, Loyd was one of the leaders of our rat pack. One gets to be a rat pack leader by being audacious, adventurous, bold and fearless. Loyd was all of these things—fearless to a fault. Fearlessness was a trait much to be admired in those days and we held him in high esteem. After his 1945 calamity at the Shuri line on Okinawa, Loyd recuperated in Hawaii then spent a postwar tour in China. He was discharged in 1946, fell in love and married in California but sadly he found, as Ambrose Bierce says—Love is a temporary insanity cured by marriage'[2].

[2] "The Devil's Dictionary" — Ambrose Bierce.

We were swimming one day at Horseshoe Bend when someone suggested suspending a rope from a giant sycamore that overhung the water—a 'Tarzan Swing'. After looking up at the upper branches of this mighty tree, it was evident that someone would have to risk his neck by climbing up to the upper branches. We permitted Loyd to volunteer. He shinnied up, tied my lariat onto a strong branch and then, while flamboyantly rappelling down the rope, lost his hold and fell about 30 feet into the water.

The water was quite deep here so he was never in danger of striking the bottom, but we dived in to help him anyway. He was OK. He laughed, "Don't worry about me, Mom said I was born to be hanged!" I pointed at the rope burn on his neck and said, "You damned near were!"

We tied a stout, two foot limb onto the rope and our swing was complete. Because it was so high we could, with a good run, swing out about 40-50 feet over the water before dropping in. Kid heaven!

RATTLESNAKE VS OL' TEX - TEX WINS!

There was, however, an incident at this swing that was a little frightening. Since the swing, while stationary, hung over the water, it had to be retrieved by using a long pole and standing as near the water as possible to snag the rope and pull it in. I was doing this one summer morning. My old dog Tex was with me. The rest of the guys were milling around and watching. As I stepped on a small shelf on the bank one of the guys said, "Lookout Sonny!"

In my path lay a 5 foot rattlesnake. Tex rushed in, grabbed it and began shaking it. He fell in the water. I was concerned, certain he would be bitten. How do you apply mouth to mouth CPR to a dog, and...what has he been eating recently?

Tex was a 4-5 year old medium size mutt of uncertain parentage, a stray that drifted in to town and helped himself to the family cats' food. I adopted him. He wasn't much but he was my dog and I didn't want him to die a snakebite death.

But, his initial attack had severely injured the snake because it seemed lifeless as he dragged it back ashore. We examined its markings and my Boy Scout training told me it was a 'canebrake' rattler. Someone (not me!) cut off the 4-5 rattles and took them home, doubtless to some questionable purpose.

I never told that story. I was afraid Horseshoe Bend would be placed off-limits, but Tex got extra table scraps that night.

A final note on the ole swimmin' hole at Horseshoe Bend. Years after we had found other diversions and drifted away, I learned that we had had unseen company at many of these skinny dipping sessions. The Stoecklein girls—teenagers at the time —had often come down and under cover of the foliage watched the cavorting little monkeys with their cute little buns. The environs of Horseshoe Bend were a part of the Stoecklein farm, so they had every right to their own private peepholes!

CAMPING OUT TONIGHT

Poor old Babe always seemed to be plowing corn and was seldom available for our Boy Scout adventures. One rare summer day, Thursday 13th July 1939 when he wasn't plowing; he, Homer Jeffress, Fred Theobald and I put together a plan to catch him up on some of the scouting he had missed. We would go for an overnight camp-out. Homer offered the ideal place—his grandfather's farm somewhere east of the Boonville road (Hwy 135) and south of the Katy tracks. Well, maybe it really wasn't ideal but at least no irate farmer would set his dogs on us.

This plan—executed on Friday, July 14, 1939—and the camp-out itself—was the worst conceived miscarriage of Boy Scout lore in the Annals of Scouting. It was so bad that it should occupy a mandatory place in the Scout Manual in a chapter entitled— "How not to do it!"

We didn't have tents. This wasn't so terribly bad. The weather promised to be dry. It was August and hotter than a firecracker. Each of us rolled up an old blanket, comforter or quilt for a bedroll. These 'bedrolls' which were never very neatly rolled, came apart a quarter of a mile down the road and we simply threw them over our shoulder and dragged them.

For food we put together two cans of Campbell soup, a can of sardines, a packet of saltines, 4-5 potatoes, a waxed paper packet of week-old Trout's bread, several packs of bubble gum and a half jar of Heinz dill pickles. Our water supply was carried in an old gallon bucket without a lid. It was gone by the time we hiked to the camp site. We drank some but it was mostly sloshed out.

Cookware was an old enamel pan that Mom was about to throw out, an old pocket knife that Homer had found, some string (always useful you know), a couple of old spoons for use as cooking as well as eating. There was one 3-tined fork with one tine missing and of course Homer's old bucket.

On the hike out Babe made the mistake of taking his shirt off 'to get a tan'. The temperature was in the 90s and the sun was unrelenting . The day was treacherous for sunbathers. It was hot but with a slight, very dry breeze. Thus, while the breeze was evaporating sweat and making you cool, the ultraviolet rays were producing melanoma or at best, a severe sunburn. We all got burned, Babe worst of all.

Those were the days before melanoma, basal cell carcinoma and actinic keratosis had been invented and a goodly tan was the mark of healthy, hearty young males (females too). Many of those sun worshipers of my era are readily discernible today, 50 years later. They are the ones with the square, mottled, leathery skin that looks like the south end of a northbound elephant.

Someplace short of the Mile Corner we thought maybe we should get off the road and practice a little scout field craft. It was also a shortcut. Several hundred yards into the field we ran into an extensive dewberry patch. We used to go dewberry picking quite often in the wild places around town. I brought in so many one time that Mom made a dozen or more pint jars of jelly and jam. I have not seen this berry offered commercially.

Of course, we fell to and gorged ourselves with the sweet berries which also, branded our clothing almost beyond redemption. The stains, however, were not the worst of it. Chiggers by the billions hang out around dewberry bushes. If there ever were a laboratory study that required great quantities of these microscopic little red bastards, I'd tell researchers, "You can find at least one million of them on each leaf of a dewberry vine!" The chiggers began kicking in around sundown that night.

Right here I'd like to digress for just a moment to say something on the subject of chiggers. I have been taught since an early age that God created heaven and earth and all the creatures therein and to each creature there is a reason and a purpose. I generally accept that except for chiggers. There, I think that God may have made one of his very few mistakes.

Chiggers are a kind of a mite, or rather a kind of mite larvae, only a hundredth of an inch long. It's hard to keep an eye out for them. They crawl on your body and find some hot, damp spot (which, in Missouri in the summer time, is every place) and there they release an enzyme, the evolutionary purpose of which is to make you tear your Boy Scout membership card into small pieces and resign forthwith.

The only thing you can do about chiggers is *not* scratch them. And you can drink three six-packs of beer and not take a whiz while you're at it. No Sirens calling to Ulysses, no Lorelei enticing Rhine boatmen to destruction, no pink mermaid breathing heavy at the local swains ever produced a desire as wild and overpowering as the yen to scratch a chigger bite. And never has there been such delight in surrendering to a temptation or achieving a goal. The next thing you know, you've been scratching for two hours and your legs are blood salad.

Chiggers are supposed to drop off after about four days. But mine seemed to migrate north instead and establish themselves in a less socially acceptable area for scratching. And my chigger itches persisted for weeks so that, when I was back in the real world, engaged in the ordinary activities of kidhood — attending Sunday School, accompanying Mom to Warnhoffs for shopping, starting back to school — I would be suddenly overwhelmed by an uncontrollable desire to thrust both hands down the front of my trousers and make like I had a bad case of Arkansas pants rabbits.

Our camp site was between a cornfield and a small branch with a piddling amount of water running through it. Homer, who was always the most gung ho of scouts, took charge of the evening meal. I went exploring.

He got a fire going (no flint or a friction stick, just a kitchen match) and put his bucket on it. I checked the cornfield and gave a triumphal yelp, "Roastin' ears!" I ripped off a few ears and returned to camp shucking the corn.

Everyone gathered around. We were all tired and extremely hungry. The water was boiling so we tossed the corn in. Fred said, "Look guys, we ain't got the time nor equipment for any fancy cooking. Lets just throw everything in Homer's bucket then we can eat sooner."

"Brilliant idea," we all agreed. In with the corn went the sardines then the Campbell's Soup. The pot boiled for a while then the fire went out. Fred and Homer got to work on the fire while I poked around in the melange to see if anything was edible yet. Some of the lumps of meat in the soup were warm so we fished them out and ate them.

"These sardines are already cooked anyway. They just need warming." We fished them out and ate them with the crackers. Only the corn was left and we found that it was far too mature for roastin' ears. They simmered the rest of the night but were still inedible in the morning.

We found what we thought might be a good place for our bedrolls and bunked down before dark. We were still on Central Standard Time in those ancient days before the great war taught us how to take an hour off the front of the day and tack it onto the end for higher productivity. At 39° North Latitude and 92.8° West Longitude on July 14th, 1939, sunset occurred at 735 PM. "EENT", the "End of Evening Nautical Twilight" came 30 minutes later. The moon was new and wouldn't rise until 2:44 AM so EENT brought down the suffocatingly humid, black, curtain of night.

The passing of the day brought two more discomfort factors. The thermal turbulence ceased and with it the gentle, cooling breeze. The warm air, however, continued to suck up moisture from the small branch converting our camping environment into that of a miasmic swamp.

The second factor was signaled by the buzzing of a myriad of tiny mosquito wings. I heard the slapping and swearing before the first one nailed me. Within an hour or so one would have guessed that we had camped in the United States National Mosquito Hatchery .

We could not protect against these vicious, blood-sucking predators. Rolling up in our blankets would merely have insured our suffocation. I laid there thinking about my Scout training: two types of mosquito are primary vectors of some pretty nasty diseases: the Anopheles carries malaria and the Aedes Aegypti carries "yellow jack". I didn't think we were in much danger of those killers so much as being simply devoured with our bones left to bleach in the sun.

At 4:00 AM I gave up trying to snatch moments of sleep between battling the mosquitoes and scratching chiggers. I got up and, stirring up the embers of the campfire, replenished it to drive away the tormentors. Sitting there quietly I began hearing some extremely spooky sounds. Probably owls out for their night hunting, but thoughts of ghosts, disembodied apparitions and spirits flooded my fertile imagination. I heard Babe slapping and spoke to him. He joined me and the spookiness subsided somewhat though I saw him looking over his shoulder as a howl echoed from the woods. A dog working the hedgerows, we hoped.

At about 0430 AM we experienced BMNT "Beginning of Morning Nautical Twilight", and breathed a silent prayer of thanksgiving as we knew sunrise would follow in 30 minutes or so. I began getting my gear together for immediate departure as soon as everyone was up and ready.

However, the arrival of daylight began to restore confidence and Babe said that he was so miserable, hot and sweaty, he was going to strip and wash in the one little pool that would had a little depth. All soon joined him. I began laughing when Babe got naked.

"What's so funny, Sonny?" He asked.

"Looks like you got the measles," I chuckled. His back and shoulders had about third degree sun burn, but his buns were as white as snow except for a dozen bright red chigger blotches. The chiggers had feasted for 15 hours.

"Check your own butt," he advised.

So we straggled back home arriving at my place at about 10 o'clock. "Did you have a nice camp out?" Mom asked. "I thought you were going to stay out *two* nights."

"It was absolutely super, Mom. Couldn't a been better!" I assured her.

Fig. 5-5. Edward C. "Toby" Ward, wife Lucille and little Wanda Marie -July 1939. Princess Stock Company flyer, right, was from the 1940s (Bonnie Rapp and the Blackwater Preservation folks.)

THE 'TOBY' SHOWS

The 'Princess Stock Company' was an improvement over the occasional medicine show which found its way to Pilot Grove. Toby was the comic relief (and owner of the enterprise). He was an early day Norman Nichols, the proverbial lout, buffoon, clown, joker, village idiot, and stand-up comedian. The Impresario, Toby, was held in high regard and he and his wife stayed with the Burgers (erstwhile town councilman) when the show came to town. Although there was a lot of buffoonery in his shows, they were essentially morality plays. In the end the good guys always won and the bad guys got a satisfying comeuppance. In order not to overburden the mental capabilities of the audience or strain young intellectual facilities, the good guys were always solid good and the bad guys were rotten to the core and they were carefully differentiated by white hats and black hats. Also, since the average vocabulary of many in the audience topped out around 20-30 words, the story was told in action—not dialogue. The company used a circus sized tent and set up in what in those days was Ries' field. They did six shows a week plus a matinee on Saturday, then knocked it all down to move to the next town on Sunday. They had a candy concession—at the intermission the members of the troupe, still in costume, passed through the audience offering boxes of 'gen yew wine Atlantic City salt water taffy'. It was terrible stuff and not at all a bargain at 8-9 pieces for 10¢. The hooker was that there was guaranteed to be in one box during the week a prize certificate good for one 'gen yew wine diamond ring'.

Some town kids always tried to slide under the tent and get in without a ticket. This scam seldom worked. They were collared and led off. Vern Klenklen used a more direct (and honest) approach. He sold nickel bags of peanuts for Toby and got in free. The drama was an acceptable level of entertainment compared with watching trains rattle through town. Pilot Grove, in those days, could have been a candidate for the "Center for the Easily Amused".

Toby was good. He had been in this line a long, long time and understood his craft and his audiences well. His antics did not draw on any heavy philosophy nor require any arduous mental processes. It was just good clean fun.

Fig. 5-6. Harris Street Gang conspiring to hang out. L-R Jerome Kempf, LeVern Klenklen, Corene Kempf, Pete Meyer, Rita Kempf, Bonnie Klenklen and Ferdinand Meyer 1944. Photo-Bonnie.

Fig. 5-7. Pilot Grove Baseball Fan Club - 1941. Front Row L-R: Doris Quinlan, Jeanette Wittman, Maxine Kempf, Corene Kempf, Back Row L-R: Lou Ellen Zeller, Sylvia Kempf, Janelle Wittman, Bonnie Klenklen, Mary Margaret Muessig. Photo - Bonnie.

Fig. 5-8. Joanne Poindexter, L.J. "Smokey" Zeller, 1947. Photo - Daisy Corbin Salmon.

Fig. 5-9. Charley, Janie and Dutchie Brownfield - the core of the PG Town baseball team in 1947.

Fig. 5-9. Boating and baseball, yes—but also a lot of hanging out in the 1940s. L-R Lou Ellen Zeller, Corene Kempf, Geraldine Lang, Doris Quinlan, Bonnie Klenklen, Imogene Kempf and Marceline Brunjes. Photo - Bonnie

Fig. 5-10. Wilbur "Charles Atlas" Quinlan, Goose Lake, early 1940s. Photo - Bonnie (Klenklen) Brown

Margie's Dance Class

Margie Ellen Babbitt's 1949 Pilot Grove Dance Class.

Margie's 1949 Dance Class: 1. Joe Schlotzhauer, 2. Butch Heinrich, 3. Marvin Lewis, 4. Wilbur Schuster, 5. Dutchie Brownfield, 6. Joe Fahrendorf, 7. Esther Gerke, 8. Charley Lammers, 9. Carol Schlotzhauer, 10. Betty Lou Young, 11. Jimmy Krumm, 12. Janie Brownfield, 13. Leroy Ries, 14. Raymond Lang, 15. Joan Lammers, 16. Leslie Chamberlin, 17. Norman Gerke, 18. Ralph Esser, 19. Jenn Rose Neckerman, 20. Charley Brownfield, 21. Donnie Lammers, 22. Kenny Kempf, 23. Wilma Quinlan, 24. Jerry Quinlan, 25. Jerry Schupp, 26. Bill Coleman, 27. ?

Fig. 5-10b. Do-si-do and around we go!

MARGIE'S DANCE CLASS

She may not remember it but, Marjorie Ellen Babbitt was in my primary Sunday School class. She was a pretty, but very demure and shy young girl, characteristics which accompanied her into high school. Imagine my surprise when Janie (Brownfield) Goehner told me about Margie's Pilot Grove Dance class. My admiration for my distant cousin went up immensely. I asked her about her dance experience and here is her reply:

"All through high school I was very self-conscious about not being a good dancer since it seemed to be the main pasttime in Pilot Grove. So when I saw an Arthur Murray ad in the Kansas City paper for dancing teachers, I went to Kansas City was interviewed and was included in a class. I had no intention of teaching but thought it was a good way to learn to dance. It was a 12 week course. We danced from ten in the morning until six at night with only two small breaks and a lunch hour. After the first week we had calluses, corns and about every foot ailment you could think of but we were lucky! All teachers prior to this class had paid several hundred dollars for their training to become Arthur Murray teachers and our class didn't pay anything. Actually, Arthur Murray paid us $1.50 per day. They were pretty desperate.

"We had to learn 20 steps in Foxtrot, Waltz, Jitterbug, Tango, Samba and Rhumba. One actually had to know 40 steps because a teacher had to know both the man's and woman's steps. After training I was sent "on the road". We went to Warrensburg on Monday, Clinton on Tuesday, Marshall on Wednesday and Sedalia on Thursday, then to Lexington on Friday and yes we had to work on Saturday in Kansas City. We would have a class for young people at 5-30 p.m. and adults at 7:00 p.m. After the class was over, I was transferred to St. Joseph, which I hated — too far from home and Bud. We had to sign a contact with Arthur Murray not to teach dancing within 80 miles of Kansas City for a year, but Pilot Grove was outside that radius we started a class there.

"I should say that Janie Brownfield started a class as she did all the work. It was a very large class and the boys outnumbered the girls nearly 3 to 1. The girls really had to do a lot of work. We divided the boys according to how many girls there were and they would dance with each group of boys which meant they danced all the time.

"There were some people who were interested in square dancing and Hap Eckerle taught that as I didn't know anything about square dancing. We only taught American dances, who in Pilot Grove would want to do South American dances? We had a lot of fun and I hope some students learned something about dancing."

DELIVERING THE MEAT (WINK, WINK)

During the 1920's and the depressing 1930s, rural pastimes—barn dances, chivarees, auctions, corn huskings and barn raisings demanded a little liquid refreshment to get the fun going. The 1919 Volstead Act which became the 18th Amendment to the US Constitution, had put the quietus on legitimate whiskey but the indominable American spirit soon found other ways. Local entrepreneurs picked up the challenge. This is a story of one of them.

Fred Eckerle hitched up old Henry to his buggy but left it in the driveway and returned to the steamy warmth of the kitchen. He sat down to a second cup of coffee. "Honey," he addressed his wife, "I reckon I'm gonna have to get onto sellin' the rest of that calf we butchered last week. Weather forecast this morning says it's gonna be a lot warmer after tomorrow. There's a few pounds left and I don't think we'd oughta risk havin' it spoil on us. I guess we butchered a few days too soon."

"You think you can get rid of it?" she asked.

"Yeah, I think so. At 15-20¢ a pound, it's a bargain that's gonna be hard to pass up. The only problem is that ever' since the bottom fell out of the economy, there's not a lot of folks who got the geetus." He set his cup and saucer in the sink, grabbed his mackinaw and went out the door.

In the smokehouse, he grabbed some old butcher paper and wrapped the bit of remaining veal quarter and dropped the package into a feed sack. He put it in the boot and drove to the rear of the barn well out of sight of the kitchen window as well as the lane that passed his house. In the barn, he took a pitchfork and carefully lifted the straw from a cache of glass in a darkened corner. He began carefully filling a wooden box, gingerly placing 12 quart mason fruit jars.

Old Fred had the good fortune to own a very fertile and productive farm in Clear Creek. In normal times this farm would have produced a fine cash income, but these were not normal times. By 1931, farm prices were so low some crops did not yield the cost of producing them. For Fred there was an option to stave off the wolf from the door. There were the continuing effects of the Volstead Act—Prohibition. Regardless of the views of the Carrie Nations of the country, there just seemed to be a strong demand for a little of John Barleycorn's magic elixir for the lightening of life's depressing realities. Fred's holdings included a heavily wooded area several miles from his farmstead which handily concealed a pot-still for the production of his most excellent "corn squeezin's". This "value-added" processing of his corn crop yielded a much more acceptable rate of return on corn.

So Fred peddled his veal about Pilot Grove and at certain stops mentioned that he might also be able to furnish another commodity much in demand in view of the upcoming holiday season. Near the south end of Harris street he greeted 'Tater' Coffman just coming out his front door. Tater was a valued customer (he paid cash) of long standing. 'Tater', I got some meat here and some other produce ya might be interested in—if ya catch my drift." Fred looked up and down the street as he went to the back of his buggy and slipped a quart of his finest into the veal package.

In the kitchen 'Tater' says, "Fred, now don't get me wrong, but that last batch you brought me just warn't up to yer usual standard. They ain't nothin' we can do about that but, if'n it's OK with you, I'd like to try myself a little taste of that there stuff afore I pay good money fer it." He pointed at the mason jar.

Fred hesitated, "Why, of course, Tater. I'm mighty sorry that last batch didn't suit you. I guarantee you that this'n will. Get yerself a little glass." He screwed the jar lid off as Tater rummaged through his kitchen cabinet.

"Damnation," he thought, "If everybody demands a sample, I'm gonna have to bump my price up a little, maybe a buck a quart." Fred frowned at the old peanut butter jar that Tater was holding out hopefully.

Tater caught the hesitation and said, "Look Fred, I want to do right by ya. Gimme a good shot in here and I'll either buy the quart or give ya a quarter for the samplin'." Fred glug-glugs in two fingers of 'white lightnin'.

The jar goes to Tater's lips where he made the terrible mistake of taking a deep breath in anticipation of a long draw on his jar. He sucked in a little corn whiskey but inhaled a lung full of pure alcohol vapors which temporarily paralyzed his pulmonary system. He turned red in the face—then blue. Finally catching his breath he look up at Fred through watering eyes and as the fiery liquid gurgled down his gullet, croaked, "Smooooth! Fred, ya kin get me another jar of that stuff," he pulled out an old wallet and dug up two one-dollar bills.

Fred was sold out by noon and putt-putted home again to proudly display his wad of cash to his wife. "I got rid of all the veal and I was surprised that nobody tried to barter me somepin' or other."

"You got all that money for that little piece of meat?" She asked straightening out the wadded old bills.

"Well, you could say that," was Fred's Clintonesque answer..

[Author's Note: The skeleton of this story was told me by a usually reliable source that wishes to remain anonymous. I have fudged in a few details. 'Tater' Coffman did indeed live toward the south end of Harris Street in those days and would have been a likely customer for someone purveying home made whiskey. As for the alcohol vapor paralysis of the pulmonary system—I personnally observed such an episode in North Carolina which was then and presumable still is, the national center for the production of white lightnin' (bootleg whiskey). It's tax free thus cheaper, it's 100 proof and some people just seem to prefer it.

The moonshine distillation process is simply the separating the portions of a fermented "beer" by utilizing the different boiling points of water and alcohol called fractional distillation. In practice the first 20% or so of the run, called "headings" is highly volatile from 180 to 120 proof—90 to 60% pure alcohol (C_2H_5OH). 180 proof alcohol is about as strong as you can get because pure alcohol sucks up water and thus dilutes itself. I heard when I was at Missouri University that a popular frat party drink was "Purple Passion" made of grape juice and 180 proof grain alcohol. Don't try this at home!

[Tater may have imbibed a bit of the headings. The other end, tailings, is much lower in alcohol and include fusel oils, complex esters and a lot of other stuff you don't want to know about. Mike Murphy, a Kansas City radio personality told how his wife chastised him about "...drinking that cheap whiskey!"

Mike replied, "$2 a gallon, I don't call that cheap!" Mike may have been into the "tailings".]

ALL YOU WANT TO KNOW ABOUT WHISKEY

Whiskey (or whisky), from the Scottish Gaèlic uisge beatha, "water of life," is a distilled alcoholic beverage. Percentages of alcohol commonly range from 40 percent to 50 percent, expressed as proof. In the United States a spirit with 50 percent alcohol by volume is termed 100 proof. Along with other distilled spirits, whiskey consumption has been decreasing markedly since the 1970s.

Whiskey is distilled from a fermented, or alcohol-containing, mash of grains, which may include barley, rye, oats, wheat, or corn. Because distillation requires an alcohol-containing liquid, it is necessary to ferment the grain. Part of the process of whiskey production includes converting the starch in the grain to sugar so that fermentation and ultimately distillation can take place. The grain is first milled, or ground to a meal. It is then cooked until it is gelatinous, releasing the starch from its tough coating. Barley malt is added because it is rich in amylase, an enzyme that enables starch to be converted to sugar. The mash is now ready for fermentation, and laboratory yeast is added. It ferments for 72 hours, creating an alcoholic liquid known as beer. The beer undergoes selective distillation to become whiskey.

Distillation may be carried out in either a batch process, using a pot still continuous process, much favored by Moonshiners, or by using a patent, or Coffey, still. The pot still is uniquely suited for full-flavored spirits, such as malt whiskey and Irish whiskey. The continuous process is best suited for light whiskeys. The product of either process is colorless and of varied flavor. Fuller-flavored whiskeys mellow with wood maturation. This aging will vary with the spirit (higher-distillation-proof spirits need less age because they have less flavor), the material of the cask (whether it is new or used and how deeply the interior is charred), the size of the cask (which determines the wood-to-liquid ratio), and the storage conditions (which are affected by temperature and humidity). The common amber color and some of the flavor of the matured whiskey are acquired from the storage cask.

The predominant ingredient in light whiskey is corn; the more corn, the lighter the flavor. Bourbon, the most popular whiskey made in the United States, must have at least 51 percent corn in the mash; it may have as much as 79 percent. Other grains present are rye and barley malt, which also contribute flavor. Light whiskey is stored in seasoned charred oak casks, which impart little color or flavor.

Blended whiskey, erroneously called rye whiskey, is a combination of straight (at least 20 percent) and light whiskey. The final product may have as many as 40 to 50 different components. Tennessee whiskey is usually made from corn, but any grain may be used. A bourbon-type whiskey, it is very full because it is treated with maplewood charcoal to remove the lighter flavors. Canadian whiskey is always distilled in the patent still and is always a blend. Most Canadian whiskey is at least 6 years old when sold.

Fig. 5-11. Gene Autry was an odds on favorite. He could shoot, act and sing (sort of). He kissed his horse, but never a girl!

Fig. 5-12. Betty Boop—a cartoon favorite of the 1930s.

Fig. 5-13. Pilot Grove High School Band, directed by Byron Morton, PGHS Director of Music. Spring 1941. (Photo - Irene Felten.)

Fig. 5-14. Byron Morton, PGHS Music Director (RIGHT) with some of his star students — (Unknown), Marjorie Burger and Enslie Schilb.

THE MOVIES

There was a struggle during my boyhood to provide the town with movie entertainment. I say struggle because we never had a permanent movie house. I can remember wintry Saturday evenings as a child of 3-4 braving arctic winds and crunchy snow while walking to the old school building north of the Katy tracks for a movie.

J.D. Heinrich used to have a small movie house above the store ostentiously named "The Gem Theater". It was at the Gem that I saw Henry Fonda and Tyrone Power in "Jesse and Frank James". The "Gem" was also used for town events and it was there that Margie Ann Brownfield, the town's *unofficial* "L'il Darlin'" was crowned the *official* "Miss Pilot Grove 1938". See Fig. 5-15. That theater was condemned as unsafe by State safety inspectors in the 1930s and for some time we had no movie house.

During all this time there was one and later two movie houses in Boonville—the Lyric and later the Casino. But, without transportation as we were, Boonville may as well be on the moon.

Finally, around 1939-40, an enterprising young couple, Bob and Bill (Wilhelmina) Egender came to town on a weekly circuit and we had movies until well into the war years. Favorites ran mostly to westerns (Gene Autry—See movie poster above, Ken Maynard, Bob Steele) which like the Toby shows were simple morality plays—white hat, black hat. At the approach of war, a few Grade B international spy thrillers were added to the offerings. Here, since the "black hat, white hat" cue was not appropriate, the bad guys were always Asians or had a heavy German accent.

TOWN BAND

In the mid 1930s the city fathers spent a bit of money and effort to build a bandstand. Saturday night band concerts had long been a tradition in the town and a bandstand was thought to be a good investment for the downtown merchants. The bandstand was constructed in such a way that it could be easily assembled and dissembled. Four individual platforms were built on 8 foot, square 2 x 8 frames. These platforms could be mounted atop sturdy four foot tall 'sawhorses'. The bandstand was painted a very serviceable shade of dark brown.

MISS PILOT GROVE

Fig. 5-15. Miss Margaret Ann Brownfield daughter of Mr. and Mrs. Jake Brownfield of Pilot Grove, who was selected as "Miss Pilot Grove, 1938" last week at a beauty pageant held in Heinrich Hall [Gem Theater]. (Rehmeier Photo - Daily News Engraving.)

William Deck, the town pharmacist and proprietor of Deck's Drug Store, was the Director and there were ample opportunities for anyone to play. Three of the slots were filled by Dr. E.I. Schilb, the town dentist (cornet), and his two children, Enslie Jr. (clarinet) and little Patty (snare drum). The younger Schilbs, like many of the other musicians, were also in the high school band. The merchants got extra trade on Saturday night and we all had a small break from the depressing times.

The High School Music Director, Byron Morton (see Figs. 5-13 & 5-14) directed concerts on Saturday afternoons.

AEROPLANES[3]

AUNT GRACE AND THE "SPIRIT OF ST. LOUIS"

My fascination for airplanes started early. One of my earliest memories was a fit that I threw over a toy airplane—a model of Lindbergh's "Spirit of St. Louis"—in F.W. Woolworth's Dime Store in Sedalia in the summer of 1930. Mom took Bob and me on a train trip to Sedalia to visit her childhood chum, Grace Mersey. I was about three. Grace was a schoolmate and so close to Mom the whole family called her *Aunt* Grace. "Auntie" Grace had gone off after her formal schooling in Pilot Grove to marry a Missouri Pacific RR roustabout working at MoPac's Sedalia roundhouse.

Dad, then a 15 year veteran of the Katy, had the dubious fringe benefit of virtually unlimited rail travel on the Katy. Dubious because: 1. The Katy didn't go anywhere we were interested in going; 2. Dad had to apply for a pass for a specific trip, and 3. The two daily passenger trains serving Pilot Grove were terribly inconvenient. The Southbound Katy Flyer No. 5 departed at 6AM and the Northbound Katy Bluebonnet No. 6 departed at midnight.

Arriving in Sedalia at 7:30AM, we spent the morning in the modest Mersey home. But late morning brought a trip to the dime store! It was at F.W. Woolworth that I saw the brightly colored airplane suspended from the high, stamped tin ceiling. My demand that Mom buy it for me was summarily dismissed. I screamed, bawled, held my breath, threw myself on the floor to no avail.

Following a burger and ice cream at White Castle I became resigned to my fate. Lunch was followed by the movies—my very first! The regular feature—silent and in black and white—was forgettable, but the 'Felix the Cat' cartoon was delightful.

Aunt Grace and her husband lived on Engineer Street only 3-4 blocks from the Katy Station. So, it was an easy walk to the station for our return trip. Although it was only 24 miles, the train would take an hour and a half. It stopped at every tiny burg to take on and deliver the mail, Railway Express, cream cans and baby chickens from the Smithton Hatchery and—on rare occasion—a paying passenger. The fare—Pilot Grove to Sedalia was 25¢ but not a lot of people had that kind of money in 1930. We had passes.

We sat on a stone ledge in the cool summer night. Bob snoozed in Mom's arms while she and Grace nattered on. It had been an adventuresome but long, long day for me. I had been up since 5AM. I went to sleep and fell off the ledge on my head. It didn't even wake me up. Mom finally got me back on my feet as the Bluebonnet pulled in and we swung aboard for the journey home. I hadn't gotten my heart's desire—the bright little biplane—but long before we ended our journey I had forgotten the Woolworth incident.

LUCKY LINDY

In the summer of 1933 before I began my distinguished scholastic career at Pilot Grove Public School I spent a lot of time at the schoolyard. It was convenient. We lived only 1/2 block away. The schoolyard offered the irresistible temptation of swings, seesaws, and a sandbox—if you could beat the cats to it. A lot of Miss Madge Goode's first graders-to-be hung out at the school that summer.

Homer Jeffress and I—trying to buck one another off the see-saw one glorious afternoon—heard a powerful roar overhead. A butterscotch colored biplane, just missing the tree tops, soared over the schoolyard. Something's up!

This schoolyard was notched out of Mr. Seltsam's cow pasture back in 1922, occupying the northwest 40 acres and the pilot seemed interested in this pasture.

[3] The novel 'flying machines' of the Wright Brothers, and others gained much celebrity in the 'Great War'. During this era, the British and the French, in unusual agreement, called them 'Aeroplanes'. Thus, it was the 'aeroplanes' of Richthofen, Rickenbacker, Bishop and Guynemer that first intrigued me.

Fig. 5-16. Even a decade later, Lindbergh's flight was much on folks' minds.

The plane was so low we could plainly see the pilot. He was leaning on the cockpit coaming, conning the pasture. At an altitude of about 50 feet he made a sharp banking turn over Schuster's farm and came roaring back. We heard his engine throttle down and thought he was going to crash. Instead, he flared out and sat the little biplane down gracefully about 75 yards from the fence where we now stood transfixed. The prop wash fanned the high grass as he taxied up to us. There was a lot of excitement all over town and the people came flocking. "What the hell?" "What's wrong?" "Who is it?" "Looks like Lindy!" Lindbergh's flight was only a few years in the past and was still much on folk's mind.

And indeed, as the tall, slim pilot climbed out of the rear cockpit, we could see that he did look a little like Lindbergh. He was dressed in khaki jodhpurs, an old but well polished pair of brown Pershing riding boots, a brown leather flight jacket and a fur lined leather helmet with genuine aviator goggles. He was lugging a five gallon gas can.

"Reckon a fella could get hisself some gas around here?" he smiled at the rubes. Earl Lockridge, the squat, dark-suited superintendent of schools was just leaving his office and came over to investigate.

Mr. Lockridge volunteered, "Sure come on. I'll run you up to Kempf's station." Mr. Lockridge had a brand new Model A Ford and was happy for any opportunity to show it off. As they walked to the car I saw "Lucky Lindy", "Eddy Rickenbacker" or who ever he was, exploring his pocket and examining his find.

When he made the mistake of leaving his plane unguarded, the little kids, me in the van, took off like a herd of goats. Screams from the parents and adults stopped most but not me. I was on the other side of the plane and somewhat out of sight. I saw the stirrup at the bottom of the fuselage and up onto the wing step I went to look into the forward cockpit. It was disappointing. "There was the joystick. Those things down there must be the rudder pedals. Looks like Patty Schilb's peddle car", I thought. There were 2-3 gauges on the tiny instrument panel—one of them presumably a gas gauge bumping on empty. There was an empty key slot for the ignition key—at least he had had the foresight to take the key with him.

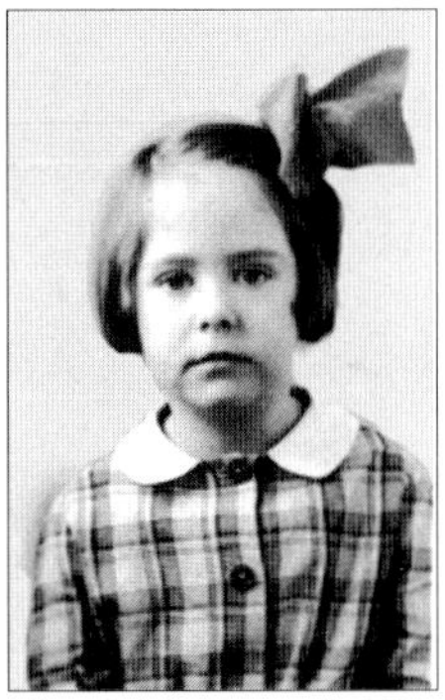

Fig. 5-17. Patty Schilb 4, drove a new, blue 1932 model Cadillac peddle car with controls as advanced as Lindy's biplane. Some may recognize Patty's Shirley Temple hair bow. Patty and Shirley are about the same age.

"Lucky Lindy" returned, gassed up and announced he was available for rides. "How much?" someone asked.

"Five bucks and I'll take you for the ride of your life!" he promised. Most of the bright, eager faces dropped at mention of that princely sum.

But one young man stepped up and says, "OK, I'm game but just don't turn that sucker upside down!" Lucky Lindy helped him into the front cockpit—the one that I had just memorized. Belting his daredevil passenger in, he explained the sequence for firing up the engine and trusted his passenger to leave the switch off as he pulled the prop through a couple of turns.

Then he says "Contact!", the daredevil turns the ignition on and Lindy slams the prop through. The engine roars into life and Lindy jumps into the cockpit of the moving plane and they roar down the impromptu pasture-runway.

As they returned Lindy flares out to another perfect landing and taxies up the silent, awe-struck crowd. The bumpkin pulled a wad of crumpled, sweaty dollar bills out of his bib overalls and counted out five. He was beaming. "Well, I did it! I don't give a damn what the old lady sez, I did it and it was worth it!"

Lindy came through the crowd again, "Who's next? Who wants a plane ride? The ride of your lifetime?" He found Mr. Lockridge and handed him back the dollar he had borrowed for his gas, waving off the change. Five gallons of gasoline would run you around 75¢ that summer. There were no further takers and finally he took off for the east delighting us with a beautifully executed Immelmann that scared hell out of Mr. Seltsam's cows. Mr. Seltsam bellyached about this incident for weeks.

We all lived very close to the edge money-wise. Lindy did too, but he also lived close to the edge with his life.

THE HARLAN BOYS

The Harlans were among the leading citizens of Pilot Grove. In 1934 they lived on the south end of Harris street. G.B. Harlan was the owner, editor and publisher of the Pilot Grove Record, our own little weekly newspaper. His two sons, Ridge and Lane were model airplane buffs. They were high school students at PGHS when I was receiving second grade tutelage from Miss Madge Goode.

Late one summer afternoon I was, as usual, hanging

Fig. 5-18. Ridge Harlan and Curtis Brownfield, PGHS Students ca 1934. Ridge got my attention when he tested his homemade balsa, paper and rubber-band model planes at the school yard.

Fig. 5-19. The Red Baron flew the twin of this Fokker Tr.1 Triplane - 1916-1918.

Fig. 5-20. The British Sopwith "Camel" was also flown by US pilots. This plane was my second model airplane project.

out at the schoolyard. Lane and Ridge came to fly their homemade model planes. The schoolyard offered an uncluttered area for flight testing. These balsam and tissue paper model planes used a rubber band as motive power. Connected to the propeller spinner, the rubber band is wound up several hundred revolutions and then allowed to unwind to spin the prop. The Harlan boys had an invention to bypass the onerous rubber band winding task. They had taken an old egg beater from the kitchen, removed one paddle and opened the end of the remaining one. Thus, fitting the beater paddle over the prop they could spin the beater a few times and voila—the rubber band motor is ready for action. I'm sure they never knew how their flight testing delighted the heart of a little ragamuffin 7 year-old.

FOKKER TRIPLANE

I began making my model airplanes in the late 1930s under the expert instruction of Wallace "Chappie" Chapman. My greatest triumph (with a lot of help from Chappie) was a 20:1 scale model of Richthofen's Fokker Dr. 1 Triplane. See Figure above.

Model airplanes in the 1930s replicated the famous Spads, Nieuports, Fokkers and SE5s of the Great War now less than two decades in the past. See Figs. 5-19 & 5-20 at right. The Red Baron's Fokker was powered by a Oberursel Rotary[3], 110 horsepower engine and had a range of about 300 miles. My Fokker was powered by a wind-up rubber band and had a range of about 50 feet!

The real Fokker Tr.1 had an enormous airfoil—three full wing surfaces which made it the most agile and maneuverable plane of its day. It could turn 'inside' any allied fighter and get out of the way of anything it couldn't outrun or out-gun. It could land at an amazingly low speed of 30 mph.

But, it was slow. The expansive airfoil that enabled it to be airborne at 50 mph also contributed to drag. Its top speed was estimated 80 mph—no aircraft of the day had any type of airspeed indicator. This slow speed led to the development, again by Tony Fokker, of the Fokker D-VII which became the primary aircraft of German air fleet after 1917.

Ironically, Anthony Fokker the designer and head of Fokker manufacturing was a 26 year old Dutchman! His factory was in Haarlem, the Netherlands. Obviously, he was primarily a businessman amorally taking his profit where he could. To be fair—he had offered his planes and designs to both France and England and received scornful rejection.

[3] The maker of the engines that powered WWI German planes was the Bayerische Motor Werken - known today as BMW.

THE 'RED BARON'

Kids today can be forgiven if they think the 'Red Baron' was a fictional character. He was not. He was one of thc most colorful figures of World War I. Born May 2, 1892, he was a German flying ace. The triplane, Fig. 5-19, is a twin of the Baron's machine which was destroyed when he was shot down and killed on April 21, 1918.

Freiherr (Baron) Manfred von Richthofen[4] (Fig. 5-22) was to live into eternity as the "Red Baron" fabled in Charles Schulz's Peanuts" comic strip where Snoopy occasionally flies his Sopwith Camel' (which looks like a dog house)—see Fig. 5-23—in search of the Red Baron and in pizzas (See Fig. 5-21). His moniker "Red Baron" came from his *red* Fokker and from the fact that he *was* a Baron. A fighter pilot from 1916, he was credited with shooting down 80 Allied planes in dogfights. In 1918 his success had brought him command of his own Jagdstaffel (Squadron)—JG-1.

Introduction of airplanes as a faster means of scouting the enemy (traditionally the role of cavalry) gave an adventuresome Richthofen the opportunity to learn to fly.

He had painted his Fokker red as a challenge to French, British and later American pilots wanting to 'give him a go'. The other members of his Jagdstaffel then followed his lead and decorated their machines in wildly bright colors. An English pilot said disdainfully, "It looks like a Flying Circus!" This was the origin of the name for the English TV comedy—Monty Python's "Flying Circus".

An interesting note on these beginnings of aerial warfare: It all started quite innocently. Early pilots went innocuously about their business of observing enemy troop dispositions and movements as well as message delivery. Legend says that a fuss developed between a German flyer and a French flyer whereupon the German threw a brick shattering the Frenchman's propeller. The nastiness escalated to pistols and rifles then machine guns.

Mounting machine guns brought a technical problem. The ideal placement would be forward of the cockpit where the pilot could aim the guns (they were mounted in pairs) by pointing the aircraft. This caused him to fire through the arc of his own propeller and risked shooting himself down. The English 'solved' the problem by affixing heavy metal deflectors to the propeller.

Fokker came up with a superior fix by mechanically linking the main engine drive shaft to the guns with an 'interrupter gear'. The guns were then synchronized so as to only fire when the propeller was safely out of the way.

An interesting coincidence: The day after von Richthofen was killed, another ace of his Jagdstaffel became JG-1 leader —Herr Kapitan Herman Goering!

For those who missed their history lessons, Herman Goering became Hitler's head of the Luftwaffe 1939-1945.

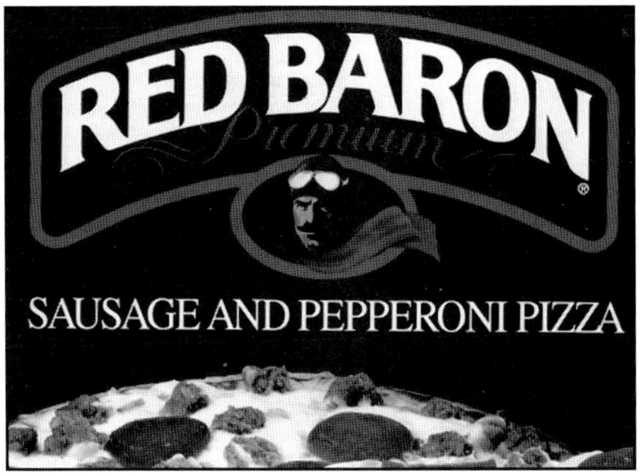

Fig. 5-21. The Red Baron is even into Pizza!

Fig. 5-22. The 'Red Baron' (center), commander of Jagdstaffel 1 with some of his pilots. His wolfhound, Onkel is at lower left.

Fig. 5-23. The Red Baron shoots down Snoopy's Sopwith Camel...again!

[4] Bibliography: Burrows, William E., Richthofen: A True History of the Red Baron (1969).

The smiles, the tears—of boyhood years,
The words of love then spoken.
The eyes that shone, now dimmed and gone,
The cheerful hearts now broken.
Thomas Moore, "Oft in the Stilly Night."

MISS MADGE GOODE

ON THE FIRST DAY OF MY SECOND YEAR OF school—the Tuesday after Labor Day, September 4th 1934—I pushed into the packed cloak hall and gagged at the stench of moth balls and wet wool. Obviously many Moms had made emergency trips to the attics to find winter clothing for their little darlings.

The freakish weather that Missouri is often subjected to had brought us an unseasonable Labor Day cold front, dropping the thermometer 40° along with 5 inches of rain. I felt lucky that Mom had done our school shopping early and found my coat on sale at Warnhoff's.

On that shopping day, anticipating my objections, she assured me, "It'll be warm, Sonny, when the winter winds start howling". But, I didn't object because the fake leather matched my "authentic aviator's helmet with goggles" that had survived from last year.

I hung up my simulated leather, sheepskin lined coat and took my assigned desk in the center of Miss Madge Goode's elementary school room next door. Miss Madge had the first, second and third grade. Miss Madge—and this is what her students called her all her life—was a maiden lady, daughter of the proprietors of the Goode Hotel which stood across Second Street from Pop Tracy's Cafe and was no longer much of a going enterprise. She was tall and slender, her narrow face framed by the severely tight coiffure-with-bun that is stereo-typically assigned to unmarried females of a certain age. She was not at all unattractive, though by 1933 when I started school, the bloom of youth was gone from her face. (Madge A. Goode was born August 31, 1883 and died January 27, 1964. She was the daughter of Thomas B. and Anna (Chamberlain) Goode.)

Fig. 6-1. Miss Madge Goode, Pilot Grove elementary teacher 1942.

She could be quite stern when necessary, but she had the patience of Job and temperamentally suited to start us off on the right foot.

Fig. 6-2. Bright young faces—eager young minds.

She had had an accident in her youth. She had, in some manner, driven a steel needle into her hip joint. At any rate she walked with a severe limp. She was a martyr. She was one of those thousands of un-bespoken women who, unrewarded, under-appreciated and unsung, dedicated their lives to other people's kids.

In Miss Madge's classroom were five files of desks, 6-7 desks per file. See Fig. 6-4 next page. First graders were assigned the leftmost file. Actually, these were the best seats because they were next to the windows. When you stood up, and there were a myriad of pretexts for doing so, you viewed a bucolic panorama of Mr. Seltsam's jersey cows grazing contentedly in the pasture below.

I no longer had the windows, but my new desk assignment conferred some status. I was no longer classed among the first grade 'babies' that cried when Miss Madge disciplined them or who, having not yet mastered the permission procedure, had accidents which left puddles on the floor. I was now 7 years old and a 'big kid'.

Later in the week, in my official capacity of blackboard monitor, I would show some of the new first graders around the room. There was a "hygiene roster" on the wall between the end of the blackboard and the door. A 'hygiene monitor' inspected each pupil and marked squares in the daily matrix to certify that he/she had: brushed teeth, cleaned nails, combed hair, etc. This monitor job was rotated so we each had an opportunity to 'put the finger' on someone who had displeased us. Thus there was a lot of surreptitious spiffing up just before class.

There also was a library roster. When we (2d and 3rd graders) finished reading a book we marched ceremoniously to the roster where Miss Madge duly affixed a gold star crediting us with our momentous achievement.

In the back of the room was a sand table and various tableaux were constructed during the year to symbolize the appropriate season. It included a set of Lincoln logs over which there was a continuous fight when inclement weather kept our recess inside. There was also a kiddie size library table that often served as a focus for learning games.

Fig. 6-3. Barbara Coleman - 1945.

Fig. 6-4. The desks in Miss Madge's primary classroom had not changed in a decade.

"CONTRACT HIT"

In January of my second year, the snow was piled high and those who ventured out for recess played "Fox and Goose" as well as snow fort and snowball wars.

Charley Brownfield and I were cautiously treading the packed snow walking home after school when we came upon Charley's little sister, Janie, wailing in distress, her face awash in tears. Charley rushes to her, "Whassamatter, whassamatter?"

"Barbara Coleman beat me up!" she wails.

Mary Jane "Janie" Brownfield was Mary and Dee Brownfield's gift to the world of Kewpie Dolls. It is a testimony to our innocent childhood that "Mary Jane" would be the name of a pretty little girl and not something that you would smoke—Marijuana.

Janie was the youngest and the smallest member of Miss Madge's first grade and had barely made it over the bar in age. She couldn't have weighed more than 50 pounds, so, if Barbara did indeed "beat her up", it would not seem like a fair fight. When all the facts came out the next day, it seems that the girls had argued, Barbara had pushed Janie who lost traction on the uncertain, snowy footpath and fell. Her main injuries were hurt feelings.

But we didn't understand this at the time and set off to avenge the little darlin' sister. We ran to catch up with Barbara and while Charley held her arm, I pushed a handful of snow in her face. This was a traditional schoolyard tactic called "washing your face in the snow."

Barbara, very assertive[1] for a six year-old, did not meekly accept this retribution and fought back announcing, "I'm gonna tell! I'm gonna tell!" And she did.

The next morning, Miss Madge called Barbara, Charley and I aside and instructed us to join her at Mr. Lockridge's office at the afternoon recess. Somehow, Janie was completely overlooked in this judicial process.

At the afternoon high tribunal, we each told our stories and awaited the Superintendent's judgement. Barbara was given a mild reprimand but Charley and I got an hour of detention after school that day.

But the memory that most sticks with me is his commandment: "Boys don't beat up on girls!" I have diligently followed that rule and I am sure Charley has too. I would like to report that I never again reported to the Superintendent for a "Captain's Mast", but that would not be strictly true. I report elsewhere the story of my three co-hookey players and I receiving "non-judicial punishment" at the hands of E.M. McKee some years later.

It was, however, the last time that I assaulted a member of the fairer sex. I will confess though, as Barbara flowered into the beautiful young woman that she was to become, I did have fantasies about her. Not snow in her face this time but kisses on her pretty, freckled, brown-eyed face. Sadly for me, this was never to be.

GOOD CITIZENS

"What is so rare as a day in May?" What indeed! It was one of those days in May in the year of our Lord 1936—Friday May 15th to be exact. We were at the end of our final year in Miss Madge's room.

After three years of being subjected to her secret, patented techniques for converting little savages to good citizens, we could now—read a little (if the words were little and the pictures were big); do a little arithmetic ('add 'em ups' and 'take aways' were easy though we would not claim complete mastery of 'times' and 'goes-intos').

Our self discipline was strengthening, we could sit still, keep quiet and speak when we were called upon. We said, "Sir, ma'am, please and thank you"; our Spencerian script was barely acceptable—my 'push-pulls' were greatly improved but Charley's 'whirly-loops' left much to be desired. Our personal hygiene was better though the hygiene monitor and roster certainly made us much more aware of the need for clean fingernails, combed hair, brushed teeth, etc.

We had had our final picnic in Ries' field and would no longer be subject to the derision of the big kids who went to exotic places for their school picnics—Chouteau Springs, Harley Park, etc. The high schoolers even made field trips to Sedalia to tour a box factory! But we had trekked across the road to Ries' and had our Kool-Aid and cookies on Thursday and today were cleaning out our desks in preparation for the summer vacation.

Miss Madge: "Now the first and second graders are dis-

[1] This assertiveness was much in demand when Barbara was a member of the champion PGHS Girls Basketball team in later years.

missed. You may collect your things and go home. I want the third graders to stay for a moment. I was a third grader and wondered what we had done to be held back. It was her 'graduation' speech.

"I want you to know," she began as the little kids filed out, "I have enjoyed having you in my room these past three years. Next year, as you know, you will go to Miss Nelson's room."she pointed to the next easterly classroom. "You won't be back in here, but you are always welcome to stop by and visit with me. I'll be very pleased to see you. But just remember—I'll not be with you next year."

"But Miss Madge! Miss Madge!" Charley Brownfield interjects, "We'll be good citizens!"

"What's that Charley?" Miss Madge looked puzzled.

Charley explains, "We won't be with you but we'll still be good citizens!"

Miss Madge smiled, "Yes, Charley. You will indeed!"

So we marched forth on that rare May day armed with Miss Madge's teachings. Strong in mind, body and spirit, we resolved with an iron will to face that upcoming summer vacation as "Good Citizens."

WARM MORNINGS

It was the first really cold and crisp fall day of the school year—October 1909. Dee was up early—long before his siblings. He sought out the warm kitchen stove to complete his dressing.

"What are you doing up so early, Dee?" His surprised mother was starting the bacon and eggs. "You don't need to start off to school for another hour!" Dee Brownfield was the oldest of ten children and later the father of Charley, Janie and Dutchie. He had just started his education under the instruction of 26 year old Miss Madge Goode at the one room Becker School.

"Mom, I'm going to walk over to Becker and start a fire for Miss Madge," he explained.

Mrs. Brownfield frowned. "Did she tell you to do that?"

"No, Mom. But mornings are cold now and I want Miss Madge to have a nice warm schoolhouse when she gets there."

Janie (Brownfield) Goehner said about her father—"Dad never was a child. He was born a little man. Maybe it was because he was the oldest of ten children but he was always very serious about his responsibilities. He always did what was right but he was particularly concerned about the welfare of those he was fond of and Miss Madge was certainly one of those!"

BOARD MEETIN' TONIGHT

Dee Brownfield's fondness for Miss Madge brought him terrible anguish nearly a half-century after he had warmed her country schoolroom. In the spring of 1944, he was a member of the Pilot Grove School Board and there was an agonizing issue on the agenda. Dr. Boley felt that Miss Madge was too old and should retire. Dee mentally reviewed his half-century acquaintance with her. She was his first teacher but was also the elementary teacher of his three children. But at this point the more heartless among us would say, "That was then. This is now."

She was well along into years and should have retired but adamantly refused to do so. "It's the only thing I do! It's my life! I've never done anything else!" All this was true.

At the board meeting, Dee's preliminary chat with other members made it clear that the votes were not there—Miss Madge's contract would not be renewed. So, when the board turned to personnel matters, Dee said, "I'll excuse myself when you vote on Miss Madge."

Dr. Schilb, the Board President said, "Now Dee, we know how you feel. You are free to make a case and vote as you please. We want to be fair about this."

"No," said Dee, "The votes are not there. What's more, you are right—she *should* retire. I'll not vote for her—but I'll not vote *against* her either! I want no part in her termination." he left the room. When he returned with moist eyes ten minutes later, the members had gone on to other business and Miss Madge was not mentioned.

Several years later, Miss Madge visited Miss Harris' Beauty Salon where Janie Brownfield did her hair. Madge, remembered her dismissal with emotion. "I just told myself that I would not accept it! I'd devoted my entire life to teaching those little people and I was not ready to quit!"

And she didn't. She offered her services to the Blackwater School when that High School was consolidated with Pilot Grove and, commuting on the busses for the high schoolers, taught the elementary grades there for a number of years before accepting her "Golden Apple".

MACHO PERM PLEASE

Janie tells about 3 special perms: "One cold day in January 1947, school was closed early because of a snow storm. Before she left school, Miss Harris phoned me and asked if I would give some boys perms. I told her that we had had lots of cancellations and that I was planning to close early." I told her, "I'll do the perms if you'll help me."

Bud Kempf, L. J. Zeller, and Chief Lewis come to the shop and we gave them permanents. They were having a ball and continued their "party" while under the hair dryer. Of course they thought they had to shout while under the dryer. The shop was next door to Beau Warnhoff's grocery store and the walls must have been thin. Mildred Warnhoff heard the voices and came rushing over to see what kind of a riot we were having. We reassured her that everything was under control, of course. She got a giggle out of seeing those three boys with their hair in curlers.

Fig. 6-5. Janie Brownfield makes an appointment at Miss Harris' Pilot Grove Beauty Salon, 1949. Photo Janie B. Goehner

Fig. 6-7. "Are you sure you want to fill 'er up? It's 12¢ a gallon you know!" Dee Brownfield operated the Schweitzer station at the northwest corner of Second and Roe Streets, ca 1922. Photo — Charley Brownfield.

Fig. 6-6. Marvin "Chief" Lewis LEFT, L.J. "Smokey" Zeller and Bud Kempf (not shown) had 4PM appointments to get their hair coiffed. 1947.

Fig. 6-8. Smokey, Bud and Chief thought, being lettermen, a perm would not degrade their machismo.

SCHOOL CHUMS

Many of my school friends appear in stories throughout this work. Some whose tenures were fleeting do not, so I will include them below.

BOGEY CRENSHAW

It was on the first day of 2d grade that Miss Madge introduced a new kid to the class. His real name was Herman but to all who knew him he would always be "Bogey". Bogey was about 4 feet tall and 4 feet wide. He must have weighed 125 pounds at age 7. He wore the same 'uniform' as all the rest of us, Oshkosh overalls, blue chambray shirt, high top shoes and knee socks that scrupulously obeyed the laws of gravity and were always down around his shoe tops.

We were released for recess at 10 o'clock that day and, anxious to get acquainted, everyone made a beeline to the playground to surround Bogey. Charley Brownfield began the interrogation: "Where y'all live?"

Bogey indicates the tiny white house across from the school at the southeast corner of Third Street, "Rat over thair."

Charley, looking at the amazing girth of this 7 year old: "What y'all eat anyway?"

Bogey: "Well, I reckon mostly 'taters. We eat lots a 'taters I reckon, 'taters fried up in bacon grease. I reckon we eat 'em ever' day!"

Charley continues the inquisition: "Yeah, I can see. Whatcher Daddy do?"

Bogey: "He's a tie hacker."

Charley, "Tie hacker? Whatsat? Who does he work for?"

Bogey, proudly: "He don't work fer nobody. He's a contracker. He works fer hisself. He cuts down trees and then makes railroad cross-ties with 'em. He gets four bits a tie!"

So, we find, the senior Crenshaw was an independent contractor doing folk sculpture—in a primitive art form, hewing oak logs into railway cross-ties. Paraphrasing Michaelangelo[2]—Mr. Crenshaw just started with an oak log and chipped away everything that didn't look like a cross-tie. These cross-ties, commanding a princely 50¢ per copy, were delivered to the creosoting plant in Franklin. The creosote protected the ties from termites, fungus and the like, but any contact with these treated cross-ties by an insect (or, as I found years later, a naive 16 year old kid) would result in third degree chemical burns.

The tie hackers made these ties with only two tools—ax and adz. I can picture Mr. Crenshaw standing with aching back and blistered hands at the end of the day looking over his day's production—probably 3 cross-ties. He might have thought: "Three ties @ 50¢ a tie = a buck and a half. And in only 12 hours. Not a bad day's work. It feeds the kid, clothes the old woman and keeps a roof over our head!" Ten years later, in 1943 I was to make personal acquaintance with some of these 'homemade' cross-ties.

In England most of the forests were chopped down in 1666 to build Drake's mighty fleet against the Spanish Armada. The forests never recovered. Therefore, cross-ties (which the Brits call 'sleepers') are made of concrete.

Mr. Crenshaw's homemade cross-ties had the *heft* of concrete. Further, they were crudely shaped, roughly finished, ugly and harder than the hammered hinges of hell. When I joined the Katy as an apprentice gandy dancer in the summer of 1943, I found driving a spike into one of these ties was an experience you don't soon forget. Each blow of my ten pound spike maul seemed to advance the spike about 1/32 inch into the oaken heart. But—these old handmade, oak cross-ties laid down in the 30's—were still in place and doing their duty when the Katy folded 30 years later. I now know why a ship made of this hard and strong native oak was called "Old Ironsides"[3].

NORMAN NICHOLS

By the late 1930s Pilot Grove Public School had been slightly reorganized to recognize that there was some middle ground between elementary school and high school—the 7th and 8th grades were designated as Junior High. In the spring of 1940 I was in the seventh grade and enjoying this exalted Junior High status. That spring the Nichols brood immigrated to Pilot Grove and our august Junior High assemblage was introduced to the scion of this family—Norman.

Norman, then about 13 years old, was about six feet tall and weighed in at about 170-180 pounds. He had red hair that looked like someone had mucked out the barn and carelessly piled a heap of manure-flecked straw on his head. He had a freckled face. He had a light complexion on those days when his face was clean enough to tell it. His hulking presence would have been somewhat intimidating if it were not for his easygoing nature. He was easygoing but essentially clueless. Norman Nichols might be accurately described as the dictionary model for the word "LOUT". Well, maybe he'd have to bathe to qualify as a lout.

The living paradox of Norman Nichols was that while he was without a clue in respect of his educational subjects, he had an astonishing ability to memorize extremely long prurient poems and bawdy ballads. He spouted these word for word, word perfect and accompanied by precisely choreographed gestures and body language.

Norman often brought Miss Roxie Hayes, our teacher, to near terminal frustration. Here's an example: One day we were reciting in American History class. She asked him (did she mean this as a joke?): "Norman, can you tell us the approximate date of the War of 1812? That is, when was that war fought?" (She surmised he would not know what 'approximate' meant.)

Norman: "I dunno whatcha mean, ma'am."

Teacher: "What year Norman?"

The other students were snickering and Norman's face got red. He was being made the butt of some kind of joke but for the life of him he couldn't figure out what it was. He said, "Miss Hayes I didn't know that there was on the homework assignment. I just didn't study that. What was the question again—did you say the War of 1812?" The class broke out in open laughter.

Teacher: "All right Norman. The War of 1812 was fought in 1812. Try to remember that." The class was now roaring but Norman never got it.

He looked at me scowling, "How the hell was I suppose to know that?"

But a week later he gathers his classmates on the playground to recite for us his latest memorization entitled "Here's to Hitler". The poem went on for about 20 stanzas ending: His [bleep] will hang like a rotten banana when we start to play the Star Spangled Banner. From the land of the free and home of the brave, we'll all march down and [bleep] on his grave. Norman was one of those creatures who marched to a different drummer.

HAWGLEG

That winter Norman sees me on the playground and calls to me. "Come 'ere, Sonny, I got somepin to show ya!"

I thought, "Some dirty poem he has copied out for us."

---

[2] Michaelangelo was once asked by a fawning admirer, "How do you carve a lion?" He answered, "I start with a block of marble and chip away everything that doesn't look like a lion!"

[3] The USS Constitution, now lying at anchor in Boston harbor.

Some of the other miscreants saw us and came charging over. Norman reaches into his waistband and pulls out a giant .45 Caliber revolver. It looked something like Dirty Harry's .44 Magnum except this gun was a cheap, nickel-plated Saturday night special. It was old. The nickel plating was worn off on several spots and the milled bakelite (plastic had not yet been invented) grips were worn smooth. It was not the .45 'hawgleg' the cowboys twirled in the Saturday night movies, see Figure 6-10. It was more like a big brother to Dad's old .32 break-open revolver.

Fig. 6-9. Norman Nichols, age 13 in 1942.

"Where'dja get it? Is it real? Is it yours? Is it loaded? Can I play with it?" The babbling idiots went on.

"Naw, it ain't loaded. Naw you can't play with it. It's my ole man's." He carried it around all day demonstrating his quick draw from his waistband. No one finked on him. No teacher or administrator ever knew he had it. He took it home that evening and to my knowledge never brought it back. Thus, the 'gun in the schoolhouse' sensation, thought to be a 1990s phenomena was predated by Norman Nichols by 50 years. Fortunately no one was ever shot at the Pilot Grove school, at least while I was there.

Norman did bring Miss Strickfadden to terminal frustration one day. She lost it! Janie (Brownfield) Goehner remembers a special trigonometry lesson in the spring of 1941.

"That year the seventh and eighth grade math classes were doubled up and Miss Strickfadden dealt with them simultaneously, spending half a period with each.

"The lesson this day was on isosceles triangles and Miss Strickfadden demonstrated some sort of geometric construction with ruler and compass that would 'solve the triangle.'

"She then outlined a problem for the combined class and left the room. Some of the eighth graders understood the technique and rapidly solved the problem. Norman Nichols hadn't a clue, nor did any of the other seventh graders. The seventh graders, desperately fearing Miss Stickfadden's temper, quickly copied the work of Becky Meyer. Norman was too dull witted to even do that.

"Miss Strickfadden returned in a few minutes and went from desk to desk looking at the work of each. When she got to Norman, he was sitting with hands folded in his lap and with a silly grin on his face. A few words were exchanged and Strickfadden lost it! She put her knee on his leg, pinned him in his desk and grabbed his mop of unruly red hair. She pulled and shook his head and screamed at him, "Why do you even bother coming in here? Why do you even bother coming to school? You're only wearing out the seat of your pants!"

"All the other students were terrified. What will she do

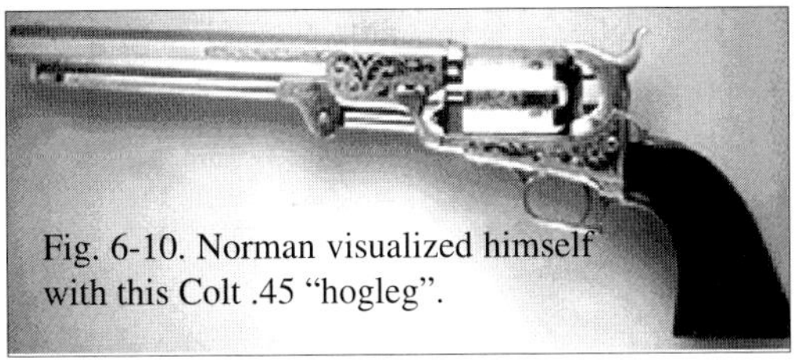

Fig. 6-10. Norman visualized himself with this Colt .45 "hogleg".

to us when she finds out that all of us seventh graders just copied from Becky? Some were at the point of wetting their pants.

"Well, she didn't find out and we all got off scot free, but we all felt guilty. Of all the dummies, at least Norman was honest."

HOMER ETSON JEFFRESS JR.

Homer's parents, Homer Sr. and Willa started him in the first grade in the fall of 1932. He was only 5 years old but they apparently were anxious to launch his education. He flunked clay class or something and was held back. We know in this more enlightened age that some kids are simply not ready for school at age 5. In those days it was considered a dishonor equal to having a funny uncle chained in the basement. At any rate we started first grade together in the fall of 1933. He was an invaluable pal to me because he was a veteran who had been through all this stuff before.

I can remember the first time I met him. He and his older sister, Winnie, were coming through Mame Chapman's yard—a shortcut to downtown. He saw me and charged like a varsity linebacker. From that day in the summer of 1933 until the day he died he and I were best of friends.

One of Homer's anomalies was his obsessive adoration of his father. His dad was a painter of no particular skill and not of exemplary morals. In my humble estimate he was not a good father. This opinion is based on his abandonment of the family upon the birth of his fifth child. It is reinforced by an incident that I personally witnessed just after Christmas in 1937.

After my sister Dixie had won her bicycle in a Capper's Weekly contest in summer of 1937, I had whined until my old man conceded to lay out $2 for an ancient, high pressure tire bike for me. Thin, narrow tired bikes had been in fashion, then back out again as the 'balloon' tired bikes like Dixie's came to the fore. My bike was a piece of junk that you might expect to get for $2—but it did all the things a bike must do! I got into some of Mom's pea green paint and gave it a couple of coats. As trashy as it looked, it was more than Homer had and he began putting pressure on his dad to get him a bike for Christmas.

On Christmas day Homer came racing over to our place to show me what his beloved father had given him for Christmas—a brand new, shiny, red, balloon-tired bike! He and I were now inseparable with our bikes. Then came a frosty

Fig. 6-11. Loyd McCreery, PGHS Class of 1943. Merchant Mariner, US Marine and mentor to the Juvenile Delinquent Apprentice Boys. He insisted, and this is his official Senior photo.

Fig. 6-12. Thelma Fredrick and Mattie Jo Heim - 1941. "Girls just want to have fun!" Photo—Norb Zeller.

January morning in 1938.

It was just after Homer's eleventh birthday and we were riding our bikes on College Street. We were heading east in front of the Wallace Burger home when he sees his dad's car approaching. His father, with his new wife and two sickly-looking step-kids, had been looking all over town for him. Homer was excited. He hadn't heard from his father on his birthday and his eyes were glowing with anticipation.

Homer Senior lays hold of the handlebars of the bike and says, "Junior, I'm gonna hafta take this bike back." Homer Junior's face fell. His dad went on, "There was something wrong with the paper work or something. I'll take it back and get you a lot better one. I'll bring it down to you (he lived in Kansas City) next time we come."

Homer Junior, brightening, says, "Oh, OK dad. Here, I'll help you load it in the car." As the old Dodge touring car disappeared around the corner, I looked at Homer. His face held great disappointment, he held back a tear. But it also glowed with adoration for his father.

You will have already guessed the rest of the story. There was no better bike nor any other bike forthcoming. One may find any number of excuses for this. Times were hard. His new wife may have berated him, "How can you spend $12 on a bicycle when we don't know where the rent money is coming from? etc, etc."

I don't know what caused this blatant travesty on an eleven year old child. I only remember that Homer Senior lost any stature he may have had in my eyes.

But 'Dad' lost nothing in Homer Junior's eyes. Indeed until the day the old man died, Homer Junior revered him—a sentiment that in my opinion was greatly misplaced.

LOYD MCCREERY

My neighbor, friend and mentor— Loyd McCreery was a senior in high school and was preparing to go into the Merchant Marine. It was the spring of 1943 and the great war was approaching a crescendo. The Merchant Marine was an honorable quasi-military option that some fellows contemplating the draft thought might improve the odds of surviving the current unpleasantness. The fact that the Merchant Marine often faced far worse hazards than the Army or Navy did not become well known until after the war. Perception was everything.

Homer, Loyd, Babe and I were sitting on the front porch of the Heim place a mile southwest of town just past Mt. Vernon Road—"the house on the hill" as Babe called it. Loyd spent a bit of time with Babe primarily because of Babe's older sister, Mattie Jo. Mattie Jo (PGHS Class of 1942) not only looked like a real doll, she had an effervescent personality that charmed everyone who came within her orbit. This pixie-faced cutie with the curly black hair and sparkling disposition—held a contingent of slack-jawed swains in thrall. Loyd was no exception. His mother confirmed to me years later that the pair sometimes cut classes together.

In retrospect, I can understand how the attributes that made us love him like a big brother—spontaneity, audacity, unpredictability—might also appeal to Mattie Jo's exuberant and carefree spirit.

On this radiant spring day, to lubricate our learned discussion on baseball, basketball and other important world matters, Loyd pulls out a pint of bourbon and offers it around. Now, while Loyd was 18 and maybe up to bourbon, Homer and I were 16 and Babe was 14 or 15. We expressed some mild reservations and I carefully examined the bottle as a means of stalling. Real whiskey was as scarce as hen's teeth in that era and I was expressing understandable curiosity.

I read the label aloud, "Hmm, Black Beauty — Distilled Pure Bourbon Whiskey, Aged in Copper Vats 6 Months, Flavored and Colored With Wood Chips. Damn, Loyd! this stuff is a real find, where dja get it?" I unscrewed the cap and pretended to take a drink.

"Never mind," he retorted, "Pass it to Homer."

I passed the bottle, and—from all the gagging and semi-retching—I think they actually drank some of it. At any rate we didn't get any high marks as bourbon aficionados in Loyd's eyes.

"Here! Gimme the damned bottle, you bunch of pansies!" He snatched the bottle back.

Homer, trying to regain lost esteem says, "Loyd, I just got choked trying to taste it. Really, it's real good whiskey. Excellent hooch."

Unmollified, Loyd says, "Watch me, you candy-asses!" He tips up the pint, very little diminished by his fellow bourbon connoisseurs , and chug-a-lugs it down as though knocking back a Griesedieck lager. He tossed the empty bottle into the yard. "Now that's how a bourbon drinker has his bourbon!"

Since Loyd's pint of Black Beauty was the sum total of the refreshments available, we continued the bull session dry. Loyd kept up with the discourse for a while, his speech becoming more and more slurred. Then he looks at me and I saw for the first time the definition of the color: bilious green. His eyes glazed over and he toppled off the porch backward. The soft earth of the lawn caught him as he measured his length on the grass.

We had engaged in an illegal activity: underage drinking—so I figured it might be prudent if I were to put some space between me and the party scene. I took off for home with Homer yelling, "Wait up, Sonny. I'm comin' too."

I don't know what happened to Loyd that evening, I assume Babe dragged him in the house to sleep it off, but that first meeting of Loyd's Bourbon Connoisseurs Club was also the last.

There is a little epilogue. Loyd did join the Merchant Marine and went off to the Merchant Marine Academy at Sheepshead Bay, Long Island for training. Upon graduation, he drew a berth as a fireman on an ancient, coal burning, 'bucket-of-bolts' merchant vessel. First voyage: New York to Halifax, Nova Scotia and return.

His duties were to man a No. 9 scoop shovel, transferring a 50 ton pile of coal to the insatiable hell of a boiler which drove the antiquated old boat. Upon his return he got a short leave and came home to show us his hands— nearly destroyed by blisters. His blisters had blisters. He never made another voyage. He resigned the Maritime service and joined the Marines saying, "If I'm gonna die, I want it to be all at once and not be tortured to death!"

He almost got that preference. In the Marines, he was severely wounded in the battle for Okinawa (June 1945). He carried Japanese shrapnel in his chest for the rest of his life. **Semper Fi!**

TEACHERS

MISS MARGARETTE VINEYARD

—was the red headed High School English teacher. She was in her early 30s and quite attractive with the pale Irish complexion to match her Irish hair. It was said by some of her detractors that the red in her hair came out of a bottle. I don't know about that. I liked her very much—partly because English Literature was among my favorite subjects.

Fig. 6-13. Miss Margarette Vineyard, English Teacher '41.

What really attracted me was her decision to organize a French class. In hindsight this was probably a mistake—the textbooks that we were given were atrocious and she found that while she was quite adequate to the grammar, she really was not very good at spoken French.

That's where I made my grades. By mimicking French movie and radio actors, I came off with an acceptable French accent. Well, anyway it was acceptable to my peers. I also remembered—with no help from the formal course material—a few things that I found useful 40 years later when I had to deal with the language.

A more immediate reward for my interest in French was a spot in the our class play as Pierre the French butler. Earlene Schlotzhauer (now Loesing) had the more difficult part of an Aunt Jemima cook/maid whose character was continually in conflict with the butler. Earlene still remembers most of her lines in this play and has been known to recite them at class reunions at the slightest provocation.

MISS LIDA HARRIS

—was another redhead—forty-ish, well proportioned, single lady of slight build—but a professional dynamo. I doubt that she ever knew to the day of her death what tremendous value her personal self-sacrifice added to the later lives of the little snots that she was afflicted with during her long tenure at Pilot Grove. She was another of the many females who ultimately gave up hope of a life of her own to dedicate herself to the (mostly thankless) children of others.

She taught history, civics and sociology. She also coached the girls basketball team. She was a queen among teachers and probably the longest tenured teacher at PGHS. She was a revered teacher of my sister Dixie during her PGHS education beginning in the late 1930s and she was there long after brother Bob graduated in 1947.

Civics was the most boring. There was little she could do to juice it up though she tried. The reward was history. I loved her history classes. I regarded the course as a series of spellbinding stories and hung on her every word. Lida Harris made a history buff of me in 1942. My fascination with the subject endures to this day.

Fig. 6-14. Miss Lida Harris-taught history and civics.

MISS BERTHA STRICKFADDEN

—had a reputation which preceded my association with her in 1941-1942. She taught mathematics and was reputed to be an ogre in regards to homework and classroom recitation.

Sending someone to the blackboard to work through an algebra problem was the equivalent of Torquemada and the Spanish Inquisition in 17th century Spain—or so I was led to believe. It was said her real name should have been Strictfadden, that she did not suffer fools. I found this to be true.

But, I aced all her math quizzes except one on the Pythagorean Theorem[4]. On the fateful day that Miss Strickfadden covered Pythagoras, Dorothy Prewitt had missed a button on her blouse. Dorothy Prewitt was—let me consult my Dictionary of Euphemisms. Here we go—Dorothy was busty, bosomy, shapely, chesty, full-bosomed—to be crude, she was breathtakingly top-heavy.

Fig. 6-15. Miss Harris in her salon - 1948. Fixtures were from the old Pilot Grove Bank. Photo—Janie.

At the end of the Pythagorean session, Miss Strickfadden focused our minds when she announced that this material would be on the next quiz. Most of the boys were sure to flunked it.

After class, Babe, Charlie, Homer and I got our heads together. What did she say about this Pythagoras Theorem, Babe? Somehow I missed it.

Babe, "It was like: 'A square hippopotamus is the same as two other things in a square.' Or somepin' like that."

I shook my head, "That don't make no sense! Guys, we are going to have to grovel here —ask the girls. They weren't as distracted as you were Babe."

Homer says, "Let's ask Dorothy ." He was figuring on more peep show.

"Naw," I said, "I don't think 'Mathematician' is among the multitudinous career choices open to Dorothy." So the deputized committee asked Rebekah Meyer but she didn't understand it either and that is why I flunked Pythagoras.

Fig. 6-16. Miss Bertha Strickfadden taught math and other tortures.

It was a great surprise to me but I enjoyed the math classes. It was an eye-opening experience and I never lost my fascination for mathematics. She was not oblivious to this and often—after berating one of my less math-oriented colleagues—called on me to work problems on the board. She was refreshing in her inspiration and introduction to a world of mathematics that was completely foreign to me and I was happy to hear many years later that—after her decades long courtship with local farmer Roger Weamer—she escaped the enervating sisterhood of old maid school teachers.

MISS ROXIE HAYES

—like all other female teachers at Pilot Grove, (and everywhere else for that matter) was never permitted much of a life of her own. They were required to be single. Marriage would constitute grounds for immediate dismissal. They could date, but tongues were sure to wag and they might be questioned at annual contract time. That's the way it was in 1941 when Roxie Hayes had the Junior High all in one room at the northwest corner of the lower classroom floor.

In the spring of that year, March or so, we began noticing how Miss Hayes was putting on a little weight. Miss Hayes was then in her mid 30s. She was quite attractive, well proportioned and had lovely complexion and hair. Her tastes in clothing ran to the darker hues or conservative black. It was her favorite black dress that seemed to be giving her the most trouble. Buttons were straining and the zipper would occasionally give way under tension. By April she was really having difficulty fitting into her clothing and had to run to the teachers' lounge every hour or so.

Finally, in late April and only 2-3 weeks until the end of the school term, she gave up and went into a maternity smock. We were shocked. Pregnancy out of wedlock was much less accepted in 'decent society' back then. She told us she would tell us a secret after the after-

[4] Pythagorean Theorem - The square of the hypotenuse of a right triangle equals the sum of the squares of the other two sides.

noon recess. We all thought we knew what it was. The more mature students had long since put 2 and 2 together. We had trouble with long division but we understood addition—family additions.

We were surprised. At 2:30 PM after the final recess bell had recalled the louts and ne'er-do-wells in from the playground we sat expectantly at our desks. For the first time since I had been in Junior High there was total silence. Miss Hayes then entered the classroom beaming. Standing behind her desk she motioned to someone in the hall, "Come in, Freddie!"

Fig. 6-17. Miss Roxie Hayes was having trouble keeping this dress buttoned by April '41.

In marches this little guy, about Miss Hayes' age, slender, well groomed, well dressed, with his face red as a beet. "Children, I want you to meet my husband, Fred Neuenschwander! We were married secretly last summer. As you know I can no longer teach here, so I'll not see you again after this year. Superintendent McKee has agreed to let me finish the school term. Mr. Neuenschwander will probably not see you again so he wants to say hello and good-bye." Freddie mumbled something and hurried out the door. Roxie, all aglow, watched him and waved a little good-bye as he disappeared down the stairs. Two weeks later the term ended and I never saw her again.

Fig. 6-18. Miss Doris Nelson, taught 4-5-6 grade 1936-1939. Photo—Janie Goehner.

MISS DORIS NELSON

—was my fourth grade teacher. I only had her that one year. She was probably around longer but I just do not remember. She was important to my education because as a part of her general objectives of 'readin' 'riting and 'rithmetic, she taught music appreciation.

I can still see her winding up the old Victrola then Walter Damrosch conducting the New York Philharmonic Orchestra playing Wagner's "Hall of the Mountain King". I really did not care for this Teutonic chant but she made it interesting by stopping at key places to explain the operatic action.

Another of her innovations was Tea Parties. They injected a little class and culture into an assemblage that was woefully ignorance of such niceties. At her own expense she brought in 3-4 little glasses of Old English processed cheese spread plus a box of Nabisco saltines. As a part of our study of the Scandinavian countries that year, she highlighted the lesson with tea which Bob Chastain make down in the furnace room. It went down quite well with the cheese and cracker dainties.

Fig. 6-19. Bob Chastain was PGHS janitor for decades.

BOB CHASTAIN

Bob Chastain was middle aged when I started to school in 1933. His headquarters was in the basement where he tended a giant furnace. The first time I had occasion to look into his domain, the fire was going full blast and he was stoking it with coal. My Methodist Sunday School teacher, Frances Brownfield had given us some descriptions of hell—and this looked a lot like it!

Bob Chastain never reported us for anything we got up to—he corrected us on the spot. He never laid hands on anyone but when one got a scolding from Bob Chastain, one was loath to repeat the offending act. He was a prince of a man and when he retired long after I graduated, dozens of 'his kids' wished him the very best for his golden years.

SCHOOL ACTIVITIES

School activities at PGHS were of four types—*sports*, which usually meant basketball, *drama* which was the annual Junior and Senior plays, *vocational* activities associated with agriculture (mostly boys) and home economics (mostly girls) and certain *unsanctioned* activities most (but not all) of which shall forever remain unrecorded.

THE TATLER, reported these activities—at least the sanctioned ones. Juniors and Seniors made up the bulk of the staff. 'Cub' reporters were designated for the lower grades. Publication was fun and the practical work was a good learning experience.

I have included on the next two pages a sample of one issue plus the staff that wrote and edited it. Get out your magnifying glass.

Editor------Charlotte Heinrich
Assist. Editor-----Betty Judy
Prod. Mgr.---Clifford Ashcraft
Typist------Charlotte Heinrich
Artists--------Dorothy Stevens
Jeanne Davis
Nell Porter
Adv. Mgrs.---Rosaline Schuster
Margaret Cullen
Circulation Mgr.---Betty Judy
Sports Reps. Beulah Brownfield
Wallace Burger
Music Reporter------Jane Wolfe
Social Rep.--Rosaline Schuster
Literary Editor-Margaret Cullen
Grade News---Rosaline Schuster

Editorial

FEATHERS AND FALSEHOOD

A peasant with a troubled conscience went to a monk for advice. He said he had circulated a vile story about a good friend, only to find out later that the story was untrue.

"If you want to make peace with your conscience," said the monk, "you must fill a bag with chicken feathers, go to every dooryard in the village, and drop in each of them, one fluffy feather."

The peasant did as he was told. Then he came back to the monk and announced that he had done penance for his folly.

"Not yet," replied the monk. "Take your bag and go the rounds again, and gather up every one of the feathers you have left."

"But the wind must have blown them away," said the peasant.

"Yes, my son," said the monk, "and so it is with gossip. Bad words are easily dropped but no matter how hard you may try, you can never get them back again."

From the SCHOOL MIRROR
Seligman, Missouri

CHARACTER SKETCH

Subject: THE LITTLE MAN WHO WASN'T THERE
Who were his parents? Transparents.
Where does he live?-----In the 2nd floor over a vacant lot.
What does he eat?-Sliced dough nut holes and vanishing cream.
Where does he keep his horse? In a Table.
His favorite song.----All the things you aren't.
His hobby.-Collecting smokerings.
His pets.------Pink elephants.
What does he say to his love? Sweet nothings.

Do you remember way back when Confucius didn't say anything?

From the SCHOOL MIRROR

Social Events

CENSUS

In the American History class a census was taken and here are the results:

Favorite
1. For President--Thomas Dewey
2. Movie Actor----Mickey Rooney
3. Movie Actress-----Alice Faye
4. Movie---------Swanee River"
5. Columnist-----Walter Winchell
6. Sports Rep---Grantland Rice
7. Radio Program------Kay Kyser and Fred Waring
8. Radio Star--------Baby Snooks
9. For Govenor of Missouri----- Allen McReynolds
10. Book----"Gone With the Wind"
11. Poet----Henry W. Longfellow
12. School Subject--------History
13. Occupation-----------Farming
14. Foreign Country--------France
15. Political Party---Republican
16. Pet-----------------------Dog
17. Athelete-------Paul Chrisman
18. Popular Song--"Scatterbrain"
19. Orchestra Leader-Guy Lombardo
20. Food-----------Fried Chicken
21. State------------Missouri
22. University-----------Missouri
23. Sport----------------Baseball
24. Painting------"The Windmill"
25. Automobile---------Chevrolet

SENIOR TRIP

Friday, April 12, the Seniors were invited to Sedalia to be the guests of the Chamber of Commerce. There were two other schools there also. We went through the Missouri-Pacific RR shops in the morning. Then we were taken to the Central Business college for a most delicious luncheon. As we had to be home by four o'clock, we did not get to go with the rest of the groups in the afternoon. The most interesting thing to the Seniors was the sight of Robert Waldo, the giant boy. A very enjoyable day was spent.

P.T.A. PARTY

The P.T.A. held a party April 18 in the high school auditorium. Everyone was invited with a plate of sandwiches as their admission. Everyone seemed to enjoy it immensely.

The second Junior play "Trouble in Paradise" was a huge success

Both the girls and boys have started softball practice. We hope to "bring home the bacon" from the tournament at Bunceton April 26.

MUSIC & COMMERCIAL CONTEST

At the Music & Commercial meet held here April 19, Pilot Grove, as in previous years, took top honors. Much improvement has been made since we had the contest here four years ago. The students and Mr. Mc'ton are to be complimented on their splendid work in the music department and Mr. Cole and his students in the commercial department. Most of our ratings in the music meet were Excellents. In music the results were: First-Pilot Grove, Second-Boonville Catholic, and Third-Bunceton.

In the commercial department. Typing-First-Otterville, Second Pilot Grove, Third-Boonville. In Shorthand-First-Pilot Grove, Second-Prairie Home, Third-Otterville. In Bookkeeping-First-Pilot Grove, Second-Prairie Home, and Third-Boonville.

The people of Pilot Grove are very proud of their young people standing in the county.

DON'T FORGET THE SENIOR'S PLAY
"FOR PETE'S SAKE!"
MAY 3rd

Jokes and Exchanges

DAFFINITIONS

Gossip---when nobody does anything and someone goes and tells about it.
Modern Girl---a vision in the evening; a sight in the morn.
Vaccuum---Nothing shut up in a hole.
Tangerine---a loose-leaf orange.
Banana Peel---food article that brings down the weight.
Echo---the only thing that ever cheated a women out of the last word.
Grapefruit---a lemon that has been given a chance and took advantage of it.
Steam---water gone crazy with the heat.
Laugh---showing in one place how you feel all over.
Saxaphone---an ill wind which nobody blows good.
Conscience---an inner voice that warns us someone is looking.
Boy---a noise with dirt on it.
Middle Age---when you begin to chance your emotions for symptons.
Telephone Booth---a sort of a vertical coffin where sweet dis positions are buried.
Detour---the roughest distance between two points.

A sandwich at a tea party reminds us of a basketball game; nothing between halves.

You can always tell a Freshman By the foolishness in his eyes.
You can always tell a Sophomore By his grin and gaudy ties.
You can always tell a Junior By the smile he has and such.
You can always tell a Senior But you cannot tell him much!!

HAVE YOU HEARD??

About the dumb wagonmaker who picked up a hub and spoke.
About the blind carpenter who picked up a plane and saw.
About the deaf sheepherder who went out with his dog and herd.
About the baldheaded man who went into the fur business and raised hairs.
About the noseless fisherman who caught a barrel of herring and smelt.

DAFFINITIONS CONTINUED

Rank---A place where you skate
Sentiment---What you feel for someone you love.
Hobo--An instrument of the wood wind family.
Tank-----Garbo's favorite word.
Specific--An Ocean of the west coast.
Epistle----An Apostle's wife.
Chivalry---The attitude of a man toward a strange woman.
Cymbal---A musical instrument of spain.
Neighbor--A man who makes faces and ...
Kissing----A tickilish feeling.

A terrible thing has come to pass,
I woke up twice in American Problems class!!
Flunk now------Avoid the rush.

I'm through with the women!!
They cheat and they lie.
They tease and torment us
'Til the day we die.
They prey on us gents.
They drive us to sin------
Say!! Who was that blonde
That just walked in!!!!!

Fig. 6-20. April 1940 issue of The Tatler. Courtesy Les Chamberlin.

THE TATLER - ISSUE OF APRIL 1940

HERE IS SOME OF THE STAFF FOR THAT ISSUE

Charlotte Heinrich - Editor

Clifford Ashcraft - Production Manager

Margaret Cullen - Literary Editor & Advertising Manager

Rosaline Schuster - Social Reporter & Advertising Manager

Nell Porter - Artist

Photos this page are graduation photos. Courtesy Les Chamberlin.

EXCERPT FROM THE MARCH 1944 PGHS TATLER

HUMAN INTERESTS

by DUKE SHOOP*

Ye old editor, in his many ramblings through the large and magnificent halls of my dear old alma mater, Pilot Grove High, discovered many groups of students in many interesting places. "Very curious indeed." Says I to myself, "I'm going to have to get to the bottom of all this mystery, yup, yup."

So I proceeded to the first objective, using my best keyhole technique. (I'll bet a nickel I misspell that word, and I'm going to murder the bum that swiped my 10¢ dictionary.)

Miss Vinyard's room is the first objective and I approach the advance guards with all the strategy possible. Under the pretext of getting a book from the library (sometimes called liberry) I gained admittance. After gazing about me with many sad shakings of the head, I was reminded of my days in Washington, D.C.

Not only was there a serious manpower shortage, (about ten girls to every boy), but the racket and confusion would put the OPA to shame. No one heard what anyone said, but they laughed because they knew it was funny. Most of the noisy little rascals were lower classmen. It surprised me how such little girls as Patty Schilb, Mildred Schlotzhauer and Barbara Coleman could make such a big noise. They seemed to have the floor and no one disputed them. (After all, who wants these splintery floors anyway?)

Lillian Lammers and Doris Hurt seemed to be very bewildered by the whole thing. Margie Hoff was there with dear Homey. Smokey Zeller and Herbie Ratje gazed about the room in open-mouth stupefaction. (Six bit word.) They didn't completely understand what was going on, but they were all for it. Unfortunately I wasn't able to stay long as I had forgotten my thirty-cent ear-plugs.

I beat it and after two aspirins and a bicarb for a headache, I was on my way again.

The next stop was the Hall of Fame, otherwise known as the study hall. There, I saw, among other things, Mary L. Gerling and Doody Bauer "battin' the breeze." I wondered what they were talking about? (Maybe they did too.) Marjorie Babbitt and Eddie Klenklen sat in the corner. I judged they were both mind-readers as they didn't ever say anything. Henry Stegner sat looking at Charlene Farrell and with a romantic, far-away look in his eyes, sighed.

Then came the executive staff in the office. Kathryn Haley, Virgil Schupp, Dorothy Spence, Paul Schlotzhauer, Patty Simmons and Eugene Schupp were "runnin' da joint" in the absence of the Chief Executive. After being gypped out of 1/2¢ worth of candy, I went on the group of amateur beauty contest judges. As each girl goes by, Alban Bauer frowns thoughtfully, nods, and says to Son Klenklen, "What's the verdict, Jackson?"

Son answers enthusiastically, "At's all right, Jack, Ahaa." (Bob Wills accent.) About this time Doris (you can pick which one, personally, I'd take both) comes along and Sonnie Salmon says, "Ah, ze vairy peak of pairfection, wee, wee!"

John Lorenz and Billy Stewart, hurriedly agree as they don't want to dispute the word of an expert on the subject.

As I have now worn out my last pencil, I'll have to say, "Buenos Noches, Amigos, au revoir mon amis, auf wiedersehn komrads, goodbye, good luck and also nuts to Hitler.

---

*nom de plume of Sonny Salmon

BASKETBALL

There was a great deal of interest in sports. We played pickup games of softball and volleyball at recess and noon break. There were occasionally organized intramural softball tournaments. Track was a big thing until the country got well immersed in the great depression. Then the 440 low hurdles, pole vaulting, high jumping, broad jumping, etc., came to a halt.

The game that survived was basketball and it became *the defining activity*. The game and Pilot Grove's position among the CCAA's teams became a town obsession that continues to this day.

ABOVE Fig. 6-21. PGHS Girls Basketball Team 1940-41. REAR L-R Lyda Harris, Coach; Mary E. Cordry, Erma Vonderahe; Marjorie Burger; Esther Gerke; Doris Quinlan; Bonnie Klenklen; Gladys Prewitt; Katherine Haley. FRONT L-R Irene Gerke; Sue Coleman; Viola Twenter; Beulah Maude Brownfield; Agnes Bauer and Edna Davis. These are some of the attractive young women who answered a question for me: "Why do the boys find girls' basketball so interesting?" Photo —Irene Felten.

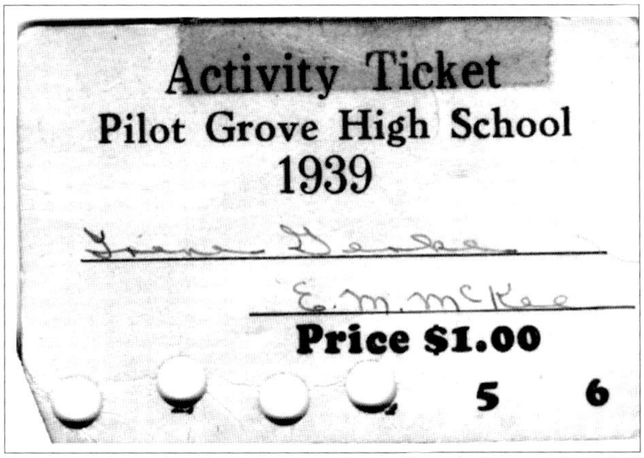

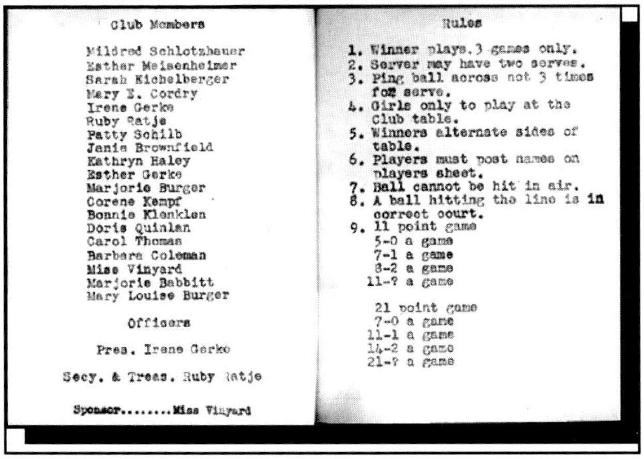

Club Members

Mildred Schlotzhauer
Esther Meisenheimer
Sarah Eichelberger
Mary E. Cordry
Irene Gerke
Ruby Ratje
Patty Schilb
Janie Brownfield
Kathryn Haley
Esther Gerke
Marjorie Burger
Corene Kempf
Bonnie Klenklen
Doris Quinlan
Carol Thomas
Barbara Coleman
Miss Vinyard
Marjorie Babbitt
Mary Louise Burger

Officers

Pres. Irene Gerke

Secy. & Treas. Ruby Ratje

Sponsor........Miss Vinyard

Rules

1. Winner plays.3 games only.
2. Server may have two serves.
3. Ping ball across not 3 times for serve.
4. Girls only to play at the Club table.
5. Winners alternate sides of table.
6. Players must post names on players sheet.
7. Ball cannot be hit in air.
8. A ball hitting the line is in correct court.
9. 11 point game
   5-0 a game
   7-1 a game
   8-2 a game
   11-? a game

   21 point game
   7-0 a game
   11-1 a game
   14-2 a game
   21-? a game

Fig. 6-22. Basketball wasn't the only athletic activity. In the late winter of 1943, PGHS girls organized a Ping-Pong Club to fill in the dreary winter afternoons after the basketball season. Who remembers the Ping Pong Club of 1943? How about the members, players and officers?

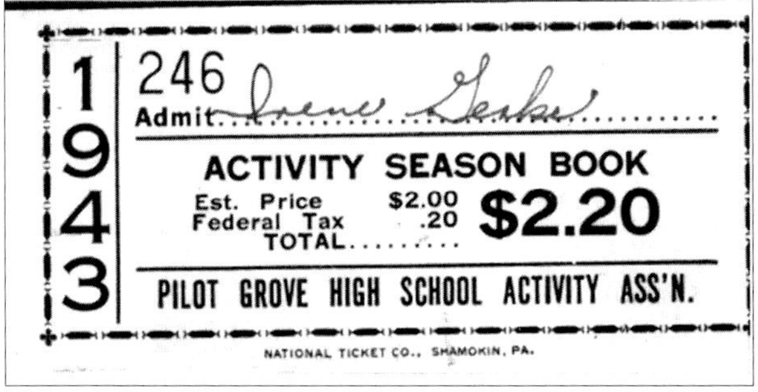

Fig. 6-23. Season Activity tickets cost a buck in 1939. By 1943 they were $2.20. Were the teams winning more? Irene was carefully keeping the won-lost score in 1941. She was a Junior and a star hoop shooter that year as well as the next.

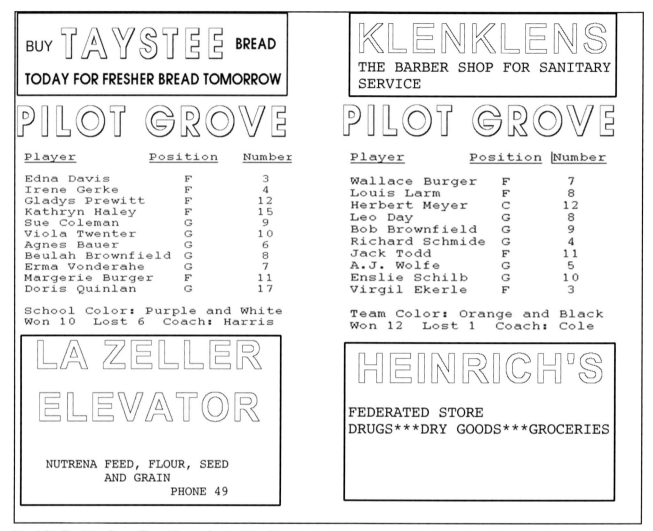

BUY TAYSTEE BREAD
TODAY FOR FRESHER BREAD TOMORROW

KLENKLENS
THE BARBER SHOP FOR SANITARY SERVICE

PILOT GROVE

Player	Position	Number
Edna Davis	F	3
Irene Gerke	F	4
Gladys Prewitt	F	12
Kathryn Haley	F	15
Sue Coleman	G	9
Viola Twenter	G	10
Agnes Bauer	G	6
Beulah Brownfield	G	8
Erma Vonderahe	G	7
Margerie Burger	F	11
Doris Quinlan	G	17

School Color: Purple and White
Won 10 Lost 6 Coach: Harris

PILOT GROVE

Player	Position	Number
Wallace Burger	F	7
Louis Larm	F	8
Herbert Meyer	C	12
Leo Day	G	8
Bob Brownfield	G	9
Richard Schmide	G	4
Jack Todd	F	11
A.J. Wolfe	G	5
Enslie Schilb	G	10
Virgil Ekerle	F	3

Team Color: Orange and Black
Won 12 Lost 1 Coach: Cole

LA ZELLER ELEVATOR
NUTRENA FEED, FLOUR, SEED AND GRAIN
PHONE 49

HEINRICH'S
FEDERATED STORE
DRUGS***DRY GOODS***GROCERIES

Fig. 6-24. The Pilot Grove Tigers' line up for the 1941 CCAA basketball tournament. This is a replica of the original game program and authentic to include misspelled names. Thanks to Irene Felten for searching her attic for a mass of memorabilia including this program.

[Excerpt from the "TATLER" November 1942.]

GIRLS
COOPER COUNTY TOURNAMENT

The Cooper County Athletic Association held its annual tournament Nov. 5-6-7, Pilot Grove High School. Pilot Grove girls did not participate until Friday evening, at which time they met Prairie Home. In general the team played good ball, but were unable to stop the scoring done by L. Burris, Prairie Home's tall forward, who made 31 of the 38 points.

Pilot Grove players tied the score at the 3rd quarter but were unable to hold the tie and thus were defeated 38-31.

This defeat put us in the semifinals for consolation Saturday afternoon, at which Boonville Catholic were our opponents. It was an easy victory the score being 57-8. The good playing that was shown in the afternoon, was kept through the final game that night. Irene Gerke was high point having 18 points to her credit, Margie Burger having 16.

The victory in this game brought us into the finals for consolation Sat. night. We met and defeated Otterville 34 to 22. Great enthusiasm was shown over the game by the crowd as they watched the second team play the last 4 minutes of the game.

The three high point girls of the tournament were, Burris of Prairie Home with 65 points, Gerke of Pilot Grove with 56 and Brandes of Bunceton with 45 points.

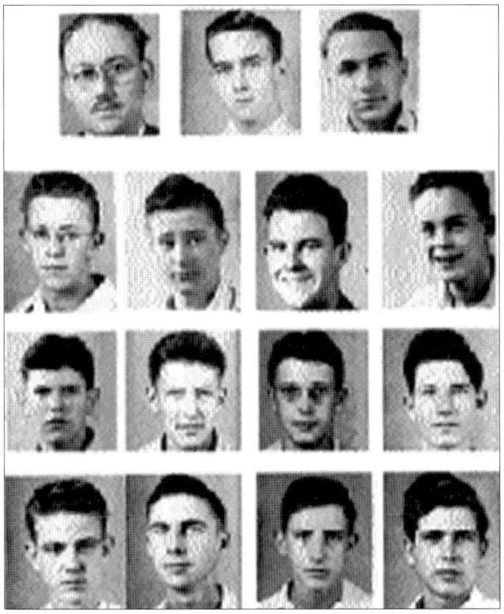

Fig. 6-25. Boys Basket Ball team, '44-'45. L-R Coach Laughlin, Capt. H. Jeffress, Asst Coach C. Brownfield, H. Ries, M. Lewis, G. Heim, R. Salmon, W. Betteridge, J. Caton, C. Schlotzhauer, E. Spence, B. Stevens, E. Loesing, R. Eichelberger, L. Zeller.

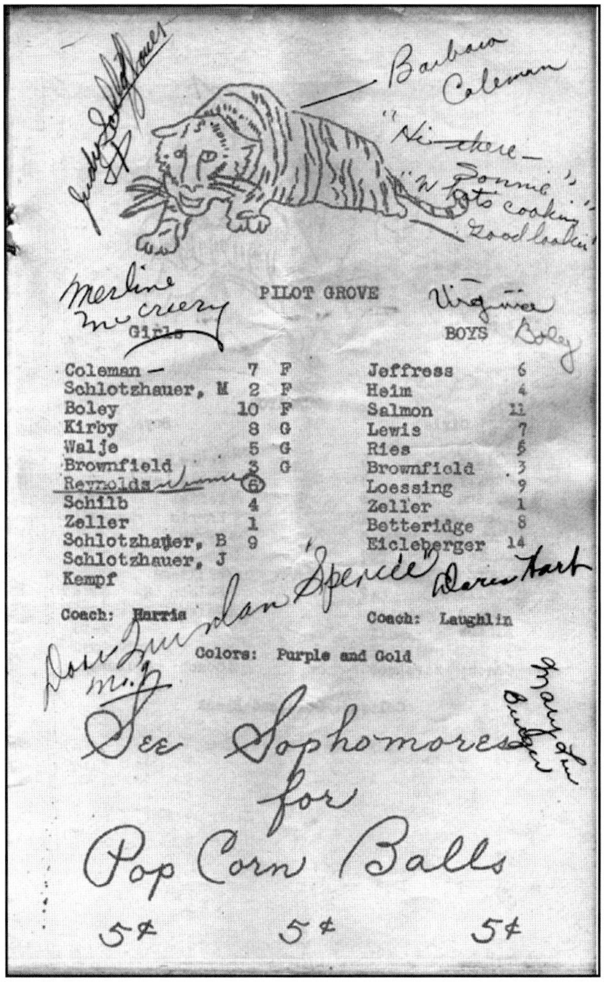

PILOT GROVE

Girls			Boys	
Coleman	7	F	Jeffress	6
Schlotzhauer, M	2	F	Heim	4
Boley	10	F	Salmon	11
Kirby	8	G	Lewis	7
Walje	5	G	Ries	5
Brownfield	3	G	Brownfield	3
Reynolds	6		Loessing	9
Schilb	4		Zeller	1
Zeller	1		Betteridge	8
Schlotzhauer, B	9		Eicleberger	14
Schlotzhauer, J				
Kempf				

Coach: Harris Coach: Laughlin

Colors: Purple and Gold

See Sophomores for Pop Corn Balls

5¢ 5¢ 5¢

ABOVE Fig. 6-28. Souvenir program—1944 NCAA Tournament (held at Pilot Grove, Thur, Fri, Sat Nov 30, Dec 1 & 2, 1944). Pilot Grove boys won county championship and four PGHS starters (including the author) were chosen County All-stars and have pretty much rested on these laurels ever since. This is the program I mention in the section on the Colemans. This old program was among my souvenirs for over 50 years and looks it. Note that student spelling was no better then than now, e.g., "Loessing", "Eicleberger".

Fig. 6-26. **ABOVE** Blackwater didn't have much of a team but they had terrific uniforms.

Fig. 6-27. **BELOW**. Snack offerings at the 1944 Tourney. Three years of World War II had driven up prices.

MENU

Hamburger	15¢	Pie	10¢
Hot Dogs	10¢	Coffee	5¢
Cheese Sandwich	15¢	Hot Chocolate	5¢
Chili	15¢	Milk	5¢
Cheeseburger	20¢	Egg Sandwich	10¢

Sponsered by the

PTA

of the

PILOT GROVE HIGH SCHOOL

Fig. 6-29. David Brunjes, PGHS Class of '42 and PFC, 5th Marine Div, was awarded the Bronze Star posthumously on Saipan, July 1944.

Fig. 6-30. Bronze Star.

DAVID BRUNJES 1924 - 1944

David Brunjes was the first born and only son of Mr. and Mrs. Gus Brunjes who lived on the southwest corner of Third and Roe in Pilot Grove. The Brunjes came to town in the late 1930s when Mr. Brunjes took up Bob Zahringer's blacksmith shop which I described earlier.

I first met David when we became charter members of the Wolf Patrol, Troop 76 of the Boy Scouts in 1939. David was a Senior in 1942 and a member of the PGHS basketball team see Fig. 6-29. I was a Freshman and trying out for a spot on the team. We freshmen scrimmaged a lot but admittedly weren't all that good. One of my problems (I told Mom) was the lack of a good pair of basketball shoes.

David had an excellent pair of all-leather shoes and when an important game came up for the second stringers, I borrowed them from him. He and I wore the same size 12. (My size 12 feet attracted comment from time to time when the Tatler reporters had space to fill up.)

Our changing room was in a loft above and behind the stage in the gymnasium and it was there, on the floor, that I negligently left David's shoes in my excitement at having actually won on place on the scrub team. The next day, I saw them laying there and started to place them in my locker. Omigosh, what's this? A mouse had eaten two strips from the leather upper. Guiltily, I took them to Mr. Schmidt's shoeshop and he did as good a job as possible in patching them. I apologized profusely to David. I might want to borrow the shoes again unless I could scratch up the $8-10 I needed to buy my own. He just waved it off.

A couple of weeks later, the scrubs had another important game and I again approached David with my hat in my hand. "OK," he said, "But, please remember to put them up in a locker when the game is over!"

You may not believe this but that night the same mouse worked on the same shoes that the same nitwit kid left laying on the same floor. There was another trip to Mr. Schmidt. [Mr. Schmidt was Richard's father. The Schmidts lived on the northwest corner of Fourth and Roe and the shoe shop was next door to Klenklen's Barber Shop.]

This time I handed David's shoes to him sheepishly. He looks at the new patches, one of them on top of an old patch. "Tell you what, Sonny," he says eyeing me closely, "You been wanting a pair of shoes, haven't you?"

"Yes," I answered but I ain't got the money yet."

"How much ya got?"

"About $6.50."

"Sold," he said and held out his hand. I paid up and those were the shoes I wore for basketball the next two years. I was finally sufficiently in the chips to buy a new pair when I was a senior. Since nobody had a foot that size, and since the uppers looked like lace filigree by 1944, I threw the old ones away. David was wearing these shoes in Fig. 6-31 below. This was before the mouse worked on them.

David Brunjes graduated in 1942 and joined the Marines. Two years later—July 1944—he died a hero in the battle for Saipan and was posthumously awarded the Bronze Star Medal.

Here's the letter from his Company Commander:

PILOT GROVE-A letter dated August 10, was sent to Mr. and Mrs. Gus Brunjes whose son, Pfc. David W. Brunjes, was killed in action on Saipan. The letter was written by the officer in charge of the company in which Pfc. Brunjes was serving. Mr. and Mrs. Brunjes, former residents of Pilot Grove, are now residing in Fayette.

The letter states: "Pfc. David: W. Brunjes, Marine, was killed in action June 28, 1944, but I want you to know how he died. Our company was in the attack on the 28th of June.

Fig. 6-31. PGHS Team of '41-'42 BACK ROW L-R: Coach Paine, Robert Jones, Henry Hoff, Glenn Neckerman, Jerome Kempf, Ernie Mellor. FRONT ROW L-R: Enslie Schilb, David Brunjes, Herbie Meyer (Captain), Virgil Eckerle and Richard Schmidt.

Our objective was a ridge about half way up Saipan. We were within 500 yards of this objective, in a jungle area, when we were ambushed. Dave set up his machine gun and commenced firing and continued this fire so as to enable our medical personnel to attend the wounded. He put this gun in action without orders because he knew that he was the only one that could cover those men. He was killed on his gun, a grenade hit the gun and killed him instantly. You lost a fine son and also a hero. He has been recommended for an award for his bravery and the fine job he had done throughout the operation. Every man and officer in A Company considered Dave as their friend. He was a fine marine in camp and in combat. He gave his life to protect his buddies, no man could do more."

David graduated from Pilot Grove High School in 1942. He enlisted in the Marines August 20, 1943 and went to the South Pacific in January 1944. His last letter was received by his parents May 3.

David was born in Tipton, May 13, 1924, and besides his parents, he is survived by three sisters, Marceline, Vita May and Martha Belle.

"DRAMATIS PERSONAE"

Casting for the annual Junior and Senior plays was not an onerous task for the class sponsor. Since classes were only about 25-30 in number, nearly everyone who cared to got a shot at one play or the other. Most everyone who had a role remembers it with some nostalgia. It was great fun—after the performance was "in the can".

I was in three—both Junior and Senior plays in the Spring of 1944 and my own Senior play in 1945 and I can report that—as an unusually shy fellow—I suffered a thousand deaths in rehearsals and the final performance but when we took our final bows, I was euphoric!

THE ACCIDENTAL STAR

I was honored with a role in our 1944 Junior Class play and also, as an emergency substitute, lent my talents to "O, Promise Me", the *Senior* Class play of that spring. Here's how this came to pass: The Seniors were in evening practice at the auditorium in the run-up to their presentation. Some members of the cast, Vern Klenklen, and certain other unnamed[3] co-conspirators got the idea that a jug of wine would go down real well before this practice. They reasoned that a quart of the magic elixir of Bardenheier's Burgundy would relieve the tension, clear the tonsils and generally convert school boys into silver tongued superstars.

The funds required (45¢) were assembled and Vern was sent for this 'mood mellowing mixture'. Ummie Kimberling, who had been instrumental in similar past situations, agreed to get a bottle from Ikey Schweitzer's Liquor Store and the conspirators were soon set for the evening of play rehearsal.

THE JUNIOR CLASS OF 1941-1942 PRESENTS

MAMA'S BABY BOY!

THE CRITICS SAY—

PILOT GROVE STAR Oct 30, 1941
The Junior play, "Mama's Baby Boy", presented at the high school auditorium Tuesday night October 28, drew a very large audience that filled both the chairs and bleachers. A considerable sum, approximately 70 dollars was taken in. The play seemed to be well enjoyed by all. Each character played their part very well. The following Juniors were in the play: Mary Elizabeth Cordry, Glenn Neckerman, Junior Mellor, Gladys Prewitt, Erma Vonderahe, Jerome Kemp, Thelma Frederick, Esther Meisenheimer, Sarah Eichelberger, Enslie Schilb and Betty Waller. Irene Gerke was prompter.

[3] That is, *unnamed by me.* I regard the incident as a youthful indiscretion but recognize those involved may hold it more serious—thus, though a half century in the past—I shall draw the gentle curtain of anonymity and spare more embarrassment.

- CAST -

Mrs. McLean.................................Mary E. Cordry
Shepherd McLean........................Ernest Mellor Jr.
Luther Long.................................Glen Neckerman
Juliet Long...................................Gladys Prewitt
Mrs. Blackburn............................Erma Vonderahe
Wilbur Warren.............................Jerome Kempf
Sylvia Kline.................................Thelma Frederick
Mrs. Anglin.................................Sarah Eichelberger
Max Moore..................................Enslie Schilb
Minnie...Betty Waller

Irene Gerke - Prompter
Miss Vinyard - Sponsor

SCENES

The entire action of the play takes place in the living room of Mrs. McLean's home in Fort Wayne, Indiana.

Act I - An afternoon

Act II - A little later in the same day

Act III - Still a little later in the same day

SPECIALTIES

Sunbonnet Sally & Overall Jim - Sally Hunt & Linda Heinrich
Soap..........................- Billy Hoff
Orchestra.....................- Mr. Morton, Director

Unfortunately, while the Bardenheier's probably did have some positive effect in lubricating tongues, it also had other, less desirable effects. In the spirit of the "Government Warning" required on all liquor containers, it would have been better if the Bardenheier's had one that said:

GOVERNMENT WARNING.

The Surgeon General has determined that school boys chugging down this wine run a serious risk of making asses of themselves!

Because that's what happened. The faculty advisor and drama coach was Miss Eager, a shapely redhead of 30-something. The two unnamed co-conspirators, under the influence of the grape, made a pass at her. She resisted and slapped one. They scattered with her in pursuit. Running through the folding chairs, they tossed some into her path. The tactic was successful, Miss Eager came to grief among the chairs.

She was not hurt, but E.M. McKee, the Superintendent, had all concerned in his office the next morning and the two boys were ejected from PGHS forthwith.

Fig. 6-32. Both LaVahn and twin LeVern Klenklen had roles in the Senior Play of 1944. Photo—Margie Schmidt

Having had no part in the amorous advances, Vern Klenklen came out unscathed. However, there was a period of several weeks in which he sweated blood. If anyone seriously investigated the source of the liquor he might be faced with an even more serious charge. During this time Ummie begged several times, "Don't rat on me, Vern!" In the end Vern and Ummie lucked out and nothing further came of the incident. But, that is how I came to be in both the Junior and the Senior plays in the spring of 1944!

In the aftermath, Vern lost any interest he may have had in a stage career and after a tour of Belgium and France courtesy of Uncle Sam, settled down to the barbering profession in Kansas City. In October 1997 he celebrated 50 years as a clip artist at his 39th Street shop and was duly celebrated by the Kansas City Star, Kansas City Live! and Hallmark See Fig. 6-34 next page.

Fig 6-33. Miss Margaret Eager had the task of Drama Coach for the Senior Class play 1944. Photo—Janie Goehner.

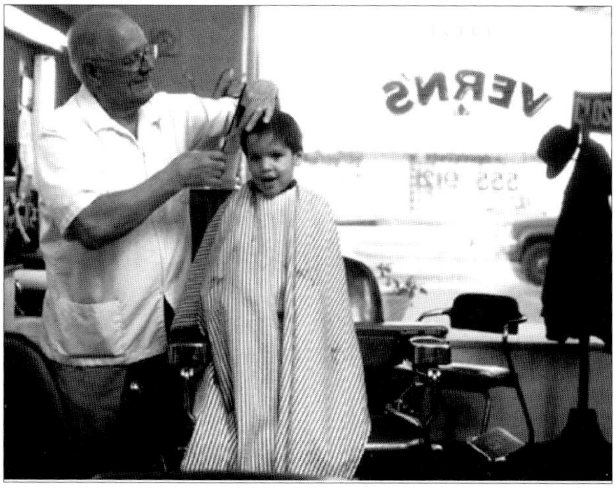

Fig. 6-34. **A CUT ABOVE**. Barber Vern Klenklen has given a lot of haircuts since 1948. He was 22 when he began trimming hair, bought his three-chair in 1953. He charges a bit more for haircuts now than when he started: from 75¢ to $8. Vern has help: daughter, Nanette has taken up the scissors. Photo - Hallmark Cards.

Vern says that insurance men have approached him over the years nagging him to set up a retirement plan. After hearing out their Plan A, Plan B, etc. he told one, "I think I am going to have to opt for Plan C!"

"And what exactly would that be?" the salesman asked.

Vern answered, "Drop dead behind the barber chair!"

"MISS HONEY"

A more formal form of address for"Miss Honey" was Mrs. A.R. Warnhoff. She born Ellen Elizabeth Gibson and came to her marriage just after WWI already wearing the nickname "Honey". She was the wife of "Bob" Warnhoff, the 'diplomat' of the Warnhoff Bros trio. After Bob passed away in 1943, she mourned a few months then renewed her dedication to the PGHS dramatic and musical productions, particularly the Junior and Senior plays.

Miss Honey had a dynamic personality. She was in her 60s and a very talented 'natural' in drama and theater. She directed a large portion of the plays presented by PGHS thespians in the 30s and 40s. She directed the two plays I was in the Spring of 1944 and our Senior play in 1945. When I returned to Pilot Grove on military leave in the fall of 1945, I ran into her at Deck's and we went on about our plays.

Miss Honey was also an accomplished choreographer. Janie (Brownfield) Goehner tells how she, as a pre-schooler, nagged her parents to distraction for tap dancing lessons. "The deal was struck," Janie said, "When I offered to give up all ice cream money for the summer in return for weekly tap lessons with Miss Honey. She had a small class and gave the lessons in her home. The class consisted of Barbara Coleman, Patty Schilb, Mildred Schlotzhauer, Virginia Boley, Marion McCutcheon and myself. Lessons were 25¢ each. Miss Honey would also let us go through her trunks of clothes

THE JUNIOR CLASS OF 1944-1945 PRESENTS

SO HELP ME HANNAH!

Johnston's Paint-Wallpaper-Glass Boonville, Missouri	Standard Drugs Boonville, Mo.
Gamble Store Boonville, Mo	Heinrichs Drug The Rexal Store

PLAY CAST

Mrs. Bascombe..........A Harassed Mother......Janie Brownfield
Willie Bascombe........Her Ambitious Son...........Harold Ries
Joan...................The only daughter..........Patty Schilb
Willie ....The Whisper..........Grovenor Windsor
Annie ....The cook...............Betty Kramel
Freddie Baldwin.......A young man in lov.........Bobby Twenter
Claudette..................A neighbor..........Lillian Lammers
Mabel....................Country cousin.........Barbara Coleman
Hannah Waters...........Willie's fiance..........Marjorie Hoff
Mrs. Van Astor..........A social light..............Doris Hurt
Deanna Van Astor..........Her daughter.......Mildred Schlotzhauer
Officer...................A policeman.........Clarence Bergman
Sergeant Devine...........A Detective...........Albert Imhoff
George.....................A milkman..............Wilbur Lammers
Lula Bell Cinders.........A negro maid..........Mary L. Gerling
Director..................................Mrs. A. R. Warnhoff
I. Story Book Characters ....Intermediate Room
II. Girls Quartet ....Little Bluebird 2. Old King Cole
Girls Trio...................................Don't Fence Me In

Spic & Span Cleaners Boonville, Mo	O. B. Franz Phone 180 Poultry Co.
Compliments of Frank Fable Attorney-at-Law	Clem Twenter Trucking Phone

Fig. 6-35. Cast of the 1945 Junior Class Play — "So Help Me Hannah". It is likely that Doris Hurt was a "Socialite" and not a "Social Light" as indicated.

and props she used for plays she directed. Miss Honey had great dramatic talent. For our senior play she wrote in parts for Betty Kramel and me. We were old maid twin sisters and did everything in unison. But, it was the tap dancing that nearly led Marion and I to disaster.'

Fig. 6-36. Mildred Schlotzhauer (left) and Patty Schilb were graduates of Miss Honey and Miss Vinyard's tap dancing classes. Photo—Janie G.

Fig. 6-37. Janie Brownfield (left) and Marion McCutcheon about the time of the Shoemaker Disaster. Photos—Janie Brownfield Goehner.

DISASTER AT THE SHOEMAKERS

Janie continues, "Now that they were in Junior High, the tap dancers were in the advanced tap dance class taught during the lunch hour by Miss Vinyard, a high school teacher (English etc).

"One windy March day in 1942, Miss Vinyard asked Marion and me to take all the dancing shoes to Mr. Schmidt's (the shoe shop was a couple of doors north of Pop Tracy's Cafe) to have toe plates affixed.

"When we arrived at Mr. Schmidt's shoe shop, the door was locked and a sign said — Out to Lunch. Since it was already well past noon, we reckoned we might as well wait for him to return.

"We stood on the sidewalk before the shop, gossiping and discussing the tap classes. Suddenly, a strong gust of wind pushed Marion off balance and she fell against the large plate glass window. It broke and came crashing down with large shards falling on the sidewalk. Some pieces were the size of guillotine blades and just as dangerous. We were in shock. We didn't know whether we were hurt or not.

"Miraculously, neither Marion nor I were hurt. My uncle, Ikey Schweitzer, ran the Dixcel station across the street and had witnessed the whole thing. He came running over to see if we were okay. Assured that we were, he recommended that we immediately walk down to the Schmidt's and tell him what happened. The Schmidt's lived on the northwest corner of Fourth and Roe.

"Mr. Schmidt went into orbit. He screamed at us and was so angry he called Marion's folks and demanded they pay for the window. They did.

"Marion and I were so upset, we walked back to Uncle Ikey's and he told us to go to my home. He called Mom and explained what had happened and that when he started his school bus route, he would pick up Marion there. Mom got us into the kitchen and busy making fudge to try to get us settled down. It worked, but I'll never forget the incident.

"When Marion visited for her Aunt Mary Burger's 100th birthday celebration in 1995, I mentioned this. She said, 'I've never been so scared in my life. I'll never forget it.'"

Richard "Dickie" Schmidt, the Schmidt's only child, had transferred into PGHS at the Sophomore level when his family moved to town. He graduated in 1942 and, like so many of his cohorts, went off to war. In a reunion letter he told of his service in the Americal Division (the only unnumbered Army Infantry division) in the south Pacific. I know he was pleased to learn in 1991 that General Colin Powell is a fellow-alumnus of the Americal.

Fig. 6-38. "Dickie" Schmidt, the shoemaker's son - 1944. Grad Photo.

THE PROMPTERS

Ralph Esser loaned me his scrapbook which included the play bill for "For Pete's Sake". This flyer, like most everything in his scrapbook was in unusually good condition, protected in most cases by glassine sleeves. This says something about Ralph and his school experiences. It appears that he was a 'happy camper'.

Irene Felten sent me most of these play bills. In reviewing them, I noted she was often the Prompter but not in the play. I thought, "This is odd. Irene was a most attractive young woman and she certainly was up to memorizing the lines."

Then it struck me. The most important person in the *actual presentation* of a high school play is THE PROMPTER! If I were the director or play sponsor, knowing the competency and stage-fright vulnerability of most high school students, I would sweat blood unless I had the most competent person available in that job. From my memory as well as the opinions of others, Irene was that person.

Fig. 6-39. Charles Curry Brownfield. I think he had seen too many Jeeves and Bertie Wooster movies. Photo—Janie Brownfield Goehner.

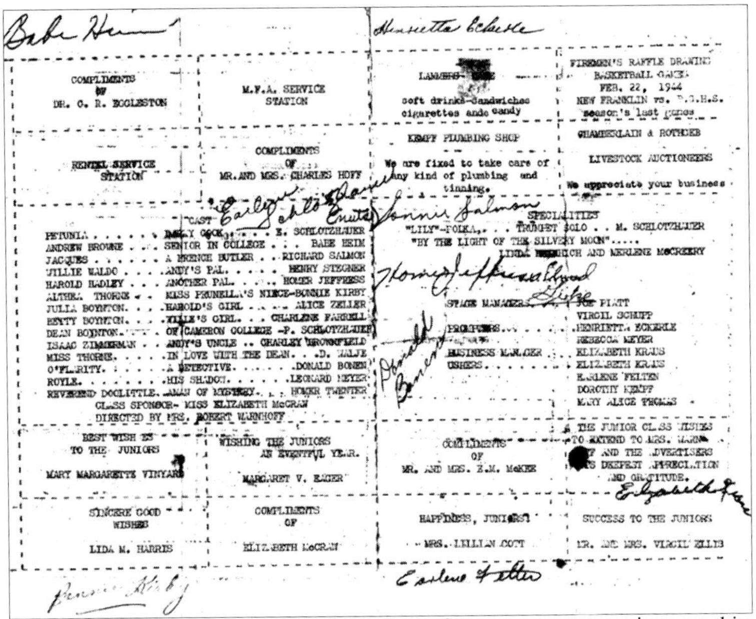

COMPLIMENTS OF DR. C. R. EGGLESTON

M.F.A. SERVICE STATION

LAMMERS-

soft drinks-sandwiches cigarettes and candy

FIREMEN'S RAFFLE DRAWING BASKETBALL GAME FEB. 22, 1944 NEW FRANKLIN vs. P.G.H.S. season's last games

SERVICE STATION

COMPLIMENTS OF MR. AND MRS. CHARLES HOFF

KEMPF PLUMBING SHOP

We are fixed to take care of any kind of plumbing and tinning.

CHAMBERLAIN & ROTHER LIVESTOCK AUCTIONEERS

We appreciate your business

CAST

PETUNIA	DARKY COOK	E. SCHLOTZHAUER
ANDREW BROWNE	SENIOR IN COLLEGE	BABE HEIM
JACQUES	A FRENCH BUTLER	RICHARD SALMON
WILLIE WALDO	ANDY'S PAL	HENRY STEGNER
HAROLD HADLEY	ANOTHER PAL	HOMER JEFFRESS
ALTHEA THORNE	MISS PRUNELLA'S NIECE	BONNIE KIRBY
JULIA BOYNTON	HAROLD'S GIRL	ALICE ZELLER
BETTY BOYNTON	WILLIE'S GIRL	CHARLENE FARRELL
DEAN BOYNTON	OF CAMERON COLLEGE	P. SCHLOTZHAUER
ISAAC ZIMMERMAN	ANDY'S UNCLE	CHARLEY BROWNFIELD
MISS THORNE	IN LOVE WITH THE DEAN	D. WALJE
O'FLARITY	A DETECTIVE	DONALD BONEN
ROYLE	HIS SHADOW	LEONARD MEYER
REVEREND DOOLITTLE	A MAN OF MYSTERY	HOMER TWENTER

CLASS SPONSOR- MISS ELIZABETH McCRAW

DIRECTED BY MRS. ROBERT WARNHOFF

SPECIALITIES

"LILY"-POLKA. . . TRUMPET SOLO . . M. SCHLOTZHAUER

"BY THE LIGHT OF THE SILVERY MOON"..... LINDA ICH AND MERLENE McCREERY

STAGE MANAGERS . . . . JOE PLATT, VIRGIL SCHUPP

PROMPTERS . . . . HENRIETTA ECKERLE, REBECCA MEYER

BUSINESS MANAGER . . . ELIZABETH KRAUS

USHERS . . . . ELIZABETH KRAUS, EARLENE FELTEN, DOROTHY KEMPF, MARY ALICE THOMAS

BEST WISHES TO THE JUNIORS MARY MARGARETTE VINYARD

WISHING THE JUNIORS AN EVENTFUL YEAR. MARGARET V. EAGER

COMPLIMENTS OF MR. AND MRS. E.M. McKEE

THE JUNIOR CLASS WISHES TO EXTEND TO MRS. WARNHOFF AND THE ADVERTISERS ITS DEEPEST APPRECIATION AND GRATITUDE.

SINCERE GOOD WISHES LIDA M. HARRIS

COMPLIMENTS OF ELIZABETH McCRAW

HAPPINESS, JUNIORS! MRS. LILLIAN COTT

SUCCESS TO THE JUNIORS MR. AND MRS. VIRGIL ELLIS

Fig. 6-40. The drama critic of the Pilot Grove Star gave us rave reviews on this three act farce. Charley Brownfield was the unreconstructed, unhousebroken, tobacco chewing uncle who juggled the several romances in the play. He, Homer Jeffress and Henry Stegner (see photo below) carried off some scenes in women's clothing that were particularly hilarious. Earlene S. and I conducted a running battle while impersonating an 'Aunt Jemima-like' cook and a French butler.

Fig. 6-41. Homer Jeffress (left) and Henry Stegner dressed for their roles in the 1944 Junior play, "Antics of Andrew". In one of Charley B.s female dress scenes, his mother whispered to Dee, "Who is that cute little girl?" Dee answered, "Mary! That's your son!" Photo—Marie Jeffress.

THE CRITICS SAY—

[Article in the Pilot Grove Star, March 1945.]

JUNIOR PLAY

The junior class presented a play, the "Antics of Andrew" before a large and enthusiastic audience Friday evening [Mar 13th]. This was one of the best plays to be presented in Pilot Grove in recent years. Every character was a star and together they formed a galaxy rarely found in a high school play.

The antics of Young Andrew, Babe Heim, and his two college chums, Homer Jeffress and Henry Stegner, kept the audience in an uproar of laughter from beginning to the end of the performance. The French butler, was exceptionally well played by the school's brilliant impersonator, Sonny Salmon, while the fault-finding darky cook, Earlene Schlotzhauer, kept him in constant trouble. Dean of the college, Paul Schlotzhauer and his girl friend Miss Purnella Thorn, played by Dorothy Walje, formed a romantic team which provoked much fun. Uncle Isaac, Charley Brownfield, was a leading master of ceremonies and promoted the romances throughout the play.

Miss Elizabeth McCraw is the sponsor of the junior class and Mrs. A. R. Warnhoff was the capable director of the play, The class, the sponsor and Mrs. Warnhoff are certainly to be complimented.

Casting "For Pete's Sake" required much of the class of 1940. To attach a face to the names of these super-star thespians, see above. Class photo from Les Chamberlain.

L-R Charlene Farrel, Gertrude Kraus, Jo Ellen Coley. Mr. Morton's Trio sang "Three Little Maids from School" 1941.
Photo - Trudy (Kraus) Knight.

(Below) "For Pete's Sake was presented again as the 1945 Senior Class Play.

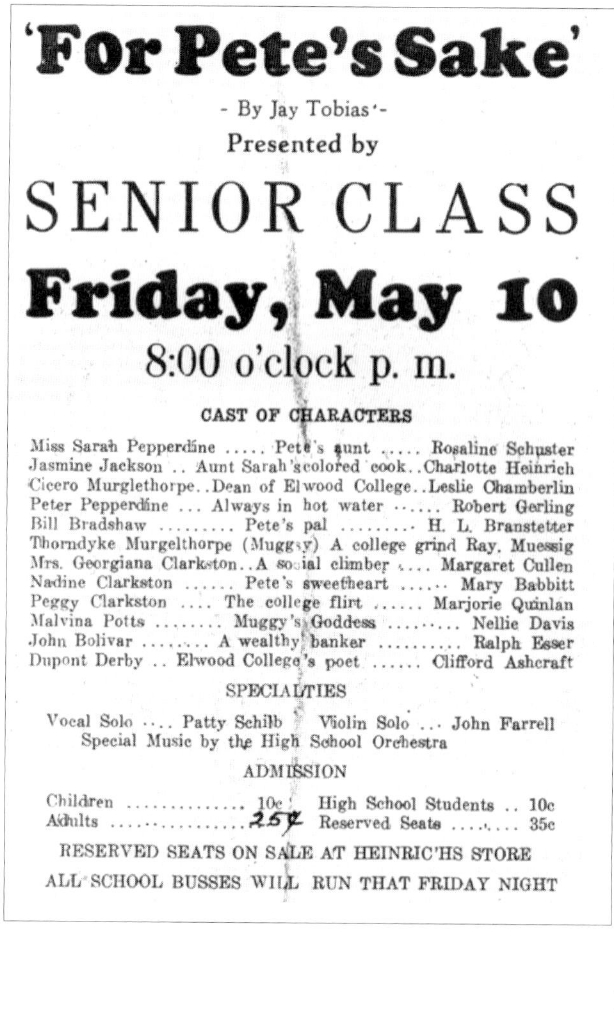

'For Pete's Sake'

- By Jay Tobias -

Presented by

SENIOR CLASS

Friday, May 10

8:00 o'clock p. m.

CAST OF CHARACTERS

Miss Sarah Pepperdine ..... Pete's aunt ..... Rosaline Schuster
Jasmine Jackson .. Aunt Sarah's colored cook .. Charlotte Heinrich
Cicero Murglethorpe .. Dean of Elwood College .. Leslie Chamberlin
Peter Pepperdine ... Always in hot water ...... Robert Gerling
Bill Bradshaw .... Pete's pal .... H. L. Branstetter
Thorndyke Murgelthorpe (Muggsy) A college grind Ray. Muessig
Mrs. Georgiana Clarkston .. A social climber ..... Margaret Cullen
Nadine Clarkston ...... Pete's sweetheart ...... Mary Babbitt
Peggy Clarkston .... The college flirt ...... Marjorie Quinlan
Malvina Potts .... Muggy's Goddess .... Nellie Davis
John Bolivar .... A wealthy banker .... Ralph Esser
Dupont Derby .. Elwood College's poet ...... Clifford Ashcraft

SPECIALTIES

Vocal Solo .... Patty Schilb Violin Solo ... John Farrell
Special Music by the High School Orchestra

ADMISSION

Children .... 10c High School Students .. 10c
Adults .... 25¢ Reserved Seats 35c

RESERVED SEATS ON SALE AT HEINRIC'HS STORE

ALL SCHOOL BUSSES WILL RUN THAT FRIDAY NIGHT

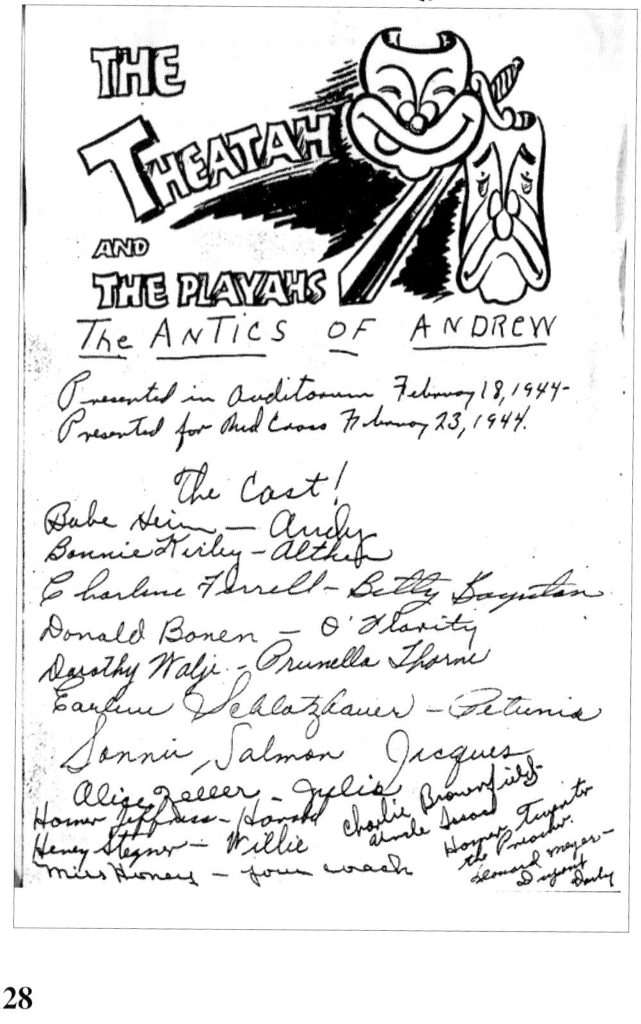

SENIOR CLASS PLAY

"pleased ta meetcha"

A MYSTERY COMEDY
MARCH 5, 1943

CHARACTERS

Martha Bixby, Mother ---------------------- Mary E. Cordry
Henry Bixby, Father ------------------------------ J. L. Babbitt
Patty Bixby, Daughter ---------------------- Jeanne Chappes
Binks, Butler ------------------------------------- Estil Loesing
Marie, Maid ------------------------------------- Betty Waller
Elmer Hicks, Fresh From The Country ----- Jerome Kempf
Seevy, Detective ------------------------------- Jakie Bergman
Archie, Betty's Boy Friend ------------------- Roger Twenter
Andrew Grimes, A Fraud --------------------- Leroy Stegner
Helen Maxwell, Girl Friend ---------------------- Ruby Ratje
Ruth Adams, Girl Friend ----------------- Thelma Frederick
Howard Willis, Boy Friend ---------------------- Babe Heim

TIME: The Present
Place: Living room of Bixby's house.

Prompter: Irene Gerke
Lighting Effects: Cleo Ratje
Ushers: Sarah Eichelberger
Esther Meisenheimer
Irene Gerke
Mary K. Ries

Fig. 6-42. Jerome Kempf. Six months after his "Elmer Hicks" role in "Pleased ta Meetcha"—the U.S. Navy said, "Pleased to Meetcha, Jerome!" Photo—LaVahn Klenklen Brown.

SPECIALITIES

ACT I— "My Heroes"
Soloist: Linda Lee Heinrich
Soldiers: Bobby McCreery
Glen Schlotzhauer
Homer L. Babbitt
Billy Godsay
John Allen Heinrich

ACT II.— "A Musical Romance"
Reader: Virginia Boley
Chorus: Mary E. Weekley
Sarah Eichelberger
Margie Burger
Doris Quinlan
Bonnie Klenklen
Rebecca Meyer
Patty Schilb
Esther Meisenheimer
Mildred Schlotzhauer
Charlene Farrell
Earlene Schlotzhauer
Mary M. Muessig

Solos: "Sylvia" Charlene Farrell
"I Love You Truly" Patty Schilb

Violin: Miss Eager
Piano: Miss Vinyard

High School Orchestra
Director: Miss Eager

Fig. 6-43. Mr. Morton's Opus — Margie Burger says, "Maestro Morton's magic turned our squeaks and screeches into sweet symphonies and made magnificent musical memories." Photo—Margie Burger Schmidt.

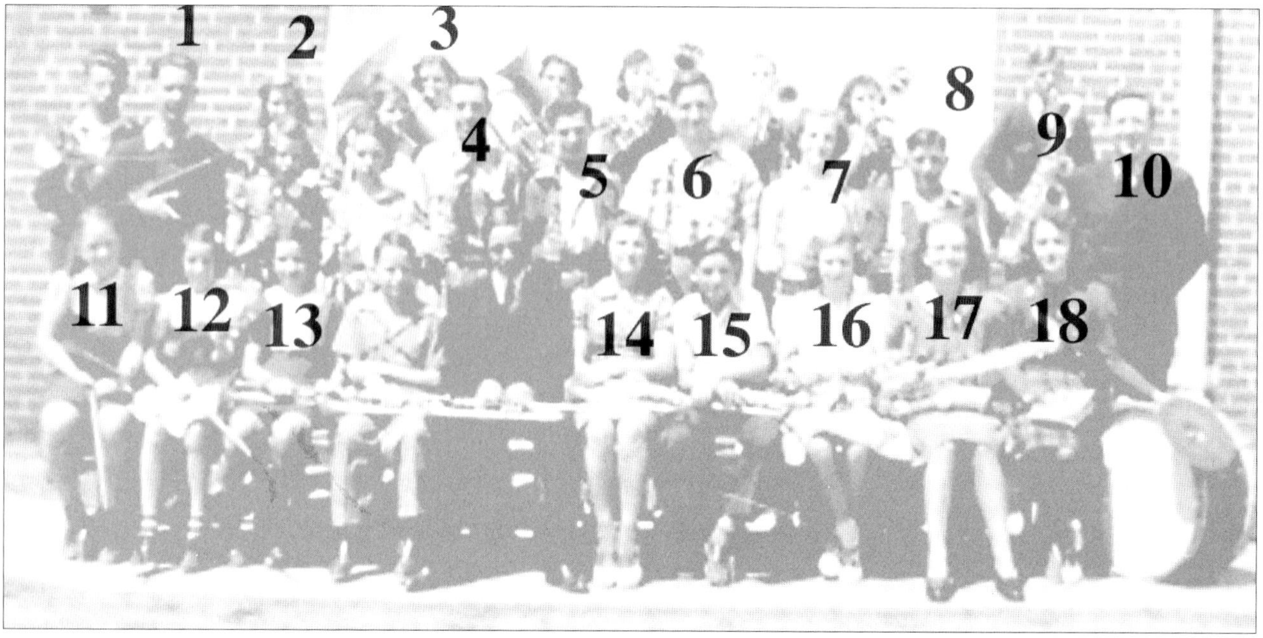

1-John Farrell, 2-Dorothy McCutcheon, 3-Betty Judy, 4-Clarence Ries, 5-Junior Mellor, 6-Enslie Schilb, 7-Marjorie Burger, 8-Joe Lee Caton, 9-Glenn Neckerman, 10-Byron Morton (Dir), 11-Patty Schilb, 12-Virginia Boley, 13-Mildred Schlotzhauer, 14-Edna Grace Davis, 16-Esther Meisenheimer, 17-Jane Wolfe, 18-Jo Ellen Coley, Also, I believe Marion McCutcheon, Marjorie Babbitt, Robert Jones, Juanita Jones, David Schlotzhauer, and David Brunjes are in the photo.

CASTE

Henry Dodge	Carl Day (a leading Citizen)
Betty	Jeanette Lammers (his sister)
Josephine	Carol Coleman (his wife)
Jane	Carol Rae Schlotzhauer (his cousin)
Samuel	Lowell Schlotzhauer (his butler)
Mrs. Wiggins	Mary Lou Burger (his Mother-in-law)
Alfred Dukes	James Robinett (who lives next door)
Geranium	Helen Bergman (the cook)
Matilda Tucker	Esther Walje of the Mayfield Purity League)
Philip McGrath	David Mellor (himself)
Spasm Johnson	Jack Poindexter (his servant)
Mr. Sylvester Scraggs	Sonny Heim (a neighbor)
Elmira Scraggs	Kathryn Winkler (his wife)
Napoleon Nettlerush	Banty Rooster

The Senior Class

presents

"Phillip for Short"

A Farce — Directed by Mrs. A. R. Warnhoff

Pilot Grove High School Auditorium

8 p. m. — April 29

SYNOPSIS

Henry Dodge, a young business man and reformer and the leading citizen of the small town of Mayfield, finds himself really involved when he hears that his sister, Betty has gone to Yellow Stone National Park unchaperoned and has become interested in a guide there. Then things really start poping when he discovers a fighting chicken right in his own house. Complications develop fast and faster, but all is well that ends well!

Specialty between Acts!

Fig. 6-44 His Honor, Charley "Magook" Brownfield, 1945.

CHARLEY "MAGOOK" AND THE MASSACRE OF THE ENGLISH LANGUAGE

If murdering the English language was a statutory crime during our PGHS school days, Charley "Magook" Brownfield and I could be indicted on charges of manslaughter at the very least. I only tell this story now in the sure knowledge that the statute of limitations has long since run out. Forgive me for finking, Charley! For some examples, see Magookspeak Glossary next page.

MAGOOK'S GLOSSARY

Magookspeak	Meaning
ARSH	Pertaining to the nation or people of Areland (country off coast of Whales).
BOB WAR	Fencing material with sharp barbs.
BUTTER	Ought to, as "The tardy bell has rung, we **butter** go in!"
CALVARY	Horse mounted army unit, ex: Custard's 7th **Calvary**
CHEER	A piece of furniture, as in "pull up a **cheer** and sit a spell."
CHEER	In this place, as in "set that six-pack rat **cheer**."
CUSTARD	Colonel commanding the 7th Calvary at **Custard's** last stand.
ET	Past tense of the verb to eat. Ex. I done **et** my supper.
EYETALIAN	Native of It'ly.
FAMBLY	A collection of kin, ex: "...we're having a **fambly** reunion."
FAR	Combustion of a flammable material, ex. "Let's build a **far** and warm up."
FRAINCH	Pertaining to or native of France, as in **Frainch** fries.
HARD	County north of Boonville, e.g., "Fayette is in **Hard** County."
HARD	Employed, ex: "...we **hard** two new guys today."
IT'LY	Country dangling down into the medarainean sea.
LIBERRY	Pron: lie´ berry. Repository for books.
MESSICANS	Our neighbors south of the Rio Grande.
MOTORSACKLE	Two wheel conveyance, a motorized bysickle.
NEW-BRASKA	A state north of Kansas.
NEW-VADA	A state bordering California.
OINKMENT	A medicating salve as in "cloverine **oinkment**."
ONCET	One time only, ex: "...in life you only go around **oncet**."
ONDIAN	A spicy vegetable good sliced on hamburgers.
RAT	Correct, ex: "Yer **rat** about that Jody."
RAT	Immediately, as in "...get yer butt in here **rat** now!"
SAMMICH	Two pieces of bread with meat between. (Or jelly or butter.)
SILVER WAR	Conflict between North and South 1861-1865.
SOUR-DEANS	Tiny fish tightly packed into small cans.
TAR	Pneumatic tube for a wheel, ex: "I gotta get a new **tar** for my pickup."
TATER	Vegetable tuber loved by all Arshmen.
TWICET	Two times, ex: "I done been to St. Louis **twicet**."
WAR	A metallic strand, as in bob **war** fence.
WARSH	To clean. Pronounced as though spelled with 3-4 r's, e.g., **Warrrsh**.
WARTER	The liquid H_2O. Also pronounced **warder**.
WRAINCH	A tool for turning nuts and bolts.
WRENCH	To warsh lightly or dip into warter, e.g., **"Wrench** yer hands afore meals!"

VO-AG AND HOME EC ACTIVITIES

I made some critical remarks about the VO-AG teacher, Mr. Maurice W. Shier in this work. When I was a sophomore, he collided with me and drove my face into the tile wall under the goal. I shattered the gold inlay that Dr. Schilb had used to repair my two front teeth.

That accident was probably the 10th collision with that tile wall under the goal, so some brilliant school administrator got the idea that a collision mat might be a good idea and would save any number of teeth. However, about two weeks after Dr. Schilb had repaired by dental work, Shier did it again. We were scrimmaging under the goal and his left elbow drove Dr. Schilb's prize work into my tonsils.

But, to show that I harbor no grudges, I'll say something good about this outstanding teacher. I don't know if Shier was the first Vo-Ag teacher in PGHS, but he probably was the best. He loved his work and tirelessly assisted his students.The articles on this page attest to that.

He was an avid farmer. Though I was a townie with no such ambitions, he continually offered me opportunities. He once had a giant tomato patch in the southeast quadrant of the town and hired me to help tend these plants. He dreamed of a tomato processing plant in Pilot Grove. This never happened but not due to his lack of trying. My gang cut and shocked corn for him one crisp October Saturday.

He gave me enough of an insight into farming that I knew that it was not for me—but I did gain great respect for those hardworking folks who followed this calling.

He had two children of whom he was extraordinarily proud. His continuous talking about them earned him the nickname "Papa" Shier. They lived down the alley from us (southwest corner of Third and Roe) and I often saw the two

Fig. 6-45. Lamb show Pilot Grove 1939. Contestants RIGHT TO LEFT: 1,2 Unknown, 3 Ferdie Meyer, 4 Unknown, 5 Cletus Felten, 6 Clemus Felten, 7 Gene Schlotzhauer, 8,9 Unknown, 10 Herman Meisenheimer. Photo—Irene Gerke Felten.

PILOT GROVE STAR 1943—

Shown here with their instructor, M. W Shier (in foregromd) are twenty-one Pilot Grove ligh school graduates who are putting their agricultural training to good use on farms in the Pilot Grove area. They are. left to right front row: Herbert Gerke, Marshal Haley, Glen Harold Eichhorn, Roger Twenter and Adolph Gramlich Second row: Marvin Schupp, Clarence Loesing, LeRoy Stegner, Herman Meisenheimer and Clarence Ries. Third row: William Lee Kramel, Silas Wessing, Wilfred Gerke, Ralph Esser, and Cletus Felton Fourth row: Kenneth Tally, Jimmy Lorenz, Kenneth Young, Clemus Felton, Kenneth Kempf and Ralph Felton. Clipping—Ralph Esser.

PILOT GROVE STAR 1941—

John Gerke of the farm four miles west of Pilot Grove in September 1941, started a purebred Hereford herd and today has four registered cvows, a registered bull and four registered calves. Shown above with the herd are, left to right, John Gerke; M.W. Shier, Pilot Grove vocational agriculture teacher who has worked with the Gerke youths in high school and the Gerke sons, Norman, Wilfred and Elwood. Clipping—Irene Gerke Felten.

children. I remember them when they were 3-5 years old and they were indeed healthy and handsome kids.

Mr. Shier was a good man, a splendid role model and dedicated to agriculture and the teaching of agriculture. He's gone now but all those who came into contact with him will never forget him.

Fig. 6-46. HERBIE'S HOGS

PILOT GROVE STAR 1939—Herbert Gerke of Pilot Grove, is one of two vocational agriculture students who, developed a Spotted Poland program that clicked. Gerke is shown hero, With his 5-year-old purebred, which with that of Marshall Haley was start,of purebred Spotted Polands in the Pilot Grove area.

In the fall of 1938, two Vocational agriculture students, Marshall Haley and Herbert Gerke, of the Pilot Grove high school decided to start a purebred hog project. These boys were in their Sophomore and Junior years in high school.

They chose two purebred Spotted Poland gilts from the Neal brothers herd at Otterville,, These gilts were bred to a purebred boar named Pilot, owned by Charles Hoff of Pilot Grove. This boar was from a vocational agriculture student's project at Higginsville, Mo.

Since the beginning of these projects each sow has farrowed 9 litters and 154 pigs have been saved and raised to maturity, all being purebred Spotted Polands. Of that number 26 have been kept for breeders, part of them on the home farmers, the rest being sold. Some other farmers having stock of this breeding are John D. Meyer, B. J. and Ralph Esser, Charles Hoff, Walter Kraus, Leo Bonen, LeRoy Stegner, Lawrence Gerke, and Robert Gerke.

Proof that these hogs are the kind farmers like and stay with is not only borne out by the foregoing but is also proven by the market show records made by these hogs at the national stock yards vocational agriculture fat hog show. For instance the Pilot Grove boys took 6 of the 10 prizes offered in the litter class for Spotted Poland last September.

Both Herbert and Marshall are increasing the blood line of this family on their respective farms by keeping back their outstanding six or more yearling gilts in their yards now. Both are purebred boars. These boys have not emphasized animals for breeding but rather raising animals for market. Each of the original sows, which are now 5 years old, are still on the home farms and doing well. (Clipping from Irene Gerke Felten)

PASS THE PORK CHOPS!

[Ralph Esser saved this souvenir of a momentous evening—an excerpt from The Pilot Grove Star, Spring of 1939. Pilot Grove's CCC Camp—where I hung out to mooch cokes, watch movies on Saturday nights, learned to shoot craps and play poker—also hosted FFA Banquets! I do declare! Note that Mr. Jones, publisher, editor, reporter, typesetter, printer and distributor of the Star seemed to dwell a lot on the menu—possibly a phenomenon of the times—the "hungry 30s".]

MANY ATTEND FATHER AND SON BANQUET

CCC Camp Was Setting Of Gathering Monday Night - Third Such Affair

More than ninety men and boys attended the third annual Future Farmer Father and Son banquet at the CCC Camp here Monday night. besides members of the local FFA classes, their fathers or other relatives, and several other guests were present two of whom made a very fine address.

A very fine menu was prepared by the cooks at the Camp, to which all did ample justice. It consisted of: Breaded pork chops, brown gravy, mashed potatoes, lettuce salad, buttered peas, mixed pickles, celery, bread and butter, tomato juice, orangeade and cherry pie with whipped cream.

Following the banquet, Lieutenant W.W. Bodus and C R Cross of the camp, members of The Board of Educaton a few special guests, and the father and sons were introduced, Charlie Callison, edition of Boonville Advertiser, Robert Kaye, Assistant County Agent, and H L 'Puny' Barrett. Vocational Agriculture Instructor of Boonville were present, the latter two being on the program.

Mr Kaye announced two very important farm programs for the very near future. Tuesday, May 21, will see two barley meets. First on the Bruno Loesing farm in the morning and the Victor Klenklen farm in the aftenoon. The next, or Wednesday May 22, fertilizer demonstrations will be held on The Morton Tuttle Farm near Prairie Home and the Edgar George farm.

Morton Tuttle, farmer of Prairie Home, then took the floor to tell of his experience as a farmer. His talk was along the subject of soil conservation. During his discussion he urged the farmers to raise Atlas Sargo, a very profitable crop very well suited to this community. He also very highly recommended terracing, as well as the use of lime.

These boys were present: Gilbert Bauer, Leslie Chamberlain, Glen Eichorn, Ralph Esser, Cletus Felten, Ralph Felton, Herbert Gerke, Marshall Haley, Louis Larm, Clarence Loesing, Herman Meisenheimer, Marvin Schupp, William Cullen, Clemus Felton, Adolph Gramlich, John Hoff, Harold Kempf, Gerald Larm, Clarence Ries, Gilbert Schupp, John Earl Young, Kenneth Young, Ferdinand Meyer, Wilfred Gerke, Jerome Kempf, Estil Loesing, James Lorenz, Raymond Schneck, Roger Twenter, Syl Twenter and Bill Todd. Clipping from Ralph Esser.

HOME EC GIRLS

The Boonville Daily News article (page at right) serves as an epilogue for thc Home Ec girls of PGHS. Although Irene is one of the overachieving Gerke family, many others also benefitted from their Home Economics experience. I do not normally bandy this about but I took a boys Home Ec class in the spring of 1944 under Miss Elizabeth McCraw. The training has saved me from starving many times and I would recommend it for any guy.

Fig. 6-47. Demonstrating that Home Ec isn't all hard work, here are: Irene Gerke, Marjorie Burger, Gladys Prewitt and Erma Vonderahe relaxing on a picnic at Boonville's Harley Park, spring 1941. Photo—Irene Felten.

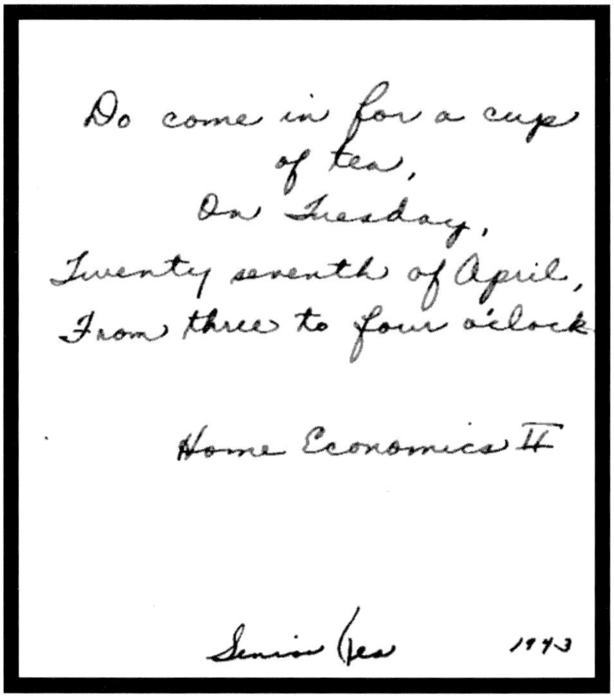

Do come in for a cup of tea,
On Tuesday,
Twenty seventh of April,
From three to four o'clock.

Home Economics II

Senior Tea 1943

Fig. 6-48. Senior Home Ec girls serve high tea to the Juniors. Spring 1943. This Fig. as well as Fig. 6-49 from the scrapbook of Irene Gerke Felten.

Eleventh Annual Spring Meeting

Missouri Home Economics Association

March 27, 1943

Jefferson City, Missouri

Program

Governor Hotel, Parlor "A"

SATURDAY MORNING

Presiding—Mrs. Nell Wright

9:00 Special Music - - - - A Cappella Choir
Jefferson City High School

RATIONING AND CONSUMER RESTRICTIONS—D. C. Wood, Extension Associate Professor, Agricultural Economics, University of Missouri, College of Agriculture

PANEL DISCUSSION: The Contribution of Home Economics to the Building of Family Morale in Wartime

Panel Leader: Dr. H. R. Meyering, Professor of Education and Social Studies, Junior and Teachers Colleges, Kansas City, Missouri

Panel Members:

Miss Anna E. Hussey, City Supervisor, Home Economics Education, Kansas City, Missouri

Miss Mary Inez Mann, Teacher of Home Economics, Cleveland High School, St. Louis, Missouri

Mrs. Rachel Owens, Home Management Supervisor, Farm Security Administration, Marshall, Missouri

Mrs. Atlanta Pummill, Teacher of Vocational Home Economics, Houston, Missouri

Dr. Lucile Reynolds, Farm Credit Administration, Kansas City, Missouri

Mrs. Kathryn Zimmerman, Home Demonstration Agent, Extension Service, Memphis, Missouri

12:30 Luncheon - - - - - Governor Hotel

SATURDAY AFTERNOON

Presiding—Mrs. Lillian W. Duncan

1:45 BUSINESS MEETING
Report of the Nominating Committee—Introduction of New Officers - - Miss Jane Hinote

2:45 PERSONAL MORALE IN TOTAL WAR—Dr. Fred McKinney, Associate Professor of Psychology, University of Missouri

4:00 RECEPTION - - - Governor's Mansion

Fig. 6-49. Ruby Ratje and Irene Gerke are chosen as PGHS Delegates to the Home Economics Association's annual Spring Meeting, and meet the Governor!

Mrs. Clemus Felten

Seamstress doubles efforts to outfit twin daughters

by SUSAN DONLEY
Community Living Editor

Page 4 Monday, January 3, 1972 Boonville Daily News

Seamstress of the Month Mrs. Clemus Felten models a suit she made and displays some garments she sewed for her twin daughters. The Pilot Grove housewife and mother of five is clothing leader for the Clear Creek 4-H Club. (Daily News Photo)

Seamstress of the Month Mrs. Clemus Felten, Pilot Grove, literally works doubletime when she makes clothes for her 20-year-old twin daughters.

"When I make one garment, I always make another one just like it, if I know the pattern fits both girls," she said.

Mrs. Felten explained that it is not as hard as it may seem to sew for twin daughters who have always dressed alike: "I always keep each outfit up with the other when sewing-for instance, I will cut both out at the same time, sew up the darts on one and then do the same to the other. I can work quickly since I can use the same thread on both and do steps such as pressing all at one time."

Sewing for two has been a part of her role as seamstress for many years, as she said, "You know, I don't think I could go into the girls' closet and find a ready-made dress! "

The fact that it is often hard for the girls to find something they both like in identical sizes in stores is a major reason why they like to have their clothes "custom made."

The girls shop around for styles they like and then pick out patterns. Mrs. Felten said she has become adept at adding to, taking. away from switching around patterns to suit their taste.

She added that she was not without help, since both girls, who now work in Columbia, had sewing training in home economics and 4-H.

Not to be ignored, Mrs. Felten's three sons, ages 21,13 and 8, want some "custom made" clothes also. "I've been hearing that I'm going to have to start making shirts," she smiled.

The seamstress would like to take a course on making men's clothing. "I don't think it would be that hard," she said, "because the major difference in construction of men's and women's clothing is in the use of innerfacings."

She admitted that she has taken the plunge and already cut out a shirt for her oldest son. "I am bound and determined it is not going to look homemade," she declared.

Although Mrs. Felten spends quite a bit of time sewing for her children, she also manages to turn out a wardrobe for herself. "I prefer to sew for myself since I am tall and hard to fit," she explained. She especially enjoys making and wearing suits because "they are so easy to dress up or down for any occasion."

The seamstress of the month keeps up with the latest clothing styles and sewing techniques by "taking all the sewing classes I can which are offered by the University of Missouri Extension Division.,, She finds these courses particularly helpful in her role as clothing leader for the Clear Creek 4-H Club.

"Extension center guidelines keep up with the styles, and the girls have leeway in what they want to make as long as they show they have learned the techniques," she said. "I enjoy working with them because I always learn with them."

Mrs. Felten has served as county clothing chairman for the Youth Fair and 4H achievement days. She has also been a clothing judge in similar Howard County events. This involves summing up the total effect of a garment and then going over it in detail with the girl who made it.

Her hands are never idle as Mrs. Felten said she relaxes in the evenings with her family while crocheting, an art she taught, herself after she was married. Here again, when she crochets something for one daughter, she has a duplicate on another set of needles for the other daughter.

She also finds time to do needlework and quilting when she isn't involved in Pilot Grove PTA activities or helping her husband on the farm.

Mrs. Felten offered this advice to beginning and veteran seamstresses as a key to successful sewing: "Learn to read directions carefully and learn how to use pattern guides."

SCHOOL ACTIVITIES OF THE 4TH TYPE (UNSANCTIONED)

PLAYING HOOKEY

When I was 13, my 8th Grade cohorts and I were promoted upstairs to join the big kids in the "Study Hall" —the top floor of the old 1922 Pilot Grove School building. It was true that we had pretty well outgrown the small desks downstairs, but we weren't really all that mature in other ways as will be evidenced by the following story.

At lunch time, the country kids retrieved their 'brown bags' or lunch pails and ate in small groups wherever the season permitted. This being a languorous, beautiful, warm, spring day—April of 1941—lunch for most was outside. Homer Jeffress and I, living less than a block away, ran home for a quick sandwich and then rushed back not to miss the playground camaraderie. We often had a quick game of softball. But as often as not we simply caucused for an exchange of jokes, riddles, stories or just to pool our ignorance.

On this day, four of us—Babe Heim, Homer Jeffress, Fred Theobald and myself—lamented that such a nice day as this was to be wasted on school. Homer says, "Let's play hookey!"

This suggestion started a buzz. I wasn't too gung ho, it seemed to be rash but, "...if you guys are for it, let's go!"

At that time Babe lived with his family on the old Brownfield place north west of town. I think this was Curry Brownfield's farm and probably where Dee (Charley Magook's dad), Jack, Bobby, Frances, et al were born.

Babe says, "There's an old abandoned house a mile or so behind our house and on our farm. It might be fun to explore". So, skulking along with heads down, trying to stay out of the visual range of anyone that might be on hookey-patrol, we headed off for a great adventure! Down Slaughter Pen Hill, past the old town dump and the new sewer treatment plant, we stepped along with all the enthusiasm (and mindlessness) of young boys on the green edge of manhood.

At the old house we thought there might be an ancient, hidden cache of valuables in the walls and proceeded to rip out a few. Disappointed at finding no hidden treasure, we soon tired of this and went for a hike in the woods. It was a lovely day and we rejoiced in all God's Creation.

At the end of the day, when the sun was well down in the western sky, we started home. The shortest route was across the Heim farm but on this course we observed Babe's father coming in our direction! Dora Heim was of the stern stuff of the lifelong farmer and did not condone the kind of nonsense we had been up to. Noting that if we continued our present course we would intercept him and collect a lot of grief—so, Homer, Fred and I peeled off to an 'escape and evasion 'course and stepped up the pace.

Babe was already nailed. Dora was now within IFF (identification) range and called out to him. Babe surrendered meekly and, after a short inquisition which confirmed his suspicions, his dad said, "That man," pointing toward town and school, "Will talk to you in the morning!""That man" was Superintendent E.M. McKee, another stern disciplinarian. See Fig. 6.-50.

Fig. 6-50. E.M. McKee, Supt. laid on the stick.

The next morning the 'fearless four' were shaking in their boots awaiting the call of the Lord High Executioner. At about 10 o'clock Miss Lida Harris the school principal walked to the wide study hall door and announced in a stern voice, "Mr. McKee wants to see Homer Jeffress, George Heim, Fred Theobald and Richard Salmon in his office!"

We all stood up and started toward the door. She stopped us and said, "One at a time. George, you may go first." If there had ever been any doubt as to what punishment was to be meted out, it was soon dispelled by the sounds of "Whack, whack, whack ..."!

For some reason I was last. I entered the Superintendent's office with grave trepidation, but then his smile and questions disarmed me, "Did you play hookey yesterday?"

"Yeah."

"Did you have a good time?"

"Yeah."

His smile disappeared and my heart sank, "Well, now you're going to pay for it." He pulled out his desk drawer , "Assume the position!" I bent and he used his short paddle. "Whack, whack, whack...!" I didn't count the strokes.

The pain was of little consequence but the public humiliation was severe—his office was just off the study hall and though out of sight, events were not out of hearing. The study hall, which normally sounded like New York City's Grand Central Station, was as silent as the grave. Everyone strained their ears not to miss anything juicy. I learned the definition of "Schadefreude" that day! Some of my schoolmates took a bit too much pleasure in my humiliation. I was angry but powerless!

I struggled to control the tears in my eyes as I left McKee's office and vowed I would die before I permitted the assembled study hall crowd see a tear from me! Hell, I was 13 years old!

So, as I walked into the study hall, I rubbed my backside with great exaggeration as I passed in front of the gloating mob and returned to my desk.

If you can't be a hero, be a clown!

The whole assembly broke up with laughter as I mentally gave the gloaters the finger. Miss Harris came hurrying down the hall to see what had happened. Of course, she missed the show.

At our 25th anniversary reunion (1970), Homer Jeffress commented, "My happiest moments were here in school. I remember four of us deciding to play hookey one day."

Mr. E.M. McKee was the keynote speaker at that reunion. He retorted, "Yes, and what did you get? I remember taking you one by one and applying the 'Board of Education' to your bottoms!"

LEAVE A NICE TIP

In the 1944 spring semester Miss McCraw (Home Ec) had a brain storm and offered a boys home economics class. Not at all afraid of the derision I might stimulate among my rough and uncultured peers — I signed up. I was then followed by 15-18 other guys and we formed the largest boys home economics class in the state. I not only found the course interesting, it was extremely useful and I value the experience to this day. This crude and crass rabble of teenage boys had a darling little blonde teacher barely out of the teens herself. See photo nearby. (Miss Elizabeth McCraw will be mentioned elsewhere in these chronicles). In addition to all the rascality we got up to, we actually learned some bachelor survival skills—at least, I did. One of the things on the syllabus was cooking and baking simple recipes.

Fig. 6-51. Mattie Jo Heim, Johnny Farrell and Thelma Fredrick, hanging out at Harley Park, Boonville, 1941.—Photo—Norb Zeller.

Fig. 6-52. Mattie Jo and Ernie Mellor Jr. 18 years old and with the keys to his old man's car. Photo—Norb Zeller.

Fig. 6-53. Elizabeth (McCraw) Drake attended many of our Class Reunions.

One of these recipes was peach pie. The class was arranged in teams of 5-6 each and, in a team effort, we managed one day to assemble and bake some. These pies were a subject of conversation one night when the 'young ruffians club' had assembled to chat about important goings-on. If I now tell you that Loyd McCreery was a member in good standing of this informal club you will immediately suspect some nefarious activities were about to be launched. And you would be correct.

Loyd was two years older than Babe, Homer and I. He was sufficiently influential, in a somewhat negative way, in the informal part of my tutelage that I relate additional stories about him elsewhere. He was not a member of the Home Ec class but was decidedly interested in our activities, particularly the pies.

Loyd had served a short stint with the Merchant Marine and was home on leave. Listening to our chatter, he says, "I really don't believe that you dumbasses could make a pie—at least not one that anybody could eat!"

Now, while we were sometimes a bit defensive about taking a course that was so obviously a girls option, we nevertheless knew that: the course was specially designed for boys and furthermore, what we were actually learning something pretty useful. The arguments and defenses continued for a while, then Loyd says, "Let's go try one a them pies, then I'll decide."

It was only necessary to slide the Home Ec room window up and step inside. The moon and the streetlights gave enough light, besides, I knew where the pies were and the table was quickly set for four. Loyd, Babe, Homer and I scoffed down one peach pie with great relish. I turned to Loyd, "OK, wiseass, what do you say?"

"Not bad, Sonny. Not at all bad! You'll make somebody a good husband."

Well, anyway we had made our point. Loyd was a tough judge and I felt good about our handiwork. As we got up to leave, I happened to have a dime in my pocket which I laid by my plate, "We really should show our appreciate for a fine repast!"

The next day at a routine assembly of the study hall denizens, Superintendent Laughlin brings up the subject of the missing pie. Since there was no evidence of illegal entry, he thought it might have simply been done surreptitiously while the room was unattended late the day before. He harangued on and on and ended by saying, "...then, adding insult to injury, someone left a dime tip!"

The intrepid Babe held up his hand, "Sir, what should he have left?"

Laughlin went along with the spirit, "Well, he'd ought to have left at least a quarter!" He knew Babe pretty well and thought he might have been the cheapskate in question. He almost had it right!

Fig. 6-54. PGHS Class of 45 Reunion - 1970. Seated in front - Homer Jeffress, Sonny Salmon, John Lorenz, Homer Twenter, Charlene (Farrell) King, Elizabeth (McCraw) Drake. Standing - Joe Piatt, Harold Kempf, Rebekah (Meyer) Whiteaker, Dorothy (Kempf) Young, Henry Hoff, Alice (Zeller) Bestgen, Henry Stegner, Elwood Gerke, Paul Schlotzhauer, Charley Brownfield, Virgil Schupp, Billy Stewart, Earlene (Felten) McKinzie, Earl Kammerich, Elizabeth (Kraus) Norman, Earlene (Schlotzhauer) Loesing Photo—Sonny.

PETE'S PRANK

It was this Boys' Home Ec Class that nearly led me to disaster later that spring of 1944. For the most part the boys were reasonably well behaved but one day got out of hand. This April incident was a near catastrophe for me.

The classroom was in essence a dining area adjacent to the kitchen in the Home Economics Department. Students sat 4-5 to each round dining table. We cooked a lot of stuff and actually ate our own cooking right here.

Pete Meyer was the class prankster, but his childish practical jokes weren't very funny even by our immature standards. One day Miss McCraw was talking to the guys at the next table — her back to us. As a prank, Pete turned in his chair and pretended to jerk up the back of Miss McCraw's skirt. Busy watching the rest of us to be sure we saw this hilarious stunt, he misjudged the dynamics and by pure accident caught her skirt and he jerked it up 12-15 inches.

EXPELLED, EJECTED AND EXCOMMUNICATED!

Furious and humiliated, she whirled on our table and looked right into my eyes. I was on the opposite side of the table and she could plainly see that I could not have had any part in this dumb stunt. "All of you," she commanded, indicating the guys at our table, "get out of here! Get out of this class! Go back to the study hall! I'm reporting this to the Superintendent! I'll have you all expelled!"

She was completely justified in laying on the stick. It was an asinine prank, accident though it may have been! However, I was incensed! I had had no part of this stupid prank and the way she looked at me I felt that she was holding me personally responsible! I retired to the study hall, cleaned out my desk and went home where I stayed several days stewing myself into a high dudgeon.

I talked to some guys about enlisting in the Army or Marines. Finally, Babe Heim and Bonnie Kirby came by and said, "Sonny, you really should go see Mr. Laughlin (the Superintendent) and get back in class! We've only got a few days left 'til summer vacation! Don't throw away your diploma! There isn't going to be any hanging after all! McCraw has cooled down and knows that you weren't a part of Pete's dumb joke."

I returned and tried to make up my lost work. I slunk into Home Ec class. Miss McCraw looked up at me and smiled. At the break she apologized for over-reacting and particularly striking out at me. I told her, "You had every right to be outraged. If I had done it I would not have blamed you for having me expelled, but I had nothing to do with it. I have always thought the stuff that Pete does was childish."

Fig. 6-55. Beulah Brownfield and Suzanne Coleman at Pop Tracy's Cafe - 1940.

So we made amends. C'est la vie!

HANGING OUT

See pictures, preceding page, this page and the next 2 pages. (Credit most of these to Norb Zeller). The cheapest form of entertainment was just hanging out—shooting the bull—entertaining yourselves. Clearly, there was a lot of this going on back in them days.

Fig. 6-56 Thelma Fredrick. 1940.

Fig. 6-57. Now you girls try it! Mattie Jo Heim and Thelma Fredrick. 1940

Fig. 6-58. Rita Kempf, Ruth Nelson, Gertrude Kraus, LaVahn Klenklen, Doris Quinlan, Unk, Unk and Joe Cullen 1940.

Fig. 6-59. Betty Eckerle and Norb Zeller, 1940.

Fig. 6-60. Herbie Meyer, Harris St. 1940.

RIGHT Fig. 6-61. Joe Cullen, 1944.

Fig. 6-62. Viola Mae Twenter, Mattie Heim, Thelma Fredrick, Elaine Hull and Agnes Bauer at the Burial Mound, Harley Park, 1940.

Fig. 6-63. Johnny Hoff and Chris Straub plinking turtles with their Winchester .22. One box of .22 shorts cost 20¢ in 1940.

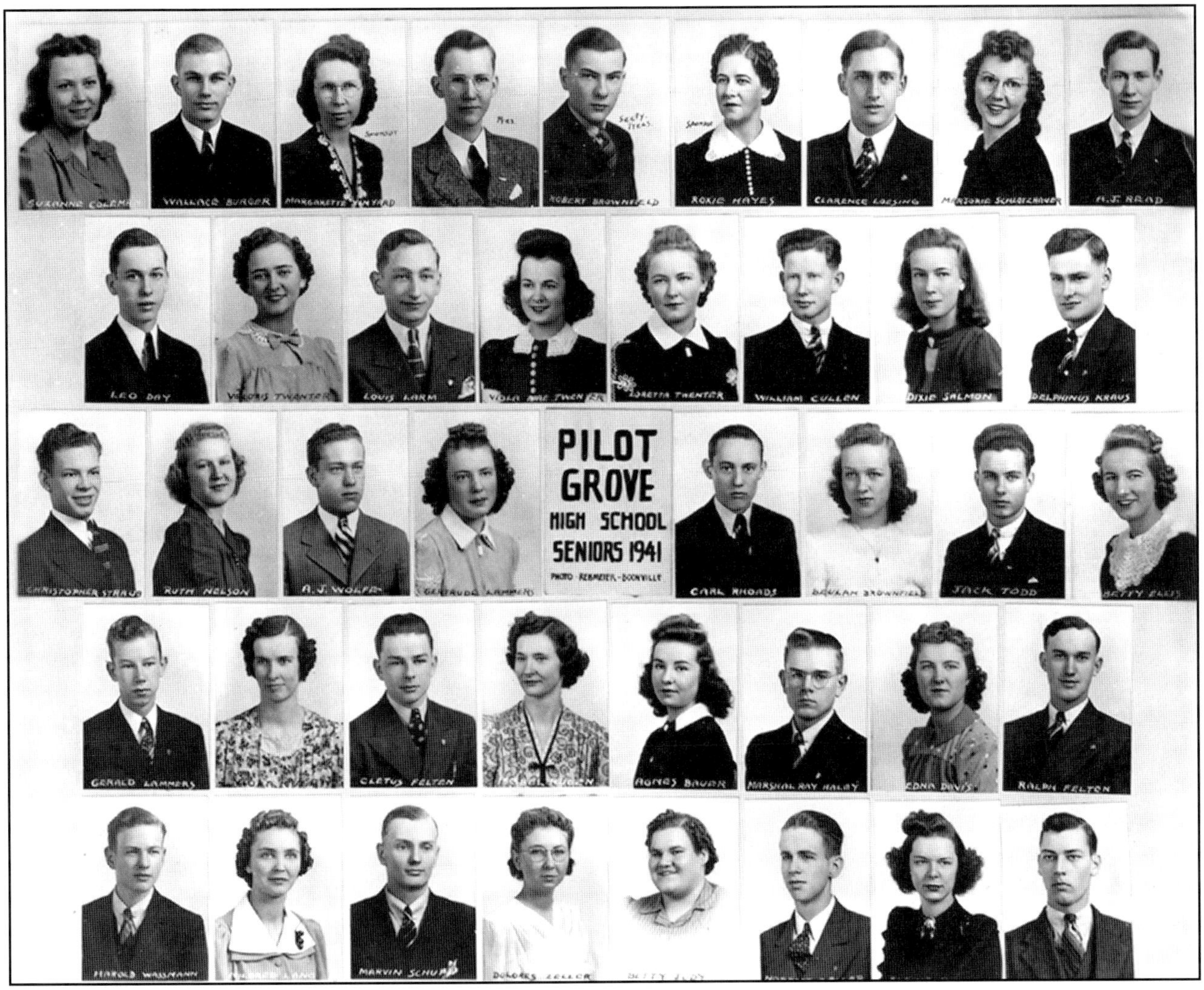

Fig. 6-64. Graduation Photos—PGHS Class of 1941. Class members are identified on next page.

Fig. 6-65. Dewey C. Hickman was Superintendent PGHS in the two year interregnum between Lockridge and McKee—1935-1937.

RIGHT—Fig. 6-66. Norbert Zeller provided most of the photos on these two pages. Norb worked on a farm for a year after graduation then served a hitch in the U.S. Navy. At war's end he took a job with Wilcox Electric in Kansas City where he worked until his recent retirement. He says, "At Wilcox, I was surprised to meet a supervisor—former PGHS Superintendent Dewey Hickman (1935-1937)."

KEY TO PHOTO- PREVIOUS PAGE

Fig. 6-67. PGHS class-1922-23. GIRLS L-R Unk*, Unk, Clara Brown (Mrs. Chas. Hoff), Unk, Unk, Florence Stoecklein, Sophia Immele, Isabelle Immele, Francis Krumm. BOYS L-R Harry Bail, Alfred Lammers, Jake Schweitzer, Roy Bail. *Unk - Unknown. Photo—Janie (Brownfield) Goehner.

Fig. 6-68. 50th Reunion - PGHS Class of 1941. Pilot Grove 1991. See key below for identity of attendees. Photo—Norbert Zeller.

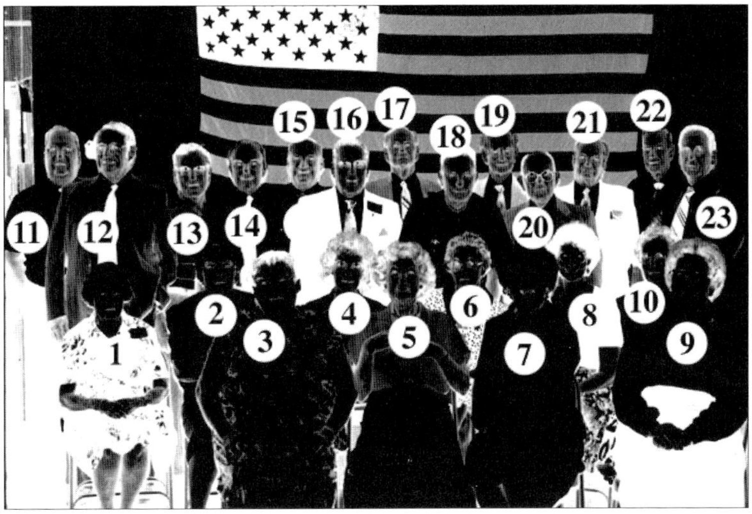

1-Roxie Hayes (Teacher), 2-Gertrude Lammers, 3-Betty Judy, 4-Dixie Salmon, 5-Viola Mae Twenter, 6-Mildred Lang, 7-Beulah Brownfield, 8-Mabel Rugen, 9-Veloris Twenter, 10-Viola Rugen, 11-Leo Day, 12-Clarence Loesing, 13-Delphinius Kraus, 14-Cletus Felton, 15-Ralph Felton, 16-A.J. Wolfe, 17-A.J. Read, 18-Jack Todd, 19-Bill Cullen, 20-Marshall Haley, 21-Marvin Schupp, 22-Gerald Lammers, 23-Norbert Zeller.

Fig. 6-69. Pilot Grove School 1928 Grades 5 -6. Top-Bert Wells; Back -Evelyn Phelps (Teacher), Robert Mowrey, Ridge Harlan, Hall Judy, Kenneth Quigley. Front-Ann Kimberly (Kimberling?), Meredith "boy", Ruth Hays, Opal Branstetter, Clara Wilson, Lucille Wells and Doug Brownfield. Photo—Ruth Hays Wood.

Fig. 6-70. 1931-Under the direction of Father Joachim, this band from St. Joseph Parochial school performed Saturday night concerts in front of the Brownfield Elevator. They were good enough to be invited to Tipton and other nearby towns. Photo—Mrs. Sarah Coleman.

LEFT Fig. 6-71. St. Joseph graduating class of 1940. Photo—LaVahn Klenklen Brown.

Fig. 6-72. Mount Vernon School 1914-15. Miss Gertie Moore (extreme left) was the teacher. Students were (L-R): Front row-Bert Harriman Jr., Vernon Tavenner, Aubrey Schlotzhauer, Bernita Mowrey, Edne Earl Brownfield, and James Curry Brownfield. Second row-Dee Brownfield, Mary Margaret Harriman, Mabel Schlotzhauer, Dorothy Tavenner, Isabel Brownfield, Wilma Mowrey and Hazel Brownfield. Back row-Emma Haley, Ella Lymer, Willa Moore, Zula Huckabay, John Haley, Herbert Schlotzhauer, Forrest Schlotzhauer, Raymond Mowrey and Riley Huckabay. Clipping from Janie Brownfield Goehner.

Fig. 6-73. Cottonwood School 1906. L-R Back row-Gertrude Eichelberger, Ida Quint, Florence Quint, Lula McClain, Oakie Mowrey, Evert Oswald, William Eichelberger, George Oswald, William Quint, Mr. Annen (Teacher). Second row-Frank Wesselman, Walter Brauey, Lawrence Brauey, Alferd Quint, Richard Salmon, Cecil McClain, George Quint, Jim Eichelberger. Front Row-Virginia Harriman, Effie Bail, Hulda Salmon, Flora Wesselman, Maria McClain, Edna Bail, Rosie Wesselman, Lorene Bail, Nadine Salmon, Lucy Weamer, Lizzie Oswald, Not present-Blanche Salmon and Henry Quint. Clipping—Sonny.

Fig. 6-74. Boys 4H. Front row, W. J. Keegan county agent, H. L. Branstetter, Milton Heims, Robert Brownfield, Leslie Chamberlain, Dick Wilson, Wallace Burger, Junior Krumm, J. B. Loesing; Second Row-D.C. Hickman, J. A. Wolfe, Ralph Esser, Glenn Eichhorn, Wm. Shipp, Morris Coleman, Jack Heims, Charles McCutcheon, Vernon Mowrey, R. P. Hartman; Third Row-Kenneth McCutcheon, Eugene Schlotzhauer, R. T. Schlotzhauer, R. A. Schlotzhauer, Anthony Samer, John Stegner, John Becker. Wallace Chapman. Photos above and below from 1937 Issue of Rural Life Edition, Boonville Newspaper -Courtesy Wally Burger.

Fig. 6-75. Pilot Grove Girls 4-H Clubs, Front Row-Dixie Salmon, Marjorie Theobold, Marjorie Quinlan, Jean Davis, Beulah Brownfield, Suzanne Coleman, Lucille Bottoms, Helen Ries; 2d Row-Ruth Hayes, Catherine Enos, Rosaline Schuster, Margaret Cullen, Isabel Lorenz, Merle Eichelberger, Marjorie Ann Brownfield, Lorene Zeller; 3d Row-Joe Ellen Coley, Rosaline Gerke, Edna Ruth Eckerle, Mary Margaret Babbitt, Imelda Kraus, Mary M. Dilthy, Lorene Gatewood, Grace Dwyer, Merle Sandy, Dixie Platt, Julia Kraus, Frances Snapp, Nell Porter, Mary Ellen Haley, and Francis Phillips.

St. Joseph School 1937

Fig. 6-76. 1937 Students at St. Joseph's School, Pilot Grove, left to right-
Top Row: Julia Margaret Kraus, Sister M. Gregory, Irene Bock, Alfreda Kempf, Mildred Gerke, Irene Schulte, Ella Young, Isabelle Kempf, Sister M. Mercedes, Grace Gerling.
Row 2: Martha Schweitzer, Francis Lammers, Gilbert Walje, Max Shay, Wilbur Quinlan, Charles Stoecklein, John Becker, Angela Gramlich, Frances Lorenz.
Row 3: Imelda Kraus, Raymond Muessig, Robert Gerling, Joseph Fahrendorf, Henry Twenter, Catherine Gerling, Virginia Widel, Gerald Day.
Row 4: Lorene Zeller, Anna Mae Imhoff, Bernardine Stoecklein, Mary Ruth Fitzsimmons, Ralph Nelson, Eugene Hoff, Junior Krumm, Rita Kempf.
Row 5: Leo Day, Herbert Meyer, Norbert Zeller Georgia Widel, Frank Imhoff, Harold Kemp, Glenn Neckerman.
Row 6: Marjorie Quinlan, Loretta Shay, Herbert Gerke, Wilbert Twenter, John Imhoff, Gerald Lammers, Isabelle Lorenz, Margaret Cullen.
Row 7: Ernabelle Mellor, Clara Salmon, Gertrude Kraus, Geraldine Klenklen, Mildred Kempf, Ferdinand Meyer, Sylvia Kempf, Anna Fahrendorf.
Row 8: Betty Jo Meyer, Edna Stoecklein, Florence Salmon, Joanne Salmon, Raymond Meyer, Junior Mellor, Charles Zeller, Jerome Kempf, William Cullen, Virginia Gramlich, Ruth Nelson, Mildred Lang.
Row 9: Mary Helen Imhoff, Dorothy Gramlich, Joseph Cullen, Erma Vonderahe, James Lorenz, Catherine Day.
Row 10: Roy Day, John Imhoff, LeVern Klenklen, Esther Gerke, Henry Hoff, Leonard Meyer, Earl Quinlan, Kenneth Kempf, Ray Stoecklein, Francis Vonderahe, Donald Bonen, Roy Stoecklein.
Row 11: Father Richard Felix, O.S.B.; Imogene Goth, Imogene Kempf, Mary Margaret Muessig, Doris Quinlan, Esther Gerke, Lou Ellen Zeller, Dorothy Muessig, Geraldine Lang, Corene Kempf, Joan Gramlich, Sister M. Constance.

Fig. 6-77. PGHS Class of 1932. 1- Helen Meisenheimer (Mrs. Paul), 2- Edgar "Red" Painter, 3- Mickey Meisenheimer, 4- Russell Schlotzhauer, 5- Eddie Ries, 6- Mrs. Henry Jeffress. Photo - Martha Sandy (PGHS 1932).

Fig. 6-78. Miss Madge Goode's First Grade 1929. Back row L-R Eugene Kimberling, Bobby Brownfield, Warren Wilson, Wallace Burger, Harold Wassmann, Clarence Ries. Front row- Martha Wilson, Beulah Brownfield, Suzanne Coleman, ? Cox, Betty Judy, Marjorie Talley, Dixie Salmon, Sarah Eichelberger. Miss Madge in rear. Photo - Wally Burger.

O, what a fair and noble city
This memory of mine evinces—
Whose folks are wise and witty,
Whose girls are gay and pretty
And whose merchants are all princes!
—Sonny Salmon

OVERVIEW

ALADDIN'S CAVE DID NOT HOLD ALL THE WONders I saw at my mother's skirts when we went Christmas shopping in Pilot Grove in the 1930s. She went store to store trying to find just the right gift or toy for each one on her list. Money was scarce and she was determined to strike the best possible bargain.

I marvelled at the sheer magnitude of "stuff". Surely these merchants must be as rich as princes. I think I reflected the attitude of all the town's little ragamuffins, "These folks must be the richest people on earth." This view of the world, coming from a guy 3 years old and 3 feet tall—was the inspiration for the title of the chapter.

I am now older and wiser. The storekeepers weren't all that rich but Sarah Coleman's story of the end of the Heinrich's store points out some of the riches that they *did* enjoy. They had a family enterprise and most of them found working together richly rewarding. As Jennette Bosch, one of the 'Heinrich kids', recalls below, it was "...thrilling to be asked to help at the store at Christmas time!"

HEINRICH'S COUNTRY STORE CLOSES AFTER 54 YEARS

BY MRS. J.H. COLEMAN- BOONVILLE DAILY NEWS

PILOT GROVE-Friday July 25, 1969-After 54 years of continuous service to the Pilot Grove community; Heinrich's Store closed its doors to business July 1.

Almost an institution in the town, the store has been owned and operated by the Heinrich family since 1915. John Heinrich Sr. was the first owner and operator, his son John took over as proprietor and operator in 1945 and then formed a partnership with his son, John A., in 1968.

The property where the store is located was purchased by John Sr. and his wife, Clara in 1915. A one-story building housing Sites and Ross Dry Goods was razed from the property and replaced by a two story structure.

The bottom floor housed the general store and the top floor was turned into the Gem Theater.

The grand opening of the store—October, 1915, was a gala affair. The outside display windows showed the newest merchandise available and inside flowers congratulating the Heinrich family on its opening, were displayed.

"Many of the lovely bouquets and pots of mums," said Mrs. Herbert Bosch, a daughter of the Heinrichs, "were sent by well wishers from all over the area.

"Inside the door visitors and customers were greeted by mother and father, Mr. and Mrs. Heinrich and their well trained staff. Guests were invited to have coffee and homemade cake while looking over the store."

Fig. 7-1. Heinrich's Mercantile in the 20s. Note the two small trees in front. These trees were full grown when Jim Sousley leaned on one to serenade us with his guitar in 1937. Photo—Charlotte Heinrich Savee.

Among the first employees of the store were—Jack Ross, Miss Pearlie Dwyer, George Weamer and the four Kistenmacher sisters, Martha, Frieda, Elsa and Betty.

"George (Weamer) was here when the first cement was poured years ago and he worked for the store until it closed this month," John Jr., the second owner of the store, said.

The interior of the store in its early years had an attractive display of the latest store fixtures and newest merchandise. The counters displayed attractive ladies blouses, cuff and collar sets, purses, gloves and Jewelry.

At the front of the store stood a large plate glass men's hat case with a full length mirror. Toward the rear of the store was the shoe department complete with high ladder which glided along a track making the stock at the top of the shelf easily accessible to employees.

"Unfortunately, that ladder was very inviting to unattended youngsters. They occasionally took a ride on it," Mrs. Bosch said.

The stock in the shoe department provided footwear for everyone from baby to adult and a wooden shoe stretcher was always available to break in those new shoes.

A wooden counter across the front of the store housed the hosiery and glove department. It also served as a favorite spot for social visiting.

"The counter height provided a good leaning place and afforded the customers a good view of the store and the street," Mrs. Bosch said.

Opposite the hosiery counter was a hat case with a large display case containing crochet thread, embroidery thread, crochet hooks, needles of all kinds, safety pins, scissors, tape measures and all other notions.

Reaching from this counter to the men's overall section

in the rear were shelves stocked with yard goods from utility materials to the best dress materials of the day-lace, embroidery edgings, ribbons and buttons.

Setting at the end of the dry goods counter were cash drawers for depositing sales money. Also on the counter was the sewing thread case with its rotary column offering a rainbow of colored thread.

Buying, selling and delivering groceries in the early years of the store was quite different from the present trend. It was possible to telephone orders to the store and it would be promptly delivered to the home. Or one could visit the store, place an order and George Weamer would deliver it to the home.

The farmers were Heinrichs' best customers in the beginning and in the end. In the early days they would come to the store in wagons drawn by two work horses.

"They hitched their team at the hitching rack conveniently located near the store on what is now Highway 135. The rack reached the length of the block and on a good trading day it would be filled, John Jr. recalled.

"When their purchases were ready the farmer merely drove to the side of the door and George would load their wagons. And John Jr. held the team for the farmers," John Jr., said.

The Heinrich family was a happy family at home and running the store. Jeanette Heinrich recalled how each member of the family helped out at the store.

"At Christmas time my father always had a complete line of toys and we would be thrilled when he asked us to help him at the store. Mother especially liked making a display in the front window," Jeanette said.

"John (Jr.) would do the advertising on large placards. Mother and I would try to place each toy to its best advantage. The display window, the first in Pilot Grove, featured articles for every holiday. I remember we had a mannequin, and I loved to help mother dress her," she added.

Through the years the store has been remodeled several times. In 1939, six years before he bought the store from its founder, John Jr., bought a drug store from the late Mr. and Mrs. Deck.

The drug store was operated along with the general store until 1964. In 1941 a food locker and processing plant was installed. In time all these buildings were joined to make one large store.

While the store grew, Pilot Grove's main entertainment center—the Gem Theater located on the top floor of the store—also prospered. "The opening night of the theater a special melodrama, "Deep Purple," starring Clara Kimbell Young and John Gilbert plus a comedy were the attractions," John Jr. said. At the entrance of the theater large posters and wooden display boards advertised coming attractions. In between reels of the movie, slides were flashed on the screen to advertise local businesses.

"In the summer the theater was cooled by six paddle fans. In the winter George (Weamer) fired the huge coal burning stove early in the morning for the evening show," John Jr. said.

Admission to the theater was an expensive 15 cents for adults and 10 cents for children. The ticket window still stands and so does the sign advertising the prices.

Pearlie Dwyer was the first person to sell tickets for the Gem. Miss Freda Kistenmacher was the first pianist for the silent movies and often was accompanied by John Meredith on the violin or mandolin.

Butch Zahringer and George Weamer operated the projection room. In the later years of the theater John Jr. helped George with the projection duties.

When the "talkies" came in the Gem Theater closed down as a movie house, but was still used for high school plays and commencements for a number of years.

The Gem featured several great stars of the silent movie, era. Abbot and Costello, Our Gang, Charlie Chaplin and Harold Lloyd provided comedy. Buck Jones, Tom Mix, Gary Cooper, Douglas Fairbanks Sr. provided the best westerns.

Other favorites box office attractions were Mary Pickford, Pauline Frederick, Ramon Navarro, John Gilbert, Clara Bow, Lon Chaney, Sonja Henie and Paul Robeson.

Although not as well-known nationwide as the silent screen stars, several Pilot Grove High School students became famous actors at the Gem Theater.

Their plays and the cast roles were written on the wall after each play. Many of the names are still legible. One of the stage doors has this play inscribed on the woodwork:

"The Feast of the Red Corn" — one act opera Tuesday, March 4, 1937."

The list of characters includes Queen, Betty Barnes; Old Squaw, Martha Schweitzer; Impee Light, Charlotte Heinrich; Fudgee, Lorene Zeller; Wudgee, Nancy Mae Wolf; Fudgee, Margaret Ann Brownfield, and Maidens, members of the Glee Club; director, Byron Morton.

The theater is now a dusty store room. The old community bulletin board is piled among some old display counters and boxes. The projector used for those early films is in a corner covered with cobwebs.

The interior of the store is now also abandoned. All that is left are the empty shelves and cabinets. The onetime center of trade in Pilot Grove is no longer bustling with activity.

The day the store closed John Jr. looked around the store and said, "I wouldn't take anything for my work here. We've served so many people and all of them are our friends. The association in Pilot Grove has meant a great deal to me."

And the people of Pilot Grove echoed Heinrich's sentiments. Everyone hated to see the country store close.

Fig. 7-2. Presbyterian Church, Hall Street, Pilot Grove. Caption (on back) "Charlotte and Ken were married here 4/18/49." The building was razed and building materials sold at auction. Les Chamberlin carried a load of bricks to Martha Sandy in Kansas City for a patio. Photo—Charlotte Heinrich Savee.

Fig. 7-3. From an article by Mrs. J. H. Coleman. Mrs. Walter Warnhoff displays some of her prized antique plates. Her collection consists of over 100 plates from rare RS Prussian place settings to English Flow Blue plates. (Daily News Photo) Fri July 25, 1969 [Mildred is the widow of Beau Warnhoff.]

EPILOGUE - HEINRICHS

Charlotte Heinrich Savee says, "Of we seven Heinrich siblings, only Karl and I are still alive. Karl lives in Lexington, Kentucky, retired after a long career with IBM. Karl and Leo had enlisted in the peacetime Navy when jobs were so scarce in the depression. This experience may have influenced Leo later.

"Leo and I were enrolled in the University of Missouri when the war broke out. Leo was a fanatic about flying and found that with a certain number of college credit hours he could qualify for the Navy's flight training program. He quit school and went for the Navy immediately when he had sufficient credit hours. He was quite talented—I suppose anyone who loves something as much as he loved flying would be good at it. He was a flight instructor at Pensacola Naval Training Station and was with a student when an accident took their lives. That was December 23, 1942. The war was just one year old.

"After his death, I volunteered for Navy service and served as a Senior Yeoman in the Chaplain's Office, 11th Naval District. Coincidentally, my boss, Capt. William Maguire, was the Catholic Chaplain who inspired the song, "Praise the Lord and Pass the Ammunition!" [For the little ones: In the attack on Pearl Harbor in December 1941, many heroic stories emerged. One was of the Chaplain who, in the heat of battle, threw himself into the defense, assisting an antiaircraft gun crew by handling ammunition. In the aftermath, contrary to his popular, heroic image—he was roundly chastised by the hierarchy of the Catholic Church as having crossed the line—Catholic priests do not "pass the ammunition".]

Charlotte continues, "My mother was a avid gardener who furnished flowers for Pilot Grove events and sold tomato and pepper plants in the spring. Our yard was a showcase of her prowess as a cultivator of flowers.

"My sister Jennette [she is the one Sarah Coleman quotes frequently in the article above] lived at home while her husband, Colonel H.M. Bosch served in the Army. After the war, he returned to become a professor at the University of Minnesota but died tragically of a heart attack while on a World Health Organization (UN) consulting mission to the Soviet Union in 1962.

"My sister Dorothea lived on a farm near Billingsville with her husband and children. Sister Margarete lived on a farm near Odessa.

"I am a retired Children's Social Worker—County of Los Angeles."

WARNHOFF BROS

Pilot Grove Weekly Record

VOLUME 55, NUMBER 23 PILOT GROVE, COOPER COUNTY, MISSOURI FRIDAY, MAR. 27, 1936 $1.50 A YEAR, IN ADVANCE

THIRTY-ONE YEARS OF

PUBLIC SERVICE HERE

Warnhoff Mercantile Company Has a Fine Record of Service Over Long Period.

Warnhoff's general merchandise store, one of the substantial and well known firms of Pilot Grove, is celebrating its 31st year of continuous business in this town.

In 1905 R.A. Warnhoff, a merchant at Wright City doing

Fig. 7-4. About 1914. Prior to opening Heinrich's Mercantile in 1915, John D. Heinrich Sr. owned a saloon. Shown above are: Alex Givins, J.D. Heinrich Sr., William Dwyer and Elmer Veal. Elmer Veal was the brother of Ben Veal who married my aunt Allie Kendrick. Photo - Charlotte Heinrich Savee.

Fig. 7-5. Heinrich's Mercantile interior late 1920s. Shown are J.D. Heinrich Sr., Stella Marr and George Weamer. George was employee number 1, joining the store when it opened in 1915. He was such a fixture, us kids called him George *Heinrich*. Photo - Charlotte Heinrich Savee.

Fig. 7-6 Beau and Mildred Warnhoff had a small grocery store in the old Pilot Grove Bank building in the 1970s. Photo—1973 Centennial Book.

business, under the firm name "Warnhoffs" located in Pilot Grove to establish himself and sons under the same business head. Of the four sons, the two elder ones, Frank and Robert, were operating a clothing store In Boonville and remained there when the father transferred his business to Pilot Grove. Walter and Harry, the other two sons, were associated with Mr. Warnhoff but a third son's aid was required in the new business and after a period of about two years Robert Warnhoff joined the firm in Pilot Grove, leaving the elder brother Frank in Boonville. Here the father and three son jointly and successfully conducted the business until about 1922, when Mr. Warnhoff retired from the firm and with Mrs. Warnhoff went to live in San Diego, California, both dying at that place several years later.

Under the cooperative efforts of the three Warnhoff sons the business has continued to thrive, and the beginning of this new year finds them celebrating, thirty-one years of successful mercantile business. In fact the firm "Warnhoffs" is rounding out its eightieth year, for it is about that length of time since the family launched the business firm.

The grandfather of the present Warnhoff firm was a locksmith of St. Louis and under his tutelage his, son, R A. Warnhoff, when a young man, built for himself a strong iron safe. During the long business career of the Warnhoffs, this same safe has done duty first in St. Louis, then in Wright City and now in the store in Pilot Grove where it meets all the requirements of its proud possessors, two generations removed from the one who established a firm of "Warnhoffs".

END OF A DYNASTY

The above article appeared in the Pilot Grove Weekly Record in 1936. Warnhoffs continued to serve the community through the war years though Bob died in 1943. After the war they continued to prosper but gradually things changed. First there was no "Dynasty" — the brothers had only two male descendants, Walter's Walter Jr. "Beau" and Ralph. As the brothers passed from the scene there was no one waiting in the wings. Ralph had departed upon graduation from PGHS and made a long and successful career for himself in the Western Auto firm in Kansas City. He died recently in Columbia, MO where he had retired.

Fig. 7-7. Ernest and Sarah Mellor celebrated their golden wedding anniversary just before the 1973 Pilot Grove centennial.

Secondly improved roads made trips to Boonville feasible, so they were competing with merchants even at a distance.

So the big store wound down. Beau and Mildred ran a little store for a while in the former Pilot Grove Bank building, but I had the feeling that Beau's heart was not in it and soon even that small reminder of the great mercantile empire was gone.

ERNEST MELLOR'S MEAT MARKET

I have not been able to turn up much on Mellor's Meat Market. I remember it of course. I used to go down to Mellor's on Sunday morning with Dad to buy the Sunday dinner. We would often get a huge slice of round steak—50¢ would feed the whole family with leftovers for Dad's dinner bucket. Mom would cut this into 4x4" pieces, pound the hell out of it, flour it and fry it in deep fat. This was my introduction to "Chicken Fried Steak" and could have been certified as authentic by any "Good Ol' Boy" of the current era.

GERKE'S GROCERY

Elwood Gerke, my classmate PGHS Class of 1945, decided in 1969 that he would buck the trend and open a grocery store in Pilot Grove. This would be a grocery store only, not the general store format that Warnhoffs, Heinrichs and the MFA had followed.

Fig. 7-8. Gerke's Grocery 1970. Front- Alma Bader, Mary Lammers, Mary Wilson, George Weamer, Back- Elwood, Charlie Hoff, Earl Reuter. Photo - Pilot Grove Centennial Book.

Fig. 7-9. Earl Hays shows the new "Cyclomatic" refrigerator ($399.75 delivered and installed) to Mrs. Jennie Larm and daughter Hedwig. Ca 1940s. Photo—Ruth Hays Wood.

There was a lot of clucking of tongues. Everyone "knew" the wave of the future. The citizens of Pilot Grove were a very different lot from those of the 30s and 40s. To some, Pilot Grove was a commuter community with Dad and sometimes Mom, commuting to Boonville or Columbia for work but favoring Pilot Grove as a nice place to live and raise kids. In addition, as noted above, the greatly improved roads made the time-distance to Boonville much less onerous. Also, it is difficult to compete on price with those stores, for example—Walmart, who buy their product by the trainload.

What the nay-sayers missed was the large number of folks who did not really care to, or couldn't drive to Boonville for grocery shopping.

Elwood determined that if you don't pretend to be a general store like Warnhoffs of the olden days—stocking everything from canned green beans to wedding gowns—you can indeed compete on price—and he has.

Elwood bought out Heinrich's buildings and hired some of the help. You may note in the picture that George Weamer, who was present at the "laying of the keel" of the original Heinrich's store, moved over to Gerke's . Old George is gone now and many have forgotten (or never knew) what an institution he was at Heinrich's. He served three generations.

I am personally proud of my classmate for the success that he has made of the store and wish him decades more. Elwood cut down two trees in 1969 and called down the wrath of town preservationists on his head. These trees are shown in Charlotte Heinrich Savee's picture above. One of these trees was the prop for Jim Sousley when he whanged on his guitar on Saturday nights in 1937. I am, however, not certain that this would rate a historical plaque and eternal preservation. I would not have voted for Elwood's lynching.

Fig. 7-10. Barber George Klenklen in front of his shop - 1940s. Photo - LaVahn Klenklen Brown.

HAYS AND STOECKLEIN

The Meisenheimer Brothers are the successors to Hays and Stoecklein, later Hays and Painter.

Pendleton Earl Hays, when partnered with George Stoecklein and later with Bob Painter, did a significant business in furniture and appliances even then though, their mainstay was funerals. Hays and Painter directed my father's funeral in 1940.

Fig. 7-11. The Friendly Tavern—successor to the Tip-Top Cafe of my era, ca. 1960s. Photo—A.J. Wolfe.

Fig. 7-12. Helen Ries in front of Deck's Drug Store, 1938. Photo—Janie Brownfield Goehner.

Fig. 7-13. Koolaid Krew. Inset: Sonny Salmon, L-R: Charlie Brownfield, Helen Ries, Dutchie and Janie. 1934. Photo—Janie Brownfield Goehner.

Fig. 7-14. Young Wayne Roach at his Standard Station, ca 1940s. News Clip—A.J.Wolfe.

KOOLAID KID KREW

In the summer of 1934, after completing Miss Madge Goode's first grade, Charley Brownfield, his sister Janie and I (with Helen Ries as advisor) initiated what was my first venture into the world of the Merchant Princes—a Koolaid stand. See Fig. 7-13 at left bottom. Charley made a sign:

ICE COLD KOOLAID 1¢

He and Janie put the stand on the sidewalk in front of their house. They were then living on the southwest corner of Harris and Fourth Streets across from St. Joseph School.

Mrs. Brownfield advanced the Koolaid, water, ice and, most importantly, the pitcher and glasses. Plastic cups were still waiting to be invented.

The word got around and we soon had customers. On our second day, Mom told Dad about it and on his way home from work, he and Louie Walje, one of his crew that lived on our street, walked the block or so to our stand and enjoyed a refreshing glass or two.

Unfortunately, on the fourth day we could see the stand was headed for bankruptcy—so, we burned it down for the insurance! I'M JOKING! Actually, Dutchie (a bit bigger than in this picture) had discovered an old truck tire and was trying to roll it around as he had seen the big kids do. It got out of control and slammed into the stand. The Koolaid pitcher and glasses disappeared into a thousand glass shards on the sidewalk. Our enterprise crashed like Wall Street on "Black Thursday"! That was my first and last attempt to become a "Merchant Prince".

Pilot Grove High School Starette

Pilot Grove, Mo. May 16, 1940 Vol. 3, No. 21

In the late 1930s and early 1940s the Pilot Grove High School Starette was written, assembled and edited by Pilot Grove High School staff and published by the Pilot Grove Star. It was supported by the Pilot Grove "Merchant Princes". See Earl Hay's ad below. The following four pages are reproduced from the issue of May 16th 1940 (Graduation Issue). Special thanks to Ralph Esser PGHS 1940 for these pages from his well preserved scrapbook.

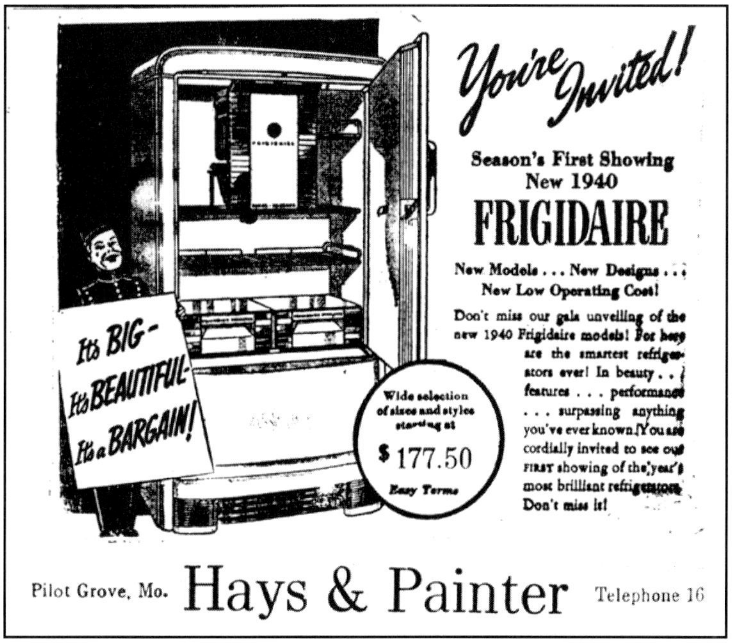

For those who read the ads included in this issue of the Starette and think the prices are just wonderful (Warnhoffs had bananas for 5-1/2¢ per pound)—keep in mind that the average starting wage for semiskilled labor in 1940 was less than 50¢ per hour!

Pilot Grove High School Starette

Pilot Grove, Mo. May 16, 1940 Vol. 3, No. 21

STAFF

Editor	Mary Margaret Babbitt
Assoc Editor	Rosalind Schuster
Departmental	Nell Porter
Sports	H.L. Branstetter
	Billy Judy
Music	Isabelle Lorenz
Social Editor	Margaret Cullen
Vocational Ag	Clifford Ashcraft
CLASS REPORTERS	
Senior	Ralph Esser
Junior	Agnes Bauer
Sophomore	Juanita Jones
Freshman	Dolly Day
Rooms I-II	Rosalind Schuster
Sponsor	Mr. Morton
Grade News	Rosalind Schuster

COMMENCEMENT
May 17, 1940 8:00 PM

Processional	High School Orchestra
Invocation	Rev. Sampson
Salutatorian "Human Relations"	Charlotte Heinrich
Girls' Trio "Green Cathedral"	Jane Wolfe, Jo Ellen Coley and Marjorie Schlotzhauer
Valedictorian "Appreciation of Government"	Mary Margaret Babbitt
Girls Ensemble	"A Song of Farewell"
Introduction of Speaker	G.B. Harlan, Pres. Board of Education
Class Address	Dr. W.W. Carpenter, Prof. Education at M.U.
Presentation of Class	E.M. McKee, Supt. of Schools
Presentation of Diplomas	G.B. Harlan
Recessional	High School Orchestra
Benediction	Dr. A.I. Jones

INTRODUCING THE SENIORS

So the General Public May Better Know The Graduating Class, Here They Are.

As a general custom with the Star, this newspaper again this year will attempt to introduce the graduating class of the Pilot Grove high school. They are:

(Compiled by Marjorie Quinlan)

CLIFFORD ASHCRAFT

Clifford Ashcraft, son of Mr. and Mrs. E. D. Ashcraft, was born at McCune, Kansas, September 2, 1920. During his Freshman year he was secretary of his class and a member of the Junior Civic club. In his Sophomore and Junior years he was a memer of the softball team. He was business manager of the school paper. In his Senior year he also was a member of the bookkeeping team, and a member of the Senior play cast.

GILBERT BAUER

Gilbert Bauer, son of Mr. and Mrs. Joseph Bauer, was born May 19, 1921. He attented St. John's parochial school the first eight years of high school and entered Pilot Grove high school in 1936. He was a member of the one-act play cast in 1940, a member of the softball team, member of the Junior play cast in 1939 and vice president of the FFA.

MARY MARGARET BABBITT

Mary Margaret Babbitt, daughter of Mr. and Mrs. C T Babbitt, was born at Pleasant Green February 19, 1923. During her high school attendance she was member of the pep squad for two years, Glee club and mixed chorus three years, student council one year, member of the Junior Booster club last year, in one-act play, member of Junior and Senior play and entered the commercial contests two years. Was a member of the Tattler staff two years and valdictorian of the Senior class of 1940.

H. L. BRANSTETTER

H. L. Branstetter was born November 1, 1922 at Pilot Grove. He is the son of Mr. and Mrs. Lester Branstetter During his 4 years of high chool he was, during his Freshman year, member of the Glee club, member of the Junior basketball team, member of band and orchestra as well as being member of the basketball team, member of softball and volleyball team, and was in the Negro minstrel cast. In his Senior year he was in the class play and a member of the basket ball team.

MARGARET CULLEN

Margaret Cullen, daughter of Mrs. John Cullen, was born January 7, 1922 at Nelson. She attended St. Joseph's parochial school for eight years and entered this high school in 1936. She was a member of the Glee club for three years, member of the play cast in 1939 and a member of the Senior play cast this year.

LESLIE CHAMBERLIN

Leslie Chamberlin, son of Mr and Mrs. H. L. Chamberlin, was born at Boonville February 16 1922. He attended school at Spring Creek, La., for six year and attended Boonville high during seventh year. He entered Pilot Grove high school in the eighth grade and has completed four years of high school here He was a member of the FFA play, one-act and Senior play and was vice president of the Senior class.

NELLIE MARIE DAVIS

Nellie Marie Davis, daughter of Mr. and Mrs. John Davis, was born September 26, 1920 near Blackwater. She attended Chouteau school eight years and Blackwater high school three years. She did her Senior work in Pilot Grove high school. While here she was a member of the band, orchestra, Glee club and a member of the Senior play cast.

DOROTHY DAVIS

Dorothy Davis, daughter of Mr. and Mrs. John S. Davis of Blackwater, was born February 27, 1921. She finished her eighth grade at Chouteau and began her first year of high school at Blackwater. The following three years

Pilot Grove High School Starette

Pilot Grove, Mo. May 16, 1940 Vol. 3, No. 21

she attend the Pilot Grove high school. Here she has been a member of the Glee club and has attended the music contest every year. She also belongs to the band ant orchestra. She was a very active member of the basket ball team during her Junior and Senior years and was co-captain of the team during her Senior year. She was also captain of the softball team this year.

RALPH ESSER

Ralph Esser, son of Mr. and Mrs. Bert Esser, was born March 11, 1922 on a farm near Pilot Grove. He attended St. Martin's parochial school for eight years then entered Pilot Grove high school which he has attended the past four years. While in high school he was treasurer of the Sophomore class, charter member of the FFA, vice president of the Junior class member of the FFA 1938-39, member of the glee club 1938-39 and president of the FFA in 1939. He was reporter of the Senior class, member of the live stock judging team of 1939-40, member of the one-act play this year, member of the Junior play cast, member of the FFA play cast 1939-40 and a member of the Senior play cast.

GLEN H. EICHHORN

Glen H. Eichhorn, son of Mr. and Mrs. A. W. Eichorn was born September 22, 1922. He attended grade school at Harriston and high school at Pilot Grove. He became a charter member of the FFA in 1937-38 and is now vice president of the FFA

ROSELYN GERKE

Roselyn Gerke, daughter of Mr. and Mrs. John Gerke, was born near Pilot Grove, November 14, 1920. She attended the St. John's parochial school and later Pilot Grove high. During the four years of high school life she was secretary of the Junior class and a member of the glee club in her Senior year.

HERBERT GERKE

Herbert Gerke was born April 20, 1922 at Pilot Grove. He is the son of Mr. and Mrs. Herman Gerke. He attended the first years of school at St. Joseph's school and started to Pilot Grove high in September 1936. In his Sophomore year he entered the FFA and has been a member for three years. In his Senior year he was elected treasurer of his class

ROBERT GERLING

Robert Gerling, son of Mr. and Mrs. Henry Gerling, was born January 18, 1921, two miles south of Pilot Grove. During his Freshman year, he was member of the Junior Civic club. He was a member of the softbal team during his Sophomore, Junior and Senior years. He was class reporter during his Junior year. He was a member of the baseball team during his last year. Was president of the Senior class and a member of the Senior play cast.

BILLY JUDY

Billy Judy, son of Mr. and Mrs. L. H. Judy, was born March 15, 1922. He has attended Pilot Grove school twelve years. During that time he was a member of the band and orchestra, Glee club and Junior Booster club. was also a member of the basket ball team, took part in the Negro minstrel two years,. and was a member of the softball team. He was president of the Junior class of 1939 and a member of the Junior play cast for that that year.

CHARLOTTE HEINRICH

Charlotte Heinrich, daughter of Mr. and Mrs. John D. Heinrich, sr., was born at Pilot Grove October 6, 1922. She has attended the Pilot Grove school for twelve years. During the last four years she was president of the Junior Booster club, president of the Freshman class, president of the Sophomore class, treasurer of the Junior class and member of the basketball team from 1935 through 1940, She was a member of the track team of 1936-37, and volleyball team and a member of the Showboat minstrel cast 1937-39. Member of the one-act play 1937-38, member of the Junior play of 1938-39, Senior play of this year, member Glee club 1936-39, member of the band 1936-39, member literary contest team 1938-39, president of Home Ecnomics club 1939-40, c-captain of the basketball team of 1939-40, leader of the pep squad in 1935-38 and was voted best citizen of high school.

DOROTHR KRAMEL

Dorothy Kramel, daughter of Mr, and Mrs. W. L. Kramel, was born at Blackwater June 7, 1922. She attended school for eight years at Peninsula. She attended her first year of high school at Blackwater and the next three years came to Pilot Grove. She was a member of the Glee club in her Junior year and was a member of the music contest at Otterville in 1939.

ISABELLE LORENZ

Isabelle Lorenz, daughter of Mr. and Mrs. Leo Bonen, was born at Pleasant Green September 24, 1922. She attended St. Joseph's school for eight years and her last four years at Pilot Grove high. She was a memebr of the girls Glee club for two years and mixed chorus for one year. Was member of the Junior Booster club, in the Junior play and a member of the softball team two years. She was also a member of The P. G. Starette staff.

RAYMOND MUESSIG

Raymond Muessig, son of Mr. and Mrs. F. L. Muessig, was born at Pilot Grove July 22, 1922. He spent most of his life on the farm and when the time came for him to begin his education

Pilot Grove High School Starette

Pilot Grove, Mo. May 16, 1940 Vol. 3, No. 21

he started to school. During his first eight years he attended St. Joseph Catholic school. During the next four years he attended the Pilot Grove high school. He played basketball for two years and was a member of the typing team in the contest of 1940. For two years he was also an active member of the Future Farmers chapter.

HERMAN MEISENHEIMER

Herman Heisenheimer, son of Mr. and Mrs. P. G, Meisenheimer, was born April 17, 1920 near Pilot Grove. He attended school for eight years at Vollmer school and the next four years at Pilot Grove high school. While in high school he was a charter member of the FFA 1937-38, member of the FFA 1938-39, member of FFA play cast of 1939-40 and a member of the FFA class of 1939 40.

DIXIE JUNE PIATT

Dixie June Piatt, daughter of Mr. and Mrs. William Piatt, was born near Pilot Grove November 21, 1922. She attended Buffalo Prairie school during 1928-36, and did her high school work at Pilot Grove.

NELLIE PORTER

Nellie Porter, granddaughter of Mrs. Mary E. Zinn, was born on a farm near Nelson. She went eight years to Postal grade school and began her first year of high schol at Pilot Grove. She was a member of the basketball team and won second place in high in track at Kemper Business academy. She was also a member of the girl's 4-H C club. The second year she attended Smith Cotton high school at Sedalia

softball and volleyball team and was chosen as the outstanding volleyball player in her class, also being chosen captain of the team. She went the last two years to Pilot Grove high school. During her Senior year she was art editor of the Tatler.

MARJORIE QUINLAN

Majorie Quinlan, daughter of Mrs. Raymond Quinlan, was born near Pilot Grove August 18 1922. She attended the St. Joeph's parochial school and later the Pilot Grove high school. She was a member of the Junior Booster club, vice presidnt of the Sophomore class, member of the track team in her Freshman year, member of Tattler staff in her Junior and Senior year, member of the pep squad and softball team, secetary of the Home Economnies club in 1939-40, vice president of the Glee club 1939-40, secretary of Senior class 1939 40, member of Junior play cast and was in the Senior play cast. She was also a member of the mixed chorus, sextette and quartette.

ROSALINE SCHUSTER

Rosaline Schuster was born December 3, 1922 near Pilot Grove. She is the daughter of Mrs. Frank Schuster and attended St. Martin's school before entering Pilot Grove high school. During her presence she was a member of the Junior Booster club in 1936-37; member Senior play cast,; member of the literary contest team in 1937-38 and a member of the Tattler staff of 1939-40. She completed high school in three years.

SHOW TICKET WINNERS

Mrs. Herbert Loeffler and Mrs. Vanie Shay will each receive two tickets this week to the Roxy theatre. One ticket each goes to Mrs. Herman Horst, Mrs. Julia Stoecklein and Gerald Lammers.

Mrs Cora Allen and Mrs E B McCutcheon had as their guests Friday Mr and Mrs Marvin Moore of Los Angeles.

Mrs Pete Muntzel and daughter Helen were Pilot Grove visitors Monday.

Pilot Grove High School Starette

Pilot Grove, Mo. May 16, 1940 — Vol. 3, No. 21

Check ✓ FOR VALUES AND VARIETY

WARNHOFF'S

Check ✓ FOR VALUES AND VARIETY

BANANAS	pound	5½c
LEMONS	dozen	19c
Lighthouse Scouring Pwd.	3 cans	10c
COOKIES	pound	10c
Quick Arrow Soap Flakes	25c size	15c
Peerless Hardwater Soap — With this coupon Limit 2 bars		3c
Kelso Vanilla Extract, and 8 oz. bottle Lemon FREE	8 oz. bottle	25c
All White Shoe Polish	10c bottle	5c
SUGAR	10 lb. bag	50c
Rice	fancy factory packed, 3 pounds Regular 25c bag	19c
J & P Coats Thread — with this coupon - limit 2 spools		3c
Toweling, unbleached, yard		5c
Ribbon, new dotted pattern, yd.		5c
Doilies, large size, 6 in pkg.		5c
Anklets, Terry Cloth,	25c value, pr.	10c
Turbans, wrap-around style		25c
Satin Slips,	$1.00 values	48c
Carpet Beaters		15c
Step Ladders, 5 foot size		$1.29
Screen Wire, 24 in. width, yd.		15c
Milk Pails, 10 quart tin		19c

Coffee- Remember-Buy 2 pounds and get one pound FREE. Biggest coffee value in Cooper County.

SENIOR PLAY A SUCCESS

The senior play "For Pete's Sake" was an overwhelming success, both figuratively and financially. The class is very pleased with the outcome, and wishes to thank the following people: first, Mrs Robert Warnhoff who so willingly contributed her time and energy, Mrs Mary Briggs who kindly volunteered her services in time of need, John Ferrell who rendered two violin selections, Patty Schilb who sang delightfully, the orchestra which played tirelessly, Hays and Painter for stage furnishings, the United Telephone company, and everyone who helped to make this play a success.

PILOT GROVE LOCALS

Mrs H M Howe and Miss Helen Howe of Northfield, Vermont were guests Saturday of Mrs Cora Allen and Mrs E B McCutcheon.

Miss Roxie Hayes was hostess at dinner in Columbia Thursday evening to Mrs Mary Briggs, Mr and Mrs M W Schier, and Robert Frazier of Boonville.

Mr and Mrs Henry Fuser and daughter of Boonville and Mr and Mrs Mike Meyer spent Sunday in Sedalia visiting Mr and Mrs Joe Meyer and Mr and Mrs Geo Robb.

Mr and Mrs Russell Schlotzhauer spent Sunday with Mrs Schlotzhauer's parents Mr and Mrs Luther Rhodes.

Mr and Mrs Clarence Harold Stegner of Arrow Rock spent Sunday with Mr and Mrs Clarence Stegner and son Wilbur.

Miss Dorothy Stegner, who is attending school at Warrensburg spent the week end with her parents Mr and Mrs Elliot Stegner.

"Hey—deedle dee dee, it's the railroad life for me!"

—With apologies to Pinocchio.

HOME AGAIN, HOME AGAIN, JIGGETY JIG!

ON THE 10TH OF JULY 1965 AFTER 20 YEARS of wandering around the world aimlessly, I returned to my native Missouri with my family. We had just moved to Kansas City from Lawrenceville, New Jersey. I served a two year tour at Western Electric's Princeton Research Laboratories. Prior to that we had lived six years in North Carolina where Karen, our youngest, was born.

I told my colleagues upon my arrival at the Princeton Labs that, like the Pilgrims' experience in Holland, we had to get out of Carolina because the kids were forgetting how to speak English. When Karen started to kindergarten at the Ben Franklin school on Princeton Pike, the other kids crowded around her and gave her nickels to hear her say, "Hot dawg" with a pure North Carolina Tarheel accent.

Daisy and I had just paid off a promise. We bought the kids a beautifully marked Dalmatian puppy and christened him Duke. Rick called him Dukey Dukey Diamond. Feeling altogether well pleased with ourselves in our new home in Kansas City and my new job in Lee's Summit, we decided to celebrate our homecoming. We chose a pleasant weekend to drive down to Pilot Grove and indulge a bit of nostalgia. Interstate 70 is the most direct route from Kansas City, but we chose 'Memory Lane'.

TAKE MEMORY LANE

'Memory Lane' was: Highway 50 through Sedalia and Smithton to Cooper County E then to Clifton City and Pleasant Green finally joining up with Route 135 and on into Pilot Grove.

I used to hitchhiked home along this route from Camp Crowder in 1945. Then, Cooper County E was a gravel road. I was happy to find that it is now a paved, all-weather highway. The route recalled with nostalgia my experiences of 20 years before.

Several miles after leaving US 50 we topped a hill near the old Young place and there—spread out before us like an old cat basking in the morning sun—was the little village of Clifton City where—according to local history—nothing much ever happened. Although Clifton City was the official name of the town, when we lived there we called it 'Clifton'—the City part seemed a little pretentious. Memories of our short residence there in 1932 came flooding back.

CLIFTON CITY LIFE IN 1932

I was a pre-schooler in the summer of 1932 when dad was 'bumped' to Clifton. He was a section foreman on the MK&T Railroad (the Katy) and this was the third, but thankfully the last time we had to move. When the Clifton stint ended we returned to Pilot Grove in 1933 in time for me to register for the beginnings of my education at Pilot Grove Public School.

Since bumping was a widespread practice in the radical downsizing of U.S. industry during the great depression, maybe I should explain it. To be bumped meant that someone with more seniority took *your* job when he lost his. The bumpee, of course, could then bump someone junior to him. This chain reaction continued until the most junior man lost his job with no further recourse. In this scheme every termination of a position would initiate a cascade of employee bumping and associated family moves. Uprooting families brought emotional and economic stress—all moves were at the expense of the affected employees.

Mom had to go to Warnhoff's and get kerosene lamps for there was not electricity in Clifton City. The days of the REA were far into the future. She got three "Aladdin" lamps and though they represented a cultural move backward, they were quite handsome and even after our tour in Clifton, I enjoyed seeing them when they were occasionally used during power outages in Pilot Grove.

Another memory of Clifton City was the general store. It had a particular smell, not unpleasant, which I now realize was from the use of a petroleum based floor sweep compound. It is surprising the whole place didn't burn down from the years of accumulation of petroleum distillate. In front of the store were two gasoline pumps, a minor concession to the automobile and the possibility that it might catch on after all. A giant of a man—nicknamed 'Heavy'—presided over the automotive department. 'Heavy' was about 5 ft 10 inches tall and about the same width with no fat. It was a town legend that he had once—lacking a handy jack—lifted the front end of a Ford Model A, holding it until a block could be placed.

While passing through Clifton in the summer of 1996, Bob and I spent a moment looking for the place we lived in 1932 and the old general store. The house is still there but the commercial buildings have long since been abandoned and now look like Roman ruins.

Dad's job here in Clifton City was that of 'Section Foreman'. The Katy mainline ran from St. Louis, MO to San Antonio, TX. That part from St. Louis to Parsons, KS was the Eastern Division. St. Louis, Franklin and Parsons were crew change points and trains were dispatched from those terminals. For railway maintenance purposes, the Katy was divided into 6 to 10 mile Sections. The 'right-of-way' of each Section was maintained by a section gang composed of a Foreman and 2 or 3 Section Hands.

The section gangs used a little 'motor car' as well as a trailer-like 'push car' to get to a work site with tools and materials. They replaced cross-ties, checked rails, etc. In the fall they burned off weeds including a wild strain of hemp called cannabis sativa, a.k.a. marijuana. Thus, during summer burnings it was often not necessary to stop by the saloon for the usual relaxing beer or two, the crew had been inhaling marijuana smoke all day.

In 1932, Sherman Todd was one of the Clifton hands. The Todd family lived in a company house by the tracks. The Katy still owned quite a number of these 'company houses'. They were little two bedroom bungalows, painted in standard Katy livery and located on the railroad right-of-way. We had lived in one in Deerfield, MO, in 1928.

Tragically, one of the Todd girls, about Dixie's age (8 or 9 years old), had tuberculosis and died in 1933. Before Mom found out about the 'TB' we used to play with them. 'TB' was still a killer in the 1930's, so our association with the Todd kids was terminated.

A favorite play place in Clifton was a culvert under the Katy tracks near the Todd home. It was 5 feet high with a grate under the rails. When a train came we ran into the culvert and peeped up through the grate. It took every bit of my 5-year old courage to stand there as 100 tons of locomotive crashed by—three feet overhead. Flames flashed from the firebox and steam roared and chuffed through the cylinders with the massive drive rods clanking out the time. These were the magnificent, the mighty 'Mikado' locomotives. Railroad guys called them 'Mikes'.

We lived in Clifton about one year yet I will always remember laying awake late at night listening to the trains whistling for the crossings and then rattling through the little village. That lonesome train whistle, is one of the most nostalgic sounds I've ever heard.

THE MIGHTY MIKADO

Until the late 1940's the 'Mikado'[1] was the Katy's main freight locomotive. It was a massive, 2000 horsepower, coal burning, 900 class, model 1923 steam locomotive built by Lima Locomotive Works, Lima, Ohio. These locomotives were type 2-8-2 which means 2 bogey (non-driving) wheels, 8 drive wheels followed by 2 more bogeys under the engineers cab. They looked something like Fig. 8-1.

Fig. 8-1. The 2-8-2 'Mikado'.

I was to get better acquainted with these monsters in the years to come.

Fig. 8-2. A 900 Class Mikado in Franklin yards. The little house on the tender was the 'office' of the front end brakeman.

Fig. 8-3. 700 Class Mikado with 16" shells for the US Navy on the West Coast emerges from Missouri River fog near Rocheport—1944.

[1] The 'Mikado' was originally designed for the Japanese National Railway hence it's name. Lima Locomotive Works adapted the design for American use in 1921 and began making them at their Ohio plant.

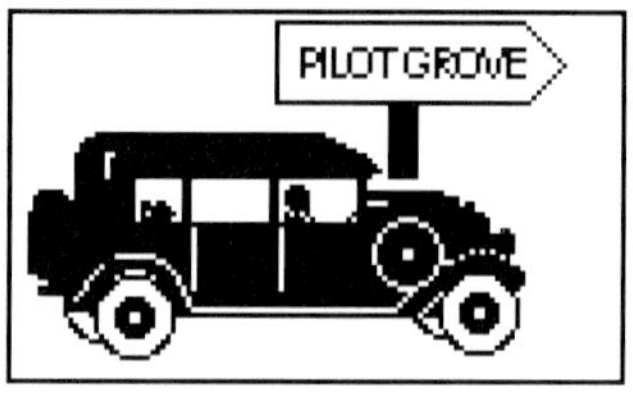

Fig. 8-4. Like Goethe's race with Death (described in "Der Erlen König"), we galloped off to Dr. Barnes and diphtheria shots in our 1929 Chevy.

PLAGUE AND PESTILENCE

My most vivid memory from Clifton involved a tragedy. I was a pre-schooler but sister Dixie attended third grade in a two room school house. This school house sat at the corner where westbound Highway 135 now makes a sharp right turn.

One cold winter night I heard Mom and Dad muttering in the kitchen. The little school had an epidemic of diphtheria! In those days diphtheria was deadly. Indeed, in this outbreak the first child to contract it died, while several others were very ill.

Mom, Dad, Dixie, Bob and I piled into the 1929 Chevy and rushed 12 miles through the darkness for Pilot Grove and Dr. Barnes. We got shots and returned home with sore arms but breathing easier.

Dr. Barnes lived in and served Pilot Grove nearly all his life. He practiced out of his home at 501 College Avenue. After his death his widow was Pilot Grove's Postmistress for many years. Dr. Barnes was the Katy's contract physician and delivered my sister, my brother and me at our home at 110 Fourth Street where Mom was also born. Dr. Barnes is the subject of a formal biographical sketch in Chapter 2.

A RAILROADING FAMILY

Dad worked for the Katy from 1915 until his death in 1940. He was never unemployed although he—like most other workers of his day—lived a life of agonizing insecurity. In the words of Thoreau, he was one of the "...men living out their lives in quiet desperation."

The Katy fared no better than any other businesses in the great depression. Rail traffic was so light in the 1930's that a double header train (two big 'Mikado' locomotives) passing through Pilot Grove was an event noted by all the kids and loafers at the Katy depot. Things were so dull in those days we used to count the cars (mostly empty) and verbally note car markings—"...103 cars and I saw a Great Northern boxcar!"

"That's nothing, I saw some Aroostook & Northerns!" (Potato cars from Maine).

DER ERLEN KOENIG[2]

Who rideth so late through the night wind wild?
It is the father with his child
He has the little one well in his arm;
He holds him safe, and he folds him warm.

My son, why hidest thy face so shy?—
Seest thou not, father, the Erlen King nigh?
The Erlen King with train and crown?—
It is a wreath of mist, my son,

"Come, lovely boy, go, go with me;
Such merry plays I will play with thee;
Many a bright flower grows in the strand,
And my mother has many a gay garment at hand."

My father, my father, and dost thou not hear
What the Erlen king whispers in my ear?—
Be quiet, my darling, be quiet my child;
Through withered leaves the wind howls wild.

"Come lovely boy, wilt thou go with me?
My daughters fair shall wait on thee;
My daughters their nightly revels keep;
They'll sing, they'll dance, they'll rock thee to sleep."

My father, my father, and seest thou not
The Erlen king's daughters in yon dim spot?—
My son, my son, I see and I know
'Tis the old gray willow that shimmers so.

I love thee; thy beauty has ravished my sense;
And, willing or not, I will carry thee hence"—
O father, the Erlen King now puts forth his arm!
O father, the Erlen King has done me harm!

The father shudders; he hurries on;
And faster he holds his moaning son;
He reaches his home with fear and dread,
And, lo! In his arms the child was dead.

[2] For the little ones—Der Erlen König (The Alder King) is an allegorical poem by Johann Wolfgang Goethe about a father's race to save his son from death (the Alder King) and the king's attempt to entice the son into going with him. My thanks to Jack Schmidt for finding the English translation for me.

Fig. 8-5. The Katy Flyer passenger service was discontinued in 1948.

Fig. 8-6. Katy train 77 passes through Pilot Grove, 1949.

When I was in Miss Madge Goode's elementary classes, recess play was halted when a train rattled through town. The school playground was a perfect viewing point as the locomotive chuffed into sight from behind Ries' grove of ancient cedars. I remember the flaming fire box and the black smoke as the mighty Mikados pulled long trains through Pilot Grove. We could see the engineer and sometimes the fireman stoking the boiler.

In those days the Mikados were coal burners. It appeared to me that this life—the life of a trainman—had to be the most glamorous vocation that anyone could possibly aspire to. I resolved that that would be my life work when I grew up!

PILOT GROVE, NOUS SONT ICI![3]

'Memory Lane' from Clifton City comes into Pilot Grove on College Street. I continued to Roe. College and Roe is sort of the epicenter of downtown Pilot Grove. In 1945 this corner had marked the sites of Pop Tracy's Cafe; Goode's place (Madge was my first grade teacher); Hays and Stoecklein Furniture and Undertaking and Schweitzer's Gas Station.

I then turned north to the once bustling Katy depot where I did my 1944 swing shift railroad telegrapher apprenticeship while in my PGHS Senior year. See Fig. 8-6.

Sadly, by 1965 the old depot was shoddy and dilapidated. Paint peeling, windows broken, platform and track unkempt, it mourned, "The old Katy is gone." My lovely chats[4] surface laid down in 1943 with my sweat and that of a hundred others was now overgrown with weeds. The rails were rusted with disuse.

Passenger service had been terminated in 1948 and the Katy Flyer and Texas Bluebonnet (see Fig. 8-5) were no more. Freight service ended in 1985 when all operations ceased and rigor mortis began. Pilot Grove folks tried to save the old depot but there was little practical use for such a building. Shortly, it would be gone too. Then the last physical vestiges of my career with the Katy would disappear.

JACK ON TRACK

It was during this moribund period of the Katy , the late spring of 1949 that Jack Schmidt was a guest in the Burger household and was assigned an upstairs bedroom. It was a warm evening and a gentle northerly breeze wafted the curtains through the open window.

Note Fig. 8-6 above. About 20 yards to the left rear of the spot where the photographer was standing for this photo there stood a black steel pole mounting a rectangular plate. This white plate had a simple black "X" on it. This "X" was a signal to all trainmen — "grade crossing directly ahead, begin warning signals". The warning signal is two long hoots from the train horn, then a short, then one very long hoot. This hooting is audible for 3-4 miles.

Lucky Jack, his upstairs window was about 100 feet from, and faced the railroad track near the Hall Street crossing. The next morning he came down with bleary and bloodshot eyes. Over breakfast he complained to Marjorie— "You didn't tell me the railroad took a shortcut through the guest bedroom!"

"Well," said Marjorie, "It was a good thing I had made up some Denver biscuits—after several helpings, Jack seemed to be coping again."

BEGINNINGS OF A RAILROAD CAREER

There were a number of distractions from my budding railroad career. During the war years, jobs were rather easy to come by although not all of them were guaranteed to set your foot on the road to riches. I regarded farm employment one of this category.

My dad grew up on the family farm but left when his family went west (Montana homestead) in 1912. He never

[3] In 1917 upon the AEF's arrival in Paris, General Pershing exhausted his entire fractured French vocabulary with this speech: "LaFayette, nous sont ici!" (Lafayette, we are here!)

[4] Chats - The fine rock waste from zinc mining and smelting.

Fig. 8-7. I never learned to drive the Payne's tractor.

completely got farm life out of his system. In the 1930s whenforeclosed and abandoned farms were dirt cheap, we spent many Sundays visiting and inspecting the offerings. Dad would walk the land, test and sniff the dirt. It was clear what his longings were. It's just as well he never mustered the nerve to actually revert to his roots. In those days it would have been like buying a ticket on the Titanic.

This was my unspoken attitude on farming when, in the spring of 1943, I was approached by Mr. Paine our commercial arts teacher and basketball coach. He was an excellent commerce teacher but no hot-shot as a coach. Vernon Paine was a medium built, nonathletic, forty-ish, bachelor who dressed in the standard style for school teachers—shabby gentility. He always wore a white shirt with tie, a dark suit which he pressed each morning. But the knees and seat of his trousers were shiny and his shirt cuffs were frayed.

I returned to the typing room after class one day to retrieve a notebook and found him scissoring his shirt cuffs. He was, I discovered, a never-married, devoted, only son of well-to-do but aging parents who were trying to work a rather extensive farm southwest of Emporia, Kansas.

The problem that his parents were having and which he put to me was that by 1943 the draft had exhausted the ranks of potential 'hired hands'. The farm desperately needed help for the upcoming summer. Vernon Paine thought he had a possible in me and invited me to spend a weekend with him and his parents on the farm.

I felt intimidated. The Extra Gang job with the Katy was not a dead certainty. I didn't want to lie and tell him that it was. I would like to please him, but unlike my father, I was never infected with the romance of farming.

DUDE FARMER FOR THE WEEKEND

I couldn't think of a diplomatic way out, so I agreed to accompany him to his family farm for a weekend in March 1943. We departed Pilot Grove after school Friday March 19th at about 500PM. At about 1100PM we passed through Emporia and near midnight we arrived at the farm. I was shown every courtesy and fixed up with a very pleasant upstairs bedroom. I conked out at about 0100AM and was awakened what seemed like 5 minutes later (actually about 0530AM) by Mrs. Paine banging on the door and cheerfully calling me to breakfast.

FARMING LESSONS

I tried to milk a cow—Grade F (I got some in my eye). I pitched some hay—Grade C. I tried to drive their ancient tractor—Grade B. This tractor was ready for the Smithsonian Institute in 1943. I was 15 years old and had never been much concerned with driving anything. I had had no instructions, but tractors in those days were designed for people of very modest skill. Apparently, my skill level was not even 'modest'.

On Sunday we followed a similar schedule. What, no Sunday School? In lieu of the farm chores I could have faked a few hallelujahs. I got the impression that for the Paines, farming was a 7 day a week job. The family was a credit to their pioneer forebears. Senior Paine was well into his 70s but still quite active and held up his end. Vernon Paine was a klutz but he worked hard. Mrs. Paine restricted her duties to the kitchen and playing Lady Bountiful (with great success, I should add). While working (and starving) in St. Charles two years later I was to remember the immense and tasty meals that she put on the table that weekend.

KATY EXTRA-GANG: HELP WANTED

In the end, the Katy saved me from a summer of serfdom on a Kansas farm. Elon 'Slim' Wassmann ran the section gang working east out of Pilot Grove—my Dad's old section. He had been selected as general foreman of an 'Extra Gang' based in Pilot Grove. Otto Stoecklein was assistant foreman. The gang would rehabilitate Katy track from Boonville westward and would start hiring in May. A week or so after my excursion into Kansas agronomy, Slim suggested that if I started to work with his section gang, I'd have Katy seniority and be a cinch to get an Extra Gang job for the summer of 1943. Consequently, although I was only 15 years old, I inaugurated my Katy railroad career on Saturday 10th April 1943.

In the event, the concerns about getting hired were absurd. By 1943 the nation had been almost completely denuded of potential workers by the armed forces. An able-bodied man getting hired was about as difficult as feeding red meat to hungry wolves.

WARNHOFF'S MERCANTILE

To be properly fitted out for my entrée into this brave new world of work I went with my mother to Warnhoff's store.

In those days, Warnhoff's was one of Pilot Grove's premier emporiums. Three brothers ran it—Harry the shrewd one, Bob the jolly one and Walter the politician. We 'ran a bill' there and in the 1930s I often accompanied my mother on payday to 'pay the bill' and buy $20-25 worth of groceries. Twenty dollars worth of groceries required a truck for delivery which Warnhoff's delivery driver 'Mac' undertook in a 1932 green Model T pickup. Dad could feed and cloth a family of five for about $50 per month.

Walter or Bob would give me a bag of candy in appreciation of our business. Harry was always able to contain his enthusiasm and keep a tight lid on the candy jar.

While glad-handed Walter and Bob Warnhoff made the business work, Harry made it profitable. My friend Vern Klenklen occasionally worked at the store weekends and after school. He worked with Henry Simmons, a guy who strayed into town from somewhere. Vern and Henry often did some roustabout work in the warehouse. Vern told me a story that epitomized Harry Warnhoff.

"Harry put us to a task in the warehouse one Saturday. We quickly finished the job— a big mistake—and were sitting on our duffs shooting the bull when Harry caught us. 'What the hell do you think you're doing sitting around on your butts!' he erupted, 'Do you think I'm paying you two loafers ten cents an hour to shoot the bull?'

"Sorry, Mr. Harry. We got finished and no one told us what to do next." Vern says wringing his hat. "Whatcha want us to do then?"

"See them bags of sugar?" he jerked his thumb toward an 8 ft by 8 ft by 10 ft stack of 100 pound bags of sugar. "I want them stacked at the other end of the warehouse. And by dam you come and tell me when you're through. You got that?"

"Yessir, Mr. Harry", and they laid to with a will. Three hours of backbreaking work later they finished and Vern was elected to find Harry and report. "We're all done Mr. Harry. Whatcha want us to do now?"

Harry accompanies them to the warehouse to verify the task and then says, "Okay, Captain Buddy. You done good. Now move all that sugar back to where you got it and don't you lazy loafers *ever* let me catch you goofing off again!"

SUITED UP FOR ACTION

April 1943 was exceptionally cold. There had been a hard frost the first week of April, thus I had to have a lined jean jacket. This was in addition to the standard Levi jeans, blue chambray shirt, striped railroad cap, leather gloves and heavy, high top Wolverines. The Wolverines were just like my Dad used to buy from Snoddy's store just across the Boonville Bridge in Howard County. These Wolverine high top shoes were "...the finest product of the shoemaker's art and the pride of Michigan." See, it says so right here on the box. The Wolverines completed my 'uniform'.

Donning that uniform was a major milestone in my life. I pondered on this when I put on a khaki uniform at Ft. Leavenworth two years later. All suited up to face a big and

Fig. 8-8. The Katy depot in 1944. I was swing shift telegrapher operator my Senior year at PGHS.

perilous world. Such was life in Pilot Grove in 1943.

THE EXTRA GANG

Slim was true to his promise and upon completing the school year I started on the Extra Gang full time. We worked six days a week, ten hours a day for the handsome remuneration of 48-3/4¢ per hour. Payday was on the first and 15th of each month. Payroll withholding was insignificant so I usually took home a king's ransom of $55 per payday. That's about $110 per month for those of you who flunked Miss Strickfadden's math class.

I gave Mom $20 per month and the rest was mine. Fortunately three factors prevented me from blowing it all. 1. I worked six days a week. On Sunday I was so tired I only wanted to rest, and 2. With the scarcities of wartime there wasn't much to buy. 3. All the temptations of the big city—Pete's Pigpen, Green Pastures in Sedalia, The Bloody Bucket, Taylor's, The Big Apple, Al's Place in Boonville were all off limits to 16 year olds and beyond my transportation range anyway. My transportation in those days was via Shank's Mare (walking) or bumming a ride with a schoolmate.

RECRUITING - 'THE CASTING CALL'

Recruiting for the gang was just getting started in May. I knew Slim was expecting to sign up a lot of high school boys. He wasn't disappointed. Joining me on the gang were Homer Jeffress, Marvin (Chief) Lewis, L.J. (Smokey) Zeller, Billy Stewart, Billy Joe Piatt came with his dad, Clifford Ashcraft, Alonzo Kempf and his dad. Because of the draft there were only three sources of manpower: 1. Underage guys like us, 2. Overage guys like—Jake Brownfield (60s), Todd and 'Tater' Coffman (70s), Joe Piatt (50s), Joe Wright, Willie Walker and Earnest Chastain (40's with a family), and 3. Draft exempt guys like Milton Moore who had lost an eye in a knife fight and Billy Joe Piatt whose vision was probably 20/4000—nearly blind. Slim says, "So far as physical requirements is concerned, applicants ought to be able to see lightning and hear thunder, lift a bar and tote a cross-tie. That's about it!"

Slim was a good boss but he was extremely busy with

recruiting, ordering materials, liaising with Mr. Brant the Roadmaster and the foremen of other resurfacing gangs. Otto Stoecklein, his assistant foreman was a wonder at dealing with people. He was a very likable fellow, in fact the men liked him better than Slim. However, Otto was no great shakes on paperwork. So Slim dumped it on me. I had to oversee the signing up of new workers and see to all the endless paper shuffling.

I especially remember one rainy day in early June. Because the rain didn't look like letting up, Slim dismissed the crew at 1000AM and started processing the 2-3 dozen applicants who were standing around the depot. They were standing on the platform under the lee of the wide eaves of the station until the slashing rain drove them into the waiting room. C.E. Lange the station agent stood in the door of his office arms akimbo like a prissy old maid and stared in disgust at the wretched figures filing into his once immaculate waiting room.

The rain ran off their raincoats, makeshift canvas covers and tattered coats making little puddles on the floor. Lange had built a fire against the unseasonable cold that had blown in with the rain that morning. The applicants huddled around the stove.

Slim sat on one of the benches and, balancing papers and a big zippered notebook on his knee, began interviewing the applicants. At 1030 he handed it over to me and said, "Here, you can do this crap as well as I can, Sonny. Just don't let them give you any bull. And here are the time books. Give everyone that showed up for work this morning 2 hours credit. That's the rainy day policy." He disappeared.

The scene looked like central casting for "Tobacco Road". These job-seekers ran the gamut from high school kids to some ancient gandies that wouldn't pass inspection to get into a homeless shelter today. Filthy, ragged overalls, rough-and-tumble coats and shoes in dire need of mending were the costumes of this Coxey's army. This depression era movie set had sound, motion, color and uniquely, one additional dimension—smell. When those soggy clothes got close to the roaring fire, the fragrances wafting through the room would have stopped a charging rhino.

EXTRA GANG 'CHARACTER ACTORS'

There were some very unusual characters here, too. There was Jake Brownfield in his spanky new stripy overalls, blue shirt and new straw hat. Jake was in his 60s. He considered himself a cut above this riffraff that he had been thrown in with, and, he certainly was. He also felt somewhat demeaned by being questioned by a 'snot-nose teenage kid'. He didn't say that but his attitude did.

Next was Todd Coffman. Todd was reputed to be, well...fond of drink. He was accompanied by his brother, Tater. Todd was already on the payroll but was accompanying (and translating for) his brother.

I asked, "Birth date?"

Todd answered "Don't know. Me brother was born in 'tater' digging time in 1875 or '76. In the remainder of the interview Todd did all the talking but details were similarly imprecise. But Mr. Coffman, whom I found was dubbed 'Tater', did have a Social Security number, he was at or above room temperature, could see lightning and hear thunder, so I personally fixed all the details by arbitrarily assigning him a specific birthday, birthplace and placed him on the rolls. 'Tater' Coffman would be over 120 years old as of this writing which is to say he very likely has assumed room temperature. I wonder if his tombstone says, "Tater Coffman"?

Next, comes Milton Moore. Mr. Moore was a giant black man—about 44 years old 5 ft 9 inches tall x 5 ft 9 inches wide, about 300 pounds and missing his left eye. Mr. Moore already had an extremely apt nickname—Bear! Bear was hired and I later saw him in action. He was the epitome of the legendary character John Henry. The 300 pounds he carried around included not one ounce of fat. I once saw him pick up a cross-tie (about 150 pounds), put it on his shoulder and run with it! He teamed with Earnest Chastain and Willie Walker in driving spikes. Earnest was the son of Bob Chastain the Pilot Grove Public School maintenance man. Bob's other son, "June" (Junior) worked as a mechanic for Barney Wessing.

The spike driving act that Bear, Earnest and Willie put on was worth an Oscar. They swung their 10 pound spike mauls with faultless timing, arcing down to strike the spike—bing, bing, bing! This was the very work that legend says killed John Henry[5] when he competed with a steam driven spiking machine.

Jim Albert Miller was another powerful black man. He was a good worker, had a good temperament and was nicknamed "Bo Jack".

Doing the paperwork that day got me the permanent job of keeping all the books: the time and payroll records, the daily work reports, the weekly narrative, the employment applications which continued all summer, albeit at a much reduced rate. Shuffling the paper did not take all my time so I always pitched in for special tasks.

Unloading cross-ties or ballast was one such task. A work train—in railroad parlance, an "Extra"—was used for this work. With the heavy war production traffic on the single-track Katy, the track had to be kept clear as possible. Everyone, including me, hopped-to on these tasks so the extra could finish and get out of the way.

SNAKE IN THE GRASS

[5] "John Henry was a legendary black man famous for his strength, was celebrated in ballads and tales. In one version of the story he outworks a steam drill, but dies from the strain. The legend may have some historical basis.

At noon some of the gang would grab one or two large tarpaulins, find a smooth place and stretch them out for a picnic-like sitting and eating space. Others would drift off to a quiet or shady place for a little solitude. Jake Brownfield always disdained the common site of the riff-raff and went off by himself. Jake's aloofness was finally broken at lunch one day.

He carefully spread his denim jacket on a small pile of leaves and sat down with his lunch pail for a little al fresco lunch. I saw a startled look on his face, then he went up into the air like a jack-in-the-box.

"Snake!" says Jake. Everyone had to run over and look, of course. Jake had sat on a 6 foot black snake that was just as startled as he was. There was a mighty uproar of laughter and Jake took a lot of ribbing from then on. Jake softened up a bit and eventually even laughed at himself.

RUN FOR YOUR LIFE!

There was an incident in late July that was not at all funny. First, a little background on the dangers of unballasted trackage: To resurface the roadbed, first the track is jacked up about 6-9 inches so the cross-ties clear the old ballast. The old ballast is pushed back underneath the cross-ties and tamped. This leaves 'skeletonized' track, i.e., there is no ballast to hold it in place. A train can safely pass over this skeletonized section if it does not exceed 3-5 mph. Train orders thus routinely noted the location of the skeletonizing work and ordered speed reduction to 'dead slow'.

In late July we were working at the bottom of the Pleasant Green hill. This hill is one of the steepest on the railroad. It and the hill at Lick (Prairie Lick) were the reasons most trains dispatched south out of Franklin had to be doubleheaders (two locomotives). It was about 330PM, the hottest part of the day and we were working at a gentle curve near the bottom of the hill. We heard a train coming out of Hoffman (now called Harriston). It was time for No. 81 which was a high speed daily freight to Texas. The crews of the daily No. 81 never took kindly to delay.

There is a rather steep downgrade coming south from Hoffman and when a train crew had a particularly heavy load, they would build up all the speed they could going down hill in order to make it up the next hill. We were working in between.

As he got closer, we could tell by the sound that, contrary to his orders, old No. 81 was *not* slowing. He either didn't read his orders or didn't give a damn. The double header was within a half mile and still pouring on the coal when we heard a loud 'SPROING!'

Fig. 8-9. "Run for your life!" Katy No. 81 gallop at us and the sun kink in the summer of 1943.

A 'sun-kink' is a hot weather hazard. Iron rails subjected to excessively high temperatures, 90°-100°, expand and when the ballast is no longer holding it in place the built-up pressure may be irresistible. The rails may jump completely off the road bed—SPROING!

No need to look, we all knew exactly what it was—the kink had flipped the track six feet to the east of where it was supposed to be! I was at the south end of the strung out gang, Slim was in the middle and Otto Stoecklein was nearest the oncoming train. I heard Slim yell at him and Otto ran to the motor car to pick up fuzees (flares) and torpedoes (an M80-like explosive affixed to the track as a danger signal) and ran in the direction of the train. When he rounded the curve he could see that he had no time to fasten the torpedoes so he struck off both fuzees and waved them in both hands.

That got the engineer's attention but what really scared the living hell out of him was the sight of about eighty guys throwing down tools, jumping the fences and running for their lives. Both engines threw the air brakes full on. A shower of sparks showed that all 16 driving wheels were locked up tight. They even reversed the drive and all drive wheels were spinning backwards when the lead engine got stopped about 30 feet from the kink.

Since there is no way this '90 pound' iron can be manhandled back to its original position—both rails must be disconnected at a joint and a hack saw used to manually cut out about 6 inches. The extra gang came back from the woods and Otto immediately set up two teams to do the cuts. The head end train crews dismounted and came over to watch. It took over a half hour.

Normally, stopping one of these trains for five minutes would result in scathing abuse from the train crew. Not this time. The crews were silent. I don't know whether this was because they obviously screwed up in not obeying the train order, or whether they were just happy to be alive.

BLOWING OFF STEAM

Not all misadventures of train crews had such a fortunate ending. The wartime traffic on the Katy, like every other railroad, stressed men and materiel to the breaking point. Train crewmen were often worked until they were ready to drop. An ICC regulation from the 1930s—the 'Hogue Law' (always referred to as the *Hog* law)—provided scant relief. The 'Hogue Law' required that crewmen not work beyond 16 consecutive hours and required at least 12 hours of relief. The 16 hour rule was scrupulously obeyed. The 12 hour rule often was not. It was not the railroad that was so demanding as much as the war effort.

If there was a trainload of ammunition that must be expedited from Weldon Springs Ordnance, to an west coast port, train crewmen, many of whom had sons, brothers, kinfolk fighting in the Pacific knew that lives might depend on the freight moving with speed. They didn't complain. It was probably this work habit that led to a terrible, fatal locomotive accident in the Campbell yards near the Sedalia State Fair Grounds.

The Katy crew roster put Herb Twenter with Earl Renfrow once back in the 1940s. Earl told me of his experience many years later. He said, "Herb was looking out the window at the lush Missouri farmland whizzing by on a beautiful summer day. The billowing, fluffy clouds set off the pure blue sky.

Earl said, "I asked him, 'Herb, whatcha think of them clouds up there?'"

"Herb says, 'Very pretty.'"

"I says, 'Glad you like 'em Herb because we're goin' to be up there among them if you don't get some water injected into that boiler!'"

On the fatal day—Sunday 7th November 1948—Herb Twenter was firing for Charles Perry. As the big Mikado helper engine rolled north into Campbell Yard (south edge of Sedalia), the down hill coasting obscured the fact that the locomotive had no power. It had no power because it had no steam. Water had not been injected into the boiler for 12-15 minutes and the boiler was dry.

All these old steam engines had been upgraded, evolving from scoop-shovel coal firing to auger feed and finally to oil burners where the old coal tenders were converted for bunker oil. But the careful control of water injection depended upon the particular operational needs and had been left as a manual responsibility of the fireman. Apparently when Herb first noticed his gage indicating dead empty, he overreacted. Though a white-hot, dry boiler is mortally dangerous, he tried to fix his oversight by opening the injector full on.

It was too late. The boiler was not only dry, it was heated to about 1200° F. This is the temperature at which hot steel passes through the color spectrum from red to orange to white-hot.

When the water hit the white hot boiler steel it flashed instantly to steam. Boiler pressure shot from nothing to 1000 pounds per square inch. The result was approximately the same as setting off a 500 pound bomb in the boiler. The explosion was so powerful that the main part of the cab (containing Charles Perry the engineer and Herb Twenter the fireman) was lifted 40 feet in the air and fell across the track. Miraculously, Perry survived. Sadly, Herb did not.

THE KATY TRAIL

The mission of the Katy Extra Gang was to resurface the road bed from Boonville to Sedalia. During my tenure we made it as far as Clifton City. This 'resurfacing' was to replace the old ballast with new, finer chats. Chats packs more solidly than the old, coarser rock and in time forms a rock-hard, impervious surface.

So when you hike the Katy Trail between Boonville and Sedalia today you are walking on a surface that Sonny Salmon help lay down in 1943—a little respect please. Figure 8-11. illustrates the extent of the trail as of 1996.

TELEGRAPHER-CLERK

"BE PREPARED"—SCOUT MOTTO

My next Katy job started in September 1944 and is a lesson on how major consequence often flow from small beginnings. The 'small beginning' was in 1939. I was 12 years old that year and my major interest was the town's Boy Scout Wolf Patrol. The 'major consequence' was my assignment 6 years later, to the Signal Corp rather than the Infantry.

In 1939, I read the Kansas City Star every day. I knew that war clouds were gathering in Europe but that was far away and the Wolf Patrol was here and now. There were about 12 scouts in Pilot Grove—Ernie Mellor Jr., Bobbie Jones, David Brunjes, Homer Jeffress, Neil Coley, me and some others. In the Scouts, I learned knots, 'boxing' the compass and a lot of other stuff most of which I forgot but some of which I still remember. One of the remembered things was Morse Code—dot-dash is A, dash dot dot dot is B, etc. I got a merit badge for Morse Code.

This Morse Code skill led to my job with the Katy 5 years later as a 'Telegrapher-Clerk'. I was 17 years old that fall and the station Agent, C.E. Lange, with some misgivings, tested me and, flummoxing him somewhat, I passed! What was really amazing to me was—this job paid $7.00 per day, 87.5¢ per hour—an absolute godsend for a high school student, son of a widowed mother. Before snickering, remember that $7.00 a day would—in 1944—buy the equivalent of 48 Big Macs. You figure out the dollar equivalent.

In September 1944 I had just started my senior year at Pilot Grove High School. Pauline McCreery who normally worked the 'swing' shift (4PM to Midnight) needed relief. She had four kids, two in service, two in school. Her husband, 'Mac' was a train dispatcher at Franklin. All in all she had about as much as she could handle.

MRS. MAC THE TEACHER

Mrs. Mac, as we called her, was an excellent teacher and I soon mastered the job—primarily copying 'Train Orders' and delivering them 'on the fly'. Train Orders were instructions, written on flimsy multi-copy green tissue paper, strung in hoop-like brackets and held up to be snatched by the engineers and conductor.

Train orders were a bit nerve wracking. Here's the way it worked: When the dispatcher called with an order to be copied and handed up, a STOP signal (Order Board) was set to stop all oncoming trains. No train may pass such a signal without his Orders and Clearance.

The Train Order was then dictated over the phone by the dispatcher and read back for verification. When a particular train approached, say No. 71, the dispatcher was notified, he verified that you had all relevant train orders which were listed in the Clearance then three copies of those orders with the signed Clearance were put in three hand-up hoops

Fig. 8-10. The Katy Trail at Rocheport 1996.

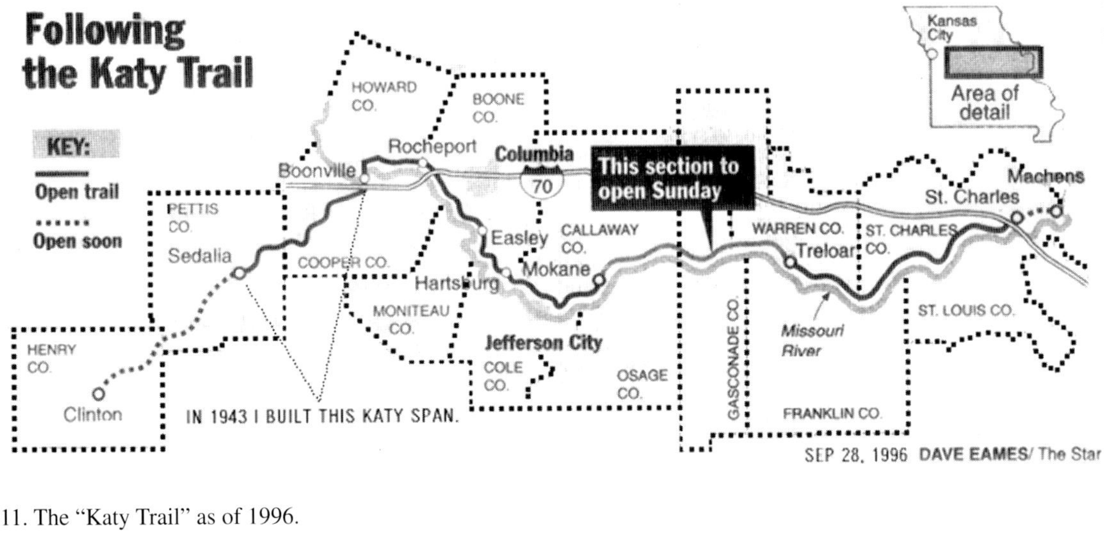

Fig. 8-11. The "Katy Trail" as of 1996.

and rushed out the door. If there was any time, you gave a visual signal ('high-ball') indicating 'get orders on the fly'.

Standing 18-24 inches off the path of the onrushing locomotives, the telegraph-operator would hold the hoops as high as he could and the two engineers (on doubleheaders) would reach down to snatch his orders from the hoops. The third copy went to the conductor riding in the caboose.

While I was working there, C.E. Lange upgraded the train order delivery process. I suppose he was scared witless a time or two when he rushed out the door almost in the path of an onrushing 100-ton locomotive to hand up—on tiptoe—orders to the engineers. He had someone construct a gas-pipe frame to hold the three order hoops. You can see this device in Fig. 8-13.

Fig. 8-12. Katy Flyer arrives Pilot Grove 6:06 AM.

At night, lights of the oncoming train were often visible when the dispatcher started dictating the order. You could hear the train whistling for Talley's crossing. As they rounded the curve behind Ries' house the train crew could see the red Order Board signalling him to 'get orders at Pilot Grove'. Expecting a 'highball', they whistled for signals...four short whistle blasts: toot toot toot toot. A few times I didn't finish the order in time and stopped the train. Stopping a 100-150 car, 60 mph train rushing 10,000 tons of war materiel was not to be taken lightly. It takes about a mile to stop such a train and half an hour to back up. I caught hell from the train crew. I took comfort in the knowledge that a train wreck would probably cause them even greater grief.

CHRISTMAS 1944—"THE SECRETARY OF WAR REGRETS ..."

I had to perform a grim 'Telegrapher' task on Christmas Day 1944 as a result of events half a world away.

Christmastime 1944 saw a ferocious battle in the snowy Ardennes forest of Belgium around Bastogne—the 'Battle of the Bulge'. On December 16th a German 'Panzer' army launched a surprise attack and decimated the American 106th Infantry Division. By Christmas Day the attack was being contained, but not before the Americans suffered severe casualties and one major atrocity. At Malmedy, Belgium, several dozen U.S. POW's were herded into a field and shot. Sepp Dietrich's 6th SS Panzer Army was guilty of this atrocity. At the Nuremberg war trials he was one of the Nazi war criminals tried, found guilty and sentenced but released after ten years.

I was working on that Christmas Day relieving C.E. Lange. As Mrs. McCreery, ever the mother hen, came in the telegraph office with my holiday dinner, I heard the Western Union telegraph calling Pilot Grove. When I answered, the St. Louis operator began rattling off a telegram to me. He was using a semiautomatic sending key called a 'bug'. I finally got him to slow down and began copying casualty telegrams. There were three messages beginning "...the Secretary of War regrets..." and signed by "J. Ulio, The Adjutant General". This was Pilot Grove's share of the butcher's bill for the 'Battle of the Bulge'.

Fig. 8-13. Conductor, Katy Train No. 77, takes his orders on the fly at Pilot Grove.

I don't remember all the names of the killed, wounded or missing. I do remember one—Wilbur Twenter. He was reported as missing following the initial German attack. Weeks later a fuller story came out. Apparently a German artillery shell had knocked down a tree which fell, pinning him. Since the enemy infantry were sweeping through the position he remained quiet and was recovered several days later in a counterattack—with a broken arm, but thankful to be alive.

Over the period of the war years many other telegrams were received at the Pilot Grove depot and local ministers and friends made sad visits to next of kin, telegram in hand. Fortunately for me, the three on Christmas Day were the only ones I personally copied.

GOODBYE TO THE KATY

After two years in the Army, I returned from service in the Pacific and was discharged in March 1947 and tried to reconnect to the Katy. I went on the Clerk-Telegrapher Extra Board. In 4 months I had 4 weeks of work at Franklin, Lynndale and St. Paul, Kansas 'riding' this Extra Board.

My swan song was a two week assignment to relieve the stationmaster in St. Paul, Kansas. See Fig. 8-17. The old town celebrated its centennial in July 1947 and the Katy stationmaster was the Grand Marshal for all the festivities. Two months later, after a few days of trying my hand at assembling Fords at the Leeds Plant in Kansas City, I was back in the US Army at Ft. Riley Kansas. I was 20 years old and had completed another life's lesson: "What ever my calling was ultimately to be—it would not be railroading!"

Thus ended forever my illustrious career as a Katy Railroad Baron and Boy Telegrapher.

Fig. 8-14. Katy Bluebonnet Special crosses the Kansas plains scampering for Texas. ca 1944.

Fig. 8-15. The Mikado 700 Class Locomotive, Franklin Yards ca 1932.

Fig. 8-16. Katy Texas Special pulls out of Parsons, Kansas.

Fig. 8-17. St. Paul, KS was my final assignment on the Katy.

Fig. 8-18. The "Mike Morfa" pulled the Katy president's private car from St. Louis to St. Paul for the Centennial celebration, 1947.

Fig. 8-19. Old Number 5 - The Texas Special passenger train leaves Parsons for St. Louis.

Fig. 8-20. Katy passenger train No. 6 rolls into Pilot Grove - 1944.

When grass starts eating cows
'Stead of t'other way 'round—
When we bow down to the Yankees,
The <u>whole world's</u> turned upside down!

Ancient English folk air played at Cornwallis' surrender, Yorktown - 1781. (Words by the Yankees).

OVERVIEW

NOT PONDERING ON IT TOO LONG, ONE MIGHT assume that history—of nations, of communities and of personal lives—is a gently unfolding highway of smooth curves and pleasant hills leading to the sunlit uplands. As we grow older, we learn that reality may be different.

The evolution of time does indeed include long periods of ennui but these intervals of monotony are often interrupted by abrupt and violent spasms of change. Such was a formative period of my life—the Spring of 1945. A period of just over 90 days encompassed momentous world events which had great effect on everyone and affected me in unique ways. In addition, some personal incidents were to have consequences on the later course of my life. It was a period when "my world turned upside down"

As often happens in real life, these events occurred randomly in time and with no logical connection, or so it seemed then. Thus, with no better rationale, I'll summarize them in simple chronological order and then expand on some of the themes in subsequent chapters.

PRAYER FOR DIVINE INTERVENTION

Friday 16th March 1945

In the spring of 1945 Reverend William Ratje, the Methodist Minister, and his family lived in the Roe Avenue church parsonage with his family. His family was—his wife, his daughter Ruby (PGHS '43) and son Herbie (PGHS '46). Older son Cleo (PGHS '44) was in the Navy.

On Friday evening the 16th of March he sponsored a meeting. I wasn't a member of this Methodist Youth Group but had been invited probably with a thought to my recruitment. I was seventeen years old, a PGHS Senior and, not having yet been convicted of a felony, was possibly thought to be a good candidate.

The Reverend said an opening prayer and at the meeting conclusion — a benediction including a request for divine intervention for those who went in harm's way. I'm sure his mind was on son Cleo serving in the Pacific.

Although we would not know it until much later, Cleo was at that moment aboard the minelayer USS Lindsey, a part of Admiral Fletcher's Task Group 58.1 making flank speed for Okinawa — directly into harm's way.

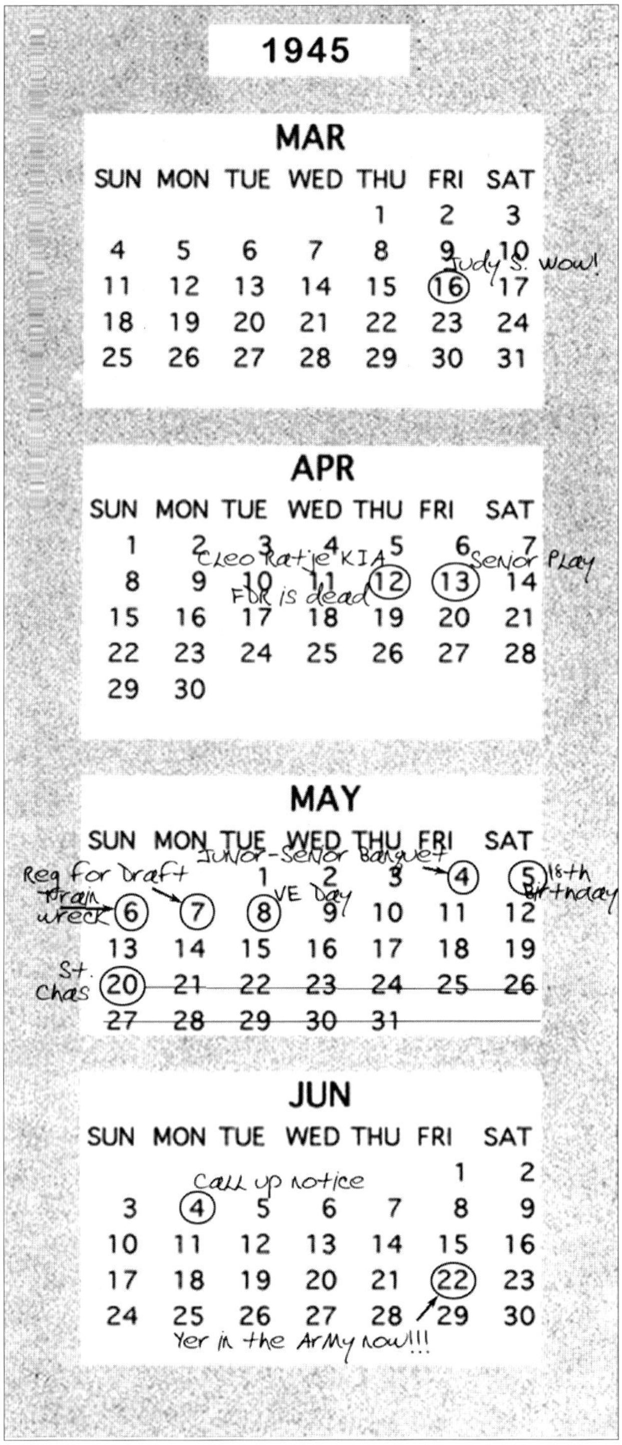

Fig. 9-1. Calendar - Spring 1945.

THE REVEREND AND THE COACH

This was the second time I had witnessed the Reverend intercede for his son. On the first occasion he had a set-to with the basketball coach, Mr. Irwin Laughlin. Laughlin was also the School Superintendent, so the Reverend's verbal assault was particularly courageous.

The incident occurred at Otterville during a regional

basketball tournament in the '43-'44 season. Rev. Ratje felt that Mr. Laughlin didn't sufficiently appreciate Cleo's talents and demanded that Cleo be put in the game. There were angry words and Cleo was between them saying, "Now, Dad! Now Dad!" and trying to get him to be, well... more reverential.

LEMME AT THEM JAPS AND KRAUTS!

The group discussion that late winter evening swerved to the war. Things in Europe were reaching a climax. The 9th Armored Division had captured the Ludendorff Bridge at Remagen and American armor was pouring across the Rhine. The Russians in the East were crashing westward across Prussia straight for Berlin and General Bradley's objective was changed from Berlin to the River Elbe.

I sometimes held the floor in the discussion of these events because I followed newspaper accounts assiduously and tried to be well informed. Samuel Johnson commenting two hundred years earlier, had caught the essence of my interest. He said, "Nothing so concentrates a man's mind as the knowledge that he is to be hanged in the morning." I had thoughts of my upcoming birthday when I would be subject to an invitation to join that valiant band with the promise of three squares, a bunk and a military funeral (as required).

It was during this discussion that I made the stupidest statement I've made in my life. "I just hope the war lasts long enough for me to see some action!"

No sooner out of my mouth and I was embarrassed that I said it and have never mentioned this to anyone until right now. I am sure those who heard me have long since forgotten it, but, in hindsight it was not such an extreme attitude for the times.

I came across the same spirit in a book my son Jeff loaned me recently. Jeff is a member of a history book club and thought I might be interested in a German paratrooper's war journal. Here's what Oberleutnant Martin Pöppel said about himself and his fellow trainees on September 1st 1939. "We were awakened at 0700 hours and told about the incredibly rapid advance of our army units [into Poland] and the daring feats of the Luftwaffe. Although genuinely enthusiastic, we were also secretly afraid that the whole war would be over before we could get into action. That would be unbearable!"[1]

I would today, in explaining this stupidity, offer four points in my defence: 1. Those were very patriotic times — Studs Terkel called World War II "The Good War", 2. I was only 17 years old, 3. Contrary to recent political correctness, there are essential differences between the male and the female of the species homo sapiens. One of these differences is the presence, uniquely in the young male, of a gene for knocking down buildings and killing foreigners, and 4. Buried deeply within the psyche of *all* teenagers is the unarticulated but nonetheless absolute faith that they are — invincible, invulnerable and immortal. A chart of casualty rates versus age for any war will show that it is these young idiotic but altruistic 19 and 20 year olds that do the dying.

O Death, where is thy sting-a-ling-a-ling,
O Grave, thy victoree?
For me the angels sing-a-ling-a-ling,
They have no room for me.
The Bells of Hell go ting-a-ling-a-ling
For you but not for me!
Popular BEF Song, WWI

YOUNG LOVE

The group convening that chilly March evening included Wanda Stegner, Herbie Ratje, Judy Schlotzhauer, myself and several others. Judy, only 16, was, nevertheless, in the "mature, suave, worldly sophisticate" class not only because she was a Junior — she was also blossoming into full fledged womanhood. I had known Judy for some time but being a very young Junior she was somewhat peripheral to my usual circle of chums (Mom would have called them accomplices), most of whom were guys. I had always thought Judy was quite pretty but that evening she was a knockout.

Fig. 9-2. Judy Schlotzhauer - 1945.

Fig. 9-3. Herbie Ratje - 1945.

She had a petite figure, but this newly nubile nymphet filled out her polka dotted navy dress very nicely indeed. She had a jade barrette curbing an unruly wave in her honey blonde hair. It matched her hazel-green eyes. She was a budding rose debuting to the world. I was not the only one that noticed. Herbie tried to move in but she elected to sit by me. She once accidentally touched my hand and I felt a 10,000 volt surge. Gulp!

I *felt* **immortal**. I *knew* I was **invincible** — I was the County All Star Basketball Center. But, maybe, just maybe — I was not **invulnerable** to Cupid's shaft. Twang!

After the concluding benediction the group dispersed and I found myself with Judy on the front porch. We chatted

[1] "Heaven and Hell" Martin Pöppel, Spellmount Press, 1996.

for awhile hitting on all those deep philosophical issues upon which teenagers are so learned and wise. We ran out of conversation but were reluctant to end the magical moment. There was a nearly full moon but it was intermittently obscured by low scudding clouds. Judy was half sitting, half leaning on the porch rail at the newel post. I stood facing her. She said something in a low voice and I leaned forward to hear better. Judy was about 5 ft 6 and I was 5 ft 11. She turned her face up to me just as the moon popped out and the effect was right out of the movies. Bright eyes, burning like fire!

She said, "Sonny, I just think you're wonderful!" Again I thought of a rose opening its petals to the sun. She cocked her head as though listening. We even had some background music for this little scene — Herbie had turned on the radio in the living room and Jo Stafford was singing 'It's Been a Long, Long Time.'

Kiss me once and kiss me twice
And kiss me once again.
Its been a long, long time.

I was 17, shy and a little naive — but I wasn't stupid! I'd seen a lot of movies and — *This is the cue for the kiss scene!* As I bent to kiss her, her arms went around my neck and I hugged her tightly. WOW! After a few more words I reluctantly broke the spell, "I gotta get to the depot, Judy. I'm to relieve Mrs. Mac at 9 o'clock and its 9:15 now."

I took leave and danced down the sidewalk doing mental cartwheels and backflips. I looked back. Judy was standing on the top step wiggling her fingers at me.

As I hurried north two blocks on Roe Avenue to the Katy depot and my swing shift job—I had a strange sensation.

"I have often walked down this street before,
But, the pavement always stayed between my feet before.
Now I seemed to be three feet above—
I can't believe it! Can it be—I'm in love?"

When I floated into the telegraph office Mrs. Mac picked up on the mood and smiled at me. "What's in the world has happened to you?"

I answered, "Nothing fatal — I hope!"

The beginning was *triumph*. The ending was *tragedy*. But that would be over a year later.

THE 'DIVINE WIND'

Thursday 12 April 1945

At 8 PM Saturday, 14th April 1945, my teacher and mentor, Mrs. Pauline McCreery, night shift operator at the Katy depot, temporarily closed the office and carried a telegram to the Ratje family. "The Secretary of the Navy regrets to inform you that your son Seaman 1/c Cleo Ratje was killed by enemy action on Thursday April 12..."

LEFT Fig. 9-4. Cleo Ratje at San Pedro, CA Nov. 1944

By mid-April, General Simon Bolivar Buckner commander of the Tenth Army understood the light opposition. For the first time in all the Pacific storm landings, the Japanese had elected not to strongly defend the beaches. Instead, relying on a mass of intricate, interconnecting trenches and tunnels they would defend in depth to draw in and annihilate the Americans.

In addition, the Kamikaze attacks had begun. Over 2,000 poorly trained but fanatical pilots volunteered to make suicide attacks on the U.S. Fleet around Okinawa. They flew "Baka Bombs"—oneway Zeroes, Zekes and Bettys carrying 500 or 1000 lb bombs. (In Japanese, "Baka" means crazy.) Nearly 45,000 Americans and 100,000 Japanese would become casualties. This was just on the ground. Navy casualties added thousands more. Even the overall commander, General Buckner was killed. "Buckner Bay" off the southeastern Okinawan coast is named for him.

By the 12th of April 1945, the Easter Sunday invasion landings which were only lightly opposed, had been successful and the minelayer USS Lindsey (PM32) had completed its task of mining the northern sea approaches to Okinawa against surreptitious Japanese reinforcements.

The Lindsey had then been relegated to duty as a 'picket ship'. The Kamikaze attacks had become so devastating that all smaller, support vessels had been assigned duty as either antiaircraft fire support or as long range lookouts to warn of approaching Japanese aircraft.

Following is a news account of the fateful day.

BIG LOSS ON MINELAYER

Twin Jap Suicide Attack Cost
the Lindsey 114 Casualties

WASHINGTON, SEPT. 13 (AP)—The 2,200 ton minelayer Lindsey suffered 114 casualties and was blown in two more than 70 feet back of the bow in a double suicide attack by Japanese planes last April 12, the navy reported today.

Of her total complement of 320 men and twenty-one officers, fifty seven men were killed and fifty seven more were wounded.

The attack occurred near Mae Shima, southwest of Okinawa.

One plane dived into the ship's starboard side, and a minute later, the other crashed into the port side near a gun mount magazine.

Approximately a third of the vessel, or more than 100 feet, was either blown away or torn and wrecked. Watertight bulkheads remained intact, and two-thirds of the ship remained afloat.

A new bow was well under construction at the Norfolk navy yard when the ship arrived for repairs.

Skipper of the Lindsey was Comdr. Thomas E. Chambers, 36, of Dyersburg, Tenn. who took command of the ship when she was commissioned at San Pedro, Calif., in August 1944.

In prehistoric times Druids built Stonehenge[2] on Salisbury Plain, Wiltshire, in the south of England to accurately determine—for religious rites—the exact day of the beginning of spring. Cultures world wide still celebrate Easter and the beginning of spring as a renewal of life.

Tragically—in the midst of that 'Renewal of Life' season in 1945—the Lindsey's Chaplain recited The Office Of The Dead, the bugler sounded taps, the firing squad fired three volleys in the ancient tradition of fending off evil spirits and the mortal remains of Cleo Ratje and 56 shipmates were committed to the earth on the island of Ulithi, the Fleet Anchorage. The severely damaged Lindsey then continued its painful 8,000 mile retreat to Norfolk navy yard for repairs and refitting.

A "Divine Wind" (Kamikaze[3]) had struck 27 days after the Reverend's prayer for "Divine Intervention". On Saturday, 28th April a Remembrance Service was held for Cleo at his father's church. I attended with Coach Laughlin and the rest of the 1944 (NCAA Champion) basketball team.

So much for teenage immortality.

ROOSEVELT DEAD IN GEORGIA

"All human things are subject to decay,
And when fate summons, even monarchs must obey."
John Dryden 1670

Another of the cataclysmic events of that spring was

Fig. 9-5. Roosevelt's funeral procession, Washington, D.C. 14th April 1945.

the death of President Roosevelt on the same day Cleo Ratje died—Thursday April 12th[4]. The Kansas City Star ran a special section in the following Sunday paper. I remember a photo on the front page. An old black man was clutching his hat over his heart as the train bearing the President's funeral entourage rolled, Lincolnesque style, through a Georgia railway station bound for Washington, D.C.

The great leader who had brought the country through years of depression and over three years of war was gone! How would we fare without him? Missourians, of course, were pleased that one of our own—Harry Truman—would now take the reins, but everyone knew that Harry had had little experience in the politics and diplomacy of the war. Had we known then that the Roosevelt Whitehouse had had such disdain for Harry, they had not even bothered to keep him abreast of things—we would have been even more concerned.

In this light, it was surprising that the decisions that he took in the months to come were so well advised. I personally think he saved tens of thousands of American lives with his Hiroshima decision. I am further convinced that one of them may have been mine.

ROMANCE ON A HARLEY DAVIDSON

Following our meeting at the Ratjes, Judy Schlotzhauer and I dated—mostly school activities, Deck's Drug Store and Pop Tracy's Cafe. During the war years many teenage romances were greatly frustrated by the perpetual lack of "wheels". I was no exception, but I was somewhat in luck. After working in a war plant during my "Super Summer in St. Louis" (1944) I had saved enough to buy a 1937 Harley Davidson 74 OHV.

I say 'somewhat' because this motorcycle had no pillion seat. On our many tours of the countryside, Judy sat in

[2] Stonehenge - A group of standing stones on Salisbury Plain in southern England. Dating to ca 2000-1800 B.C., the megaliths are enclosed by a circular ditch and embankment that may date to 2800 BC. The arrangement of the stones suggests that Stonehenge was used as a religious center and also as an astronomical observatory.

[3] Kamikaze translates from the Japanese as "Divine Wind" and alludes to a miraculous event in 13th century Japan. A giant Mongolian armada was on course to attack Tokyo when a typhoon struck sinking or scattered the attackers — thus the Japanese regarded the typhoon as a "Divine Wind".

[4] Cleo died 4 days before his 21st birthday. After the war, in the 'Great Repatriation of the Dead' that I write about elsewhere, the Ratjes elected to have his body repatriated and he is now buried in the family plot at Smithton Cemetery, near Sedalia.

Fig. 9-6. Ace Twirler Judy Schlotzhauer 1945. Judy rode the pillion seat of my Harley.

the back of the saddle and I tried to sit forward. It was not a perfect solution and she must have spent most of the spring with creases on her bottom. It wasn't any easier on me but when you're 17 what the heck!

When the weather was good and I could get a few gallons of precious gasoline, we had fantastically good times—picnics, movies at the Lyric in Boonville and just cruising around aimlessly. Judy had me out for meals where her father, Leonard sized me up with a suspicious eye.

For years Leonard had 'followed the wheat harvest' Texas to Canada. He needed someone to drive and Judy, his oldest, got a driving license at age 14 (in Kansas). In that distant spring, Leonard often let her use the family car—a giant, gas-guzzling, "four holer" Buick. My guess is that he thought this might be preferable to having a surgeon pick gravel out of Judy's backside. To be fair to myself, I never had a serious accident on the old Harley.

We had joy! We had fun!
We had our season in the sun!

DECK'S DRUG STORE

Deck's Drug Store was a teen hangout and when I had a few coins, Judy and I hung out there. Deck's featured a super soda fountain — 15¢ for an ice cream sundae but if you were financially strapped, a cherry coke was only a nickel. Fudgsicles and Smoozies were favorites. A "Smoozie" was ice cream on a stick with a thin chocolate coating. Even better than scarfing down a Smoozie was the possibility of getting a free one. If — on your Smoozie stick you found the magic words: "FREE SMOOZIE" — you were in luck! To this day after eating a Haagen Daz ice cream on a stick, I still find myself looking at the stick for the magic words: "FREE SMOOZIE"

Marjorie Burger worked the soda fountain evenings and weekends and for a time after she graduated in 1944. She not only made a superb ice cream soda or chocolate malt—if Bill Deck wasn't watching, she'd add an extra scoop.

As an adolescent I hung out in the comic book section of the drug store where I learned from Charley Brownfield how to nurse a nickel coke for hours while reading all the latest comic books, Captain Marvel, Superman, Spiderman, et al — never dreaming of buying one. Bill Deck the proprietor was rather easy going. He died along about this time and his widow, Marie Deck then ran the store. J.D. Heinrich Jr. served as the pharmacist and later bought the drugstore.

POP TRACY'S CAFE

Another hang out for the teeners was Pop Tracy's Cafe — later the Pilot Grove Cafe. Pop's sundaes weren't as good as Deck's and he didn't have a rack of comic books, but you could get a good hamburger or hot-dog at Tracy's and get change back from a quarter.

Throughout that delightful spring I knew, of course, that the days of this our romance would soon be interrupted. When I graduated I would have to do my duty. In the spring of 1945 there was no honorable way that a healthy 18 year old could do otherwise. What is more, I looked forward to the Army as a great adventure.

"FOR PETE'S SAKE"

Friday 13th April 1945 "You were wonderful, Sonny!"

School was still on of course and I continued on my 'swing shift' at the Katy depot as well. The Senior Class went to Marshall to have their photos taken and I gave several to Judy. I was seventeen years old and not dry behind the ears—that photo showed it! See picture, page 1.

I had a role in the Senior play "For Pete's Sake" presented Friday 13th of April. There was consideration for changing the date. It seemed bad form because of the President's death and also Friday the 13th seemed portentous. In the end it was left standing and actually was a relief to all the gloom and doom. Judy though I was pretty good and ought to take up drama. Small chance! But I appreciated the flattery.

18TH BIRTHDAY, SATURDAY 5TH MAY 1945

"Celebrated with a 7 course dinner - six pack and a hotdog!"

Normally in those days, one's 18th birthday is celebrated by reporting to the draft board and filling out a stack of forms regarding one's suitability for cannon fodder. Mine came on Saturday, so my registration was deferred until Monday.

On that Monday, I inquired as to volunteering. "Too late, son." The clerk told me, "Ya can't enlist after you have registered. But, if you're in such an all fired rush, we can sign you up for immediate induction. Normally a fellow is called up for a physical and then given 6-8 weeks to settle his affairs. If you want, you can waive that 6-8 week delay."

I said, "Make it so."

TRAIN WRECK! SUNDAY, MAY 6, 1945

"The ole Katy starts coming unstitched!"

I was well into a nice Sunday afternoon nap blowing Z's after a 'swing' shift at the depot. At 2:30PM I was awakened by a earth shaking Whoomp! Train No. 72 had derailed at the Pilot Grove's north switch and 23 cars piled up behind Ries' house. The front cars were tankers carrying Oklahoma crude to the Whiting, Indiana refinery. They ignited. The rear cars, filled with artillery shells from the Parsons, Kansas Army Ordnance Plant, piled on top of the burning tankers!

It was later learned that a brake beam had broken and hung like a vaulters pole bouncing along at crosstie level. By luck it missed the south switch 50 yards from the depot near the main town crossing. Had it hit there the cars would have gone into the depot, tumbled into the town square and possibly wiped out much of downtown.

Thus began three days of desultory explosions as the shells 'cooked off'. The town watched at a respectful distance as the 3-ton 4 wheel carriages were hurled 100 feet into the air. Amazingly, there were no fatalities and only three injuries. Two trainmen were hurt.

During the cleanup a 'genius' signalman picked up a fuze to toss back into the bonfire and it exploded. There is a small initiator charge in a fuze which this de-fingered signalman now knows.

I sometimes thought of that train wreck as an omen for the Katy. The physical breakup and wreckage on that day would be more than matched a few years later with a corporate breakup and wreckage. Even I suffered from that wreck.

After the trainwreck, I continued normal work but because all traffic had to be routed over other lines, we had no trains and no duties for the next three days. The wreck was quickly cleaned up and the big doubleheader Mikados were back hauling oil and ammunition again. Today, few people remember or even knew how close the 'war' came to destroying the town on that warm spring Sunday long ago.

The swing shift was usually very quiet at the depot so I didn't discourage my schoolmates from coming down for bull sessions. I remember Homer Jeffress, Babe Heim, Winnie Reynolds and others. We entertained each other with jokes, tall tales and teenage banter on those long winter nights.

Two years later the true value of my telegraph experience paid off. In the spring of 1945 I went to Ft. Leavenworth for induction into the Army. We suffered through a battery of tests to separate the sheep from the goats. Actually for branch assignment and training. After 100,000 casualties on Okinawa, the Army wanted Infantry. My Morse Code test said Signal Corps instead! I became a 'radio telegrapher'.

"GOODBYE HITLER. HELLO TOJO!"

Tuesday, 8th May 1945—VE Day!

The collapse of the Nazis in Europe and the end of the war there was celebrated in Pilot Grove by a school holiday. Everyone was happy at the news, of course, but VE Day did not mean the end of the war. There were still the Japs and they were resisting fiercely. The fighting on Okinawa was beginning to make folks apprehensive. If they would defend Okinawa with a thousand kamikazes (even a kamikaze battleship—the 18" gun Yamada), how much more would they defend their home islands? Cleo Ratje's fate was a hint.

Fig. 9-7. Paratroopers display a captured Nazi flag—1945.

D-Day for Okinawa was Easter Sunday the first of April 1945. By May, the island was still far from secure and American casualties would prove to be the highest of any single battle in the entire war. Loyd McCreery was one of these. In the 5th Marines, he was seriously wounded at the Shuri Line by Japanese shrapnel. The Navy took more casualties than it had accumulated in its previous 150 year history.

Samuel Johnson was right, it does wonderfully concentrate a man's mind to know that he will be hanged in the morning! And it looked like the class of '45 might be elected to be the spearpoint into Japan proper. The Army Quartermaster was rumored to have ordered:

> Coffins, wooden, 6 ft, complete w/cross, wooden, white — 300,000 each.

COMMENCEMENT - WED 16 MAY 1945

"The class of '45 now belongs to the ages!"

The senior class of 1945 was feted to a banquet by the esteemed Junior Class on Friday night, 4th of May and marked our Baccalaureate the next evening, my birthday.

On Wednesday, May 16th we marched in to Pomp and Circumstance (Patty Schilb and Mildred Schlotzhauer on two pianos), honored our Salutatorian and Valedictorian—Alice Zeller and Mary Alice Thomas respectively and accepted our hard earned diplomas from Dr. E.I. Schilb, President of the school board. We switched the tassels of our mortarboards. Which was it, right to left or left to right? I've forgotten.

Father Leo Gales O.S.B. pronounced a benediction and we marched out at the recessional to duly assume our appointed place in history— a dusty and faded old class photo from whence we would forever glowering down on the unworthies in the halls of PGHS.

FIRST REAL JOB

May 20th 1945 - The money's good, you can spend it anywhere!"

The Sunday after graduation — May 20th — I went to St. Charles to work two weeks for the 'graveyard shift' Katy operator who was getting married. The 'Graveyard shift' is midnight until 8 AM or in this particular case — 11PM to 7AM. Judy and I enjoyed a farewell Smoozie at Pop Tracy's Cafe on Saturday night May 19th and at about 1AM she saw me off on Katy No. 5.

"Goodbye, Judy. See ya in a couple of weeks." I promised. I arrived in St. Charles at dawn. It was not that the train was slow — it was just that it stopped at every little town along the way to exchange mail, pick up Railway Express shipments, cream cans and occasionally a passenger.

WELCOME TO ST. CHARLES!

The managing station agent, William Howard, met me at the St. Charles depot and drove me to his home. His light brownish hair was beginning to thin a little and he was growing a small paunch. Mrs. Howard was an attractive, slightly plump, well dressed lady. I think she made a lot of her own clothes because you couldn't buy clothes that nice in the stores. They — to their eternal credit — recognized that here was a young man who was away from home among total strangers for the first time in his life and might be subject to some apprehension and misgivings.

Mrs. Howard — one did not call married ladies by their first name in those days — called us from our chit-chat in the parlor, "Come on to breakfast." She had prepared ham and eggs plus toast with real butter. They tried to make me feel welcome. After breakfast, we took a sightseeing tour of the area the high point being Lambert Field. Lambert Field — now St. Louis' prime air hub — in those days was dominated by McDonnell Aviation. McDonnell made a lion's share of the Navy's carrier fighters including the F6F Wildcat.

In all honesty, despite the greatly appreciated efforts of the Howard's, I did not much enjoy my sojourn in St. Charles. The sleeping accommodations which they had found for me were quite adequate, comfortable and inexpensive. My room was a walk-up, second floor bed-sitter on Front Street easy walking distance from the depot. My real problem was getting something to eat.

SULLIVAN'S CAFE

At 6 PM that first day, after getting myself settled into the bedsitter, I had my first taste of gastronomic austerity. I walked down the street a block or so to Sullivan's Cafe. Sullivan's was a little like Pop Tracy's Cafe, maybe a bit

Fig. 9-8. The Katy's St. Charles station in the 1940s.

larger. Apparently, it was a designated hangout for old geezers. Three or four were there — striped bib overalls, checked cotton flannel shirts, 'hunting' caps of brown corduroy with turndown ear flaps (I suppose these caps were the forerunners of 'CAT' hats). They gave me a careful up-and-down as they sucked on their toothpicks. Not too many strangers around these parts obviously. The matronly waitress was kind enough, "What'll you have kid?" I ordered a hamburger.

She looked amused and the bystanders snickered. "I ain't gonna tease you, kid. What I can give you is an egg sammich or a cheese sammich! That's it. That's all we got!"

ANOTHER CENTER FOR THE EASILY AMUSED

I looked at the local yokels and they weren't having *anything* so I had no basis of protest. "OK, you can unbait your rat traps and give me the cheese 'sammich' with a bottle of Nu-Grape." The old gandies got a real charge out of this and I realized that I was providing them some rare entertainment. Apparently St. Charles was also a Center for the Easily Amused. I scarfed down the cheese sandwich — knocked back the Nu-Grape and for the finale — let off a giant burp.

I have not often pondered on this trivial incident but then something similar happened at the 'Bobber' Restaurant on I-70 near Boonville a year ago. I was describing how I had checked the air in my tires with my own gauge. Some old gandy in the next booth was hanging on to my every word. I got a flash of insight! There are obviously some people in the world whose lives are so dull that eavesdropping on someone telling of airing his tires is entertaining!

My work hours at St. Charles also made meals a problem. I came off duty at 7 AM and was too tired and sleepy to go foraging for food. The Cafe wasn't open yet. I wondered why they opened at all, they had so little to offer. I often skipped breakfast and went to bed hungry. After a week of this, my starveling countenance must have tweaked the conscience of a waitress at Smitty's Bar which I passed on my way home. The waitress was the owner's wife I found later.

CONTINUED ON PAGE 180

CLASS PROPHECY 1945

by Sonny Salmon

Somewhere in the dim, mystic realm of the future, ye olde prophet takes a speedy "Katy" flier to a large Midwestern city where he has business with a racketeer. I beg your pardon—a printer who has just bought plates to print imitations of Ten Dollar bills for Amusement Purposes only, of course.

As I step off the Twenty-First Century Limited, I am met by cheers and cries of greetings. "Oh, what joy to be famous," I think, but soon discover they cheer not for me, but for two beautiful young actresses behind me. To my great surprise, they are Misses Bonnie Kirby and Alice Zeller two of my PGHS classmates. I am struck dumb and before I can speak they are surrounded by a cheering mob and I walk away amazed at their success and me—only a curator of government works of art such as appear on various denominations of currency.

It is hot and dusty and when I see a cop—beg your pardon—a policeman, I decide hurriedly to enter the first door at hand which turns out to be a refreshment bar. I order a double Positive Chocolate Banana Split with an accent on the Positive, when I find myself looking into the face of my dear old buddy, Silas E. Brownfield Jr. I'll never forget his greeting, "How's about that two bits you owe me?"

I gave him two bits, my last two bits I might add and we had a drink on the house—Pink Lemonade.

I had spent too much time and it was getting late. I had to hurry. I called for a cab and a beautiful little racing model glided up to the curb. I said, "Eighte Amoun Shalf Tane and step on it Buddy! I'll pay the fines." Then I noted the cabby's wavy hair and well shaped head and it stirred memories—I thought, "Oh yes, my old buddy from which came all the pencils, paper, etc. that I used in my Senior year, none other than Virgil Schupp." I asked him, "How'd you get into this racket, Schupp?"

He replied, "You'd be surprised at the money I pick up robbing the public."

At this point a traffic jam developed due to some, as yet unknown, obstruction in the street. I climbed out to walk and discovered the obstruction was what appeared to be a riot but was actually an American Legion Convention whooping it up. I joined, hoping to see some of my old high school buddies. I was rewarded—there was Donald Bonen, Lee Roth, Earl Kammerich, Paul Schlotzhauer, Henry Stegner, Homer Twenter and Homer Jeffress.

Donald told me he had a dairy farm back in dear old Missouri and was doing very well. Lee was in business as a tractor and farm implement salesman. He was also doing very well when he could get his foot in the door. Earl owned half interest in a billiard palace. Paul, after 20 years service with the Merchant Marine retired with a comfortable fortune of $60,000. He told me he owed his fortune to his devotion to duty, courage, heroic endurance and an uncle who died and left him $59,999.50.

As I continued on my way, I came upon a tall, dignified, elderly looking man, who, on closer observation I discover to be my former classmate, Elwood Gerke. I asked him how the world was treating him and he was astonished to find that I didn't know he was the President of the Ever Ready Peanut Butter Company. On inquiring, I found that he still liked his classmates as Henrietta Eckerle and Mary Alice Thomas were his typists, Dorothy Walje was his personal secretary and Dorothy Kempf was his stenographer.

He told me good-bye then as he was in a hurry and I went on my way. I was down in the night club district, so I decided to drop into the "Stork Club" since someone had told me that I would know the two singers who worked there. I went into the small door and a girl took my hat. As I walked on, I saw through the dimly-lit, smoke-filled room two scantily clothed night club singers giving vent to a sultry, throbbing, romantic tune. I was not too surprised to find that they were Earlene Schlotzhauer and Charlene Farrell.

I was then told that there was a baseball game scheduled for 2:00 that afternoon so I hastened to the stadium for I always had a whim for the Yankee Stadium in New York and there was a huge crowd. Charley Brownfield was the manager of the St. Louis Cardinals and they won 20-0.

As I left the stadium, I saw a long limousine cruising down the street. To my amazement, it pulled to the curb in front of me. A large, pompous gentleman opened the door and invited me to enter. I looked at him, realizing that he must know me. After looking carefully, I discovered it was my old buddy, Joe Piatt. Of course I was glad to see him although at one time that if I never saw him again it would be too soon. I inquired how he had risen so high in this world. He told me that it was due to the fact that he had inherited the largest cigarette factory in the world. He now controlled the manufacturers of Lucky Strike, Camels, Phillip Morris, Old Gold and Kools. After a long chat, I happened to glance to the front of the car. The chauffeur's head looked familiar! Could it be another of my school mates? It was John Lorenz, Joe informed me. "He's been with me for 15 years, 3 months, two weeks and 6 days. He declared that a more dependable fellow had never been seen. I remembered how Johnnie used to drive his old Chevy around back at good ole Pilot Grove High School and I wondered.

As I was passing through the underworld, I mean to say the social section of New York on my was back home, I came upon a burning mansion. A woman came running from the building with a bundle of newspapers under one arm. People began laughing and making fun of her and realizing her embarrassing predicament, quickly ran back into the burning build and returned empty handed. People said to one another, "Poor Becky, she must be nuts." As I stood there gaping, two fire engines pull up. To my consternation I saw the most fearful sight to be beheld by human (or inhuman) eyes. Could I believe it? Yes, it was true. Women drivers on fire trucks and what is more they turned out to be two of my classmates—Elizabeth Kraus and Earlene Felten. About that time up walked the Chief of Police with the firebug and who do you think it was? Sonnie Salmon. To think that he would come to such an end.

After seeing that sight I wandered on home feeling very melancholy. I turned on the radio. To my surprise I heard Billy Stewart the famous radio announcer extolling to the world at large the merits of El Stinko Cigars. The star of the program was Pete Meyer, the swooner, crooner and the ideal of all humanity. What a man! What a man! With this, the spirit of prophecy was lifted from me and a weird and poorly voice came out of the great unknown. "Tell what you have seen and heard or forever hold your peace."

GUARDIAN ANGEL

One morning—she must have been watching for me—she popped out of the bar and said, "Hey, would you like to come in for some breakfast?" I thought: "Would a starving wolf go for a lamb chop?" I had never gone into the place because I was a minor and it was counter to the law of the land. I was a bit uneasy about this, but she goes back of the bar to a small grill and made me a tall stack of pancakes.

There was no bacon, no sausage nor ham but she had plenty of maple syrup. She was a life saver, an angel and I stopped in often thereafter. A question I have often asked myself is; "Why did she do that?" I also wondered where all the food had gone. I was to find out later at Fort Leavenworth, Kansas.

Fig. 9-9. PGHS Class of 1945. Left to Right up the diagonal: Earlene Felton, Lee Roth, Rebecca Meyer, Silas Brownfield—Paul Schlotzhauer, Miss Tye (Sponsor)—Harold Kempf, Elizabeth Kraus, Earl Kammerich, Elwood Gerke, Bonnie Kirby, Alice Zeller—Mary Alice Thomas, John Lorenz, Leonard "Pete" Meyer, Earlene Schlotzhauer, Donald Bonen, Homer Twenter—Babe Heim, Charlene Farrell, Charles Brownfield, Richard Salmon, Dorothy Walje—William Stewart, Henrietta Eckerle, Joe Piatt, Virgil Schupp—Dorothy Kempf, Homer Jeffress.

STARVING IN THE SHENANDOAH VALLEY

During the Civil War the Confederates used the Shenandoah Valley as a source of provisions for men and horses. General Sheridan—a Union cavalry commander — was sent by McClellan, Commander of the Army of the Potomac, to disrupt this cozy arrangement. When Sheridan had completed his path of devastation he reported back to General McClellan: "There'll be no further provender for man nor beast in the Shenandoah Valley. After today, a crow flying over that valley will have to carry his own rations!"

In May of 1945, I thought: the ghost of old Phil Sheridan must have passed through St. Charles, MO recently. At my physical examination later at Fort Leavenworth I measured 5 ft 11 inches tall but weighed only 140 pounds.

LESSON LEARNED—The Future is something that happens while you are busy planning something else.

HASTA LA VISTA ST. CHARLES, I SHAN'T BE TROUBLING YOU AGAIN!

I finished my last shift early Saturday morning the 2d of June, scrounged around for chow, slept most of the afternoon and with thanks to all, caught the Katy at midnight Saturday . "Goodbye St. Charles. I shake your dust from my heels!" I got into Pilot Grove at first light Sunday. The old town looked beautiful — 'the green, green grass of home'.

But not for long—a letter awaited me from "...your friends and neighbors" which told me that I would soon be... in the words of that ancient ballad... "Gone fer a Sojer".

BOOK TWO

Gone fer a Sojer

"We were soldiers then, and young."

Attention Parents: Before you let your little ones start this part, you should quickly scan it and use discretion. Using categories—Sex, Language and Violence, I would rate the material as follows:

- **Sex**: G, General audiences.
- **Language:** PG-13. There is some barracks room language, about what you hear on prime time television.
- **Violence:** NC-17. There are several scenes in the "Korea" chapter that you may want to withhold from any child that is subjected to nightmares.

He's gone fer a sojer. Gone this very day!
Gone fer a sojer—over the hill and far away.
—Revolutionary War Ditty

FORT LEAVENWORTH

WHEN I RETURNED FROM MY TWO WEEK STINT in St. Charles, the fateful letter 'from your friends and neighbors at the local draft board' awaited me. I looked on it as my personal invitation to the war in the Pacific—the big kids having already done Europe. I was assured the US government would provide free meals, free clothing, $50 per month spending money, neat identification tags of genuine stainless steel with a cute little notch to stick in your teeth—in case, you know, things didn't go as planned—also I might qualify for a military funeral with free flag and headstone plus $10,000 for my next of kin.

Judy took me to catch the bus in Boonville on Wednesday June 20th and with her tearful good-byes ringing in my ears, I set off again to seek my fortune this time at Fort Leavenworth. "Goodbye, Judy. I don't know when I'll see you again. I'll write." Since I had volunteered for immediate induction, we knew I would not be back soon.

MALINGERERS, SKIVVERS, DRAFT DODGERS

Many things have stuck in my mind from the half century just past. Some will be mentioned in this book. One of those things was the attitude that people had about those who failed to serve in the country's hour of need.

During World War II malingering, skivving off, slacking and draft dodging were held in particularly low esteem. Doubtless, many a poor slob had a perfectly legitimate claim to military exemption, but was nevertheless treated very roughly by his peers.

This malingering and draft dodging came to mind when I was in the line for hearing tests. The medical examinations were done at a cavernous facility in Kansas City—U.S. Armed Forces Examining Station near the Main Post Office. The guy in front of me was a loud mouth jackass from Boonville. Johnny Imhoff knew him, I didn't. The 'hearing test' was conducted by a doctor standing about 25 feet down the hall whispering numbers.

It was now the malingerer's turn. The doctor whispers: "Thirty-seven."

With my less than perfect hearing, I heard him plainly and I was 10 feet farther away.

Malingerer: "Fifty-five."

Doctor: "Ninety-eight."

Malingerer: "Twenty-one."

The malingering was so blatant I expected the doctor to deputize a firing squad and shoot this guy on the spot. But, this was the real world. The doc said, "Have you had hearing problems?"

This, of course, gave Malingerer his opening to relate his story of how his hearing had been damaged by blah, blah, blah. He was still bending the doc's ear as they went off for 'more extensive testing'. Malingerer was classified 4F with hearing better than mine. Such is life and justice.

YOU'RE IN THE ARMY NOW

I passed my blood and urine tests with flying colors and went on to Fort Leavenworth to be sworn in on Friday June 22d 1945. A bored Warrant Officer stands on the platform and intones the oath. "Do you solemnly swear that you will bear true faith and allegiance to the Constitution of the United States and all officers and noncommissioned officers appointed over you? Signify by taking one step forward."

"The corporal commands: "One step for'ard — March!" The Corporal reports to the Officer in Charge that all have taken one step forward. "Congratulations, you are now in the United States Army!"

I thought, "And may God have mercy on our souls!"

I have always thought that the U.S. Army was a natural habitat of the adolescent and post-adolescent American male. In my experience, all males are born with a vandalism gene. They are congenital mess makers and destroyers. Sherman's March to the Sea was, as my grandfather once said, "One helluva big Halloween Night!" Put that together with the wartime mission of the Army: Destroy stuff and kill people—and you have a perfect fit!

Orientation began immediately. There were a lot of lectures and movies. For example, on the evils of consorting with loose females — • the chaplain warned of the dangers to one's immortal soul, • the doctor spoke of the jeopardy to one's health, then the • Provost Marshal listed all the "Off Limits" places thus illuminating us on where such loose females were to be found.

Probably the most effective orientation was the continuous harassment of the NCO's. I know now that in order to instill discipline and unhesitating obedience to orders, it is necessary to infuse a little fear. There are some guys who — without proper indoctrinate might find it foolish to throw himself on razor wire in a minefield and let his battalion run over his backside. Many years later at the 82d Airborne Division's NCO Leadership School I met an old Master Sergeant. As a young Corporal this fellow had acted with extraordinary heroism at Anzio for which he was awarded the Medal of Honor. I asked him why he did some things that were quite "above and beyond the call of duty." He replied, "Ah was scared to death a my platoon sarnt! Ah'd druther face that battalion of Germans than get chewed out by him!"

COURT-MARTIAL

Without letup it was, "Get your butts out here now. If you're not out here in 10 seconds you gonna get a court martial." …"I want this here barracks scrubbed down so clean I can eat off'n the floor. If I find one speck of dirt it's a court martial for ya!" "I want all the trash, cigarette butts, paper, everything picked up. If I find one butt, *yer* butt is up for court martial!" Etc., etc. We had an idea that 'court-martial' was where you were led to a wall, blindfolded, given a cigarette to await the firing squad.

All these threats of court-martial were much on my mind when I went to the mess hall one evening. There was a long serving line, hundreds of recruits shuffling through being served by disinterested mess cooks. Nonchalantly talking to one another they plonked and sploshed and splatted food onto our giant metal mess trays. I looked up to see a giant sign over the serving line: "Take all you want, but eat all you take!"

My famine plagued tour of duty at St. Charles had effectively shrunk my stomach. I left St. Charles in an early stage of starvation and I was now concerned at the growing piles of food accruing to my tray. I tried to fend off some. No one paid any attention and I wound up with enough food to feed Pilot Grove for a week. I learned why civilians had such trouble finding food!

I sat on that hard bench at the giant mess table trying to eat three pork chops, 2 pounds of mashed potatoes, a quart of gravy, one pound of green beans, five slices of bread with 1/2 lb of butter. I was feeling more and more like a python that had swallowed a water buffalo. I simply could not eat it! I began visualizing the court martial that I would now face. Pleading my case, I might appeal to the judge, "The sign says: Take all you want …Your highness, I didn't *take* anything! Them mess cooks just dumped it on my tray!"

My realistic solution was a simple tactic of diversion. I knew that sooner or later some luckless recruit would incur the wrath of a noncom and create a scene. When that happened I would proceed with utmost rapidity, without calling attention to myself, to the garbage disposal. Here one sorted and disposed of the various categories of garbage: glass, metal, paper, inedible and edible(?). (What in the world is 'edible' garbage?) Anyway, it worked exactly as I planned. While Corporal Martinette chewed out some poor recruit, I dumped my meal surplus and with great relief exited the mess hall backside intact. I skipped breakfast and lunch the next day and thereafter made so bold as to decline all servings excess to a 'normal' 5,000 calorie meal.

NEW GUYS MEET THE OLD GUYS

My other lasting impression of my first days at Fort Leavenworth was more sobering. It considerably cooled my gung-ho spirit. Most of the new recruits were only days out of high school. I was typical in this respect. These 18 year old guys were immature, overgrown adolescents. When we fell in for roll-call or to be "marched" to tests etc., there was always a noisy milling around and a lot of horseplay. Some recruits, in virtue of having arrived a week before my group, viewed themselves as "old veterans". These guys — wearing their ill fitting, unpressed fatigue uniforms, some with tags still attached — yelled at the recruits still in civvies, "You ain't a-gonna like it heeeeere!"

One morning as we stood around, hands in pockets, waiting to be marched off — herded actually — to classification testing, we observed a formation of several hundred real "soldiers" shaping up to marched to their demobilization processing.

These were the type of men Patton was talking to as they mustered for shipment to North Africa in 1942: "...after the war when you're sitting around the fire with a kid on your knee and he asks you, 'What did you do in the great war daddy?' you won't have to tell him you shovelled horseshit in Louisiana."

Why were some guys being demobilized when the war was still on in the Pacific? A little background here. When the European war ended the Pentagon wanted to immediately move these massive forces, e.g. 60 Infantry Divisions, 20 Armored Divisions, two numbered Air Forces, etc. to the Pacific and get on with the war with the Japanese. In fact, several divisions *were* moved directly from Bremerhaven, Germany through the Panama Canal to the Far East without even a stop in the US. So many families bitterly complained about this that thereafter all European returnees were landed on the East Coast, took a short "delay enroute" then reported to West Coast ports to sail for the Asia-Pacific Theater.

Upon reflection, the Army determined that maybe they didn't immediately need 3 million more troops in the Far East — they would be so numerous there wouldn't be facilities for them — so they came up with a point system. Based on the point system some of the veterans of the ETO (European Theater of Operations) would be discharged. Points were awarded for decorations, wounds, months overseas, years in service, POW status, etc. The first batch of these included the men we were observing at Ft. Leavenworth. They were *very* high point men.

These guys apparently were furnished with and required to wear all campaign ribbons and decorations. Nearly all of them had 3 rows of ribbons. On the left sleeve above the cuff, each diagonal bar indicated 3 years service — all had one, some had two; above the 'hash marks' a stack of gold bars indicated six months overseas per bar — all had four or more. I also recognized their decorations, Distinguished Service Cross, Silver Star, Bronze Star, Purple Heart (many with Oak Leaf Clusters for second awards), service medals - ETO ribbon with 5 battle stars and invasion arrowhead, National Defense Ribbon (service before 1941), etc. Above the ribbons over the left breast pocket were special qualification badges: Combat Infantry Badges, Parachutist Wings, etc. Many wore the French, the Belgium and some the Dutch fourragére (decorations awarded by those governments to units). These were the veterans of Kasserine Pass, Anzio, Monte Cassino, Omaha and Utah Beach, the Colmar Pocket, the Falaise Gap, the Ardennes, the Remagen Bridge, the Elbe. All in neatly pressed, well fitted uniforms.

With the command "Fall in" all moved silently to a place in the ranks, did a quick close order "dress right dress" aligning ranks and files perfectly. There was no horseplay, no jokes. Disdain for the recruits was shown by their disregard of the ragtags that watched them — quietly for a change.

The most sobering sight to me was the look in their hollow-eyed, haunted faces as they marched by. I've heard this look described as a "1000 yard stare." Five years later — Thanksgiving 1950 — I was to see this same haggard, haunted expression again. This time on the faces of guys of the Third Infantry Division and the First Marines during a fighting retreat from the Chosen Reservoir and Koto-Ri in North Korea.

"...SIGNAL CORPS—RIDING ON A BIKE"

So we more soberly marched off to testing and classification. In June of 1945, the Army was quite keen to make good the infantry casualties of the Battle of the Bulge and the chase across the Rhine to the Elbe. They were also anticipating about one million casualties in the upcoming invasion and final battle for the Japanese home islands. They wanted — cannon fodder.

But I aced all the classification tests, particularly the ARC (Army Radio Code) where the Katy telegraph experience was crucial. I was assigned to the Signal Corps to be trained as a Radio Morse Code Operator. Purely by chance that training would be at Camp Crowder, MO near Joplin. Camp Crowder was home for the Central Signal Corps School and 40,000 troops who were training there. Neosho, the nearest town, was of about 5,000 population.

I waved goodbye to Leavenworth never expecting to ever see the place again. But I did exactly 25 years later when my class graduated from the U.S. Army Command and General Staff College.

CAMP CROWDER - CENTRAL SIGNAL CORPS SCHOOL

BASIC TRAINING

On Monday morning 2d July, 1945 we bussed to a train on a siding at Fort Leavenworth and started an enjoyable day trip to Camp Crowder, Missouri. A delightful luncheon was served enroute. [I have tongue in cheek.]

Fig. 10-1. Camp Crowder was in the extreme southwestern corner of the state.

Actually, the canned beef looked extremely red and was unusually tough. The rumor started that it was horse meat and some wag said, "Don't say 'Whoa' or we'll all choke to death. Confronted with the horsemeat allegation, the mess cooks swore it was 'Argentine beef' and all Argentine beef looked like that. I thought, "Maybe, maybe not."

The trailer busses that met us at the Doniphan Road siding reminded me of the old WWI 40 & 8's designed for 40 men or 8 horses — but, more comfortable for horses than men. We were parceled out to companies of the Branch Immaterial Training Group for six weeks of basic infantry training. Upon our arrival at our billets we were met by a corporal who showed us to our bunks. Bunks were assigned in alphabetic order.

He showed us how to make up a bed with 'hospital' corners. He then took us to his tiny 'cadre' room where, using his own clothing rack, he demonstrated how our clothes were to be hung. "OD Wool overcoat on right, then raincoat, OD winter 'blouse', two OD wool shirts with trousers, 3 suntan khaki uniforms then finally on the left: 2 OD fatigue uniforms[1]. Have them hung up neatly before inspection in the morning!"

Reality hit us a few moments later — no one had any hangers! "Hey, Corporal, Sir — where do we get hangers?"

"That's your problem!"

"We'll have to go to the PX."

"No, no you don't. None a you recruits are to leave the company area! You heard the ole man."

"He let us stew for a few minutes and then, "Aw, listen guys, I tell you what. I think I can get you guys some hangers but they're gonna cost you a nickel apiece!"

When he returned a few minutes later, we all lined up with our nickels in our hot grubby hands thanking him for being a "savior." Two months later when everyone shipped out for their branch schools leaving hangers scattered all over the floor, I saw him carefully harvesting them for the next cycle.

[1] These were to be my total wardrobe for the next 15 months — civvies were forbidden.

BAKING BREAD BEACON

It was a very warm and sultry summer night, black as pitch. Not even a slight breeze relieved the six sweaty young soldiers as they blundered through the Ozark woods. I had concluded an hour ago that we were irretrievably lost. It was now 2AM. We had expected to finish our reconnaissance and find our way back to headquarters by midnight.

It was Friday night (actually, Saturday morning) 18th of August 1945. Dawn would bring the end of our week-long misery: a critique by the Colonel then transportation back to Camp Crowder and transfer to the Signal School.

We eagerly anticipated the Colonel's talk. He might tell us something about the rumors that had been circulating around the evening camp fires—a new kind of bomb had been dropped on two Japanese cities completely destroying them. The end of the war might be at hand!

Fig. 10-2. Pvt. Richard L. Salmon 1945. The badge is for Expert Rifleman.

We had been cut off from outside news since early August and could not credit these rumors. Some 18 year old high school physics wizard tried to explain how a small amount of special explosive (he said the size of a dime) had had the explosive power of 20,000 tons of TNT. We guffawed at such nonsense.

My 'class' of about 1,000 troops had been in the field for a week. The one-week field exercise was the culmination of the basic training that all Army recruits endure. Infantry training was 13 weeks. Signal was 8 weeks, but we did the same delightful things: Crawl through a barbed wire entanglement with live machine-gun fire overhead; bayonet a dummy where the proper scream was as important as the horizontal butt stroke; toss a grenade where some klutz inevitably pulled the pin then dropped the grenade (it happened so often the cadre would calmly grab it and toss it out of the bunker); run an obstacle course including a swing over a water hazard (this provided the comic relief—some fatso would always fall in); climb a 10 ft wall; etc.

Fig. 10-3. While Times Square celebrated the end of the war with Japan, we were totally in the dark in the wilds of the Ozark boondocks.

We all complained bitterly at the forced marches with full field packs that created masses of foot blisters. We railed at the 16 hour days of mindless repetition of rifle drill, field stripping and reassembling the old Springfield 03 until we could do it blindfolded. But truth is — it was much like the Boy Scouts and many of us loved it!

This final night we had a reconnaissance and map exercise. The classroom work on map reading and reconnoitering would be put to the acid test. Each squad was given a map, a compass and detailed instructions as to a recon route to take. Part of the route would be to observe and make notes on 'enemy' troop movements, strengths and weapons.

Since the setting of the moon this night we had suffered the bane of democratic decision making. There is an inescapable phenomenon: any time six people or more are in decision-making mode, there will be one person who will attempt to dominate. This person will be the most stupid, loudmouth know-nothing in the group. Tonight, this man was Private Aaron Miller. But, since most of us were not really all that sure about our position and direction, the one guy who was 'positively certain' often carried the decision.

Someone once defined 'being positive' as being wrong in a loud tone of voice. That was the case this night and now we all conceded that we were lost.

Finally, we had a bit of starlight but could not see landmarks more than ten feet away so a 'point' man was sent out with a tiny pocket flashlight. He illuminated his face and we shot azimuths on him.

We were beginning to make progress. At least our 'expert' had grown silent as all realized he had been mostly wrong. The squad gave him short shrift, mumbling, "Whatever Miller says, we do the opposite."

Fig. 10-4. Putting up the loaves.

It was painfully slow going so I suggested, "Look, guys—thanks to Daniel Boone Miller here we are lost and probably are not going to find our way in the dark. Why don't we just sit here and wait for the signal flares?" The training cadre were prepared for those squads who couldn't find their own backsides with two maps and a seeing eye dog. Some time before dawn they would begin firing illuminating flares to guide the lost lambs home.

There was a bit of mumbled discussion which Miller did not join. Just then my nose detected something. I was transported back to Mom's kitchen on baking day. The exceedingly pleasant aroma of light[2] bread fresh from the oven was vividly recalled to my mind.

Now, the myth that females are born with an innate ability to cook and that housewifely skills are instinctive was given the lie by Mom. She never was a good cook nor did she pretend to be — but, she could bake delicious bread. Allusions of that fresh, hot bread slathered with butter and dripping with honey were coming in on the wind. We were at the head of a draw and a southwesterly breeze was wafting the fragrant aroma up the gully. Our acute hunger sharpened our sense of smell.

I pointed down the draw, "My nose tells me we should go that way." My stomach had been rumbling with hunger for hours and I noted that the entire squad was gurgling worse than the town drains after a storm. The rest of the squad got the scent and went on point like precision-trained bird dogs.

"Yep, that's it, let's go." And off we went stopping only occasionally to re-sample the breeze like wolves on the spoor of a fat jack rabbit. Within a half hour we were in the all-night mess hall. The baker was putting up loaves in a bread case — a tall, shelved and screened enclosure.

[2] I've never understood the origin of the term "light bread". Maybe it was to distinguish it from biscuits or other types of bread. Whatever the reason, the term was universally used in my world of the 1930s and 40s.

He looked at our scruffy squad, "Breakfast is at 0500 gentlemen and..." he looked at his wristwatch, "That's about two hours from now."

"Aw, Sarge", I begged (he was a corporal). "We been out all night and are about to starve. Surely you got somepin' we could eat?"

He looked at the bread, "Well, get some butter out of the cooler back there... I just baked this here bread ya see."

"Yeah, we know", I answered, "Thanks loads!"

WEEKEND PASS

Being stationed near home didn't mean much for the first three months. We were restricted to base during basic training. We were usually so tired we wouldn't have wanted to go out anyway. We were in the final phase of this basic infantry training — the field exercise I describe above — when Col. Paul Tebbets flying the B-29 Enola Gay dropped a 20 kilo-ton atom bomb on Hiroshima (August 6th). Three days later — on the 9th — a similar bomb was dropped on Nagasaki. On Wednesday August 15th the Japanese accepted terms of the Potsdam Conference and we celebrated VJ-Day!

The Central Signal Corps School at Camp Crowder was — in 1945 — the largest communications training facility in the world. We marched from our barracks in the cantonment areas to school each morning to the 'Col. Bogey March'. 'Col. Bogey' was later to be the theme music for 'The Bridge on the River Kwai". What was impressive then was the immensity of the formations. Each formation was one battalion (about 1,000 men). We marched in battalion fronts with 12 men abreast. This filled the entire road shoulder to shoulder with rightmost and leftmost files very nearly in the ditch. As far as the eye could see there were these undulating OD colored formations marching off to school.

Six years later, when I returned from the Korea War, Camp Crowder was a reassignment center for Regular Army troops returning from the war. Nearly all the thousands of buildings were gone. With only foundations left it looked like a WWII bombed-out European cityscape. It was an eerie sight — miles of desolation crisscrossed by the macadam streets where in 1945 we marched to school by the tens of thousands singing Col. Bogey!

I started training as a "Radio Operator, Intercept - Japanese" on Monday August 20th. It occurred to many of us that the uses for an "Intercept Operator (Japanese)[3]" might be lacking after VJ Day. The only thing we cared about was that we were now eligible for weekend passes. 'Weekend', however, was defined as noon Saturday — after inspection — until Tattoo 9 PM Sunday night.

[3] A "Radio Operator, Intercept - Japanese" copies Japanese radio telegraph traffic for possible de-cryption by the "Code Breakers".

Public transportation was primitive in southwestern Missouri. Getting home to Pilot Grove for a the abbreviated weekend was so difficult I only braved it a few times. Here was the schedule:

- Saturday noon - Depart Camp Crowder on one of the frequent 25¢ shuttle buses to Neosho (I think the saloon owners subsidized these buses.).
- 2 PM - Catch the Neosho - Springfield bus. This bus made about ten stops enroute.
- 7 PM - Catch the Springfield - Sedalia bus. This bus stopped at every wide place in the road: Buffalo, Louisburg, Urbana, Preston, Cross Timbers, Warsaw, Cole Camp and Sedalia. They also handled small packages, crates of chickens, (but no cream cans).
- Midnight - Arrive Sedalia and pray No. 5 (the Katy Bluebonnet passenger train) had not pulled out. Most of the time it had.
- 7 AM - Arrive in Pilot Grove for breakfast.
- 8 AM - Fire up the old Harley and go see Judy.
- Sunday noon - Start the return journey. Fortunately, Leonard would often let Judy drive me back to Sedalia Sunday noon to catch the bus for Springfield. Reversing all the above process, I'd be back in camp for 9 PM bed check. What agony for a four hour visit! But as I often said, "...we were soldiers then, and young ."

The summer of 1945 brought in a revolutionary new idea in fountain pens — a ball point pen! I have always been a techno-freak, an early adopter, so the novel idea led me to buy one. They were available in the PX where because of the discounted prices I only had to pay $12.50. This was only 25% of my monthly pay! Converting this to today's equivalent dollars, it was about $125. It has this tiny metal ball which rolls the ink on, it writes under water, etc., etc.! I immediately applied this technology to my correspondence with Judy. Mail call and her weekly letter was much appreciated.

I don't know how Judy cajoled her mother into it, but they came down to Neosho for a visit on Sunday August 26th. We just strolled around town a bit, I was sufficiently socially sensitive to recognize that the Schlotzhauers probably would not appreciate "JOE'S BAR - LONGEST BAR IN THE OZARKS Budweiser on Tap". We had pictures taken in a dime photo booth. I still have them. See above right.

Two out of three times I missed the Katy Bluebonnet from Sedalia and had to hitchhike. Hitchhiking was more socially acceptable in those days. Gasoline was rationed — 3 gallons a week for an "A" sticker. "A" stickers, displayed in the right corner of the windshield, were for those like me, who couldn't dream up any good lies for the Ration Board and therefore got a minimal allotment. Uniforms helped in

Fig. 10-5. Dime Fotomat pictures from Camp Crowder August 1945. Judy Schlotzhauer and Sonny Salmon.

hitchhiking, but I wore mine because I was required to.

During the war years (in fact, until September 3, 1946) the wearing of civilian clothing in public by a serviceman could be taken as prima facie evidence of desertion! The maximum punishment for desertion in wartime was death! Imagine going to the wall with cigarette and blindfold for wearing T-shirt and jeans?

One night in the fall of 1945 I missed the train in Sedalia and was forlornly hitchhiking on US 50 east out of Sedalia. At midnight there was very little traffic and I was fast losing hope. Finally a couple of recently discharged GIs picked me up in a Model A Ford. These guys looked like the fellows I had seen at the Fort Leavenworth demobilization center. They still wore their khaki uniforms but with a 'Ruptured Duck' over the right shirt pocket.

This 'Ruptured Duck' addressed one of the problems associated with demobilizing millions of GIs — finding affordable civilian clothing. The factories could not meet the demand. The flip side of the regulations prohibiting military wearing civilian clothing was a regulation prohibiting civilian wearing of service uniforms. The solution was to affix an emblem above the right shirt or jacket pocket. The emblem was an eagle perched in a gold ring. This designated a demobbed serviceman and permitted him to wear his uniform for several months if he chose. GIs irreverently but affectionately termed this insignia 'The Ruptured Duck'.

Fig. 10-6. The "Order of the Ruptured Duck."

In addition to their 'Ruptured Ducks' these two ex-GIs were different from their Fort Leavenworth cohorts in another way — they were rip-roaring drunk.

So relieved to finally get a lift, I didn't notice this until we were well underway. By that time I thought it would be rather impolitic to bring it up. Furthermore, since they weren't going anywhere in particular, they volunteered to take me all the way home. I directed them through Smithton then onto County E — at that time a gravel road. We went ripping through Clifton City at 2 AM. With gravel and dust flying, it was a miracle we stayed in the road. The old Model A clipped off 40 - 50 miles per hour. We made it OK past the Wesley Chapel corner then the alcohol overcame the heretofore surprisingly good driving skills and we careened off the road into a deep ditch.

No one was hurt but the old Model A was stuck. We pushed and hauled but the driver was just not up to it. Finally he said, "You can just walk in from here, can't you?. We'll get some sleep, sober up and get out in the light of day." That's what I did. I never learned how they got out but when I biked by on the old Harley the next day, enroute to see Judy, the car was gone.

RHEUMATIC FEVER

Just after her 17th birthday — October 7th 1945 — Judy came down with a severe sore throat which was eventually diagnosed as a streptococcus infection. While the acute infection was ultimately cured, it apparently initiated an even more serious condition — rheumatic fever. It was so bad that when I came home on Christmas leave — 15-30 December — she was still convalescing. We had a little Christmas celebration in her sickroom and I gave her a small gold locket with chain. Merry Christmas 1945!

THE WINDS - 1945

Wind in my hair and bugs in my teeth
As I biked[4] out to the farm
To visit afflicted, suffering Judy
And try to cheer her with my charm.

RE-ENLISTMENT

In the new year, everyone was happily getting used to peacetime but the Army was having severe manpower problems. With the pressure to demobilize everyone as soon as possible, there were not going to be enough troops to do things that had to be done. I accepted an offer of a one stripe promotion, a 30-day leave and a $300 bonus[5] and on January 30, 1946 reenlisted for one year. I spent nearly every day of this February leave with Judy. She was not getting better. There were no more bike tours. There were no more picnics.

Finishing the radio operator training at the end of April I went into 'casual' status awaiting an assignment. I mostly pulled 'fatigue' details packing up the Signal School for transport to Fort Gordon, GA. The Army was winding down operations and consolidating. My skivving off, dodging details and general shirking came to an end when orders arrived on Tuesday, 14th May:

> 'EM listed below, Sig C, ...are placed on TDY for approx 150 days with Joint Task Force One ...WP 17 May to Hamilton Field, Calif. reporting thereat NLT 23 May for air trans to Kwajalein ...Three day delay enroute authorized... Salmon, Richard L. PFC RA 37813858 Pilot Grove, MO SSN 0740...'

[Joint Task Force One conducted the first post war atomic bomb tests in the Marshall Islands.]

I had a whirlwind 3 days leave in Pilot Grove, biked out to visit a wan and frail Judy, kissed her good-by and caught a train for San Francisco. I never saw her again.

> LESSON LEARNED: The aroma of a mother's baking bread will always guide you home but alas, it doesn't cure everything.

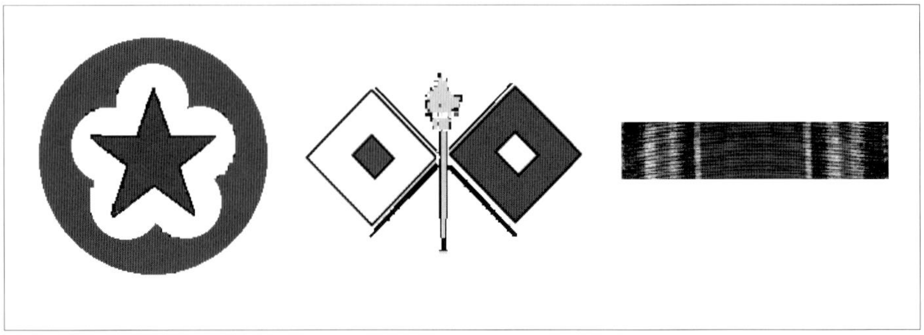

Fig. 10-7. Insignia collection - Part 1. Left to Right: Army Service Forces shoulder patch, Signal Corp lapel emblem, WWII Victory Ribbon.

[4] I had an old 1937 Harley-Davidson solo 74 OHV.

[5] In 1863, my grandfather Kendrick got a bigger reenlistment bonus than I did — $400. In 1865 he could have received 40 acres and a mule. He declined, not caring to raise corn in Wyoming.

I wanna go back to my li'l grass
shack in Keealakekua Hawaii.
—Cap'n Cook.

ATOM BOMB TESTS - KWAJALEIN

FOR FOUR YEARS AFTER THE 1945 BOMBING of Hiroshima and Nagasaki, the United States had a monopoly on atomic weapons but there was concern among the U.S. military as to how to use the new weapons, thus a need for testing.

These tests were initiated in 1946 and conducted annually for several years in the Marshall Islands. Operation Crossroads—Headquarters at Kwajalein (see Fig. 11-1.) was the first. Two bombs were detonated in and over the lagoon at Bikini Atoll in the northern part of the Marshall Islands.

It was ironic that the name of this atoll—Bikini—the site of the first post-war atomic bomb test and scene of destruction of biblical proportions should be appropriated by the fashion world for an ultra-revealing female swim suit — the 'teeny weeny, yellow polka dot bikini!'

The bombs tested on some derelict naval vessels were of approximately the size and force of those used in Japan — about 20 kilotons. They were held in great awe. However, 8 years later near Rongelap — also in the Marshalls — a 100 megaton (100,000 kiloton) thermonuclear bomb was tested that made these Hiroshima class bombs seem like firecrackers!

THE WINDS - 1946

I witnessed the terrible blast
And felt the dreadful wind
A teeny-weeny[1] atom bomb at Bikini
Upon which our peace is pinned.

OFF TO KWAJALEIN

I was so excited I forgot about my sore arms. (I had gotten immunizations before leaving Crowder — Yellow Fever, Cholera, Japanese B Encephalitis, Tetanus, Typhoid, and Smallpox — all at once.) I had just turned 19 and was excited by this part of my most excellent adventure because— this would be: 1. The first time I had been more than 250 miles from home, 2. The first time I had been on an overnight train trip, 3. The first time I had been on an airplane, 4. The first time I had been outside the country. There may have been some other firsts too.

[1] Both of the 1946 Bikini atom bombs were of 20 Kiloton size, same as Hiroshima. In respect of subsequent bombs they were 'teeny-weeny'.

Fig. 11-1. The first atom bomb of the post-war atomic testing series was detonated in Bikini bay on July 1st, 1946.

Trying to squeeze the maximum out of three days leave, I consulted C.E. Lange's train schedules (equivalent to today's OAG) and found that the Santa Fe's premier train, El Capitan, made the trip Kansas City to San Francisco in two days. Regular trains took three. I spent an extra day at home. When I departed for 'Frisco Judy was not so tearful because we could see the end — or thought we could. But Judy was still convalescing. "Goodbye, Judy. I shouldn't be too long. The orders say 150 days and then return to Camp Crowder."

Unfortunately, when I checked in at Kansas City's Union Station on Tuesday 21st May, I found that the speedy El Capitan was an extra-fare train. All deluxe, it commanded a surcharge of $100. In those days $100 to me was like $100,000 today. The agent commiserated with me, but couldn't help much. He shrugged his shoulders, "Such is life." In the event I took the UP Overland Route — Kansas City, Denver, Cheyenne, Ogden, St. Lake City, Reno and finally Oakland, California. I was going to be a day late arriving at Hamilton Field, but it was a delightful trip.

It was so enchanting I didn't even worry about the 'inevitable' court-martial. I had a comfortable Pullman berth. There was an excellent dining car with good food. They accepted my meal tickets although the meals actually cost much more. There was an older lady — probably 24-25 — who was very friendly and offered me some dates (the fruit!) But, on balance it was a great adventure for an unsophisticated country bumpkin, one I will never forget.

The next morning Friday 24th May we arrived in Oakland and figuring I would be clapped in irons when I arrived a day late I skipped breakfast to catch the first ferry — Oakland to San Francisco. I would make up a few minutes at least. There was no Oakland Bay Bridge then. My breakfast that morning consisted of a giant 5¢ Washington State Delicious apple from a vending machine on the ferry. As we cut through the smooth waters of Oakland Bay to the giant dock-

Fig. 11-2. The "Great Speckled Bird", an Air Force MATS Douglas C-54 wings westward - California to Kwajalein with the Signal Detachment of Joint Task Force 1.— May 1946.

ing sheds on the San Francisco side I found a place at the rail and took it all in. There was a beautiful view of the San Francisco from water level. In addition, as many people excitedly pointed out— Alcatraz was visible through the morning fog. There was an inmate uprising at that time. Police boats circled the island. The papers that day described a bloody scene. Half dozen inmates were killed as well as several guards.

Hamilton Field was not really an airfield but an Air Corps facility for military air passengers — sort of like a downtown air terminal. The JTF-1 Logistics Office was a temporary organization greatly disorganized and not really interested that I'd reported a day late. They were much too busy to form up a firing squad! I was bussed with several dozen colleagues to flight facilities at Fairfield-Suisun Airbase (now Travis AFB). We got supper and spent several more hours with Army red tape. Finally at 10 PM Saturday 25th May we boarded the Materiel Air Transport Service — MATS — 'Great Speckled Bird' (see Fig. 11-2.) and departed for Kwajalein. This Douglas C54 was a four-engine aircraft called a DC4 for the civilian trade. Facilities for the transport of troops was not up to the standards I enjoyed years later on commercial flights. Seating was in canvas lattice benches which folded down from the fuselage interior. Troops sat with backs to the fuselage without seatbelts. The interior space, now empty, was normally used for tied down cargo. The floors were fitted with recessed, flush rings in the floor for tie downs. We did have windows but the comfort facilities were limited to 'relief tubes' — no coed facilities here!

We arrived in Hawaii at 0620 AM Sunday morning and stopped over at Hickam Field near Pearl Harbor. We had a few hours to took around. Hawaii is fascinating even for the worldly. Imagine how it looked through the eyes of a 19 year old Missouri boy. Some of the buildings still exhibited bullet holes from the Japanese attack 4 1/2 years earlier. At 1000 hrs we were issued a boxed lunch — a cold chicken leg, a small apple, a piece of stale bread and a paper cup of pineapple juice and then departed at 1040AM for the final leg.

Fig. 11-3. Four years earlier and 1,000 miles north of Kwajalein, the U.S. Navy won the Battle of Midway and began turning the tide against the Japanese. Above, a Japanese bomber evades the fierce flak and scores a hit on the Yorktown — June 4, 1942.

After ten hours of boring flight over an seemingly endless Pacific Ocean, the pilot began his landing approach — a turning descent from 20,000 feet — we could see Kwajalein off the right wing. It was just after 7 PM on Monday May 27, 1946. Sunset was at 702 PM and EENT (End of Evening Nautical Twilight) was at 735 PM. This in-between time the old Scottish poets called the Gloaming. The Mills Brothers called it "Twilight Time". Whatever you may call it the light at this hour causes illusions.

From 5000 feet the lines of colored runway lights plus the outlines and lights of the control tower and associated buildings gave the illusion of a giant aircraft carrier. The warm waters of this part of the south Pacific supports a rich nutrient 'soup' of phyto-plankton. This plankton is the bottom of the food chain. It feeds small marine life which feeds small fish which feeds — etc, etc. An unusual phenomena of phyto-plankton is its extraordinary absorption of phosphorous. When plankton is exposed to oxygen it fluoresces. This natural phosphorescence of the surf breaking on beaches of the island completed the illusion of the frothing wake churned up by a aircraft carrier making a hard-port turn into the wind to "launch all aircraft!".

Our first week on Kwajalein marked the fourth anniversary of the pivotal Battle of Midway fought in the seas 1000 miles to the north. See Fig. 11-3. This battle was unique at the time in that it was fought totally in the air. The battleships never saw one another. It was a great American victory but costly. The USS Yorktown was lost as were several hundred Naval Airmen including Lt. "Butch" O'Hare for whom O'Hare Field at Chicago is named. Butch O'Hare won the nation's highest award for valor — the Congressional of Honor for his heroism in that battle. It was awarded posthumously. The Japanese Fleet was so badly damaged that they never fully recovered. It was the desire to acquire 'unsinkable' aircraft carriers that led the Naval strategists to seize

BREAKFAST ON A SOUTH SEA ISLAND

Orange Juice, with acidity that could remove the enamel from your teeth.

Egg Omelette from powdered eggs left over from the WWII Italian Campaign.

Bacon unblemished by one fleck of lean.

Baked Beans with the density of lead. Heavy enough to bend the metal trays.

Toast with texture of a shingle.

Margarine, from an OD can, so parafinized it won't melt on a hot stove.

Coffee, strong enough to float horse-shoe nails.

Peanut butter that will remove loose teeth.

"Strawberry" Jelly unsullied by any acquaintance with a real strawberry.

the Marshall Islands in early 1944 — Rongelap, Majuro, Roi, Eniwetok, Carlos, Ebeye, etc. Kwajalein was the southernmost of these islands and afforded the best airstrip as well as a small but ideal harbor.

Touch down on the tiny atoll was at 720 PM Monday — we had crossed the International Dateline and gained one day. As we debarked from 'The Great Speckled Bird' we were hit in the face by air that felt like a wet mop. The inevitable Olive Drab 1940 Chevy bus was waiting for us as we shouldered our duffel bags and musette bags containing all our worldly goods. Years later when a ten ton moving van was required to move our family's 'worldly goods' from New Jersey to Kansas City, I remembered those many moves where I carried all my "worldly goods" on my back. For example, at the Inchon landing in Korea September 1950, I carried on my back all my 'worldly goods' plus a carbine, 200 rounds of ammunition, two grenades and three days rations.

Another first impression of Kwajalein was the pervasive smell of diesel fuel and diesel exhausts. All island electrical power came from diesel generators which roared away endlessly near the Task Force Headquarters. Later, the periodic mosquito suppression program added petroleum based DDT spray to the island's special bouquet. A weekly Navy R47 flew over at 100 feet spritzing us liberally. Bugs were never a problem on Kwaj.

Enroute to our billets in the fading light, we could barely make out three B-29s (see Fig. 11-4.) of the 509th Composite Bomb Group parked on aprons just off the main runway. The 509th was the Group that delivered the two atom bombs on Japan from Tinian. I correctly assumed these aircraft would be used in the upcoming tests.

Our billets were Quonset huts. Quonset huts are formed from semicircular steel ribs fitted with 4 x 8 corrugated steel panels which formed both roof and walls. The bulkheads of these huts were screen only so as to catch the slightest stray breeze. Average daytime temperature was about 85°. Not too bad but the humidity never fell below 80 - 90%. We had departed San Francisco wearing woolen OD uniforms which were prescribed for that area. We wasted no time getting into lighter clothing stowing the woolens in packing crates that we used for lockers. The effect of the extreme humidity was demonstrated upon our departure 10 weeks later when I pulled my woolen ODs out of storage and they disintegrated!

Fig. 11-4. A B-29 heavy bomber of the 509th Composite Bomb Group dropped the test bomb.

KWAJALEIN

Kwajalein lies at 8°41' North Latitude, 167°43' East Longitude. It is just west of the International Date Line thus is one day ahead of the continental US — 18 hours ahead of US Central Time. It is only 135 miles from the equator. The heat would have been unbearable if it were not for the constant ocean breezes. It is one of thousands of atolls in the southwest Pacific that resulted when — 100 million years ago — volcanoes sank under the ocean and then in another geologic age were heaved back up to expose the old volcano rims. If these rims had been perfect they would have formed circles of land surrounding a lagoon.

The atolls—viewed from the air—look like a cast off string of iridescent pearls lying on the azure velvet of the sea. During the geologic age when these atolls were under the sea, trillions of small crustaceans lived out their lives then endowed the atolls with their tiny calcified remains (diatoms). These diatoms, along with the coral, make up the top stratum of these small islands.

Two characteristics gave the atolls military importance: the partially enclosed lagoons made excellent natural harbors, and their level coral surface eased construction of airstrips. A bulldozer could scrape out an airfield in a matter of hours. Such was the case with Kwajalein. Kwajalein had been a small, relatively deserted Pacific Island until the war. The Marshall and Gilbert Islands had been mandated to Japan by the League of Nations in the 1920's. Contrary to this mandate and international law the Japanese began fortifying them in the 1930's. This is roughly the area where Emilia Earhart disappeared in 1937 and a number of theories have connected her disappearance to the Japanese and these island fortifications. In June 1946 this tiny island, smaller in area than Pilot Grove was home to Joint Task Force 1 and 11,000 men of 'Operation Crossroads'. There may have been some women too, but in the three months I was there, I never saw one.

LIFE ON KWAJALEIN

After a minimal amount of in-processing we were given work assignments. I went to the Atoll Commander's Headquarters - Communications Section as a teletype operator. The Atoll commander was Commodore Wyatt who had been here before all the atom bomb testing project started. I met him one night when — upon returning from the Officers' Club — he stopped by to chew out the hapless navy signalmen that I worked with. It was embarrassing because the poor signalman really hadn't done anything wrong and Commodore Wyatt was drunk. My humble opinion was: Commodore Wyatt would have been out of his depth managing a news stand. A real officer does not show up drunk to harass the troops in front of their colleagues.

The Signal Detachment was augmenting the Navy communications facilities. Thus, we were given passes for the US. Navy Mess. This lead to a variant of the St. Charles Starvation Syndrome. Here, however, the problem was not quantity but quality. A typical breakfast menu is illustrated above. See 'Breakfast on a South Sea Island".

To be fair to the US. Navy, they dealt with a logistic nightmare. Everything except the air we breathed and the water we drank (distilled from sea water) had to be transported from the continental US. 6,000+ miles away.

The US. Army Air Force fared better. After all, they controlled the air. If the mess cooks wanted to lay on a fresh tossed salad for lunch — they'd radio MATS Honolulu and have them put the materials on the next flight from Hickam Field. Although the US. Army Air Force would not become a separate service (US. Air Force) for three years — 1949 — they were already getting uppity. On many of their organizational signs they 'forgot' to include 'Army' the parent from whom they had sprung. But they ate well and — whenever we could sneak into the Air Force mess — we did too.

Off duty, there was really not a lot to do. We could enjoy swimming at an excellent coral beach but showering later never fully removed the sea salt. While drinking water was completely purified and desalinized — water for bathing and washing was not. We had an open air movie two nights a week. I remember seeing Rita Hayworth in "Gilda". We also did a lot of beach combing. We found some beautiful seashells and using paper clips for connectors, strung them together to make necklaces. The Air Corps guys bought them.

It was during a solitary expedition one July morning in search of these shells that I had a chilling experience. I walked along the beach with the surf lapping at my bare feet. The action of the waves often tossed up beautiful and exotic shells. We all wore shorts (actually fatigue trousers hacked of above the knee and hemmed up with varying degrees of skill. We all looked like Robinson Crusoe). I saw a particularly large wave approaching and stepped back to the beach so as not to be inundated. As the wave crashed on the sandy beach, a silver-gray cloud catapulted out of the wave top. A school of fingerling size fish — sardines without the can — cast themselves onto the beach and their silvery undersides flashed in the sun as they flip-flopped and thrashed wildly to get back into the water.

I wondered what could have caused this attempted mass suicide. Then I saw it! In the shallows 15-20 feet away a distinctive dorsal fin sliced the water's surface as a 8-10 foot blue shark herded the tiny fish toward shore. Although it was a hot day, I broke out in goose flesh as I scampered to higher ground. This was our swimming beach and we had never thought of shark danger. I never went swimming again.

We had no quartermaster support for fixing clothing so we had to improvise some emergency tailoring for ourselves. I mentioned above that we found necessary was to hack off the legs of our trousers to make our own shorts. I'm surprised that the Army let us get away with this. It was so hot and humid, shorts were mandatory. Another break from normal Army discipline was beards! I never saw such atrocious looking mustaches and beards in my life. However, there was no barber and it was inevitable that we end up looking like castaways. Spare time was devoted to letters. Reading and re-reading letters from home and writing to loved ones.

Insofar as real disciplinary problems there simply weren't any. Part of the reason for this was the total lack of any alcohol for the enlisted men. In mid-July a ship came in with beer. Not only would there be a ration of two bottles for every man on the island — it would be cold. I remember coming off my 'dog watch' at 2000 hrs (8PM) and going straight to the Navy Mess where it was being doled out. The line was 3/4 mile long and took 2 hours. I got two bottles of cold Carlings Black Label, popped the caps, sat down on the coral ground and drank them in two long draughts. Aaaaah!

LETTER EDGED IN BLACK

Working in a Navy environment I had to conform to their weird work scheduling. I had the 'dog' watch from 1600-2000 hrs then the 'first' watch from 0400-0800. Thus, at 1000 hrs Monday, July 29th I had my Navy breakfast of baked beans and toast and was off duty when the Detachment clerk held mail call. I sat on my bunk in the Quonset hut that was our barracks and read the letter from Mrs. Schlotzhauer, Judy's mother. My initial apprehension at getting a letter from her was justified. Judy was dead!

There had been a epidemic of polio in central Missouri. Judy's sister Carol Rae had had it and suffered damage to nerves in her legs, but Judy, her body weakened by her long bout with rheumatic fever was unable to cope. She died Wednesday 17th July 1946. Drs. Salk and Sabine were 10 years too late in getting that monster caged.

Mrs. Schlotzhauer had enclosed a clipping from the Boonville Daily News — the death notice and a memorial program from the funeral at Wesley Chapel. She wrote, "You'll remember the locket you gave her last Christmas. Judy fitted your graduation picture into it. It meant a lot to her so we buried her wearing your locket and picture."

THE MOUND

I read and re-read the letter and pondered the details. I was devastated! What ever happened to immortality? I really needed to go somewhere private get my mind back together. Finding privacy on Kwajalein was going to take some doing. Kwajalein is tiny, only 2 miles long by 1/2 mile wide with a population density to challenge New York City.

But a place did come to mind, isolated if not too quiet. There was a small parklike spot at the north end of the island. It was under the landing path for the airfield so it wasn't all that quiet but it was isolated. There was no transportation available, but since it was only a mile away I could easily hike it. I started walking along the road, lagoon side... past the swimming beaches... past the wharf where three ships were tied up. The first ship was the USS Albemarle, the laboratory ship where the atom bombs were being assembled. The US government is quite touchy about atom bombs. There were at least four guards from FMF-PAC[2] wearing full battle dress with slung Thompson sub-machine guns. They eyed me as I walked northward.

The next ship was the USS Betelgeuse which served as logistic support and housing for the 100 or so atomic scientists from Los Alamos and Sandia, NM. Very few of the GI's knew what "Betelgeuse" is (a star in the constellation Orion) and in mockery of the pretentiousness of the scientists, called the vessel: "Beetlejuice". The third vessel was the USNTV[3] Spindle Eye. The sight of it was a humorous distraction. I was needing all the distraction I could get.

One of my Signal Detachment colleagues, PFC Francis Coelho of Vallejo, California had been assigned as a communications technician on this vessel upon our arrival. The Spindle Eye cruised the islands the first three weeks he was aboard making poor Coelho seasick as a parrot. He wasn't much of a sailor. He told me if they hadn't finally docked at Kwajalein he would have died, or committed suicide.

My destination, the deserted little park, was not much trafficked because it was a graveyard — of sorts. A mound of coral about 50 ft in diameter had been shoved together by bulldozers. It was topped by a large white ship's anchor. The anchor faced northwest toward Japan. On the opposite side near the top of the mound was a brass plaque. It faced northeastward toward the US. There was a coral ramp rising to a small platform in front of the plaque. I had read the plaque before but tried distracting my mind by reading it again. Not until the third time did the words begin coming through: "In this burial mound are the remains of 4,938 of the 4th Imperial Japanese Marines who died on this island 31st January to 3rd February, 1944 ..."

The Japanese defenders had chosen to fight to the death and the U.S. 7th Infantry Division had accommodated them. At the end of that battle, nearly 5,000 Japanese bodies were deposited here, cremated with aviation gas and had 20 feet of coral bulldozed over them. The burning was not meant to be disrespectful — hygiene dictated that 5,000 dead bodies on a tropical island had to be disposed of quickly.

Ironically, at the moment that I was reading this inscription, the 50 or so Japanese survivors were prisoners of war at Fort Shafter, Oahu, Territory of Hawaii. They were working on the largest military cemetery in the Pacific area — the Punchbowl. The Punchbowl was then in the process of receiving remains of US war dead retrieved from all the Asia-Pacific battle areas including the 157 US infantrymen killed on Kwajalein that had been temporarily buried on Carlos Island — a pleasant, green, palm-fringed island nearby. The Punchbowl is regarded to this day the most beautiful military cemetery in the world.

[2] FMF-PAC - Fleet Marine Force - Pacific.

[3] U S Navy Training Vessel. The Spindle Eye was a 1920's era four masted, steel hull sailing vessel. After Pearl Harbor sails were stowed and it was converted to a diesel powered communications vessel. The communications gear and a photo section were manned by US Army Signal Corps. This vessel had covered the surrender ceremony in Tokyo Bay ten months before — 12 September 1945.

The Japanese Burial Mound was at the extreme northern end of our crescent shaped island. At this point the island is only 200 yards wide. And since the island was only 8 feet above sea level at high tide, the mound's extra 20 feet provided an observation point. Standing before the bronze plaque I could see the nearby island, Ebeye, where the natives — former residents — of Kwajalein were now living — wards of the US Government. To the east the sun reflected off the sea with a million flashing pinpoints of light. The whitecaps looked like sea gulls flashing their white wings angrily. All on a gentle sea. Here, and at this time of year, the Pacific Ocean was living up to its name. It was very pacific. But mostly I saw the immensity of the endless ocean. Standing here on the grave of 5,000 Japanese soldiers, a thought came to me: this ocean is like the ocean of sorrow this war has exacted from America and the world. My tears and personal grief are but a tiny contribution.

THE CHAPLAIN

It is now 1130 and although under somewhat better control, I still didn't know what I should do about requesting leave. Another hot dusty walk back down the lagoon road, this time to see the Chaplain. His assistant, sensing my distress, let me wait in the Chaplain's Quonset hut office. I'd never met the Chaplain so he introduced himself when he returned from lunch — Captain Somebody or other. I explained the situation and he said, "Shall we say a prayer?"

"Yes, sir." I said. Actually, I would have much preferred a stiff jolt of Jack Daniels but if he had any it never occurred to him to break it out.

He went on, "I do sympathize with your situation, but I don't know if an emergency leave would do you any good. Let's think this through. First, we are 6,720 miles from Pilot Grove, Missouri. If you were to get a leave you'd have no flight priority. How long did it take for you to get out here from Crowder?"

"Ten days." I answered.

"OK, it took ten days when the Army urgently wanted you out here. Going back they don't really care, so what would it take? Three weeks? Four? Besides all that, I can tell you that no one will move on this until the Red Cross has investigated and verified the circumstances of your case. There are just too many fellows out here who want to go home now the war is over. They pull all kinds of shenanigans. Including time for the Red Cross what are we up to? Six weeks? Eight? Operation Crossroads will beover before you even get a decision on this don't you think?"

Fig. 11-5. The Punchbowl National Cemetery at Ft. Shafter, Hawaii was built in 1946.

"I guess so," was all I could say. And that was the end of it. I wasn't going home. I wrote to Judy's mother with condolences and explained all this. I really don't think she expected me to come.

The Chaplain had been right. At the end of Operation Crossroads, the Army was in no great hurry to get us home. On Wednesday 7th August, 1946 The Signal Detachment boarded the troop transport APA33 USS Bayfield and began a three day voyage to Pearl Harbor.

DUTY IN THE SANDWICH ISLANDS[4]

NOON SATURDAY 11TH AUGUST, 1946. The sea was living up to its name — Pacific. Swells of 2-3 feet were no inhibition to our white bow-wave as we made 20 knots heading for Pearl. I was leaning on the starboard bow rail watching the flying fish. Were they being disturbed by the Bayfield's prow cutting through their habitat or were they just curious and flying up to get a look at us? Large schools exhibited their astonishing ability to fly and glide for 100s of yards, lightly skimming the gentle waves. They were so numerous that the fluttering of their fins (wings?) was audible above the southerly breeze in the ship's rigging.

It was high noon and first call for the noon meal had just sounded. Since the sun stood broad on our starboard beam, I could reckon our course as due east. I had just started toward the hatch leading to the galley when someone on the port side sang out in an amateur imitation of some ancient seafarer, "Land Ho! There's Hawaii!"

Of course, all the deck loungers — including myself — immediately rushed over to the port side and saw the self-appointed lookout pointing at something about 3 points off the port bow. We watched as the green headland of Barbers Point clarified itself through the shimmering haze. Within a few minutes the green hills of Oahu west of Pearl Harbor showed themselves and the excitement mounted. It would be an absolute delight just to get off this miserable cattle boat. The troop compartments, all on the lower decks, were stifling with the heat and humidity. After lights out I usually took my GI blanket up the ladders and gangways to the open deck to try to sleep. You could at least breathe. On every hatch and clear space on the deck were semi-naked bodies glistening with sweat in the moonlight. It looked like some giant cans of sardines had been decanted and silver fish strewn randomly about.

[4] When Captain James Cook discovered these islands in 1778, he named them "Sandwich Islands" in honor of his sponsor the Earl of Sandwich (Yes, this was the same guy who invented the 'sandwich'—pronounced 'sammich' in some parts). For Cook's kind consideration, in 1779 the natives killed him (but did not eat him!) When King Kamehameha unified the islands in 1810 the islands were renamed the "Hawaiian Islands".

We were sustained by thoughts of our destination—Hawaii! It would be a dream compared with the primitive life we'd lived over the past months! We still had illusions of going home, but a short stopover in Honolulu would not be at all disappointing.

Being a PFC I had to pull all kinds of fatigue duty although to be honest the KP was not bad — lots of extra eats! What was bad was guarding our cryptographic equipment. This crypto equipment — 20-30 crates — was stowed in a bow compartment and was required to be kept under armed guard 24-hours a day. Although I have always had the good fortune of not being susceptible to sea sickness, this bow compartment guard duty was an acid test. This part of the ship was like an elevator. Even in calm seas I rose 15-20 feet then dropped in a free fall as the bow fell off the swell. This was my first experience at weightlessness and it was extremely disconcerting to the stomach. To cap it off, the compartment bulkheads had just been painted and the paint fumes were almost overpowering. It was all I could do to hold onto my meals.

Fig. 11-6. On my first pass in Hawaii, I had to see Waikiki Beach! September 1946. Diamond Head is in background.

As were pulled into our berth at Pearl we could see a Matson Liner arriving at a Honolulu pier across the bay. The hula dancers and leis were much in evidence probably welcoming home those folks who had retreated to California for the war years. We were as elated as they were to be arriving in Oahu — for different reasons.

THE TENTH ARMY REPPLE DEPPLE

The Signal Detachment retrieved personal baggage then was segregated into one of the '40 and 8' trailer buses that the military used for short hauls. We were off to the Tenth Army Replacement Depot just outside Wahiawa 10-20 miles north of Pearl. The Tenth Army never existed except on paper. It was the massive Army that was to be formed on Okinawa in 1945 and carry out the final campaign of the war in the Pacific — the assault on Japanese Home Islands. This Hawaiian 'Repple Depple' was to be a part of the Tenth Army, serving as a pipeline to feed troops into that sausage grinder when things got going good.

Normally, the first impression of this Repple Depple would have been crushing to the spirit. Hundreds of tar-paper barracks (shacks, really) were set up on stilts to keep the termites and tropical rot from devouring them. A slum-lord who lodged tenants in such housing today would be subjected to the most severe of sanctions. We were not concerned in the least. We're off that troop transport. The weather was—cooler and not so humid as the Honolulu-Pearl Harbor area. Wahiawa is several hundred feet above sea level—critically important elevation for comfort. We had room to spread out—no more slave berths. No more salt water showers for the first time since May. We had real folding cots for bunks not hammocks. The food was good and plentiful. The Quartermaster facility—whose staff was looking at demobilization with a great deal of trepidation— were unbelievably accommodating with new clothing. Further, these new uniforms would be tailored to an exact fit by soon-to-be-laid-off seamstresses. Gotta look good on Waikiki! See Fig. 11-6.

For most of us this form-hugging tailoring turned out to be a big mistake. Months of bad Marshall Island chow, debilitating heat and humidity had caused many of us to drop 10-20 pounds. The good food, invigorating climate and inactivity of the Wahiawa Repple Depple soon restored that avoirdupois plus a little more. Sheepishly some had to go back to the seamstresses to 'just let out a little in the waist'.

Unsurprisingly, there was still a wartime-like regulation of the troops in the Repple Depple. It had been necessary during the war to stringently control personal movements of troops who were bound for battle areas. Many of these troops had puzzled out that their next sea voyage would take them to regions that would be extremely hazardous to their health and well being. Some took it in mind to forswear this great honor and seek sanctuary in a more hospitable place like — say — Pitcairn Island[5]. The MPs who regulated the orderly to-ing and fro-ing from the Wahiawa camp were still of that wartime controlling mindset.

We noted the concertina barbed wire and guard towers that surrounded the camp and complained to the camp com-

[5] Pitcairn Island, 25° South Latitude, 130° West Longitude, near the Tropic of Capricorn and well out of harm's way in any age. Pitcairn was colonized (1790) by mutineers from the British naval vessel Bounty and Tahitian women whose descendents still inhabit the island. Capt. Bligh and the 18 loyal crew members were set adrift in a small boat; they sailed 3,618 miles over open sea to Timor, a feat that stands unmatched in world naval history.

Fig. 11-7. At the WTJ transmitter site in Upper Kipapa Gulch (Oahu, Hawaii) our billets were disguised as plantation worker housing. Sonny Salmon 1946.

mander. It was mentioned that the war was well over now. We won and had been at peace for over a full year. He relented. The fence and towers remained but we all got passes to go to town — Wahiawa. But, "You gotta be back in camp by Call to Quarters!" That was 2300 hours—11PM.

Our increasing fear that we weren't really going home was confirmed just after Labor Day. The 972d Signal Operations Battalion personnel officer and some of his staff whistled us out of our tar-paper billets at Wahiawa and announced that we were hereby and henceforth assigned to the battalion at Fort Shafter.

An interesting non-sequitur: just before we moved to Fort Shafter, the Army issued an order permitting the wearing of civilian clothing while off duty. This was the first time since 1941 that the wearing of civilian clothing was not treated as prima facie evidence of desertion. We all celebrated by rushing to Honolulu to shop for the brightest, gaudiest, most outlandish luau shirt we could find. How strange it seemed to wear such clothing without danger of being arrested! However, in a more just world some of us would have been arrested by the fashion police for displaying such appalling taste!

THE PINEAPPLE PLANTATION

My stay at Fort Shafter lasted only overnight. I drew an assignment with the Army Radio Station WTJ Transmitter Detachment in the pineapple fields of Upper Kipapa Gulch in the Waipio area. This facility was supposed to be secret so there were no signs or other evidence that it existed. The bus driver who had never been there spent the whole morning looking for it — and didn't believe it when he found it.

In 1942 when Hawaii was considered vulnerable to further air and naval attacks, the military radio transmitter facility was moved from Headquarters Pacific in Fort Shafter to the boondocks. The entire facility was hidden in a giant tunnel in Upper Kipapa Gulch in the Waialae Mountains. There was a small farm road that left Kamehameha Highway (Hawaii Route 1) the main road between Honolulu and Wahiawa. This dirt and gravel road wound for 5-6 miles through sugarcane fields finally debauching into a giant, red-earth pineapple field. In the midst of the pineapples was the transmitter facility.

The transmitters themselves were buried in a tunnel under a mountain well protected from air attack. The antenna fields had to be above ground of course. They were dispersed and from the air would not have been obvious to 1940s era spy technology. Finally, to disguise the living facilities for the 30-40 man operating staff —a Hawaiian pineapple plantation was replicated. There were 6 houses that looked like plantation worker cottages. See Figs. 13-7 and 13-8. A large metal building housed the messhall, orderly room and dayroom and looked like a processing plant.

For the first time in my service, I worked a very decent 40 hours a week. The work was under ground in giant humidity controlled, air-conditioned tunnels. This unparalleled lavishness on working environment was not for the benefit of the troops. It was the expensive equipment that was being protected. The only drawback to the work was that we had to take our turns on the day, the swing and the graveyard shifts. Manning was 24 hours a day, 7 days a week.

Originally the billeting assignments — the ersatz workers homes — were according to shift. Since shifts continually changed, we ended up bunking wherever we wanted. The "tenant" cottages had three bedrooms, a dining room, a living room and one bath. We bunked two per bedroom, two in the dining room, three in the living room and one in the kitchen. The kitchen had no equipment other than a refrigerator which was — as you might guess — kept filled with beer — in this case Tecate.

GLOSSARY OF HAWAIIAN TERMS

Aloha	uh LO ha	Greeting: hello, goodbye, howdy, kiss off, etc.
Haole	ha OH lee	Mainlander, non-Hawaiian, Anglo
Kanaka	kuh NAK uk	Wooly headed, dark-skinned, betel nut chewing, aboriginal native of a micronesian island about one generation removed from cannibalism. A perjorative that GIs called native Hawaiians when they wanted to have their hair parted with a sugar cane machete.
Kane	KAH neh	Man, boy, male.
Wahine	wah HEE nee	Woman, girl, female

Fig. 11-8. Our billets were in the middle of a giant pineapple field. Near Wahiawa, Oahu, Territory of Hawaii Sep. 1946.

TAVITAS AND HIS MUCHACHOS

I initially shared a room with T/4—Technician 4th Class Carlos Tavitas, (see Fig. 11-10.) a moody Chicano from Los Angeles. Carlos was a lead cook and had a hoard of Tecate in the kitchen and refrigerator. Everyone liked Tecate okay so we chipped in with him and maintained a perpetual inventory.

I soon had to forego Tavitas as a roommate. His shift never corresponded with mine. In odd weeks he had to arise at 4AM and get breakfast started at the messhall. He was never overly careful about the racket he made upon arising. Most annoying, however, was his phonograph and his Mexican records. The music was OK, I liked most of them. As a matter of fact many were classics and are still popular in the Texicano genre to this day. It was just that he played them all night and into the early morning hours while forlornly sucking on his Tecate.

I came to the conclusion that all popular Mexican songs are ballads recounting death of loved ones, unrequited love and other heart-rending tragedies that afflict the poor campesino. "Adios Muchachos" is an example. I knew very little Spanish but I could follow, roughly, the theme of this ballad. There's this poor mother dying of God-knows-what. She calls her little boys to her side to say goodbye. The way she goes on is pitiful. It would bring tears to the eye of a potato.

The last time such melancholy ballads dominated American music was during the Civil War[6]. And then, there was an abundance of things to be sad about. But I will not judge. There undoubtedly is a lot of sad stuff in the Chicano experience also.

Fig. 11-9. Me and King Kamehameha. We kept things under control in Honolulu - 1946.

A FIFTY YEAR OLD JOKE

The photo at right, Fig. 11-10, hid a latent practical joke that escaped me for over 50 years. In 1946, as "Red" Atchison was getting me posed, Tavitas wanders out onto the verandah and unzips to expose himself. Archie Bunker called this "full frontal nudididitty!" The joke failed because no one noticed until I enlarged this picture X 8 to prepare it for the book. Don't fracture your eyes—I've retouched it to restore full respectability.

Fig. 11-10. Sonny in front of Hawaiian billets. Tavitas the cook in background. 1946.

PINEAPPLE RUSTLERS

It was not long until some larceny arose in our hearts concerning all those pineapples. It was nearing harvest time and we felt that a few fresh pineapples would go down very

[6] You want Civil War melancholia try "Faded Coat of Blue", "The Vacant Chair", "Tenting Tonight" or the magnificently maudlin "Lorena".

Fig. 11-11. Waikiki Beach and Diamond Head in 1946. The only Japanese here then were Prisoners of War.

Fig. 11-12. The beach at Ft. DeRussy in 1946. DeRussy was at the western end of Waikiki and was an "R&R" post in WWII, Korea and Vietnam.

well indeed. Three of us chose a moonlit night to search out the perfect pineapple. We found 4-5 that were close contenders and keeping a sharp lookout cut them off at the ground and slipped them under field jackets. We smuggled them into the messhall cooler. We never had any room in our refrigerators for anything but beer.

Over the next few days we peeled these stolen treasures and munched our way through 2-3 of them. One thing I learned: when you peel these suckers, do not be greedy and peel too thinly. The pineapple has tiny spines on the skin that, if not peeled off, will make your mouth and stomach think you've eaten shards of broken glass.

Two weeks later a gang of Filipino farm workers harvested the crop. We had harvested about 5. They got about 500,000. As their trucks passed through our cantonment area loaded to the gunnels with delicious, ripe, fat pineapples, the workers tossed them off to us by the bushel! But, they didn't taste quite as good as those we had rustled!

THE TEE-SHIRT BIDNESS

PFC Waxman, a fat Brooklyn kid, who had never driven a car in his life until entering the army, was driving a 3/4 ton weapons carrier to Wahiawa one morning on an errand. He hailed me and my pal "Red" Atchison, "Want to go to town?" We were off duty so we piled into the back.

Too late I realized that while Waxman may have convinced the army driving instructor that he could drive — he would have to improved mightily to convince me. He took off across the now harvested pineapple field on a 'shortcut'. Now, the regular dirt track that served as an access road was bad enough, the furrowed pineapple field was like corduroy. In some kind of convoluted logic he just drove faster. I was bounced off the seat to strike my head on the wooden frame and fell back on the seat. I had my left hand extended to break my fall and instead of breaking my fall I broke my hand.

We went directly to the Schofield Barracks Army Hospital and reported to what passed for an emergency room. The PFC Medic asked, "Can you move your finger?" I could and did. He said, "Well, it ain't broke, probably just sprained bad." But it hurt like hell and I protested. "OK," he says, "I'm gonna send you over to Orthopedics and they'll take a picture of it."

I saw the X-Ray and the diagnosis was clear even to me: "Full fracture third metacarpal left hand." I was fitted with a full forearm cast and wound up confined[7] to hospital for nearly a month.

The food was good. I had a lot of time to read. I was responsible only for making my bed, so it wasn't a bad life, but the boredom of confinement was deadly. It was the boredom that drove me to the Occupational Therapy workshop. I screwed around with some stuff — sketched some, tried to paint and did some linoleum block printing.

The linoleum block printing turned me onto an idea. I was permitted to have my underwear and had a extra tee-shirt or two. I got a new linoleum block, drew up a Signal Corps crossed flags design, added "Waipio Army Radio WTJ 972d Sig Opns Bn and gouged out a printing plate. Yes, I knew the lettering had to be carved backwards. I wasn't a complete dolt.

I rolled the orange ink on the plate and carefully placed the linoleum plate on a new tee-shirt. I let the ink soak in a little, then — voila, a souvenir tee-shirt. I should have patented the whole idea because — believe it or don't, in 1947 no such thing as a tee-shirt with a message existed!

I took the linoleum block plate with me when I was discharged from the hospital. I bought tee-shirts from Navy Stores in Pearl Harbor for 20¢ each. I put my stamp on them in orange ink and sold them for $1. I could have gotten more because I couldn't make them fast enough. Sales were terrific. I was a bit apprehensive and indeed after a few washings the orange ink faded badly. I might have had to refund some money if I'd charged more. But for $1—tough noogie!

[7] Confined is a deliberate choice of words here. I did not have access to my clothes. I had to wear a dark wine colored pants and jacket suit that clearly identified me as a patient (inmate?).

ALOHA TO HAWAII

My enlistment ran out on 14th March 1947 and I was feeling more and more like a short timer. I spent weekends and off-duty hours catching the sights and delights of Hawaii, well, Oahu at least. I saw surfing for the first time at Haleiwa Beach. The vision of the waterfall at Pali Pass will remain in my memory forever. The white sands of Waikiki were delightful. See Fig. 11-11. The Army maintained a recreation center—Ft De Russy—at the western end of Waikiki.

Fort De Russy was a study in contrasts. The Royal Hawaiian Hotel (see Fig. 11-13.) was then the premier resort hotel in Hawaii if not the entire U.S. One had to be a millionaire to afford a stay there. Fort De Russy (see Fig. 11-12.) shared Waikiki Beach with the Royal Hawaiian. Right next door, it housed raggedy-assed GIs who had only seen a twenty dollar bill in the movies. The beach itself was commons and we mingled freely with our more affluent countrymen (and countrywomen). Like my friend the distinguished philosopher, PFC 'Red' Atchison said, "Once we're in our swim trunks, they can't tell us riff-raff from royalty."

I was just 19 years old and the Territory of Hawaii required one to be at least 20 to enjoy the delights of adult beverages. There was a minor amount of 'carding' in the Honolulu saloons but the Black Cat Bar on South Beretania Street never bowed to such governmental intrusion on one's manly right to get blotto. My co-conspirators and I—all underage—often hung out there for that reason. The Black Cat offered some exotic drinks—Honolulu Holocaust, Singapore Sling, as well as all the tropical rum drinks— Fog Cutter, Sailor's Revenge, Zombie, Mai-Tai, etc., but it was a 'going home' celebratory Singapore Sling that did me in.

As expected, in late January a number of us JTF-1 guys simultaneously got orders for reassignment to the 'Zone of the Interior' for discharge and resumption of the haole life.

SCHOFIELD BARRACKS

Schofield Barracks was the setting for James Jones classic tale of pre-Pearl Harbor army life, "From Here to Eternity". Many of the 'location' shots for the movie were made there. On 1st February when I moved bag and baggage to Schofield for out-processing — the bullets holes from the Japanese raid were still in evidence on some of the barracks. That small part of the stage setting for "From Here to Eternity" did not have to be faked.

Schofield Barracks is only a few miles west of Wahiawa and has always been considered a plum assignment. When I was there the 24th "Taro Leaf[8]" Division, America's "Foreign Legion"was being rebuilt there. The 24th Infantry Division was nicknamed 'Foreign Legion' because, as of that time, it had never been stationed in the continental U.S.

Compared with what I had seen of army facilities heretofore, being ordered to Schofield Barracks was like orders to the Ritz Carlton! We were in permanent barracks with fans although it never got all that warm. Even the latrine floors were of marble tile. The food was excellent and although they tried to get some fatigue work out of us, we had so many conflicting out-processing appointments, we only worked when we wanted to. Mostly, work was cutting grass.

Processing out with us was a few old veterans who had somehow got lost in the shuffle. I met one fellow, Sergeant Mickey Owens who told a story of unbelievably bad luck. When President Roosevelt had Federalized the National Guard in September 1940, Owens was in a Wisconsin Guard unit. He told me, "In my town the National Guard was like a country club for the working stiffs. We had a heck of a good time — camp every summer, hiking, swimming, marksmanship training, camping out, it was just a overgrown Boy Scout troop and we loved it."

But then Uncle Sam called in some of his chits and his unit was called up in September 1940. They were dispatched to Schofield Barracks. At that time he was having an appendectomy and did not go with them. In late December 1940 he had completed his convalescence and joined his unit. In September 1941, having served their one year tour, his unit was ordered home. There was argument as to whether he would go home with them since he had not served his full year. In the event, he did not and on 7th December, 1941 he was in this very facility being out-processed when the Japs attacked Pearl Harbor.

After a few beers one evening he walked me around the quadrangle to point out the bullet holes and describe how the Zeros strafed the barracks. He said, "I thought at the time —good news — they didn't hurt anybody, but—bad news, I'm afraid this is gonna crimp my discharge plans!"

"I argued that my time was up and I had to be discharged. There was so much confusion for a while, I thought maybe I had convinced them to send me home. Finally, the decision: I could either enlist in the U.S. Army reserve for the duration of the war plus six months with immediate active duty, or I would be drafted with all the same terms. I really didn't want to do either. Finally I made a virtue of necessity and enlisted. Then I got an idea. They had to give me a physical examination. If I failed it, I'd be discharged! I set about trying to find some way to flunk my physical."

"Some yard-bird told me that if you take some of that GI soap in the latrine and rubbed it thoroughly under your arms it would temporarily raise your blood pressure. Well, I don't know — maybe I did something wrong, but it didn't do a damned thing for me! I was getting pretty desperate when some ex-medic showed me what to do." Owens demonstrated in pantomime with his cigarette, "You take a little bottle of iodine see, you can get that in any drug store. You get out your needle and thread. Dip the thread in the iodine. Soak it real good. Now use the needle to pull the thread through your cigarette, light 'er up and inhale deeply."

[8] The Taro is a Hawaiian native plant like a banana plant without bananas.

Fig. 11-13. Grounds of the Royal Hawaiian Hotel 1946. Here I am a trespasser. Thirty years later I stayed here on a Citibank assignment. ("Assignment" sounds better than "boondoggle, doesn't it?)

"This here medic guy says that iodine is 'radio-opaque' and the vapors will show up as spots on your lungs. At the time I didn't think that it might also kill me, I just did it. And it worked! Well, it kinda worked. After my chest X-Ray I did some other tests. The next day they called me from the orderly room to report back to the doctor. 'Hot dam! It worked! Now I'll puff another iodine cigarette and if I can just BS my way through this meeting maybe I'm out."

Owens takes a long swig on his Tecate and shakes his head mournfully. "What happened?" I cued him.

Owens says, "Well, the doc thumped my chest, made me cough and listened all over my chest and back with his stethoscope. He asked me all kinds of questions about TB and lung disease in my family. Then, shaking his head, he sent me down for another X-Ray. I cool my heels for about an hour. Finally the doc sends for me. He's got my two X-Rays on his viewer thing. I see him there looking at both of them together. He looks up at me with a furrowed brow and says, 'The spots on your lungs have moved since yesterday! Now I don't know what the hell you're up to, soldier, but it looks suspiciously like malingering! I'm thinking of certifying you as fully fit for duty and recommend you for the Philippines with the 26th Cav. They're leaving Pearl in a few days. You want to tell me what you're about?' He scared hell out of me so I just gave up and told him everything. I've been out there in the Pacific 'til two weeks ago."

HOME AGAIN, HOME AGAIN, JIGGETY JIG

A farewell quotation and memento from Hawaii:

Ie luna kau,
puuni kakeke,
miha ke holahola
na makau.

On 11th February we were trundled off to Pearl Harbor and boarded the USAT W.G. Haan for a cruise to San Francisco, or more precisely, Oakland Army Base. This cruise seemed not quite so distressing — we were going home, the heat was not quite so blistering, and we'd be in Frisco in just over four days.

Generally, the voyage was uneventful. I read a lot. I finished "The Man with the Golden Arm." The last night out I found a rip-roaring crap game in progress on F Deck. My billeting compartment was on F Deck so I had no way to avoid the game. I figured if these guys are going to disrupt things such that you can't read, I might as well join in.

Except for some penny-ante poker games among shift mates at the Upper Kipapa Gulch Gentlemen's Club and possibly a few small bets on our endless games of 8 Ball, I really hadn't much experience at gambling, especially craps. There are a number of things about the game that I do not understand to this day. But, what the hell, I dived in and—miraculously—won some big money.

There was another guy who had also won big. As the clock moved toward 2100 hours and lights out, he announced that he was going to retire and start getting his stuff ready for debarkation tomorrow. An immediate growl went up! "What you think you're doing? Give us a chance to get even here!" There was such a air of malevolence I think some of those guys might have done him injury. He relented and got back in the game.

Now I was concerned because I was just about to do the same thing—pull out of the game. 'How in the hell am I gonna get outa here with a whole skin?' I thought. I thought about just losing down to my original stake but when I began placing big bets—I won again! Not all of my sweat was from the temperature in the crowded, malodorous troop compartment.

Suddenly, a cry came down the companionways—"Frisco, Frisco, there's the Golden Gate!" Everyone grabbed their money and the lower decks exploded with troops boiling up onto the main deck. We were passing under the beautifully illuminated Golden Gate Bridge — Thanks Be Unto The Lord From Whom All Blessings Flow!

FORT SHERIDAN, ILLINOIS

Our troop train rattled out of Oakland early Thursday morning 20th February 1947 bound for Fort Sheridan, the demobilization processing point for the Fifth Army area. This train was strictly 'GI Class'. The 'sleeping cars' had triple stacked metal GI bunks bolted together. We had a kitchen car in which, for once, I didn't get selected to serve on KP. There were several 'lounge cars' — simply old chair cars. The chairs were reversible so that, with the addition of a table, we could play cards. I mostly sat up there and read my Ellery Queen stories.

With no civilians to trifle with, the train whipped across states like a banshee. I could estimate our speed by timing the mile posts—85 mph!—90 mph! Telegraph poles zipped by like a picket fence. We hardly ever stopped. Thus, on the third day we pulled into Fort Sheridan right on time.

A slower trip might have been more to our advantage. We came from balmy Hawaii. We processed in the cooler but still pleasant climate of San Francisco. We still wore our khaki uniforms. When we hit Illinois we found 3 feet of snow and subzero temperatures. As Shelley Winters once said, "It was so cold I almost got married."

On 26th February I was discharged effective 14 March 1947 with 14 days of terminal leave and two days travel time to Pilot Grove, MO. The next morning I took a train down to Chicago, had a wonderful civilian lunch at the Union Station and bought a ticket to St. Louis. With several hours to kill, I tried out some of the lovely local Chicago beer. Although Illinois law prohibited me from drinking a beer (I was not yet 20 years old), the legendary Chicago hospitality for GIs only prohibited me from paying for it. I had heard GIs tell stories of the friendly Chicagoans who habituated the bars. To them the GIs were all heroes who must not be permitted to pay for a beer. I found these stories were true!

I changed trains at the Union Station in St. Louis to catch the old Katy Flyer for home sweet home. It was nearly midnight when the Flyer left St. Louis. I slept fitfully for several hours, waking up at first light when we pulled into Franklin. Franklin was a division terminal where locomotive and crew were changed. It also was a breakfast stop. Dining cars had been long since removed from Katy passenger service.

I must have presented a scruffy picture to the poor, hassled waitress as I sat down at the counter to get my SOS[9] and coffee. I looked up at the menu posted above the backbar. SOS and coffee, I calculated, was going to cost me a lot more than the 25¢ my military meal ticket allowed. "Oh, hell," I said to myself.

The middle-aged waitress looked at me with concern, "What's the matter soldier (I had my uniform on as I had no other clothing save my luau shirt) are you short on money?"

Actually, I wasn't, but before I could say so, she went on, "Order anything you want, honey. It'll be all right!"

I was very touched by her attitude. It was similar to the good folk of Chicago. Maybe I should not have been, but I was surprised at these people treating me, a total stranger, so kindly.

Fig. 11-14. This is Waikiki Beach in 1996. We just can't keep anything nice anymore can we?

My belly full of SOS, home made biscuits, milk and a cup of coffee, I answered the hooting Flyer and re-boarded. In less than an hour I stepped down onto the station platform at Pilot Grove and again surveyed the 'Green, Green Grass of Home.' I said good morning to Lon Judy who was collecting the mail. Lon mumbled something as he eyed me carefully— with no recognition. I shouldered my duffle bag and began the three block walk home.

LESSON LEARNED: Pacific Islands are nice to visit. You wouldn't want to live there.

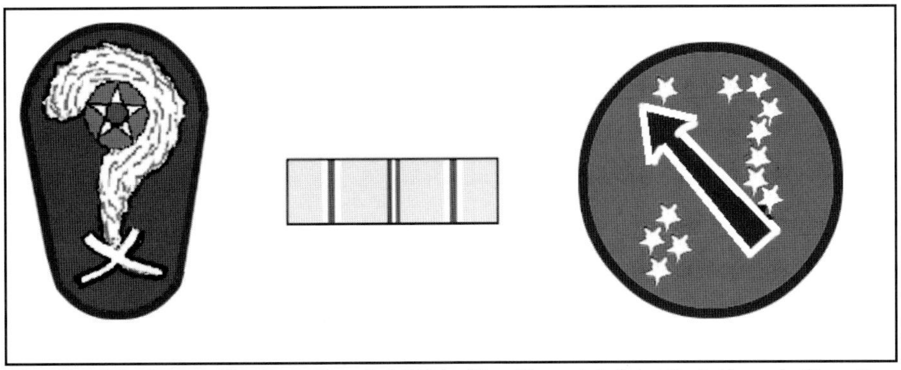

Fig. 11-15. Insignia collection - Part 2. LEFT—Shoulder patch Joint Task Force 1, Operation Crossroads, Kwajalein; MIDDLE—Asiatic-Pacific Campaign ribbon; RIGHT—Shoulder patch US Army-Pacific. Red arrow points to Polaris the North Star. Lower left stars are the Southern Cross. These stars have been Pacific mariners' guides for 2000 years.

[9] Kids, get your daddy to tell you what SOS is.

EPILOGUE - SAYING GOOD-BYE

Contrary to my promise to myself, I did *not* visit the Wesley Chapel Graveyard to say good-bye to Judy. I was unsure of the protocol of belated condolences. Time and opportunity drifted away. I felt guilty whenever I thought of it in the passing years. Then came—

LEONARD'S WAKE

Bob called me Friday evening 4th of June 1993. Leonard Schlotzhauer had passed away. Leonard had been a resident at the Katy Manor as was our mother. Bob knew Leonard well. Both lived in the Senior Housing nearby until Leonard's health no longer permitted him such independence. Like Mom, Leonard did not go gladly to the Manor. But, I suppose, also like Mom, he was eventually happy about 'his' choice to do so.

Leonard L. Schlotzhauer

b. Pilot Grove, Missouri Dec. 3, 1907
d. Columbia, Missouri, June 3, 1993

The Kansas City Star said friends would be received at the Meisenheimer Funeral Chapel 6 to 8 PM Saturday June 5th. The weather was very sultry that evening. Dark rain clouds threatened as Daisy and I drove from Boonville. Inside, air conditioners fought the stuffiness.

Joe Schlotzhauer greeted us at the Chapel entrance. I must have look puzzled. He said, "Sonny, I bet you don't know me, do you? "I'm Joe Schlotzhauer."

I knew *Joey* Schlotzhauer—a preteen imp that delighted in driving his sisters up the wall. But, that was 48 years ago.

We caught Carol Rae's eye (she's been known as Carol for a long time but to her friends who knew her and loved her 'way back', she'll always be Carol Rae). She escorted us to the flower laden bier to view her Dad. She explained his final illness while lovingly patting his cheek. He had deteriorated rapidly at the last and all the heroic efforts to fix his problems were to no avail. You really can't cure old age and in my view we sometimes try too hard. Maybe when a loved one has had a long and productive life, they deserve a rest.

I was surprised to see so many people at the wake. Many I knew, though some had to give me a cue. Growing older we find cued memory is superior to uncued memory. I read somewhere that when you hit 50, three things happen to you: 1. You begin losing your memory and 2… well, I've forgotten what the other two were. The medical term for this is "CRS" — "Can't Remember Stuff".

I should not have been surprised at the crowd. LBJ caught the essence of small towns when he left Washington, D.C. in '68—"I'm going back to the Pedernales where: when you're sick, people know it and when you die, people care."

The chapel was full of soft-spoken stories of the life and times of Leonard Schlotzhauer. I told how I regarded Leonard in those bygone years (1945-46) as the watch dog guarding his chicks. I think he regarded me as the one of the foxes. When I dated Judy, I had a 1937 Harley Davidson motorcycle. After biking Judy around the countryside for a few weeks in the spring of '45 we were pleasantly surprised to have Leonard volunteer Judy the family Buick. She had celebrated her sixteenth birthday the previous November and could—with some difficulty—keep that 1941 "four holer" Buick between the fences. It was somewhat out of character for him to do this and I didn't catch on for a some time. His probable motivation: He didn't want the doctors picking gravel out of Judy's backside. He viewed me with some suspicion in '45 and I don't think he regarded my prospects with great enthusiasm. In his place, I wouldn't either. In early 1945 the pall of war hung over the nation. Young men of 17 weren't into long range planning. When you are knee deep in alligators, you're not interested in plans to drain the swamp.

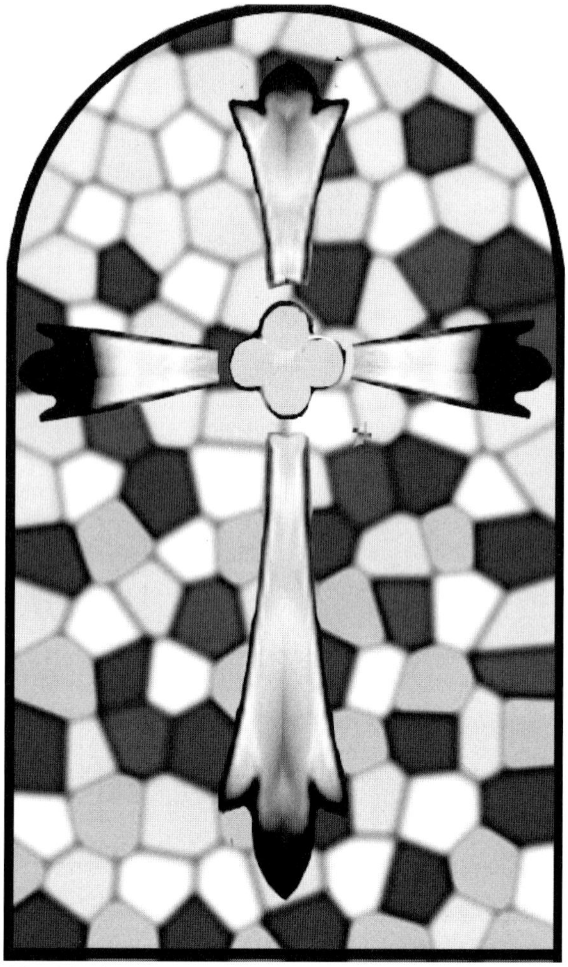

Fig. 11-16. In nominee Patria et Filii et Spiritus Sancti — Requiescat in Pace.

There were many poignant stories told, Leonard might have chuckled. Altogether, it was not a bad sendoff—a last rendezvous with good friends…good memories of good times. This is the way it should be — a celebration of a life well lived

THE BED AND BREAKFAST

At about 830PM, concerned about the threatening rain and noting the House of Meisenheimer diplomatically consulting their watches, I began thinking of an exit line. Here comes Carol with daughter Julie (named for her Grandmother?). Carol asked, "Who does she look like?"

I thought I was suppose to say "Judy" but judging from the frown, that was not the right answer. Julie is a beautiful young woman but she really doesn't look much like her aunt Judy. This exchange put Judy in my mind.

With farewells said we were about to depart for Boonville. However, Clarence offered, "How about a cold beer at the Bed and Breakfast?" The family was staying at the B&B across the street. A cold beer sounded pretty good to me and since Daisy and Carol go back many years to High School and Methodist Youth Groups they also needed a bit more 'catching up'. In addition, I wanted to check the B & B for possible future use.

The B & B sits next to the former site of the Methodist Church. This old church played a memorable role in my childhood. My mind was casting back to the 1930s. I attended kindergarten and elementary level Sunday School there — taught by Francis Brownfield Rybak. My father's funeral was in this church Wednesday, April 22nd, 1940. But the old church had been pulled down long ago and the artifacts moved to other churches or sold off. Mom bought me one of the little Sunday School chairs that I had sat in at age 5-8. Without really giving it much thought, I had assumed the parsonage had been demolished with the church.

This B & B, Pilot Grove's first and only, is a two-story frame house with green asbestos shingle siding. It has a high hedge in front which cuts it off from the street. Negotiating a parting in the hedge, we followed the walkway to a small front porch. It was on the porch steps that recognition hit me like a load of bricks! This is the old Methodist Parsonage! This recognition triggered a flashback to vivid memories of that certain night in March 1945—memories that had been buried for nearly 50 years—came flooding into my consciousness like a time warp! It was an epiphany!

I have read about such strange tricks of the mind. They're usually associated with post-trauma shock or sometimes the use of some sort of dope — Mescal, Peyote, LSD, etc. I had not even had a beer, yet. I was recalling — virtually re-experiencing the events of that Friday evening March 16th, 1945.

I was standing again with Judy on that chilly evening. With misty eyes, I examined the porch floor. I saw clearly in my mind's eye like an Arthur Murray dance instruction diagram—two sets of footprints; size 11 loafers and facing them—oh so close, size 6 saddle oxfords. I could visualize precisely where

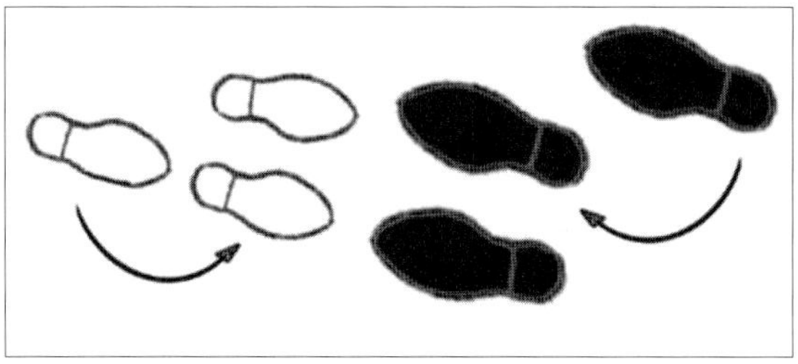

Fig. 11.17. Two Hearts in Three Quarter Time.

we stood as I looked down into her bright eyes on that spring evening long ago.

Bright eyes burning like fire.
Bright eyes how could you close and fail?
How could the light that burned so brightly
suddenly turn so pale?

'Bright Eyes' from Watership Down.

A wave of nostalgia engulfed me and I got a baseball sized lump in my throat. I hurried on in for the promised beer but I was so shaken, Clarence looked at me strangely and asked if I were all right. I said yes, I had just thought of something that I had to do. I vowed to myself to visit Judy's grave—47 years late but I would apologize and explain.

PENANCE AT A COUNTRY GRAVEYARD

A few weeks after Leonard's funeral I went out to Wesley Chapel, the church from which Judy was buried, to say my last goodbye and, as a small penance for my procrastination, try to mentally recreate the day of her funeral— Friday, 19th July 1946.

Bob told me that he knew the pastor and could conveniently get the Chapel opened. I decided not to do so. Forty-seven years would have brought a lot of change. I preferred to resurrect a memory from the spring of 1945 when Judy and I had attended Vespers. That memory was a bit misty and vague but it was from the right period and a more accurate picture of the way it looked then.

I pictured what that day, 47 years in the past, must have been like. The coffin would be before the pulpit, loaded with flowers… the minister would be saying the prayers, the eulogy (I wondered who read it?), there would be comforting words for those who would not really be comforted. Now the familiar old songs are sung. Finally the six pallbearers (who were they?) carry out the mortal remains.

Judith Nan Schlotzhauer
b. October 7, 1928
d. July 17, 1946[6]

[6] This date is correct. Judy's gravestone says "1928 - 1945". The 1945 is an error.

Fig. 11-18. Rosebud, Goodbye.

Fig. 11-19. Judy age 17, winter 1945.

Fig. 11-20. Watercolor of Judy, Spring 1945.

Play the pipes lowly, beat the drums slowly.
Play the Death March as they carry her along.
Ancient Scottish Funeral Song[10]

I thought of the sad cortege lead by the Hays and Painter hearse as it moved through the graves to that one that was to receive Judy. Again, the words, the crumbled earth, the flowers, the tears. Then—it's all over and I am alone at the grave thinking of the words of that sad letter Judy's mother had written me on Kwajalein in the summer of 1946: "...buried her wearing your locket and picture."

THE LAST GOODBYE

Well here I am finally—young Judy the Bright Eyed.
Do you mind if I sit down here by your side,
And rest for awhile in the warm summer sun?
For years I wandered and now I'm near done.

In those years when I was lonely or the road was too long
And I thought love was only for the lucky and the strong,
I remembered in the winter, far beneath the bitter snows:
There lay a bud, which in a distant spring, became a rose.

The sun, how it shines on the wheat fields and stands.
In a warm summer breeze—the wild flowers dance.
Oh how the sun shines from under the cloud,
There's no pain, no suffering, no misery now.

But here in this graveyard on this consecrated land
The tombstones and crosses in mute witness stand,
To all those loved ones—passed on before,
Along with a precious one we'll see nevermore.

But, among the loved ones that you left behind,
Your memory in their hearts is forever enshrined.
Now, I'm an old man, gray and solemn of mien,
While you, lie here, forever seventeen.

Now, sadly I leave you—I've finally said goodbye.
Now I feel redeemed, now my eyes are dry,
For there on your breast, in your locket's gold sheen,
Is the boy who loved you—also, forever seventeen.

We had joy. We had fun.
We had our season in the sun.
But like the wine and the song—
The season is now gone.

Thus, I said goodbye to Judy, goodbye to our season in the sun, goodbye to the final season of my youth and to the village that I called home but would never see again in the light that I saw it in the long ago Spring of 1945.

[10] These words are from "Streets of Laredo", but were originally a Scottish dirge. The term "pipes" refers to bagpipes. When did you ever see a cowboy funeral with drums and bagpipes?

"In winter out there on the Kansas Plains, there ain't nothin' between you and the North Pole but a one-strand barb wire fence—and sometimes it's down!"
Will Rogers

FOR ALL TIME

FORMER ENGLISH PROFESSOR CHARLEY Kempthorne left his sinecure at the Kansas State University (Manhattan) to found the Family History Institute (also in Manhattan). He teaches and coaches folks—mostly old gandies like me—to write family histories and autobiographies. His book, "For All Time" is an encapsulation of some of these sessions.

Evidently he is quite successful in this training. One of his students of several years back—Jessie Brown Foveau, a eighty-something Kansas farm divorcee—auctioned her story to a New York publisher for $1,000,000 the winter of 1996.

In Kempthorne's encouragement to his students, he points out the objective insight, the introspective self-administered psychoanalysis that is a priceless by-product of committing the events, people and feelings of your own life to paper.

I had never entertained any such desires but—after the word processor got cold on these next four chapters of my life: Plains of Kansas, Fort Bragg and Randolph Field (I left this stuff to work on "Cousins" and didn't get back to it for a year)—a lot of underlying turmoil in my life becomes evident.

In a space of about 24 months, I—gave up on civilian life and reenlisted; started to Officer Candidate School then resigned rather that take an accident induced 'wash-back'; tried a few months of paratrooper life (82d A/B Division); started Air Force pilot training but was washed out on a physical after I had soloed in the T-6 Texan; got engaged and shipped out for the Far East.

Diagnosis: A young guy—adventuresome, energetic, ambitious and gung ho—very dissatisfied with his lot but without a clue as to what he wanted to do with his life.

I am reminded of a 'good news, bad news joke. An Alitalia airline pilot comes onto the intercom: "Folks, I have good news and bad news! The good news: we are making good time—about 800 knots. The bad news: I haven't a clue where we are!"

Like Luigi's 747, my life was moving ahead at flank speed, but I hadn't a clue as to where I was going.

Fig. 12-1. Wheat is the flower of the Kansas Plains. More than 10% of wheat in international trade comes from Kansas.

FORT RILEY

The bus roared and rumbled ever westward on US 40 enroute from Kansas City to Fort Riley, Kansas. It is Friday 12th September 1947.

A radio could be heard from the rear...

> "Try to remember that long ago September,
> When life was slow and oh so mellow.
> Try to remember that long ago September,
> When grass was green and grain was yellow."
> Adapted from "September Song" with apologies to "The Fantasticks."

It was a sweet, nostalgic melody particularly appropriate to the moment. The grass was indeed green on the well manicured lawns of Lawrence and...the fields near Topeka were yellow with corn awaiting the harvest. But, the stubble fields of the now-harvested wheat were brown and dry as tinder. Mid-September is an inter-seasonal time in Kansas. The summer winds—dry, furnace hot, desiccating blasts off the deserts of New Mexico and Arizona were now attenuated—but the gentle autumn rains and their accompanying cool breezes had yet to begin.

Because so few trees grow to obstruct the view, Kansans grow up expecting to see every sunrise from its exquisite beginning and every sunset until its brilliant end. The plains west of Lawrence are taxing as well as brilliant. The summer heat is searing, the winter cold biting. And it is dry, only 22 inches of rain annually. The one physical constant is the wind which can make either the heat or the cold cutting.

Fig. 12-2. Sept 2d, 1945, Japan surrenders on the foredeck of the USS Missouri.

THE WINDS—1947

Kansas, lovely Kansas
Where the wind never lays
Thunder storms and funnel forms
On muggy summer days.

The date was just after the second anniversary of the formal end of the war with Japan. Almost exactly two years ago on this day in 1945[1], on the foredeck of the USS Missouri, in the shadows of the "Mighty Mo's" 16 inch guns, the emissaries of the Japanese Empire bowed to General MacArthur and threw in the towel. I wasn't there but I did have vivid memories of and graphic detail from a guy who was.

ON THE FOREDECK OF THE MIGHTY MO

I met Technical Sergeant Sandoval in July 1946 on Kwajalein in the Marshall Islands. I was visiting PFC Jimmy Coelho. Jimmy—a fellow alumni of the Central Signal Corps School at Camp Crowder—was one of the Task Force Signal Detachment working radio links on the USNTV Spindle Eye and providing communications support for Joint Task Force 1. JTF-1 was conducting the first post-war atom bomb test.

Coelho had been on the Spindle Eye since the day of our arrival in May. He had also been seasick from that same day but now that the ship was tied up at the Kwajalein quay, he was beginning to revive. Jimmy was from Vallejo, California and of Portuguese descent. Short and bandy legged with high cheek bones and deep dark eyes, he was not a great gift to the ladies. I counted him a good friend because he had helped me in my radio code practice at Crowder. His current scruffy appearance gave no evidence of it but he was quite a bright fellow.

PFC Klaus, who had been to see him a few days earlier, lead the way to his bunk. He was billeted in the fo'csle (crew quarters) on C Deck. If anyone had been misled by the yacht-like exterior of this vessel he would have been sorely disabused at the cramped, dark, dingy EM billets.

Coelho looked like hell. His sunken cheeks accented his already oriental looking facial structure. His pallor had a bilious green tinge—a leper without his bell. He said he had not been able to get to the galley (mess hall) while the Spindle Eye was at sea—over two weeks. He was fortunate to have had some very good mates who brought snacks to him and tried to make him comfortable. The military has never considered seasickness as a real illness or disability and he had received no medical help whatsoever. "Thank God", he said, "At last we're tied up here at Kwaj and I'm beginning to think I may survive!"

After commiserating on his weak stomach for a while, we got around to other topics and a tour of the Spindle Eye. The Spindle Eye had been MacArthur's floating communications center throughout the Pacific campaigns and was with the USS Missouri in Tokyo Bay on the historic day of the Japanese surrender.

Coelho insisted we see the photos Sgt. Sandoval had taken of the surrender ceremonies. Apparently Sandoval was the official Signal Corps photographer for the event.

Ducking through the companionways, we entered the even dingier looking Photo Lab. The lab featured the sickening, acrid stench of the photo developers and hypo 'fixative'. While T/Sgt Sandoval sorted out his portfolio, I looked over the shelves of photo supplies—"ferricyanide, sodium sulfate, stannous chloride..." No wonder it stank like a backed up sewer!

Sandoval was a tall, slim, 30 something guy of dark complexion—Hispanic or Indian. However, judging from his excellent language, if he was of Spanish descent, his ancestors must have preceded the Anglos in his native New Mexico by several centuries. Sandoval, at Jimmy's urging, then began painting us an animated word picture of the events of that day 9 months before. As we passed around the 10 x 12 glossy prints, he demonstrated how the frail General Wainwright had stood beside MacArthur trembling with emotion at key points of the ceremony. He mimicked the Japanese officials as they came aboard the Missouri from their launch. "There was not one of them that would not have preferred being tortured to death", he conjectured. "It was only the authority of the Emperor himself that forced them to it. In Japanese culture the Emperor is a god and not to be disobeyed."

Sandoval demonstrated MacArthur's stance as he somberly concluded: "These proceedings are now closed." It was obvious from the excitement in the Sergeant's voice and in his demeanor that he was still deeply moved by the memory.

TRANSFORMATION TO PEACETIME

Thus, on September 2d, 1945 the USS Missouri put into Tokyo Bay providing the stage for the formal surrender of Japan. The rest is history. There followed weeks of joyous, unbounded, euphoric celebrations—the country saw the beginning of transition to peacetime. After four years of blood,

[1] Actually Tuesday 2d of September 1945.

sweat and tears, the transition was very welcomed.

However, this transformation was not without gut-wrenching problems, particularly for me. While congress had guaranteed the rights of veterans to get their old jobs back, this guarantee meant little to me because I didn't really have an 'old job' to go back to. I only had a small claim to a telegrapher-clerk job at the MKT Railroad (I had worked in the position less than a year) and anyway the Katy was in initial stages of rigor mortis.

Since the day I lugged my old OD duffel bag back to Pilot Grove in March of 1947 with a Fort Sheridan discharge in my hand, I had worked 'extra-board' as a Katy Telegrapher-Clerk. When permanent employees took vacation or were off sick I got a few days of work. As of July 1947 I had worked three weeks total. A week at the tiny village of Linndale and two weeks at St. Paul, Kansas during their centennial celebration. Pay was good, but work was scarce. A $1.25 per hour rate (good rate) times 0 hours (bad hours) = nothing.

I was a twenty year old untrained, uneducated and unemployed veteran—a young and callow fellow. The Fantasticks continued:

> "Try to remember the kind of September
> When you were a tender and callow fellow
> and if you remember, then follow."

I faced the problem of the younger members of the 'Order of the Ruptured Duck'—no job seniority and no military experience marketable in the unfolding peace economy. Precisely who uses tank drivers, machine-gunners or—in my case Radio Telegraph Operators? I had assumed—without really pondering it very much—that I would follow in my father's footsteps and the Katy would be my career. Clearly that was not to be .

My radio operator experience was of no great value on my resume. I verified this at Western Union in Kansas City in July. There, I was interviewed by a senior telegrapher, a grandfatherly old gandy right out of a John Wayne western—watch chain across his dark vest, green eye shade, sleeve garters and thick glasses. He tested me on the chattering telegraph sounder. I had mastered the 25 words per minute required for Radio Telegrapher certification in the Signal Corps. But that was International Morse code and was a chirping, musical tone. Western Union's clicking, rattling tintinnabulation sounded nothing like that and moreover, it was coming at me at about 30 words per minute. I surrendered with what dignity I could retain and returned to my pad at 3616 Holmes and went back to the Kansas City Star's help wanted pages.

MAKING FORDS

I have always consoled myself on failing to make a go of the telegrapher jobs. After all, telegraphy at the Katy and Western Union disappeared forever within a few months—displaced by new technologies: teletype and voice radio. My final attempt at civilian life ended with a disastrous job slapping '48 Fords together at the Kansas City Leeds Plant. This job involved disassembling the body sides of the new '47s. While a workmate used a pneumatic wrench to unscrew a door, I grabbed it and carried it to an adjacent conveyor line. These doors weighed about forty pounds and after hoisting several dozen over my head my arms and shoulders were aching. In addition, these body sides were fresh out of a scalding, live steam, degreasing bath. They were not only hot, but dripped greasy water on the floor.

Some brilliant factory engineer had designed a fix for the poor guys wading in 1 to 2 inches of this greasy muck—duct boards. This fix presented a slatted floor, probably warehouse pallets, for our working comfort—except, it didn't work for me. On my first day I had made the mistake of wearing an old pair of combat boots—this seemed appropriate since I had already seen this workplace and knew that it was a swamp. The disaster came when the sole of my right boot ripped loose. With my every step this loose sole found its way between slats and—twisting my ankle—and occasionally dropping me on my butt. This happened several times. Finally, I began raising my right foot to an exaggerated level to clear the duct board.

My impromptu choreography was a terrific hit with the Neanderthals on the factory floor. They broke up with laughter, nudging one another and pointing at me. That was really just the frosting on the cake! The job paid pretty good. There was even a chance that with several years seniority I might be entrusted with pneumatic wrench and some other jerk would tread the duct boards. But I felt like there just had to be a better life than this. I resigned, drew my final pay nevermore to trod the boards.

I dragged my aching body back to my bunk at Holmes. I was glad to have it over. Just getting to and from Ford was a challenge. It was public transportation all the way and I had to change buses twice—a commute of nearly two hours each way. I had considered riding my big white 1946 Harley 74 OHV to work. This would have taken only 20-25 minutes but discarded the idea. I would have had to park it in the huge employee parking lot, entrusting my most prized possession to the mercies of the troglodytes who were my shop floor colleagues.

GOTTA BE SOMETHING BETTER

I ascended the driveway and checked the Harley, then climbed the front steps, entered and checked for mail on the hall table. I looked up to see our 'beloved' landlady Mrs. Hartman. A 60-something shrewish, ferret eyed harridan, she epitomized the stereotype of a landlady. She eyed me with suspicion. My heart in my mouth, my thoughts raced. "Had I left the hall light on when I left this morning? Illumination of the upper hall and stair-

Fig. 12-3. I moved the Harley Hog to Ft. Riley in September '47. Shown are the ruins of a WWI division headquarters at Camp Funston.

way was from a bare 20 watt bulb with a pull string, but at Mrs. Hartman's rooming house 'burning lights in the daytime' was a capital crime. Had I used more that my allotted one gallon of water when I queued 15th for a bath last night? I probably did but how the hell would she know that?" I felt a wave of relief when she whipped a letter out of her apron pocket and handed it to me. "Here's yer mail." She handed me a letter from U.S. Army Reserve confirming my March 1947 enlistment—five months after the fact. No wonder they were called the 'Disorganized Reserve".

In my relief I never thought to ask her what she was doing with my mail—probably trying to read it since it was an official letter.

Mrs. Hartman ran a taut ship. Her old two story house—originally a very comely, turn of the century mansion built for some long gone Kansas City gentry—had gone to seed. She had—without benefit of any remodeling—taken on about 24 roomers. All were, like me, bachelors and mostly veterans. Virgil Kempf, my next door neighbor in Pilot Grove, lived here. He hired on at Ford in mid-summer 1947 and was a primary motivator for my applying at Ford. He moved out of Mrs. Hartman's in August when he married Margaret Young of Clifton City.

In the small upstairs bedroom—about 10 x 10 feet—which I shared with three other guys, steel Army cots lined each of the four walls. There were three more such bedrooms on our floor and two down stairs. Second floor denizens shared one bathroom at the end of the hall. There was a commode, a wash basin, no shower but an ancient bathtub that stood on four iron lion paws. The bath was used by at least 16 people and cleaned by Mrs. Hartman about twice a year. None of the roomers would ever stand accused of cleaning anything.

SURRENDER AT 3616 HOLMES

I gathered my wardrobe from an orange crate under my bunk, packed my worldly possessions in the saddle bags of my Harley Hog and headed home to Pilot Grove and the next day to the Recruiting Sergeant in Boonville. I elected to re-up for three years, thinking, " I'll sit out this dance and try again in '50." I put a tarpaulin over the bike and parked it beside Mom's garage. She was renting the garage to a neighbor for the princely sum of $2 per month. I was reluctant to leave the bike to the weather like this but reasoned that I'd move it out to Fort Riley as soon as I got settled in.

This big Harley was my most expensive possession. It was the third of three Harleys that I owned 1944 to 1948. In the summer of 1944 between my Junior and Senior years at PGHS I was making big bucks at Emerson Electric 18th and Washington in downtown St. Louis and living with Dixie. By August I had saved $300 and realized my boyhood dream of owning a motorcycle. Bike shopping on Delmar, I put the 300 down on a seven year old 1937 Harley Davidson 74 OHV.

I re-upped at Camp Crowder in January 1946 on the promise of a 30-day furlough, $300 bonus and promotion the Private First Class. I used this bonus to trade in the old red Harley on a newer 1946 blue Harley 45 (the numerical designator: 74 or 45 refers to the size of the engine—74 cubic inches and 45 cubic inches respectively). Finally, I had a bike with a pillion seat much more suitable for a passenger particularly of the female persuasion. The blue Harley 45 languished at the homestead until I returned from Hawaii for discharge in March of 1947. With an imposing $300 mustering out payment plus pay for accrued leave and travel home, I had enough to trade the little blue 45 on a big white Harley Hog. This machine was about as far as you could go in a Harley in the year 1947. It had chrome fog lights, chrome fender guards, chrome decorated saddle bags, all Lucite windshield with chrome trim and white metal sidewalls. I took it to Harriman Hill and speed tested it. Speed had been a big disappointment on the under-powered '45. Headed east, I reached the bottom of the hill and lined up for the Lamine River bridge. I noted the speedometer—120 miles per hour! This was my primary mode of transportation between Pilot Grove and Kansas City during my job seeking period and later the reactivation of my military career at Fort Riley.

I felt I'd better not take the bike to Fort Riley until I had had opportunity to check out the territory. So here I am on a Trailways Bus, duffel bag overhead, traversing Kansas wheat fields on my way to again seek adventure and fortune with Uncle Sam. As was said of army recruits in England during the Napoleonic Wars: 'Married to Brown Bess', 'Took the King's shillin', 'Followed a drummer boy, a dancin' bear and a recruitin' sergeant.'

It was hot. The westbound Trailways bus was two hours out of Kansas City and the air conditioner had already crapped out and poured out 'conditioned air' remarkably like the insufferable, humid soup outside. A handful of my fellow travelers joined me in manhandling the windows open increasing the chance of surviving the oven the bus had become. Thank God, I was not yet in uniform. I have been in some commands where winter uniform is mandatory after some arbitrary date like lst September regardless of the actual weather and temperature. The Armed Forces had authorized the wearing of civilian clothing while off duty just one year ago September 1946. I usually exercised the privilege.

My seatmate, a grizzled old farmer-type in bib overalls and a battered, dirty straw hat gave me a hand with the window then after giving me a careful up and down and not connecting my GI duffel bag stowed overhead, asked, "Where you off to there young feller?"

"I'm off to Fort Riley", pronouncing it Fort 'Raleigh' as some of the locals called it. He puzzled on this for a while, then, "Why, young feller, the war's over you know. Wuz you drafted?" I explained my difficulty in managing the transition to peacetime and how I decided to sit out civilian life for one hitch (3 years).

He cut to the essence, "Couldn't gitcher self a job, eh?"

I took this as an affront, "Not so. I had myself a job awright—Ford Motor Company—I reckon you heard tell of them haven't you?" He nodded allowing as how he had indeed 'heard tell of Ford'. "As a matter of fact I outwitted their whole Personnel Department to get it!" I couldn't help smirking over this bit of chicanery. Answering his quizzical expression, I explained—"This past summer Ford was hiring a lotta new people for their Leeds plant. I took a bus over to Leeds on a Thursday morning early and took my place at the end of a four block long employment line. I shuffled along for 4 hours taking lunch from an enterprising hot-dog vendor working the line. At about 1 PM I finally made it in to the Personnel Office and learned why the process was taking so long: one old, white-haired gandy was doing all the interviews—probably His Eminence the Personnel Officer himself. I handed him my little scribbled out application card. First question: "Any mechanical experience?"

"Why no, I was into radios and stuff in the Army."

"OK, that'll be all. We may call you. Next!"

"I knew I had struck out because the people who were hired immediately continued with their in-processing. It was also pretty clear to me where I had screwed up—I'd told him I'd had no mechanical experience. What to do, what to do. I made my way, somewhat distressed, along the applicant line toward the bus stop and a trip back to the rooming house. It was about 3 PM and the line now was greatly reduced—only 75 - 100 applicants. "What the hell"—I thought—"I'll just get back in line and this time lie about my experience." I thought, "Honesty and truthfulness is a luxury for those who already have a job. After seeing 4-500 people today, the old geezer won't remember me." And, that's precisely what happened. Only one glitch: when I told the bald face lie—'Yes, I've had some mechanical experience.—the old Gandy says, 'OK gimme your employer's address and we'll get a letter out to them for a reference.' He called my bluff! Thinking quickly, I says, 'Actually it was with my uncle Bob who has a motorcycle shop in Pilot Grove.'

'That's OK says he. Just give us his address and we'll get a reference from him. You go on in the next room there and begin filling out your employment forms.'

"On Saturday I whipped down to Pilot Grove and checked the mail first thing off. A.G. Olsen the Postmaster said, 'Sonny, I got this here letter to Bob that's addressed to 'Bob's Motorcycle Shop'. Is that for your brother or has this thing been misdirected?' 'Oh no', says I, 'Its for Bob awright. He's into some kind of correspondence course or something. He asked me to take care of this.' I took the envelope to the lobby desk, ripped out the form and, using the cheap Post Office pen, proceeded to scratch out a glowing commendation of this sterling fellow Richard Salmon. Mr. Olsen sold me a three cent stamp and the enthusiastic recommendation was dispatched in the return mail all official and proper."

'But I hated the job with a purple passion. My work mates were dolts. If their collective brains had been dynamite they would not have enough to blow their noses. The job was dirty, repetitious and so dull it would glaze the eyes of baboon. I put up with it for three days and quit. Gotta be a better life than this.'

So, I was very dissatisfied with life in general and my lot in particular. I really felt quite lost in the chaos of a return to peace. Give me murderous, well ordered war anytime.

I thought of that August of '45 when Judy and her mother visited me at Camp Crowder. We just walked around Neosho. If you weren't going to a beer hall to hoist a few, there wasn't a lot to do. We came upon a photo booth. Judy insisted I get a picture taken. Then she popped in for hers. It must have been a low tech setup. Judy had fabricated a school pennant with her name on it. The pennant was affixed to the front of her dress. When her picture came out—her name was backwards! The machine used a simplistic though undetected shortcut—it printed a mirror image. When I saw her at Christmas time 1945 she said she kept my picture beside her pillow on her night stand. It was a budding romance but destined forever to be unfulfilled.

> Try to remember when life was so tender
> That dreams were kept beside your pillow.
> Try to remember when life was so tender
> That no one wept except the willow
> Some more "Fantasticks

During the summer of '47 Smoky Zeller offered to fix

me up with a friend of his girlfriend Joanne Poindexter in Blackwater. I had never met Daisy Corbin but she had seen me at a Pilot Grove High School basketball game just after I was discharged in March. I was at that time still in the role of the returning war hero—campaign bar for the Asia-Pacific war and two gold overseas bars signifying one year overseas duty. Making a virtue of necessity, I was still in uniform. The uniform offered a certain panache but, truth to tell, I had no decent civilian clothes that would fit me.

From the first date, Daisy and I clicked. I have always regretted that I could find no acceptable work so that I could have stayed in Missouri and developed this relationship more rapidly at the time. The story of my life would undoubtedly be very different.

The old Trailways bus had just passed through the little village of St. Mary's when a boiling cloud of black smoke appeared on the horizon. The eternal Kansas wind was fanning the flames of a racing prairie fire. Some eager farmer clearing his stubble field had let his work get out of hand. I wondered whether we would be able to get through.

Straw hat says, "We'll get through there awright. These dumb bastards have been burnin' off after the wheat harvest since the beginning of time. These fires gets out of hand sometimes, but it'll be awright. It's just wheat straw and dried out Johnson grass. The county agents try to get them to stop it but the old guys claim this burnin' returns somethin' to the soil—potash or somethin' and they'll likely keep on adoin' it until they burn their damned farmsteads down and put themse'ves out of bidness entirely." He was right of course.

The Trailways bus whipped safely through the smoke, leaving the good farmers of Pottawatomie County to the gentle mercies of the prairie fire.

Ten years earlier—in the summer of 1937, my sister Dixie won a prize. This win ended a record of two centuries standing. Since my ancestors combed the burrs out of their hair, put on shoes and came down from the Scottish Highlands in the mid-1700's there has been no evidence that anyone in that lineage had ever won anything, anywhere, anytime.

Then—Capper's Weekly, a newspaper mailed from Topeka, Kansas and subscribed to by Mom for reasons that escaped me—had a contest! 'Name the bicycle and win it!' Dixie offered the name: 'Prairie Fire' and won first prize, a brand new, blue, balloon tired, 26" bike. Until this day I had been completely baffled as to why that particular name struck a cord in Topeka. On September 12, 1947 I got the answer—I *saw* a 'Prairie Fire'.

As we passed through Wamego, the open windows sucked in the most awful stench I'd ever smelled. Gagging, I got some of the windows closed and asked my strawhatted seatmate, "What the hell is that God-awful smell?"

"Aw", says he, "That's the new alfalfa dryer. Its been a blessing for the folks around here trying to get in a wet alfalfa crop. Used to be if was a little wet you waited 'til it dried and as often as not, it rotted before it dried. Them dryers is lifesavers for the hay farmers."

Thereafter, every time I passed through Wamego whether the alfalfa dryer was operating or not I remember the sweet essence of scorched alfalfa. Memories of the town were further enhanced by a bizarre experience I had there one crisp evening that October.

TWIRLER QUEEN IN TIGHT FITTIN' JEANS

On the weekend of October 17th the commander of 1st GGSD went nuts and canceled the regular Saturday morning inspection. Here it was only two years after the end of the war and the Army was beginning to slip back into slothful, peacetime mode. Without Saturday morning inspection I could bike out of Fort Riley Friday after duty and enjoy a weekend in Kansas City.

I skivved off early, packed up my Dopp Kit, a set of skivvies, fired up the Harley and at 1700 hours (5PM to civilians) I was headed for Kansas City 125 miles to the east. Now US40 was a good route but it was two lane which meant you might get behind some farmer's manure wagon and not be able to pass for miles because of oncoming traffic. US40 also toured the downtowns of every little jerkwater town in Kansas. These factors were slowing me down and it looked like I'd not make my planned 2000 hour (8PM) arrival in KC.

It had been an unseasonably warm day and I enjoyed the scenery—typical pre-Halloween fields of shocked corn—probably even some pumpkins in there though I didn't see any. The particular angle of the sun made a beautiful picture. As the sun sank lower at my back the wind in my face started getting a trifle nippy. I had on a field jacket over civvies as well as my W.W.I style leather flying helmet, leather gloves and goggles. I could stand much colder temperatures.

The sun was casting very long shadows as I approached the tiny burg of St. George. Here's where I began sensing trouble. I was losing power and the Harley gave off an occasional backfire. I was running along what passed for main street in St. George and could see my reflection in the store windows. What gave me great concern was a rocket of fire coming from the exhaust pipe. My stomach dropped because I didn't have the slightest idea where I could find mechanical help. I also didn't have a lot of money. I thought, "I'll just ride on and hope to hell it doesn't get worse."

I only made it another 6-8 miles. By the time I came into Wamego, the little town of stinky alfalfa fame, I was barely making headway. Sputtering up to a drug store/malt shop/cafe I dismounted and began looking over the Harley. I had stopped at this cafe because there was an old Indian motorcycle parked in front.

My exhaust pipe was cherry red. Obviously I had a major problem in the ignition or timing system. The gasoline vapor, passing through the cylinders unburned, was being cooked off in the exhaust system. I popped the distributor cap and there it was! The breaker points used a tiny phenolic card, the size of a thumbnail, to ride the cam—opening and closing the points. This card was broken but had not separated. Thus it worked but only at about 10% efficiency. It was a simple part, cheap and easy to replace but it had to be an exact replacement—and I had to find one in Wamego—at 6PM on a Friday evening. I went in and a waitress pointed out the owner of the Indian. He was sitting in a booth alone nursing a coke and flirting with a couple girls in the next booth.

I approached him, introduced myself and told him my story. He was very friendly and said, "I'm Freddie. Have a seat here and we'll talk this over." He patted the seat beside him. He ordered another coke and then told me, "I'm afraid we got a little problem here!" That put slush ice in my kidneys but I liked they way he said '...*we* gotta problem...'.

"Ya see," he continued, "There ain't no bike shop here in town. There's a shop in Manhattan but you probably don't want to go back there—probably not open at this hour anyway. Simmons Chevrolet here in Wamego has a guy who works on bikes and he's not too bad but the helluvit is—they're closed and there's no way we can get them to open up. By the way, you had your supper yet?"

"No, I haven't. I was planning on hitting up a friend in Kansas City (Vern Klenklen) for a little late snack. They got anything decent here?"

Freddie said, "Not really but it may be a long night and you'd ought to get yourself something."

"OK, I'm going to play it safe and have the hot roast beef sandwich", I said. The service was pretty fast. Probably because Freddie and me and the San Quentin quails were the only ones in the place.

Now you build a hot roast beef sandwich by slapping down a slice of white bread, then a slab of beef, then a dollop of mashed potatoes and cover it all with a quart of brown gravy. The gravy was OK. It was tender with no lumps. The potatoes were good too. The bread always turns to goo so no surprise there. However, the 'beef' could have been called the 'piece de resistance'. Food rationing had been on in the USA from 1943 'til the end of the war. Red meat had been extremely scarce and one was not wont to ask too many questions as to the origins of any that one might come into. But the war had been over two years now and most places were serving up something a bit better than this. I visually examined the gray, sinewy, tire boot-like slab. It had obviously been excised from the flank of an elderly bullock.

I had a vision of an ancient ox pulling a manure wagon through the streets of Wamego. He drops dead of old age one day and all the local restauranteurs rush out to slice him up into hot roast beef sandwiches.

As I was struggling with the rump of bullock, I noticed the two cuties peeping over the back of the booth at us. Both were quite young, the older, a blond, was about 16...17 tops. I watched her as she took 10 fairy steps over to the counter. She wore a white, short-sleeve, eyelet blouse which enhanced her apparently newly discovered nubility very well. Her exaggerated posture puffed up her front assets and the tight jeans fixed up the rear. The outfit was completed with white cheerleader boots. This might have been the first time I had seen jeans that tight—and—well filled. Cutie pie watched me out of the corner of her eye and made a dramatic scene of her ice cream cone order.

Freddie poked me and asked, "Are you game for a little midnight requisition?" He had been nattering away as I watched the Twirler Queen in her Tight Fittin' Jeans and I really hadn't exactly followed his tactical plan.

"First," I said, "Tell me who is the nymphet?" I nodded toward the Twirler.

"Oh, that's Jenny Thornton. She's a Junior at Wamego High. She was selected for the Pep Squad this year. The Pep Squad wear white cowboy hats and them white boots and jeans. She has worn those boots and jeans every day since she joined the Squad, probably wears them to bed!" Freddie said.

"She your girl?"

"Naw, she's just a kid. She hangs around a lot and is often in the gang when we go off to drink beer at the park and stuff, but I been out of school since last May and..." he eyed my field jacket, "I'm thinking about joining the Army or something. Anyways, she's too young for me."

This disdain of the 18 year-old for the 17 year-olds stunned me. I thought, "What does that make me...a senior citizen at 20?" "Anyway", I said, "Tell me again about what you are suggesting for my problem."

He said with a sigh, "I told you that I know a guy who has a bike—a Harley—about the same year as yours. What we can do, see, is go out there—he parks it in the street—and 'requisition' his points. He's going to have a spot of trouble tomorrow but those points only cost 89¢ and he can get 'em at Simmons." He studied my face carefully.

"OK", I said, "I don't have the money to spend the night here and the guys in Kansas City will be wondering where the hell I am. Let's go!"

When we got up to leave, Jenny the Twirler moved out of her booth and—looking at me—said to Freddie, "Freddie, where you'all going?"

Freddie answered in exasperation, "Jenny, we are going to do some work on a bike over on Broad Street. We're going to bike over on my Indian. In case you thought you wanted to go along—you can't."

"I'm driving Mom's car, she answered, "Can I come along and watch?"

Freddie, "Oh, hell. I don't care. We need someone to hold the flashlight. You can do that." He looked at me. I

Fig. 12-4. Col. George Armstrong Custer led the 7th Cavalry out of Ft. Riley in the spring of 1876 to chase down Sitting Bull. He is shown as a Civil War Brevet Major General at age 32.

shrugged my shoulders. 'What the hell does the Twirler Queen want anyway', I thought.

Freddie and I were unlatching the distributor cover as Jenny held the flashlight. Freddie snapped at her, "Dammit don't flash that light around like that. Keep it right here where we're working!" Freddie was worried that we might alert the owner. I was squatting beside him very concerned that this part be very similar to the one I needed.

The Twirler moved closer with the flashlight and accidentally(?) fell onto my neck and back. Trying to recover her balance she held my shoulders tightly and incidentally attempted to impress me with her feminine assets. She did make a couple of points.

I thought, "Wondered what's the age of legal consent in the state of Kansas? Then she then leaned over farther and turned her face until we were approximately nose to nose. "I'm so sorry," she cooed. Ewwwgh! Her breath would stop a charging rhino. I pushed her away, grabbed the points and jumped on the Indian with Freddie. We raced back to malt shop looking over our shoulders for flashing lights or anything. Again I'm kneeling, this time at my bike and we are changing out the points as quickly as possible. I had one thing on my mind—get this sucker fixed and get the hell out of Dodge!

Undaunted Jenny and her sidekick followed us and came to watch the conclusion of the repairs. Jenny said, "You said you were stationed over there at Fort Riley, right? Why don't you bike over here to Wamego on Saturdays? It's really not all that far—30 miles or so. We can have a good time hanging out here at the malt shop and there's other things to do."

"Yes, I'll consider that. "I said kicking over the old hog and sighing in relief as she roared into life. I thought, "'... other things to do' probably means a free tour of the alfalfa drying plant—and betting which made you puke first: Jenny's breath or that scorched alfalfa." I thanked Freddie again, looked back for the cops or an irate citizen and burned rubber east on US40. Splitting the chilly night air on my dash to Kansas City I pondered on the nymphet Jenny.

She's headed for a lot of trouble, I thought. I visualized her standing before the justice of the peace with some young dope while her father waited in the wings with a 12 gage buckshot-loaded Winchester. Then I thought: "But then... maybe not! Her dragon breath will probably keep her safe!"

WELCOME TO FORT RILEY

Fort Riley was established after the Civil War to control the plains Indians who were beginning to get uppity about the white settlers pushing westward. The Fort was hard by the confluence of the Republican and Kansas Rivers and commanded the flint hills of central Kansas with its famous 7th Cavalry Regiment. It was from Fort Riley that Colonel Custer led his cavalrymen on forays against the pesky redskins including his legendary and final expedition against Sitting Bull's Sioux at the Little Big Horn in Montana territory in 1876.

In 1947 the Indians were not much of a problem anymore—boredom was. This isolated and desolate part of Kansas could accurately be titled, "The back of beyond". The fact that Kansas was a dry state mitigated not at all against the use of booze to breakup the monotony. Made it cost a little more but it was still plentiful. It was said that Kansas preachers and the bootleggers were dead set against renouncing Prohibition. President Roosevelt had reopened the saloons in 1933 but Kansas—the home of Carry Nation, the national nag—promptly closed them down again. Fulfilling an obvious economic need was a disused Conoco station midway between the Fort and Junction City. Here one could drive onto the forecourt of the station, extend a ten dollar bill from the car window (it was always ten dollars—no negotiating) and receive a fifth of whiskey. There was no choice as to brand and it usually was "Ten High"—not really rotgut but not on the menu at the White House either. Ten High seems to have been a favorite—at least of the bootleggers.

As we approached our destination that warm September afternoon, we passed Camp Funston. An eastern 'suburb' of the main Fort, Camp Funston was a sprawling complex of low, mostly tarpaper barracks originally built at the start of 'The Great War' of 1917-1918. My namesake, Uncle Loyle Edwin Kendrick, was inducted and received his training here in 1917 with Company H, 89th Infantry before going off to France and glory. He ultimately attained the rank of Corporal at St. Mihiel and thus matched his father's meteoric rise to celebrity at Chickamauga in the Civil War 53 years earlier. Corporal John Henry Kendrick had held this illustrious rank since Shiloh. Then some Johnny Reb fired a Minie ball at him, opening up some daylight in his chest during a skirmish at Allatoona (north of Atlanta). This ended grandpa's military career.

Fort Riley proper was a pleasant surprise. The heart of the post featured a cluster of field stone buildings which were quite pleasing to the eye. Architecturally, they were standard 19th century Great Plains government buildings. Though somewhat austere, the use of native field stone nevertheless gave the assemblage of structures a certain panache not shared by many military facilities.

It was a small post. The only combat organization was the 11th Armored Cavalry Regiment whose rough troopers were in exile at Camp Funston and thus did not clutter up the main post amenities like the movie house and post exchange.

Ever reluctant to give up its historic precedence as a cavalry post, Fort Riley, even in 1947, still maintained connections to its past. Custer's horse—stuffed, of course—was duly enshrined at the Cavalry Museum. The Officer's Quarters where the Custers lived is preserved much as it was in 1876. The parlor, where his widow, Libby, on that September morning 71 years before received the sober delegation bearing news from the Little Big Horn, looked as though it had been undisturbed from that day. There was even an equestrian training course among the miscellaneous schools at Fort Riley the Army still participated in its horsy events worldwide.

The guys (including me) that did all the grunt work for these miscellaneous units were assigned to an amalgamated organization called the 1st Ground General School Detachment. The 1st GGSD was responsible only to feed, house and pay us. Operational control and daily tasks came from the functional unit for which we worked. My initial functional assignment was the Post A&R (Athletics and Recreation) Office.

The Post A&R Officer was a round, pudgy faced lst Lieutenant Walter Thomas. Lt. Thomas was about 5' 9" 180 pounds and beginning to run to chubby. If one were searching for an athletic role model he wasn't it. He was relatively recently married, no kids and lived in Post Housing. I met his wife later under very exasperating circumstances which led to my decision to ask for transfer out of the A&R Office. Marilyn Thomas was a rather attractive, if mousy woman of about 30. Several months later I was destined to learn of her pitiable fate.

Lt. Thomas hardly ever showed his face at the office—not that anyone cared. The functions of the office were quite adequately, efficiently and effectively supervised by Technical Sergeant William T. "Jughead" Collins a gregarious Irishman. Collins was quite competent and a good soldier except that he suffered the curse of the Irish—an over fondness for strong drink. To be fair, I never saw him drinking on duty nor did his after-hours drinking ever affect his duty.

Two other lushes—Sergeant Bradshaw and PFC Gilmore along with PFCs Johnson and Salmon made up the rest of the military contingent. We had a young woman assigned as an accountant. Normally, a dinky little operation like ours had no need for an accountant. However, we dealt with Non-Appropriated Funds. NA Funds transactions are derived from things like ticket receipts from Post Athletic Events, purchase of athletic equipment, etc. These transactions do not come under the supervision of normal military appropriations, are occasionally subjected to 'funny things' and are consequently watched like a hawk over the chicken coop.

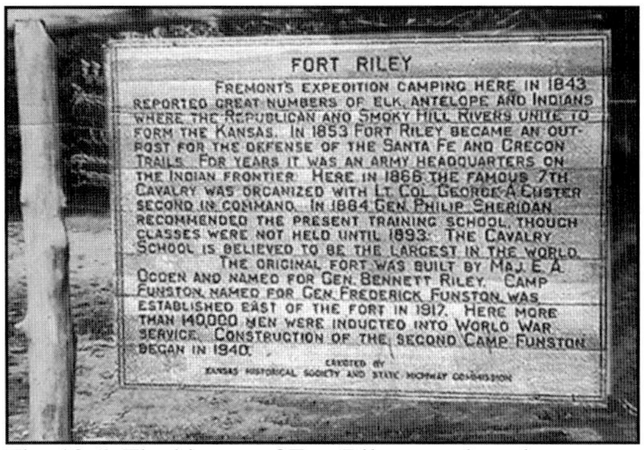

Fig. 12-5. The history of Fort Riley on a board.

I never learned the accountant's name. A week after I joined, a couple guys from CID came to the office and she went away with them never to return.

DOC BLANCHARD

Doc Blanchard and Glenn Davis were the stars of the West Point football team of 1946-1947. They were not only stars, but had individually broken several long standing records: yards rushing, etc. Even though I had not been a extremely avid football fan, even I knew of Blanchard and Davis.

My game was basketball but I was more interested in playing than watching. My military duties at the Post Athletic and Recreation Office brought me in frequent conduct with the Post basketball team. It was a natural then for me to join the post team.

I was quite surprised at practice one afternoon at the Post Fieldhouse. A handsome, athletic looking guy in basketball togs was observing intently. He had been watching me practicing free throws. He approached me. "Would you be interested in a pickup game with a pro-team?"

"Sure," I answered, thinking about the days—not that long ago—when I was the Center for Pilot Grove High School basketball team. In 1944 we won the County Championship and I (among others) was named to the County All-Star team. I hadn't yet gotten over that heroic era.

"OK", he said, "Give Sergeant Bradshaw your name." He jerked his thumb toward Bradshaw who happened to be a friend and colleague from the A&R Office. "By the way, I'm Lieutenant Blanchard. On the field you can call me Doc." My God, THE Doc Blanchard!

We practiced diligently at the Field House under the coaching of Doc Blanchard. Since the A&R Office was composed of jocks, ex-jocks and sports nuts, I was able to get almost unlimited time off for basketball practice. Four weeks later at the Kansas State Field House in Manhattan we played the Phillips 66 Oilers! The 66'ers ranged from 6 foot 6 on up. I stood at just under 6 feet. At the tip-off I looked at the navel of the 66'ers center.

It was a disaster! We lost 99 to 24. As we dispiritedly

trudged back to the bus for the sad trip back to Fort Riley, Blanchard was trying to cheer us up. "Hey, guys it was at least a moral victory for us. Do you know that this is the first time the 66'ers have been held under 100 points?" The personal lesson I took out of this was: "Don't get too cocky, you may not be as great as you think you are."

WAR STORIES

Sgt. Bradshaw was a veteran of the Battle of the Bulge and had been seriously wounded there. He was an excellent yarn spinner and contributed more that his share in our many after-game 'postmortems'. The postmortems always started with the dissection of the game but then usually moved on to other topics of interest including the inevitable war stories. These sessions were at the office late at night and although it was frowned upon, there was often strong drink present. Like I say, we never, ever saw hide nor hair of Lieutenant Thomas.

I learned of the Conoco "Gas" station during preparation for such a session. Jughead sent me out to get a jug of Ten High on the afternoon of a big game. Jughead knew the postmortem would be long-winded. I protested, "Jughead, I can't buy liquor, I'm not of age. I'm only twenty!"

Jughead laughed, "Salmon, for Chrissake, the whole transaction is illegal. It's bootleg. The bootlegger ain't going to check your friggin' ID!"

That was the night that Bradshaw, after sucking up a snoot full of Ten High, got started on his experiences at Bastogne in December 1944—the Battle of the Bulge. "The fog was so damned thick you couldn't see ten feet in front of your nose. The CO sent me out with my squad to see if we could see, or more likely, hear anything. Well, about 4-5 miles out of town we damned near ran into this colored outfit—the 820th TD Battalion. Well, it wasn't really a battalion we ran into. It was a half-track with a 75mm anti-tank gun. It was colder than hell and they had made a little fire and had some coffee brewed up. It was about time for a break so we joined them. We swapped some K rations—I could never stand those damned things anyway—for some of their hot coffee. I gotta tell you it tasted pretty damned good! I could feel my guts thawing out as it went down."

"After we drank our coffee and shot the bull a little, we headed on down the slope toward the woods. We still couldn't see diddly squat for all the fog. We had just started into the woods when we heard this Godawful racket right dead in front of us. I estimated tanks at 5-600 yards. We had heard all kinds of rumors that Patton was sending an armored column north to relieve us and at our briefing for this little patrol the CO had confirmed this. Man, would it ever be good to see those guys from 4th Armored Division. I figgered we should go down to meet them and guide them in—they were most likely lost in this damned fog.

"I signaled the squad and we moved forward abreast toward the sound of tanks knocking down trees and brush. We were damned lucky. A little breeze momentarily cleared some of the fog in front of the leading tank. It was a German Mark VI Tiger! [This was the Mk VI König (Royal) Tiger officially designated the Panzer-Kampfwagen VI, 8.8 cm gun.]

"From the noise there must have been two or three more behind him. You rear echelon screw offs never saw one of them but let me tell you about the Tiger. They got 4 inches of armor in front. It'd take a direct hit from the USS Missouri to stop one. They also mount an 88 as the main gun. You heard the old song—them 88's are breaking up that old gang of mine? Well, they got it about right!

"Suddenly—the fog we'd been cussin' was now our friend. I was sure they didn't see us because they continued on course. I signaled the squad at first to take cover. Then recognizing that although they couldn't see us now, we didn't have any good cover and if the fog cleared we would be in deep doo-doo. We did not have so much as a bazooka—not that that would a been any great influence on 'em.

"Of course I thought of the TD guys on top of the hill. I got the squad together and told them to separate so that whatever happened at least some of them would get back to battalion in Bastogne to warn them. I told them I'd get back to the anti tank guys and see what they could do.

"All out of breath, I told this colored Lieutenant about the two or three Tiger tanks rumbling in our direction. Luckily, the top speed of the Tiger is only 4-5 mph—it weighs around 75 tons—and in the wooded terrain they weren't going that fast.

"The Lieutenant says, 'We got some stuff here just over from the States—this stuff's got a shaped charge in the nose and a PDSQ fuze (Point Detonating, Super Quick). We'll fix them suckers! Sergeant! As soon as you can lay that gun give that mother three rounds of that new ammo as fast as you can load and fire!' The gun crew—with eyes like saucers—didn't need encouragement to move quickly. They were already optically tracking the Tiger's radio antenna. We could hear the ominous rumble but could only see the antenna as yet. I put a respectable distance between me and the TD and stood to watch the fun. Finally, the snout of that mean looking 88 stuck out of the fog. About three seconds later the TD fired three rounds so fast you could tell that gun crew was terrified.

"At 5-600 yards they couldn't miss, but the Bam! Bam! Bam! was immediately followed by Boing! Boing! Boing! All three rounds hit home. And all three rounds bounced off. The lead tank slammed on his brakes and the tank rocked back and forth as the turret gunner and assistant gunner desperately cranked their handles to traverse the gun onto us. That's all that saved our lives—the turret of the Mark VI is hand traversed. I later thought of that very pissed off, deafened gunner frantically winding his crank to lay that 88 on us before we got off something serious. As far as the crew of the TD—well, their Mammas didn't raise any fools. They bailed out and split the air for cover.

"I was following them when the first Tiger round hit the TD and it disintegrated. A piece of the tread landed on my legs and pinned me. I couldn't move and I figured I was one dead duck. The only thing I could think to do was lay there quiet-like and maybe they'd think I was dead, or—and this is what actually happened—the fog enveloped the whole scene again bringing down a curtain of mercy on half a dozen scared GIs. I could hear a helluva battle going on around me but didn't have any idea who was winning. It got dark and I tried to get that damned tread off me but I was weak I thought my leg was broke and by now I was damned near frozen. My feet were totally numb.

"I guess I passed out because the next thing I knew I was in a hospital. Anyways, I got the Purple Heart for two frozen feet which are still numb to this day."

There followed a long argument about the requirements for award of a Purple Heart. "I thought you had to show blood. I thought you had to be struck directly by an enemy projectile—a bullet or shrapnel, you don't get no Purple Heart from having something fall on your ass, do you? When you went to school, didn't you have to read Red Badge of Courage by Steven Crane? If them old guys were caught moving toward the rear they had to show blood! That's the way its always been."

Everyone had a skin full of Ten High by this time and though it was good-natured, Bradshaw got a lot of ribbing. I thought Jughead went too far. "If your feet are still numb how the hell can you walk? You don't even limp." Bradshaw took this as a challenge to his veracity and jerked his brown GI brogans off. Removing his socks, he took a deep drag off his cigarette then applied the burning end to the bottom of his right foot. Twice. Then three times on the left. I could smell the burning flesh. "I ain't feeling a thing. Now do you SOBs believe me?" He looked at us in triumph.

The next morning I made it to the office on time. There was ole Jughead yacking it up with someone on the phone. Bradshaw was not in sight. I crept by Jughead to my 'office'—a battered old desk in a small room formerly used for office supplies. Jughead hung up and I prayed he'd find something else to do. I really didn't feel up to one of his BS sessions. No luck.

"Salmon," he sat on my rickety desk to tell me of the terrific opportunity he had developed for me—"That was Lt. Thomas on the phone. He's just now moving into new Post quarters and would like some volunteer help to do a little redecoration. It would be a good opportunity for you to make a few brownie points with the old man!"

I groaned, "What did he have in mind?"

"He's on the way over here. I told him you were here and might have some spare time on Saturday."

"Jughead, you bastard." I saw my weekend disappearing. "What's he going to pay?"

Fig. 12-6. German Mark VI Tiger Tank. This tank weighed 75 tons, had heavy frontal armor and a 88mm gun. It was first used in 1944.

"Salmon my laddie, he's not paying anything! These are the sorts of things that Army folk do for one another. Think of it as a visit from Welcome Wagon with you as the host." Jug was having a good time with this. Lt. Thomas came in the door about then and, hearing us in the back room came back to play the beloved commander visiting his loyal troops. There was a desultory discussion of last nights game. It was clear he wasn't even there but was faking it from what he had heard elsewhere.

Then, "PFC Salmon, Sergeant Collins says you are single and probably not doing anything this weekend. My wife and I have a lot of work to get our quarters ready to move in and wondered if you might like to volunteer to help?"

"Exactly what type of assistance were you looking for, sir?" Maybe it was something that I could claim total ignorance and incompetence.

"What I'd like you to do is help paint the kitchen."

I couldn't weasel out of that and did indeed "volunteer" to contribute such assistance. As Lt. Thomas left he passed Bradshaw in the doorway. Bradshaw was limping badly. Jughead started to say something. Bradshaw scowled, "You said I didn't even limp. How about this?" He exaggerated a limp but we knew he wasn't faking it. We said nothing further.

As I suspected, I didn't *assist* at the Thomas' redecorating. I did it all. Mrs. Thomas often came in to see that I was diligently at work and not splattering too much paint. She could see I was steamed and didn't say much to me. And, Jug was right, there was not even a offer of payment. This entire episode really frosted me and I vowed it would never happen again. In the old Army back in the 1930s, enlisted men were often used as servants and 'step-and-fetchits' by some officers. Under cover of the authority of their office they abused subordinates for their own gain. It was penny-ante crap but still demeaning. Those old days were now past, at least they were supposed to be. I harbored a great deal of ill will toward both Lt. Thomas and his wife. "I hope the bastard gets RIFed and has to shine shoes for a living!"

This incident influenced my decision on an OCS opportunity that arose several weeks later.

IQ TESTS

Among the bureaucratic folderol that a rookie is subjected to is a general classification test. Prior to being assigned to a training regime, it is necessary to separate out those who would best be hewers of wood and drawers of water. In 1947's Army this test was the AGCT (Army General Classification Test).

The AGCT was composed of three elements: Arithmetic Reasoning, Logical Reasoning and Spatial Cognition. Such tests attempt to eliminate bias and do not depend upon actual knowledge in a particular subject. The idea is to measure one's *ability* to learn not what one has *actually* learned.

Because these tests adhere to well established tenets of Galton, Spearman, Binet and other pioneers in the field of measuring intelligence, it is, in Army circles, thought of as an IQ test and is so called by many. It is often misunderstood and sometimes misused by some in authority. So it was with me. My unusual score cause me a great deal of grief.

In October 1947 the Detachment clerk called the A&R Office and left word for me to see the Post I&E (Information and Education) Officer at 0800 the next morning. I told T/Sergeant 'Jughead' Collins what was up and he said, "OK, Salmon. But, while you're over there tell that dumbass Sgt. Jenkins to get that baseball equipment back to us. The I&E Section borrowed that stuff a month ago for their picnic and ball game and if he doesn't get them back here, the I&E Officer is going to have to reply by endorsement to the Post Commander. I'm getting damned tired of calling him on this!"

The Post I&E (Information and Education) Officer was delegated the responsibility for all the testing on the Post. AGCT as well as branch training school entry examinations were administered by his office. I could not fathom what he wanted to see me about. I had taken the AGCT some few days before and was worried that he thought I had cheated or something. It would be like cheating on a urinalysis, i.e., impossible. But any EM ordered to report to an officer is primarily wondering if he is going to get a chewing out for an unwitting infraction of some obscure rule.

Lieutenant Taliaferro was a ring knocker. When I stopped precisely one pace short of his desk and saluted he snapped a return salute and rapped his ring on my 201 File. I thought, "Lieutenant, I am fully cognizant of the fact that you are a graduate of the 'trade school'—the United States Military Academy at West Point. It will not be necessary for you to break your knuckles banging that ring." He must have had the same thought. He didn't do it again.

"Salmon, I have your 201 File here and I'd like to go over some of your test results." He indicated a wooden chair beside his desk. "Have a seat." He opened the manila folder and extracted the yellow 201 Form. "Your composite score, that's the average of your scores on the three elements, is 163. We've never seen a score quite like that. Don't be offended, but we've investigated this very carefully and it seems to be correct. Anyway, we've looked over your 201 file. You have a good clean record—no Article 15's, and graduated high in your class at the Signal School and you're a high school graduate (somewhat of a distinction in 1947). I'm surprised that you've even done an overseas tour. How old are you?

"Twenty, sir."

"Well that's a full record for a twenty year old. What I got you in here for is this: I've talked with the Selection Board out at Camp Forsyth and they agree that you should be encouraged to apply for Officer Candidate School."

So, that's what this is all about. I sighed with relief. Then I thought of the exceedingly disparaged '90 day wonders' of World War II fame. There was not much prestige associated with OCS. On the other hand I had just committed myself to three more years of Army life. OCS could be a significant step in the direction of an Army career. Maybe I should consider the proposition—at least the pay ($215 per month plus allowances) was a lot better than my $54 per month pittance.

"Two questions, sir: What do I have to do to apply and when is the next course?"

"Next course starts in about 6 weeks but there is no way in hell you have all the bureaucratic crap done by that time. They do a full FBI security check, etc. I would recommend you start on the application as soon as possible and aim for the May '48 class. I can have someone at the Board send you the whole kit if you think you want to go?"

"Let me think about it. Could I get back to you, sir?"

"Sure but don't procrastinate. Get on this right away!"

POST SIGNAL OFFICE

I enjoyed the camaraderie at the A&R Office. Jughead was a great guy, Gilmore was a real clown and quite competent when sober and we all loved Bradshaw. But I detested Lt. Thomas so much I set about getting a transfer to the Post Signal Office. A bunk mate at the 1st GGSD had told me there was an opening as a teletype operator and the Post Signal people were 'good folks'. The Signal Officer himself,

Captain Clark, was somewhat of a prick, but he was never around. Operations were supervised by a Civil Service lady—Mrs. Spence. She was in her early forties, quite pleasant and easy to deal with. There was a 30 something WAC, Cpl. Maude McClardy who would be somewhat attractive but for her eagle beak. A young PFC Smith short, heavy set with a receding hair line (at age 21!) completed the complement. Smith was a very intelligent fellow but very reclusive and thought to be some kind of weirdo. I was not willing to await the outcome of the OCS application next class would be in May so—a week later, Monday January 26th, 1948, I reported for duty at the Post Signal Office. I never forgave Lt. Thomas for the personal servant incident but just a few weeks later one of the first Western Union telegrams I handled completely changed my attitude toward his wife.

I was a summa cum laude graduate of the Signal School and had worked at the Atoll Commander's Signal Section JTF-1 Kwajalein as a teletype operator. Therefore I was assigned to the military traffic section teletype. But the office was small. The traffic was light and the Western Union section had to be manned 16 hours a day. With no seniority I found myself doing some night shift work with the Western Union. Actually, I rather enjoyed it. I was all alone. Not much to do. I got a lot of reading done.

I was working that shift—1500 to 2300 one night in mid-February. The Western Union teletype began clattering.

The WU machine printed on a narrow (1/2 inch) pre-gummed yellow paper ribbon which could be torn off between telegrams. One message might consist of 2-3 feet of this ribbon.. The message was from J. J. Gilliam, Colonel MC, Head of Pathology, Fitzsimmons General, Denver and was addressed to H. E. Larned, Capt MC, Pathology, Post Hospital, Ft. Riley.

"...REUR SPECIMEN CONTROL NUMBER 826583N, PATIENT NO 34587FTR: MARILYN N. THOMAS. SPECIMEN RECEIVED 1400 HRS 5 FEB 48. OUR LABS CONFIRM YOUR DIAGNOSIS—CERVICAL SQUAMOUS CELL CARCINOMA..."

My God! This is Lt. Thomas' wife. I had to go to the dictionary for "squamous": flattened or scalelike. The rest I knew. Mrs. Thomas had cervical cancer! In 1947 such a diagnosis was a death sentence. I had wished them bad luck but not a disaster. I knew that I must not reveal private information like this under penalty of a court-martial so I never contacted anyone at the A&R Office and though I watched the Post newspaper, I never learned the outcome. Thank God I had never shot my mouth off about the kitchen painting incident, I would have been full of guilt.

Mrs. Spence our supervisor nearly gave me another opportunity to embarrass myself. She was a very pleasant woman and a delight to work with. One day in March we were working on the weekly work schedule. She felt bad about having me and Smith carry the whole load on the swing shift. She said that she had to be there during the day to interface with the Signal Officer and that she didn't like have a woman—Cpl. McClardy working at night. Actually I didn't really care. I could sleep late, didn't stand inspection, didn't have to deal with the martinets and got no grief from Captain Clark. "I'll be going to Lansing this weekend to see my husband..." she said.

Curious, I asked, "What does your husband—"

McClardy cut me off, "Salmon could you come here a moment please?" She was holding a teletype page off the military network and rattling it urgently. I hurried over.

"Don't ask about her husband!" she hissed at me. "I'll tell you later." Then in a louder voice: "Where in hell is WTJ? Some screwball has misdirected this Urgent message to us and I've got to re-direct it in a hurry!" I looked at the message and none of that was true. But I caught her drift and went into a long winded explanation of how to re-direct to WTJ which is Honolulu, which she knew very well.

At lunch time I returned early and McClardy asked: "Do you know where Lansing is?"

"Yeah, its between Kansas City and Fort Leavenworth."

"And, do you know what's there?"

"No, what?"

"The Kansas State Penitentiary. Now you got a whole bunch of questions haven't you? I don't have any answers but something real dramatic happened about a year ago. My old man got shipped off to Germany. I didn't want to go so I came out here from the Signal School at Monmouth. I'd just been here a week or so—there was a guy, a GS-9 in charge then—when there was a lot of commotion in the office. I saw His Eminence the Signal Officer himself come in here with Mrs. Spence they looked around quickly but by the time I could think of an excuse to get near and eavesdrop, they left. Later Captain Clark's clerk and factotum came to fetch the GS-9 and the three of them were in Clark's office for about an hour. I strolled to the water fountain several times and could hear them but couldn't make out what was said. Two weeks later Mrs. Spence was introduced around as the new supervisor and the GS-9 disappeared. It was only a couple of months ago that I found out about her old man being in the slammer. Listen, if you find out something on this, let me know. I am dying with curiosity."

Since gossip was not a big thing with me, I didn't bother doing any detective work on this. However, I was in the PX beer hall (3.2 % Falstaff was 15¢ a bottle) with some friends one evening. At the next table were two or three 11th Cav guys also swilling down some of Falstaff's finest. The guys from 11th Cav seldom came to the main post so I was giving them the once over. My ears pricked up when the Sergeant mentioned Spence. Was Mrs. Spence's husband a GI?

I counted the empty longneckers on the 11th Cav table—only 4-5 for 3 guys—obviously they hadn't been at it long enough to be drunk and belligerent. I got another beer and came back by their table. "I couldn't help overhearing you mention the name Spence. I work with a lady by that name and was curious if there is any connection?"

Sergeant Murchison—so his name tag said—looked at me with narrowed eyes. "You work at Post Signal?" I allowed as how I did indeed. "And you don't know the story of Master Sergeant Spence and that son of a bitch of a judge in Junction City?"

"No. I just reenlisted in September. I only been here at Riley less that six months."

Murchison says, "Sit down here and join us. You need to be indoctrinated on the slimy bastards down there at Junction City." He took a long pull on his Falstaff. "Sgt. Spence was absolutely railroaded. When it happened the 11th Cav guys wanted to go to Junction City and tear the damned place to pieces." He was getting more and more animated.

"Tell me what happened, I haven't an inkling of any big fracas between the GIs and the Junction City civilians."

"It ain't the civilians. It's that bastard Gutfreund. He's a traffic court judge. The son of a bitch ain't really a judge, you know, not like he's a lawyer or something. I doubt if he's got a high school education. He may be a 'good friend' to some of the people of J City, but he sure as hell ain't no 'good friend' to the 11th Cav."

I was very curious but could see I'd have to get him calmed down to get the story. "You're sucking bottom on the Falstaff, Sarge. Let me buy you another (remember, it was just 15¢) then I hope you can enlighten me with this Sergeant Spence story."

I hand Murchison the Falstaff, he takes a slug, wipes his mouth with the back of his hand and begins. "Master Sergeant Spence was...still is ...one helluva guy, a real soldier. I knew him. Knew his wife. He was a pre-war soldier. Enlisted back in the Great Depression. He spent the entire war with Patton's Third Army in Europe—4th Armored Division. He and I came up here from Ft. Hood, Texas in the summer of '46. The 11th Cav's Regimental S-3 was beefing up the training program and we got selected because we been around the barn a time of two."

"How old is Sergeant Spence?" I was trying to get some picture of the guy.

"Hell, I don't know. He's a couple years older than me. Probably 37 or 38."

"Anyways, Sgt. Spence was involved in an auto accident and ended up getting three years up there at Lansing Penitentiary. An unbelievable miscarriage of justice as they say in the movies."

I was incredulous, "How in hell could he have gotten three years for being in an accident?"

"Well, there was this here young girl that got killed. And...it turns out that this young girl was the daughter of that the 'hanging judge' Gutfreund."

"Still," I insisted, "That's no basis for three years in the slammer!"

Murchison explained,"Well the judge was out for revenge. Let me tell you what that bastard Gutfreund did. First, he ain't never had any great love for the inhabitants of Fort Riley anyways. Maybe you can understand that. As Municipal Judge the only GIs he ever came in contact were the snot nosed young punks who drink a couple bottles of 3.2 beer, think they are drunk and wreck a bar or something...and traffic violations. He was hell on speeding and stuff like that. Since the Army population is probably greater than the civilian population in these parts, most of the offenders were GIs."

"Anyways," he went on, "Here are the absolute facts. There was a collision involving Spence—he was alone—and a carload of teenagers. The Gutfreund girl was killed. Judge Gutfreund vowed to 'hang' the GI involved. I can understand his grief. But his revenge was not the law. There was one other fact that the judge used to succeed in 'hanging' Spence: Spence had had a coupla beers."

I asked, "Was he drunk?"

"Look," he peered at my nametag, "Salmon, would two 3.2 beers make *you* drunk?"

"I really don't think so—particularly this thin stuff" I waved my Falstaff bottle."

"Well, Spence has about 50 pounds on you and what's more—at the trial he had some guys who'd been at the bar testify that he only had two beers. Gutfreund engineered the whole thing. Spence was tried for manslaughter at the Circuit Court in Topeka, but Gutfreund, the little SOB, he knows all the people in the judicial system. He'd been in politics all his life. Too incompetent to do anything else."

Murchison goes on, "No one ever claimed Spence was drunk. He was never tested or anything. They just had the police who worked the accident testify that they had smelled alcohol on his breath. They were good, I'll give them that. I sat in on this trial as they painted a picture of the drunken sot of a GI who ran a stop sign into the path of the other car brutally killing this lovely young woman in the flower of her youth. There wasn't a dry eye in the courtroom."

"Spence testified that he did not run the stop sign and further that the oncoming car with the teenagers was speeding well over the limit which caused him to misjudge the leeway. There were no credible witnesses, just a couple of old ladies. It was hard for them to judge the speed of a car that they were not even paying any attention to. There was never any investigation as to whether the teenagers had been drinking although there was some talk that they had."

"When they found him guilty of manslaughter and sentenced him, Elizabeth—that's his wife—went into shock and they had to carry her out. She was under doctor's care for a month. I'll say this though—our Colonel tried real hard to help Spence. He knew it was a railroad job—totally unfair. Gutfreund—caused all this. That's how Liz got the job there at Post Signal. Our Colonel Hansen had her in his office several times that I know of. He knew that she had some experience in administration. She'd been a GS 5 or 6 before she and Spence got married. She's competent."

"But couldn't the Army do something about this obvious screwing Spence got?"

"It's all politics. The Army ain't got the chance of a snowball in hell against these damned politicians. That there is in the Constitution. Maybe if all this had happened on post or even in some other town, he'd have gotten a fair shake. But, no, as a matter of fact the Pentagon wanted to go strictly by the book and give him a Dishonorable Discharge. Colonel Hansen went to bat for him on that. He got his discharge upgraded to General. But that was the end of his career—eleven years down the drain, no pension, no nothing. And when he gets out of prison what can he do? Know anybody looking for an expert tank gunner?"

When I reported in for work at the Post Signal Office the next morning I greeted Mrs. Spence with a bit more deference. She responded as always with a pleasant "Good morning Cpl. Salmon." I had finally gotten my promotion to Technician 5th Grade which rated corporal's stripes over a "T". "Captain Clark was in earlier and wants to see you."

"What about, do you know?"

"I don't know. He didn't say." she answered.

I had just started working the military TWX circuits when His Grace the Signal Officer appeared. "Salmon, you've been selected for Officer Candidate School. Let me be the first to congratulate you! They're going to want you out at Camp Forsyth on Monday." Thus endeth my career at Fort Riley Post Signal Office.

CAMP FORSYTH

Camp Forsyth lies 4-5 miles to the south of the main post (Ft. Riley) and is the ancestral home of the famous 10th Cavalry—one of the celebrated 'Buffalo Soldiers' regiments. (The 9th Cavalry Regiment was the other.) The 10th Cavalry was once commanded by John J. (Blackjack) Pershing during the 1916 unpleasantness at the Mexican Border. After the incursion of Pancho Villa into New Mexico and the massacre at Columbus, the 'Buffalo Soldiers' chased him all over Northern Mexico to little avail.

In 1948 there weren't any Buffalo Soldiers but there were some leftovers from WWII training days. They didn't know Blackjack Pershing but did know another celebrity. Mickey Rooney had been a soldier at Camp Forsyth. Although Mickey's acting career came after WWII, he had been a child star in the 30s. It was this affluence that attracted such disdain from his fellow trainees. They claimed he was an arrogant, egotistical, self-centered, insufferable bastard. They were particularly contemptuous of his hiring fellow troopers to do all the scut work that is the lot of all recruits—shining shoes, cleaning the barracks, doing KP, etc.

OFFICER CANDIDATE SCHOOL

My barracks mates at the 1st GGSD teased me that "OCS" (Officer Candidate School) really stood for "Organized Chicken Shit". How very right they were.

Fig. 12-7. Beetle Bailey captures the essence of my OCS experience.

Fig. 12-8. Camp Forsyth was a satellite of Ft. Riley, and in 1948 the home of the Branch Immaterial Officer Candidate School.

Fig. 12-9. "Blackjack" Pershing commanded the Buffalo Soldiers at Ft. Riley. Pershing commanded American troops in France, WWI.

Fig. 12-10. The 9th and 10th Cavalry (Black Soldiers) based at Ft. Riley in the 1870s were called "Buffalo Soldiers" by the Indians. They fought the 'Messicans' in the 1916 Mexican border troubles.

But, I enjoyed the rigors of the training—lectures, demonstrations, do-it-yourself exercises and the extensive physical conditioning. I learned to drive an M24 tank, dissemble an M1917 A6 light machine gun, identified all the war gases then in existence, fired virtually every small arm the Army used, adjusted artillery fire, studied and practiced small unit tactics—river crossings, assault on fortified positions, etc. Artillery simulators, blank ammunition and practice grenades made it a kids dream. More fun than Fourth of July and Halloween night combined! I loved it.

The practical training was good—and it was fun. I remember one practical field exercise that everyone screwed up. It seemed silly to the point of infantile at the time but later the lesson came through. The instructor says: "In this situation you are a captain. Your task is to erect the post flag pole. You have a 20 ft length of rope. A ten foot hole is already dug. You have detailed to you one sergeant and one private. How do you get the flagpole up?"

Of course everyone took this as a problem in trigonometry and struggled with it as such. No one came up with an acceptible solution.

The correct solution: You command, "Sergeant Jones, put that flagpole up!"

The lesson? Give missions, objectives and orders but *do not micromanage* the troops.

I was twenty years old, healthy, active, adventurous but extremely raw. I fully acknowledge I was an uncut gem totally bereft of the social graces that might be expected of "an officer and a gentleman". The particularly unkind critics had a saying: "Raised by wolves!" All this became painfully evident at the Officer Candidate Banquet Saturday night July 10th, 1948 at the Aladdin Hotel, Manhattan, Kansas. The cumulative effects of the events of the evening were *not evident* at the time.

My father died in April 1940 leaving a widow and three minor kids. In May and June 1945 I graduated from high school and entered the Army respectively. Between those two dates there was considerably more concern in our family about surviving than there was, say, the proper utensil for dishing up caviar—or the precise placement of the fish knife with respect to the salad fork. In short, while I never considered myself a complete barbarian—I would admit to what a sympathetic observer would have termed "a certain charming rusticity".

The OCS Banquet—which was billed as a stress relieving night out for the boys—was exactly the opposite. The real purpose was to bring a little couth to the essentially uncouth. There were a number of us "diamonds in the rough." Unfortunately, by mere chance one of the TAC Officers was sitting next to me. I became the target of opportunity for Lt. Tice to show all the wannabe Officers and Gentlemen the wrong way to hold your pinky while drinking tea or the proper manner to slurp soup. We had a separate banquet room and ladies were not invited. We were at least spared that humiliation. The TAC officers knew this was going to be a social disaster and didn't want their wives to be embarrassed.

At this banquet there was a Tactical Officer at each table of 5-6 Cadets. We all ate our soup with exaggerated care, offered one another the salt with ponderous politeness, and carried on 'learned' conversations so lofty that by comparison a discussion in congress would sound like a quarrel in a gin mill. All the while our TAC Officer, a smooth, beady, fuzzy cheeked 24 year-old Second Lieutenant kept his eye on us, sizing us up while pretending to be a boon companion.

What a social disaster it was! There was no pretense of enjoying the conversation, food or drink. Since Kansas was dry, the drinks were Coke or Pepsi. We might have known there would be no wine with these tight sphinctered bastards. We might not have been so upset if we'd had a couple of snorts of something. To be fair I must admit that the objective was good: give the candidates some opportunity to mill around in a setting somewhat more refined than the beer gardens we were used to. But the execution was terrible. It was an unmitigated goat slaughter!

The final curtain of charity fell on this catastrophe at 10PM and we were dismissed to our beddy-byes. I joined several others in seeking the solace of a bottle of Ten High in Mr. Warmbrodt's room. Any bellhop could have one in your hand in 5 minutes for $10. As the hours crept by and the bottle slowly emptied, our resentment grew. But, of course, any rational and logic disappeared into inanity. We were fortunate I suppose that everyone crapped out before we could do something really stupid.

I got up at 9AM the next morning, hung over pretty badly and tried to remember whether I had done anything particularly half-witted the night before. I got into the shower hoping it would help clear some cobwebs. I must have been especially clumsy because as I climbed out my foot slipped and I hit my neck on the edge of the tub.

It hurt so badly that I thought maybe I had busted something. By the time my friend Warmbrodt helped me back to the hospital at Fort Riley, my neck was swollen and very tender. I underwent a series of Xrays and consultations with orthopedic surgeons as well as a neurosurgeon. All this attention was beginning to worry me. The neurosurgeon asked, "Do you feel any prickling in your legs or arms? Let me see you clasp your hand. Now the other one. Etc, Etc."

I thought, "These guys think I've broken my neck!"

I spent 2 weeks in the hospital undergoing tests and just generally "under observation". The distressing fallout from this hospitalization was that I would have to restart OCS. Back to square one. Do not collect $200.

Fig. 12-11. OCS sleeve patch.

My decision to not start over was also based on the loss of the comrades I had met in the program so far. Our small cell had been of great mutual benefit.

After a final weekend of agonizing reflection I submitted my resignation on Monday 28th July 1948 and moved to the casual barracks at Camp Forsyth to await further orders. Then, on Friday July 23, 1948. ..."T/5 Salmon, Richard L. RA37813858 is reld of duty and asgmt Ft. Riley, Kansas and is reasgd Co. B, 4th Sig Bn, Ft. Bragg, NC rptg thereat NLT 2400 hrs 15 Aug 1948. Fourteen (14) days delay enroute auth. Tvl via POV auth. Four (4) days tvl time auth. $9.00 in lieu of meals payable in adv...etc., etc."

The POV (privately owned vehicle) referred to my '46 Harley but I deemed a 1,500 mile trip to North Carolina too much for biking. I traded off my Harley Hog for a red 1941 Studebaker 4 door sedan in Sedalia while on my 'delay enroute'. This Studebaker proved to be a wreck-on-its-way-to-happen—a piece of scrap iron.

Thus ended—thwarted and frustrated—my first attempted penetration into the world of my betters. In later years I occasionally thought on this ignominious departure from the field of glory—

I *passed* M1911A3 .45 Cal Pistol, M3 .45 Cal Submachine gun, M1 rifle, M2 Carbine, M1918 BAR, M1917A6 Light Machine gun, M1918A1 Heavy Machine Gun, M1 Grenade, Jeep, 2-1/2 Ton Truck, 5 Ton Truck, M24 Tank, 105mm artillery fire control, map reading; field demolitions—dynamite, TNT, prima-cord, nitrostarch and PETN.

BUT...I *flunked*: fingerbowl.

There was blood upon the risers,
there were brains upon the 'chute;
his intestines were dangling
from his paratrooper boot.
Old Paratroop Ditty

WELCOME TO FORT BRAGG

This hearty welcome to Bragg (see Fig. 13-1) was greatly diminished by the three DRs (Delinquency Reports) I collected in my first 90 days at Bragg. Departing Fort Riley, Kansas, I had traded my beloved Harley 'Hawg' for an ancient (1941) Studebaker junker because I didn't think my backside would stand up to a 1400 mile motorcycle ride. But, 1948 was still the era of a sellers' market in autos and this was the best I could do. I was never able to get everything fixed and have it stay fixed while I passed North Carolina state auto inspection. The DRs were the result.

A "DR" is a sort-of traffic ticket issued by Military Police and is referred to the evildoer's commander for action.

Fort Bragg, North Carolina at Fayetteville was named for Braxton Bragg, 1817-1876, Confederate general; b. Warrenton, NC. As commander of the Army of Tennessee, he tried unsuccessfully (1862) to invade Kentucky. In the Chattanooga Campaign (1863), he was defeated by Gen. Grant. He then became military adviser to Jefferson Davis. Apparently President Davis figured he could keep his eye on him better in Richmond.

With inferior numbers, inferior equipment, inferior artillery support—he believed the superior élan, discipline and morale of his troops would prevail. It did not and half of his command was slaughtered by Union artillery at Chickamauga. Slavishly following a flawed strategy is not a virtue. Or, as Mark Twain said: "The battle does not always go to the strongest—but that's the way to bet!"

It was a blisteringly hot and humid day in August. I had driven all day through the Smokey Mountains then down into the sultry Carolina Piedmont with all windows rolled down. Air conditioning for autos in 1948, was a luxury far into the future. My sweaty shirt, windblown hair, rumpled trousers were quite appropriate for the old Studebaker I was driving. The gate MP looked at my orders suspiciously...

The MP handed my orders back. "The 4th Signal Battalion is out on Smoke Bomb Hill. You go right on to the main post, whip a left on Anzio Drive and follow it on south about 3-4 miles to Smoke Bomb Hill. You'll see the organizational signs out there and you can just follow your nose or ask again."

I got my gear stashed in the Radio Platoon Barracks and phoned my brother Bob. He had just made S/Sgt at the AGF Airborne Materiel Test Board #4 down the Main Post.

Fig. 13-1 In 1948, Fort Bragg was the home of LEFT TO RIGHT: XVIII Airborne Corps, 4th Signal Battalion of V Corps, 82d Airborne Division and Board 4 of the Army Ground Forces.

He had a pretty cushy administrative job and was in the midst of some very interesting testing programs for airborne operations. He told me that our old Pilot Grove comrade Earl Davis was in the 82d Airborne Division's Signal Company.

PFC Earl Robert Davis Jr. "Cooter" was the grandson of Fred Rapp, the Pilot Grove constable with whom he and his divorced mother were living when we were in high school. Old Fred's house was directly across the tracks from the Katy depot. The old man was helping support them as best he could. He was town constable, Post Office employee (he met the two daily passenger trains which were the primary mail carriers into Pilot Grove) as well as whatever other odd job came his way.

Grandpa Fred took himself very seriously. He was waiting for the Katy's Blue Bonnet Special one night. The eastbound Blue Bonnet was due in Pilot Grove around 1245 AM. My old friend and schoolmate Vern Klenklen, was working as the graveyard shift telegraph operator at the Katy depot. Vern asked him facetiously, "Do you check out the people getting off the train, Fred?"

Fred was offended, "Look here, you little wise ass," he dug into his overall pocket to produce his .32 caliber nickel plated revolver. "Do you realize that if any desperado gets off that there train, I'm all that stands between him and the citizens of this here town?"

Earl "Cooter" was a year or so younger than Bob and was a part of our gang. We had engaged in a lot of lunatic antics as teenagers in PG—on Halloween mostly, but one of the zaniest and certainly the most dangerous was the blasting cap caper.

Homer Jeffress and I met Cooter at the depot one summer morning. I suppose we were about 12-13 years old then. Cooter called us around the corner out of sight of his granddad sitting on the front porch. "Lookit what I got!", he said showing us a small, shiny brass tube.

"What is it?" Homer asked.

"It's a blasting cap. Let's go set it off!"

We took off down the railroad track passing by Homer's house and looking nonchalant as his mother eyed us from the backyard. Over the cattle guard and on toward Dead Man's Crossing About a half mile out of town Cooter stops, "Far enough. Gimme a match and I'll shoot this sucker off."

Fig. 13-2. Earl Robert "Cooter" Davis Jr. - 1945.

Both Homer and I had had initial misgivings which had grown as we walked down the track. We both were shaking our head. "Cooter", I said, "Just how are you going to set it off without blowing yourself up?"

"Look", he said, "This here is a cap, it's not explosive. It just sets off the dynamite. Since we ain't got no dynamite, it ain't gonna explode." Thus was demonstrated the danger of a little bit of knowledge.

Holding the flange end of the blasting cap he applied a match to the insert end. Nothing happened and he struck another match. Two seconds into the second match there was a loud pop. The fulminate of mercury, becoming more and more agitated by the heat, had done it's job. The blasting cap vaporized—along with the end joints of his index finger, middle finger and thumb of his left hand.

We were stunned and when he looked at the remains of his left hand, I thought he would pass out with shock. Homer and I got beside him on either side and we double timed back to his home. Under the cover of the ensuing pandemonium we tactfully got the hell out of there.

Bob and I went to visit Cooter at his barracks at the 82d Airborne Division's Signal Company. He was working on his Corcoran jump boots. He had a shine that you could look into and see for a mile! Jump boots were issued in parachute outfits but nearly all the troopers disdained the GI model for a pair of expensive Corcorans. Even the Division Commander, Major General James M. Gavin wore them!

Earl put his boots away and we sat around on footlockers and regaled one another with PG stories. I noted that his hand had healed nicely and he seemed to do OK without 20% of three fingers. He showed us a big, wicked looking K-Bar knife he'd just purchased. "What do you do with that?" I asked. He told us of a recent incident that had caused many of his platoon to obtain similar knives.

"One of the guys in the 504th had a real bad experience last week. They were jumping on Normandy LZ at about 1000 feet. This guy's main chute streamered. He fought it a few seconds then pulled the ring on his reserve 'chute. The reserve snapped out properly but then the reserve lines tangled with the main chute. He couldn't get it straightened out and hit the ground pretty hard. He's alive but has broken bones where he didn't even know he had bones. I decided I ain't going to have that problem. I got me this here K-Bar and I sharpen it before each jump. Ya see, if my main chute streamers, I'm going to cut that sucker loose before I go to my reserve! Jumpin' from 1000 feet only gives ya a few seconds."

"General Gavin recently had a contest for a Division song. Here's what some funny guy in DivArty submitted." He handed me a mimeographed sheet. " It follows the tune of Battle Hymn of the Republic."

BLOOD UPON THE RISERS

Stand up! Hook up! Follow yer sergeant out the door!
Feel that blast of wind, hear the mighty engines roar!
Snap went the static line and pop went his chute,
But the shroud lines got tangled, the streamer was a beaut!

He grabbed his D-ring with knuckles turning white.
'If this reserve don't work they'll dig for me all night!'
His reserve popped out and promptly tangled up
With two chutes a-streaming he hit with a mighty WHUP!

There was blood upon the risers, brains upon the chute
His intestines were dangling from his paratrooper boot.
Gory, gory halleluyah. Gory, gory halleluyah.
He ain't a-gonna jump no more!"

[NOTE: I have adapted the original airborne marching song slightly to fit the reserve chute concept.]

The 82d has its own march—"All Americans", so far as I know, it is still in use today. Here's all I know of it:

"We're All American and proud to beeee,
Defenders of our country's liberteeee!"

Cooter was getting married! It turned out to be a 'marriage of convenience'— a disaster for him. Cooter was about 18 then and a gullible young trooper—easy prey for camp followers. As soon as the new bride got an expensive operation at government expense, she and her mother said goodbye. I took my undelivered wedding gift to sister Dixie next time I passed through St. Louis.

Trooper Davis finished his tour of duty with the 82d, went on to enjoy a long career and retirement from the Kansas City Police Department. In the summer of 1954, while I was attending MU, someone (Ralph Warnhoff?) got up a 'Pilot Grove Reunion' at Wildwood Park for all the Kansas Citians who had emigrated from Pilot Grove. Earl was there and regaled us with some of his motorcycle traffic cop stories. Here's one:

"Genessee Street in midtown Kansas City is one-way between 39th and 43rd Street (Westport Road). Being in the area of Vern's Barber Shop one day (Vern Klenklen is the son of Pilot Grove barber George Klenklen), I dropped in to share a joke with him. When I departed eastbound on 39th street, I whipped a right on Genessee and headed for Westport Road. Then I see this car parked—headed in the wrong direction on this one-way street. Well, I'm sworn to uphold the law and ordinances and there is a little known ordinance that says that you must not only not *drive* the wrong way, but must not even *park* the wrong way on one-way streets.

I parked my bike in front of the illegally parked car and began writing a traffic ticket. I had nearly finished when this guy and his girlfriend or wife or something comes rushing out of the house. 'What have we done? What's wrong, officer?' they demanded.

As I looked up at them, my eye caught the sign with the one-way arrow and, believe it or not, it was *me* that was going the wrong way! Thinking fast, I put my ticket book away and told them, 'I'm gonna let ya go this time, but don't ever let this happen again!'

I wheeled my bike around and raced back to 39th street. In my rear view mirror I saw this guy looking at his car and scratching his head."

Last I heard, Earl "Cooter" Davis was in the private security business in Jefferson City.

CAMP MACKALL

It was my own foolishness that got me onto a very uncomfortable detail. It all started at Camp Mackall. Camp Mackall[1] was a semi-dilapidated, tarpaper shack 'Hooverville' cantonment area in the piney woods of the vast acreage of Fort Bragg. It had been the home of the 17th Airborne Division in 1943. It is separated from 'downtown' Fort Bragg by 20-25 miles thus a safe distance from the 82d Airborne Division. The 17th got more injuries from the 82d than they did from the Germans!

In January of 1949 the XVIII Airborne Corps ran a maneuver in the Mackall part of the Bragg military reservation. The 4th Signal Battalion was billeted in Camp Mackall proper. I was now a Sergeant and Section Chief of the Radio Section. Our equipment was four SCR 399 radios, 2 or 3 SCR 197s and a whole lot of ANGRC9s. We provided radio communication links between the main Corps units—XVIII Corps Hqs, 82d A/B Div., 325 Tank Bn, 504th Regimental Combat Team, etc.

I was in the orderly room talking to the Top Sergeant one morning when the company clerk asked Top what to do with the bugle he had just unpacked.

"I don't know", he answered, "Let the supply sergeant worry about it."

"Lemme see if I can still blow a bugle", I reached for it.

He handed it to me and that was the beginning of a lot of misery for the guys back in the billeting area. I practiced all the daily bugle calls I remembered from Camp Crowder. Camp Crowder was like most military posts during the WWII —the entire schedule of troop activities was regulated by traditional bugle calls. From First Call at 0530 to Reveille 0600 to Mess Call 0630 to Sick Call 0700 to Mail Call 1100 to Fatigue Call 1800 to Taps 2100 and finally Call to Quarters 2300—there was a bugle call for everything. I practiced on all these despite the threats. The brass bugle was very resonant, but, there are very few of those calls that really have any redeeming musical value even if the bugler were an accomplished musician which I was not.

At any rate, either because someone wanted to get revenge on me for disturbing their peace at Mackall or just that the CO had heard me tootling the bugle—I got assigned to a Burial Detail. But first, some background.

REPATRIATION OF THE DEAD

The trauma of the war was far from over in 1948. Grief and bereavement were still raw and open wounds in America. There was a national debate concerning repatriation of American war dead for re-burial in hometown cemeteries. It was no secret that American war losses had been horrendous but, as yet, there had been no opportunity for the home folks to see the magnitude of this horror with their own eyes, no graphic personal experience for the home folks. The government was loathe to provide one now.

The Truman government wanted to leave the bodies in European Cemeteries as an eternal reminder to the Europeans of American sacrifice. But the politicians couldn't put off bereaved relatives. The issue was resolved in 1948. Those who chose could have the bodies of their kin repatriated. Many did but thousands did not. Those then were left in American Cemeteries in Europe. To this day the nation can be proud of the immaculate care of these cemeteries.

Many American servicemen were buried in England. Some died in flying accidents. Some air crews were killed over Europe but returned with their damaged B17s. Some of the D-Day dead were returned to England for burial before cemeteries were established on the continent.

Another major contribution to the toll of war dead resulted from one of the best kept secrets of the war—a pre-D-Day training catastrophe. Nearly 500 GIs died one horrible night in April 1944 during landing maneuvers near Slapton Sands on the south Devon coast.

Green US troops were rehearsing predawn beach landings. Troop ships sallied into the Channel, off-loaded the Infantry onto LCIs bobbing in the Channel swells just as they would a few weeks hence at the Normandy invasion. Two German motor torpedo boats sneaked into the confusion of these operations and torpedoed 3-4 troopships. Dead bodies washed up on Slapton Sands for several weeks thereafter. The ancient, tiny churchyards of most Channel ports —tiny fishing villages really—had new sections set aside for hundreds of American dead.

An interesting sidelight was a major diplomatic problem that arose from repatriation of these American dead from the United Kingdom. It was anticipated that the American project would cause emotional appeals for similar treatment of British dead. Britain was broke, demoralized and dispirited. American Lend Lease had been abruptly terminated. As Attlee complained, " The aid stopped ten minutes after the last shot was fired". They couldn't even feed themselves. There simply would be no way that the United Kingdom

[1] Camp Mackall was named for Pvt John T. Mackall, 2d Bn, 503rd Parachute Inf Regiment, one of the first paratroopers killed in action (in North Africa).

Fig. 13-3. The National Cemetery at Salisbury, NC originated as a prisoner of war camp for Union soldiers in 1863.

Fig. 13-5. Sgt. Salmon of the Burial Detail (without bugle). Ft. Bragg, NC 1948.

could repatriate it's worldwide war dead.

Prime Minister Clement Attlee intervened with President Truman directly. Getting no satisfaction on his appeal to leave the cemeteries as they were, he finally extracted a promise that all the disinterment would take place at night. So, this melancholy task was executed by US Army Graves Registration, a small army of local workmen and a top-secret train surreptitiously moving about the lush green countryside of England collecting the American dead under cover of darkness—with all the modus operandi of grave robbers.

SALISBURY NATIONAL CEMETERY

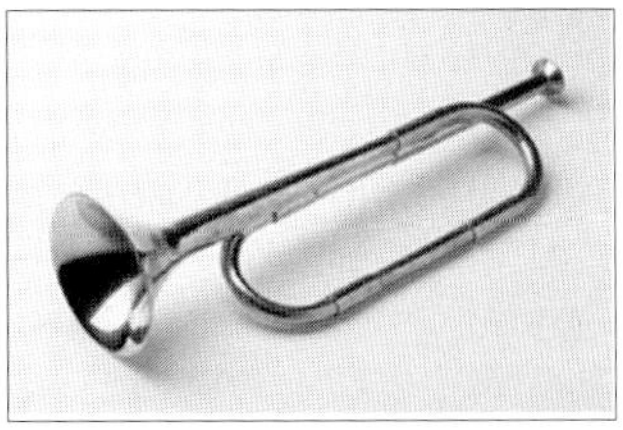

Fig. 13-4. "Day is done. Gone the sun..." Taps, Gen'l Daniel Butterfield, 1862. My battered old bugle never looked this nice!

The Burial Detail was composed of the bugler (me), a 6 man firing squad and a Lieutenant who was Detail Commander. We journeyed to Salisbury, NC, about a two hour drive, in a Carryall[2]. Arriving there on a beautiful sunshiny, if muggy, day. We had an hour or so to mosey around, which I did. I learned that the Salisbury National Cemetery had been a prisoner of war camp for Union prisoners during the Civil War. Several thousands of the graves were for Union prisoners of that era. Years later I read MacKinlay Kantor's "Andersonville", a story of a similar hell hole in Georgia.

We carried off our duties with dignity and decorum, so much so that we were drafted for one more of these details. I sounded Taps, my colleagues fired the three volleys and the lieutenant awarded the flag. Tens of thousands of the boys were coming home' like this and it was the least we could do—but I never pretended that I liked it.

AIRBORNE!

I visited with Cooter Davis at the 82d Signal Company often. I felt somewhat duty bound to a schoolmate particularly after the local strumpet had done a number on him. We spent a lot of time at the NCO Club knocking back Falstaffs. Cooter was drowning his troubles. Soldiers are peculiarly unaware that troubles are excellent swimmers and cannot be easily drowned. But, we tried.

We had always been fast friends but my bucking him up in his personal difficulties made us even closer. He suggested on a number of occasions that I transfer to the 82d and join him. Of course, we both knew that one does not just 'transfer' to an airborne unit. I would have to go through the special training—jump school. Jump School was at Fort Benning, Georgia, a place in which I was quite disinterested. Fort Bragg climate was bad enough. Fort Benning was much worse, but the real disadvantage was the harassment and chastisement that went on at the Infantry School. Although I was Signal, I would have to go through a part of the infantry training. I just didn't want any part of it. Besides, I didn't want to be away for six weeks now that I had re-connected with Cooter and Bob.

Cooter called me one Saturday after inspection: "Guess what, Sonny! Gavin[3] is going to start a jump school here at Bragg! The division will run the school and it is designed exactly for guys like you. The infantry guys will still have to go to Benning but the service troops like engineers and—SIGNAL—will go through a shortened course without all that chicken at Benning. Whatcha say? Come on over here and see the signal company commander, Captain Mabbett, if he OKs it, you are in like Flynn." So I did, Captain Mabbett did, and I was indeed 'in like Flynn'. I believe "Fortune favors the bold" (SAS motto), i.e., 'tis better to be killed by an

[2] The Dodge 'Carryall' was a predecessor of the 4x4 sport vehicle. Painted olive drab and clunky looking, it did not look very sporty.

[3] Major General James Gavin, 82d Airborne Division Commander, later US ambassador to France.

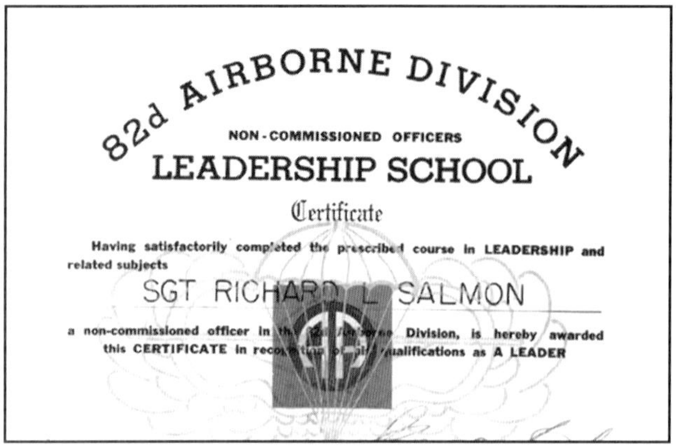
82d AIRBORNE DIVISION
NON-COMMISSIONED OFFICERS
LEADERSHIP SCHOOL
Certificate
Having satisfactorily completed the prescribed course in LEADERSHIP and related subjects
SGT RICHARD L SALMON
a non-commissioned officer in the 82d Airborne Division, is hereby awarded this CERTIFICATE in recognition of his qualifications as A LEADER

Fig. 13-6. My 'diploma' from 'All American' 82d Airborne Division.

eagle than nibbled to death by a duck. Thus began my short[4], though exciting, career with the 'All American' Division[5].

Fig. 13-7. Parachutist Wings.

Ironically, Bob's enlistment ran out and he was discharged to return home and before I started jump school, Cooter also was discharged and returned to civilian life.

LEADERSHIP SCHOOL

I was already a Sergeant, but the OIC of the training program insisted that I attend the 82d Airborne Division's NCO Leadership School. I reported for school on Monday 28th February 1949 and graduated on Friday 11th March.

Times must have been hard in civilian life in those days because there were 5-6 senior NCO's in my class who had just reenlisted. Amazingly, two of these guys were Medal of Honor winners! One was a Filipino—Padilla. In a bull session someone asked him about his medal and he just brushed it off. I have forgotten the other guy's name but he was with the 82d (504th Parachute Infantry) at Anzio and had captured, single-handedly, a German infantry battalion.

While I was attending this class, several 'technical advisors' returned to Bragg. Paramount had borrowed these five or six guys who had been with the 101st Airborne[7] at Bastogne. These 'volunteers' went to Hollywood for two months as 'technical advisors' for the movie 'Battleground'

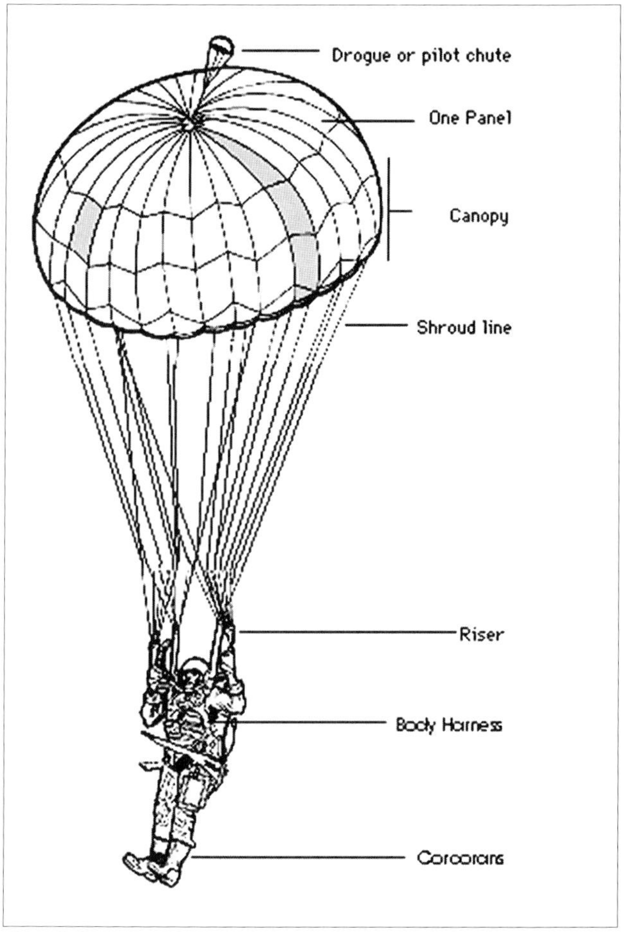

Fig. 13-8. The M-92 tactical parachute, ca 1948.

(starring Van Johnson) which pretended to be the story of the Battle of the Bulge.

I talked to them and got the impression that their main duties were to slurp frozen daiquiris and flirt with the starlets around the swimming pool. I saw the movie some months later and—based on the accounts of the guys I knew who had been there—any similarity between 'Battleground' and the Battle of the Bulge would have been purely accidental.

A brief summary of the Fort Bragg 'jump school'—First lesson: How to hit the ground. At Benning there are a number of 30 ft training towers with steel cables sloping off to earth. You climb the tower, attach your harness to a rolling block, jump out the door, free fall for 5-6 feet simulating an opening shock, then go gliding down the cable to hit the ground like a flop from a tall cow. Proper procedure: with knees slightly bent, as you hit the ground, ball yourself up and tumble. This is supposed to dissipate landing shock. Watch the landing gear on aircraft making carrier landings and you see this 'knee-action' concept which converts a 'controlled crash' into an acceptable landing.

Here are the parts and functions of an M92 military parachute. See Fig. 13-8. At the top is a **drogue** chute which is a little toy parachute like I used to make with a handkerchief

[4] Four months, February through May 1949.

[5] In World War I, most Infantry Divisions were derived from National Guard units indigenous to specific states…40th of California, 69th of New York, etc. The 82d Division however, was drawn from all over America—thus the nickname: 'All American'.

[6] Even ex-members of the 82d were required to attend this jump school as a refresher.

[7] It was the 101st Airborne Division, the 'Screaming Eagles' that were the heroes of Bastogne, but the 101st was not active in 1949. Many 101st veterans had transferred to the 82d and that is why Paramount Pictures came to Ft. Bragg.

and a rock. When the end of the **static line** releases the backpack cover the drogue chute deploys and pulls the **main chute** out. The **main chute** is composed of a **canopy** made up of 32 **panels**. A **shroud line** attaches to the edge of each panel and in turn is attached to one of four **risers**. Risers are attached to the **body harness**. This harness may be released by a **quick-release buckle**—a round brass plate that you rotate then strike with the ball of your hand.

At Bragg's new school they only had one tower which was insufficient for the number of retreads being run through. The Army expediency—load up a six by six GMC truck without canvas cover. While driving at about 25-30 miles per hour on a dirt road the trainees squatted on the two benches facing forward. As the jumpmaster hits you on the shoulder, you vault over the rack, landing on the roadside. Don't forget: knees bent, hit the ground and roll! This expedient training was fairly effective.

Ultimately my squad did get to go off the tower. Not that I was all that gung ho about it, but there was one important lesson to be learned on the tower—snugging up your harness in the crotch area. I learned to my cost that if that part of the harness is not cinched up tightly, you can get some of your favorite body parts crunched.

Benning had several 60 ft captive-chute towers. These parachute towers are essentially the same as those you see at some of the bigger amusement parks—Coney Island for example. The trainee is rigged into a conventional parachute, except the chute itself is pre-deployed. The chute is attached to a cable which lifts the trainee and open chute to the top of the tower. He is then released and descends freely—wheeeee! The simulation is almost complete, only the actual exiting of the plane and parachute opening shock are missing. Unfortunately, the Ft. Bragg quickie school did not have a parachute tower thus the first air drop under a real canopy would be out of the back of a C-82 at 2000[8] feet.

Naturally, integrated with all the parachuting instruction was the usual standard harassment: double-timing everywhere with full field pack. The full field pack included about 100 pounds of field gear—shelter half, entrenching tool, blanket, mess kit, etc. Plus the basic weapon and 2-300 rounds of ammunition. My assigned weapon was the M1A1 Carbine which was identical to the M1 but with a folding metal frame stock. With folded stock the carbine was only about 26 inches long and could be strapped across the chest under the reserve parachute.

All the retreads also had to visit the parachute rigging facility. The rigging sheds had very high lofts to accommodate parachute inspection, repairing, cleaning and drying. We packed a chute but I'm sure that as soon as we left it was handed to the regular guys to re-do. As a souvenir of our lesson each student got a shroud line salvaged from a discarded parachute. Nearly everyone dyed their nylon cord brown[9] and cut them to size for boot laces. I braided part of mine into a lanyard and still have it.

At Division level there is a parachute riggers platoon. These are the guys who retrieve, repair, dry and repack the parachutes. Since the functioning of each parachute is a life and death matter, the riggers are carefully chosen and supervised. In addition, on unannounced inspection visits to the rigging sheds, a divisional staff officer would randomly select parachutes and require the working riggers to use them on a jump. "Keeps 'em on their toes!"

BUTT BUSTER

More background for a little story about a bone crushing jump I made in May 1949: On average, a trooper descends at about 18 feet per second[10]. Under ideal conditions this is about the same as jumping off a ten foot platform. Conditions however are seldom ideal—sometimes unanticipated surface winds are present in the drop zone and the 18 ft/sec velocity is modified by a horizontal wind motion of equal or higher velocity—like jumping backward off the top of a 18 wheeler moving at 15-20 miles per hour.

In combat jumps a platoon of Pathfinders jump an hour or so before the main force, examine the drop zone and local weather conditions. This up to the minute intelligence is radioed back to the main force and adjustments made.

In addition—in a tactical or combat jump—you are not guaranteed to land in a nice cushy meadow. For example, the 82d did a tactical jump on the island of Vieques, Puerto Rico in the summer of 1948, where a drop zone covered with tree stumps put one-third of the troops in the hospital with broken bones. On D-Day morning behind the Normandy beaches, one trooper of the 504th Airborne Infantry landed on the roof of a church at Ste. Mere Eglise.

Thus, on descent, there is an occasional need for a mid-course correction[11]. This is accomplished by a pulling on the risers. This nudges the descent path by spilling wind out of the opposite corner of the canopy. This seems very simple—pull the two right risers, wind is dumped from the left of the canopy and you sideslip to the right, etc. The catch is—if you don't have a lot of experience doing this sort of thing—and I didn't—you can go into oscillations with your body acting like a pendulum. This is what happened to me. I actually had no need to make a course correction. We had just been taught these maneuvers and I wanted to try them.

[8] Combat jumps are from 1,000 feet or lower. Our extra 1,000 feet was a safety factor—more time to figure what the hell to do if something goes wrong!

[9] 1949 was the era of the 'brown shoe army'. Black boots came later.

[10] 18 feet per second is about 15 miles per hour. Descent velocity may vary 20% depending upon weather. A hot and dry day makes for 'thin' air and a fast descent. On cool, muggy days descent is soft and easy.

[11] The 82d now uses the T-10M steerable parachute, which greatly improves mid-course corrections.

I pulled on the forward risers, probably too hard, and collapsed the chute. I experienced a 45-50 ft. free fall. I then over-corrected with the rear risers and began oscillating wildly swinging in an arc of about 20 feet. I was on an upswing when I hit the ground, free-falling from 20-25 feet. I landed on my rear-end and legs with all the grace of a brick outhouse. No bones broken but my tailbone was sore for a week. The Jumpmaster, a tall, lanky Alabama Master Sergeant grinned at me rubbing my back, "What's the matter Salmon—you bust yer butt? Heh, heh, heh!"

Here is a doctoral dissertation idea for a social psychologist: When a guy breaks a bone, he gets concern and sympathy from his comrades; soft, fragrant, pretty nurses hover about caring for him—unless that bone is the coccyx, the lower four, fused vertebrae called the tail bone. Then he gets derision, bad jokes, sniggers and guffaws. Explain that please.

THE WINDS - 1948

The wind sighs through the canopy
And strums the taut shroud lines.
Mother Earth looks possessively up at me
Through the beckoning Carolina pines.

The 82d used the big twin-boomed C82s as the main troop delivery aircraft in those days. It was a lot different, much easier actually, than the old C47s. On the C82s you exited two doors in the rear, that is, two sticks were dropped simultaneously. The one disadvantage of the C-82 was that you exited backward. When the static line snatched the main chute open, the harness and shroud lines came out over your head and if you weren't prepared for it—you get 'rope burn' on your neck. You could pick out the guys who were new to the C-82 by the neck burns.

Our Signal units used special C82s which had the rear cargo doors removed to drop heavier equipment. The Signal equipment in use in those days was all WWII vintage and really did not lend itself to airborne operations. It was bulky, heavy and very unforgiving of, say, a drop of 1000 feet or so sans parachute.

The field wire teams could train realistically. They could parachute in, retrieve their wire and telephone equipment pallets and actually install some communications. I used to marvel at the pole climbers. These guys were absolutely nuts. They would put on their tree climbing spurs and with a running leap, jump 4-5 feet up on the trunk of a pine tree and then run up the trunk like a monkey.

It was frustrating that my Radio Team had nothing realistic that we could do for training. For the most part, if we were to use our radios at all they had to be landed—that is, air *lifted* not air *borne*. My specialty, the heavy, long range radio equipment—Systems SCR399, SCR 197, etc.—saw little use. Truman's new SecDef, Louis Johnson was already in the saddle, cutting appropriations and we simply could not afford to risk air-dropping our radio equipment. Anything lost would never be made good.

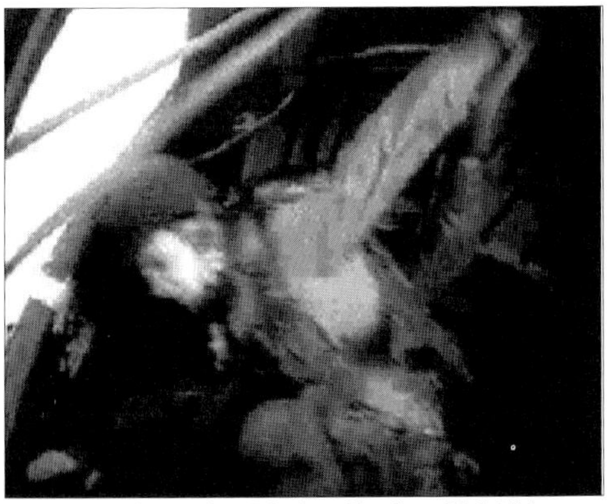

Fig. 13-9. Operation Market Garden. 82d Airborne Div jumps on Nijmegen in Holland.

Fig. 13-10. British "Red Devils" (5th Para) jump on the Rhine bridge at Arnhem, Holland; which was the "Bridge Too Far."

In an Infantry unit in those days, only the PRC-6 'Walkie-talkies' and PRC-9 'Handi-talkies' were of great use. These were low power, but heavy, man-packed, radio-telephones. All officers above lieutenant had an 'RTO' Radio Telephone Operator, who was simply a flunky who packed a 10-20 pound radio for the convenience of his commander. This 10-20 pound load, by the way, was in addition to his own gear. Being Division Signal, we had responsibility for the supply and maintenance of these radios, but thank God, we did not have to provide the troops to carry them.

As a part of our 'jump school' training we also had some demonstrations mostly by the AGF Board. The AGF Board were the guys who developed and tested military materiel especially for airborne units. I remember one demo particularly: The FMC[12] tested and demonstrated a self propelled 76 mm combination antitank/assault gun. Fully tracked, this assault gun was capable of about 50 MPH, was air droppable and fired 6-8 rounds per minute of armor piercing antitank ammo. It looked strange because it was like a tank totally without armor. The commander, the gunner and assistant

[12] FMC - Food Machinery Corporation. Belying their name, FMC was a major defence contractor and their materiel was held in high regard.

gunner/driver drove, managed and served the gun from a small, rear platform completely open to weather, hostile fire, snowballs and everything else. All this in order to radically reduce weight to airborne specs. I later understood the grave concern in providing airborne units with armor defense when I saw the movie 'A Bridge Too Far' based on Cornelius Ryan's excellent book of the same name[13]. See Figs.13-9 & 13-10, previous page.

APPENDECTOMY

I had an acute attack of appendicitis in late April and Captain Lindsey, 82d Medical Battalion removed my appendix on Sunday afternoon 1st of May. I was convalescing a few days later when General Canham the Assistant Division Commander came through the hospital with the Hospital Commandant and the Chief of Surgery reviewing the patients for fitness. He dismissed nearly all the airborne troops but not me. The Division was preparing for a Division CPX with a massive airdrop of troops and materiel. I guess he decided 3 days was not quite enough for my appendectomy to heal up, thanks be unto the Lord.

I did welcome the time away from day to day duty to think about my life—where I was in my career and where I was going. I really had to admit I hadn't spent a lot of time thinking about my future and needed to consider the possibility that I couldn't spend the rest of my life playing sojer boy as much as I enjoyed it. During my enforced idleness at Munson General Hospital I had come across some info on the Aviation Cadet Program in the new U.S. Air Force. The one year Program at Randolph Field near San Antonio, Texas would entertain applications for the class beginning in June.

Fighter pilot training had been a dream of mine so lofty and unreal that I never had any hope it might be achieved. But, what the hell, I've done everything else I wanted to, why not give it a try? I'd have to hurry, I understood military and government red tape all too well and since this was early May, I would have to hustle to make that June class. So, I hustled.

TONSILLECTOMY

One of the fall out difficulties I had had with the appendectomy was a severe allergenic reaction to some of the medication. I was treated for the allergy for a few days and then was to be released, so I thought.

[13] Briefly, in the greatest airborne operation in history, the British 5th Para Division was dropped right into the operational area of General Bittrich's II SS Panzer Corps—two Panzer Divisions and ancillary units. The result was a disaster—airborne troops were not then equipped to defend against armor.

[14] EENT - Eye, Ear, Nose and Throat Clinic.

By coincidence the Head of EENT[14], Major Horvath, did my final checkout. Major Horvath was a Hungarian with such an accent I had a hard time understanding him but he was friendly and we established an easy rapport. He found my allergies cleared up but tsk, tsked at my tonsils. "Zem tonzils vil haf to come oudt!" With no consultations as to my wishes in the matter he booked me for a tonsillectomy on 11th May.

I had had an unusually rapid response to my Aviation Cadet application and was scheduled for a board hearing on the 13th of May, two days after a tonsillectomy. The tonsillectomy was worse than the appendectomy but I was glad to have it over and Major Horvath was important to me because of a terrific favor he did for me a few days later.

FORM 1 PHYSICAL

The Aviation Cadet application consists of a long written form with all of ones vital statistics, military history, etc. This form is the basis for a meeting with a board of Air Force officers for an intense grilling. A few days after the Boarding I was notified to report to the Base Hospital at Pope Field[15] for a "Form 1 Physical Examination" on Thursday the 19th of May.

The "Form 1" is an extremely thorough examination. The findings that I remember were: 1. Pes Planus 3° (severely flat feet); 2. Vision - 20/15 both eyes (i.e., surpassing normal vision) and 3. Audiometric - 20 decibel hearing loss in right ear at frequencies above 6 kilocycles.

Apparently flat feet do not disqualify flight trainees, so, no problem. The 20/15 vision was good news. The hearing loss was not! In fact it was disqualifying—but just barely. In a panic, I hastily hunted down Major Horvath and told him what I was doing and how much it meant to me to pass this physical.

He looked at the charts. "Hmmm, vell you don't miz it far. Hokay, I'll fix." And he did. He got clean charts and duplicated the marks, 'improving' the right ear enough to pass me. I was elated. On 28 May 1949 I got my orders to the "3510th Pilot Training Wing, Randolph Field, Texas. Reporting thereat NLT 16 June 1949." A 13-day 'delay enroute' was authorized.

> LESSON LEARNED: Keep on a-temptin' fate and you'll need more that a razor-edged, 18 inch K-Bar!

[15] Pope Field is adjacent to Fort Bragg and is the base for all airborne flight support operations.

Fig. 13-11. Insignia collection - Part 4. LEFT - Shoulder Patch V Corp, MIDDLE TOP - Battalion Crest, 4th Signal Battalion. MIDDLE BOTTOM - Parachutist Wings, RIGHT - Shoulder Patch 82d Airborne Division "The All American Division".

Fig. 13-12. Gen'l Braxton Bragg CSA 1864, namesake of Fort Bragg. His generalship was one of the reasons the Yanks won!

Fig. 13-13. Yes, the "All American" Division is now coed. Them girls is just a-ruining ever'thing!

"Off we go into the wild blue yonder,
climbing high into the sun—"
US Air Force Song

SAN ANTONIO

FORT BRAGG SUMMERS HAD BEEN MY PICK for the hottest in the United States. On Thursday the 16th of June when I arrived there, San Antonio, Texas easily surpassed Bragg. I had had a 13-day 'delay enroute' in Pilot Grove before catching the Katy Flyer literally to the end of the line—San Antonio, Texas. See Fig. 14-1. Even in Missouri, an unusually hot June had driven me to sleep in my skivvies on the front porch, but this Texas weather was much worse!

Fig. 14-1. The San Antonio Katy Station. It was much more chaotic on the day I arrived, Thursday 16th of June 1949. This photo was taken 3 years later after the Katy discontinued passenger train service.

Clambering down from the chair car, I must have looked like a bum. The Katy had no Pullman cars. I couldn't have afforded a berth if they had. I had been sitting in a 'chair car' for about 18 hours trying, with little success, to get some sleep. Air conditioning was unknown to the Katy and I was hot, sweaty and grimy. I needed a shave. I needed a bath. My khakis were wrinkled — worse than the standard 'barracks bag press. They were flecked with diesel locomotive soot. It was a very inauspicious beginning.

I shouldered my duffel bag and pushing my way onto the main concourse of the station proper, found the Base Transportation booth. San Antonio's Katy station was an architectural classic. Like many of the city's public buildings, it followed the lovely Spanish Mission style even to include twin bell towers. But on this day my appreciation for this architectural beauty lost out to the heat, sweat and a concourse crowded with the unwashed masses (including me). I never saw so many 'Messicans' in my life. They gave me a momentary panic, "Had I overslept San Antonio and gone on to Mexico? Naw, too many signs in English."

San Antonio was a military town — Kelly Field, Lackland Field, Fort Sam Houston, Randolph Field and several lesser entities assured that all major city entry ports would be manned by representatives of the Area Transportation Officer to rescue lost GIs.

I showed the TO's Sergeant my orders. He grunted, "They's a shuttle bus out to Randolph ever' hour or so. He's due about now so you'd better get out there onto South Flores. The pickup point is just outside there." He pointed to the south exit. "It's a GI bus with signs front and sides that says 'Randolph Field'— you can't miss it."

COLLEGE DORMS

Randolph's billets were much like college dorms. There was no air conditioning but giant fans at the end of each floor circulated air. The Field was very old in terms of the newly minted U.S. Air Force and reminded me a little of Schofield Barracks in Hawaii. The architecture was tropical Spanish colonial with red tile roofs and the wide eaves typical of public buildings in the tropics. Wide eaves were a functional necessity since—without air conditioning—the windows had to be open much of the year and torrential rains were frequent in the rainy season. In the billets proper, the lower half of all the doors were louvered. Student rooms were all double occupancy. I was fully prepared for the immaculate state of the common areas as well as the individual rooms. I knew full well who kept them that way!

HELL WEEK

What I was not prepared for was the intense hazing — 'Hell Week'. It began as we were dismounting from the bus. The lower classmen (me, for example) were treated to an unceasing stream of verbal abuse from the upperclassmen. Hazing has always been common in college frat houses and certainly in West Point and Annapolis. What I did not realize at the time was that the Air Force, now less than one year old, was feeling its oats as a separate service and anxious to establish its own traditions. My class was to be one of the last at Randolph. Work was even now underway for a full fledged four year Air Force Academy near Colorado Springs.

Mostly the hazing was in good spirit. I quickly learned what a 'brace' was, how to 'cage my eyeballs', how to eat a 'square meal' and how to reply to a request for the time (Sir, the exact and precise measure of sidereal time at 90° west longitude is 10 hours, 14 minutes and 7 ticks!).

I was also surprised at how quickly we got into the program. Formal classes began before we even got all our uniforms and equipment issued. The 'ground school' started in basic subjects like trigonometry. Although many of these topics were high school level, the settings for class problems were realistic. For example trigonometry lessons were integrated with complicated navigational exercises. Incidentally, one of the subjects was radio code. This was quite difficult for most of the cadets but a snap for me. I had passed 25 words per minute at Crowder in '46 and it was only required that we do 5 wpm here. My proficiency at Radio Code

Fig. 14-2. North American's AT-6 Advanced Trainer.

brought my tests average near the top of the class. Unfair, maybe but all's fair in love and war and this was not love.

FIRST FLIGHT

Best of all, the second week of the course put us in the cockpit of an AT-6 Trainer. The AT-6D which was then the aircraft of choice for pilot training and was the latest in an evolving line of training aircraft. In the early days of WWII, pilot training started with a Primary Trainer — the Stearman PT-13. The Stearman was an ancient biplane with a Pratt and Whitney radial 'Wasp' engine and two open cockpits. It was reminiscent of the old WWI Spads. In earlier days it offered preparation for the Advanced Trainer — the North American AT-6. See Fig. 14-2.

In 1949, only the AT-6 was used. The North American AT-6D Texan (also called the Harvard) was powered by a 550 HP Pratt & Whitney R1340 AN-1 engine capable of roaring along at 212 mph for a range of 870 miles. It appeared huge to someone who'd never been close to anything bigger than a Piper Cub. It had a 42 ft wingspan and was 30 ft long. It was, of course, dual controlled, student in front and the instructor in the rear seat each with a sliding Plexiglas canopy.

I had been assigned a locker in the Flight Operations Building and went there to suit up for my maiden flight. When I finished I stopped at a full length mirror near the exit. I just had to admire reflection there — khaki cloth flight helmet with real aviator goggles, tan canvas one piece flight suit with neat pockets all over the place and a seat-pack parachute which would bang on the back of my legs as I waddled out to the flight line. I thought of the day that I had watched the itinerant pilot bring his little butterscotch colored Jenny biplane into Pilot Grove and landed in Mr. Seltsam's cow pasture. How many little kids dream of walking out to the flight line to climb into their aircraft like this. How many of them actually achieve those dreams?

I felt one disappointment: I had thought that the flight boots I saw everyone wearing were government issue. They were not. Like the Corcorans at Fort Bragg, I would have to buy my own half-Wellington flight boots. I made a mental note to ask around for the best deal. In the meantime I wore my jump boots.

This first flight was nothing more than accompanying the instructor in his preparation and filing of a flight plan, his preflight check and a 'tour' of the cockpit. The instructor talked me through all the things he was doing with little tips like, "One of the things a guy might forget particularly on a hot day like today — turn on the carburetor heat as soon as you start the engine. You tend to forget that only a few thousand feet up it's colder than hell but what's more important — the carburetor is essentially a Venturi tube and that when 100 octane gas is vaporized it sucks heat out of the metal. Without adding heat, any condensate in the carburetor freezes in a few seconds. With a frozen carburetor you get no gas, without gas you got no engine and with no engine you're gonna find this beast has all the aerodynamic characteristics of a rock. You'll know you got carburetor ice problems if you see that you're pulling 30 inches or so manifold pressure but ain't getting power."

THE TEXAN

"The Texan actually has more engine than she needs. That Pratt and Whitney generates a mighty clockwise torque, so remember that when you do a bank to the right. She wants to roll that way anyway so don't give her too much stick. Rolling counter-clockwise you get the opposite effect. You'll probably have to get both hands on the stick to grunt her over. "

Of course, on this first flight I never put a finger on any control. I sat like a full fledged doofus, rigidly at attention trying to observe everything while absorbing everything he said. "Put your feet on the rudder pedals — I want you to get their feel, but for Chrissake don't put any force on them, just follow me. I looked down at the pedals. They were full size and would even fit my size 12 boot. I thought of the little biplane that had landed in Seltsam's cow pasture — the first real airplane I had seen up close. Those rudder pedals on that clunker reminded me of Patty Schilb's pedal car.

I was pleasantly surprised by the attitude of the instructor, Lieutenant McManus. We were lining up on a railway. I remembered the admonitions about buzzing but then thought, "It's McManus' ass, not mine."

His voice came on the intercom, "I'm going to simulate a strafing run. I want to show you something. If you get into fighters this is very important. Your guns are fixed. Your ballistics depend entirely on your plane's angle of attack. You have to elevate or depress the gun pattern by raising or lowering the nose. That's easy. He demonstrated. Its harder controlling right and left deflection. I'm about to show you how you do it. Put your feet on the rudder pedals." I complied. "Now look at that crossing we've lined up on. Pretend you have a gun sight right in the middle of the windshield." I could feel him gently touching the right rudder. The nose moved to the right such that we were pointed 5-6 yards to the right of the crossing. "It just takes a light touch of the rudder to get 5-10 yards of deflection. The new guys tend to overcorrect. Now you try it. We went around for another pass and I tried my light touch. "Too much, too much Mr. Salmon! Well, it's early on to be doing this anyway, you'll get the hang of it."

When we landed and did a walkaround the aircraft McManus continued his tips on ground attack. It sounded more like he was thinking aloud. "You know the guns on a fighter are aimed for the air-to-air mission. The fire pattern converges at about 300 yards. In theory at 300 yards all the rounds would go through one knothole in the fence. Ground attack may require that you hose the lead around a little. You use the light rudder touch tactic. To cover a wider area you simply wiggle your tail like a teeny bopper cheer leader."

WATCH THE HIGH WIRE

The giant Cadet mess was filled with the usual clatter and banter at the evening meal on Sunday the 26th of June. Lower classmen "Plebes" or "Kiwis" were busily scampering to the serving line for refills. Heavy crockery bowls were sluiced full of mashed potatoes, creamed corn and such that graced the training tables. Some scurried for refills of the statutory hot drink (almost always coffee) or cold drink (usually lemonade) served up in giant metal pitchers.

As a raw Cadet, I tried not to be surprised by anything — but the royal entry of the Wing Commander and his entourage startled me. Some alert upperclassman immediately spotted the Colonel and bellowed out "A-TEN-HUT!" Flatware clattered, a coffee pitcher clanged on the concrete floor, several chairs were knocked over as the Cadet Corps — as a man — leaped to a rigid attention.

There were a few murmurs, "What in hell...What's happening?..." They were admonished in a fierce whisper, 'You're at attention there, Mister!"

Colonel Gabreski was a WWII ace fighter pilot of the 9th Air Force. He made his bones — 28 of them — in the 1944-45 skies over Germany. His was one of the new legends of the embryonic Air Force Academy one learned very quickly at Randolph. Gabreski was of medium build with jet black, curly hair that was beginning to show a bit of gray. Clearly, he was one of the few fighter jocks who matured to major command.

Gabreski wasted no time: "Stand at ease!" He commanded, "I am sorry to interrupt your meal gentlemen but I have some bad news for you and an extremely important message! Some of you may have already heard that Cadet McKinley P. Sullivan was involved in an aircraft accident this afternoon. He lost his life. I am sorry to have to announce his accident in this manner."

Even from 10 mess tables away I could see that the Colonel was even more distraught than would be explained by the 'aircraft accident'. He continued, "Mister Sullivan was killed when he flagrantly and willfully disobeyed flight regulations. He buzzed the swimming beach at Lake Mitchell this afternoon. He collided with a high tension electrical transmission line and went into the lake." The Colonel drew a long breath. "Gentlemen, you are being trained to undertake operations which may some day put you in harm's way. Those are unavoidable. What are avoidable are childish stunts that violate basic flight regulations with which each and every one of you is quite familiar. I'm am very sorry about Cadet Sullivan. I've been on the telephone to his parents and you can guess how that went. Let me leave it at this: you know the regulations on minimal flight altitudes. You also know the prohibition of aerobatic flying without special permission. Don't make me have to call your parents. Remember, if you survive such nonsense, I will have you court-martialled and at the very least you can kiss your wings good-bye!"

The Exec bellowed: "A-TEN-HUT!" and the Commandant and his retinue departed.

SOLO

After a student has soloed, he had the privilege — under strict guidance and with many provisos — to check out an AT-6 and get in some extra "stick time". This was actually encouraged since everyone agreed that "the way you learn to fly is by flying". That was one element of the tragedy. The other was the typical upperclassman, particularly those close to graduation, had at least one girl on the string. Girl chasing offered no great challenge since the young 'debutantes' were often escorted to Randolph by their Moms. The Pilot Training Wing was considered prime husband hunting ground for the local gentry looking to unload a likely daughter.

Such was the situation of Mister Sullivan, an upperclassman of the class of 1949 when he checked out an AT-6 on that Sunday in June. June in San Antonio is about like August in Missouri so the swimming season was well underway. Sullivan knew that his latest lady-love would be at "The Beach". "The Beach" was a sandy, man-made swimming area on the banks of Lake Mitchell just south of San Antonio.

The Lake that day was just crammed with the delightful nymphs, nymphets and water sprites of San Antonio including Sullivan's girlfriend. It was a perfect opportunity for some fancy didoes of one of the Cadet Corps' finest, Mister Sullivan. Sullivan began his aerobatic show with some barrel rolls then looped the loop. No one knows whether there were other items on his itinerary because the next thing he did was an illegal low pass over the beach — buzzing. Flying under 500 feet except for takeoff and landing is universally forbidden. He wanted, I suppose, to see if he could identify his girlfriend in the beach throng below. Upon pullout at under 100 feet he hit high tension wires and cartwheeled into the lake while cutting off power to much of south San Antonio — Sic Transit Gloria Mundi..

DESOLATION

On Thursday the 25th of August 1949 I soloed! I really felt I had a natural bent for flying and this seemed to confirm it. I was not the first but I was among the first dozen or so. When I walked away from that old T-6 to the Operations building for my report and to change clothes, I was right on top of the world. This euphoria continued as I walked back to the barracks to crow a little bit with my fellow students.

Fig. 14-3. Headquarters, Air Training Command, Randolph Field, Texas in 1949. This was the scene of my 'boarding out'.

The notice on the bulletin board hit me between the eyes!

It is said that he who the gods would destroy they first make proud. I was very proud that day.

The notice read in part: "...following cadets will report Base Surgery for modified Form 1 physical examination 0800 hrs Monday 29 August...Salmon, Richard L...."

"What the hell is this? Had I been caught? No, there were 10-12 guys on the list." I thought. Knowing full well that my right ear had not made the grade back at Pope Field I dreaded the tests. There would no way I could fake it here. No insider help. Where is old Major Horvath now? I spent the weekend mostly in my room. I didn't eat. I tried to rationalize — "Actually I hadn't been very much under the limits at Pope. Maybe I could fake it. Maybe they won't even do an audiometric after all why beat it to death?

The audiometric test involves a anechoic chamber (small insulated booth) and a headset. A tone of precise frequency and volume are transmitted by the technician to the headset. The subject holds down a button as long as he can hear the tone and releases it when he can no longer hear it. "Hell," I thought, "I can finesse this after all. I'll simply wait a second or so after I can no longer hear the tone to indicate I've lost it at a lower volume!"

But, this was all wishful thinking. While I could credibly fake hearing the tone after it had disappeared from the aural perception of my right ear—I could not anticipate the same point as the volume was slowly increased. I could see the test technician looking at the tapes. He looked at me with puzzlement and went for the Master Sergeant section head.

The old sergeant was under no illusions as to the seriousness of what he was looking at. He looked at me through bushy eyebrows as he contemplated the graphic results, "Mr. ..." he looked at my name tag... "Mr. Solomon, we seem to have some problems with your audiometric. Have you had recent trauma to your head or have you been target shooting or something like that? Are you taking any medication?"

"No, none of the above." I figure it is too late now to be lying my way through this. I had already thought out a fall-back' position. I would use the fact that I had demonstrated a better than average academic record and had in fact soloed last week well ahead of most of my class plus the fact that my hearing loss was only 10 db worse than standard. I thanked the sergeant for his concern.

He anticipated a plea from me to 'adjust' the graphic results... "I gotta send these results over just as I have plotted them. You understand that don't you?" Another look through the bushy eyebrows.

"Yes, sergeant. Do what you gotta do."

BOARDED

I met with the board two days later and pleaded for a waiver. I cited my academic record, my early soloing and my sincere desire to continue the program.

My pleas were not rejected out of hand. I was ordered to reappear the next day. At that meeting I could tell by the demeanor of the Board what their decision was — wash out! They expressed "...the appreciation of the USAF that I had made a brave try and sincere regrets that it was necessary to board me out. Your particular physical deficiency is not waiverable, etc., etc." I expected this and was steeled for it but I have never been so crushed. On the 5th of September I was on a bus rambling back to Bragg.

EPILOGUE - CADETS

In the years and decades that have passed since that day I have pondered on it many times. I tried to console myself via a 'sour grapes' rationale — "Hell," I told myself, " If I had graduated with that class (June 1950) I would have gone straight to Korea. If I had gotten my wishes I'd have been flying P51s on ground support missions just like the 1st Marine Fighter Wing I worked with at Koto-ri. Strafing and dive bombing is the most dangerous job in the Air Force. Better a live 'wash out' than a dead fighter pilot."

But to be very honest, none of this rationalizing ever worked. Ever after that day I considered my washout a loss like losing a basketball game! Since then, I won some and lost some, but no loss did I regret more than leaving Cadets!

SCARWAFED

Immediately on my return at Bragg I requested a meeting with the company commander, Captain Mabbett. I laid it all out for him and asked for an overseas assignment—anywhere. I just wanted to get the hell out of there and start over somewhere else. I really wasn't thinking very clearly when I volunteered for a SCARWAF assignment in the Far East.

SCARWAF stands for Special Category, Army with the Air Force. When the Air Force was new, there were a number of functions that were not a part of the conventional service and had to be furnished by the Army. Aviation Engineering was one of those. Aviation Engineers build, maintain, defend and, when necessary, destroy airfields.

On the 20th of September I departed for home leave and then for San Francisco and the Far East Air Force.

Fig. 14-4. Captain Eddie Rickenbacker with his SPAD in France in 1918. Eddie was America's number one ace with 26 planes. He was also one of my pulp fiction heroes.

Fig. 14-5. Lockheed's P-38 'Lightning'. It could climb higher and faster than the Japanese Zero.

Fig. 14-6. North American P-51 'Mustang'. When equipped with a Rolls Royce Merlin engine, it was the best fighter plane of WWII. Used in Korea by 1st Marine Ftr Wing, 4th (USAF) Ftr Wing and 51st (Texas Air Natl Gd) Ftr Wing.

Fig. 14-7. Shoulder patch - US Air Force.

Fig. 14-8. The F-15 Strike Eagle, first line fighter - Persian Gulf War.

Fig. 14-9. Pilot's Wings - my hopes went a-glimmering.

Lesson Learned: Better to try and fail than never try at all, but the pain of loss is there regardless.

Lolita, from her balcony: "Come on up, I geeve you something you never had before!" GI Joe: "It would have to be leprosy. I've had everything else!"

HAMILTON FIELD, SAN FRANCISCO

HAMILTON FIELD, IN NOVEMBER 1949, WAS very little changed from my first visit three years earlier enroute to the Marshall Islands. Then I was subjected to Air Force discipline (or lack of it) because I was flying to Kwajalein. Now I was among a large draft of senior non-commissioned officers headed for SCARWAF duty. SCARWAF units were Special Category, ARmy With Air Force.

Pre-embarkation was routine—except for one process. The immunization series, shots and vaccinations were a bit daunting. We were inoculated for—Tsutsugamushi Fever, Schistosomiasis, Japanese B Encephalitis, Cholera, Tetanus, Typhus, Typhoid, Yellow Jack, TB and Hemorrhagic Fever (early Ebola), What are we getting into here?!

BETROTHAL

I had been authorized a 'delay enroute' to Hamilton Field. Technically my leave address was with my mother in Pilot Grove. Actually I spent it mostly in Blackwater with Daisy. I was now a Staff Sergeant and was beginning to show, in Roy Corbin's (Daisy's father) eyes some potential for the future. At least he didn't set the dog on me. Actually, Ole Shep had departed for doggie heaven the year before and was now getting his dog biscuits from St. Peter.

Daisy and I had been dating for about two years now and we both thought we'd do best to formalize the arrangement. Admittedly, this was a rather dumb time to become engaged—just as I was leaving for an overseas tour. Actually, I was misled by my information on this tour. It was advertised as 12 months. Twelve months was the shortest of any Army overseas tour. It was considered a 'hardship' tour which simply meant that dependents could not accompany.

So we figured 12 months was OK to think out our future, save some money and marry upon my return around Christmas 1950. But, as the Scottish poet Robert Burns said, "The best laid plans of mice and men gang aft agley[1]!"

We, of course, had no inkling of what the next two years would bring and celebrated our engagement at places like Sedalia's Green Pastures, Howard County's Taylor's and Big Apple where adult beverages were sold.

I had visited a jeweler in Sedalia and plunked down $160 for a gen-yew-wine diamond engagement ring, then a cheap

Fig. 15-1. We passed under the Golden Gate Bridge enroute to the Far East.

magnifying glass such as to see the diamond[2]. Don't laugh. Remember the Big Mac Parity rule. $160 was a lot more money then than it is now. Although Ray Kroc had not yet spread the tentacles of the MacDonald Corporation to the entire world, a Big Mac-like burger could be had for about 50¢. Thus $160 would buy 320 Big Macs. That many Big Macs today would cost about $780. Still not a lot for a diamond engagement ring but not so paltry as $160.

Now that I had secured my logistic base in Blackwater and could be assured of a stable supply of cookies, Christmas fudge and even the makin's for pizza—I could relax and prepare to enjoy this upcoming chapter in My Most Excellent Adventure—Okinawa, the mysterious Orient and the inscrutable Orientals. The "pizza makin's" is a story I present for your amusement in the "Korea" Chapter.

A CRUISE IN THE PACIFIC

The USAT General WS Morton passed under the Golden Gate Bridge at 1000 hours 15th November 1949—a chilly, foggy morning. We were still within sight of the Golden Gate when the gentle Pacific swells began to sow seasickness among the landlubbers. Iron-gut Salmon was unfazed. As a

[1] Gang aft agley - Go often wrong. That Scots-talk.

[2] Just joking, actually the diamond could be seen with the naked eye.

matter of fact as we passed directly through the eye of a typhoon on the day before and the day after Thanksgiving—even though the poor old Morton rolled, pitched, wallowed and yawed— all but standing on her stern—I suffered not a whit. I will, however, admit to sneaking up on deck (forbidden during the storm) to get a breath of air the second and last day of the typhoon. There's just so much that one can endure of the fragrance of ripe socks; sweaty, unwashed bodies and unrestrained flatulence. Ultimately you have to revert to breathing that rare substance: fresh air.

I peeked out the hatch so as to be unobserved. Waves—50 feet crest to trough—were breaking over the bow. The wind was so high the rain came across the deck horizontally and slashed at your face. Anyone exposed on the main deck would probably be washed overboard. I was never so foolish as to venture out. This 14 day voyage to Okinawa was definitely not a pleasure cruise.

I've seen the 18th century plan layouts of slave ships. Our berthing arrangements were quite similar. To be fair, I must depart from the stereotype of military life. The food was pretty good and in ample quantities. I realized later possibly one of the reasons for the ample quantities was the presence of dozens of seasick soldiers. Spewing over the rail to feed the flying fish, they often declined to dine on greasy porkchops adorned with copious toppings of gravy. Though I would never claim they were of Pierre Franey or Paul Prudhomme class, the Navy messcooks were quite competent and conscientious. So in this category the USAT WS Morton was decidedly better than the slave ships.

Okinawa lies 6090 miles west of San Francisco at 26° 12' North latitude, 127° 54' East longitude. On Wednesday night 23rd November we crossed the International Date Line and observed a rare phenomenon of time and space. We went to bed on Wednesday night the 23rd and woke up to Friday 25th! Thanksgiving Day disappeared! This raised some consternation among the troops. They thought they were going to be done out of Thanksgiving dinner. They weren't. On Friday we sat down to fresh roast turkey with all the trimmings. More accurately, we stood up to dinner—the galley was a tight collection of gallery feeding tables on stanchions designed to be used standing up. This conserves space and encourages turnover—"...eat it and beat it, there ain't agonna be no floor show today!"

WELCOME TO OKINAWA!

On Tuesday, 29th November 1949 our ordeal ended. We docked at Naha Harbor, Okinawa. Greeting us on the wharf were some of the most bizarre sights I've ever seen. There was a gaggle of costumed Okinawan female dancers performing—I presume—some kind of native dance. It was sort of a discount version of a Hawaiian lei festooned greeting. These were some of the ugliest women we had ever seen and we had been at sea for weeks! To be fair to them, after a month or two, some of the troops began to think they were pretty cute!

The second shock was the convoy of vehicles that were to transport us off to our assigned units. There were about 30-40 trucks, mostly 6x6 'deuce-and-a-halfs', some ton-and-a-half weapons carriers and a few jeeps. All were in the most appalling shape! None of the 6x6s had a full canvas cover. Most were missing all or some of their racks. Half of the dual wheels were missing. All needed painting. The budget cutting knife of Mr. Johnson, Truman's esteemed new SECDEF, had gone to the bone here. I later learned that most of the units in the Far East were similarly devastated by Defense budget cuts. We were also to learn just over a half year later that these budget savings in Washington would be paid for in blood in Korea.

We jubilantly debarked from the Morton praying we'd never see her again. The ship's crew unloaded our baggage—for my part a duffel bag containing the totality of my worldly goods—by tossing them off the ship onto the wharf. Thankfully, I had nothing breakable. We retrieved our bags and were directed to the proper vehicle for 808th Engineer Aviation Battalion. Finally, as a fitting anti-climax to this Chinese fire drill—some overzealous MP stopped the entire convoy of 40 vehicles and ticketed each of the drivers for speeding. I thought, "This is not an auspicious beginning."

AN ISLAND HARD WON

What can I say about Okinawa? Okinawa, island (1950 pop. 822,458), 454 sq mi (1,176 sq km), 600 miles SW of Kyushu; part of Okinawa prefecture, Japan. Okinawa is the largest of the Ryukyu Islands. Naha is the largest city, chief port and ancient capital. In the Pacific war, Okinawa was the last major battle and the bloodiest. Here and in the surrounding waters, the Kamikaze attacks reached their crescendo following the invasion by Army and Marines on Easter Sunday 1st of April 1945. The kamikazi attacks were aimed at the mass of U.S. Navy vessels supporting the invasion. The Navy suffered more casualties in the battle for Okinawa than they had suffered in all previous actions combined from the Revolutionary War to the present.

The Island was finally secured on June 15th 1945. The Japanese lost 103,000 troops; U.S. casualties were 48,000. The Japanese commander, General Hirago had commanded all his troops as well as the island civilian population to fight to the death. There never was any mass surrender though the defenders were outnumbered three to one. Banzai suicide attacks were the final tactic and even civilians—including women and children—committed suicide by leaping off a 100 ft cliff near Naha to the rocks below. When I was at Kadena Air Base, 'Suicide Cliff' was one of the "tourist points of interest" for island tours. The bones had long since been removed but the imagination could provide the gruesome

Fig. 15-2. TSgt. Hachtmann, Sgt. Nicolai and SSgt. Salmon at the 'Coral Castle' - Spring 1950, before the feces hit the fan in Korea.

details.

This fanatical Japanese defense of Okinawa was one of the major contributors to Truman's atom bomb decision a few weeks later. Okinawa—the bloodiest of all the Pacific battles gave portents for the coming invasion of the Japanese Home Islands.

Sadly, a beloved reporter was one of the last casualties of the war. Ernie Pyle, a famous American WWII war correspondent was killed at the final skirmish on tiny Ie Shima isle just off Toguchi Harbor at the north end of the Island.

Lloyd McCreery, Pauline's somewhat eccentric second son was here in '45. He was one of my Pilot Grove High School comrades of the 1940's. He had enlisted in the USMC (Uncle Sam's Misguided Children) in 1944 in time to participate in the invasion and battle of Okinawa in April-June 1945. In the attack on the Shuri Castle line in central Okinawa he was severely wounded by Japanese shrapnel. For him that was the end of the war. He survived but carried pieces of shrapnel to his grave (he died in 1992). Sic Transit Gloria Mundi.

BUILDING FOR HEAVY BOMBERS

Based on Okinawa was an Engineer Aviation Group (931st) composed of two EA Battalions (802d and 808th), one EA Maintenance Company (919th) and an EA Group Headquarters. The 931st Group was far behind schedule on upgrading the giant airfield at Kadena, Okinawa to accomodate heavy bombers. The heavy bombers were of the 19th and 316th Heavy Bombardment Wings (B-29) of the 20th Air Force. These were of the type that dropped the 'big ones' on Hiroshima and Nagasaki.

The 931st problems derived directly from the draconian defense cuts that Truman's new Secretary of Defense, Louis Johnson[3] had imposed. Johnson's Scrooge-like parsimonious, frugal, close-fisted micromanagement of the military had not only failed to procure the materiel and get it to the right places—personnel management was badly SNAFUed as well. The 931st not only was short of materiel, it was short of personnel, particularly non-commissioned officers. Hence, the draft that left Oakland for Okinawa had so many sergeants, we were called the zebra farm.

I got sorted out to Company A of the 808th EAB and we were treated to an orientation lecture by Col. Worthington, later to be dubbed "Great White Father" in honor of his snowy white hair. The Colonel was a martinet of the first water. His inspection visits to my company billets after I had been repatriated from Camp Motobu taught me the fine art of dissembling. He once asked me how many light bulbs were in use in our barracks. He had no interest really. He just wanted an issue to badger me. I knew damned well that he didn't know so I immediately made up a number—"128 sir!"

We were discussing the "Great White Father" one night after he had initiated a construction project — a battalion stockade. He called it a 'morale improvement project'. Hachtmann volunteers, "His tendency to make improvements is merely a natural instinct inherited from his public-spirited ancestor, the man who dug the post holes on Mount Calvary!"

Both the 802d and 808th had long WWII records. Both battalion flags sported battle streamers from 10 Pacific campaigns—from the Solomon Islands to Biak, Alaska. At the orientation I found that my assignment would be Co. A which was building a radar site for the 20th Air Force's 529th Aircraft Control and Warning Squadron (AC&W). Further, while all the other Group construction projects were in or around Kadena Air Base (near the Group cantonment area), my company was 50 miles away at the island's northern extremity. The village of Toguchi on Motobu peninsula was as far away from Kadena—and civilization—as you could get.

"Civilization" in some back-of-beyond assignments—and Okinawa was certainly one of these—may simply mean a PX, a NCO Club, a movie theater, etc. Kadena had all these, Motobu had none.

CAMP MOTOBU

On Monday, 4th December 1949 our convoy of 4 deuce and a half trucks led by Lieutenant Allen in a jeep rolled out of the confines of Kadena Air Base and wended northward toward the Motobu Peninsula and Oku-San Mountain. The day was miserable with special miseries for those of us who had spent much of the weekend at the Coral Castle NCO Club. The gloomy skies and desultory rain added to the many commiserations we had received from the old heads. "That Camp Motobu is an absolute hell-hole! It's like a penal colony! Ya ever heard of Devil's Island?" were a few of the

[3] Johnson was a political crony of Truman's and took his cues from Harry. Harry had a great deal of contempt for the military born of his first hand observations in World War I. He was quoted as saying, "It is not against the law to be stupid. If it were, most of my generals would be in the penitentiary!"

comments. We were not looking forward with joy to Camp Motobu.

The sea coast road to Motobu had been built by the Japanese in the last century and little upgraded since. The 808th Engineers themselves had had to spend a month or more on the road the year before when the AC&W project started. Prior to their work the road was virtually impassable by heavy transport vehicles. Afterward it was passable with grave difficulty. It meandered from fishing village to fishing village, from pot hole to pot hole and washout to washout. The only pleasant relief in our back-of-a-truck vista was the ancient, deformed mugho pines hugging the rocky coastline and warped by centuries of sea breezes. They looked like products of a primitive but superb bonsai artist.

ARCHITECT: THREE LITTLE PIGS

Architecture in rural Okinawa owed a lot to the three little pigs—straw, sticks and bricks. Well, it wasn't really straw, the favored construction material for native huts was thatch. This was not the romantic and charming thatched roofs on exposed timber beam walls of rural England and Wales. On Okinawa, the entire hut is made of thatch and bears little of the fanciful reminiscences of Hawaii—

> "I wanna go back to my
> little grass shack in
> Kealakakua[4], Hawaii…"

This thatch is from the natural, endemic Kunai grass (also called elephant grass) of Pacific Islands. When Daisy and I lived in southern California, these grasses were being introduced as a part of the newly fashionable zerascaping (landscaping for ultra-dry, arid regions).

Three-little-pig style stick construction was used for animal enclosures. 3-4 ft faggots were woven with crude hemp into fences for pigs, goats and the odd chicken.

As for three-little-pig brick—there wasn't any, but prefecture and village offices were housed in native, hand-cut stone. Beginning at the time Okinawa was annexed to the Japanese Empire in the last century, patient stonemasons had been at work carving stone for public works with such exquisite precision that mortar was not needed. Bridges and road abutments also got this treatment which I observed later in North Korea.

The native thatched huts stepped up the hills rising from the sea. Northern Okinawa offered little in the way of arable land being mostly mountainous. The few tiny paddies—yams were a main crop—looked like a child's portion of a family garden plot.

Each thatched hut displayed an 'anti-goblin' screen, a 6 foot square panel of thatching that defended the front door. Mischevious kazi (evil spirits), were nearly omnipotent, they strangled babies in their cribs, they stole away the virginity of young women, they snuffed old men in their sleep. However, due to some ancient and strange rules, these kazi had to enter a house by advancing through the front door at an exact angle—precisely 90°—and, they could not penetrate a flimsy panel of thatching. Thus, an anti-goblin panel would keep you and your loved ones perfectly safe. Hey, don't ask me to explain this further, I am not of the Animist religious persuasion!

The weather and climate on Okinawa belies its low latitude. Latitudes around 25°-30° North in the Western Hemisphere cut through northern Mexico and the Baja Peninsula. Therefore Okinawa should have a pleasantly mild, sub-tropical climate, right? Wrong! True, it never snows or freezes, but the winters—rightly called the rainy season—make up in howling gales, cold and wet misery what they lack in snow and ice.

With the road-dictated slow pace and innumerable 'comfort' stops required for tortured kidneys, it took nearly ten hours to travel the 50 miles of our journey into exile. There's something about bouncing around in the back of a truck that greatly stimulates the bladder. Of course, some of us were still full of the beer that we had been advised to partake of deeply, "You guys ain't going to see civilization for a while, better drink up!"

The rain and clouds parted briefly as we passed Ie Shima Bay and looked out to the tiny island where Ernie Pyle had been killed 4 years earlier in the last skirmish of the last battle of World War II.

The road passes through the last village on our route—Toguchi. From Toguchi the main road continues on to Yontan Air Field. Yontan was scraped out in 1945 but only used a few weeks before the end of the war. We left the main road at Toguchi and began the ascent up Oku-San Mountain to Camp Motobu. We were now on a road that didn't exist until the 808th Engineers carved it out last year. It was extremely crude, narrow and one lane with an occasional lay-by to permit opposing traffic to pass.

Most importantly the road had a gradient of about 8-15%. Our heavily loaded trucks had to drop down to low range and then use the lowest gear—compound low. We no longer had to stop for bladder relief, we just got out and walked alongside.

We could see that the Okinawans were already taking advantage of the new road and had planted rice and sweet potatoes in tiny paddies alongside the right-of-way. But, any Okinawan with a cart on this road was fair game, Army traf-

[4] You will think Kealakakua less romantic when you know that Kealakakua Bay was where Captain Cook, commander of HMS Resolution and discoverer of the Hawaiian Islands, first set foot on Hawaii and the place where, later, he was clubbed to death by irate natives on Feb. 14, 1779.

Fig. 15-3. TSgt. Beauchesne, FSgt. Donoho, Sgt. Johnson and SSgt. Salmon during preparations for movement to Korea - August 1950.

fic would not stop for them and often forced them off the road or into a ditch.

Okinawa was not considered 'liberated' territory. The people were enemy citizens and were treated rather firmly. Okinawa had been a prefecture of Japan for over a century (and is again today). The primary language is Japanese and the currency is denominated in yen. On the positive side, we also soon learned that they brewed a mean saki!

Oku-San[5] Mountain—at about 4,000 feet —is the highest mountain on Okinawa. That's why the AC&W site was placed there, of course. That's not a particularly high mountain compared, let's say, with the Rockies—but it is high enough to have a micro-climate all its own, in a word—bad. Year around, a cover of low clouds and rain obscured the peak even though there were often winds so high as to be dangerous to traffic on the precarious access road. In the winter it was a cold, misty rain. In the summer it was hot, sticky fog that kept everything wet.

We finally pulled into the camp proper, a sprawling collection of Quonset huts huddled in a small plateau had been created by brute force (dynamite and bull dozers) just 100 feet beneath the peak. There were about 20 huts for troop housing, a larger Butler building for the combination messhall, orderly room (company headquarters) and day room (troop lounge) plus a 30 ft trailer that was the BOQ[6]—Lieutenant Pfaehler's quarters.

There was a tiny track that continued up the mountain to the peak where the radar itself would be installed. Radar effectiveness is unaffected by fog. This track ascended at a slope so steep that—I learned later—construction materials had to be put on skids and dragged up by a D8 bulldozer! So the radar site at the peak was an ordeal to reach, but on the rare clear day it was worth the effort. You had a view over the East China Sea that seemed to go to eternity. Some claimed they could see the Chinese mainland. This was pure baloney because it is over 400 miles to Chekiang, the nearest Chinese coastal Province.

The ten or so NCOs had a Quonset of our own. It had a concrete floor, steel ribs and corrugated metal roof but the interior was not completed and there was no heater. We completed the interior ourselves on weekends and evenings and scrounged a space heater to fight off the chilblains.

RAGTAG AND BOBTAIL

OK, so Camp Motobu fell well short of the opulence and comfort of Club Med. Physical facilities gave new meaning to the term 'Spartan'. However, the physical facilities were not the real problem. A year or more of neglect and bureaucratic snafus had created a demoralized, undisciplined mob that was supposed to be a unit in the United States Army. Ragtag and Bobtail. The mood among some of the troops was, "...it can't get any worse than this! Threaten me with courtmartial and the stockade? Don't make me laugh. The Kadena stockade is a resort compared with this!" And they were right.

There were no NCOs in the unit at Motobu—none, nada, niente! The 'Acting First Sergeant' was a 19 year old PFC! Platoon sergeants were all PFCs. Little got done. Discipline was a monumental problem. Imagine taking orders for hard, arduous and dangerous work from a youngster who didn't yet shave and knew nothing of what he was supposed to be doing. The food was awful. The ration truck brought in good material but the cooks stole it for the black market and screwed up what they did cook.

The Messhall problem was fortunately, one that got fixed very quickly. MSgt. Baxter, one of our 1949 'Zebra draft', immediately took charge and, returning the incompetent 'cooks' to construction duties, brought in some volunteers to train. He did most of the cooking himself for several weeks. The food quality and morale immediately improved. There was always much to complain about but chow was not one of them.

Morale improved but in general, discipline was still far from acceptable. On the morning of the day we arrived at Motobu, someone had fired a carbine. The bullet struck the BOQ just above the door as Lt. Pfaehler was entering it. A stupid accident or an attempted murder? This incident was never solved. Lt. Pfaehler was a very young—I'd say early 20s—he was of swarthy complexion and wore a little black moustache in a vain attempt to make himself look older. He had a pointed nose like an eagle beak and bulging eyes. Of course the undisciplined mob that was his company nicknamed him "Gooney Bird". I was in the Orderly Room talking with Donoho one morning. Lt. Pfaehler came in and sat

[5] Oku-San means 'old man' or 'old one' and is a term of respect in Japanese.

[6] BOQ - Bachelor Officers Quarters.

down at a nearby desk with some papers. Soon some jerk PFC came in and said something to Donoho. Donoho leaned forward cupping his ear, "I didn't hear that. What did you say?"

The jerk bellowed, "I said—I want to request a transfer and I asked for permission to speak to Lt. Gooneybird!" Pfaehler's face went red and Donoho for once was speechless. I didn't know what to think. Was this guy insulting an officer in the teeth of the First Sergeant? The First Sergeant who had introduced himself upon our arrival by rearranging the face of just such an insolent fellow? Well, unbelievably the stupid ass had just joined and had heard Pfaehler referred to as Gooneybird and actually thought that was his name! He just barely escaped losing some teeth. Needless to say, he didn't get a transfer.

As we were dismounting from our arduous, ten hour trek from Kadena there were a large number of the troops skulking about watching. We heard 'zebra farm' and other comments less complimentary. FSgt. Donoho jumped off the truck and grabbed one of the guys in front of the pack. "What's 'at you said?" Donoho snarled, "Lemme tell you SOBs somethin'." He began a tirade: "The only difference between you jackasses and a bag of dog turds is the bag!...Beginning right now you bastards are gonna be reintroduced to the United States Army..." He went on for about 15 minutes.

The poor dimwit that triggered this had the misfortune of being placed on the spot in front of his peers. He put on a brave front and made some inane comment. Donoho hit him on the nose so hard he was lifted off his feet and rolled into a ditch. He was holding his face and streaming blood as some of his mates helped him off to the barracks.

Personally, I have never held with the old army idea of a First Sergeant who was chosen on the basis of his ability to beat the living crap out of anyone in the company—all the old tough-guy Wallace Beery movies to the contrary. However, I had to admit that what Donoho did was justified. The company was almost completely out of control. AWOL, desertion and VD[7] rates were unbelievable. Complaints against the GIs from the Okinawans in Toguchi ranged from petty thievery to rape. We had to get a grip, fast.

Donoho was the guy to do it. Baxter M. Donoho had been All Army heavyweight boxing champion in the late 30s. He looked it although he was now beginning to go to seed. He was about 6 ft 2 inches and would weigh in at about 275 pounds. His hair was now beginning to gray and some flab was showing around the middle. But Donoho still had the aggressive spirit of a boxer.

He had killed an MP in a drunken brawl in Georgia in 1939 or 1940. Donoho explained himself, "The bastard hit me with his nightstick. It hurt like hell. I took it away from him and bashed his head in! Hell, I didn't mean to kill the sum-bitch but he shouldn't have hit me like that."

Convicted of manslaughter, he served two years at the US Army Disciplinary Barracks, Fort Leavenworth, Kansas. The war got him bailed out and he served with an aviation engineer battalion in Europe coming out of the WWII as a First Sergeant. Donoho was from Red Boiling Springs, Tennessee. Red Boiling Springs is in Appalachia. I've heard it said that some of the people of this region live so far back in the sticks, the hoot owls come down at night and rape the chickens. Many of the rabble that called themselves Company A also came from Appalachia. Donoho knew how to deal with them.

Donoho said, "You've probably seen some of these shotgun shacks up in the hollow. There'll be a derelict car up on blocks in the front yard and a refrigerator on the front porch. That's a status symbol in them parts. And all them hounds under the porch—well, they all got a bunch of dogs you see. Somebody has to do the brain work." No doubt about it, Donoho knew his hillbilly brethren. When this lot left Appalachia to enlist up in the army, the average IQ of the region went up 50 points.

The poster boy representing all these lamebrained dimwits—the Neanderthal—was Zeke Carpenter.

ZEKE CARPENTER - LIVING PROOF THAT THE NEANDERTHALS STILL DWELL AMONG US!

If you think that Neanderthal Man is just a boring exhibit in some dusty Museum of Natural History, you are wrong. Slope headed, hairy nostrilled, bushy browed, knuckle dragging Neanderthals dwell among us unto this very day. I offer Pvt. Zeke Carpenter as living proof.

Zeke Carpenter was a tall hulk of a man, about 23 years old, 190^{+} pounds, over 6 feet tall; wild black hair; yellow, rotting teeth projecting from his mouth in several directions and less than fastidious in his personal hygiene. His craggy brow shadowed pale blue eyes. A careful look into these eyes would clearly reveal—nobody home. Today this guy could make a fortune on daytime talk shows—Oprah or Sally Jessy Raphael—as a living fossil.

Zeke was a Neanderthal in both looks and mentality! The first time I saw him at Motobu Camp I thought some of the more bizarre misfits of Company A had somehow captured a mountain gorilla and haphazardly hung old pieces of army fatigue uniforms on him. Physically, he was comparable to one of Diane Fosse's mountain gorillas but intellectually he was too far below the gorilla's intelligence to be considered an equal.

[7] VD - Venereal Disease. This was before the era of political correctness when such disease became STD - socially transmitted diseases.

My first substantive contact with him was in my capacity as Sergeant of the Guard (I was sometimes called the 'High Sheriff of Motobu' during this period). Zeke had had an encounter with our tailor lady, an Okinawan civilian. Company A, being over 50 miles away from any normal logistical support, had had to cut a number of private deals with locals in Toguchi. Tailoring, mending clothing, sewing patches and stripes plus some ironing of Class A uniforms was one of these services. A local Okinawan woman had been contracted to do this—the Tailor Lady.

One morning Zeke, ostensibly with legitimate business, entered her Quonset shop. Now the Tailor Lady wasn't exactly a Miss Universe, actually she was a 40 something, short, of dark complexion, moon faced woman, perfectly competent in her work but not really a Dolly Dimple, if you catch my drift[8]. It was a mark of the intellect of this guy, that he was overcome by passion and attempted to grope her. She responded with a crushing blow to the back of his right hand with a pair of heavy tailoring shears.

The fracas attracted attention and I was summoned. There was the Tailor Lady jabbering a mile a minute to the camp interpreter who was trying to calm her down at the same time he was giving us dribs and drabs of what she was saying. Zeke was sitting on the floor holding his right hand while rocking to and fro in pain and swearing at her.

After I had interviewed Zeke and Tailor Lady and completed my incident report, we helped him to the First Aid hut—to be seen by our distinguished Medic and chancre mechanic, PFC Johnson. "Doc" Johnson bandaged his ham-sized fist and said he thought there might be some broken bones. Zeke was slated for the next ration run to Kadena Air Base and treatment at the Base Hospital. That came the next day.

At Kadena, Zeke was triaged to a very busy X-Ray lab. There he handed in his papers and the technician told him, "Stand right here with your chin on the rest and press your chest closely to the plate. Take a deep breath. Hold it!"

After his chest X-Ray Zeke finally speaks up, "But what about my hand?" He waves his bandaged right hand.

The technicians stopped short. "You stupid dolt, why didn't you tell me you were in here for an X-Ray of your hand? Okay, get back in here!" Embarrassed at his own screwup, he slapped Zeke's hand down on the X-Ray bed causing all the pain he thought he could get by with and repeated the process, this time on Zeke's hand.

Zeke had a fractured metacarpal of his right hand but was not admitted to the hospital. He had a huge, heavy cast formed around a metal cylinder like a flashlight battery in his right fist. He was then dismissed to his unit and ordered to remain at Company A's Kadena cantonment awaiting any further treatment necessary and disciplinary proceedings. He was placed on limited duty. This should have been the end of the story. But not for Zeke the Neanderthal!

Zeke violated his restriction to the Company area and went off to New Koza. New Koza was the Okinawan village nearest Kadena. Available there were all the things that are not provided in the Base Exchange or Government Issue—souvenir jackets, tailor-made clothing, shoemaker shoes, sake, Japanese beer and whiskey, wild women, etc.

After taking on a load of sake, Zeke proceeds to pick a fight with some black soldiers. He then cuts in his 'secret weapon'—the heavy-weighted cast on his right fist. He later assured us that he 'laid out some of those kuhroi haitei [black soldier][9] bastards!'

Apparently his Homo Erectus tactics won the brawl. The black soldiers left. They returned to their unit where one of them who had been particularly abused by Zeke's mace-like fist, snitched a loaded carbine from a guy who was supposed to be on guard duty. He returned with the carbine and after a short search located Zeke. Zeke was celebrating his triumph against his fellow US soldiers by seeking out the arms of a convenient Okinawan Honey-ko.

The black soldier confronts Zeke. Both were totally inebriated. They wrestled and flailed around drunkenly. Zeke grabbed the carbine. The black guy wrestled it back and tried to shoot him. He succeeded in hitting the girl. The bullet passed through her gluteus maximi, both her buns and exited without hitting the pelvis. No bone damage, but the medics later said, "You could have dropped a baseball in the exit wound." This occasioned much loss of blood and in the event the poor girl nearly bled to death.

All these events began to surface to the Air Police when Zeke comes staggering into the main gate of Kadena Air Base. His cast was broken and dangling. He had Honey-ko, bleeding like a slaughtered pig, wrapped in a GI blanket and, limp from loss of blood, thrown over his shoulder like a bag of grain. He was 'taking her to the hospital', so he said and had already had carried her about 3 miles! Either because of, or in spite of, Zeke's action—Honey-ko survived. She was treated at the base hospital, patched up and released.

Zeke went straight to the Base Stockade. He was tried a week later and got 3 months hard labor and loss of 2/3 pay. He didn't lose any stripes because he didn't have any. He also did not get the Undesirable Discharge that he was hoping for. The significance of this Zeke story was that these sorts of things were happening every two or three days.

[8] In point of fact Hachtmann said if he had a bulldog that ugly, he would shave his butt and make him walk backward.

[9] This incident occurred in January of 1950. The military services were not then integrated. Integration came via a Presidential Order from President Truman about 5-6 months later.

THE HIGH SHERIFF OF MOTOBU

My basic branch was Signal Corps and I was completely out of my element among these 'gravel agitators' as they called themselves. How the hell I ever got such a mis-assignment was one of the mysteries the army is full of. It only took a few days on site at Camp Motobu to see that I really had nothing much to do. There were internal EE-8A telephones served by a Signal Corps Switchboard BD-72. The Orderly Room was connected to Lt. Pfaehler's quarters, the messhall and the motor pool. There were no external lines. We could not telephone our Battalion at Kadena. There was an ANGRC-9 radio at the radar site peak and the one code operator sent urgent messages to Battalion via Morse Code. This pittance of a communications facility could easily be managed by a trained chimpanzee and hardly required a Staff Sergeant graduate of the prestigious Central Signal Corps School!

I answered Lieutenant Pfaehler's call one day. "Sergeant, you don't have a lot to do, do you?" I admitted as much thinking he had it in mind to return me back to Kadena and civilization. "Well, how would you like to be Sergeant of the Guard?"

Guard duty is a roster duty, an extra duty assigned in rotation like Kitchen Police. Everyone has to do these crappy details some time or another. I said, "Well, of course. If it is my turn, I expect to pull my weight."

"No," says Pfaehler, "I mean on a permanent basis, sort of a High Sheriff thing." Well, I did not want to do that but, as I've said before—I was a soldier then, and young.

I didn't get a star but I got a US Army .45 Colt ACP M1911A3 pistol which was the badge of office. For the next three months I was the High Sheriff of Motobu. Some of the perks were: a private jeep with driver, coffee and snacks at any hour in the messhall, drive off to Toguchi any time I felt like it, take tours of the north end of Okinawa at my leisure. While there was very little prestige or distinction attached to this office by the G I's—the Okinawans stood in great awe of the 'High Sheriff'.

On one of my reconnaissance sweeps I once saw a crowd on a side street in Toguchi. I approached out of pure curiosity. It was a match pitting a mongoose against a Habu with wild, high stakes betting. The Habu is a poisonous rice-field snake of the neuro-toxin, venomous cobra family. As I advanced, the locals opened up a path pulling the kids out of my way while bowing deferentially and smiling toothlessly. I got the same treatment whenever I dropped by the 'teahouse' for a cold Sapporo, I was never allowed to pay for it. By the way, the mongoose won. They always do. I won 100 yen—about 80¢.

TET DRAGON DANCE

It was on another one of my solitary sweeps to Toguchi that I saw Tet (Chinese New Year, winter of 1950) being celebrated with the traditional Dragon Dance. The giant paper maché dragon's head was trailed by 20-30 feet of tissue paper 'dragon' managed by wildly enthusiastic (and saki lubricated) young men. It was a magnificent and dazzling display, but that aspect of the celebration that most sticks in my memory was the music.

It appeared that most of the island high school bands had been consolidated for this holiday. There were many western style musical instruments in evidence but most were unique to the orient.

Asian music to me seems to contain no concept of rhythm or tonal variation. The consolidated bands' rendition of the Dragon Dance music sounded for all the world like a truckload of wind chimes colliding with a mountainous stack of empty barrels during a bird call contest.

HOME MADE WHISKEY AFICIONADOES

I was again in Toguchi one Saturday when I stumbled onto a major bootlegging enterprise. Donoho had asked me to get him a bottle of saki to celebrate his first weekend off for many weeks. I came upon Cpl. Tug Rawls and Cpl. Robert Raper making a big whiskey deal. I saw them in the back of the saki shop with an old papa-san, gathered around a table talking animatedly. It is amazing how quickly a few key words of Japanese can be learned when there is some incentive.

Cpl. Robert Raper, the distinguished connoisseur of home-made whiskey (he was from the moonshine making parts of eastern Kentucky) was joined for the tasting by Cpl. Tug Rawls, the technical expert on pot stills and products therefrom. Rawls was from eastern Tennessee—from whose hills had poured forth that 'eau de vie', commonly called white lightning, which had fueled barn dances and shivarees since before the American Revolution.

Both of these guys were likable fellows and good soldiers. They were proof that the gene pools of eastern Tennessee and Kentucky had not all been polluted. They had been part of the 1949 Zebra draft, i.e., they had come over on the Morton with me. Raper was a muscular, well built, black headed fellow who had been in the 6th Ranger Battalion when it scaled the cliffs at Pont du Hoc on D-Day morning 6 years earlier. Apparently he had had some kind of disciplinary problem because he should have been a sergeant by now.

Rawls was shorter and heavier set—starting to run to a little fat. He was also somewhat of a yarn-spinner. You had to listen carefully to tell whether he was telling you something or pulling your leg. He liked his 'corn squeezins' and was an excellent raconteur in the frequent war story sessions that made for entertainment at the isolated camp. Most of his stories were of his adventures at Goose Bay, Labrador where he had served 18 months on a military construction project the first of a series of early warning radar stations looking over the pole at the Russkies. He was a heavy equipment operator and an expert power shovel man.

I walked back and joined them. I was not certain whether these proceedings were illegal or not. Army regulations prohibit virtually everything so although I was a little nervous about this, I decided to just play it through and make a judgement based on what transpired. Clearly, they saw nothing irregular about their deal. They made no attempt to hide what they were doing.

The ancient, wizened Okinawan whiskey executive (he looked 90 but was probably 40 something) handed each a tiny earthenware saki cup with a sample of his finest. Like a couple of French wine blenders or English tea tasters, they carefully sniffed the raw, rough rice whiskey, as though they were savoring the aromatic spirits. Then carefully and in unison they dumped it onto their palates to swished and gurgled it around. "You gotta get this stuff back there on those taste buds in the back of your tongue to fully appreciate the subtleties of the flavor." Rawls said, looking down his nose at me. It would then have been appropriate for them to spit the sample into a brass spittoon. Of course, they did not do so. They swallowed, made a bitter face, semi-retched and exclaimed, "Smoooooth! Nectar of the gods! We're gonna hafta have 10 or 12 cases of this stuff!"

The Okinawan papa-san who was watching their reactions carefully, now broke into a gap-toothed grin and bowed. "Ah so desu ka! Numbah one wisu-kee! Dai jobo! Jou case—jou nee case aru! Ima aru!" [Number 1 whiskey. I have 10 or 12 cases for immediate delivery.]

"Okay, Papa-san," says Tug, "Ikura dessuka? How much are you going to rob me for this sewer water?"

Papa-san gets his abacus and rattles the beads around a little, then announces, "Jou case [10 cases], jou ichi hyaku yen [1100 yen]." He holds up one finger. "Jou ichi hyaku yen." That was less than $10 US per case. A case was 12 bottles of about 24-28 oz. per bottle.

Tug says, "Okay, papa-san you got yerself a deal." He counted out a wad of Okinawan yen and tossed it on the table.

Papa-san gets out a piece of notepaper with Japanese hen scratchings on it. "You sign, Tugu-san." He poked the sheet at Tug.

"What in hell is he saying? What does he want?" I asked Tug.

"We know that this crap is just sake (rice wine) that someone has gotten the equipment to distill into a kind of rice wine brandy. It is really rough, tastes like turpentine, but we can't get nothin' better up here on Motobu. He can get us 10 or 12 cases immediately but for some reason I gotta sign for it. Apparently he is working for someone who doesn't trust him much."

Tug duly signed off for his consignment and handed the paper back. Papa-san pulled out a small, lipstick size rubber stamp, his 'han', put his chop on it and stuck it in his pocket.

He motioned to Zeke and Tug, "Koko kua... you come." They went out the back and soon were loading cases of homemade Okinawan whiskey in the back of the weapons carrier.

"Sarge," says Tug, grunting a case into the truck, "We're just grocery shopping for the guys in the barracks." We left it at that and nothing further was heard about it.

SPEAKO BOOKS

In this period of my assignment as Sergeant of the Guard, I dealt a great deal with the civil authorities of Toguchi, collecting miscreants in jail, compensating saki bars for the excesses of drunk G-Is, etc. On the north end of the island, having only minor contact with the Americans, the natives had very little English. I had to learn some Japanese. I did this mostly the way a child learns his 'mother' tongue—by listening to Japanese speakers and trying to emulate their dialect and tone.

I had some help from a 19th century English missionary, the Rt. Rev. Hepburn who, after Perry opened up Japan to international trade in 1854, set about trying to make this language translatable. His gift to posterity was a method called Hepburn spelling. It is still used. He broke down Japanese words into their elemental sounds and assembled a series of pronounceable syllables that replicated the word. Hepburn spelling is the basis of the U.S. Army's Japanese Language books. We called them 'Speako' books. These books were my textbooks for learning Japanese although the most efficient way was 'total immersion' amongst Japanese speakers.

I never attempted the written language. Written Japanese uses three types of characters, Kana, Katakana and Hirakanji all of which are pictogram-based (like Chinese, although they are not the same). A literate person would need to know 3-4,000 of these pictograms. For me—forget it! I studied the Speako books and listened to the old men in Toguchi and tried to mimic their accents. Months of this and I had a good grasp of spoken Japanese—or so I thought!

In 1950 on R & R in Tokyo (from Korea) I stayed at a hotel where most of the other guests were green troops straight from the States. Although a pidgin language[10] had evolved to satisfy most inter-language communications, these guys couldn't even do that much and I was dragooned as an interpreter. I was doing fine and getting the information that the rookies needed. However, every time I spoke in Japanese, the men would smile and the girls would titter. After the rookies were sent off I started to asked this woman what was so funny about my Japanese. Before I spoke she asked me, "Where you learn Japanese?"

"On Okinawa" was my reply.

Her face lighted up with the revelation and she said, "Ahhh sooo!"

Apparently I was speaking a sort of 'hill-billy' dialect of Japanese not held in high esteem in Tokyo. Sort of like a Louisiana Cajun escorting English tourists in New York City. It was ego deflating but I took solace in the fact that I had so accurately mimicked the Okinawans that I sounded like one.

POISON LOVE

New Year's Day 1950 was welcomed to Camp Motobu with a 50 pound cratering charge set off at precisely midnight. The F/Sgt and M/Sgt Hachtmann did the honors. I had been a little skeptical when they were assembling this bomb because they had already been partaking generously of some Real Scotch Whiskey. It was the Scots you know that first began making such a big deal out of New Years. "Hogmonay" it is called in Scotland. Donoho claimed direct descendancy from the Scottish Highlands. I don't think Hachtmann made any such claim.

I questioned their guzzling Scotch while assembling a bomb. Hachtmann looked at me bleary eyed, "Salmon, you must know—whiskey is necessary for a man so that now and then he can have a good opinion of hisself, hold hisself in high esteem undisturbed by the facts."

I said, "Hachtmann, in your case, self esteem might be defined as an erroneous appraisement."

About one week later we experienced another typhoon. This was the equivalent of Gloria that killed so many in 1945. Our huts were "typhoonized"[11] so we didn't worry about them blowing away but we had to barricade ourselves in the hut with sandbags at the end bulkheads. We had three days rations, water and a plentiful supply of likker. Unfortunately, we also had the 'benefit' of a phonograph owned by M/Sgt Charley Eaves, the Transport Sergeant. Eaves also had one (1) record—"Poison Love".

Now I have to tell you about this character Eaves. Charles E. Eaves was one of those people—everybody knows one—that did not have 'opinions'. He had Revealed Truths, The Gospel, The Orthodox Verity. Name the topic, and though he might know little or nothing about it, Eaves could hold forth for an hour, not with opinion, but with Revealed Truth. Like St. Paul's Epiphany on the road to Damascus—he received Revealed Truth. St. Peter had no *opinions* on the diety of Jesus he had Revealed Truth. In other words, Eaves was one of the most obnoxious bastards you ever would not chose to be confined with in a Quonset hut for 3 days in a typhoon.

THE WINDS

A howling, raging gale
Blowing off the China sea—
Worse by far than Gloria.
This is Typhoon Annie Lee.

The storm raged for three days. We sat on our bunks willing the roof to stay on and that no boulders would be dislodged from the peak above and crush us like worms. We could hear garbage cans being buffeted about all over the camp. We had strung lifelines to the latrine just 50 feet from our door. There was no option but to put on Sou'westers several times a day, get some help to pull sandbags away from the door, fight the door open and, grasping the life line with a vise grip, go do your daily duty. The downpour of rain was being driven horizontally by 90-120 mph winds. We took on a lot of water but kept it swept out, catching some with pans, boxes, helmets and messkits.

Eaves' bunk and his phonograph were right next to me and I simply could not escape the mournful caterwauling of his prize record: "Poison Love". On the second night, Donoho hit his limit. It must have been near midnight although it may have been noon—after days of being cooped up in this hut with only Suntory whiskey to kill the pain—night became indistinguishable from day.

About the 3,000th time Eaves played Poison Love—Donoho gets out of his sack and staggers down the aisle. Without a word he slaps the needle off the record—Screeeerup —grabs the record, throws it on the cement floor and jumps on it. Eaves, of course, was highly indignant at this boorish behavior and staggers to his feet. "Why, you sumbitch, argh showya ina Gawddamm goofsnuts!" and drunkenly swung at Donoho. Donoho brought a ham-sized fist up from the floor, caught him on the chin and laid him out.

Unfortunately, poor old Eaves' jaw was broken and in a few hours when the storm let up and things were somewhat more sober, Donoho and Hachtmann jeeped him down to the Kadena hospital.

Personally, I deplore violence except under certain cir-

[10] Example: Pure English - 'my friend'. Pure Japanese: 'anata wa no tomadachi', Pidgin: 'my tamadachi'. My best pidgin English story is from James Mitchener's "Return to Paradise". WWII American effect on the life of natives of Tulagi (Solomon Islands) led to this rendering of the story of the Crucifixion by a native minister: "Master he look down he see Picaninny belong Him in pain too much. He sing out, "Son, how's things?" Picaninny belong Him sing out, "O.K., Boss!'"

[11] To 'typhoonize' a hut, a concrete pad is poured for the floor with a 2 ft apron on all sides. Four eye bolts are set on each side. Into the eyebolts 1/2 inch steel cable is drawn over the corrugated steel roof and cinched tightly. Most of our huts survived 100 mph winds.

Fig. 15-4. After I returned to Kadena from Camp Motobu, I got so proficient at military para-legal work I could knock out a Special Court-Martial in one hour.The one I am working on here got Pvt. Billy G. Claire 6 months in the slammer. Sadly, I did the paperwork and served on the court-martial of a friend in Korea later. He was relieved to get 6 months at hard labor. Sleeping on guard duty in a combat zone is punishable by death!

cumstances. One of those acceptible circumstances is being serenading with Poison Love 3,000 times in a typhoon-barricaded Quonset hut.

COURT-MARTIAL MILL

By March 1950 with Donoho's iron grip on the company and with Lt. Allen spending more time at Motobu, the unit was beginning to shape up. A lot of the mis-fits were being boarded out, court-martialled or just slated for normal rotation. There were so many courtmartials in the mill that Lieutenant Allen and F/Sgt Donoho called me aside one day.

"How you likin' this High Sheriff job, Salmon," asked Donoho. This question was for Lt. Allen's benefit. I bunked in the same Quonset with Donoho and he knew damned well what I thought of it—not much! I said so.

Lt. Allen says, "Well, Top here said you didn't like it all that much. We've been talking and think you'd ought to go back to Kadena and be First Sergeant of the rear detachment. There were 6-12 guys back there working in supply, getting our construction materials forwarded, etc. There are also 10-20 transients back there at any given time on temporary business—sickcall, being boarded or courtmartialled—you name it. We need someone to get control of that loose tail and straighten things out. You know, kick butt and take names!"

Another sergeant who of necessity spent a lot of time at the Kadena rear-echelon was "Nick" Nicolai the Supply Sergeant. Nicolai was one of the breed that makes things work. He had the instincts of a ferret. Contrary to all the Army Regs on requisitioning and accounting for those myriads of items of supply that are a logistical nightmare but absolutely necessary for the welfare of the troops not to say the operations of a military unit, Nicolai had an informal network of friends in the supply pipeline. Other units languished for months awaiting critical items. We got resupplied overnight—nevermind that some items like lumber or cement which we had in surplus disappeared overnight.

What they were asking me was the equivalent of asking an inmate of Alcatraz if he would like a nice office job in downtown San Francisco! "I'm your man," I said hardly believing my good luck. I initially thought, "At last someone appreciates my sterling, soldierly qualities." That may have been true but another old adage also came to mind—"In the land of the blind, a one-eyed man is king!"

"Just one thing, Sergeant." the Lt. came back, "You'll have to help us with quite a number of courtmartials. We may be able to find some clerical help for you but you'll have a lot to do yourself."

So, when Spring returned with warm days and fair, apple blossoms filled the air, God was back in his heaven and justice and truth prevailed—I bade farewell and turned my back on the Institute for Incorrigible Young Offenders and Screwups—Camp Motobu on Oku-San Mountain. In the pines, in the pines—where the sun never shines. I was packed and on the ration truck for Kadena within the hour.

Lt. Allen was right on the courtmartials. He piled them on—I had a little help but did about half of them myself. I got to the point where he could give me a few details and I could have all the papers prepared for a special courtmartial in about 2 hours. It was Rough Justice perhaps but fair and from my personal experience with that rabble, richly deserved.

KING ROGER SIX EASY HOW

One of the recreations that I enjoyed at Kadena in my new found leisure was amateur radio. I had for years had the dream of getting an amateur radio operator license and surf the air waves. On Okinawa I finally did it.

For most the very difficult part of the examination was the Morse code requirement. You had to send and receive 5 words per minute. I had passed 25 words per minute at Crowder! Five WPM was a breeze.

You also had to draw an electrical schematic diagram of an acceptable 'push-pull' amplifier, a Colpitts oscillator, a testing 'bridge' and demonstrate knowledge of the regulations on use of the radio frequencies. I memorized all this and successfully passed the test under the auspices of the Signal Officer - Ryukyus Command. I was assigned the radio call letters KR6EH. This, in the phonetic alphabet of the

[12] ARRL - Amateur Radio Relay League, an association of radio 'hams'.

Fig. 15-5. My 'promotion' picture. I took this myself the night after I got my second rocker (TSgt). You can see I got the stripes sewed on within an hour. Okinawa - July 1950.

day, was KING ROGER SIX EASY HOW. Years later at Camp Carson I happened upon an ARRL[12] amateur radio operators listing. KR6EH was still in it!

Unlike CB Citizens' Band radio of a later age, the objective of most 'ham' operators was not to exchange information, although much of that was done of course. The primary objective was to make high quantity and high quality contacts or QSLs. Quality was measured by distance. My best 'QSL' was via Morse code with a ham operator in Santiago, Chile. Morse code, called CW mode, has a great advantage over voice in reaching out long distances. Though Chile is about 11,220 miles distant from Okinawa, that distance is all open ocean and transmission was particularly good at night. Of course, neither spoke the other's language so we could only exchange 'greetings and felicitations' via the Q codes.

Major Stephens, himself a 'ham', was impressed and enthusiastic about the ham radio station in general. We used an Army surplus SCR399 with a powerful 500 watt Hallicrafters Model 610 transmitter and a rhombic antenna. The fun ended when our attentions were diverted by war in Korea and I shortly thereafter discontinued the hobby. Farewell sweet youth!

Fig. 15-6. Cpl. Van De Venter, Sgt. Johnson, Cpl. Brewer and I. These guys were the first appointed gun crew for the M46 for our field exercise. They were drawn from 808th Battalion Hqs. I was the only one to go to Korea in 1950.

GOOD OLE BOY VISITS

In late July 1950 after the Korea War was under way but before we got our marching orders—who should pop into the Company A Orderly Room but my life long bosom pal, Homer Etson Jeffress Jr. now the First Mate on the SS Sea Serpent. The Serpent was a civilian vessel manned by the Merchant Marine of which Homer was a member. The Serpent happened to be in East Asia waters when the defecation hit the fan in Korea and was pressed into immediate service to move cargo from Okinawa to Japan.

Homer had had a couple of days shore leave while his ship was being loaded at Naha and came up to Kadena (20+ miles north) to see me. The jolly time we had is recounted below.

The reason for the diversion of his ship was interesting. But first a little background: After Okinawa fell in June 1945 it was the obvious place for the staging of men, munitions and equipment for the impending attack upon the Japanese home islands. By July 1945 it looked like England in the spring of 1944. The Tenth Army, the 24th Corps and a massive logistics organization were assembled there. They supervised the stockpiling of about 10,000 trucks, 15,000 jeeps, 200,000 artillery shells, 2,000 155 MM howitzers, etc.[13]. You get the idea. When atom bombs ended the war 30 days later, public opinion and political pressure forced the military to simply walk off and leave the guns and equipment for an army of 500,000 men. It sat there and rotted.

FROM THOSE WONDERFUL PEOPLE WHO BROUGHT YOU PEARL HARBOR!

Four years passed. Equipment stored in a subtropical climate for that long deteriorates badly. Now couple this with the fact that the 7th, 24th and 25th Infantry Divisions now in Korea had lost nearly everything they had in trying to stop the onslaught of the North Korean Army. There was desperate need for resupply and—guess what? Mitsubishi, the Japanese industrial giant who used to make Zeros, Zekes and Bettys allowed as how if Uncle Sam could bring this stuff up from Okinawa they would cannibalize it, make new parts where necessary and have everything up and running, good as new in a few weeks. And they did! Shipload after shipload of WWII 'war surplus' moved up from Okinawa. In 4-5 months all the supply dumps were emptied. I always think of this as the beginning of the industrial recovery of Japan. The Korea War was hell for us but an economic bonanza for the Japanese.

After Recall (the 530 PM bugle that signals the end of the work day), Homer and I dropped by my billets, I got 'dressed up' (added a khaki necktie and dusted off my low quarters) and we headed out for the Coral Castle.

The Coral Castle was a Non-Comms club for the 931st Engineer Aviation Group and was walking distance from the billets. It was a hot day and there were some cold adult beverages waiting at the end of our trek, so we stepped off gaily down the dusty road, heel by heel and toe by toe.

We rounded a hillock to see the Coral Castle sitting in a commanding position on a hillside opposite. There was a giant billboard-like sign proclaiming:

The Coral Castle
Non-Commissioned Officers' Club
931st Engineer Aviation Group
802nd Engineer Aviation Battalion
808 th Engineer Aviation Battalion
919th Engineer Aviation Maintenance Company

Homer put out his hand to stop me, "What in hell are those things below the Club?"

I followed his pointing finger. "Those are tombs, Okinawan tombs", I answered. "The Okinawans are mostly Animists. They also worship their ancestors and will bankrupt the family to build those massive, white stone tombs into natural hillsides like you see there. You'll see them all over the island. They raised all kinds of hell when the Group built the NCO Club up there among them but the Colonel said we spent 48,000 casualties taking this island and we'll build wherever we damned well please! The main portion of my company, Company A, which is on the north end of Okinawa at Motobu found those tombs to be lifesavers. When a typhoon blew down all their buildings in 1948, the troops ran for the hills and lived in those tombs for 3-4 days."

We were now at the bottom of the steps winding up to the Club. "Good God", says Homer looking up the 2-300 steeply inclined steps. "They obviously want to separate out the guys who are really thirsty!"

"Homer, you'll just enjoy your drinks all the more", I said. "Let's go."

We were going to enjoy a luxurious meal here at my expense—steak and french fries. But first we had to cut the trail dust out of our whistles. I ordered a double scotch with water and Homer ordered white wine. The waiter looked at him puzzled. Then he looked at me. I shrugged my shoulders. The clientele of this place had tastes that run more to beer or rye whiskey—neat. Some guys at nearby tables looked at us suspiciously. Homer was in civvies. I was in uniform. No one could quite figure us out.

I saw the waiter talking to the bartender then go rummaging in the store room. He finally came out with a big wine jug. There were no wine glasses, so he brings Homer a small water glass and pours from the jug. Homer eyes it then takes a little sip. He made an awful face and asked, "Don't you have anything cold?" The waiter returns with my drink and couple extra ice cubes which he drops in the wine.

Homer swirls the ice around a bit then takes another taste. He says, "Sonny taste this crap would you? This is worse than bilge water!"

"Thank you very much, Homer, I really don't care to taste it. Actually they're all thinking you are some kind of tooty frooty ordering white wine, but I'll ask our waiter if he can find something better." I signalled the waiter who was placing our steak orders.

The waiter approached glowering. Homer said, "Is this your best white wine? This stuff is atrocious. Don't you keep some decent wine in stock?"

The waiter leaned over the table to face Homer directly and said in a low growl, "Sirrr, the war wasn't won on white wine!"

Anyway the steaks were quite good and before we departed we visited the 'Class 6' stores and bought a bottle of Haig and Haig Pinchbottle scotch and a bottle of Moët et Chandon champagne. We had a weekend coming up and, without transportation, nothing much to do. I figured we would continue catching up on events of the past 4-5 years and have some French 75s[14].

We finished off both bottles on Saturday night and Sunday morning. We went to a messhall breakfast on Sunday morning late and I remarked to Homer, "Amazing thing about that Pinch and champagne—no hangover!" And it was true.

Five years later when I was enrolled at Missouri University - Columbia. Daisy, little Rick and I were living at the Taylor's place in Boonville (across from Temple-Stephens). Homer had taken a new job with National Cash Register. One Saturday he passed through Boonville on his way to training in St. Louis. I had prepared for his overnight stay by tapping our meager purse for— you guessed it—a bottle of Pinch and a bottle of Moët et Chandon.

Sitting in our modest living room with Highway 40 traf-

[13] When I was at Motobu I jeeped out to the Motobu Airfield one morning. The landing strips were still there from WWII but most of the field was used to store 500 pound General Purpose bombs. I drove for miles and saw nothing but bombs. Stacked 10 deep, they covered about one square mile.

[14] I called my own concoction a French 75. In retrospect I realize it was not. It was two parts champagne and one part scotch. Anyway, it had a kick like a French 75! Try it.

fic rumbling by outside, we recreated that long ago night on Okinawa, telling war stories and again polished off both bottles.

Sunday morning Daisy cooked up a delicious breakfast featuring a batch of pancakes, bacon and eggs. Homer comes in and sits facing me. He looks up at me through eyes so bloodshot I thought they were bleeding. He groans and said, "You know, Sonny, what I like about those French 75s—no hangover!" He choked down a few pancakes and departed for St. Louis. Apparently one's immunity to French 75s diminishes greatly over the years.

NEW BOOTS

By July 1950, the situation in Korea had deteriorated badly and the three infantry and one Marine Division were barely hanging on. I describe this war picture elsewhere. It was the motivation for the 'around-the-clock' operations of the Kadena heavy bombers. The Air Force had a precision, factory-like process for fuzing the 500 pounders and attaching fins and the three Heavy Bombardment Wings (B-29) operated like a mail delivery system. The carpet bombing of the Pusan perimeter was keeping our guys alive.

The chief of supply section noted people in the battalion street looking into the air. The North Koreans had no means of air attack on us but, we had been extremely edgy about the Chinese. We were an easy bomber run from the mainland.

We hurried out. A B-29 was flying low and slow, passing over the runway as if to land then turning for a leg over the Pacific Ocean then back again. We knew that the bombers had all returned from the regular morning bomb delivery run—what's wrong with this guy?

Sergeant Wells knew a guy in flight operations and confirmed our suspicions. "Can't get his wheels down!"

I suppose that in most cases policy would be to retract all wheels and come in for a belly landing. Always messy, but the crew had a good chance for survival and the aircraft, though damaged, could be saved.

Circumstances at Kadena made the decision more difficult. Bombs, 100 octane aviation gas, as well as the refueling and bomb arming facilities were jam-packed near the runways. More importantly, nearly two full wings of B-29s were parked on hard stands just off the runways.One screwup and a wing of B-29s could be lost.

The circling continued for half an hour then, obviously giving up on the wheel retraction mechanism, the crew began bailing out. I suppose the autopilot was set for a slow, steady course to the east and the crew began dropping out at about 10 second intervals.

We could see them plainly as they exited—a short plunge then a pop of the 'chute and a gentle drift to mother earth. All except the last guy out!

He came out wiggling and writhing and we thought he had hurt himself somehow on exiting the craft. As his downward velocity accelerated, everyone began holding their breath as they stared. "Pop that 'chute, you screwball! Why doesn't he jerk the rip cord?" Unlike the paratroopers' static line, crewmen departing their aircraft at 4,000 feet must open their own 'chute.

I was imagining the sickening thud as this guy hit the ground like an overripe watermelon tossed off a ten story building.

He dropped behind a building and we couldn't follow him anymore but no one saw a 'chute. It was not until 'Happy Hour' at the Club that night that we obtained 'closure'.

As I entered the front door, I saw a large group gathered around this runty looking sergeant-gunner. He was saying, "...after I paid $50 for these boots? You're nuts! They's a guy over at the BX that takes measurements and they hand make these suckers in the Philippines. Lookit that," he hikes his pant leg and lifted his leg to show off a beautiful, hand tooled, ornamented boot burnished to a high gloss. That there is water buffalo leather. You can't get nothing like that in the States!"

Answering another question, he said, "No, I didn't have my feet in 'em good. I knew when that 'chute popped, my boots would say bye-bye. I figgered I had time to get 'em worked back on but about 15 seconds after I popped my 'chute, I hit the ground."

"Naw, nothin' got hurt. I saved my butt *and* my boots!"

ORDERS FOR KOREA

The news of North Korea's attack on the South Korea on Sunday 25th June 1950 was all over the island within minutes. What would this mean to us? Will we be ordered up to Korea? What about the guys who are about to rotate off this overseas tour? Etc., etc. Of course no one had any answers that they were willing to share.

What we did not know but might have guessed: there was a fierce tug of war at MacArthur's Headquarters between 5th Air Force which was in charge of the Korea-Japan theatre of air operations and 20th Air Force which commanded air operations on Okinawa and was our boss. Fifth AF wanted all the Engineer Aviation troops brought to Korea immediately. There were not many good airfields in Korea and Japan was rather distant for fighter strikes. Of course, 20th AF argued that the two heavy bombardment wings (B29) operating off Kadena and at that very moment blasting hell out of the North Koreans at the Pusan perimeter[15] were also contributing to the war effort and the engineer troops were needed there.

The final solution, of which we would be notified shortly, was: 'One company brought up to full strength by drafts as necessary from other companies, would proceed as soon as possible to Korea'. The other troops would remain on Okinawa until the Kadena Heavy Bomber fa-

Fig. 15-7. SSgt Salmon sitting on the Okinawan tomb in front of Battalion HQ - Spring 1950.

Fig. 15-10. SSgt. Ratto and the M46. Ratto was my driver and assistant weapons commander when we had a harrowing experience in Korea 5 months after this picture was taken (on Okinawa July 1950).

Fig. 15-8. One last field exercise before shoving off for Korea. That's me with the BAR.

cility was complete, they would then proceed to the war zone.

A few days later (late July) Company A, 808th EA Battalion was designated the lucky company. On 25th August we got specific orders. The company and its equipment loaded out on the Assault Transport USS McGoffin on Friday 8th September 1950. We were bound for Korea and the Inchon Landing scheduled for one week later—15th September 1950. Sayonara Okinawa!

Fig. 15-9. SSgt Merrill Swann and me at the Coral Castle on "K-Day, 25th June 1950.

> Lesson learned: Hang on to your war surplus. You may have to fight a war with it.

[15] By the way, a part of the immense amount of materiel that was being rushed to Japan and Korea by Homer's ship and others was the store of 500 pound GP bombs. These however were being delivered by the two heavy bomb wings from Kadena. During the crisis of the Pusan Perimeter when US troops were hanging on by their fingernails, there was a shuttle of B29s each carrying forty 500 pound bombs to carpet bomb the North Korean forces north of the Naktong River.

Fig. 15-11. These B29 "Superfortresses" of the 19th and 329th Hvy Bomb Wings operated off Kadena AB in Okinawa while the 316th Wing flew from Andersen AFB on Guam. Like a conveyor belt, they each lugged forty 500 pound GP bombs to Korea daily.

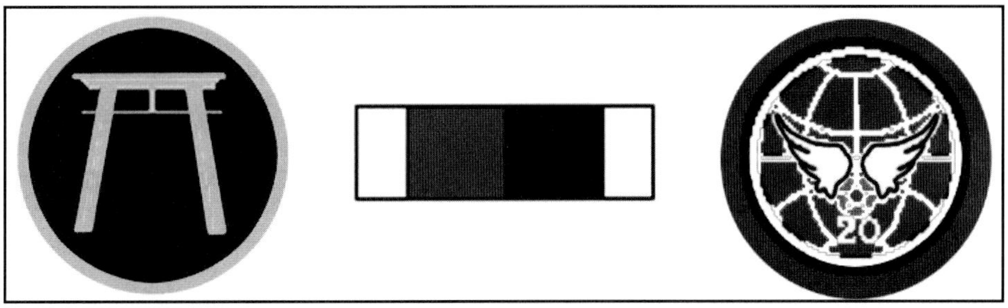

Fig. 15-12. Insignia Collection - Okinawa. LEFT - Ryukyus Command, CENTER - Occupation Ribbon, Japan, RIGHT - 20th Air Force.

"We ain't retreatin'. We are attacking to the rear!"
Colonel "Chesty Puller, 7th Marines

COMBAT BREAKFAST OFF INCH'ON

THE YELLOW SEA WAS APTLY NAMED. ON THAT cool, foggy morning, the water looked as though most of the topsoil of China had been converted to river silt and dumped into the sea. I was pleasantly surprised though, at the ultra calm of the ocean. No chops and the swells were only 2-3 feet. When I awoke in my hammock the past several nights, I could feel the vibration of the engines moving us ever northward otherwise I would have assumed we had heaved to. There was total absence of the usual wallowing heave, pitch, yaw and roll on the Assault Transport Magoffin (the Coughin' Magoffin) as we slid up the west coast of Korea. I was always surprised when I came out on deck and saw that we were making 20-25 knots, the bow throwing a bigger wave than any on the sea surface.

I had a few butterflies. The night before, Tuesday night 12th September 1950, some Magoffin crew members had come down to the troop compartment on C Deck. I heard them talking to MSgt Hachtmann. "Any yer guys know anything about the .30 cal. machine-gun?"

Hachtmann said, "Yeah, quite a number of guys do, but I'll be happy to help. What's the problem?" he asked.

"They ain't no problem really but we're getting the LCIs[1] prepared and none of the Cox'sns[2] knows crap about them there .30s in the ring mounts. Thought you army guys might be able to show us how they work."

Fig. 16-1. T/Sgt. Richard Salmon on board US Assault Transport MacGoffin in the Yellow Sea headed for Inch'on - September 1950.

Fig. 16-2. Flag of the Republic of Korea (South Korea). The Koreans call their country "Chosin - Land of the Morning Calm." We had other names for it.

Hachtmann went off with them and I asked Top, "These guys are going to take us in to a hostile landing in a couple of days, and they don't even know how their guns work?"

Each LCI had one M1918A6 .30 Caliber Browning machine gun mounted in a ring mount in the forward part of the boat. These guns are used for bug spray—they 'sanitize' the shore line and beaches as the assault wave crosses the surf. The "sanitizing spray" was about 15,000 rounds of M1 Ball from the LCI machine guns. You don't have to be an expert shot to hose the beaches but it is nice to know how to load and fire these guns.

Donoho says, "Well, you've probably noticed these guys are all Naval Reservists. Did you ever see so many bald headed Seaman deuces? Imagine, a forty year old seamen second class!"

The landing plan, as I was best able to figure it out, was to initially land a company of Marines on Wolmi-do. Wolmi-do was a fortified island commanding the harbor at Inch'on. When the island was secured, the main force, most of the 1st Marine Division would go ashore in AMTRACs and secure the port areas.

"AMTRAC" is an acronym for Amphibious Tractor. This beach assault vehicle was born as a solution to the bloody problems exemplified by Marine assaults on Tarawa and Tinian. Those beaches had gently sloping sea approaches that grounded the LCIs while they were still nearly a mile

Fig. 16-3. Marine AMTRACs at Inch'on.

[1] LCI - Landing Craft, Infantry
[2] Cox'sn - small boat driver.

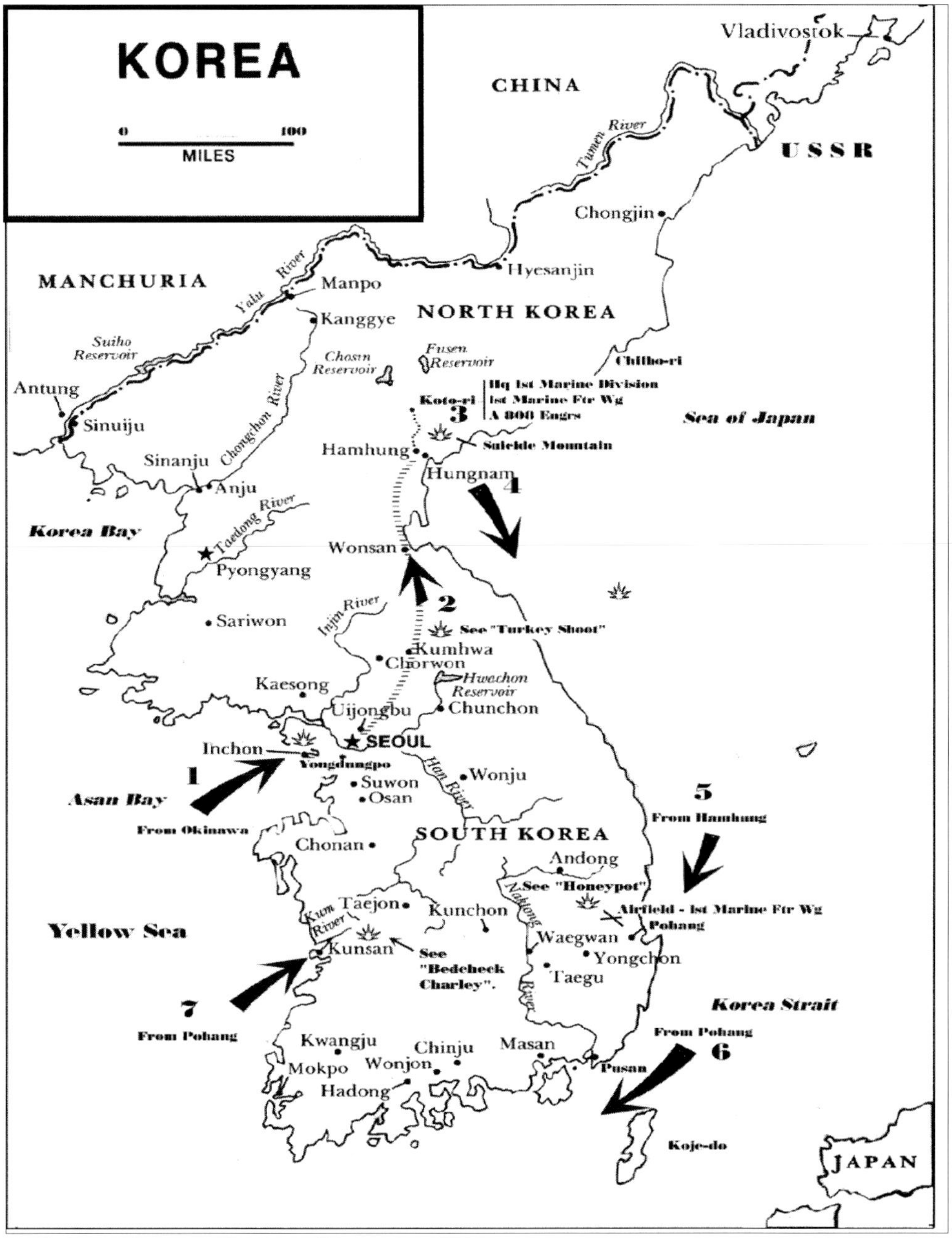

Fig. 16-4. A summary of my adventures in Korea 1950-1951.
1. Landing at Inch'on 0400 Friday 15 Sep 1950.
2. October 1950 - Built the track for the 'Chosen Choo-Choo'; Turkey Shoot.
3. December 1950 - Shootout at Suicide Mountain.
4. 15 December 1950 - Escape by sea.
5. 18 December 1951 - Land at Pohang.
6. 9 August 1951 - Depart Pohang for a trip "around the horn".
7. 15 August 1951 - Rejoin Battalion at Kunsan.

Fig. 16-5. Climbing down the cargo net to the LCI below. Assault on Inch'on -15 Sep 1950.

from shore. When the front landing ramps disgorged the first waves, Japanese Nambu machine guns raked the open craft and the troops sluggishly wading in waist high water a half mile from shore.

The AMTRACs, when combat loaded, had little free board. Gunwales were within 24 inches of calm waters and even a moderate sea would threaten to swamp the boat. But they had some protective armor and most importantly, they wallowed through the surf onto the beach and put the Marines ashore "with their feet dry." And, fortunately, the surface of the Yellow Sea this day was as placid as a farm pond.

These AMTRACs were the only new equipment I saw in Korea. This was America's first war supplied out of a national collection of Lon Judy's War Surplus Stores.

Other units such as ours would go ashore in LCIs a lá Normandy D-Day. Our heavy engineering equipment would then be landed and we would head for Yongdungpo, the western industrial section of Seoul. (Seoul was and is the capitol of Korea and had been lost and recaptured three times.)

Depending on how the fighting near Soeul went we would probably then stand at the call of the lst Marine Fighter Wing which was supporting the 1st Marine Division.

A complicating factor in the follow-up logistics of this landing were the tides around Wolmi-do. They were some of the highest in the world—30-35 feet ebb to flood. We would land on the high tide but when it went out and the sea dropped 35 feet, 4-5 miles of mud flats would be uncovered and there could be no resupply until the next high tide. That would be the next day.

The real slush ice in the kidneys came from contemplating the assault landing itself. The troops — and Colonel Robertson told me once that, "Nobody is smarter than a hundred GI's"—were assessing the tactical situation with all the facts available plus similar historical events. At Inch'on the facts were:

• We would land at high tide in an area that had the highest tides on earth.

• Once landed, those tides would prohibit us being reinforced, resupplied, evacuated or getting seaborne assistance before the next high tide.

• Most of the naval task force was composed of 'retreaded' Naval Reservists whom—as we had just discovered—didn't know how to load and fire their machinegun, had never done a landing and only barely knew how to operate the landing craft.

• The historical model—the most recent comparable event at that time—was the D-Day landings on Omaha Beach.

• Fact from Omaha Beach: There were 4,000 casualties the first day.

Of course, in retrospect—casualties were low and the sphincter tightening seems laughable now. But, there was very little laughing on that Friday morning 15th September 1950.

On Thursday night the 14th, the Marines attacked Wolmi-do. Most of our guys stayed up that night and we learned at about midnight that the island had fallen. There had been little resistance and the way seem clear for our landing in the morning. At 3AM the Top Sergeant circulated around C Deck to wake up the troops, but we were already awake. I hurried top side to look at the sea. We were stopped now, heaved to and dead in the water, standing about 10 miles off Inch'on well out of artillery range. I went to breakfast.

Some of the guys didn't have much appetite, "I just cain't eat this Navy crap, Sarge!"

I reminded them: "Except for the rations in your packs this is your last meal for God knows how long — three days at least! Personally, I ate heartily but regretted it later.

MENU FOR A COMBAT BREAKFAST

USAT MacGoffin
Friday morning,
15th September 1950

Baked Beans
Powdered Eggs
Bacon
Creamed Hamburger
Toast
Pancakes
Corn Flakes
Reconstituted Milk
Reconstituted Orange Juice
Coffee

BON APPETITE!

At first light, while we were at breakfast, the Magoffin had pulled within 6-7 miles of shore and began launching the LCIs. After breakfast we saddled up as the Coxs'ns brought the boats under the cargo nets to receive the troops. Final instructions were bellowed by Navy crew. "Put your feet on the laterals and hold get a good hand hold on the verticals. If you don't do it like we say, someone will step on your hands and you'll end up in the Yellow Sea!" See Fig. 16-5. for an example of the exercise on the "monkey ropes". One hundred twenty pounds of field pack, weapons and ammo added to the challenge and fun.

Each one of us had a full field pack with C rations for 3 days, 200 rounds of ammunition, two grenades, rifle with bayonet and gas mask. See Fig. 16-6. I reckoned the camouflage netted steel pots topped me off at about 120 pounds and I carried a carbine. Pfc. George Brunnel had all the same stuff and in addition he carried a Browning Automatic Rifle! Without regard to any weapons proficiency, the BARs were almost always assigned to the biggest guy in the platoon. The guys with size 20 neck and size 5 hat. Brunnel would dress out at about 280 pounds and had the build of a silverback lowland gorilla with an IQ to match.

He was commiserating with Hachtmann as we were awaiting boarding orders, "Sarnt Hachtmann I make just too damned big a target. I think I oughter go in on the last wave. Ya gotta pertect this BAR."

Hachtmann, busy taping his allotted two grenades to his suspenders says, "Brunnel, I grant you you're as broad as an M24 tank, but them gooks could shoot you 6-7 times without hitting anything important! You go first wave. That's final. We need your BAR up front."

As I went over the side and began climbing down the net I thought, "With 120 pounds on my back and those two pounds of baked beans in my gut—if I fall, I'd go straight to the bottom of the Yellow Sea — forever.

Thank God, the sea was very calm and there was only a minor amount of bobbing about of the LCIs. Still, some poor joker managed to fall. Fortunately, he fell into the boat and wasn't hurt badly. As the boats were filled, they circled continuously in Navy assault landing fashion to prevent enemy shore gunners getting a bead on them. Someone said, "...also to test for seasick tendencies."

Fig. 16-6. This is me the day before we left Okinawa. The 'full battle dress' was about the same at Inch'on except, at Inch'on I also had two M-1 grenades, 200 rounds of ammo and 3 days C rations.

The Marine assault wave had been landing for an hour beginning before dawn. As we got closer in and could see the sea wall more clearly, it seemed unusually quiet. This scared us about as much as if all hell were breaking loose. We all thought, "They're just waiting 'til we all get within range. Crouching on the floor of the boat, everyone tried to find a position to relieve the dead burden on their backs. Some of the more vulnerable were beginning to look a bit green around the gills. There were probably a lot of silent prayers. I personally prayed I would not puke on the back of Cpl. Brumley's neck.

Finally, the bow door dropped and we began wading the last 40-50 yards to the sea wall a few hours after the Marines. There was no serious seasickness and more importantly, I didn't hear a hostile shot fired, not close anyway. After our landing craft had 'sanitized' the beach and near shore—the Navy crew had finally figured out how to use their machine guns—we received no return fire.

We proceeded in assault formation to the main port area, requisitioned a building near the wharf where we set up the Company CP. We milled around a little and, at dusk, set up a perimeter guard, ate cold C rations and bunked down—blankets on cement floor.

The next day we learned that the main fighting had moved to the Han river near Seoul. Our equipment and hold baggage would be unloaded that day and we would report to 1st Marine Fighter Wing for instructions. The Wing was operating from inside the Pusan perimeter (200 miles to our south and east) and it was not clear what we would be doing.

The only casualty I suffered was one bottle of Scotch. I had visited the Coral Castle's Class 6 stores the night before we shipped out of Naha and laid in two bottles of Haig and Haig Pinch. I thought I had packed them very well, wrapping all my clothing around them and placing them in center of my duffel bag. When our personal baggage was unloaded at Inch'on, the bastards simply tossed it overboard to the wharf below. A war atrocity! When I got to the baggage area

Fig. 16-7. Company A's artillery—TSgt Saylor's 60mm mortar.

these monkeys were standing around grinning. It smelled like a distillery. They thought that was funny! I did, however, save one bottle. It was to be my last and only booze for one year.

CHASING THE GOOKS TO THE YALU

At FECOM, MacArthur's Headquarters in Tokyo, there were staff battles going on through September. The 8th Army under the command of Lieutenant General Walton 'Bulldog' Walker constituted the main U.S. forces and they were on the western side of the Korea corderilla (mountain spine). General Ned Almond was beseeching MacArthur to give him the command. Walker never commanded much respect and confidence from the FECOM Headquarters. Almond may have contributed to this.

In the event, a new Corps was constituted—X Corps which would have responsibility for the eastern wing. This Corps would be composed of the 3rd and 7th Infantry (Army), 1st Marine Division and several ROK Divisions. The Marine Division would be withdrawn from Inch'on and go by sea to the east coast. They landed at Wonson on October 25th.

In the meantime, we did some work around the rail yards in Yongdungpo, cleared some mines along the river south of Seoul and mostly tried to kept from being sucked into some harebrained assignment by local commanders.

THE CHOSIN CHOO-CHOO

As the eastern wing, the ROK I & II Corps, began making headway in pushing north, it appeared that there would be some kind of seaborne attack north of the current line. Accordingly we got orders in early October to proceed by train to Wonsan. Some logistics magician had found a locomotive and enough flat cars to carry our heavy stuff and we placed the company in march order in the rail yards of northern Seoul on Saturday, 14th October.

The railroad wound north from Seoul through Uijongbu, Yonchon, Pyongang and Singosan to Wonsan 120 miles northeast. "Piece of cake! Be there in a couple of days!" we were assured.

Like hell! Easy on the map, but on the ground this little logistic move actually required 19 days and the troops were so beat up they had to take 2 days off to recuperate when we finally go to Hamhung.

The railroad had just been recaptured by the ROK forces and the logistics guys at Ascom City (a giant military supply dump that immediately sprang up between Yongdungpo and Inch'on) had no idea as to the viability of the track. It was not very viable. We had to rebuild it in a dozen places. The NKA had intentionally destroyed some parts as they retreated. The ROK had unintentionally destroyed some more when they called artillery fires on NKA units near the track. So it was one long agonizing railroad building exercise. Not like the Katy of my 1943 experience because we only needed to fix it enough to get our train through and to hell with anyone who followed us.

To add to all this torment, just outside Kumhwa a Major from the Military Advisor staff of ROKs II Corps wandered over to advise us of what appeared to be a bypassed NKA battalion that was apparently trying to exfiltrate back to the north. They were following a narrow valley north of the Hwachon Reservoir and approaching the track where we were working. We were about ten miles behind our own lines and not really in a mood to put up with this crap.

I conferred with Sergeant Saylor, the ex-25th Division mortar gunner. He and Hachtmann figured these guys probably would not attack. They were most likely weak from hunger, not heavily armed, carrying wounded and would probably prefer to bypass us.

This would be particularly true—we reasoned—if they thought we were a big, heavily armed unit, loaded for bear. We presented a plan to Captain Allen. We would get all the readily available automatic weapons assembled (some of the heavy .50s had been disassembled and crated). Using the available guns and Saylor's little 60mm mortar we would make such a Gawdawful noise they would be convinced we were a full battalion of infantry and just leave us the hell alone.

We got all the troops pulled off construction work and assembled a rough skirmish line by early afternoon. We were working on a bridge and the gulch and creek it spanned would be an obvious approach route for the NKA. An American advisor from one of the ROK Corps headquarters said that a large group of stragglers had been seen at a distance of about a mile. "That's close enough for us," says Captain Allen and designating individual fire zones, he shouted "Show 'em some fireworks!"

TURKEY SHOOT!

Although there was no panic, there was a little slush ice in the kidneys. The troops let loose with a mighty roar. The one thing that I'll always remember was Saylor and his loaders firing that little 60mm mortar. He claimed later, "I had nine rounds in the air[3] before the first one hit!" That's the kind of action you get out of highly motivated troops. Never mind that their motivation was to save their backsides.

Some of the first shots flushed out some large birds from under the bridge. I don't know what they were but they gave a name to this half hour of fireworks[4]. The troops called it ever after, "The October Turkey Shoot." But, believe me—an old turkey plucker—those birds were not turkeys.

After 20-30 minutes of this 'reconnaissance by fire' Captain Allen called a cease fire and we watched and listened intently for any evidence of the NKAs. There was none. I was reminded of the Duke of Wellington's words after a British volley at the Battle of Waterloo—"I don't know how the enemy will be affected by that but it sure scares hell out of me!"

UP THE MOUNTAIN TO KOTO-RI[5]

Our little toy train chugged into Hamhung on Thursday 2d November. We off-loaded the construction equipment and placed it in march order. After a necessary 48 hours of rest following the desperate rebuilding of the Seoul-Wonsan Railway, the remaining 25 miles were negotiated up the mountain track with bulldozers and power shovel on tank retrievers.

A cursory look around at the small dirt strip on the plateau near Koto-ri demonstrated why the Marines had demanded more help on the airfield. There were elements of two combat engineer battalions there—the 13th and the 185th, about 150 men in all, but airfield construction is not a normal combat engineer mission. They were not equipped as we were and had neither tools nor expertise in laying PSP

Fig. 16-8. This narrow mountain track near Koto-ri was was used by the Marines headed north to the Chosin Reservoir - October 1950. Two months later it was our escape route.

(Pierced Steel Planking) a common material used for tactical airfields.

There was one narrow turf runway lying among the rice paddies. There were no taxiways, no revetments, no servicing aprons. Fighters don't demand concrete runways, but since "Snuffy" Smith[6] had set up his CP (Command Post) at Koto-ri, he would be getting a lot of 'fly-in' visitors. Furthermore, the road from Hamhung was so bad, a facility for urgent air resupply as well as medical evac was badly needed.

There was need for a certain amount of grading and earth-moving. Paddies would need to be filled in—'so sorry Mr. Kim—we're sure you and your descendants will not mind working another five hundred years to restore your beautifully terraced rice fields.' We were just about to tear hell out of a picturesque, patchwork of paddies and dikes—the painstaking accrual of centuries of work and with an aesthetic effect quite pleasing to the eye.

The primary impact on the senses however was not the lovely green and black quilt-like rice paddy panorama. It was the overpowering stench. The only form of fertilizer used here, like all the rest of the orient, was euphemistically call 'night-soil'. The night soil was collected and placed in wells that we dubbed 'honey-pots'. After several months of fermentation, the E. Coli bacteria worked its magic and—voila—the ancient chemical process yielded up ammonium nitrate and other assorted natural plant nutrients. It was a prehistoric but very efficient process. But when the wind was just right, EWWW! Rice paddies—pleasing to the eye but not the nose!

I told Donoho at the "Club" one night, "We wanna make sure in any peace negotiations that come out of this—the Koreans have to keep this God-forsaken place. It seems that the total wealth of the nation consists of assorted piles of

[3] The 60mm mortar shell, like most mortar shells, has six fins with a powder increment between each fin. Firing 'charge 6' at a high angle would give a trajectory apogee in excess of 3,000 feet. He might indeed have had 9 rounds in the air at one time.

[4] I had never heard of anyone doing this until I read "We Were Soldiers Once, And Young" the story of the lst Cavalry at the Ia Drang Valley in Vietnam. The Cav often began the morning by firing every weapon they had at the surrounding jungle. They called it a "Mad Minute."

[5] The suffix "ri" means settlement, village or town. Koto-ri is sometimes referred to as "Koto".

[6] 1st Marine Division Commander.

manure!"

THE ROCKER CLUB

October and early November brought periods of euphoria but also occasional unease. There was little fighting and 'home for Christmas' rumors were widespread. The work was not terribly hard—draining rice paddies and laying PSP runway augmentations. Life was settled enough that our senior non-comms created a 'Rocker' Club and used the mess hall after hours. 'Rocker' refers to rank insignia, i.e., membership required at least one 'rocker' (Staff Sergeant).

Such clubs usually feature booze or at least a small ration of beer. There was none available in Koto-ri. Instead, Baxter (Mess Sergeant) had a perpetual pot of hot, black, GI coffee and, on rare occasions, was able to concoct a few doughnuts or cinnamon rolls.

Occasionally a Marine of the 1st Air Wing was allowed in for the bull sessions. One night someone told the story of our October 'Turkey Shoot'. Gunnery Sergeant Lopez was an ancient chicano or Indian at least 40 years old. His dark, leathery face looked like the hide off an elephant's ass that had been tanned too long. He was one of the apparently indestructible survivors of Iwo Jima, Okinawa and now six months of Korea. Intrigued by the tale, he asked, "But how many gooks did you kill?"

I answered, "Probably as many as they killed of us—none. That is, unless we scared some of them to death, in which case they would be just as dead as if we'd took the top of their head off with a .50 caliber burst."

This was not a very satisfactory response and Lopez continued, "Tell me, just what the hell is it that you aviation engineers do anyways?"

T/Sgt. Hachtmann who had spent nearly all of his 10 year career in aviation engineers recited the official mission of aviation engineers: to "...secure, construct, defend and when necessary—destroy airfields". That's our mission right out of the book." He peered at Lopez combatively, "What's your's?"

"Hell, I don't know if we got any such fancy words. I just remember what the Marine Recruitin' Sergeant told me in 1942, 'Join the Marines. See the world. Meet interesting people and kill 'em!"

Hachtmann rejoins, "Well, that's why I joined the Army in '42. What other job lets you drive tanks through brick walls and kill foreigners?"

THANKSGIVING AT KOTO-RI[7]

Friday, 24th November 1950 (Day after Thanksgiving)

The wintry winds howled down from the 'roof of the world' — Manchuria. They strafed us with blasts so cold and dry they could freeze and crack exposed skin. Although Koto-ri lies on the 40th parallel of latitude—only one degree north of Kansas City, Missouri—the winter climate is much more severe. This is partly because of the 4,000 ft. altitude but mostly because of the winter storms that came swooping down from Siberia like wolves upon the sheepfold. By early November, winter had closed in with an accumulation of 8-10 inches of snow and temperatures often below zero Fahrenheit.

Thanksgiving had come and gone with no great elation on the part of the troops. The hot meal rationed out to the elements of our Company A, 808 Engineer Aviation Battalion actually included some turkey and was a decided improvement over the cold C and K rations that we had dined on the past several weeks.

But we are now back to fine dining on C rations and I'd swear some of these cans were left over from Eisenhower's 'Crusade in Europe'. Beanie Weenies was one of the favorites. At least you knew what it was. Some of those C Ration offerings looked like Kennel Ration dog chow and had a mummified brownie possibly left over from World War I.

The only problem with the Beanie Weenies is that they generated enough methane (natural gas) to heat our hooch for a week if only we could figure out how to capture and burn it.

Our company of engineers was spread out among a dozen abandoned Korean hooches in Koto-ri—the inhabitants having long since fled to relative safety in Hamhung. We were warming ourselves with improvised gasoline stoves—dangerous (we burned aviation gas because that's what was available). It was decidedly preferable to frostbite.

A pall of uncertainty hung in the air. On the 21st some of the spearhead elements of the 7th Division[8] had occupied Hyesanjin, a tiny village on the Yalu River[9]. In exultation some of the Americans had emulated Patton and Churchill at the Rhine in 1945—they urinated into the Yalu. If the Chinese were watching with binoculars from across the river—and I'm sure they were—I wonder what they thought? Our euphoria aside, the restraint of the Chinese was becoming very strange.

[7] James Michener wrote an excellent novella about Navy carrier fliers doing some close support work for the forces in North Korea. It was serialized in Life magazine and made into a movie—The Bridges at Toko-ri. Toko-ri is a fictional place. His model for Toko-ri?— Koto-ri! Get it? TOKO-RI = KOTO-RI!

[8] Ruby Ratje's first husband Paul was with the 7th Division and was lost in the subsequent Chinese attack. She later married Paul's brother Fred.

[9] The Yalu River is the international boundary with China (Manchuria).

MacArthur had promised that the troops would be home for Christmas and this seemed to be confirmed by the seeming lack of any concentrated effort to get winter clothing and cold weather gear to X Corps.

The main US fighting elements of X Corps were the 1st Marine Division with its organic 1st Marine Fighter Wing (whom we were supporting), the 3rd US Army Infantry Division and the 7th Infantry Division. Of these, the 5th and 7th Marine Regiments were in contact with some remnants of the North Korean Army near the Chosin Reservoir north of Hagaru, but there was little activity elsewhere. It was quiet, but it was an ominous quiet.

In the third week of November the logistics dam broke and the winter gear flooded in. We were happy to see the down-filled sleeping bags, arctic parkas, long underwear, gloves, etc. Someone remarked, accurately, that it was cold enough to freeze the appendages off a brass monkey. But the issue of these cold weather items seemed to added to the dread that maybe we wouldn't get out of this desolate, frozen hell-hole by Christmas after all.

Marguerite Higgins, a journalist on the New York Herald Tribune, produced notable reportage of World War II, also covered the war in Korea. She visited Koto-ri about the time the winter clothing arrived. She talked with one Marine who had just donned his new winter wardrobe. There he was bundled up like a Teddy Bear with 4-5 layers of winter clothing topped off by a fur lined parka. Trying for a human interest story, she chit-chatted with him then asked—"What's the biggest problem you have now?"

The Marine grunt thought for a moment, looked down at his new winter togs and answered, "Biggest problem I have is 6 inches of clothes and a 3 inch weenie!" I daresay this quote never made it to the Herald Tribune.

MacArthur had reassured his civilian bosses in Washington on October 15th that the CCF (Chinese Communist Forces) constituted not more than 60,000 men in Korea, probably less, and were showing no evidence of serious intervention. Wishful thinking!

THIRD CHINESE ROUTE ARMY[10]

That Friday night after Thanksgiving was cold and still. There was very little cloud cover, thus some illumination from a now waning gibbous moon. This was notable because the enemy had no air support and would rely on the cover of darkness to maneuver for attack. A full moon was usually bad news for him, good news for us. As I pulled my sleeping bag around my shoulders and settled down on the cold floor for a little sleep I could hear the Caterpillar D-8 Bulldozer idling in the motor pool. We always kept one D-8 idling overnight in case we couldn't get something started in the frozen mornings and had to jump start it by towing.

We were awakened at first light (about 0545) Saturday morning by the whoomp of artillery—it sounded like 105mm howitzers—1st Marine Division Artillery. The 105s have a very distinctive thump. The thumps were followed by a hellacious whistling and ringing of junk falling into our company area. I'd never heard the like—they were not short rounds (imagine, I thought at first, surviving this long to be killed by our own artillery). It was more like large tin cans falling on our roofs.

Sgt. Louby noted my startled look and explained, "I think them's expansion rings you hear Salmon. Them old 105s the Marines are using are World War II war surplus and have had 100,000 rounds or more through the tubes. Them tubes is wore slick—damned neart smooth bore." Noting my continued puzzled look, he went on. "They use these brass expansion rings ya see—look like a giant brass wedding bands. They pound them over the round. The ring catches what's left of the lands and grooves to give the shell a spin. It also cuts down on the blow-by. Without them it would be kinda like shooting a 22 bullet out of a 30 caliber rifle."

"Roger to all that Louby, but what worries me is this: If those expansion rings are falling on us, the artillery must be behind us! That is not exactly the way a civilized war should be conducted, is it? I don't believe it is in our contract to be in front of the artillery. What the hell you reckon is happening?" I asked. His smirk faded and a little apprehension showed on his face.

"Damn! You're right, Salmon!" he exclaimed, "I'm going to run up to the Orderly Room. Maybe Donoho knows what the hell is goin' on!"

As I said it is getting light now and we hear all the P51s revving up. The entire 1st Marine Air Wing is on a big time scramble! Before Louby could get up, Captain Allen burst in the door and orders: "Get all the troops up and stand by for orders. The whole damn Chinese army broke through last night."

Christ! We didn't even know they were in Korea! One regiment (about 2,000 Marines) had been ordered to advance to the Yalu and had run headlong into a Chinese Army of about 200,000 men at Mupyong just northwest of Hagaru. The Marines were quickly surrounded and the CG, 1st MarDiv was hastily assembling a strike force (Taskforce Drysdale) to extract them. The first of the P51s roared overhead for the Chosin Reservoir and their first strikes of what would be a long, long day.

I had occasion to go by the airfield later that day. All the 51s were committed. As they came back to refuel and rearm they were taxied to a revetment and a crew of Marine armorers swarmed over them.

[10] "Third Chinese Route Army" was a joking designation. The Communist "Third Chinese...", headed by Mao Tse Tung made the famous "Long March" into exile in the 1930s.

During WWII there had been a gradual escalation of armament for the fighters especially the P51 Mustang. From the two .30 calibre machine guns of the WWI Spads, early WWII U.S. fighters had four, then six guns. Then they found that .30 calibre rounds could spray a Messerschmitt and, unless a vital part was struck, the Me109 would fly home for supper. Messerschmitts had two 12mm (about .50 calibre) machine guns on the wings, but a 23mm (almost l inch) cannon in the prop spinner which fired explosive rounds.

The Air Force (and Marines) then upped the ante and Model H of the 51s was fitted with six wing-mounted machine guns. See Fig. 16-10. This model used the 1380 HP Packard[11] engine,

So, one of these Mustangs had 50% more firepower than our half-track-mounted M16 Quad .50.

I watched the armorer crews load one. There are slots on the top surfaces of the wings for gun access. Each gun has a channel where the ammo is laid to feed it. Each channel holds 324 rounds - 9 yards of disintegrating link-belted .50 Cal. ammo.

There is a common saying popular to this day, "...the whole nine yards" (meaning all... everything) derived from this ammo capacity. When 51s made 'fighter sweeps' in the last weeks of the war in Europe, worthwhile targets were beginning to be rather thin on the ground. If a pilot lucked out and found something to shoot at, he might be asked, "Did you shoot anything?"

He might reply, "The whole nine yards."

I was talking with one of the Marine armorers. He showed me the ammo channels and the gun-laying adjustments. He said the Air Force P51s were 'dog fighters'. Their guns were 'laid' such that the trajectories of the rounds converged at about 300 yards. That was about the optimum range for engaging enemy aircraft.

"These here guns," he showed me the adjustment screws, "are set to converge fires at 1,000 yards. That's because their targets are on the ground. Ya see, when they make a sweep, the gooks throw everything up in the air—machine gun fire, rifles, rocks, dirt, whatever. They tell me it looks like an Apache war dance. Our guys like to standoff a little bit from that so they commence firing not at 300 but at about 1000 yards."

The thought that was most on my mind though, was that if I had just been more lucky (less lucky?) at Randolph Field last year—I might be flying one of these 51s. Not with the Marines, of course, but with 5th Air Force who was also using them, e.g., 4th Fighter Wing, Kimpo and 37th Fighter Wing, Kunsan. My conclusion was that Somebody was watching over me!

It was evident within a few hours that the whole 3rd Chinese Route Army were attacking along a 100 mile front. Apparently the half-moon had given the CCF army enough light for their infiltration strategy but not enough for any significant detection by Allied Forces. This was the worst failure of intelligence since the attack on Pearl Harbor! I think X Corps was blinded by its own Pollyanna-ish view of the situation. 'The war is over!' 'The North Korean Army is utterly defeated.' They desperately wanted this to be true and were still saying it even as the long columns of gray quilted uniforms were silently padding down the dry stream beds and gullies between the widely separated US forward units.

There was a funny anecdote on the first reports of the massive Chinese incursion. A KATUSA[12] semi-English speaking soldier answered a phone call from General Chesty Puller Commander of the 5th Marines.

Gen. Puller: "We've heard you are receiving an attack by Chinese troops. How many would you estimate are on your battalion front?"

KATUSA: "Many".

Puller, sighing: "OK, but how many?"

KATUSA: "Many, many!"

Puller: "Dammit, get an American on this line!"

Marine Sergeant: "Sergeant Jones here sir."

Puller: "How many Chinese on your front sergeant?"

Sergeant: "They's a chamberpot full of 'em sir!"

Puller: "OK Sergeant. Thank God there's someone up there that can count."

Ned Almond and the X Corps staff floundered around for 3-4 days issuing conflicting orders and mostly spinning their wheels while the situation clarified near Hagaru. Finally, on 28th of November, X Corps faced up to reality. Almond realized we were very close to a disaster of epic proportions. X Corps asked for and got massive air support. By the time we were exiting the mountains, there were so many planes bombing, strafing and napalming the hill crests they needed a traffic cop. This continuous air attack plus the bitterly cold weather was so bad for the Chinese that some of them came down from the mountains to surrender to troops who were only interested in getting their butts the hell out of there.

It was during these frightening and uncertain days that I made a solemn vow to myself: If I were captured by the

[11] The WWII long range escort P-51s used a Rolls Royce Merlin engine. I don't know why the switch to the Packard.

[12] KATUSA - Korean Army Troops with US Army.

Fig. 16-9. That's me in the turret of an M-16 Quad .50.

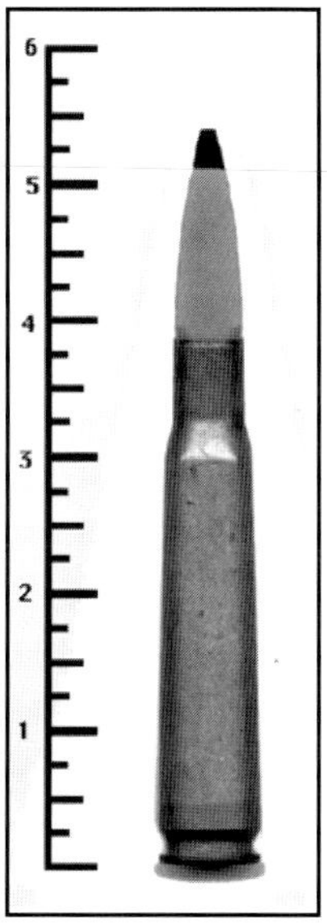

Fig. 16-11. .50 Cal. M-284 Ball, full metal jacket 260 grain machine gun round w/600 grain propellent charge.

Chinese and dragged off to Manchuria and 'durance vile', I would turn down no food that could be clearly identified as nonpoisonous and which held hope of possessing any nutrition whatsoever. This decision came from the following story.

On 20th October the 187th Airborne Regimental Combat Team (including some guys I had known at Ft. Bragg) parachuted onto Sukchon and Sunchon to cut off a fleeing North Korean POW train. The action was not a complete success but some prisoners were recovered. Some stories from these recovered American prisoners had spread by word of mouth: many Americans had died in captivity because they simply refused to eat the ghastly looking, unappetizing fare—seaweed (highly nutritious kelp); cold, gummy rice balls (high in protein), soybean curd (which is rich in protein and now favored by the sophisticates as tofu) and fish head soup (protein, minerals and vitamins).

My experience in coming out of Koto-ri set two basic philosophies that I follow to this day: 1. If hungry enough I will eat anything that doesn't try to eat me first, and 2. I will never again willingly sleep outdoors, on pointy rocks in subzero weather.

Our orders came on Sunday. Anticipating Gen. Almond's decision for an extensive withdrawal, X Corps staff had ordered all service troops including wounded and dead that could not be moved by air, out of Koto-ri. On Tuesday the 28th, Company A, 808th Engr. Avn. Bn. (our company) would depart Koto-ri following a small 'point' of Marines and clear the road south to Hamhung and its port city, Hungnam.

The M16 Quad .50 would be placed at the front of the

Fig. 16-10. 1st Marine Air Wing P-51H flying from airfield at Koto-ri.

serial one march order followed by the D-7 and D-8 bulldozers (on their transports, of course) to deal with roadblocks or ambushes. Saylor and his 'toy' 60 MM mortar would be near the rear and the heavy .50s would be equispaced in sandbagged dump trucks along the 100 vehicle serial to help deal with any flanking attack.

The battalion of Marines plus the combat engineers and our demolition squad (Sgt. Rawls and 2 other guys) would remain to defend 1st MARDIV CP until the last of the Marine infantry was extracted from the Chosin Reservoir area. Upon evacuation of the airfield, Rawls would blow it up.

THE WINDS - 1950

Shrieking down from icy Manchuria
Through the hooches of Koto-ri,
A frigid gale—froze silent bodies pale
They would not make it to the sea.

As I mentioned above, the role of Engineer Aviation Units is to "...secure, construct, defend and when necessary—destroy airfields". The 'defend' role gave us an antiaircraft as well as a heavy weapons section. The Mortar section commanded by my good friend TSgt. James P. Saylor, was composed of one 60 MM mortar and a crew of three—Gunner (Saylor) and two ammo loaders/bearers.

My 'normal' job with the Engineer Company was First Sergeant of the company's forward or rear echelon during our 'leap-frog' displacements. My 'battle assignment' was heavy weapons commander. The antiaircraft section weapons included five ancient .50 caliber M1918 water-cooled machine-guns which we mounted in dump trucks with sandbag ballast. They were so cumbersome as to be nearly useless. They made only a small contribution to our escape from the mountains of Koto-ri.

In the event, our premier weapon was an M16 Quad-50 electrically driven turret mounted in an M46[13] 'Motor Gun

[13] Many years later I learned this weapon was used in Vietnam. It was dubbed "Thor's Lawn Mower."

Fig. 16-12. Koto-ri Road heading south. 1st MARDIV escapes from Chosin Reservoir December 1950.

Carriage'. See Fig. 16-9. The 'M46' is a half-track with light armor (1/4 inch steel all around but no top). The M16 mounts four .50 caliber machine-guns in a turret with electrical traverse and elevation motors. The guns are Browning .50 caliber air cooled, recoil operated, M2, Heavy Barrel. Each gun fires about 450 rounds per minute—1800 rounds/minute from the turret. Disintegrating belt ammunition is auto-loaded from four, 500-round canisters which you can see in the picture. See Fig. 16-11. This round is about 5 inches long.

The M16 was designed as defence against strafing aircraft. The 'ring and radius' sights made it rather ineffective in that role except for throwing up a hail of lead that an attacking aircraft might (accidently) fly into. Antiaircraft effectiveness was moot anyway since we never had any trouble from enemy air. However, against personnel, targets for which it was not designed, we found the M16 in Korea to be devastating. The Chinese used a 'human wave' tactic to simply smother defenses by swarming masses of lightly armed infantry that could not be killed fast enough. The Quad .50 addressed this tactic very efficiently. In one minute it throws out 1,800 260 grain boattail, metal jacketed slugs at about 1,000 miles per hour. Anyone hit by just one of these will be explosively dismembered—with body parts returned to next of kin in a plastic bag.

DIARY OF THE ESCAPE FROM KOTO-RI

Mile 25 from Hamhung

1800 Hours Monday 27 November 1950

In preparation for our 0400 hour departure in the morning, Sergeant George Ratto, the driver of the M46 half track, was loading ammo boxes in the back. He opened one and pulled out four feet of the belt and studied it. "This is an antiaircraft belt," he announced. Ratto was a master at stating the obvious like it was an earth shattering discovery.

"Ratto," says I, "The quad-50 is an antiaircraft weapon. You would expect to find antiaircraft belts wouldn't you!"

All banter aside, we did have a concern: The Geneva Convention, attempting to make warfare slightly less barbarous, includes rules on ammunition. We knew for example that 'dum-dum' bullets were outlawed. Dum-dum bullets are soft nosed or hollow point bullets which expand on impact and cause horrible damage to human flesh. "Question Ratto: Are these antiaircraft belts legal under the Geneva Convention for use against troops?"

"OK," Ratto says, " Let's examine the facts. The sequencing of the belt is: 2 rounds of ball —black tips; 1 tracer—white tip; 1 armor piercing —blue tip; 1 incendiary—red tip and 1 armor piercing/incendiary—yellow tip. This six round cycle repeats throughout the belt."

I say, "It's the incendiary and tracer that bother me. You can see how this sequence would be OK against aircraft but—against troops?"

Ratto: "You heard what Cap'n Allen said about the Marines at Yudam-ni. I don't think any of those guys being massacred by the Chinese could care less about the Geneva Convention."

"Yeah," I said, "We're wasting time philosophizing about it. Anyway, I suspected those Chinese who are gonna be converted to cat meat by these antiaircraft rounds would not distinguish much between the M-33 ball and the M-17 white phosphorus (colloquially called WP or Willy Peter) tracer."

I had a final rationalization which made it OK: "There actually may be some redeeming medical value in these 'hot' rounds. Think about this: the tracer and incendiary rounds have a medically therapeutic effect since—while rearranging the flesh—they would at the same time close blood vessels by cauterizing them with 1200 degree burns."

Mile 24

0600 Hours Tuesday, 28 November 1950.

As a cold, gray dawn broke, the murky gray shadows behind us clarified into a long snaking column of vehicles.

This road had evolved over the centuries from a footpath to a cart track then a mostly one lane road with an occasion 'layby' to accommodate opposing traffic. There had been some improvements of the surface but not the geometrics. I heard one driver say a snake would break his back following this road.

It hugged the western slopes of 'our mountain'. The sheer rock face at our left hand rose above 100 feet at places and 'sheltered' us from the warming sun until nearly noon. But the rock face also sheltered us from Chinese enfilading fire from the heights above us—if they were up there. We were almost always in defilade and expected trouble, if it came, to be in the form of roadblocks.

Ratto was driving the M-46 half-track and I was standing up in the front seat watching as our 'elite' gun crew, Privates Incognito and Sanger in the back belting some .50 ammunition that they have failed to do before we left Koto-ri.

A Marine lieutenant had passed us in a jeep just as we turned left onto the MSR (Main Supply Route) that ran by Koto-ri and up to the Reservoir. He and a 6x6 truckload of Marines were the 'point'. They were just becoming visible in front of us.

As the valley on our right flank became more perceptible, it took on the appearance of a moonscape. Hulking mountains under 1-2 feet of snow down to the 2,000 ft. level, barren rocks, no vegetation, no trees. It was as desolate and forlorn a land as I have ever seen. A vista so desolate littering would improve the ambiance.

Mile 23

0700 HoursTuesday, 28 November 1950.

Now the light is better, I am driving and Ratto is trying to heat up some C ration coffee with an improvised gasoline stove in the rear. I pray he doesn't set us afire. We are carrying about 6,000 rounds of ammo for the Browning machine guns.

We are moving at such a slow pace I can leisurely look at the cliff on my left. Because we occasionally hit an extremely narrow portion of the road and because we are all hugging the defilade security of the rock on our left, I am often close enough to reach out and touch it.

I was surprised to see that the rock walls are not all natural. Some of them are stone retaining walls set with great precision by some ancient, highly skilled stonemason. These well-lichened rocks—moss covered on the northern exposures—were so skillfully set the seams were invisible.

I had seen similar stone masonry on Okinawa along the road from Kadena to Motobu and recognized it as uniquely Japanese. Japan occupied Korea as a colony from 1910 until the bomb at Hiroshima brought freedom to Korea. These walls must have been built during that time.

Decades of rock fall had left small piles of scree along the cliff side of the road. This scree had two effects, one good and one bad. Bad because the daily minor thawing created little rivulets of snow melt. The superficial drainage runnels were blocked by the scree and caused some flooding into the roadway. This flooding then froze at night adding even more hazard to our driving.

On the other hand, these little piles of gravel served as ready-made patches for those many pot holes that threatened to break the axles of unwary drivers. I could imagine the suffering of the poor wounded guys lying in those trucks.

Fig. 16-13. Navy F4U Corsairs gave top cover from the carriers Leyte and Philipine Sea in the northern Sea of Japan.

THE F4U CORSAIR

The Corsair, first introduced to the Pacific Fleet in 1943, has a most distinctive gull winged appearance. Here's why: After airframe design firmed, a new engine became available, the most powerful aircraft engine then made. This engine required a giant, four-bladed propeller 12 feet in arc. This size propeller required, in turn, an additional 18 inches of clearance under the nose. Adding 18 inches to the length of the landing gear was out, so the wing roots were canted downward sharply to the juncture of the landing gear raising the nose and clearing the propeller. The wings then resumed normal dihedral. Incidentally, the Corsair was the first (and only) propeller driven plane ever to shoot down a jet—a MiG 15 in North Korea.

Mile 22

0900 Hours Tuesday, 28 November 1950.

The clouds finally lifted and we take this as a good omen for DAY ONE of our exodus. But there was no warmth. You could only discern the sun by its bright rays reflecting from the snowy mountains miles to the west.

Mile 21

1000 Hours Tuesday, 28 November 1950.

Thin shafts of weak and watery sunlight continue to pierce the clouds and illuminate the western mountainsides on our right. We may get some benefit by noon.

We all had a lurking dread that Chinese strategy would be to push their assault elements down the spine of the mountain. From these mountain fastnesses they could debauch along any one of the fingers and, keeping to the high ground, take us by the flank.

Our nightmare was to look up to the commanding ridges and seeing a horde of gray cotton quilted uniforms descend-

Fig. 16-14. These are the M1 Grenades used in 1950. These 'pineapples' were little improved over the original 'Mills bombs' invent by the British in WWI.

ing on us. X Corps down in Hamhung was thinking the same thing.

Mile 19

2100 Hours Tuesday, 28 November 1950.

Through the pitch black night we hear the roar of several planes overhead. The sound gave reassurance. Someone is up there watching over us. This night it was a flight of Navy F4U Corsairs[13] from the Leyte in the northern Sea of Japan. They flew over the mountain we were hugging and dropped hundreds of magnesium illuminating flares. The mountain lit up like a bright summer day, but without the warmth.

Without orders all the gunners went to battle stations and trained their guns on the ridges above expecting an attack. A few bursts were fired before the officers and noncoms could get them quieted down. There was nothing there. Nothing happened.

Mile 17

0700 Hours Wednesday, 29 November 1950.

Results of last night's reconnaissance came to us via Captain Allen. He barreled down the road in his command jeep, 808A1. Bad news! The Chinese are indeed on the mountains above us. Good news! They do not yet appear to be in great strength. Along with this news, Allen told us that Koto-ri had been attacked by a swarm of Chinese on Tuesday night (about 18 hours after we had pulled out). The attack had been beaten off but the engineers had been particularly hard hit with 40-50 casualties.

Days later when we were safely on board the LST and making turns for Pohang Do—Sgt. Rawls and his squad gave us an informal 'after-action report' on this attack.

Sgt. Rawls began with some disparaging remarks about the guys in the 13th Engineers (Third Infantry Division). The 13th and 185th were combat engineers and the aviation engineers held them in low repute. "We're the guy that are building this airfield. You guys should really just shuck on off!" was our guys' attitude.

FRESH MEAT

Rawls: "We were expecting the gooks to hit us that night. Some of the marines up the slope were watching with binoculars and saw a lot of activity about 4-5 miles away and further up the mountain. I selected some positions and we dug in.

"We had the turrible misfortune of having some of them gravel agitators from the 13th on our right flank. They had a whole bunch of young draftees and they were scared stiff.

"After Brunnel here tried out for his Purple Heart and got hisself evacuated for the night, we tried to settle everybody down. But these guys—I'm telling you their butts were tight enough to bite the heads off of nails—didn't settle down much.

"At about midnight, there was the damnedest explosion—actually a bunch of explosions over there in front of the 13th. Everyone thought it was an attack and began firing in the general direction of Manchuria.

"A few hours later there was an attack as you know and the gooks broke through in several places. It all came right in the end though some of the guys in the 13th got clobbered. I had forgotten about the earlier explosions what with all the later commotion and me trying to stay alive and all. Then one of the guys from the 13th, laughing his butt off, called from up the hill. 'Ya wanna see somepin' funny sarge?'

"After the night before I could use a little humor so I walked up the hill a half mile or so to see what was so damned hilarious.

CAUTION: Animal lovers and particularly animal rights wackos should definitely skip this section and go on to the section "Purple Heart" below.

"A bunch of these engineers were looking down the slope which was all churned up like it had hit by one of them gook 123 Millimeters. They were pointing and laughing. I thought they were pointing at Chinese bodies which I didn't find all that entertaining.

[13] See Fig. 16-13. and sidebar previous page.

"I couldn't see much so I walk down and gazed at the dismembered body of a small deer. I had seem some of these little critters before. They ain't nothing like an American deer. It was no bigger'n a hound dog and judgin' from the big chunks it was red.

"They was all kinds of talk like 'call the cooks' and 'start a fire, Corey's got us some fresh meat'. They finally filled me in on what had happened with 'Corey' the night before: Corey was a very young white faced trooper looking over the slaughtered deer with a stupid look on his face. "Corey was so damned terrified that he got hisself a case of grenades—I mean a whole case! Theys 12 grenades in a case kinda like them old timey wooden beer cases packed in these neat little plastic tennis ball tubes, one per tube. What this terrified jerk did was to remove all them pineapple grenades and then, one by one, pull the pins and put them back in the case so that the container itself prevented the spoon handle from popping off and starting the fuze. (See Fig. 16-14.) This is what pineapple grenades look like. This Marine is missing a front tooth because he tried to emulate John Wayne and pull the arming ring with his teeth!)

"When this poor miserable little creature [indicating the deer] skittered about below his position last night, the uptight Corey grabs the whole case of grenades and tossed them at what he thought was the gook army. That was all the explosions we heard last night.

"What was the idea Corey? Was you just adding to the general gaiety of last night's frolic or what?" Rawls asked him, "Was you maybe just a tad skeert?"

Corey was defensively sarcastic, "Yeah, I'll admit I was slightly concerned at the thought of whole dam' Chinese army scrambling up this hill. Actually, I'd ought to get a metal. It wasn't more'n two hours later that the Chinese did hit us!"

"Yeah, Corey," Rawls told him, "I'm going to tell General Almond that you deserve a medal for killing a Communist goat. That goat is red ain't he?

"Tweren't no goat! There it is. A fool can see that its some kinda little deer." I suppose if you could reassemble the poor litter critter in your mind like, it might resemble a tiny deer. Corey was still defending his honor against a bunch of guys who were feeling so relieved to be alive, they were making sport of him. Then relenting a bit Rawls gave him a little reassurance. "Look Corey, its all over now and they didn't hurt us bad. What did they do to us...40-50 casualties? Hell, where I come from in eastern Tennessee, we have more casualties than that at a Saturday night barn dance!"[14]

"Yeah," says Sgt. Rawls, "You really should examine that carcass more closely. That there mighta actually been a Chinese soldier just disguised as a deer! Anyways do you think you deserve a medal and praise from your momma for assassinating Bambi?"[15]

PURPLE HEART

Rawls continues his story: "We didn't really have time to get our stuff together real good and it was dark before my guys got themselves into position. It was pitch black and everyone was relying on hearing the gooks approach.

Well, you know how it is, if you are expecting to hear the Chinks sneaking up there at night—that's exactly what a hyped up guy hears. Every mouse scurrying through the grass is a battalion of gooks bent on massacre.

"We got ourselves organized at about 2100 hours [9PM]. The lieutenant had told me to let him know when my guys were in position so I sent my little friend Brunnel here"—he nods his head at PFC Brunnel (Brunnel turns beet red and ducks his head.) Rawls was making a joke here. "Little" Georgie Brunnel was 6 ft 2 and weighed in at about 250 pounds.

"When Georgie Porgie left his slit trench and scrambled up the slope...well, Brunnel, you tell 'em what happened."

Pfc Brunnel cleared his throat and continued the story: "I was scrambling over those damned rocks and tripped. I went butt over teakettle down the slope. Immediately some Marine opened up on me with a machine gun. Somepin' whacked the heel of my left foot and I knew I'd been hit bad. It like to a took my whole foot off."

Rawls then cuts in: "We didn't know it but the Marines had set up one of them old heavy .30s. [M1917A1 watercooled, .30 caliber machine gun] on our left flank. Brunnel began screaming 'Cease fire! Cease fire! Get me a medic somebody! Hurry, I'm bad hit!' As soon as the dumb jerk Marine stopped firing, I ran over to Brunnel. He was sitting up holding his left foot and howling. A couple guys helped me and we got him back to the Aid Station. His left boot was disintegrated from the heel on up the back. We could see his leg but with all the dirt and him howling, I couldn't tell whether he had anything left of his foot or not. The Medic finally cut off his boot and—believe it or don't—this lucky bastard didn't get a scratch!"

Brunnel began defending himself, "You shoulda seen the bruises on my foot and ankle. They're still sore as hell! I thought my foot was gone. It hurt bad enough!"

"Aw come on Brunnel, I said, "You think you're going to get a Purple Heart for that?" That's called 'friendly fire'. You only get a Purple Heart from 'unfriendly fire'.

What I didn't know at the time Brunnel was having his

[14] Brave talk, but Rawls *was* with the 6th Ranger Battalion that scaled Pointe du Hoc on D-Day.

[15] I never personally saw the deer in question. Forty years later I saw a PBS show —"Realm of the Russian Bear" that identified it—a saiga, a Siberian goat/deer/antelope.

boot dismembered—was that in a matter of hours I was going to be greatly concerned about my 'friendly fire'.

Mile 16
1800 Hours Wednesday, 29 November 1950.

Orders trickle forward from our rolling company Command Post (Allen's jeep and a 6x6 truck in the rear): "Blackout discipline will be in effect until further orders!"

This was chilling. The blackout lights on these vehicles gave about one candlepower of light. Half of them were not even working. Heavy overcast had made last night positively Stygian black. Two trucks had slipped over the precipice already and had only been salvaged by moving our 10 ton wrecker forward from its rearward position and half a night's exhausting work with winches.

"What the hell is the point?" I bitched at Ratto, "We make so much racket I'm sure we can be heard in Peiping! The Chinks know we are here! Geez!"

Ratto philosophizes, "Ours not to reason why. Ours but to do or die!"

"In this case," I say, "It's do *and* die!"

I don't know where this stupid order came from. Captain Allen was too intelligent for such nonsense. One thing is for sure, this night time blackout driving was part of the reason we took over five days to drive 35 miles to Hamhung!

Mile 14
0800 Hours Thursday 30 November 1950

I am day dreaming about that delicious fresh hot turkey we had for Thanksgiving. Can it be only a week ago today? Seems like a lifetime.

The Marine 'point' is out of sight around a bend in front when we hear firing! Chug-chug-chug! Either that machinegun was one of the Marines old WWI M-1917 A2 water-cooled .30s or it was the Chinks! Ratto eased it down to compound low and crept around the bend.

The lieutenant was running hell for leather toward us. He jumped on the running board and shouted at me, "Sergeant, get this gun down there by my jeep as quickly as possible! There's a gook machine gun on that ridge—" he waved his arm toward the ridge on our left flank, "He's putting fire on my detail. We've got to deal with him quickly before the convoy bunches up. I don't know what else is up there but I'm sending a squad to try to take him out. I want you to support them."

I looked at the steep incline the assault force would have to climb. I know that machine guns, in any army's doctrine are never without at least a squad or so of infantry to protect them.

"Oh Jesus," I thought, "This is going to be suicide for those Marines!" I never learned the name or designation of that ridge, but thereafter we always thought of it as 'suicide mountain'.

While the Marines were preparing for the assault, Ratto moved us into a more advantageous position—one where we could bring fire on the Chinese machine gun but also be partially protected from return fire by a massive outcropping of rock. From this new location we could see that the situation was not as bad as it originally appeared.

First, the gunner was firing at extreme range. The shape of the terrain in front of him had an acoustic effect and made him sound closer than he actually was. Since most of the front of the convoy was in defilade, he couldn't see what he was shooting at and from the rifle fire coming from the ridge, there did not appear to be more than 10-20 riflemen in support.

Nevertheless, his rounds fell like scattershot hail, unaimed but deadly. I am informed that very few soldiers are hit by a bullet "with their name on it." Most casualties are from bullets addressed "To whom concerned."

Ratto looked at me in mock soberness, "If he keeps on like that, he's going to hurt somebody!" He sounded like my mother.

That broke the tension. We laughed and began preparing for action. I yelled at Sanger and Incognito who were crouched behind the armor plate in the rear, "Go find Captain Allen. Tell him what's up here and get me some more ammo." I had 6000 rounds but I didn't know what we would be facing this day and anyway the guys at the rear of the convoy didn't need it. I did.

Sanger and Incognito stared at me with their mouths open. Their eyes were like saucers. I shouted: "Do you understand what I'm saying to you!"

"OK, Sarge. Got it. We're off!" They took off like a coyote with a butt full of buckshot!

These two guys were the company screw-offs, slackers, skivvers and I immediately had suspicions. "Those two bastards are going to bug out!" I thought. "Well, nothing for it now. We've got 12 cannisters of ammo. If that runs out we'll just have to play it by ear. Throw rocks at them maybe. Besides, they'll find out there ain't no place for them to bug out to—kinda like the Alamo, there ain't no back door."

Some dolt who had hitched a ride in the back of the M46 heard the yelling about ammo and began rummaging through the pile of ammunition links remnants of Sanger and Incognito's catchup belting. He found one .50 caliber round and came forward to Ratto grinning like a kid with an apple for the teacher. "I heard ya say ya needed more ammo, Sarge." He held it out to Ratto.

Ratto peered at his face intently for evidence that he was being mocked. Seeing that this poor weenie was sincere, Ratto took the round, patting him on the head gently and said, "Isn't that just precious? Actually, what I had in mind was some a these." He kicked one of the 500 round cannisters. The weenie stared blankly for a moment then jumped off the half-track and followed Sanger and Incognito. I had never seen this guy before and I never saw him again.

I thought about ordering Ratto onto the gun but that wouldn't be fair. It wasn't his job. It was supposed to be the job of Sanger or Incognito but they had never been trained and the weapon was my responsibility. With my bowels doing a polka, I climbed into the turret.

Now, I never had any illusions about this Quad .50. It would indeed cut swathes in the waves of gray quilted infantry. But the first volley would attract the attention of every gook in North Korea who then would then mark us for personal assassination. We had quarter inch armor on the sides of the half-track and a Mickey Mouse quarter-inch shield in front of the turret. I thought, "This is going to be very interesting!"

The M16 turret is controlled in traverse by twisting a joystick right or left. Elevation of the guns is similarly controlled by twisting the grips up or down. The twin grips come together at an apex where the fire switch is located. The fire switch is roughly an inverted V with the bolt release in between the right and left legs. When the last round is fired from any of the four guns, the bolt mechanism is locked open to facilitate rapid reloading. Thus, in the frantic and frenzied environment that we faced, I had to remember to release any bolts that were locked open after reloading and before resuming fire.

Of course, the most grave concern here was not to fire into the Marine assault team. 'Friendly' fire kills just like 'unfriendly' fire and in addition greatly pisses off the survivors. "Fratricide" must be avoided at all costs[16]. Since the antiaircraft sights were worse than useless, I knew that the only way of aiming was to watch the tracers.

I elevated and traversed the guns to be certain of firing above and to the right of the friendlies. The Marines were scrambling up the slope taking advantage of any cover they could find. We are near the moment of truth.

Ten or twelve gray clad uniforms boiled over the top of the ridge and made for a rocky ledge from which they could block the assault.

This is it! I fired a short burst and watched the tracers. A batch of glowing tennis balls arched over the Marines. Thank God! I was not only well clear of the team but I could see precisely where the rounds were going. Now, a little depression, left traverse and another short burst. Right on!

Fig. 16-15. Marines were still retreating from Hagaru on December 1st. Temperature was below zero.

Now, fire for effect! I held the fire switch down, walked down the slope and then directly into the Chinese. At a range of about 7-800 yards I could clearly see the explosion of bits of rifles, uniforms, cotton padding, arms, legs, bone and flesh as the blizzard of .50 caliber rounds struck. It looked like a flock of gray geese flying into an airplane propeller.

Gaining a little confidence now, I switched fire to the top of the ridge, hosing the area where I had last seen machine gun muzzle flashes. The ancient Maxim machine gun fell silent. The Chinese survivors scampered back up the slope and disappeared.

Mile 14

0900 Thursday 30 November 1950

The engagement is over. After that last burst, Sanger and Incognito came running, stumbling, staggering and just about physically spent. They each had two cannisters of ammo. That's about one hundred pounds for each of them!

As I watched them in amazement, feeling guilty at my misreading of their characters, Ratto pounded on my shoulder pointing to the top right gun. I looked at him. His lips were moving but I couldn't hear a sound. I was almost totally deaf. I followed his pointing finger. The upper right gun barrel was glowing red. That last burst was a bit too long. Fire that gun one more time and we'd risk an exploding breech.

[16] At the Command and General Staff College these are called "blue on blue" casualties. Blue is the 'good guys'.

What really scared hell out of me now was that we might be disabled in the face of a major attack. I suspected that there would be a lot of very browned-off Chinese after what we had just done to their comrades.

Asbestos gloves are in the M16 accessories kit and we scrambled to find them. But by the time the new barrel was in, the engagement was over. The assault team came down off the mountain with one wounded and the toy-like Maxim machine gun with its 8 inch wheels in tow—a war trophy. We renewed our painfully-slow southerly descent out of the mountains toward the safety of Hungnam. We would run the gauntlet another ten miles.

Mile 8
0800 Hours Friday 1 December 1950

Only 20 more shopping days 'til Christmas! I can think about stuff like this now. Over those hours of flight down the mountain my emotions had run the gamut—from a initial resignation to our being killed or captured to steaming anger at X Corps and General Almond for refusing for so long to believe that he had a problem up here and, finally, to elation: we might yet make it!

On December 1st the Marines were still fighting their way down from Hagaru and Koto-ri. "Chesty" Puller was a Colonel commanding the 5th Marine Regiment. In response to a correspondent's question he said, "Retreat hell, we are just attacking in a different direction!" He was right.

My ears were still ringing as they would for days. You see, macho guys never used ear protectors in those days, indeed, none were provided. I had never seen one in my life. The M2 .50 Caliber machine gun uses a cartridge with a 600 grain propellent charge. This is the approximate equivalent of 10 cherry bombs or M80s. On the M16, the gunner sits with his ears centered between the four gun breeches. A one minute burst is the equivalent of 18,000 cherry bombs—exploding 18 inches from your eardrums.

CLEARING THE PATH

Mile 3

0800 Hours Saturday 2 December 1950

On our last day in the mountains with Hamhung in sight the convoy suddenly stopped. Something around the bend of the narrow mountain road was holding us up. I quickly counted our ammo cannisters then dismounted the M46 and walked around the bend. Two South Korean soldiers driving a weapons carrier (3/4 ton truck) were trying to go north on this narrow trail. There was no way to pass and they were arguing as to who must back up to the 'layby'. Finally, Captain Allen signalled to one of our D-8 bulldozer drivers to bring his dozer around to the front bypassing the several vehicles in front of him.

We held our breath as TSgt Marion Justice jumped up on the dozer and told the driver to hop off. Justice took the dozer onto the 30° slope in the left side and eased it around the trucks. If he had rolled it, not only would he and the dozer been lost, he probably would have taken a deuce-and-a-half with him.

Justice moved up to the Korean weapons carrier. As the Koreans argued with Captain Allen, Justice placed his blade against the front bumper. He jerks the right clutch lever, stomps the right brake and pushes the throttle to full power. The dozer spins to the right flipping the weapons carrier off the road. It seemed to be a minute before we heard it hit the bottom of the canyon. The Koreans stood with their mouths hanging open. Later that day, Justice passed us on the wrecker. He winked at me and said, "They told us that we was to clear the road, didn't they?"

We were very fortunate at having been early off the mountain. After our passage, two bridges had been destroyed by the Chinese halting the retreat. In an historic feat, the Air Force loaded up some C-82 cargo planes and parachuted two Bailey bridge spans to the engineers of the 3rd Division and the 1st Marines. With two days of desperate work, the chasms were bridged and their retreat resumed.

AFTER ACTION REPORT

In the five days we were creeping down the mountain from Koto-ri I had time to think about our chances. I never did think they were very good. If I had known then of the enormous forces of the Chinese, I would have been even more pessimistic. So how were we able to get out alive?

In retrospect, though our estimate of Chinese strategy was essentially right (take the high ground atop the mountain spine. Then launch massive, human wave assaults down the slopes), several factors diminished their ability to execute it:

• While the weather at our elevation was terrible—a foot of snow, temperatures at 10-25°, winds at 20-30 MPH—along the upper ridges where the Chinese were attempting to flank us the weather was much worse. Temperatures were below 0°, there was 2-3 feet of snow, winds were 40-50 MPH and windchills were 20-30 degrees below zero!

• The Chinese were not clothed for this arctic environment. They wore gray, light, quilted, cotton uniforms and rubber shoes. Nearly as many of them died from exposure as were killed by allied fire.

• They could only manage light arms up the mountainous terrain—rifles, machine guns and only a few mortars. All supplies were man-packed they didn't even have mules.

• Their only winning strategy was mass attack, a human wave assault. But every time they massed they provided lucrative targets for allied air—the Navy flying from carriers in the Sea of Japan and the Air Force flying from Kimpo, Suwon and Kunsan in Korea and even some attack aircraft from Japan. Air-bursting 500 pound bombs, showers of 20 pound fragmentation bombs and napalm by the ton kept them distracted.

• We had total air cover and fairly good artillery cover. We had plenty of transport although the roads were terrible and because of the rough mountainous terrain off-road transport was virtually impossible without our "Chogey Boys".

Some of these "Chogey Boys" were boys but most were old men. They had unbelievable strength and stamina. They used a three legged wooden frame to carry artillery shells, gasoline cans, rations, whatever. We were not totally 'road bound' when we had our 'Chogey Boys'.

Anyway, what the hell! We were soldiers then, and young.

Mile 1

0900 Hours Sunday 3 December 1950

From the Valley of the Shadow ...

... Yea though I walk through the Valley of the shadow of death, I will fear no evil: for thou art with me; thy rod and thy staff comfort me. - Psalms xxiii

The shadow of those mountains would fall over most of us for the rest of our days. I never contemplated much on it but in my occasional sauerkraut-induced nightmare, I saw the shadow.

As we finally cleared the mountain and passed through Oro, I stood up on the canvas seat of the half-track and looked back. The weather was clear now but still crisply cold. Visibility was, as the pilots say, unlimited. The white capped mountain peaks behind us stood out starkly and I could still see much of the tortuous road we had travelled. Indeed, as we passed into the northern outskirts of Hamhung, that tiny road was still jammed with trucks and men slowly wending their way down the harrowing route. I could see most of the hard-frozen Songchon river in the valley as it snaked its course off to the northeast.

I wanted to fix this picture in my mind forever. When the day comes that my brain has the same facility that my Macintosh has, I will punch the PRINT button and print out the picture of this valley. Caption: The 23rd Psalm—"...The Valley Of The Shadow Of Death...". It was a religious moment.

By the time we came within the 10 mile radius of the harbor of Hungnam, the USS Missouri, HMS Gloucester (British cruiser), and about 6 smaller warships were standing off Hungnam. They began raining down high explosives so intense nothing could penetrate it. This 'curtain of fire' protected the engineer troops—3rd Div., 7th Div., 1st MarDiv and our Co. A, 808 EAB as we watched the infantry pass through and board the transports as each of us thanked God for the majesty of large caliber artillery. The 16 inchers of the Mighty Mo hurled bunches of parting 'bouquets' to Kim Il Sung and Mao Tse Tung. When the low clouds lifted we could actually see the Missouri's salvoes. They swished overhead like an 18 wheeler zipping across a bridge in the rain.

We silently recited the doxology: Thank God from whom all blessings flow, thank Him all ye creatures here below.

Months later in Japan I heard a quote from one of the turret gunners on the Missouri: "...we always felt better after delivering one of these one ton 16" rounds. We knew that we had made the world a little bit better place". Amen to that!

HUNGNAM DOCKS

1200 Hours 15 December 1950

All the engineer troops stayed behind several days to rig demolitions to blow the docks, cranes and other facilities at Hungnam. We used normal construction demolitions—nitrostarch, TNT and dynamite but had to add some Air Force 500 pound GP bombs and even some naval shells—anything we could find for this immense job.

The docks were completely rigged by the 12th December and as we pulled out of the harbor on 15th we watched the dock dissolve in an atom bomb class explosion. Hungnam was our Christmas gift to the Kim Il Sung and the Commies!

I thought of my old granddad marching through Georgia with Sherman in 1864. Sherman's army burned or blew up anything they couldn't convert to their own use—railroad rails, cotton bales, railroad rolling stock, etc. Grandpa called it, "...the biggest damned Halloween night in history with 4th of July throwed in!" That's what we did at Hungnam.

Today if you look up Hungnam in the Grolier Encyclopedia, it says: "...Hungnam was severely damaged during the Korea War." I confess to contributing to that 'Mother of all Halloween Nights'.

A WHIFF OF THE GRAPE

While we set charges at Hamhung harbor—preparing to demolish the warehouses, cranes and port facilities—we had occasion to shoot the bull with some of the guys from the 1st Marine Div Arty[17]. They contributed several truck loads of 105mm ammo for the planned explosive and festive jollity. Their mission of supporting the 1st MarDiv was now

[17] DivArty - Division Artillery.

Fig. 16-16. Company A straggles into Hamhung - December 1950.

Fig. 16-17. My old pal Homer Jeffress, First Mate of the SS Sea Serpent loads part of 98,000 Korea civilians fleeing the oncoming Chinese army - Hungnam December 1950.

handed over to the Navy and they were getting their guns and vehicles in march order for evacuation.

The night before we pulled out we went over to their warehouse billets to coordinate some final details. This mission accomplished we settled in for a couple hours of sharing experiences in the nastiness of the past few days.

I told my story of the whistling and ringing of expansion bands from Div Arty's 105s had been our surprise announcement that some of the Marine artillery was behind us. It had given us tight pucker strings at the time but we could laugh about it now.

One bandy-legged little Marine gunner did not think it was funny. "That battery[18] was damned lucky to get back there! My battalion[19] was supporting the 7th [7th Marine Regiment, west of the Chosin Reservoir] and we lost about a third of our guns to the gooks. They was all over us. They attacked in waves faster than the infantry could mow them down. Several thousands of them bastards got through the grunts and went for the guns."

"I never had this experience before and can't say I'd like to see it again", he continued. "Them chinks swarmed all over Able and Baker Batteries. They lost half their guns. This has never happened before in the history of the Corps and the battery commanders might get themselves court-martialed over it. I heard though that all the breech blocks had been jerked out and thrown into the ravine so's the guns would be useless. Some guys even used thermite grenades in the tubes to spike their guns, so to speak."

"But when they came at us, Captain Lanahan says to depress the muzzles and fire canister with zero fuze setting—'give 'em a little whiff of the grape!' he sez. Hell, they was only 3-400 yards away when we began firing. With VT fuzes set at zero the rounds exploded 10-15 yards out of the tubes. They was just like 6 giant shotguns pumping out about 30-40 rounds a minute. It wasn't really grape-shot like the captain said—'give 'em a whiff of the grape'—but actually, double-ought buckshot at point blank range is worse. We shredded more'n a hundert of 'em."

"When I was a kid I seen this movie about the Civil War. The Yankees just pointed them cannons in the general direction of the Rebs and blasted away. We used our guns just like the cannons at Gettysburg. As I said, I don't think Marine artillery ever had such a fight before in history.

"It was a mess and when things quietened down a little we went out to look at the slaughterhouse. Even the ground itself looked strange. What had been frozen, rocky soil was now plowed up and harrowed like a Kansas wheat field ready for fall planting. It looked for all the world like someone had tossed a herd of cows into a tree shredder. The plowed and gouged ground was covered with arms, legs, gray uniforms tatters and body parts. I been to a coupla church socials and a county fair and I ain't never seen nothin' like that! I damned neart got sick and would have felt sorry for them but I thought of all the redlegs[20] in our battalion who got shot, bayoneted or had their skulls bashed in by these bastards. So I just sez, 'Semper Fi! you mothers'."

"...ATTACKING IN ANOTHER DIRECTION"

It was with great gratitude that what I considered a bugout, a headlong flight from the mountains (if 'flight' could be applied to a 2 MPH lurch along mountain roads) was seen as a 'courageous, action—a fighting retreat from Hagaru and Koto-ri'. Here's what the official U.S. Army Historian said,

"...seeing that the X Corps was in danger of piecemeal destruction, MacArthur ordered its evacuation. The Marines—"attacking in another direction" —doggedly fought

[18] An artillery battery is usually composed of 6 guns and the troops to man them.

[19] Artillery battalions usually have four firing batteries, i.e., 24 guns.

[20] Artillerymen are often called 'redlegs' from the red stripe on their dress trouser legs.

their way out of the mountains toward Hamhung, while a relief column [Drysdale's Task Force] battered a path inland to meet them. Aerial support and supply were magnificent, even bridging equipment was dropped to replace destroyed spans. Unlike the Eighth Army, the X Corps lost comparatively little heavy equipment[21]. It had been a major defeat, but somewhat of a moral victory. CCF casualties had been staggering."[22]

PYRRHIC VICTORY FOR THE CHINESE

I had seen some Chinese prisoners on the mountain and they were pitiable—wounded, frost bitten and even more miserable than we were. I had seen our own wounded and heard their moans while being trundled along in the freezing cold beds of cargo trucks. I couldn't have a lot of sympathy for the Chinese. However these Chinese prisoners caused me to realize that they—the Chinese—had been hurt much worse than we had. But, there was a helluva lot more of them!

When the order came to X Corps to 'get the hell out of here', the poor Chinese learned to their cost that you don't get in the way of terrified but heavily armed Yanks when they're headed for the exit. Those that got in the way were trampled in the rush. Well, not trampled really but converted into dog-meat by fragmentation bombs and automatic weapons or barbecued by Marine and Navy napalm.

The estimated 2,500 X Corps losses—killed wounded and captured at Chosin Reservoir, Hagaru and Koto-ri plus the gauntlet were more than matched by an estimated 20,000 casualties on the Chinese side.

HOMER'S REFUGEES

An interesting footnote: I learned years later that a classmate of mine, Homer Jeffress, was First Mate on a merchant ship which had off-loaded ammunition at Hungnam in early December and on-loaded some of the 98,000 Korean refugees trying to flee.

He had several thousand people jammed into a cargo ship with no facilities whatsoever for their care and feeding. On the four day voyage to Pusan dozens died and were tossed overboard, babies were born, robberies and murders were committed in a desperate struggle to survive.

Homer said, "We couldn't help them at all. There were only 22 guys in the crew of our Victory ship and the refugees numbered in the thousands. We secured all the hatchways and prayed they would not break in on us. It took us a week and a gang of a hundred Korean Chogey boys to clean up the filth after we off loaded them at Pusan."

Fig. 16-18. The M46 in defensive position with heavy camouflage. The next day Sergeant Justice dug us in with his Cat D8 bulldozer. We would fire from a 'hull down' position. In a test, our crew of four jerked off the tarpaulin, fitted the four M2 machine-gun barrels and were ready to fire in 45 seconds.

POHANG-DO

We found that we required an entire LST[23] to haul our heavy equipment and troops out of Hungnam harbor. When safely aboard, most of the troops collapsed with exhaustion and relief. For public consumption we gave Kim Il Sung the finger and the Bronx raspberry. After all we were within the shadow of Harry S. Truman's personal gunboat—the USS Missouri. We figured we were pretty safe being protected by a battery of 16 inch guns which could—and did—hurl shells the weight of a Volkswagen twenty miles inland as a parting gesture of our esteem for the gooks.

The second day at sea gave us a weather change. A warm moist wind blew up from the south Japan Sea. It brought dense fog but temperatures rose 15-20°. There was a joyful spirit of exhilaration among the troops. We acted like giddy school girls. The warmer weather contributed to this as did the realization that we were well into the Advent Season. Christmas was only a week away! But, our giddy spirits was, in Winston Churchill's words: "...the unique, exquisite exhilaration of a man who has been shot at without result." We were so damned glad to get out alive we were beside ourselves with joy.

Our situation put old Master Sergeant Marshall in mind of an incident on Guadalacanal. He had been a gun captain on a 90 MM antiaircraft gun there, defending Henderson Field. He told us a story of the 27th Fighter Squadron flying off Henderson Field in the winter of 1942-43:

"One afternoon the entire squadron of P38 Lightnings returned from a foray up Rabaul way. Rabaul was a strongly held Japanese base on the eastern cape of New Britain—about 600 miles northwest of Guadalcanal and heavily defended by Japanese fighter squadrons.

"As the Lightnings came over the field they began do-

[21] Company A lost not one jeep, truck or piece of heavy equipment.

[22] West Point Atlas of American Wars Vol II, Korea War, Map 9.

[23] LST - Landing Ship, Tank.

ing victory rolls and barrel rolls. The guys on the field ran out cheering as they landed one by one. I walked over to the nearest revetment when the Lightning was taxiing in to park. When the pilot climbed out stiff and sore from 5-6 hours in the cramped cockpit, I asked him, 'From the aerobatic display you guys put on when you buzzed the field, you must have destroyed the whole damned Japanese Air Force—how many did you get?'

"The pilot looked at me with an amused grin, 'Actually, we didn't get any. We were at 10,000 ft. approaching Rabaul from the south at about noon when what seemed to be that 'whole damned Japanese Air Force' you're talking about jumped us from out of the sun. There must have been 100 Zeros! We stood them Lightnings on their tails and climbed straight up to 30,000 feet. The Zero can't do that you know.' We gave them the slip and headed for the barn.

'We were so damned glad to get out of there alive, we did some victory rolls when we got home. We didn't kill any of them, but what's more important—they didn't kill none of us!'

It was on this sea voyage that I finally felt sufficiently assured of survival that I broke out my treasured bottle of Pinch for a celebratory thanksgiving. I saw Donoho eyeing me and explained that the Pinch was a part of a religious ceremony. "I'm popping for the Bloody Scotches", I told him.

'What the hell is a 'Bloody Scotch?" he asked.

"You know what a Bloody Mary is, don't you?" He nodded, still puzzled.

"Well, a Bloody Scotch is the same thing with Scotch instead of Vodka...and you also leave out all that tomato juice, Tabasco, celery and crap...and you just drink it straight out of the bottle."

"Oh" he said, eyeing me queerly.

'ADMINISTRATIVE LANDING'

After 2 full days at sea we pull into a tiny little harbor at Pohang-do. In another age this would be a picturesque little oriental anchorage that would offer mystery and excitement to the tourist—'...get the camera loaded Margaret'. It would offer us some respite. The Japan Sea was a bit rough even hugging the coast as we were, although we had all long since gotten our 'sea-legs'.

The living accommodations aboard an LST do not at all compare to the Caribbean excursion liners—not at all like "The Love Boat". We were past ready to terminate the cruise and get our feet on dry land.

There was a dirt field a few miles inland—west of Pohang and the First Marine Fighter Wing was already there flying sorties. One advantage of a Fighter Wing—they can get orders to clear out and in four hours be flying sorties from a field 400 miles away. The 1st Marine Division went ashore in what they called an 'administrative landing'. An 'administrative landing' differentiates the situation from a 'hot' or opposed landing. After landing, the Marines moved 20 miles or so to the west near Yongchon and became a part of X Corps Reserve.

Reserve usually means that you get to rest, resupply, relax and regroup. This was not to be. In mid-January one North Korean Army (NKA) division infiltrated through the ROK lines and penetrated to within 30 miles of Pohang Do.

The airfield at Pohang Do didn't require a lot of work for use by P51s. At the time of the NKA infiltration, we had completed installation of PSP (Pierced Steel Planking) and the field was pretty good even in bad weather. Since we were not engaged in any desperately needed airfield work we were assigned to the combat reserve to defend the airfield if the NKA got that far.

The 24th Infantry Regiment was also put into defensive position guarding the airfield and I Company was on our left flank. This relationship with I Company was how I met Sergeant Evans.

Evans came over to the company to establish liaison and coordinate the defensive line. At first he smirked at a company of Aviation Engineers being responsible for his right flank. He also was a little bit worried. I led him out to look at our prepared positions. We had one helluva advantage over the infantry—we had plenty of earth moving equipment and had built trenches, revetments, bunkers and even a firing position for my old M16 Quad-50. See Fig. 16-18. He was impressed. He underestimated the motivation to be derived from a division of North Koreans coming at us for scalps.

Our primary positions were at the military crest of an escarpment that ran generally northeast to southwest about 10 miles north and west of the airfield. Any attack from the north would be channelled down a valley of rice paddies that would be dominated by our high ground.

Unfortunately, the muzzles of the Quad-50 cannot be depressed below horizontal—it is, after all an air defense weapon. It could not be used effectively to fire into the valley. So we had a bulldozer scoop out a ramp and dug it in about 4-500 yards behind our main line of defense. Everyone was quite familiar with the massed, human wave assaults that Communist doctrine favored. We built a strong fall-back line anchored on the M-16.

Evans was a 'Lifer'. He had been in the Army for 6 years then and had some combat experience in the last battle against the Japanese—on Okinawa. Evans was a squat little bulldog of a man. Like most people who are a bit smaller than average, he felt it necessary to make it up in aggressiveness.

THE HONEY DIPPER

As the 24th was blundering around to come into position and link up with us, some of the screening units wandered too far north and ran into some elements of the NKA infiltrators near Uisong. Evans said, "We didn't actually run into them, we knew they was there, but we just didn't have our stuff together so's to take advantage of the situation."

I asked him, "How did you know the North Koreans were close by?"

"Smelled 'em!"

"You smelled 'em?" I asked somewhat incredulous.

"For Chrissake, Sergeant, ain't you never smelled the Kimchi[24] on these Koreans? Haven't you never et that stuff?" It was Evans turn to be incredulous.

"Well, sure, now that you mention it, I've heard of it, but no, I've had no desire to journey into the culinary unknown, at least in that direction."

Kimchi, is a garlicy sauerkraut mixed with a hot-pepper sauce so hot the devil could use it to paint his Cadillac. It is a breakfast, lunch and dinner condiment in Korea. Every family in Korea has a big earthenware vat used to make it in the fall when the cabbage is in. It's made up and buried in the garden to ferment (and stink) for several months.

"Yeah, well the thing is when that Kimchi fragrance arises from a coupla battalions of North Koreans in a vapor of eyeglass-fogging Kimchi breath, throat-searing Kimchi burps and terrible pants-splitting Kimchi farts—you can smell it three miles away if you're down wind."

Apparently the North Koreans were equally off-guard and did not exploit the contact. Evans was ordered to take his squad forward to 'check 'em out'. His squad tried to cross a rice paddy—they were supposed to be dry in winter and maybe even frozen. Actually, the rice paddy wasn't frozen and wasn't too dry either.

The squad was slogging through ankle deep mud when a NKPA machine gun jerked up a flurry of nightsoil divots like a deranged golfing maniac and splattered them over the Korean landscape like a malfunctioning manure spreader. The squad took off toward the rear bobbing and weaving.

As Evans makes it to a dike the machine gunner picked him up and each burst got closer. Evans sees this hole in the ground and jumps in. He told me, "As I was in midair I could see what I was jumping into—a honey pot. I bent my knees and when I hit bottom, with the 'fertilizer' nearly up to my neck, I gave a mighty leap and bounced right back out again like coming off a trampoline!"

"One of my squad says, 'Get down Sarge! They gonna shoot your ass off!' I says, 'I don't give a damn if they kill me, I ain't going back in there!' It took me a week to get the smell off me. I threw all my clothes away but I had to keep my M-1."

Now I know how GIs love scatological humor. I told Evans, "Sarge, you're never going to hear the last of this! Your troops are going to rag you about this for months. They'll call you the 'Honey Dipper'. You'll become a legend of the 24th Infantry!" This 'Honeydipper' story may be a 24th Infantry tradition to this day.

The combination of the lst Marines and the 24th Infantry stopped the NKAs, decimated them in fact and we, thank God, never saw any of them.

MACARTHUR GOES HOME

On Monday the 8th of April 1951 MacArthur's Headquarters in Tokyo received a communication from the President of the United States, Harry Truman. In semi-diplomatic words it said, "YOU'RE FIRED!" A dynasty ended and the Japanese people and many an American GI took it like the death of a great Emperor which was not far from the truth.

Truman said, "I fired him [MacArthur] because he would not respect the president. I didn't fire him because he's a dumb son-of-a-bitch but he is that too."

ANOTHER OCEAN CRUISE

In the Spring of 1951 the overall situation was such that the CCF and NKA[25] were running out of steam. After the Marines kicked the butts of the Pohang infiltrators, things settled down so much that we had no further alerts and spent our time doing a minor amount of maintenance on the field as well as the operations buildings.

By summer the field was in such shape that we had little to do. The Marine engineers took over and on Wednesday 8th August 1951 we put all equipment in march order and proceeded to the docks at Pohang Do. We would rejoin our mother battalion who had come up from Okinawa.

We loaded back on an LST to make a long sea trip to the other side of the peninsula—from Pohang-do around Pusan, up the Yellow Sea to the Kum river then offload and rejoin our parent battalion at Kunsan. This would be a 600 mile sea voyage to reach a point only 180 miles away.

The roads across the peninsula to Kunsan were very nearly impassable—one lane dirt trails—totally unsuitable for heavy equipment. Railway rolling stock was assigned to much higher priority tasks.

[24] If your winter colds block your sinuses and you suffer occluded nasal passages, try a small serving of Kimchi. Almost any Asian store now has it. Bon appetite!

[25] CCF, NKA - Chinese Communist Forces. North Korean Army.

Fig. 16-19. Co. A re-unites with 808th EAB at Kunsan Air Base June 1951.

Most importantly however, there was the presence of several thousands of the NKA in the area south of Taejon which would have to be traversed for a land movement. A large portion of an NKA Corps had been bypassed, cutoff and left to 'wither on the vine'.

So, a lovely cruise it would be, with invigorating sea breezes, epicurean, gourmet cuisine; exciting shuffleboard; and self-indulgent deck lounging[26]. We were to spend about a week sampling the delights of the lovely Sea of Japan and the Yellow Sea.

KUNSAN

THE TEXAS AIR FORCE

On Wednesday afternoon 15th of August 1951 our convoy of tank carriers (carrying bulldozers, graders, etc.), deuce-and-a-halfs[27], dump trucks and jeeps rounded the last curve of the dirt road and pulled into the main gate of the airfield. The gate guards waved us through. We passed a giant multicolored sign: "Welcome to Kunsan Air Base K-8—Home of the 37th Fighter Escort Wing (P51), Texas Air National Guard."

K-8 was set in a rice growing area. Just east of us lay a giant complex of rice paddies. The paddy dikes delineated hundreds of tiny plots each worked, I supposed, by a Korean peasant family. From a distance it made a quaint picture—the green grass of the dikes setting off the black soil of the fields like the patchwork quilt of Koto-Ri. The rice was now harvested and the fields were dry awaiting the next crop.

There before us as we entered the airfield, was an assemblage of tents and quonsets, with one large Butler building obviously housing Wing and Base headquarters. Flying proudly before the Base Headquarters was the Flag of the Lone Star State. Period. That's it. There was no U.S. flag, no UN flag, no recognition whatsoever that this war was anything but Texas versus the Commies.

Fig. 16-20. The Martin B26F was used as a 'night intruder'. This one is on the ammo apron being fitted with bombs. It had eight .50 cal machine guns in the nose.

To give them their due, the Fighter 'Escort' Wing was actually used as close infantry support just like the P51s of the First Marine Air Wing. And they rendered full service for their pay. These same airmen (probably with the same planes) had broken the back of the German Luftwaffe in Europe just 6 years back 'escorting' the Fortresses on deep penetration raids into Germany. They were among the first of the reserve units to be recalled for the Korea Conflict.

THIRD LIGHT BOMBARDMENT WING (B26)

The reason for the urgency that our Engineer Aviation Battalion faced was evident. Kunsan was a sod airfield. The P51s were flying off a cow pasture. This is OK for the light P51s but the 37th was being moved up closer to the line and the 3rd Light Bombardment Wing was to occupy K-8 as soon as possible. They were 'night intruder' attack aircraft. Since bombers required concrete runways, concrete aprons, concrete revetments, etc. we had a job to do.

The 3rd used the Martin Marauder B-26F medium bomber capable of a 2000$^+$ pound bomb load. These Marauders had had the dorsal and rear turrets removed and eight fixed, forward firing, .50 machine guns installed in the nose. The conventional bomb bay carried five 100 pound bombs. In addition, wing pylons and hard-points could accommodate rocket pods or fragmentation bombs. The crews and the planes were, as we were to find later, vicious. I can't think of a more descriptive word.

We were fortunate that our cantonment area had been prepared for us. Squad tents on wooden frames had been erected by Korean labor. It was luxurious; real wooden floors, folding cots, even JP4 heating stoves for the coming winter.

We immediately began working two 12 hour shifts, 7 days a week. We started in mid August. By late September one runway was complete and the Third Bomb Wing moved in. Their bombing missions began the next night.

[26] I'm being facetious. The 150 man company and 20-30 pieces of equipment and vehicles were crammed onto one LST. We slept on the deck, in the truck beds and in the jeeps. We ate cold C rations.

[27] deuce-and-a-halfs - 2-1/2 ton, ten wheel trucks used for general cargo as well as troop carrying.

RECYCLING IN 1951

On the 12th of September 1951 my four year enlistment (I had extended my enlistment for one year to get on a draft for Germany that never happened), would be fini, complete, consummated. However, if you believe the Army is going to send guys home whose enlistments had run out while a war was raging, you believe in the Easter Bunny and the Tooth Fairy.

A Presidential Proclamation extended all enlistments for one year—my three year enlistment which I had extended to a four year enlistment became a five year enlistment.

I thought about it carefully. I was faced with an automatic one year draft and probably another extension after that if "...the needs and exigencies of the service warrant...". I was now an E5 (Technical Sergeant) with good chances for a further promotion. I had acted as a First Sergeant when our company was echeloning forward as we supported the 1st Marine Fighter Wing and then fighting our way out of Koto-ri to Hungnam.

There was a big reenlistment bonus to be had. Besides my base pay, I drew 20% overseas pay plus $50 per month combat pay. I had a 'Class E Allotment' which deposited about $125 per month in my account at the Citizens' Bank, Pilot Grove, MO. A fantastic amount of money in those days. I figured I would probably be a 'lifer' anyway so I went for the money and re-upped for three years on 12th September 1951. I was sworn in and congratulated by Captain Sheetz the Battalion Adjutant. I was the first in the battalion to be 'recycled'. Others followed.

My real concern now was getting the hell out of Korea. My original assignment was to Okinawa for a one year tour. Okinawa, because it was 'unsuitable for dependents' was designated as a one year, 'hardship tour'. In theory my 'one year tour' expired as I was coming down the mountain from Koto-ri with half the Third Chinese Route Army trying to assassinate me personally (or, so it seemed). If Okinawa was a 'hardship assignment', what the hell is this? We in the 808th Battalion had had a load of fun, but where in hell are the other 807 battalions?

So that you don't become distressed, I'll jump ahead and tell you that this injustice was ultimately rectified at Headquarters 5th Air Force.

Captain Tanski, a real son-of-a-bitch and our new company commander called in each of us of the '1949 NCO draft' for a personal chat. "You're not going home Sergeant Salmon, we need you here!" he announced, then went on to say, "Fifth Air Force is still trying to resolve the tour and rotation policy and we think you guys will get out of here in 2-3 months. In the meantime I don't want any slacking off. We still have a war on you know!" What an inspiring speech! Anyway, a few days later he told us that December would bring the end of our misery, and it did. I can't say we liked it but we could understand the problem.

Fig. 16-21. T/Sgt Salmon in front of Co A headquarters at Kunsan Air Base. Living in these squad tents was like the Ritz to us.

KUNSAN PIZZA

One evening in early October some of the NCOs were gathered in a favorite hanging out place—the Mess Hall. The Mess Hall was open 24 hours a day to fit the work schedule of the battalion. Cooks were always baking up something, usually bread but on rare occasion, a batch of doughnuts. They went down well with the black GI coffee.

Someone said, "The thing I miss most is pizza! I haven't tasted a pizza for years."

I volunteered recklessly, "I'll get the ingredients if you will bake one for us Baxter!" I nodded at Baxter the Mess Sergeant who was not only a good Mess Sergeant but a creative cook. I thought Bob might be able to assemble the ingredients from Tsuiki, Japan.

He said, "You're on, Salmon."

Well, Bob could lay hands on a lot of esoteric things that the guys ordered but Japan was not yet into the pizza craze. I wrote to Daisy offering to pay the airmail cost if she could somehow get the stuff to us. She set to work on it.

About a month later I get this humongous package. There were several gallon metal buckets that her Dad had soldered closed for her. With help from a meat cleaver we opened them up and there it was! Roy Corbin had had great misgivings about his youngest daughter taking up with a sojer, but when push came to shove he came through. The pizza material would never have survived had it not been so carefully packaged.

The postage came to just over $40 but we had a real feast with 2-3 pieces of pizza for each of the Company A NCOs. Thank you, Daisy and Roy!

BEER RATION

By this time the battle lines had become sufficiently stabilized that longer term requirements of the troops could finally be addressed. One of these long term needs was beer. My company had been in Korea for over a year and a routine supply of that elixir of the soldiers life—beer—had not been established. That was finally rectified on Monday 17th September 1951.

I left my billet for the orderly room at first light of day as always. Looking up the battalion street I see a giant tent being set up across from battalion headquarters. I asked Donoho jokingly, "Is it Ringling Brothers or Barnum and Bailey?"

First Sergeant Donoho laughed and said, "You ain't gonna believe this but that is going to be the NCO Club!"—and it was. There were two anomalies with our club, one I understood and the other I did not. 1. Although the Club offered mixed drinks and they had all kinds of hard liquor—they had no glasses whatsoever. You had to bring your mess cup! This was understandable. 2. What I didn't understand was the beer. Plenty of it and it was cold and extremely good, but there were only two brands—Tuborg and Holsten. Further, it was bottles only. I learned later that the Germans (brewers of Holsten) who consider themselves the final authority on beer, believe that putting beer in cans is a sacrilegious and blasphemous act such as to warrant death by drowning in a beer vat! Tuborg is from Denmark but I suppose they think the same way.

I had never heard of either one of them at the time. They were both excellent beers and much appreciated. For years after I returned to the Zone of the Interior (The USA) I looked for them on grocery shelves to no avail. Don't tell me that every grocery store in the land has them now! They didn't then.

In 1952 I lived with my new bride, Daisy, in a tiny bedsitter with Murphy bed and micro-kitchen at 424 South Tejon, Colorado Springs, Colorado, (near Fort Carson) I was still in search mode for Holsten beer. Finally, giving up, I tried various other brews to try to duplicate that magic moment when I quaffed my first beer in over a year in Korea—a cold bottle of Holsten.

We finally found an obscure malt liquor called "Glueck's Stite". Not quite the same but it satisfactorily replicated that excellent bouquet and taste of Holsten. Glueck's Stite was packaged in cans with a conical lid that had a bottle cap on it. The can was decorated with vertical black and white stripes that could be confused with a Brasso can. Brasso was (is?) a brass polish much favored by those of the 'spit and polish' persuasion (myself included).

Fearing that I'd not see Glueck's Stite again, I bought a case. When I put the case on the kitchen table I noted that sealing tape concealed a portion of their admonition: "For better enjoyment, si• slowly." Daisy asked, "Are they saying sin slowly?" Maybe so, or maybe it's sip slowly. This was the first time ever I saw evidence of a brewer acknowledging that one might be better served by sipping instead of guzzling this high-octane brew.

Upon reassignment to Fort Bliss, Texas in 1953, Glueck's Stite disappeared from our table. I never saw it again. However, 40 years later, in 1993, son Rick offered me a "Mickey". Mickey is a malt liquor packaged in a squat green bottle and brewed by Heileman's of LaCrosse, Wisconsin.

The day being rather hot and sweaty I accepted. I jerked the unusual pull-top lid off the jar-like mouth and had a long pull—Eureka! That's Glueck's Stite! I researched the corporate history and voila! Mickey is a direct lineal descendant of Glueck's Stite!

KILL THE BASTARDS!

I was in the Company A orderly room arguing with the First Sergeant about our R&R policy when one of the B26 pilots came in. He said, "Sarge", referring to grizzled old F/Sgt. Baxter M. Donoho, "I been told that you engineer troops have BARs in your TO&E[28]. Is that right?"

"Yes, we do." Donoho allows, "But if you think you can borrow one to go duck hunting I gotta tell you they ain't worth a damn for that purpose."

"Naw, naw", says he laughing, "I'd like to borrow one awright and I'll sign for it all proper and everything. Let me tell you my problem. I'm sure you guys are familiar with our mission and tactics. We fly mostly at night—night intruders you know—but occasionally we get daytime strafing missions. You also may be familiar with the guns on the '26. Them eight .50 calibres can rip hell out of a lot of gooks—but, as you know they are fixed. Once I commit to a run there's little I can do about those bastards that dodge off the road or dive into a ditch. They thumb their noses at me as I rip divots outa the road."

"OK", says Donoho, "But what's that got to do with a BAR?"

"Well", says the pilot "What I'm gonna try is this: As I begin my strafing run and them sons-of-bitches start scattering, I'm gonna slide my canopy back, stick a BAR out and knock off a few of those smart-alec bastards!"

"Done and done", says Donoho and he sent for a BAR. The impression left in my mind is that these bomber pilots

[28] BAR - Browning Automatic rifle. A 20 round clip-fed gas operated rifle that fires like a machinegun but is used like a rifle. TO&E - Table of Organization and Equipment. A list of personnel specialties and ratings plus each item of equipment authorized for a specific unit.

were just as gung ho as the fighter jocks. I had never seen anyone in the Air Force quite so mercenary as this blood-thirsty B26 pilot. That is, not until the recycled beer bottle caper.

RECYCLING THE BEER BOTTLES

My shift at the orderly room was 6AM to 6PM. After 6PM I usually dropped by the Club for a cold Holsten and bull session with some of the day shift guys. Normally, an NCO Club will demand Class A uniform, tie, etc., but these guys were breaking their butts and after a few 84-hour weeks they weren't in the mood for parade ground uniforms. They came in directly from working on the airfield sometimes so dusty you couldn't identify them except by voice.

M/Sgt Beauchesne was a construction platoon sergeant. One evening I see him in the Club. He was bellyaching about the 'Indigenous Labor Relations' Officer. We used a lot of 'indigenous' labor. 'Indigenous' labor meant Koreans.

Pierre Beauchesne claimed Maine as his home, but obviously he was a refugee from Quebec—a French Canadian. Clearly one of his ancestors got tired of those 16 foot snow drifts and escaped to the balmy climes of Maine. No one knew his first name except the guys who had access to his records and it was very likely that anyone calling him Pierre would risk a split skull.

Beauchesne was a hyperactive fellow who sometimes drank too much but, for the most part was an excellent construction foreman. His personality weakness was simply that he followed the stereotype of the Latin as being excitable and mercurial as hell. He was in such a mood this evening.

Beauchesne says, "You remember last week when we caught the tail end of the typhoon? On Wednesday it was raining so damned hard you could hardly see your hand in front of your face. I had some of my crew out there in their sou'westers cleaning out some of those half finished drains so that the runway wouldn't get flooded.

Well, here comes this jeep see, an this ass asks for the person in charge. I didn't know whether he was a PFC or a general but he sounded pretty official and he had someone driving him, so I ran over to him and reported. The sanctimonious bastard chews me out good. 'Sergeant, you cannot, you must not force these indigenous laborers to work in this terrible weather.'"

"'Sir', I says. 'These people are GIs from the 808th Engineer Battalion. They are Americans, not Koreans. 'Oh', he says, 'well, I guess that's all right then. Carry on.'"

While Beauchesne was bitching about his encounter with the Indigenous Labor guy, I had noticed an Air Force officer come into the Club. He talked with the bartender and must have sent for the Club manager. I got a queasy feeling. 'Someone has got drunk and screwed up something and we're gonna lose our Club', I thought.

I dropped Beauchesne and walked over to the bar. The bartender was a SSgt who had come to Okinawa with me. "Swann", I says, "What's all the conspiracy with the flyboy? Are we in any kind of trouble here?"

Swann laughed, "Hell, no! This Captain is asking us to save our empty beer bottles." He points to the 55 gallon barrel that we had been tossing them in—"He wants us to quit breaking them and save them in some crates he'll bring over."

"What in hell for?" I asked. "I have heard some goofy stuff from 3rd Bomb, but this is the strangest yet." Swann had no idea.

A week later the mystery of the beer bottles was solved. I was at the Club bar shooting the bull with Swann when a 1-1/2 ton USAF weapons carrier truck pulls up outside and a couple of Air Force guys came in. They looked around, saw the vegetable crates of empty beer bottles and began carrying them out to the truck. I followed them out. They already had half a truck load. They must be robbing the trash dumps all over the base.

I asked one of the guys, a corporal I think though I was not too sure of the insignia, "Hey, we really appreciate you guys hauling away our trash. But, I know the Air Force. You ain't doing this out of pure kindness or obsession with sanitation, what in hell are you doing with these bottles?"

The corporal look at me quizzically, "Are you kidding or don't you really know?"

"Believe me, I have no idea", I replied.

"Look, this is our last pick up. Why don't you hop aboard and we'll show you?" says the corporal. "We're taking this stuff over to the maintenance hangar. It's only a mile or so and we'll even bring you back to the Club if you can't catch a ride."

I looked at Swann who had followed us out. He shrugged his shoulders. "OK", I said, "What the hell. Let's go."

There was a B26 pulled in to the maintenance hangar with one of its powerful[29] 2,000 HP Pratt and Whitney engines dropped onto a dolly. Apparently the USAF also worked 24 hours a day. It was 7PM but there seemed to be a full complement of mechanics and helpers. The helpers were Korean.

We backed the truck into the hangar to a work area. There were 5-6 guys sorting something into vegetable crates simi-

[29] I say 'powerful' for I had seen, a week before, an extraordinary demonstration of this engine. A fully loaded B26 (2,000 lbs of bombs) took off, one engine failed but by firewalling the other engine (max power), the pilot got it airborne and continued on the mission! He explained later that it would have been too dangerous for him to try to land with a full load of bombs!

lar to those we were hauling. I went over to look. In each crate they were placing 2-3 layers of beer bottles. Another guy carried a box of what looked like some kind of plumbing supplies. I pick one up. It looked like something from a child's set of jacks.

"Tetrahedrons", says the corporal. See, they're 1-inch hollow brass tetrahedrons with razor sharp points. Any which way they land on the road one point is always up. They'll destroy a tire. They're made of brass so the gooks can't use magnets to sweep the road. The idea is that we hope the broken beer bottles will wreck tires but we're not absolutely sure they will. The beer bottles also do something else. The brass tetrahedrons add in some insurance.

As the crates of tetrahedron-enriched beer bottle tire slashers were filled, another ingredient was added to the recipe. Two guys trundled over a case of 20 pound fragmentation bombs. These bombs looked like the World War I bombs that were hand tossed out of a rear cockpit of the old Handley Paige. They looked like toys. The final touch to the witches brew was added by the armorer. He screws out the point detonating fuzes and substitutes delayed action fuzes set for random intervals of 20 minutes to 2 hours.

The Sergeant-Armorer recaps for us with eyes gleaming: "So here is the tactic: we drop these here crates of bottles, tetrahedrons and delayed action bombs on the roads and troop areas at night. The sound of beer bottles falling on their heads will scare the crap out of them. The broken glass enhanced by these little babies —", he holds up one of the tetrahedrons, "gives their transport one helluva headache. Finally, the coup de grace [he pronounced it coop da grass]—when all the beer bottles have stopped whistling through the air and them gooks stick their heads up out of their holes like a pack of gophers, WHAM! WHAM! WHAM! These frags will trim 'em off right at the Adam's apple!"

I thought, "Mercenary, savage, blood thirsty, murderous, bloody—I love it!"

I never did get any information as to the effectiveness of the beer bottles, but when I left Korea in December, they were still collecting them.

DOING 'BIDNESS' AT K-8

While I was clearing out of Koto-ri, my brother Bob was with the 4th Fighter Wing at Kimpo Airfield near Seoul. The 4th got the message (the Chinese are coming! The Chinese are coming!) in plenty of time and cleared off to Tsuki Air Base on Honshu. Honshu is the southernmost of the main Japanese Islands. In Japan the 4th was being refitted and resupplied. They were converting from the old P51 Mustangs (Props) to F86 Sabres (Jets). Thus, his station assignment was relatively stable. This situation was the basis of our entering into a little 'bidness', mostly in 'trade goods'.

This was all strictly legit. We had a microscopic PX good for cigarettes, razor blades, soap, etc. but there were many things that a guy needs to make life more comfortable if he is to stuck in the God-forsaken place indefinitely. It was obvious that we were now in a stable situation and everyone wanted to set up housekeeping.

I got a list of stuff from my bunkmates and sent it off to Bob to see how this deal would work. I ordered brass wash basins, electric razors (we had electricity!), magazines, books, you name it. For myself, I thought an air mattress might not come amiss. Word spread quickly on arrival of our first order and I was besieged by dozens of guys who wanted everything imaginable.

A captive market is a good market. I tacked on a small fee of 20-50% for my services and we made a bit of money. I imported about 4-5 major shipments then quit.

Though Bob was perfectly willing to continue operating the logistics base in Japan, I gave it up as too much of a hassle and I had found something much more lucrative and less hassle—war souvenirs.

MERCHANTS OF DEATH - THE ARMS TRADE

In November 1951 the ROK Capitol Division was moved into our area to augment airfield security. This South Korean division was the pride of the Korean Army. They were very good troopers. However, in the early fall of '51 the South Korean high command which was always embarrassed at having US troops doing a lot of their fighting felt they had to save face.

First ROK Corps had a strategic objective—White Horse Mountain—in the Chorwon area (one corner of the 'Iron Triangle'). The Koreans sent their best, the ROK Capitol Division, to take the mountain. Twelve times they charged up the mountain and twelve times the NKA threw them back. I was told that the Division Commander reported to his Corps leader that he had lost most of his division and asked for further orders expecting relief.

His orders were to attack White Horse Mountain! The thirteenth time he succeeded but only a few hundred of his division survived. Those were placed in reserve and sent to Kunsan to help guard the airfield from the exfiltrating NKAs who had been cut off north of Pusan by the Inch'on Landing.

You can see why these guys would have all kinds of Chinese and NKA souvenirs. I walked out to a perimeter post one night. One must approach guard posts with extreme care. I spoke no Korean. They spoke no English. They were armed to the teeth and had just days before barely escaped with their lives. But, what the hell, bidness is bidness!

I had cigarettes, candy bars, soap and money. Using GI money —MPCs[30]—for trading on the economy was illegal

Fig. 16-22. ROK Capitol Division troopers. These were some of the survivors of White Horse Mountain.

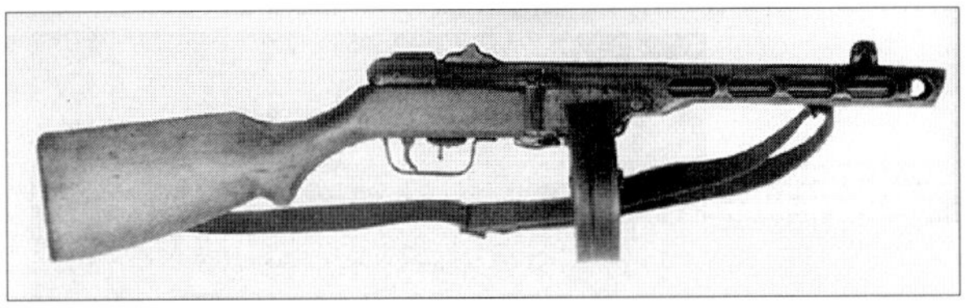

Fig. 16-23. Designated as the Type 50, this 7.62 mm submachinegun was manufactured in communist China in the 1950s and is a direct copy of the Russian PPSh 1941. This gun is still being used by the 'People's Militia'. At Salmon's Gun and Souvenir shop, I got them from the ROK Capitol Division troops for one carton of cigarettes and sold them for $125.

but everyone did it. These guys had Russian tommy guns (forerunner of the AK-47 Kalashnikov), Chinese rifles, knives, bayonets, hand-grenades, flags. I even found one with a Chinese bugle!

The most in demand was the Russian sub-machine gun. I sold them for $100-$125. Of course, I only sold them to guys who would not be rotating out of Korea for a long time and certainly not with me! Automatic weapons and grenades were prohibited and when those items showed up at the repatriation center in Yokohama they were confiscated. It would have been embarrassing if I were there when it happened.

Interestingly though, all the other weapons when duly signed off by an officer could be shipped back to the states. They probably could have been carried through Yokohoma also, but we heard tales that the MPs in Japan made up some of their own regulations and did a 'midnight confiscation' of some war trophies.

SGT. SWANN'S WOUNDED TROUSER SNAKE

I came in from the Orderly Room one evening to find my good friend SSgt. Merrill Swann sitting on the side of his bunk with some of his lower impedimentia dangling into a Planter's Peanut can. The 6 oz. size I believe. I laughed at him and asked, "Fishing, Swann?"

He looked up mournfully and said, "It's really not very funny. You won't believe the freak accident that happened to me last Monday!"

"Try me," I answered.

He explained, "We were out on the runway in a torrential downpour, the tail end of that typhoon I guess. We were helping Beauchesne's crew clearing drains and had our Sou'westers on to forestall acute drowning.

"Beauchesne told me about your tribulations out there," I said.

"Well," Swann continued, "I had to take a whiz. To display courtesy to my crew I moved leeward and stepped up on a drain housing. Well, as I finished, I grabbed the lanyard on the zipper and yanked on it. The wind whipped me off balance just at that moment and I half fell off the drain. Turns out I was not completely reeled in and that damned zipper tried to eat me!"

Now, I was familiar with these Sou'westers and as to the zippers—don't think about some dainty zipper on a ladies' skirt. These zippers had teeth like alligators. I understood what happened to my old pal.

"Hell, Swann, you better get over to the medics and get some treatment. In this filthy environment you're going to get a serious infection."

"Salmon, I don't dare do that! You know damned well if anyone shows up on sick call with any abrasion, scratch, lesion or pimple on his body between knee cap and belly button, he'll go on report for VD[31]. I'm going to use this salt water soak and get it healed up."

The terrible thing is that he did not. He got an infection much as I predicted and when we finally got him to see the doctor, it was so bad that he had to be evacuated to Japan. We were concerned the he was at risk of surgical banishment from guyhood. Sadly, we never saw him again, but when we passed through Japan on our way home months later we met a guy who knew him and he said Swann was OK. When he was discharged from the hospital he was so close to the end of his tour of duty he was sent home. We never learned whether he had been awarded a Purple Heart and, if so, how he proposed to explain it to his girlfriend.

REBURIAL OF THE DEAD - KOREAN STYLE

The Battalion operated a quarry at Kunsan. All the stone and crushed rock than went into paving the landing strips—thousands of tons of it—came from an ancient quarry that had originally been worked by the Japanese decades earlier. A Korean contractor furnished the labor and built a narrow-

[30] MPCs - Military Payment Certificates. Denominated in US Dollars, they were the only real medium of exchange.

[31] Before the Politically Correct "Socially Transmitted Diseases" the common term was VD - Venereal Disease.

Fig. 16-24. Korean kitchen helpers at Kunsan—1951.

gauge railway to handle the rock. Our guys manned the wagon drills, the pneumatic drills, the crusher itself and the blasting operations.

When the original quarry had been pretty much worked out another 20-30 acres behind the quarry face were designated as the annex and preparations were made for an initial blast. These shots entailed drilling holes and tamping in a total of 2,000 pounds of dynamite. It would be one helluva blast!

Unfortunately for the poor Koreans, this annex included an ancient cemetery. Word went out that anyone who wanted to move the bones of their departed ancestors would have to do so before a specified date. I happened to be at the quarry when one family arrived to move the bones of such an ancestor.

There was a very old man, presumably the family patriarch—he must have been in his 90s and highly revered. He was carried on a palanquin by four bearers. I had never seen such a procession.

All the family were dressed in gleaming white, the color for mourning in the Far East. The palanquin was brought to rest near the grave site and the ancient one was helped out. He stood at the grave—performing some ritual I presume. Everyone else stood in reverential silence.

Then the younger men set to with shovels and very soon were into the grave. The young women had the task of cleaning the bones and arranging them—I suppose in anatomical order—on a large white ceremonial sheet. The sheet-wrapped bones were then placed on a stretcher-like contrivance. The procession arranged itself with the patriarchal palanquin in the lead and moved off down the road.

BED CHECK CHARLEY

In the October runup to Halloween Kunsan Air Base (K8) was visited by "Bedcheck Charley'. I initially thought

Fig. 16-25. 40mm Bofors automatic cannon didn't get Bedcheck Charlie at Kunsan.

this lunatic was some kind of early Halloween prank. Bedcheck Charley, so called because he always showed up around 9PM, was an audacious North Korean or Chinese pilot who flew an ancient, World War I era biplane. He must have read all the same old pulp fiction magazines that I did—the Lone Eagle, the Red Baron, Eddie Rickenbacker, etc.

The US Air Force had absolute and total control of the air. USAF radar pickets were so thick nothing could escape their attention—well, almost nothing, Bedcheck Charley slipped under the net. He flew so low and so slow, if he was picked up at all he must have been mistaken for a large bird. Actually you had to admire the guts of this guy.

Fortunately, other than surprising us and embarrassing the Air Force and air defense guys he really did little harm. Oh, he tossed some mortar shells at nothing in particular. But, he couldn't see what he was doing so he hit virtually nothing. One exception, he hit our tire storage shed one night and ripped up one truck tire. He was, however, a nuisance and embarrassment.

It would be a nice conclusion to the Bedcheck Charley story if I could say we shot him down. Actually, we did not. What ended his nocturnal visits was a sort of replay of our "October Turkey Shoot." The formal responsibility for air defence at Kunsan was now in the hands of a battery of SP-AW AAA[32]. Sited at Kunsan were two M-16s like the one we used at Koto-ri, plus four Self Propelled Twin 40mm Bofors automatic cannon.

About the third or fourth time he came to visit, these guys opened up with everything they had. Since they had had no hopes of hitting him, they didn't even fire at him. In desperation, much as a bear swats at a bee, they put on a terrific display of fireworks. The tracers were lovely and the 40mm all were firing proximity fuzed ammo which, if it hadn't gotten in the 'proximity' of anything were designed

[32] Self-Propelled Automatic Weapons Anti-Aircraft Artillery.

to fail-safe after 30 seconds. They made lovely starbursts.

After about ten minutes of this they ceased firing. In the sudden stillness, we could hear the little biplane puttering across the rice-paddies, headed for home. I assume he escaped unscathed, but we never saw him again. I suppose he went back to his Captain Marvel magazines.

R & R

By October of '51 we were sufficiently on schedule at the airfield to begin allowing 2-3 guys at a time to go on 5 day R & R in Japan. R & R - Rest and Recuperation, was so called because it was initially a perq for the wounded later extended to all troops.

My turn came in mid-October. I began preparations by interrogating the guys who had just returned. One of the tricks: start your R & R-ing immediately you set foot in Japan.

The official 5 days didn't start until you reported into Tachikawa Barracks just outside Tokyo. Since travel was by air on a catch-as-catch-can basis, it might required 2-3 hops to get to Tachikawa with an overnight stay in intermediate points. If you have enough overnight stops on the way you can stretch the 5 days into a week. That's exactly what happened to me. I flew to Asahi first, spent one night there testing the local (Asahi) beer before going on to Tachikawa.

Funny thing happened in Asahi. I was travelling with Cpl. Brumwell, a good companion. He was a Country Music fan and had found a Japanese night club that featured country music. The entertainers were very good. It was amazing to me that in those ancient days, very few Japanese spoke English, but these performers had memorized the sounds of dozens of songs which they sang with all the right Tennessee and Kentucky accents. They did this without understanding one word that they were singing.

We found a small Japanese inn for the night. It cost the great sum of $4. I got up early the next morning to get out to the airfield and report for any flight to Tokyo. This is part of the strict regulations. When I got up I saw hundreds of dollars (in MPCs of course) scattered over the floor. It was mine. I had been given 5-600 dollars by Donoho, Hachtmann and others to fill a long shopping list. Worried about all the cash, I had stuck it in my shoes. Apparently when I took my shoes off last night the money was scattered over the floor. Not a cent was missing!

In Tokyo I visited the giant PX on the Ginza. The Ginza in Tokyo is very much the 5th Avenue of the Orient. Donoho had me order him a Browning 12 gauge automatic shotgun. Hachtmann had several smaller items on his list. I also bought some Japanese records, which I still have. They are 78 RPM of course, but some day I'll convert them to cassette.

Fig. 16-26. Gen. Douglas MacArthur issued instructions to the Emperor of Japan.

Vendor pushcarts were two and three deep off the sidewalks of the Ginza. The Korea War was a boon to the economy of Japan. Nobody wanted to miss out on the opportunity. I stopped at a pushcart featuring wallets. Leather, nice quality—I held one up and asked, "Kuri wa, ikura desska?" [How much for this?]

He answered, "Ni jou hyaku yen." [Twenty hundred yen—about $6.]

I was contemplating this when a British soldier strutted up. "How much for the wallet?" he asked.

Same answer, "Ni jou hyaku yen."

The Brit turned to me and demanded, "Wot the hell is this bugger on about?" I told him he was asking 2,000 yen. He threw the wallet back on the pile, glared at the vendor and asked "Wot the hell you think I am…a bloody American?" He stormed off.

I should have been offended. I was not. These poor slobs got about the equivalent of $10 a month walking around money. They bitterly resented the Yanks and their ability to throw around gobs of cash, thinking nothing of spending $10-20 for an evening's partying. I felt sorry for the UN troops, none of them had the big bucks that the Yanks had. As the Japanese say, "Shigata ga nai?" (What can ya do?)

THE "YANKS"

The British soldier used an interesting term, "Yank". Since World War II, many Brits have used the term to refer to Americans. Even today, if you were to drop into a London pub for a pint of warm bitter you might be so addressed. The Brits can spot a Yank at a hundred paces. Sneeze and they pick up the accent. But, it must have been particularly ironic for some of the Georgia Crackers 1942-1945 to write home to Mom and tell her that he was being called a 'Yankee!'

HIS IMPERIAL MAJESTY

It was on a similar stroll along the Ginza earlier in the year that I had opportunity to behold an almost unbelievable sight. The warm spring day was unusually beautiful.

The Ginza was crowded as always. The vehicular traffic was also heavy. The Japanese had not yet recovered from the war. There were not many gasoline fueled trucks but they were innovative. Some vehicles burned charcoal, some a blend of gasoline and sugar beet alcohol and, of course, there was massive bicycle and rickshaw traffic. The roadway was choked.

Suddenly one could sense the celerity of an oncoming wave, like a sunami. In the roadway the travellers were falling over one another getting out of the way. I thought it was a fire engine or ambulance. Finally, the nose of the procession appears—a jeep.

This jeep was lacquered to a brilliant finish and had a two pennants flying. On the right was the U.S. flag. On the left was a 18" square, gold fringed, royal purple banner that proclaimed "GHQ".

Four military policemen with white Sam Browne belts, white lanyards on their M1911A3 Cal .45 sidearms and chrome plated helmet liners sat at a rigid attention. They stared straight ahead, following their flashing red light.

Closely following the point vehicle was an auto that I couldn't call anything but royal or imperial. I don't know what make it was. Not a limosine but more like the car that Queen Elizabeth rides in—Daimler or Bentley or something. It was an automobile the God would drive if he had the money.

There were again two pennants. The U.S. flag but this time accompanied by a royal blue pennant sporting 5 stars arranged in a circle. General of the Army Douglas MacArthur in person.

Following the Royal Vehicle was another auto slightly less regal — the Imperial Toadies. Another jeepload of the Praetorian Guard brought up the rear of the royal procession and the street traffic swirled back into its wake.

Now here is the astonishing part—as the sea of Japanese pedestrians saw and understood who was commandeering the right of way, each of them stopped, faced the oncoming procession and bowed from the waist. They bowed so deeply, their upper torsos were parallel to the ground. If they straightened up to find that the procession was still in sight, they bowed again. Years later when I saw football fans doing "The Wave", I was reminded of that day in Tokyo when "His Imperial Majesty" favored us with his drive-by.

8158TH QM BATH & FUMIGATION COMPANY

Except on R & R, nobody in Company A had had a real tub bath or shower for about 14 months. How do you stand the smell? You just get used to it. Apparently, over eons of time, the human mind and body evolved a physiological self-preservation ability—the sense of smell adjusts to stink. Oh, we washed. Immersion heaters were used to heat 30 gallon cans full of water and everyone had a 'steel pot'—the M1 helmet. These 'spit baths' had to suffice for over a year.

You can imagine the delight of the entire battalion when a colored[33] outfit—the 8158th Quartermaster Bath & Fumigation Company—pulled into our battalion area one day in late September and began the construction of a real, honest to goodness shower facility. They erected all the plumbing, hot water pipes, cold water pipes, water heaters and duct boards. There was no roof nor walls, just a canvas screen. But that very night we were fully into the personal hygiene business. Even though the air was beginning to take on the crispness of fall—down into the 40s and 50s at night—a hot shower was on everyone's schedule every evening.

This QM B&F unit was one of the few non-integrated units left in the army. Truman had ordered the army integrated in early 1950 but because of the war it was not immediately carried out. But we were deeply appreciative of what these guys had done and bestowed a few bottles of our precious beer on them.

I've often thought of the irony of Truman's integration order to the Armed Forces. He was courageous and did the right thing. But, his proclamation came at a time such that the only practical effect of his 'equal opportunity' mandate was that the black troops had an 'equal opportunity' to get their butts shot off! But, such is politics.

EPILOGUE

Years after the Korea War I came across a moralistic, self-righteous criticism piece in the New York Times Sunday Magazine. It criticized all of America's foreign wars as "basically immoral."

This second-guessing, Monday morning quarterback, this armchair bound philosopher quoted John Donne, "Any man's death diminishes me ... do not send for whom the bell tolls. It tolls for thee."

Oh yes, if we could all just get along!

"OK," I thought, "Chopping up a squad of Chinese soldiers at Suicide Mountain diminished me. But it diminished them a hell of a lot more!" Every time I hear or read this kind of soppy, milquetoast philosophy, Rudyard Kipling's century old sentiments come to mind—

[33] African-Americans were called "Colored" in the Army at that time.

"It's Tommy this and Tommy that
And Tommy mind your soul.
But it's the ***thin red line****,*
When the drums begin to roll!"

Fig. 16-29. 808th Battalion Hqs. the trailer is the Colonel's quarters—Kunsan AFB K-8, Korea.

Fig. 16-27. Me and Incognito in Kunsan. Incognito is the guy I sent for ammo on Suicide Mountain…and he got it!

INSIGNIA COLLECTION - PART 5

Fig. 16-30. Campaign ribbons awarded during my Korea service, 1950 - 1951. Left—Korea Campaign ribbon (US) with 5 battle stars. Center-National Defense ribbon. Right-Korean Campaign ribbon (United Nations).

Fig. 16-31. Upon arrival in Korea we came under the USAF's 5th Air Force — a new patch for my collection.

Fig. 16-32. Shoulder patch - 1st Marine Fighter Wing.

Fig. 16-28. Pvt. Kim Sung Il ROK Army and T/Sgt Richard Salmon. This is the guy that furnished me with the Chinese Tommy guns.

> Lesson Learned: Sometimes just surviving may be a great victory.

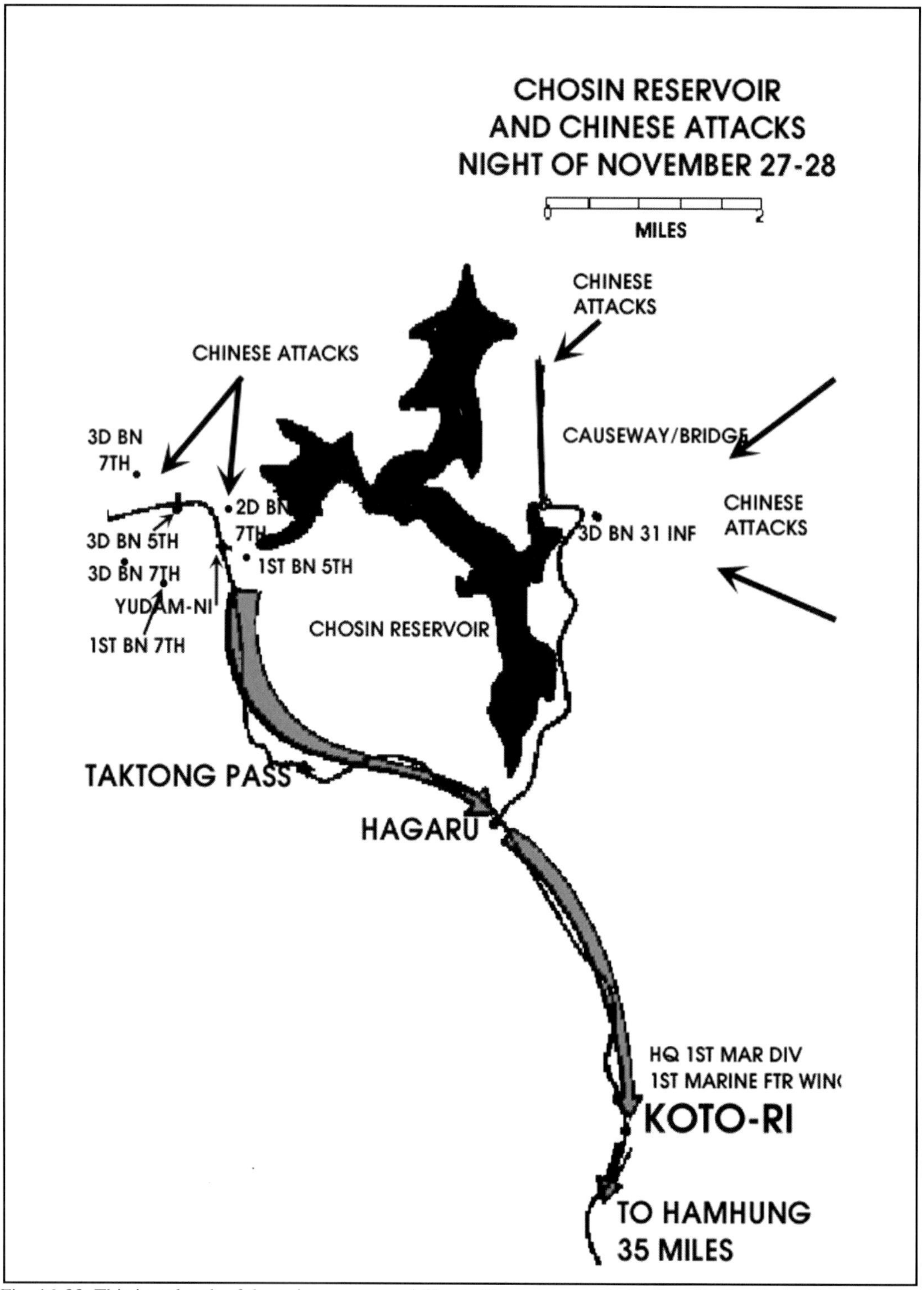

Fig. 16-33. This is a sketch of the goings on around Chosin Reservoir and Koto-ri on the day it was determined that we "better get the hell outa here!"

"Flagstaff, Arizona...don't forget Winona—
Gallup, New Mexico.
Oklahoma City...looking mighty pretty,
Then northward, on we go!"
Adapted from "Route 66" (Eastbound)[1]

HANA NO SATO

On Monday 15th October 1951 we finally got the orders we had awaited so long. "Fol EM, 808th Engr Avn Bn, 5th AF are rel duty and asgmt and w/p o/a 3 Nov to FEAMCOM, Tachikawa for processing and prep for retn to ZI for reasgmt: FSgt. Donoho, Baxter M. RA 06248931, MSgt. Hachtmann, Charles F. RA31078530,...TSgt Salmon, Richard L. RA37813858..." There were about 20 guys on the orders—all the guys who came over on the Morton. The 'Zebra Farm' was going home...a year late but we were thankful nonetheless. There would be no overworked tear ducts when our C54 transport took off for Japan.

We were still sweating on 2d November 1951. Our replacements had been processed in, our bags were packed, we had said our goodbye to all the guys, we had hoisted our last few beers down at the NCO Club—but we still didn't know exactly how we were to depart this lovely place. Early Saturday morning as we were drinking some of Donoho's reserve liquor and contemplating a mass suicide, a call came from Kunsan Traffic. "Get your guys down here, we got a C-54 going to FEAMCOM and leaving in an hour." We were at the airfield in 2 minutes hurling bouquets to the "Land of the Morning Calm".

FEAMCOM is Far East Air Materiel Command and is located in Tachikawa just outside Tokyo. FEAMCOM provided the logistical support for Far East Air Force. We checked in to Personnel, 5th Air Force. FEAMCOM at Tachikawa was to be our last connection with the US Air Force. We were given billeting assignments and—since it was Saturday—a weekend pass. We didn't know it then but this would be our last overnight pass. FEAMCOM, FEAF and FECOM wanted no untoward incidents in processing us and getting us to hell out of the country.

With very little to spent it on, most of the guys had accumulated a wad of money in Korea. Although I had been sending home a Class E Allotment of $125 per month, I had a considerable sum too—saved from my 'Arms Merchant and Souvenir' business. At 6PM we collected our weekend passes and, as Hachtmann said, "Ya can sit around reading that Gideon Bible just so long then ya gotta go to town!" Sergeant Nicolai the Supply Sergeant and ace scrounger had scrounged up civilian clothes. Well, actually a shirt. He wore this screamingly loud Hawaiian luau shirt with khaki pants and GI shoes. The luau shirt was not at all appropriate for the climate and weather but he said, "I'm just determined to get the hell out of uniform for the first time in almost two years!" He found some kind of nondescript light jacket to cover up the short sleeves.

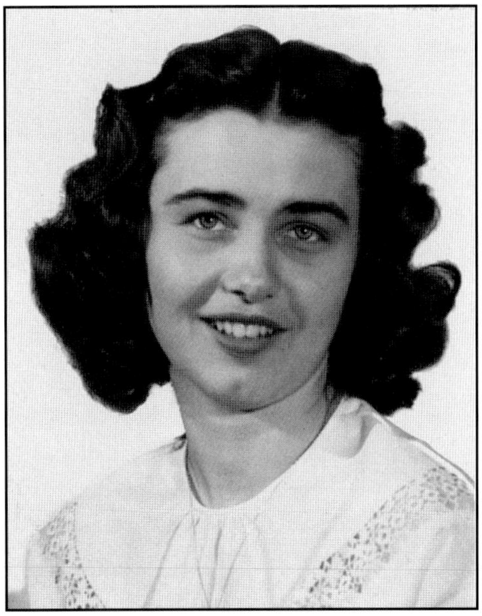

Fig. 17-1. Daisy Corbin 1948. The reason I was urging El Capitan along old "Route 66".

When he came into our billets, he said, "Ta da! Whatcha think of my evening suit?"

Hachtmann says, "Good God Nicolai, I've seen better dressed chimps at the circus! I'm not sure I want to be seen with you."

We got a cab and I acted as the interpreter (I was surprised that my mates had spent so much time over here and didn't know one word of Japanese!) The cabby took us to a resort hotel called "Hana no Sato" [The Flowers' Repose] in the western part of Tokyo. I had described to him what we wanted: a three hour hot bath, good food, at least a plateful of anything unfermented and a helluva lot of cold beer. Hana no Sato had all this in abundance. We were introduced to the "Ichi Ban Kirin"—a 22 oz. bottle of Japanese beer.

In just a few minutes after arriving, the entire Company A 'zebra farm'—5-6 or us, were in the giant hot tub each with a glass and an Ichi Ban size bottle of ice cold Kirin beer. Mama-san saw to it that this glass was never empty. We luxuriated for 2-3 hours. Our skin wrinkled up but we only got out of the bath to go recycle some of the beer. To understand the feeling, letting me put this evening in perspective:

• From September 1950 until September 1951 Company A had bathed in steel helmets.

[1] The Santa Fe Railroad route of El Capitan (my route home in 1951) parallels famous Route 66 from California to Oklahoma City.

• After September 1951 we showered in a facility open to the sky, wind and rain. As the fall winds began to carry a bit of chill and the frost line moved down the Korean peninsula, showering in our QM facility exposed some of our favorite body parts to frost bite.

• For over one year, August 1950 to September 1951 there was no cold beer.

• For one year, September 1950 to September 1951 there was no hard liquor.

We never knew or thought about this, but in the years to come—the Korea War—although it lasted longer and the US suffered more casualties than in World War I, would be termed the "Forgotten War[2]". It was our express purpose on this beautiful autumn night in Tokyo in 1951 to begin our own personal forgetting.

Fig. 17-2. In the early 1990s the "Forgotten War" was remembered. This Washington DC monument depicts a Korea era infantry squad crossing a rice paddy. Authentic details except for the stink!

The next morning was beautifully sunlit and smells of Mama-san cooking up eggs for breakfast infiltrated the entire hotel. I stepped out on the little balcony to take it all in. The sun was well up, cooking fires were sending little plumes of fragrant wood smoke skyward all over the precinct. It looked like everything was going to be OK.

It pretty much was but, any thoughts of repeating the Hana no Sato experience were to be disappointed. There were no further overnight passes. On Thursday the 8th we took a train over to Yokohama—a hour or two away. Here we went into close quarantine. We were permitted a pass good until 9PM. We were out every night and on the last night had frog legs at a Japanese restaurant. The frogs that habituate the rice paddies in Japan grow to humongous size. The legs on that sucker were the size of chicken drumsticks.

We never stayed out overnight again but very quickly learned how to thwart the 9PM curfew. The main gate was staffed by MPs and they even went so far as to put up a concertina barbed wire fence which was covered by a roving patrol. However, under the cover of darkness this fence could be breached by a team which would find a weak place, hold up the fence while all went through and then have the favor returned. We did this almost every night. We were now in a critical period. We had only MPCs—the funny money used in overseas areas. We were totally quarantined on the last day, and could exchange only $20 worth of MPCs and get $20 in Uncle Sam's greenbacks. Thus, anything more than $20 would be worthless after lockdown on 10th November. We simply had to get rid of that money! This turned out to be much less of a problem than anticipated. Good food, beer, taxis, and souvenirs did it very nicely.

Total 24 hour quarantine was instituted on Saturday 10th November. We marched with everything we owned to a giant warehouse on the wharf at Yokohama where hundreds of army cots were set up for a shakedown inspection. We stripped to our underdrawers, placed our clothing plus the contents of our bags on the cots. About a hundred MPs went over everything with a fine tooth comb. I heard the yells and arguments when automatic weapons—souvenirs—were confiscated. Thank God none of my customers were in this crowd.

This took a half day. At the conclusion, we repacked, shouldered our duffel bags and filed on board the USAT Admiral Sims—a ship that would have had a capacity of 300 people as a civilian cruise ship or 3,000 GIs as the US Army Transport that it was.

The next day as we were getting underway brought the most poignant sight I'd seen in the Far East. Let me set this up—when we left San Francisco in that long ago November (actually it was only two years—it just *seemed* like a lifetime) there had been about 5 people on the wharf. One or two were waving goodbye the rest had clipboards and were ticking off stuff. There was no band, no ceremony, no nothing. It was peacetime and our departure was much like someone going off on a business trip.

But, upon our departure from Japan was very different. The wharf was packed. With Japanese—mostly young women saying tearful goodbyes to their lovers, boyfriends, 'honeykos', husbands(?) and friends. The guys hanging over the rails yelling at them were no less emotional. I suppose most of our shipmates were long time Japan hands. It was astonishing to me that there would be much more emotion and concern for their departure from Japan than there ever was for our departure from the US. As the old Sims was pushed away from its moorings and slowly got under way out of Yokohoma harbor, some crewman who had a berth just off the main deck put a record on his phonograph and opened his porthole. We stood out to sea. As the lights of the harbor receded, the strains of *Chinanen Yoru, Kan Kan Musame, Ono Ko Kawai, Tonko Bushi*

[2] Cf. Clay Blair, "The Forgotten War".

and Ipai no Kohi Kuroi—all the Japanese tea house songs we knew so well—serenaded the night and dozens of heartsick young troopers gathered at the fantail to see the last of Japan and wipe back a tear.

CAMP STONEMAN, CALIFORNIA

On Sunday, 25th November, we offloaded the old Sims and were bussed to Camp Stoneman for processing. Stoneman had been an infantry training center during World War II and was in the process of fading away when the Korea War resurrected it for one final task—processing the Korea returnees. We got our Form 201s brought up to date and an issue of clothing to bring us up to our duly authorized allocation. We also got our Thanksgiving turkey here although we would have gladly foregone the turkey to get the hell on the road to our 30 days of home leave.

Fig. 17-3. Santa Fe "El Capitan" comin' fer to carry me home.

THE SANTA FE EL CAPITAN

By 8AM Thursday, 30th November we had boarded Santa Fe's El Capitan and were clicking out of town. Actually, it wasn't really the El Capitan, but I have always preferred to think of it as that El Capitan I couldn't afford to ride in the spring of '46.

The Santa Fe follows a southerly route—along Route 66 much of the way—Barstow, Needles, Kingman, Flagstaff, Gallup, Grants, Albuquerque, Tucumcari, Amarillo, Oklahoma City, Wichita, Kansas City. This train was a military special and had right of way over everything! We clipped along at 70-80 mph. Even the crew knew we were more than a little anxious to get home.

We had to eat in shifts, the Army was using conventional railway dining cars but they would not seat all the guys aboard simultaneously. First call for lunch came as we were clicking along through Bakersfield. I'd been watching the barren vegetable fields all morning and thought this part of our scenic tour was getting repetitive, so I headed for chow.

By mid-afternoon we whizzed through Barstow and started across the great Mojave Desert. I'd never seen so much of nothing, but the sun was shining brightly appropriately reflecting all our good spirits. By the time we got to Needles we had watched a beautiful desert sunset and went off to have cold sandwiches for our last meal of the day.

THE WINDS - 1951

Like the desert winds, El Capitan flew
Across the cold and empty land.
Bedding down in Arizona, joyously I knew
Tomorrow I'd rejoin my happy band.

There's something relaxing but also unnerving about snoozing in the Pullman as your train sways along at 70 mph. I woke up one time and thought I was experiencing the gentle wallowing of the 'coughin Magoffin' in the Yellow Sea swells the night we had hove to off Inchon. I jerked the blind up to see the reassuring lights of some unknown, little town in Arizona—thank God! We were in Gallup a little after 9AM the next day. The train stopped for some time there, crew change? Some of the guys got out onto the platform but it was a bit cold and I elected to nurse my third cup of breakfast coffee. There was an enterprising young Navajo boy on the platform with a giant Kotex box. He offered sweet rolls, cartons of milk, magazines, gum, candy bars, etc. Obviously, the troop traffic through here was pretty heavy. He did a sell out business. I was initially put off by his vending box and by the time I had got over it and decided to buy a roll, he had sold out and departed.

At about 6PM after sunset on the Painted Desert, there was another long stop, this time in Tucumcari, NM. I did get out there to stretched my legs. I returned to play a few games of penny ante poker and then settled in for my last night on the "El Capitan".

HOME AGAIN, HOME AGAIN

We had a very nice Sunday dinner, 2d December—roast pork with applesauce and roast potatoes. I finished hurriedly after a passing trainman said we would be in Kansas City in about an hour. There, I would part company with the few remnants of Company A . I hurried back to the Pullman car to get my duffel bag packed and sort myself out.

Completing my preparations for disembarking, I returned to the lounge car and saw the old 'Zebra Farm' gathered to say goodbye. The six remnants were a diverse group. Ratto was a Philadelphian, Donoho and Justice were from the little town of Red Boiling Springs, Tennessee, Hachtmann was a New Yorker, Baxter was a lean and lanky Kentuckian. We ranged in age from Donoho's grizzled 45 to my 24 years.

There was a lot of jokes about the Hana no Sato, the October Turkey Shoot, Camp Motobu and the fireworks at the Hungnam docks. I accused the old Top of planning to pack it in now, but he denied it. "No, no. I'll stay in for my full 30," he said. I then went around to each of them and shook hands. We were all 'Lifers' and could pretend that we'd likely be together again some day.

We had been together just over two years. But the intensity of our shared experiences in those two years would never be matched in any ordinary lifetime. We all said things like, "…see you around", "…ya get to Tennessee, look me up", etc. It was all brave talk. In our hearts—we knew we'd never meet again.

KANSAS CITY

I had written to Vern Klenklen and he said he'd meet the train in Kansas City and, after we'd hoisted a few for all times sake (the Christmas season had already started), he'd take me home. I had no idea when the train would be in and said I'd call him. I called and then went into the Fred Harvey restaurant.

Fred Harvey Restaurants were fabled in song and movies but I'd never been in one. It looked just like the old black and white movie version, bentwood chairs, marble top counter, white tableclothed tables with a bud vase and rose. Except the waitresses dresses and aprons were about a foot shorter than the old, turn-of-the-century, movie version. I ordered a cup of coffee and watched the front door.

Fig. 17-4. Sonny is home and dry—Christmas 1951 with gifts and treasures from the Orient.

Vern Klenklen, my lifelong friend from Pilot Grove, was now a distinguished graduate of the Moller Barber College, was gainfully employed in his father's occupation, living the life of a carefree bachelor and sporting a new red Ford convertible. He picked me up before I had finished my coffee and I went with him to his digs. He called Babe Heim, another PGHS alumni and we made plans for a few brews and dinner.

I had nothing to wear but my Class A Winter Olive Drabs so I decorated my battlejacket with the multi-colored ribbons we had been issued at Camp Stoneman then polished by jump boots. I experienced my first inkling of what Blair called "The Forgotten War" when Babe looked over my sartorial splendor with obvious disapproval, "Why are you wearing that monkey suit, Sonny?"

I explained to him that I had just returned from nearly a year and a half in Korea where I had not had the benefit of my tailor. I had no civilian clothes. In the case of Babe, he wasn't forgetting the Korea War—he never knew there was one. He was far from alone.

We had a beautiful KC steak as well as lots of good Kansas City Muehlbach beer. The evening was a complete success—basketball stories, high school sweethearts, and 'what ever happened to…' questions. However, the next day as Vern and I zipped down Highway 24 to Marshall, the real world began closing in on me. A niggling concern was working its way into my consciousness. I suspected that I was not totally at one with the society which I was reentering. Two years of exile from my homeland—indeed, from civilization—would itself be somewhat estranging. With most of that being in Korea, I felt extremely alienated.

I heard the plaintive wail of a train steam whistle miles away. The sound put me into a more subdued mood. There is just something about the sound that is emotionally evocative. Movie makers have exploited this phenomena from the advent of the 'talkies' to the end of steam locomotives in the 1950s. It efficiently and non-intrusively set a background mood of leaving, loneliness, loss and longing.

This is the reason I became more and more nervous as we approached the moment-of-truth when I would be re-united with my beautiful, beloved and af-fianced Daisy. I felt like I was coming in from outer space. What might I expect after being away for more than two years? Will she have lost interest? Will her ardor have cooled? Will she now have second thoughts about the commitment we made when I gave her an engagement ring in the fall of '49?

We had to inquire to find Mac's Market just off the main square in Marshall. Daisy had acceded to her sister Lucille's plea for help and had joined her in Marshall. Lucille's husband, Lee McClure, a Navy Reservist had been recalled for the war and was a radio operator on an LST in Korea waters. We found the little store and with heart in my mouth, I entered. A comely, if plumpish young woman bearing all the earmarks of a high school kid looked up, I asked for Lucille McClure not sure she would know Daisy. "They're up on the square doing some shopping."

Marshall, being the Saline county seat, was laid out around the obligatory town square. The 'better stores' were clustered on that square, so that's where we went. Vern parked and we began peeking into some of the stores. There was a semi-shout, semi-scream and Daisy, leaving Lucille and 2-year old niece Cindy standing slack-jawed, came dashing across the square to enter a rib-crushing clinch. "This might work out okay after all," I thought.

"Oh that we could fall into a woman's arms without falling into her hands!"—Ambrose Bierce.

> Lesson Learned: After two years bathing in a helmet and sleeping on rocks—hot showers and warm beds take a little getting used to.

"Yon peak will never be scaled by mortal man!"
—General Zebulon Pike,
commenting on Pikes Peak in 1810.

CAMP CARSON

VERN JOINED US AND ACTED AS REFEREE TO break the clinch. We had some desultory conversation then Vern begged off dinner and returned to Kansas City, his good deed done. A couch was prepared for me at Daisy's sister's home and I spent the next two nights living over the store at Mac's Market, Marshall.

There was one thing I needed to get squared away right off—wheels. My life had been greatly restricted in years gone by because of my being 'wheelless' in mid-Missouri. Daisy and I had written on this subject and she had visited the Pontiac showroom in Marshall, sending me some of the literature. I had one picture of a sea-green Pontiac 'Catalina' that I kept with my junk throughout my Korean travels. That green Catalina would be it.

Daisy borrowed Lucille's car the next day and we went to see the Pontiacs. There, in the featured position with all the spotlights on it was the very car whose picture I'd been carrying around for months! I, in effect, said, "Wrap 'er up." I got my checkbook out.

The dealer was very gracious. "...But, it seems, er that is, why we, you must understand—this is our featured show car and we are having our showing in ten days and would really like, you know, to keep this car until then. Would that be okay with you?"

The answer was, of course, "Hell no!" but since I was feeling my way back into civilized society I was much more courteous than that. I was going to leave there that day with a car! Daisy helped me pick out a blue one somewhat similar to the Catalina[1]. I wrote out a check for the full amount. The dealer noted the bank (Citizens' Bank of Pilot Grove) and after I signed off 120 pieces of paper, said, "OK, everything seems to be in order. "We will, of course, have to service the car but it'll be ready for you in the morning!" I'm sure he got right on the 'phone to Citizens' Bank and got an OK.

GET SOME WHEELS

Paraphrasing Tevye in "Fiddler on the Roof", I've been wheelless and I've been wheeled. Believe me, being wheeled is better. In retrospect, this long home leave was an extremely valuable time of decompression. The term 'decompression' is used advisedly, I sometimes felt like a diver coming up from a very deep dive and having need of a hyperbaric chamber. I got it through Daisy, her family, my Mom and sister. One incident did brown me off somewhat though.

Fig. 18-1. New wheels! 1952 Pontiac. Photo taken in summer of 1953 at the Malpais in New Mexico.

It was visiting in Blackwater one evening when a bad storm hit the area. Freezing rain and then freezing temperatures were beginning to put a glaze on everything. Daisy and her family insisted I stay with them for the night. I demurred because my sister Dixie, Leonard and daughter Pat were visiting with Mom and I had sort of made a promise to see them off the next day. It was a mistake. I got out onto Highway 40 but could see that there would be no way I could negotiate some of those steep hills on the road into Pilot Grove. The highway didn't seem too bad, so, I thought by driving very carefully I could make it to Boonville and put up there. The ice got progressively worse and I only made it to Sale Barn hill. After swapping ends several times and duly noting that there was no traffic whatsoever on the road, I gingerly pulled to the side of the highway and parked. I slept fitfully most of the night and at first light was awakened by a state highway cinder truck spreading cinders. Hooray, the cavalry is here!

The ice was still bad but I finally made it in to Pilot Grove to find everyone very tense and worried. They weren't worried about me. Leonard had to be back to work the next day and busses were not running. Leonard starts on me. I must drive them home!

I protested, "If busses can't make it, how can I?"

"Of course you can," he looked at me like a stupid dolt. "You just need to get some chains. No problem."

We went on about this for some time. Finally, realizing that it was only my stupid obstinacy that was placing Leonard's job in jeopardy, I relented, bought and attached some chains and we were off. Ask an auto mechanic if he

[1] This buyer timidity may seem strange today, but some will remember that for 7-8 years after the end of WWII, autos were a seller's market. "Object too much and we may not sell you a car at all!"

would recommend driving a car 150 miles with chains. Upon arrival in St. Louis, the chains were ruined, cross-links worned out. The rear tires looked like they had been attacked by a school of alligators with rips and missing chunks. The lesson I learned: One way of solving your problem is to just award it to someone else and demand that they solve it.

Although Daisy and I had planned to be married we had never decided on the details. I didn't know where I would be stationed after my leave. I was also still suffering from decompression as of the end of thirty day leave and we had not set a date. My orders were to "...report to Camp Crowder, MO NLT[2] 2400 hrs 20 Jan 1952 for reasgmt..." Also, Lucille was very concerned that she be left in the lurch with responsibility for the store as well as the care of little Cindy. We tacitly agreed to postpone the nuptuals until 'things settle down around here.'

DEJA VU—CAMP CROWDER

We had just had another winter storm as I drove into Camp Crowder, found a one parking space not quite knee deep in snow, parked at the 5028th Personnel Administration Center and handed in my orders. The Adjutant said, "Just leave your car here, Sergeant Salmon. There's no place to park over at the NCOQ. You'll just be here a day or so anyway." I grabbed my AWOL bag leaving my duffel bag and other stuff in the trunk of the Pontiac. I caught the shuttle bus to my designated quarters and checked in.

The Winds - 1952

"Report to Camp Crowder NLT..."
Now under two feet of snow
The bus growling and the wind howling
Through the pines I knew so long ago.

At the next day's processing session I experienced one of those encounters that life is full of, what I call an asymmetric relationship encounter. A captain wearing Medical Service Corp insignia rushed up to me, grabs my hand and says, "Sergeant Salmon! I never thought I'd see you again. How are you? Where've ya been?" He jabbered on about people that were presumably mutual acquaintances. Some I vaguely remembered, most I did not. He looked somewhat familiar so I knew it was not a case of totally mistaken identity. I stood there, mouth hanging open and with a dazed look on my face while I frantically searched memory for a glimmer of who this guy was. I never got it and he soon hurried off on his task. He knew me quite well—I hadn't a clue as to his identity!

My assignment? The 529th Signal Operations Company, Camp Carson, Colorado. Camp Carson is near Colorado Springs and sits amidst some of the most beautiful scenery in America. "Hey, not bad!" I thought. "Not terribly far from home. I'll get out there and get the lay of the land, get some living quarters arranged then Daisy and I can set a date."

On the last day at Camp Crowder, I drove through the areas that I remembered from my 1945 sojourn. There was little left. Nearly all the two storey, Truman era barracks had been demolished, sold off for the lumber. Grown up in weeds were the wide asphalt streets that we had marched in battalion front to the tune of the Col. Bogey March. A few more years and the entire post will have disappeared.

In my new Pontiac, I buzzed along retracing the route I had made so many times before, going home on 72 hour passes—Route 60 out of Neosho through Monett and Aurora to Springfield. Route 65 north out of Springfield past the Veteran's Hospital which was now a medical facility for Federal prisoners. It sat on the southwest corner of the junction of Route 65 and old Route 66 fabled in legend and song. As I continued my trek northward and passed through those little towns, I could hear the bus driver announcing: Buffalo, Louisburg, Urbana, Preston, Cross Timbers, Fristoe, Warsaw, Lincoln, Cole Camp and Sedalia. In 1945 it took about 5 hours. I made it in two. Continuing on Route 65, I intercepted Route 40 at Marshall Junction and bore off east to Blackwater junction then made my triumphal entrance to Blackwater bearing glad tidings.

I had a limited time to report to Camp Carson so I had to leave early the next morning. Beginning a long tradition, I drove Blackwater to Camp Carson in one non-stop, 15 hour day. Showing my orders to the MP at the gate, I received a temporary permit for the car and proceeded to 529th Signal Company. It was quite late therefore I didn't particularly notice the unusual lack of activity in the billeting area. I checked in with the CQ who eyed me curiously. He had keys to the supply room and issued me a mattress, pillow and linens. "You can find a bunk in that first barracks on the right, Sarge," he suggested. I carried my stuff into a completely empty barracks and made up the first bunk I came to. I was too tired and sleepy to notice anything strange. That came the next morning.

I woke up at First Call and hurried to the latrine to get cleaned up. Don't want to make a bad impression on the CO and Top on my first day. At Reveille I saw no one in the company street. At Mess Call I followed a crowd of guys two streets over and got in line for my SOS and coffee. I asked one of them, "Is this the 529th Mess?"

WAR GAMES

A Staff Sergeant looked at me strangely, "Are you just reporting in, Sarge?"

"Yeah, I just got back from Korea and Fifth Army Personnel at Camp Crowder assigned me to the 529th."

He looked at me then looked down. "Well, Sarge, the 529th is on maneuvers at Fort Hood down in central Texas."

I said, "Arwwwwgh sheeeeit! Two years I been in the

[2] NLT - Not later than.

Far East, in some of the worst crap-holes in creation. Fifteen months in Korea sleeping on rocks, freezing my ass off, getting shot at—and now I gotta go play war down in central Texas!"

But that's the way it was. I talked with some officer who was taking care of the 529th's business at Carson and got a partial pay, some extra time to get to Texas. I drove the car back to Blackwater to leave with Daisy and flew a DC3 Kansas City to Colorado Springs. The next day I left with some other guys who were in precisely the same situation I was. At least we flew down to Temple, Texas and were met by some jerks from the 529th and carted out to North Fort Hood to join the company. I was one browned off GI.

A week later, even before I'd gotten acquainted with anyone in the company, I was sent out to take charge of a communications facility serving some of the 33rd "Dixie Division's" support units. The 33rd Division Hq (Louisiana National Guard) was out in the boondocks between Lampasas and Copperas Cove. This area was not even on the giant Fort Hood military reservation. The Army had leased land from surrounding ranchers for this massive, three division (60,000 man) maneuver.

Our commo facility was right next to the 33rd Quartermaster Ration Breakdown Company. This company, like all the rest of the division was composed of a bunch of Louisiana Cajuns and red-necks. They were good ole boys and God knows they fed us extremely well. I characterized them as treating everyone equally—their 100 man company took half the rations and gave the 15,000 man division the other half.

The 33rd was, like most National Guard units, a nest of incestuous relationships. The Tank Battalion Commander is the Division Commander's brother-in-law—the DC got him the job; the Regimental Commander's cousin is the Division Artillery boss; the Assistant Division Commander's son-in-law is an artillery battalion commander; and—well, you get the picture.

I point this out because the 529th, my unit, was an Army National Guard company that had been activated in upstate New York early in the Korea War. We were to come to grips with the shortcomings of this company when we got back to Carson. First we had to suffer the Joranado del Muerto (Journey Of Damned), a 750 mile motor trek from Ft. Hood to Camp Carson. The 529th vehicles reminded me of what we found on Okinawa and what we fought the Korea War with—old junk that would be unfit for the War Surplus Store.

Two days of 30-35 mph crawl along secondary roads through Raton Pass and finally reaching Walsenberg, CO where we holed up for the night in an Armory. We had an indoor toilet, showers and a roof over our head but the sleeping accommodations were blankets on the cement floor. The troops were so fagged out that when the inevitable carloads of young cuties began buzzing around throwing notes with their telephone numbers, most of the troops said to hell with it and collapsed into bed.

Fig. 18-2. It's right here in the UCMJ. AR615-369 says any cook that burns the oatmeal may be exiled to Tinian, Marianas Islands. Cpl. Brooke and F/Sgt Salmon prepare to Shanghai a screwup cook.

My Fort Hood observations of our esteemed company leaders, both officers and non-coms, indicated a slackness and lack of discipline that was inviting lightning to strike. Therefore, I was not at all surprised upon our return to Carson that a new company commander had been assigned. The current company commander had been an Air Force officer and clearly had no concept of command. He was a tall, cadaverous looking fellow about 6 ft 2 inches tall and weighing about 110 pounds. I had noted somewhat of a resemblance to the first sergeant thus was not surprised to find they were brothers.

NEW FIRST SERGEANT

In late April, I had noted the comings and goings at the Orderly Room and was just a little bit apprehensive. I knew that some real powerful kicking of ass and taking of names would have to take place. I was concerned that everyone would get lumped together and we'd all pay the piper. My nervousness doubled when I got a call to report to the new company commander. I really was beginning to feel bitter. I had been in this route-step, shiftless, indolent, ill-disciplined company for just over two months and here I am about to get my butt racked with the rest of them.

I dressed in my Class A Winter uniform and reported to Captain Sullivan precisely according to the manual if a little defensive. He said, "Relax, Sergeant, have a chair. I got you in here to offer you a job."

"And what job would that be, sir?" I couldn't imagine what he was talking about and since I'd never met him, I thought he might be saying something sarcastic.

"Sergeant, I've looked at your record and from your experience, I'd say you know what a slip-shod way this company has been run in the past. Am I right?" He looked at me intently.

"I've seen better organized Cub Scout Troops." I replied.

"Well, I want you to be the First Sergeant and help me whip these jackasses into a military unit, OK?"

So that was it. I was to be the Top Kick. I would like to say that I whipped that miserable company into shape in short order. Indeed I did kick ass and take names. But what really solved our problem was that over the next 2-3 months the old NG guys finished their tours and were discharged. The replacements were all Korea War returnees, most Regular Army and many 'lifers'. Welcome back to the United States Army!

THE END OF THE BEGINNING

I had often, in the past three months, compared the 529th Signal Company with the way we had found my old alma mater—Company A of the 808th Engineers—in the winter of '49. Slack discipline, don't give a damn attitude, dereliction of duty. In fact the 529th was not nearly so inadequate. The troops weren't all bad, their poor showing was mostly due to extremely poor leadership and management. Unfortunately, this made my job harder because as the First Sergeant I had to show an example. I was with the company for reveille and saw to it that they all got out of bed in the morning. I was the Physical Training Instructor putting the entire company through the army's 'Daily Dozen' each morning after breakfast.

I had full backing from Captain Sullivan. Here's an example: He and I went in to breakfast one morning. This was an event because the old NG officers never ate with the troops. They never got up that early.

"I LIKE BURNT OATMEAL"

We had oatmeal, among other things. I heard one of the troops in line complain about the oatmeal being burned. It *was* burned. The wiseass cook said, "Well, just get used to it! Some people like their oatmeal burned." I caught the cook up short, "How would you like a transfer out of this unit, Corporal?"

"Be just fine with me. I don't care about this outfit anyway. It's getting far to chicken for my taste!"

I sensed someone behind me and turned to find Captain Sullivan taking in the situation. He said to the cook, "Okay. You've got it! I have a request for personnel on my desk right now. It's for the Mariannas Islands, Tinian I think. You'll be on that draft this week!" And he was. The cook with the lip shipped out to exile in the 'Back of Beyond' within the week. That was the end of burned oatmeal.

The infill of Korea veterans also helped mightily. One of those guys was TSgt Richard Farr who took my old job as the Radio Platoon Sergeant and who was to become a fast friend.

PLAN A MAY WEDDING

I called Daisy in late April. She had had to have some surgery and I was concerned that she was convalescing okay. I told her about the First Sergeant job. This was not all good news. The demands on my time would be double that of a Platoon Sergeant but we could handle it. I had talked to the CO and cleared Saturday, 17th May. The day was Armed Forces Day and a holiday for all troop units that were not committed to parades, demonstrations, open-houses, etc. The 529th was not so committed. I offered Daisy this option for a wedding date. She had a lot of arrangements to make but in the end that was it.

Her sister, Bernice and brother-in-law, Charley Poindexter would leave Boonville after Charley got off work Friday the 16th. Driving all night, they would be in Colorado Springs by midmorning Saturday. They would be coming out in my car and Lee, who had now been released from his Navy Reserve service, volunteered to buy Bernice and Charley's bus ticket home. He and Lucille were feeling a little guilty that we had delayed our wedding so Daisy could stay longer and help Lucille.

Thanks for all favors but the way my situation turned out it was very good that we had not gotten married during my home leave. Daisy would have been left marooned while I went off to Texas to play war. Daisy wasn't quite up to that at the time.

I had leased an apartment in Colorado Springs. This took some doing because Colorado Springs had already become a resort mecca for the upwardly mobile. I found a second floor, walk-up bedsitter, with microscopic kitchen and a share-the-bathroom arrangement at 424 South Tejon. It was dollhouse size but in an excellent location, just a short walk from downtown. I was there when the wedding entourage pulled up at 9AM Saturday.

There was a lot of catching up to do and everyone talked at once. Daisy said, "I'm sorry I didn't get anything for your birthday. We've just been so busy."

Bernice said, "Well, it's a little late but you *know* what you can give him for his birthday. Giggle, giggle. Wink, wink. Nudge, nudge." Daisy gave her a dirty look.

I had ordered some orchid corsages that we would have to pick up. I had delayed final arrangements with the Methodist Church until I saw the whites of their eyes, so I now had to get on with this. Daisy and her family had insisted that she be married in the Methodist Church.

Pastor Lemburg of the First Methodist answered the phone and I told him what I wanted. He said, "Gee, I'm sorry. I have to spend the next few hours getting my sermon ready for tomorrow." I explained how the wedding party was from out of town and had to leave tomorrow, etc. He relented, "Look, if you could get over here later this afternoon, I'll get things together for you. I'd like to have some time to talk to you, so be here around 3PM."

A WEDDING AMONG MULES

After a lunch of cold cuts—we were too busy and nervous to go out for a meal—we searched out the church. There was a major celebration being staged in Colorado Springs for Armed Forces Day. I was surprised. The 4th Field Artillery (Pack) complete with mules, 75mm mountain howitzers and mule skinners were getting themselves sorted out on the street alongside the church. They were to be followed in line of march by the 35th Quartermaster Supply Company (Pack) with their mules. These were old and historic units remaining from the days of the 10th Mountain Division which had trained in the mountains back of Camp Carson and had fought WWII in the Italian Alps[3].

Reverend Lemburg met us in the sanctuary and there were introductions all around. Daisy was the radiantly beautiful bride-to-be in her powder blue suit. I had on my best (and only) suit, a Botany 500 number that I had acquired before I went to Okinawa for what purpose I do not know. Bernice clutched her orchid corsage. Charley looked duly somber and nervously kept his hands on the ring in his pocket.

The good Reverend was prepared for a lengthy counselling session. I'm sure he had had experience with young soldiers who fell in love on Friday night and wanted to get married the next day before they had completely sobered up. He began a series of questions which quickly led him to the knowledge that this was not a Friday night romance. "Oh," he said, "So you've known each other for years! And have been engaged for two years." There was the obvious question of why then the sudden rush. All four of us collaborated on the story of why the affairs of mankind sometimes do not assiduously conform to convenience of the individuals involved.

Through all these preliminaries there were shouts from the mule skinners, sergeants and officers outside. "Get that damned mule up here!" "Look at that gun tube sergeant. Get your guys to cinch that pack board up better than that. It looks like hell!" "Hey, who's the jackass here and who's the gun section leader? The trail has to go on a separate mule. Get old Sam over here, dammit!"

The Reverend began the ceremony, "Dearly beloved we are gathered here in the sight of God..."

Outside, the troops were completing their shuffling around and about to step off on parade: "BATTALION!" Then the echoing, "BATTEREEE! BATTEREEE! BATTEREEE!" as each subsequent battery commander alerted his troops. Then, "ATTEN-HUT! For WARD, Harch!" Clomp, clomp, thromp, thromp, jingle, jangle—the mules and their handlers stepped off smartly.

Mrs. Lemburg, who had been hovering around in the background, preparing the taped Lohengrin March and fussing with the flowers, threw up her hands in disgust and rushed over to the window to slam it down. Too late now.

[3] Ex-Senator Bob Dole was one of the alumni of this Division.

Fig. 18-3. Daisy Eleanor Corbin and Richard Loyle Salmon on their wedding day—17th of May 1952 (Armed Forces Day) at Colorado Springs, Colorado.

Charley produced the ring on command and after the "I do's" and the soulfelt kiss, it was all over. I don't know what was going through Daisy's mind. I was thinking—I have a feeling things is agonna to be a lot different in my life now!

HONEYMOON (SORT OF)

In late summer, Daisy's sister Marie with husband Jerry and 3 year old daughter Sandra came out to Colorado for a visit and an overnight in Estes Park. The trip up through Leadville where we were treated to a small snow squall was delightful. An overnight in a rustic log cabin in the national park was beautiful and the fresh morning mountain air built a terrific appetite for a Marie's combat breakfast. We had stopped for breakfast fixin's the day before and the crisp bacon aroma drew us back in for bacon, eggs, toast and coffee. All save Daisy that is. Daisy was suffering a bit of morning sickness, confirming our suspicions of a forthcoming family addition. First born Rick was to make his appearance in El Paso in the coming year.

We enjoyed our downtown bed-sitter. It was ideal really. Who needed a honeymoon trip when we lived in the midst of Rocky Mountain splendor? Garden of the Gods—the Pikes Peak zoo—Manitou Springs and the cog railway—the beautiful drive along Rampart Range. Life was good!

But, this second floor walkup was very nice only if you compared it with what I had become accustomed to in Korea. In my estimation, a folding cot in a tent with ten other guys in Kunsan was heaven compared to sleeping on the cold ground in a pup tent. Daisy was more accustomed to civilization and in September we moved to better accommodations on Camp Carson. We no longer strolled to downtown Colorado Springs for Chinese and a movie, but we had two full bedrooms, our own bath, a separate dining room and a fully equipped kitchen.

A SALUTE FROM THE MULE ARTILLERY

Activities at Camp Carson were mostly routine and immensely boring training. Truman's SecDef, Louis Johnson was still in charge of the Army's purse strings so we were restricted to WWII surplus for communications equipment.. We were not capable of anything very sexy.

This monotony was broken by a funny incident in August that not only gave us all a chuckle, but inflicted some poetic justice on some stuffed shirts from Fifth Army.

Major General Keane, Commanding General, Fifth Army scheduled a visit in late August. Since the 4th Field Artillery Battalion (Pack) was a unique organization, it—as usual—was designated to do the honors. "The honors" was a 17 gun salute[4].

To do this up right, the mule artillery would go through a formal gun drill. As General Keane entered the post in his staff car with flags flapping, they would lead the mules to their designated firing positions, unload the parts of their 75mm Pack Howitzers and assemble them (they were disassembled in to 4 parts—the tube, the trail, the 2 wheels and the trunnion assembly). Each gun crew then would load the first round (blank of course) and upon orders begin firing the salute. All of this was done in a rigidly choreographed ritual, in cadence and so stylized that it is called the "Cannoneers' Hop." Even the mules performed splendidly.

The artillerymen were perfect, not a glitch! The problem came when the first rounds were fired. Blank rounds are nothing but a small powder charge. With no projectile, the burning powder sprays out of the tube and—in this case—onto a field of tinder dry grass.

You guessed it. In a few minutes we were treated to a prairie fire that ultimately required the entire post to be engaged as firefighters. It took several hours of the camp fire companies as well as GIs flailing away with wet sacks, to get it under control. I noted General Keane and entourage slinking off to Post Headquarters.

VENISON SAURBRATEN

Sergeant Nielsen, a native Coloradan, came by our quarters in early November with some of the fruits of the beginning hunting season—fresh venison.

Neither Daisy nor I knew much about preparation of game of any kind much less venison. Nielsen gave us a sketchy outline and Daisy thought we might try to combine his ideas with a more familiar recipe—sauerbraten.

Fig. 18-4. Insignia collection Part 6- Shoulder patch, 5th Army. In WWII, 5th Army was in Italy and commanded by Gen. Mark Clark.

I'd like to report a delicious meal of venison sauerbraten, but in reality, it didn't turn out quite that way. We ate it but cannot enthusiastically recommend vension sauerbraten. You will have noted that this dish did not appear in the "Cookbook..." section.

MOVIN' ON

One morning the eastern, early morning light twinkled off the newly whitened peaks of the distant Front Range with the first snows of the winter season and the winds off the eastern slopes began to carry a slight nip of fall—a signal that it was time to move on. My orders came in early November.

'Par. 50. Salmon, Richard L. F/Sgt RA 37813858 Pilot Grove, MO SSN 0766, Sig C, ...is reld pres asgmt, First Sergeant, 529 Signal Operations Company, Cp Carson, Colo and reasgd 1st Anti-aircraft Artillery Brigade (Guided Missile) Ft. Bliss, Tex. for tng and subsequent deployment....EM WP o/a 17 Nov 1952 reporting thereat NLT 2400 hours 28 Nov ...Ten day delay enroute authorized. ...Tvl via POV auth.'

This was not a surprise. Most of the personnel of the entire army had been screened in the summer of 1952 for potential trainees for the army's new air defense umbrella which would use the revolutionary new Nike guided missile system developed by the Bell Telephone Laboratories and manufactured by the Western Electric Company.

Nearly one thousand guys had been selected, mostly signal and antiaircraft artillery and would train at the Army's Antiaircraft and Guided Missile School at Fort Bliss, Texas and in the nearby desert at White Sands Proving Grounds, New Mexico and environs.

> LESSON LEARNED: If you are posted to a beautiful area with nice living and duty—don't unpack your bags, you'll be moved soon. This is Murphy's Law.

[4] There is an elaborate and detailed protocol for visiting dignitaries by way of "ruffles and flourishes" by the band as well as "salutes" by cannon fire. Heads of state get 21 guns plus 4 ruffles and flourishes, Major Generals get 17 guns, etc.

"Out in the west Texas town of El Paso,
I fell in love with a Mexican girl..."
—Marty Robbins, "El Paso."

EL PASO

EL PASO, ORIGINALLY EL PASO DEL NORTE (Spanish, "the pass to the north") received its name in 1598 from Juan de Onate, a colonizer of New Mexico. It lies in extreme western Texas, on the north bank of the Rio Grande at an altitude of 3,762 ft opposite Ciudad Juarez, Mexico.

It's at 31° 55' N Latitude and 106° 30' W Longitude in case you want to set your Lincoln Navigator GPS System to find it in the dark. It is as far west as you can get in Texas but shares the climate and topography of New Mexico to the north and west and Mexico to the south. These three regions also share topsoil (actually top-*sand*), trash, McDonald wrappers and everything else than can be blown away—on a periodic basis. The midwestern United States has *thunder* storms—El Paso has *sand* storms. The climate is dry—average annual precipitation is 8 in—and warm—the average annual temperature is 63 deg F. The University of Texas has a branch there, as does the Federal Reserve Banking system. Fort Bliss (established 1849), home of the U.S. Army's Anti-aircraft Artillery and Guided Missile School, is nearby. Fort Bliss was the cavalry post from which "Blackjack" Pershing launched his "Buffalo Soldier" (9th and 10th Cavalry Regiments) punitive raids against Pancho Villa in 1916.

We drove a spanky new Pontiac to El Paso in November 1952. When we departed in the spring of 1954, the sandstorms had taken the paint half way down to the metal. The windshield was so sand pitted, oncoming headlights caused it to scintillate like a 4th of July fireworks display.

THE WINDS - 1953

Screaming down from the desert,
Comes a raging fury of silicon and sand.
It's a natural hazard of El Paso
That scours this empty land.

Four or five miles out of town in any direction and you see the definition of *desolate*. In Salmon's illustrated dictionary under the term "back of beyond" is a picture of El Paso. Not to be too hard on the place, there were some nearby areas that were quite beautiful. The Organ Mountains standing behind the White Sands National Monument and the National Forest around Ruidoso, NM come to mind. The latter is actually an Indian reservation for the Mescalero Apaches. The Mescaleros were the last tribe to come to a sort of peace with the palefaces. I say 'sort of' because, at least when I was there, there was little love lost between the Mescaleros and the local 'Anglos'.

Fig. 19-1. A NASA Space probe with the giant Saturn booster. This and other US rockets were descendants of Wernher von Braun's V-2 experiments at White Sands, New Mexico. See Figs. 21-2 and 21-3 next page.

As for precipitation, a little anecdote captures the essence better than the almanac's "average annual rainfall".

> An Englishman, unfamiliar with west Texas, was looking at a ranch. In his tour, he found himself momentarily alone with the rancher's ten year old son. Hoping to get unembellished truth from the child, he asks him, "Jimmy, your father said it never snows in these parts. Is that right?"
>
> Little Jimmy replies, "Oh, yes sir. It's never snowed here, but I saw it rain once way back before I started to school!"

The characterization is accurate. Locals call a 6 inch rain one where the drops fall six inches apart. This was not altogether a bad thing. Daisy used to hang her wash on the clothesline outside our backdoor. When she finished the basket of wet wash, she went back to the first thing hanged and began gathering it in. The wash would dry in about 5 minutes.

Air conditioning in the early 1950s was something that one might read about in the Sunday supplements, "Lookit here, honey—there's a guy that has invented something that will cool down the house in summer—Mr. Carrier or somebody. It'll never catch on though, summer's is just supposed to be hotter'n hell!"

Unthinkable in civilian life meant *inconceivable* to the military. However, in especially hot and especially dry regions there was a very simple device that would do a passable job of cooling a dwelling—a "swamp cooler". We bought an 4-5 year old swamp cooler from some GI who was shipping out and installed it in the dining room.

I don't know exactly where the name came from but it worked! It was installed in a window much like a window air-conditioner. It required a source of water which fed in-

Fig. 19-2. ROCKET SCIENTIST—Wernher von Braun (pictured above) was in residence at White Sands Proving Grounds while I was in training there. He was a driving force in the development of manned space flight and directed the development of the rockets that put humans on the Moon. Von Braun headed the German team that developed Hitler's "Vengeance Weapon 2 (V-2) See Fig. 19-3. After the fall of the Third Reich, von Braun and more than 100 top engineers of the German Peenemunde rocket research facility on the Baltic coast, surrendered to the U.S. Army. After interrogation they were offered (1945) contracts to continue their research in the United States. This research was done first at Fort Bliss, Tex., near the White Sands Missile Range, N.Mex., and then at Redstone Arsenal at Huntsville, Ala.

Fig. 19-3. The V-2 was a liquid-propellant rocket developed at Peenemunde, Germany between 1938 and 1942 under the technical direction of Wernher von Braun. The V-2 was eventually used against targets in Britain and other countries. The V-2 stood over 46 ft tall and weighed 28,380 lbs at lift-off including a 2,201 lb warhead. Propellants were liquid oxygen and a 75%-25% ethyl alcohol-water mixture. The V-2 reached a maximum velocity of about 5,200 ft/sec and had a range between 190 and 200 miles. Much rocket technology after the war was based on the V-2. The US brought dozens of these rockets from Peenemunde to White Sands. While I was in training there, one of the experiments malfunctioned and a V-2 landed in a cemetery in Juarez. There was no warhead on it but there was nevertheless a great deal of diplomatic scampering for a few weeks. I think the Mexicans got a few new tombstones.

ternal nozzles. The nozzles continuously emitted a fine spray into absorbent material over which a stream of air was fanned into the house. This evaporative cooling principle was even applied to large buildings and while we were in residence at Fort Bliss, troop billets were built and equipped with such air-conditioning. This was the first time in my life I had ever seen anything done for the comfort of the troops.

Summer daytime temperatures often were above 100° F. You could get a nice tan in 3-4 minutes and a third degree sunburn in 15. Desert heat exhibits a strange phenomenon—the sun can grill bare skin in a few minutes, but the air is so dry that a sweaty person can stand in the shade and an evaporating breeze will give him goose bumps. The air is thin with virtually no moisture in the air to retain heat. After sundown, the temperature in the desert plummets and a blanket feels quite cuddly.

POST QUARTERS

Daisy and I enjoyed a holiday Thanksgiving with her folks and her mother's excellent cooking during our "Delay Enroute". In continuing to Ft. Bliss from mid-Missouri, we followed US65 to Springfield and thence "Route 66" through Joplin, Tulsa and Oklahoma City. We took 277 south to Chickasha and Lawton in order to stop by Wichita Falls AFB and visit with Daisy's younger brother Johnny who was on a 4 year Air Force enlistment.

Probably President Eisenhower's greatest contribution to the nation was his determination to build a national system of "Defense Highways". The Interstate Highway System did not long retain that name, but it was ultimately a crowning glory of national infrastructure.

Unfortunately, in 1952, virtually none of this system was in place and major cross country trips were great adventures that most people would prefer to skip. Such was the trip to El Paso.

At the end of the first day we found ourselves tired and hungry at a small roadside restaurant near Lawton, OK. We looked over the menu. This was my introduction to "Chicken fried steak" which must be the national dish of Oklahoma. The topper on this menu however, was the "Wine List".

Apparently, to belatedly recognize the repeal of the 19th Amendment, Oklahoma had grudgingly permitted local option on the sale and drinking of adult beverages. This locality included Fort Sill, the home of the Army's Artillery

School and probably a number of folk who liked to cut the accumulated trail dust with a good snort.

The "Wine List" attested that they had not been into this "hard likker bidness" very long. Here is a replica of that 1952 Wine List—

WINE LIST
1. White wine.
2. Red wine.
3. Rose wine.
Order by number, please.

Surviving the Chicken Fried Steak and the wine, (Bin 1, please)—we put up for the night and continued to Wichita Falls and El Paso the next day. We made the trip a little bit touristy by stopping at Judge Roy Bean's courtroom (The Law West of the Pecos). Said Judge Bean to the unknown man found dead on street in Pecos, "I'm fining you that $20 gold piece you got in yer pocket for littering our streets with your carcass! Bailiff, drag him out and send it the next case."

About the time I was certain that we were going to drive off the edge of the earth and be devoured like the ancient mariners—"There be monsters here!"—we sailed through Van Horn, Fabens and on into El Paso to bunk down in one of the original Motel 6s. In our case, they really meant it—it was $6 a night, but it was grossly overpriced.

The next day we were assigned on-post quarters and our furniture was shortly delivered. Billets weren't much but we were to find they were ideal because later in the training phase we were to spend months in the desert and the families were all together for mutual support.

NEED FURNITURE ? MAKE YOUR OWN

When Post Transportation folks came out to our Camp Carson quarters to pack up our household goods, Daisy and I were struck dumb in amazement at what they did.

First of all you must consider what they were packing. Our little bedsitter in Colorado Springs was mostly furnished. We supplied some bedclothes and kitchen utensils and old man Brackett, our landlord, supplied the rest.

When we took Post housing at Carson, there was no furniture and we had to buy a few things. We probably paid $100 total for a bed, mattress, box springs, kitchen table, kitchen utensils, a winged back and a lounge chair, floor lamp and some odds and ends. Even though $100 was much more money then than it is now, it still wasn't much.

To pack us out, Post Transportation brought a pickup truck full of grade A lumber (mostly 1 x 4s) and set two carpenters to work making wooden crates for each major piece of furniture. They told us that regulations required them to ship by rail and household goods had to be packed commensurately. For our $100 worth of furniture, the Army used $200 worth of lumber, $100 worth of carpenter time, $100 worth of local transportation on each end and then $100 or so for railway shipment. We told them, "Give us $100 and you can throw the damned stuff away!" That, however is not the way bureaucracies work.

Our household goods were delivered to our Post quarters at Ft. Bliss. I could see that the workmen doing the uncrating were going to destroy the lumber, so I told them, "Thank you very much fellows, you've done an excellent job. Now you are released from any further responsibility, we will complete the unpacking ourselves. They were quite happy to get out of an afternoon's work and did not argue.

I went to Sears Craftsman shop and bought a hammer, a saw and a box of nails. Over the next few days, using the dismantled packing crates, I constructed a dressing table for Daisy, a coffee table, a lamp table, a wash bench for our new Sears wringer washing machine, two night stands for the bedroom and two flower boxes. I would estimate the value of the furniture constructed from the packing crates was 2-3 times the value of the furniture it had contained.

GROUND SCHOOL

The classroom facilities of the Anti Aircraft and Guided Missile School were excellent. I was reminded of ground school at Randolph Field, Texas.With the Russkies breathing on our necks in both atom bombs and long range bomber capabilities, Uncle Sugar was willing to cough up a few shekels for a state-of-the-art air defense training facility.

We didn't really understand this at the time, but there were two problems lurking in the background. Western Electric was not able to meet their schedule of delivering these Nike Ajax systems. This caused us to have a lot more classroom lecture type training than had been anticipated.

This redounded to my personal benefit because all the instructors were rocket and electronic engineers and scientists and were extremely capable. They began presenting the fundamentals of electronic computers, rockets and radar—the bases of the Nike system we were learning. I got so carried away with this new world, I went over to the School Book store and bought a "Hyperbolic, 4 Vector" slide rule. I'll freely admit I hadn't a clue as to what a Hyperbolic 4 Vector was but I eventually learned to use the slide rule there and used it for 3 years of Engineering school at MU a few years later.

The other lurking problem was the difficulty the army was having in getting money appropriated for a firing range for these Nike Ajax missiles. When you build a firing range for small arms, you are dealing with a few acres. The Nike had a range of 28 miles so you must deal with an area the size of a small state. New Mexico had that but then came the question of roads and troop billeting facility. With a range camp this remote, troops would be in residence for weeks at a time. In the event, as you may have guessed, the decision was to let the training troops build the camp facility. But that would start in the summer of 1953.

After 2-3 months of this "ground school" I came to realize—this is it! This is what I want to do with my life. After years of blundering about aimlessly for years, I was hooked on electronics and engineering. A pity it took so long but better late than never. I still had 18 months to go on my service obligation but I resolved that I would begin preparations for college. I recognized that insofar as formal high school credits for the pre-engineering courses I would need—they just weren't there and I would have to make them good somehow. The answer was the US Armed Forces Institute, USAFI.

The months I would later spend in the New Mexico desert would be put to use taking correspondence courses.

But it wasn't all work. The trainees lived together and there was good camaraderie. The young singles had Juarez across the river.

CIUDAD JUAREZ

Juarez is larger than El Paso and sits directly south just across the Rio Grande. The two cities are linked by a bridge and a railroad. In 1888 it was renamed for Benito Juarez who had his headquarters here during his exile in 1865. Juarez was a hero of one of the innumerable Mexican revolutions (this one against Maximilian).

I never cared much for the ambiance of Juarez and hardly ever went there. Daisy said there were just too many foreigners to her liking. But the unmarried troopers loved the place. Bull fights, good lookin' wimmen, cheap likker, etc.

One thing Juarez had was cheap liquor—that is if you like tequila or mescal. Even today you can buy good quality tequila for just over a dollar a liter. In those days it was much cheaper. A perennial GI problem has been running out of money before you run out of month. Thus, the last few days of a month tend always to be impoverished.

In these situations, one could always catch a ride with a friend, go to Juarez and get straight shots of tequila [two oz.] for 10¢. Pfc. Floyd and Cpl. Bennett found themselves in such circumstances one weekend and pooling their combined treasury of $2-3, they drove over for the tequila and lime shooters. As the evening wore on and they were downing their tenth or so tequila, they got the idea they'd better be getting on home while they could still stand. So far, so good.

But just outside the bar they bump into a street vendor selling chiles. "Jalapeños, seniores? Habañeros? Muy bueno chiles. Habañeros muy caliente! You buy?"

Now right here's where their tenuous grip on reality snapped. Floyd said, "Bet I can eat more a them chiles than you!"

Bennett says, "You're on." They stood there and spent the remainder of their $3 treasury dining al fresco on a couple of pounds of Mexican chile peppers. The name of the winner was lost—forgotten when their gastronomic depth charges hit.

Dr. Sullivan, a California chemistry professor several years ago devised a scale and rated the level of capsicum[1] content and thus the incendiary power of various types of peppers. With common household black pepper at 10, jalapeños rate a 100, but the habañero comes out at about 5,000.

The next day after trying everything including sitting on a bag of ice cubes, Floyd shows up in class to tell the story and said, "Last time I saw Bennett, he was sitting on the commode praying, '...come on, ice cream!"

When summer returned with clear days and fair, and cactus blossoms filled the air, our classroom days were nearly done and we would now toil in the desert sun—at Red Canyon Range Camp. RCRC for short. We would be there for nearly 8 months and the family separations were very trying.

AERODYNAMICS OF THE OLDS 98

The route home from Red Canyon Range Camp was: range road north to US380 then 20 miles east to Carrizozo and US54, thence straight south to Ft. Bliss and home. It was a total of about 160 miles. US54 was—and is—a well maintained highway in a state that, at that time, had no effective speed limit.

In the summer of 1953 about 200 men—students and cadre—of our battalion (four firing batteries) moved to a tent city at the firing range. We would construct the range facilities. "Troop labor" was the only alternative when the remnants of the Louis Johnson Defense Department still had their foot on the neck of the military budgets. Ultimately we were to spend most of the next 8 months in this desolate, desert camp among the sidewinders and coyotes. There was such pressure to complete the range, we worked 7 days a week with only alternate weekends off duty—Friday evening to Monday morning.

[1] Capsicum is the "hot" in hot peppers and is the active ingredient in pepper spray.

Many of these guys were young marrieds like myself and the extended time away from wives and family was a real hardship, and certainly made the heart grow fonder if you get my drift. Thus, you can imagine the hustle on those weekends we were given passes. There was an old master sergeant, the Camp Fire Marshal, who brought his personal plane up to Red Canyon and flew off an impromptu desert airstrip to get home to Bliss in a hurry.

It happened that one weekend, a carpool of which I was a part—Sgt. Roach driving that week—passed the airstrip outbound just as Sgt. Thomas took off for Bliss in his Piper Cub. We were restricted to 30-40 mph on the range-road connector to US380 but went to "flank speed" as soon as we hit the hard surface of the highway. We screamed through Carrizozo at 80-90 mph to join US54.

In many western regions, rainfall is so sparse that an opportunity is taken to save on culverts and bridges. Since the streambeds are nearly always dry, engineering design must only accomodate the 10 year or 100 year floods. To do this the highway is simply gently sloped to the bottom of the dry stream bed and then back up to grade. Driving at less than breakneck speed, you might barely notice these swales. Driving at "Flank Speed" was another matter.

Roach is peering at the sky on our right, "There he is!" He points and we can barely make out the tiny Piper Cub heading south in the lea of the Oscura Mountain range. As he tried to get a few more revs out of his Olds 98, someone cautioned about the dry washes. "Yeah, I know. Sarn't Russell here is ridin' shotgun. That means he is also the navigator. He's going to navigate them dry washes."

This worked pretty well. As we zipped through Oscura, Three Rivers then Tularosa, Russell, apparently from memory, coached Roach on these hazardous washes. Roach would ease off to 50-60 mph. Even at that speed we got a sensation much like a roller coaster. Going into the approach slope, you momentarily feel semi-weightless. You then hit the bottom, the springs compress, your weight goes to about 300 pounds then about 100 pounds as you exit the wash.

As the western Organ Mountain peaks began pointing their long shadowy fingers toward us, we cruised through Alamogordo the last major town on our homeward route. Roach returned to flank speed. We could catch the glint of the dying sun on the Piper Cub's wings as it bounced on the mountain thermals. I actually think we were gaining on him!

South of Alamogordo, I must have dozed off in the back seat. The 98 was a luxurious automobile and rode like a dream, which is probably what I was doing. It had been a long, frustrating week of hard work and I was just impatient to get home to my young bride and a cold beer. Suddenly I had a sensation of total weightlessness. This lasted about 3 seconds then we bottomed out the springs, hitting hard. I pancaked a T-6 like this once at Randolph and caught hell for it.

Fig. 19-4. A German WWII "V-1" Buzz bomb". The Brits called them Doodle-Bugs. About 1,000 of them dropped 2,000 lb warheads on southern England. They used a very rudimentary inertial guidance system. They could hit countries and states but cities were iffy. However, the ram-jet engine was 5 years ahead of the Allies.

Another 3 seconds and we were not only weightless, we were airborne! I snapped fully awake to see Roach's white knuckles in a death grip on the steering wheel. This shock induced catatonic state probably saved us. If he had even slightly turned the wheel we would have landed and rolled.

We finally regained contact with terra firma and only to fishtailled badly. Roach got it under control and spoke angrily to Russell, "Dammit ta hell, you didn't tell me about that one!"

Russell, sheepishly, "I miscounted, Jack. I miscounted. I'da swore there was only three of them suckers! OK, so there was four. I swear they ain't no more of 'em. It's straight sailin' all the way home now."

Indeed, US54 was straight, dry, clear, lightly travelled like so many New Mexico's roads—one of the reasons one-car, fatal accidents are so high in that state. Roach responded by putting the pedal to the metal once again and as we went through Oro Grande as a bluish blur, we heard Thomas in his little Piper. He had seen us and came down to waggle his wings. OK, so we didn't beat him to Bliss, but we kept up with him!

Classroom lectures were getting more rare now, but the following week, Lieutenant Vitelli gave us two hours on the aerodynamics of the Nike missile. The lieutenant was an aeronautical engineer and gave a good lecture. Afterward he asked if there were any questions or comments. Sgt. Russell held up his hand and volunteered, "Lieutenant, if you ever need any input on the aerodynamics of a 52 Olds 98, Sgt. Roach here can tell you plenty. He raced Sgt. Thomas in his Piper Roach from the range camp to Bliss and beat him!

It was only a slight exaggeration.

Those odd weekends were blissful but most evenings we had to provide out own entertainment which was mostly bull sessions.

Fig. 19-5. Sidewinder, Crotalus Cerastes. One of our pets in the New Mexico range camp.

DINING AL FRESCO IN NEW MEXICO

Lying on my folding cot one night with the tent flaps rolled up, I noticed a campfire near the range road. Bored, I drifted on down to participate in what I assumed would be a bull session. I assumed correctly although a couple of the guys had sticks and it looked like they were roasting wieners.

"Whatcher got there, Crawford?" I recognized a young draftee, one of the very few in the Nike program. Crawford was a back-east college guy who had, by some monumental personal screwup, let himself get drafted. Making the best of it, he understood the opportunity in the guided missile program and had volunteered.

"Here you are, Sarge." he disengaged his roasting stick and handed me something rolled in a slice of white bread. They were all peering at me intently and I knew damned well they were up to something!

"But, what is it?" I insisted. They all rolled their eyes, laughed and watched me.

"Rôti de Sidewinder," said Crawford, eyeing me uneasily as I peeled open the bread.

They were expecting a violent reaction and I will admit I was somewhat stunned. But, old Colonel Robinson said, '...never let 'em see ya sweat!'

I took a bite and said, "Needs a little salt Chef Crawford. You seasoning leaves something to be desired!" But I ate the rest of it to the disappointment of the campfire boys. Not to let them down on their little prank, I told them, "I'm sorry to deflate your joke but you see I made a solemn committment to myself in Korea some months ago that, if necessary, before I starve, I'd eat anything that didn't eat me first."

Crawford then told me how he had almost stepped on the rattler just after sundown and had killed it in what he considered self-defense. He showed me the skin which he had stripped to dry and make a belt. I often wondered if he did and also if he ever told this story to his kids and grandkids. I don't think they would have believed him.

The Sidewinder (Crotalus Cerastes) was the most intriguing to me among the flora and fauna of the New Mexico desert. It's called "sidewinder" from its sidewinding locomotion—an efficient method for escaping over soft sand by looping the body forward in the shape of an S that contacts the ground at only two points, then "rolling" each loop ahead by shifting those points of contact back along the length of the body, by which means the snake may reach a top speed of about 2.5 mph. Sidewinders average less than 2 ft long and are generally a sandy color with grayish or brownish blotches, and the scale above each eye is developed into a hornlike projection. See Fig. 19-5. Sidewinders are primarily nocturnal and feed on lizards and small rodents.

If you look a sidewinder square in the eyes (kids, don't try this at home!), it looks like a horned toad—so ugly as to be bizarrely striking. Of course they will strike, although, being on the small end of the rattlesnake family lineup, they don't carry much venom and might not kill you.

Since that lovely, crisp evening in the New Mexico desert—Daisy and I have dined aboard La Perouse anchored on the Schelde in Antwerp—feasting on *eel* (Paling en ter Groene), I've savored sautèed baby *eels* (Anguilles Sautèe), while gazing over the Prado in Madrid, dined on *squid* (Calamari Fritti) at the Principia de Savoie in Milan and *conch* (Scungili Salata) at Les Madrigals in New York City as well as dispatching some other disgustingly delicious delicacies—but none would ever compare with Rôti de Sidewinder à la New Mexico!

FIRST BORN

The days dwindled down, shorter and shorter and we celebrated Christmas with a few days off in Ft. Bliss. But as winter solstice passed and we looked toward the vernal equinox, we knew when it came there would be three of us to celebrate the rites of spring.

Indeed, I was on a few days break in early March when the appointed time arrived and we made a dash for William Beaumon Army Hospital, maternity ward.

Since the 7th century, millions Tibetan Buddhists believe each Dalai Lama is the reincarnation of his predecessor. They are taught that at the Dalai Lama's death, the incarnation is to be sought among newly born boys.

At 1700 Hrs (5 PM) 5th March 1953, Conrad Richard Salmon checked in at 6 pounds 11 ounces— a fine healthy, lusty, baby boy. Just one sinister shadow fell on this otherwise blessed event—Joseph Stalin[1] died at precisely the same hour. What if...?

So that you may sleep better tonight, I should report that after carefully monitoring Rick over the years we are certain there are absolutely no tendencies toward genocide,world domination or totalitarianism and...not only is he not a Communist—he even listens to Rush Limbaugh.

[1] Joseph Stalin, the dictator of the USSR, was born Joseph Vissarionovich Djugashvili on Dec. 21, 1879 and died suddenly on Mar. 5, 1953.

Fig. 19-6. Daisy and Rick on our back stoop at Fort Bliss, 1953. Rick is about 4 months old. The 'swamp cooler' is behind Daisy.

Fig. 19-7. Here is the little man again in Ruidoso amongst the Mescalero Apaches. Neither Rick nor I flinched at the scalp dance consequently we were spared some hair.

KNOB TWIDDLERS

It was October 1953 and the blistering New Mexico summer sun had burnt everything at White Sands Proving Grounds black and was beginning to relent. Me and the other cadre of the transitioning 86th Anti-Aircraft Artillery Bn (GM-Nike) had joined the "old" battalion for their final Annual Gun Practice on the AA ranges. The "old" 86th was a 120mm gun battalion which was based at the old WWII Libertyville Naval Air Station, northwest of Chicago. All anti-aircraft units in the continental US came to White Sands each summer for service practice. The good folk at home would not appreciate the fireworks of live firing over their heads.

We were invited to wander around and familiarize ourselves with battery operations as well as get acquainted with the current members of the battalion but had no role in the firing practice. The "old" 86th was equipped with the latest equipment for gunfire control—the Air Defense Fire Control System M33 designed by Bell Telephone Laboratories and manufactured by the Western Electric Co. at Winston-Salem, NC. The radar antenna is mounted on the roof of a 25 ft van which otherwise housed the entire system—computer, video displays, computer driven map plotters, optical tracking facilities and communications. I was quite impressed with the setup. There was nothing obsolete about the equipment. What *was* obsolete was the concept of conventional guns against 1950s era aircraft. Guns just couldn't cut it anymore. This was the reason for the development of the Nike guided missile system and the 86th's transition to missiles.

Captain Novak had his six 120s laid, nervous cannoneers were in position on the gun platforms and live firing would begin momentarily. The 356th Tow Target Squadron flying out of Biggs Field 20 miles south of us would furnish towed sleeve targets[2]. Two other alternatives were "RCATS"—Radio Controlled Aerial Targets and "virtual target engagements" which fed dynamic electronic simulations of engagements into radar and computer circuits. Virtual targetting involved actual firing but the scoring was done by radar and theodolite assessment of the airburst and the redlegs didn't like it much. "It's much more satisfying to see something blown to hell!"

As the target towing aircraft made its first pass to show itself and hopefully reduce chances of accident, Novak stepped out of the door of the fire control van and, standing on the small metal rear platform, watched the target with one hand on a computer control just inside—"Fuze Spot". Throughout the engagement he continuously "twiddled" this knob.

The battery fired in salvo. Six 120mm guns going off simultaneously makes a thunderous boom. Firing in salvo attempts to bracket the target and at the very least, scare hell out of the crew.

After the first day of annual service practice, we retired to the Club since "After Action Reports" are always

[2] To be fair to the gunners, these targets were enhanced by addition of "corner reflectors" to give the radar echo of a full size Russian bomber.

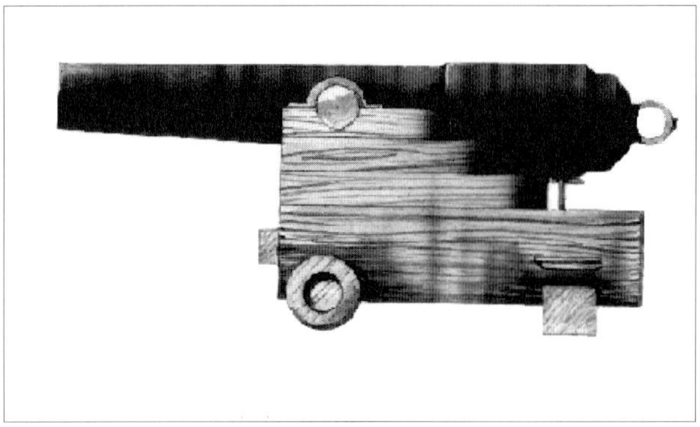

Fig. 19-8. Ole Betsey, handmade, 240mm, smooth bore black powder cannon. Shoots cannonballs, rocks, dead animals or cans of garbage. Castles knocked down. Butts kicked. Rent is 10,000 ducats per month with skilled artillerist. Satisfaction guaranteed.

Fig. 19-9. The Parrott cannon of Civil War fame looks over the old battlefield at Chattanooga. The artillerist-artist elevated the gun with the screw just under the rear of the barrel. To traverse, he had to pick up the trail and move it.

more productive when accompanied by copious quantities of cold beer. I brought up the question of Captain Novak's knob twiddling. After much discussion, I formed a picture that was really quite sad. Let me explain—

Saint Barbara, the patron saint of artillerymen—or artillerists, as they were called in the Middle Ages—smiled with favor upon many of them. Some artillerists developed their skills to such a degree that, operating free-lance, they were in great demand. Scene: The Chamber of Counsellors at the local castle where King Ludd and his counsellors are talking with a famous artillerist.

Artillerist: Yes, your Honor—your royal Luddness, me and old Betsey out there...(jerks his thumb toward his 10" cannon parked out front see Fig. 19-8.)...can certainly help you if, say you wanted to kick a little butt over there at Ol' King Ludwig's. Them walls that your guys are going to take 2-3 years to batter down—me and Betsey can do it in a week. My fees are fair and you will actually save money! I want 1,000 ducats up front and 10,000 more upon the smashing of the walls. But, your Grace, I must point out, this is a limited time offer." Thus, the artillerymen of the Middle Ages were highly esteemed, highly paid, ate higher off the hog and had a warm bed by the fire.

Look at them now. It's all science and very little art. Consider the skill requirements of the cannoneers on the platforms of those 120mm guns. Watch what they do—at the command "Load" one ammo handler grabs a 40 pound projectile and tosses it into the loading cradle, another adds a 30 brass cannister, the propellant charge, behind the projectile. Noting the placement of the semi-fixed ammunition, the gun captain (a sergeant) hits the big red "Load" button. The rolling breech block unlocks and rolls open. A hydraulic arm (Thor's biceps) then sweeps the ammunition into the breech and the block automatically re-closes and locks. Internally, the fuze cutter is positioned to grasp the ogive-shaped nose of the projectile and, receiving time signals from the fire control computer, adjusts the Variable Time fuze to the latest computed time value.

The M33 uses an analog fire control computer. Far from eyeballing along the barrel of a Parrott gun[3] then adjusting the elevation screw before firing a 24 pound shot at Pickett's Gettysburg charge—the artillerist now sits with hands folded in lap and watches the computer continuously solve 400-500 differential equations to compute the X, Y, and Z space coordinates of a predicted intercept point and send this information to the gun platform to spin the electrical traverse and elevation motors of the gun and the fuze cutter.

When the fire control chief hits the "FIRE" switch, the fuze cutter is retracted, the firing pin strikes the initiator and 40 lbs of high explosive erupts from the muzzle and starts on a ballistic path to the computed intercept point.

In the fire control center: three radar operators control the radar and thus the computer input for azimuth, elevation and range. Most of this is in "Auto" mode. The operators seldom touch the controls. The fire control chief watches the Plan Position Indicator and the auto-plotting maps. He chooses a time such as to not down the aircraft on top of the local elementary school, he flips up the safety cover and thumbs the red switch to "FIRE".

What art has come into play here? Very little! The technology has sucked all the art out of it . I sympathize with Captain Novak and his twiddling with the only control he had over firing his battery—the VT fuze spot.

[3] The Parrott gun was the most commonly used cannon in the Civil War and was named for its developer. See Fig. 19-9.

BACK TO THE DESERT

Although the weather did not show it, technically fall had arrived in El Paso del Norte—it was early October 1953. We had celebrated the end of our ordeal ("The Bridge on the River Kwai" often came to mind) at that hot, dry, dusty summer—building Red Canyon Range Camp. Battery D was reveling in unaccustomed luxury back at the AA and GM School at Bliss. That we all regarded Fort Bliss life as luxury says something about our months of living in the desert. Frustratingly, we were now looking at our first anniversary at Bliss on what was billed as a six months training tour. The delays were due to manufacturing glitches at Western Electric's plant in Winston-Salem, NC but now rumors were rife. The manufacturing bottle-neck was now broken and trainloads of Nike Ajax Systems were streaming westward.

Western Electric had assigned a dozen or more field engineers to the AA&GM School. These fellows would liaison with the troops and, after qualification firing, would accompany the battalions to their deployment sites—one engineer per battalion. I hung around a lot with these guys and picked their brains when I could[4]. All bright young guys, most with families, I sympathized with their plight. They had no idea how long they would be in residence in El Paso, consequently, some brought their wives, some brought preschoolers while others lived as bachelors. What neither troops nor engineers knew is that we and they were about to undergo tribulations that try men's souls.

By mid-October we no longer needed rumors. As we did our rotating shifts on the two sets of Fire Control equipment in the radar park, we could see the Ft. Bliss railroad sidings begin to fill with masses of Nike equipment. There were mixed emotions. We were elated to get the equipment and we would very soon go do our mandatory three rounds of live fire and be on our way. But, we were depressed that this qualification firing would be at Red Canyon Range Camp. "Oh well, it shouldn't take more than a couple of weeks," we thought.

Daisy and little Rick were getting re-acquainted with me and life was at least tolerable. Our quarters was half a ward of the WWII Fort Bliss Post Hospital converted to a two bedroom apartment. Daisy learned to stuff cotton into keyholes and tape around the windows and doors when sandstorms threatened. She missed the keyhole in the front door once and about a bushel of sand filtered in like a skiff of snow. She was even happy to hear the news of the equipment arrival. "You're going to have to be gone again but at least we can see the end of this West Texas stay."

The 1st Guided Missile Brigade Commander, Brigadier General Martin, accompanied the troops and equipment in his chauffeured staff car as we convoyed up to Red Canyon. We should have been more apprehensive at what transpired on that 160 mile trip—portents of future agonies.

General Martin acted as though we were hauling loose eggs. He stopped one prime-mover[5] after another to berate the driver, call the NCO in charge to account for permitting reckless driving, etc. When one prime mover stopped, all stopped. After all these interruptions the convoy was 3-4 hours late and got into the Range Camp well after dark. Moving these trailers over that range road nearly drove the General (and drivers) nuts. General Martin was up tight.

Initial installation of both Fire Control and Missile handling facilities took three weeks. It should have taken one. Again, General Martin was all over the place—commanding and demanding.

"Well, it's just one more ordeal that we must endure for our ultimate redemption—shoot three missiles and get the hell out of here!" was the prevailing attitude.

In the Fire Control section our work was repetitive and frustrating as we assisted the field engineers in getting all the electronic circuits through "ring out". But this work was not particularly dangerous. The guys in the Missile Section could not say that. Here's what they had to contend with:

Warhead handling. The main Nike Ajax warhead was a watermelon shaped core of PETN[6] tightly wrapped with 100 yards of piano wire[7] of 0.5 cm square cross section which was scored, also at 0.5 cm intervals. This main warhead is located amidships with smaller warheads just aft of the forward canards and just forward of the missile boat tail. The total effect of these warheads was to spray 10,000 steel cubes into a spherical volume at a velocity of about mach 4 which is 3,000 ft/sec or about the speed of a rifle bullet.

> Looking back on these words, I realize that some gentler souls may be put off by hints of horrible explosions, shrapnel flying, aircraft torn apart and falling from the sky. I apologize, but ask them this—if a Russian bomber had penetrated all the US outer defenses and was proceeding toward *your* city with an atomic bomb in his bomb bay and mayhem on his mind—would you prefer a prayer from Billy Graham or the ole 86th AA Battalion salvoing missiles at him?

These warheads are always stored separately in blast

[4] Three years later, after a BSEE at MU, I would join Western Electric in North Carolina as one of these Nike Field Engineers.

[5] A Prime Mover is a large, powerful military spec tractor much like the tractor of today's 18-wheelers. They pulled the equipment trailers.

[6] PETN - Pentaerythritol Tetranitrate $C(CH2OH)_4$ A high explosive of extremely high brisance or shattering power.

[7] "Piano wire" refers to the type of steel used—cold drawn with extremely high tensile strength. It has nothing to do with pianos.

proof bunkers but had to be manhandled into the Ajax missiles to prepare for a shoot. Actually PETN is as stable as TNT and I have never known of an accident with it. What was a lot more scary than the high explosives was the fueling operation.

Missile fueling. In the years to come most of the Army's rockets and missiles were to be propelled by solid fuel. Even then the booster used Thiokol solid fuel. But, the Nike Ajax was a pioneer and used liquid fuel. Let me lecture a bit on how a liquid fueled rocket works then you'll see why fueling these suckers made folks a bit uneasy.

LAUNCHING

The "boost" phase pushed the Ajax missile from zero to about 2,500 miles per hour in about ten seconds (kids, don't try this in your Camaro) after which it was burnt out and disengaging the missile, fell back to earth. In all cases the boost phase was unguided and the missile was launched almost straight up to about 60,000 feet. Upon booster separation, the booster collar slipped off the rear end of the missile and actuated the "boat tail switch".

The Ajax missile had a small, "sustainer" rocket engine, a ceramic lined chamber about 18 inches long and 6 inches in diameter. It had the classical shape, a combustion chamber, a narrow throat for compressing the gases and then a venturi nozzle for the exhaust. It generated about 1 to 2 g's of thrust and burned for about 20 seconds. Remember, the missile is at 60,000 feet and moving at 2,500 miles per hour. It doesn't need much thrust to maintain its velocity since at the "7-g dive" command its belly is rolled to the azimuth of the predicted intercept point and it then dives in that direction. In all cases it *dives* onto its target much like a falcon stoops[8] to its airborne prey.

At "SUSTAINER MOTOR IGNITION"—inhibited red fuming nitric acid (IRFNA) is injected into the combustion chamber to mix with a like injection of methyl alcohol. This is a hypergolic[9] mixture. (The GI's called this mixture "Paregoric" see below.) The primary fuel, JP-4, is metered into the resulting flame front and provides the propulsion. JP-4 is simple jet fuel used by thousands of commercial and military jets.

JP-4 is innocuous, very similar to kerosene. Methyl alcohol is medical (rubbing) alcohol. It's the IRFNA that is scary. I went into the launching area one day and watched my old pal Sergeant Roach manage a team fueling a missile. The entire team donned their "space suits" of specially formulated polypropylene with glass visors. I saw Roach pretest the emergency shower. He stepped under it with his suit on and yanked the big metal ring. A hundred gallons of flushing water fell on him before he could get it turned off. I said 'so long' to Roach and got the heck out of there. That red fuming nitric acid is baaaad stuff!

ZERO TOLERANCE

Our optimistic "two weeks in the range camp" had started in late October. It was now late February and there were rumbles of mutiny. The basis of the distress was not so much living in the desert again, this time in the bitter winter of 1953-'54. The joking about applying for mutiny permits was caused by the General. He was obviously out to make a name for himself and was totally impervious to the technical advice of a hundred Ph.D. scientists at Bell Telephone Laboratories and of the Field Engineers. He demanded that each and every pre-firing test of the equipment show perfect results. Although tolerances must be and are applied to every manufactured item in the world, he would not have it. He demanded absolute *zero tolerance*.

Let me try to illustrate the stupidity of such orders—lets say your State Auto inspection specs demanded that—say, tires must be aired to exactly 32 pounds per square inch. And, further, the inspection station had the equipment to measure tire pressure to one millionth of a PSI. You say, 'It's no problem at all to air up tires to 32 PSI. I say it is *impossible* if the inspector insists on *zero tolerance*. If he says, "Mr. Smith, you may not drive this car until it meets tire pressure requirements with no tolerance allowed. I will not accept 32.000001 PSI. I will not accept 31.999999999 PSI. Pressure must be exactly 32.000000000000 PSI

Do you understand what our beloved general was doing? And all the frustrating while, we were separated from home and family, living in squad tents where the frigid desert winds sucked the heat out of a tent in 3 minutes. We broke ice in our wash basins to wash and shave while this asinine jackass played his zero tolerance game. My mind went back to the incident at Motobu Camp on Okinawa where Lt. Phaehler was narrowly missed by a carbine round that ricocheted off the door above his head. I thought that was horrible. But I was now wondering...

Ultimately the general management of the Bell System—Bell Labs and Western Electric— went to the congress and to the Pentagon. They contractors were being made to look like absolute incompetent fools by this martinette in New Mexico. I think he must have been dressed down by the Army Chief of Staff personally. Whatever caused it, his foot came off our necks and firing schedules were beginning to be met. It is now March.

There was such a logjam of firing batteries lined up to get off the three qualifying rounds and get out of there that scheduling was a nightmare and sections chiefs (e.g.,

[8] "Stooping" is an effective falcon tactic for catching prey on the wing. High over the target, the falcon folds its wings close to its body, retracts its legs and free falls on the target. At the instant of impact, it flares and strikes the bird at 60-80 mph—talons first.

[9] Hypergolic mixture - two liquids which ignite spontaneously upon contact.

me) had to sign off in blood that the system was ready to go. Finally in early March we were on! RCATS were revving up 20 miles south at the Oscura RCAT Launch facility and we would shoot at around 10AM.

Like the gun practice at White Sands, the RCATs carried corner reflectors so that they gave off the radar signature of a Russian medium bomber. The RCATs were launched in a peculiar manner. The launching runway was circular with a 6 ft solid steel post in the center. I visited the facility once and was impressed by the resemblance to model airplanes. They used a small, two-stroke gasoline engine and gave off the same annoying whine of power models. The plane's right wing tip was affixed to a restraining cable from the center post. The engine was started and the captive plane circled the center post wildly, gaining speed. When they got up to 50-60 mph, the controller hit the release, the restraining cable was disconnected and off he went. They were controlled by radio and visually observed by powerful theodolite optics.

By the way these RCATs were the granddaddies of the drone observation aircraft that were used extensively in the Gulf War. For example, a pilotless observation drone was launched from the foredeck of the battleship Wisconsin to examine an area that had just been salvoed by cruise missiles. As this drone careered around probing the battlefield, a group of Iraqis emerged from their bunker and waved a white flag! This was the first "toy" airplane to take prisoners on the battlefield!

FINAL EXAM 1 OF 3 - ACED IT!

The word came from Oscura, "Your target is on the way!" My position was at the PPI where I would first see the target as a blip on the acquisition radar screen. The acquisition radar had a range of over 100 miles and continuously swept the area. The RCAT blip shows up and I immediately place an electronic cross on it to designate it as a target and tell the target tracking radar operators, "TARGET!" They confirm the command and the range operator pushes the "ACQUIRE" switch which takes information from the acquisition radar to guide the initial acquiring of the target. In a hot engagement, I would have actuated the IFF (Interrogation, Friend or Foe) circuits and watched for a correct response from the designated target.

I took the target tracking radar operators about 3 seconds to lock on the RCAT (range was about 15 miles) and flip all controls into AUTO mode. Immediately I flipped the ENGAGE switch and heard the computer behind me slew its potentiometers into prediction mode. The guys down in missile launch area were, of course, listening to all this on the intercom. The Battery Commander issued Roach the command, "PREPARE TO FIRE".

The launch crew had long since added fuel and warheads to one of the Ajax missiles and at this command, they simply rolled it onto the launching arm, actuated the erector arm to point it up at an 85° angle and reported "MISSILE READY". The next command initiated the final task in the launching area—"ARM THE MISSILE". Roach then physically screwed an initiating squib into the rear of the booster and reports, "MISSILE ARMED". The launching crew now make a dignified retreat into the bunker and swing the heavy door shut.

In the Fire Direction Center, Captain Novak asks each of us in turn if we are ready for launch. I look at the horizontal automatic plotting board—whose two plotting pens are off the paper but hovering over the target and the predicted intercept point respectively. The motors of the plotting arms whir as the target bounces around at 10,000 ft. The pen plotting the intercept point is like a cat with the target as the mouse. Each time the target changes direction, the intercept plotter quickly moves to "head him off".

The Missile tracking operator has acquired the erected missile and reports "LOCK ON, STRONG RETURN". Novak lifts the safety cover and holds the FIRE switch. On the intercom he now counts down backwards, ...3, 2, 1 Fire! He flips the switch. For two seconds nothing happens this delay permits the last calculated intercept azimuth to be sent to the missile control gyro. The gyro is pointed to that azimuth then uncaged and will provide the base course from which all guidance corrections will be issued. Then WHOOOM! and the game commences.

Normally, my position would be to remain before the plotting boards and monitor the engagement. (At launch both the plotting pens drop to the board and begin plotting the course of the engagement. The "Intercept Point" pen now switches input to plot the missile position and in the first few seconds did not move much. That was because it is launched almost straight up and its ground track was barely moving. However, on the ALTITUDE PLOTTER, the pen was heading for the ceiling. Novak spoke to me just as the DIVE COMMAND LIGHT went on. The missile had now quit climbing and was diving toward the target at a breathtaking rate. Novak said, "Go outside and watch, Salmon. I don't think the booster has landed yet and we have a strong southerly wind." Hard to believe only 15-20 seconds had elapsed.

I stepped out the door and quickly closed it (the interior is kept in darkness such that the tiny ultra violet lamps can cause the controls, dials and indicators to fluoresce with a faint green glow. I searched the sky to the south and saw the dark streak of the booster casing falling well within the safe zone. Novak will be pleased to know we haven't killed anyone on our side yet.

It was a clear day and the chilly wind was beginning

to lay. I thought I might be able to see the missile miles away but I knew it was now swooping down on the target, only seconds to intercept. All the missiles were painted white and in the clear desert sky could often be seen by the naked eye up to 10 miles away.

I did not see it but because I was focused on that part of the sky, I saw the intercept, and the orange and black explosion of the warheads. We would have to examine all the recorders to evaluate the shoot but it looked good to me!

Both Fire Control and Missile Launch sections were huddled in the messhall with our third cup of black coffee when the Battery Commander finally showed up. He came in with a solemn look on his face and our hearts dropped. Then with a big grin he announced, "Best shot so far. We actually hit the RCAT!" No one expects to do that, indeed it isn't necessary. The game is like horseshoes and hand grenades—getting close counts.

EXAM 2 OF 3 - BUST!

With all the above-mentioned hazards available to be loosed on us by one screwup —150 lb. of PETN, 50 gallons of fuming nitric acid, you would never guess the cause of a real accident that occurred on our second shoot. A careless habit of a "shadetree mechanic" scrubbed that shoot.

Everyone knows a "shadetree mechanic" indeed, at one time or another most grown American males have *been* shadetree mechanics. Shadetree mechanics helped win WWII. Rural folk and especially farmers must learn at least some rudimentary mechanics in order to keep things in repair. Most do it quite well and some extremely well.

When such soldiers are given special mechanical training, they often excel. However, there is one bad habit these skilled craftsmen often find difficult to get rid of—the desire to tighten screws and bolts to the very limit of their strength. You hear—"I don't want to see this darned nut come lose and cause the blade to take my leg off." or "I've tightened this darned thing three times and it comes loose each time. Hand me that humonguous wrench there would ya Jody?"

The "skin" on the AJAX is made up of 20 mil magnesium body moldings. Magnesium is lighter than aluminum and is more ductile thus easier to shape into some of the unusual forms that missiles require. Virtually everything that was done to the missile required removal of some access plates. On our second shot, one of Roach's missileers was dreaming of home and fireside (I suppose) and lapsed into old habits. On replacing a panel, he screwed it on with a regular wrench (forbidden) and—worse—he "...tightened that sucker down so she'd never fly off!" All this we learned at 1400 hours that afternoon.

Again, Novak got the jitters about dropping the booster on someone's head. He had absolutely no control over the booster impact point other than to delay firing momentarily if there were heavy or gusty winds from the south. Again, he sent me out to the rear deck to watch. I thought this was pretty neat since we had already proven there was very little danger from missile blastoff—a lot of sand, dust and a few pebbles flying harmlessly. Now, I'd be able to follow the entire engagement, or at least until the missile streaked downrange and out of sight.

The launch was awesome. Even though it was a mile away, I felt the blast and the rush of air on my face. The Ajax was still well within sight when it popped the sound barrier and sent a startling BOOM downrange. I saw the booster separate at the extreme range of my naked eyeball. But, something was radically wrong! There was 1-2 seconds of sustainer motor burn then the rocket exhaust disappeared then reappeared—the missile was tumbling. About 2 seconds later it looked like a giant bag of confetti exploded. MISSILE BREAKUP! MISSILE BREAKUP! I ran in to tell Novak what had happened and he immediately got on the intercom and passed the warning to everone. He didn't need to. There were dozens of onlookers in the open on the slopes behind us. They saw what happened and headed for cover!

Fortunately, the ground track of the missile was already miles to our south and after the initial few seconds of reaction, everyone came out to watch the debris fall. We were again lucky in that most of the main chunks were retrieved and more importantly, the cause of the breakup was clearly evident to the Douglas missile engineers. These screws were to be torqued at 25 ft-lbs. The investigator said, "Some of these screws were torqued down to about 300 ft-lbs. He musta used a pipe wrench!"

We were permitted to fire again the next day and achieved another bulls-eye. It was getting routine.

PAREGORIC

While were waiting our turn for our final shot, I wandered down to the fuel dump. There was a giant dump with dozens of barrels of methyl alcohol. This alcohol was one half of the HYPERGOLIC (called, colloquially, PAREGORIC) mixture that was the oxidizer for the JP-4. Stenciled on each was a warning skull and crossbones:

DANGER - WARNING - POISON

METHYL ALCOHOL - NOT POTABLE
THIS ALCOHOL CANNOT BE MADE POTABLE
BY FILTERING OR CHEMICAL PROCESS
DRINKING THIS ALCOHOL WILL RESULT
IN SEVERE GASTROINTESTINAL DISTURBANCE,
BLINDNESS AND POSSIBLY DEATH!

DANGER - WARNING - POISON

I thought, for Pete's sake—I can understand the concern about having alcohol around the GI's—and the long explanation that it cannot be made "potable". There is a myth that will not die about submariners straining torpedo (methyl[10]) alcohol through a loaf of bread and making it drinkable. But these signmakers really screwed up. They used the word "potable". Not one GI in five knows what the word "potable" means.

FINAL EXAM 3 OF 3 - ACED IT!

After our third successful launch we celebrated with a cup of black coffee in the mess but then immediately ran to our tents and began packing up our duffel bags to exit Red Canyon Range Camp never, ever, ever to return.

Little Rick had been born and had celebrated his first birthday while I was on this extended desert tour. In early March we went to Juarez to buy him a pair of cowboy boots for his birthday. With new cowboy jeans and jean jacket he was ready to visit with his grandpa and other relatives in Missouri. See Fig, 19-10. No grass would grow under us. We were very anxious not to suffer one more sandstorm.

There were graduation speeches, awarding of certificates and then the formal "PASS IN REVIEW". We stomped by General Martin in the reviewing stand kicking up as much dust as possible while flipping him a one-finger salute. Our household goods were packed and loaded, our autos were loaded and we were ready to go. Immediately off the parade ground—everyone rushed to their cars and took off like banshees. So looong El Paso! We shan't be bothering you again.

LAST TEST—A BLUE NORTHER'

Since we were headed for Pilot Grove and Blackwater, we layed out a different route—we went up US54 (at less than flank speed) through Alamogordo then connected with US70 through Ruidoso where we saluted the Mescaleros (once we had a clear path out of town). On we went—to Roswell, through Area 51, to Portales where we had been stranded once in a deluge that put 5 feet of rushing water in the dry washes. We departed New Mexico at Clovis and headed up the Texas panhandle hellbent for Amarillo.

Little Rick, now one year old, was a good traveller. He snored away in his little car bed and we stopped several for snacks and diaper changes. He got plenty of fluids to counteract the dessicating winds that were starting to blow. At Clovis, I stopped for gas and had to hang on to the car to keep from being blown away. But it was still pleasantly warm,

Fig. 19-10. Conrad Richard "Rick" Salmon, Ft. Bliss, Texas 5th March 1954 (first birthday). "Now that I gots me a cowboy suit, you're headed for Chicago!"

a normal New Mexico spring day.

As we approached Amarillo, the northern sky was turning dark blue and looked threatening. "Too late for snow," I thought. But, as I gassed up in Amarillo, the wind which had not moderated in intensity, turned cold. It felt like it was right off a glacier. I was reminded of Will Roger's comment on Oklahoma weather, "There ain't nothin' between Oklahoma and the North Pole but a one-strand barbed wire fence and that one is often down."

That day brought our introduction to the "Blue Norther". In the space of 3 hours, the temperature dropped about 40°, 70 mph winds shifted from Oklahoma back to Texas the geography that had been last shifted from Texas to Oklahoma and we began receiving stinging sleet.

Fortunately, once we hit Route 66 in Amarillo, we tacked hard starboard set a heading for Oklahoma City, put the pedal to the metal and fled the hostile realm of the "Texas Blue Norther".

LESSON LEARNED: Inspiration for some life decisions may come from very strange places.

[10] Methyl alcohol—CH_3OH—is the secret ingredient added to ethyl (drinkable) alcohol to "denature" it and make it poisonous and undrinkable. The process is irreversible, so you can just forget about filtering it through bread.

EL PASO EPILOGUE

In 1974, 20 years after our sojourn with the sidewinders, cactus and coyotes in Ft. Bliss and New Mexico, I had occasion to fly to El Paso on a consulting project. I took Daisy along and we did a nostalgia tour of some of the places of our early years of wedded bliss at Fort Bliss. We saw William Beaumont US Army Hospital where Daisy presented me with our first born—Rick. I saw the old radar park where my team ran exercises on the first Nike training system. We visited Swanky Frankie's and had batter fried shrimp. The shrimp was good but it was $2.50 instead of the 50¢ we had paid.

Probably the strangest sight I saw was upon our arrival. The airport is one of those where the gates are about 3 miles from the main terminal—or at least it seems that way. As we strolled down the corridor following the signs to the MAIN TERMINAL, the PA system had Marty Robbin's "El Paso" on a loop.

I heard the distinct cadence of troops marching in step and it is easy to tell, they are marching to that tune. We rounded a corner and here they came—about 50 troops of the *Deutsches Luftwaffe*. I remembered that the Anti-aircraft and Guided Missile School at Bliss, my alma mater, enrolled students from many NATO countries[11]. But it was was a very strange sight.

WELCOME TO CHICAGO

THE WINDS - 1954

Pixilating, fenestrating, ventilating,
Icy winds blew straight off the lake.
This is Springtime in Chicago?
With frosted nose, frozen toes
Feels like my bones gonna break.

The calendar said it was springtime when we exhausted our few days of "delay enroute" (vacation). PawPaw said good-bye to his favorite grandson and we set course for Chicago in our 3-shades lighter Pontiac Catalina. Apparently, the good folks of Chicagoland take instruction from a different calendar. The winds off Lake Michigan were so icy and cutting, I suffered a relic of my childhood—otitis media—inner ear inflammation.

After I got Daisy and Rick ensconced in temporary quarters, I went to the Libertyville Naval Air Station to report for duty, Battery D, 86th AA Missile Battalion (Nike). Several other members of the Ft. Bliss cadre—my classmates—had reported in on that day, so Captain Novak took the occasion to introduce us to the somewhat bewildered former gun crews. We also toured the temporary installations of the Fire Control Center, Tracking Radars, and Missile Launching Facilities. They were set up on the old NAS hardstands and landing strips without any attempt at blast-proof bunkers. These would come later via a contract with a major construction firm. This site-hardening work was already underway but would take months to complete.

Fig. 19-11. North Chicago, Spring 1954. Rick said he was happiest when he was an only child. Here he is in the first of his three year reign in that position. Indeed, he does appear quite satisfied with his lot doesn't he?

Troop billets, as well as administrative offices were housed in Nissen huts. A Nissen hut is a Quonset hut with canvas replacing the corrugated metal of sides and roof. These buildings would be my habitat for the remainder of my tour, indeed the remainder of my active duty Army service. With the unending Lake Michigan winds, the pictures in my memory are much like scenes from the Antarctic.

OUR LITTLE HOME BY THE LAKE

We drove up to the last address on the list. It was a quiet North Chicago street but maybe that was just because it was Sunday. We were dreading to look at another one of the dog kennels that we had visited that day looking for quarters. Daisy was demoralized after driving all over the northern suburbs of Chicago and being shown apartments

[11] The Deutsches Luftwaffe also had and still has a major contingent of pilots training at Holloman AFB in New Mexico. They can't get their required flight training in the crowded airways of continental Europe.

that she would not judge suitable for old Spot. Hard eyed landlords had given us the up-and-down, checked out the car, the uniform, the baby and then with a straight face asked for a rent you would expect on the French Riviera. If this last one didn't do it, we might have to consider Daisy and Rick returning to Boonville to stay with her sister until I was discharged. I had started the paperwork for an "early out" to make the summer session at MU. I would not particularly relished staying in the BNCOQ—pretty sterile ambiance—but it would only be a few weeks.

Daisy was using Rick's fretfulness as an excuse to procrastinate—to build up the courage to face one more of these fleabags. He was probably hungry. He had inherited a transmogrification gene from his mother. Unless he was fed within 5 minutes of his stomach's precise mealtime alarm, the gene kicked in and he was transmogrified from a sweet, cuddly, darling little boy to a screaming and snarling monster. Fortunately, one peanut butter filled cheese cracker completely reversed the process. I looked around for a store to get him a snack but Daisy had packed some things for him and was rummaging in her huge rucksack. I should have known she'd be prepared to deal with him.

So here we are— 1 bdrm, furn, kit w/all appl,TV,
fans, nr trans, no pets. HI6-6239

Steeling ourselve to mount the stairs and ring the bell, we checked out the neighborhood—not too bad. There was an ancient oak in the front that lent a certain panache. The lawn looked like it hadn't been mowed since President McKinley visited Chicago last but there was a cheerful rose garden at the side of the house. The older, 2-3 storey houses reminded me of my short 1947 stay at 3616 Holmes in Kansas City. Large, comfortable, single-family houses built years ago for some long dead Chicago executives, had been broken up into small apartments with skimpy planning by craftsmen of indifferent skills.

Here we are. The landlady was a surprise. She was personable, fortyish, plump but dressed semi-fashionably and spoke English with only a trace of her native Armenia, or Bulgaria or one of the other -garias. The apartment on offer was on the first floor (thank goodness) and was overall of reasonable size except for the bedroom. It was fitted with a double bed but was so tiny that when you rolled out of bed you were in the living room.

The bathroom had a nice tub and commode but no washstand. "Do that in the kitchen sink," she said. She showed the washing facilities in the basement—which was a dungeon. She took us out back to the gas meter feeding a hot water heater dedicated to the washroom. "You just insert one or two quarters into the meter and you'll have hot water in 15-20 minutes."

"Lemme get this straight. If we want to do laundry we gotta come out here in back of the house and insert money into that parking meter looking thing—is that it?" I asked her.

"Yes, of course," she looked at me as though I had just fallen off the pumpkin wagon. In my life to that time, I had not seen or even heard of selling gas or electricity in that manner. Years later in England, I learned that practically every low to middle priced home in the country built from the turn of the century until the 1950s had just such an arrangement. English screenwriters universally use the "shillin' in the gas meter" to evoke that particular era.

The kitchen was adequate and "all appls" were there. The "fans" in the ad worried me. We had just come from Texas and wondered about summer heat. "You won't be bothered with heat up here on the north shore. We get a cooling lake breeze all summer. The fans will be enough." she reassured us. I had already spent a few days on the Libertyville Nike Site and had experienced that "lake breeze" she alluded to. I was thankful that there was a flip side to this unending wind. Chicago is not called the "Windy City" for nothing.

There were many negatives but the TV compensated. It had a screen of about 7 inches but was enhanced by a Rube Goldberg rigging that held a large magnifying glass in front. In addition, though color TV would not be widespread for a decade, you could visualize color on this set, with a little imagination and the assistance of a transparent plastic film stuck on the back of the magnifying glass. This film was blue at the top, fading to transparent then to green at the bottom.

"OK," I thought, "Lemme see here. We are being offered adequate if not exactly luxurious quarters. The environs are a little scruffy, probably working class, second generation immigrants—the very people whose boisterous hospitality I had gratefully accepted when I returned from the Pacific. Most important of all, the rent quoted was well within our means!"

A niggling little voice asked, "What's the catch?" But we were nearing the end of our tether and so we signed on for one month. That was on Sunday.

On Monday, broad shouldered, workaday Chicago and environs returned to its grind and the niggling little voice said, "I told ja so!"

The "catch" was the noise...and the smell.

A fish processing plant on the lake about 2-3 miles away favored us with its fragrance—wafting in on the famous lake breeze. Skokie Highway—invisible to us but only 2-3 blocks away—carried a raging torrent of auto commuters to the city spewing clouds of nitrous oxide, carbon monoxide, sulphurous particulate as well as a noise level just under the threshold of pain. Abbott Laboratories—a giant pharmaceutical firm—had a plant which must have been engaged in rendering the essence of skunks. A major truck route 2-3 blocks to our west had recently been criss-crossed with new gas lines and the backfilling and restoration of street surfaces left much to be desired. Eighteen-wheelers hauling loads of junk and scrap metal bounced along at 50-60 mph and sounded like riveters in a boiler factory. The earsplitting clamor was accompanied by clouds of diesel exhaust.

In 1968, the Congress passed the first "Clean Air Act" and the environmentalists began their ascendancy. Not everyone was at one with this noble purpose and a number of curmudgeons commented on it. My favorite curmudgeon of the era was Jonathan Winters[12] His quote was: "Clean air my foot. Where I come from, we just don't trust air that you can't see or smell!"

Winters would have been right at home in North Chicago in 1954. And as for the smell—one of God's manifold gifts to mankind is the gift of olfactory habituation—you just get used to it. Your nose gradually normalizes to whatever scent of the day drifts in on the wind and that stench becomes normal. I think that a full breath of fresh air would have startled us. "What in the world is that strange odor?"

But, in the days to come, we tried out the smoked and dried fish in the local ethnic delicatessens and found we liked it. I still regard smoked Lake Michigan white fish a treat.

AMOR VINCIT RAZORWIRE

Monday, 24 May 1954—Received my orders to report to the Fifth Army Personnel Processing Center at Ft. Sheridan on Wednesday 2 June for out-processing. I had taken a risk and pre-registered for the summer session at the University of Missouri (Columbia), praying my "early-out" request would be approved.

I received a fat student packet (Student No. 40721) in early May and now Fifth Army Special Orders 154 completed the requirements for my "Sojer to Student" transformation. The 3-day Memorial Day holiday would give us opportunity to rent a trailer and load out our few household effects, kiss the landlady good-bye, clear our apartment before the June rent was due and zip down to Boonville for the weekend. Daisy and Rick would again impose on the kind hospitality of her dear sister Marie and brother-in-law Jerry McClure while she looked for suitable digs in Boonville for our new married-student life. (I had decided to locate in Boonville and commute to Columbia because there was a higher probability of finding part time work in Boonville. MU students glutted the labor market in Columbia.)

[12] Years later I learned that one of the reasons this guy was so funny was that he suffered bouts of insanity.

Tuesday, 1 June 1954—I never had any misgivings about this major change in career and family direction but I would confess to a bit of nostalgia. I had spent nine years in military service and it was a familiar if strictly regimented life that I would be leaving. It was with these feelings that I said good-bye to my cohorts at Battery D then drove down to take leave of a few particularly close friends at Battery C. I would move into the Ft. Sheridan BNCOQ the next day.

Sgt. Jones was a likable fellow, but he was one of guys who tended to be described as 24 going on 6—not very responsible and subjected to frequent "iron whims". "Yep, I'm a-gonna buy me that little red convertible and I don't give a damn what *you* say!"

It was he, his wife and all their troubles that caused Daisy and I to try to be "Dutch Uncles" to them. I wanted to see how they were doing in their marital war. Jones met me at the main gate and signed me in.

"What the heck is that?" I pointed at the massive amount of razorwire forming "aprons" on both sides and sitting atop the chain link security fence. This was the first time I had seen razorwire and on more careful examination, I thought— 'I wish we had had that vicious looking wire at Koto-Ri! Well, maybe not. If we had had razorwire, we'd probably still be there!'

Battery C was subject to all the security surrounding the Nike Missile Defense System. It was located on the grounds of Argonne National Laboratories. Argonne was a facility of the Atomic Energy Commission and was a major player in the development of the atomic bomb. It also rated a high level of security. But this construction was new and massive, not in evidence at my last visit.

I felt a cold finger on my spine. To understand this concern, you must remember the national obsession with the Communists in the early 1950s. In 1954 US Senator Joseph Raymond McCarthy was riding high in the saddle, conducting televised senate hearings on his allegations that the Army was infested with Communists, Communist sympathizers and other assorted pinkos and fellow travelers. Careers, reputations and lives were being destroyed on prime time television. His activities gave rise to the term McCarthyism, referring to the use of sensational and highly publicized personal attacks, usually based on unsubstantiated charges, as a means of discrediting people thought to be subversive. In December the Senate voted to condemn him, 67-22. Thereafter, McCarthy's influence declined sharply—but, in May, he was charging forward, all guns blazing.

In early May, 86th Battalion officers and non-coms were assembled for an orientation by the Fifth Army Office of Counter-Intelligence. For a half day, we were familiarized with several actual espionage attempts to penetrate US

Fig. 19-12. Insignia collection - Part 7. LEFT - The 86th AA Artillery Battalion insignia (Battalion Crest). Metal, it is worn on uniform epaulettes,CENTER - Shoulder patch - The Air Defense Artillery Command worn on left shoulder and RIGHT Collar brass - Air Defense Artillery Branch worn on left shirt collar or blouse lapel .

air defenses, to exploit seemingly innocuous contacts with servicemen. We were admonished and instructed on all the standard counter-intelligence measures to protect Chicago Air Defense integrity. Clearly, from all the new razorwire barriers—some type of overt attempt must have been made on physical security at Argonne! Senator McCarthy's fulminations may not be all scare tactics.

"Jones," I asked, "Have you guys experienced some penetration of security here?"

"Whatcha mean?" He looked puzzled.

"All this," I waved my hand at the bristling fence with its sparkling razor points along the new fence.

"Oh, that," he replied smiling, "Yes there was a penetration awright! A couple of high school girls!"

"Girls! What? Girls?" I was amazed.

"Oh, yeah. Salmon you apparently you ain't been down here in early evening. It's now..." He consulted his watch. "...eighteen hundred [6 PM]. Take a look at the street out front."

And there it was! A unending parade of cars each with two to six young women cruised slowly before the daunting fence. They apparently were circling the block, I saw one group several times as we watched. There was also a gaggle of "honeykos" pedestrians at the fence—talking with the troopers inside.

"Well tell me about it," I urged Jones, "Did they actually penetrate the fence? What did they do? Were some of your guys involved?"

"Sure, our guys were involved. About two weeks ago the OD [Officer of the Day—in charge of the interior guard] found two a them little quails in the Fire Control bunker with their boy friends."

"Doing what? Why have we not heard about this?"

"I think they were drinking a Pepsi Cola. You ain't heard about it because all the brass is so embarrassed at them teeny-boppers breaching our security that they are keeping it quiet. Believe it or not the troopers who helped them in will not be court-martialled or even seriously disciplined!"

I looked at the passing parade and the razorwire fence, "There is an Latin saying, 'Amor Vincit Omnia' [Love Conquers All]. Apparently here in Chicago, we can also say ***'Amor Vincit Razorwire'.***

Jones: "Huh?"

ENDGAME

My frenetic activities of March, April and May of that last year—preparing for a drastic career change— reminded me of that part of a Nike air defense Fire Mission called "ENDGAME".

Picture this: In a darkened Fire Control Center, greenish dials glow under the ultraviolet lamps while seven actors play out the final moments of what could be a life and death game. Four tense radar operators monitor their CRT displays, ready to manually intervene if this "bogey" shows any ECM[13] capabilities. The computer guy stands by the massive analog computer listening to the click of zero-set switches to anticipate any fault. The Fire Control Chief (me) sits in front of the Horizontal and Vertical Plotting Boards to determine where this "Bogey" is going to be splashed. The Battery Commander sits in front of the Plan Position Indicator and the security covered FIRE Switch.

ENDGAME begins about ten seconds before pre-

[13] ECM - Electronic Counter Measures.

dicted intercept. You can sense it . Potentiometers whir at a frantic rate as the computer speeds up calculation of a new intercept point. Missile guidance commands are doubled in intensity. On the Horizontal Plotting Board, the Missile pen begins vibrating as the missile violently maneuvers to more urgent commands.

Finally—INTERCEPT—both target and missile echoes break up and the game is over. ENDGAME—a few taut, frantic and tense seconds followed by sighs of relief and wiping of sweaty brows.

FINAL EPILOGUE

So, that's about it. I drove off into the sunset, was discharged and paid off at Ft. Sheridan and started classes at MU on Monday 14th June. I'd like to say that everyone lived happily ever after. I can't—because we have not yet arrived at "ever after". But, let me assure everyone concerned about my personal stories—wandering around clueless for so long. I deeply appreciate your concern but, the stories (not yet written) change after 1954. Your CARE packages may not be required after all. Before retiring to California in 1988, I was Vice President for Planning of Citicorp's European Division headquartered in London (and ineligible for Food Stamps).

When one reaches that Biblical "three score and ten", one is permitted to philosophize and pontificate. One proviso—do it in writing so your audience may, without giving offense, quietly skip to the next page. Here's my pontification.

I've learned most of my lessons by making mistakes. I certainly do not hold myself as any example to be emulated by my descendants or other impressionable young "skulls full of mush". But there are some attitudes I think are useful. I would admonish a young person—

• Don't be paralyzed by fear of failure. I failed many times and was chagrined, embarrassed, humiliated and devastated. But I never obsessed on it. I tried to puzzle out what these failures told me abut myself—weaknesses and strengths of which I was oblivious at the time.

• Don't be a smart-ass. The fact that you aced all the hard subjects in school and are held in some esteem as a nerd, may not mean much when "when the drums begin to roll." Mastery of difficult skills is valuable but so are personal and social skills. Try real hard to be a little humble.

About growing up in a small town—best place in the world to raise a family! Even in terrible economic times and in the shadow of the onrushing World War, I luxuriated in the freedom that I enjoyed as a child. Even my school homework, my chores as well as the few wage producing jobs I held as a child and youth left me lots of freedom to explore and pursue my dreams of the moment. Of course, one advantage of growing up during the Great Depression, it was difficult to get into serious trouble.

One thing I suffered was lack of a mentor. I mention elsewhere that in 1954, on the MU Library steps Mr. Shier said about me, "In Pilot Grove, even fatherless boys can get themselves prepared for college!" He was only partially correct. He inferred that had my father been alive, I would have gotten guidance toward a career or vocation. This was not true. The late 1940s were a period of such rapid change, virtually no one could predict with much confidence, where the future would lie for a young guy.

My Dad could not have helped much, but then, neither could anyone else. In hindsight, I sometimes cringe at the advice I heard my cohorts receiving from their parents. The old folks were trying to be helpful but were pontificating from personal experiences that had been scathing and scarifying—the Great Depression.

I have no overarching wisdom to offer on this problem but suggest that it is a *big problem* for many young people.

When he was about seventeen, older son Rick started on his mother and me about getting a motorcycle. We gave him a firm no. "But, Dad, I'm not asking you to buy me one! I've got the money." But all he heard was NO! NO! NO!...Until the day he found a picture of me astride my big white 1946 Harley "Hawg". Parents have difficulty defending themselves from charges of hypocrisy. He got his motorcycle.

This story is by way of addressing those who might be intrigued by "Gone fer a Sojer". I would advise that while long term military service was a part of my "Great Adventure", I would *not* recommend it generally. For anyone that wishes to argue that I am a hypocrite on this, I would point out that the national and world situation was very, very different in 1945. I would point out that the alternatives open to uneducated, untrained but adventuresome young men was somewhat limited in those days.

But, a short tour of military duty just for the travel and adventure of it, for the self-discipline that every young man needs—would not come amiss. It might lead to a "Most Excellent Adventure"!

Oh yes, you want to know what ever happened to Sgt. Jones and his wife. I returned to the old battalion the following summer (1955) for a two-week tour of reserve duty. Jones was glumly living the bachelor life in the barracks—his wife had split.

APPENDICES

Appendix A — The Burnhams

Stories of my ancient ancestors—some from as far back as the Norman Conquest, 1066. The poignant story of my Great Grandfather and his younger sister occurred just prior to and during the Civil War. The setting was Pilot Grove, Boonville and environs.

Appendix B — Cpl. John Henry Kendrick

This is a concise story of my maternal Grandfather and his four years of service in the Civil War. He was mustered out at Boonville in 1865.

Cape Ann, Massachusetts. The first of the Burnhams to come to the new world were cast ashore here in 1635. Three brothers, John, Thomas, and Robert, sons of Robert and his wife Mary (Andrews) Burnham, of Norwich, Norfolk County, England, came to America early in 1635 in the ship Angel Gabriel, in charge of their maternal uncle, Capt. Andrews, master of the ship. They were wrecked on the coast of Massachusetts about 30 miles from Boston. Family tradition has it that a chest (containing valuables) belonging to the three boys was thrown overboard with the freight to relieve the vessel at the time of the disaster.

The boys settled in Chebacco, in the colony of Massachusetts Bay, with their uncle, Capt. Andrews, who having lost his ship settled there, the boys remaining with him. John and Thomas served (boys as they were) in the Pequot expedition against the Indians in the late 1600s.

From quiet homes and beginnings, out to undiscovered ends.
There's nothing worth the wear of winning, but laughter and
the love of friends. —*Belloc*

OVERVIEW

IN THIS APPENDIX I RELATE THE ORIGINS OF the Burnham family (my maternal ancestors) as well as stories of distant relatives in their early days in the new world. In addition I relate a poignant story of the death of my Great Grandfather's younger sister who was Marjorie (Babbitt) Brown's Great Grandmother

I must thank Marjorie for the loan of an extremely unusual book—Roderick Burnham's compilation of genealogical records and stories of the early Burnham's. The Burnhams were among my maternal ancestors. (I completed a book on my *paternal* ancestors last summer.)

There are several aspects of Roderick Burnham's work that you may find fascinating. They are:

• The (1080 A.D.) origins of the name "Burnham" which can serve as an example of the origins of surnames. Surnames (last names) were little used before the middle ages.

• The story of the traumatic arrival of the Burnham brothers in the new world in 1635. They were shipwrecked at Cape Ann, Massachusetts Bay Colony.

• The story of one of the brothers (Thomas, 1662) who, in trying to save the neck of a client accused of blasphemy—Abigail Betts—placed his own neck in jeopardy.

• The religious fanaticism of some of the people of the Bay Colony who seemed to insist on freedom of religion for themselves but denied it to others.

• The arcane, barely decipherable language, spelling and terminology of the day (1662). I reproduce the court records of the Betts affair in their original form.

• The "Burnham Estate" of £70,000,000 or so awaiting the valid claims of "North American Burnhams".

•The terrible anguish that the author of the Burnham book must have felt when his only child—a 21 year old Lieutenant of Artillery—was killed at the Battle of Chickamauga in 1863.

THE BURNHAM FAMILY GENEALOGICAL RECORDS

By Roderick H. Burnham, Longmeadow, Mass. Publ by Case, Lockwood and Brainard of Hartford, Conn, 1869

Bio-sketch of author—Roderick Henry Burnham devoted much of his time—five or six years—to the compiling and publishing his History and Genealogy of the Burnham Family. He represented the towns of Longmeadow, East Longmeadow, North and South Wilbraham, in the Legislature of Massachusetts, the memorable winter of 1861-2.

His wife, Katharine Livingston Burnham, was the daughter of Samuel Mather of Middletown, Conn., and Katharine, daughter of Capt. Abraham Livingston, of Stillwater, N. Y. Samuel Mather is descended from Rev. Richard Mather (and his wife Katharine, daughter of Edmund Holt, Esq., of Bury, England), who came to this country from Lancashire, England, in 1635, and settled in Dorchester, Massachusetts.This family of Livingston is descended from Lord Livingston, Earl of Linlithgow.

Roderick and his wife Katharine were devastated when their beloved only child, 21 year-old Lieutenant Howard M. Burnham died at the Battle of Chickamauga in 1863. See "Roderick's Son Howard Killed at Chickamauga" below.

Fig. A-1. Burnham Coat of Arms— "Four crescents argent on a sable field and divided by a Cross argent." From the Encyclopedia of English Heraldry.

ORIGIN OF THE BURNHAM NAME

Walter Le Veutre, came to England at the Conquest, (1066), with William of Normandy, in the train of his cousin german Earl Warren; and at the survey (1080), was made lord of the Saxon villages of Burnham, county of Norfolk, (and of many other manors). From this manor he took his surname of De Burnham, and became the ancestor of the numerous family of the name, that have lived through the succeeding generations.

To the Normans belongs the credit of having first regularly instituted and employed surnames in the present sense of the word; and they may be said to have been formally introduced into England at the Conquest. It appears, however, on good evidence, that they were not wholly unknown there prior to that event. The feudal system naturally tended to create surnames out of landed possessions, and at the same time to limit their use to the upper classes. For a long time, therefore, they were the privileged titles of the few, and the means of family distinction, employed by the people in general. It may be said that five centuries elapsed between the date of their importation to that of their general adoption throughout the country, during which interval they were slowly spreading downward through society.

BURNHAM BROTHERS 1635

From the best information obtainable at the present day, it would appear that the three boy brothers, John, Thomas, and Robert, sons of Robert and his wife Mary (Andrews) Burnham, of Norwich, Norfolk County, England, came to America early in 1635; that they came in the ship Angel Gabriel, in charge of their maternal uncle, Capt. Andrews, master of the said ship; that they were wrecked on the coast; that, with the freight thrown overboard to relieve the vessel at the time of the disaster, was a chest (containing valuables) belonging to the three boys; that the boys came to Chebacco, in the colony of Massachusetts Bay, with their uncle, Capt. Andrews, who having lost his ship settled there, the boys remaining with him. John and Thomas served (boys as they were) in the Pequot expedition.

John was appointed deacon of the church at Chebacco. He became the owner of a large tract of land, lying on the east side of what is now known as Haskell's Creek. Many of his descendants removed from Chebacco and settled at other places.

Thomas was commissioned as Lieutenant, was Deputy to the General Court, was Selectman, and on town committees. He owned much land both in Chebacco and in Ipswich, and a sawmill on Chebacco river.

COURTS —THE BETTS CASE

1662. Abigail Betts, wife of John Betts, was accused of blasphemy, in saying that "Christ was a bastard, and she could prove it by scripture." Thomas Burnham attempted her defence, and in "saving her neck," drew down upon himself the indignation of the Court, and suffered accordingly, as will be seen.

At a Quarter Court held at Hartford March 10: 1662, Thomas Burnham's Accusation in the Case of Jo: Betts; That ye said Burnham's carriage therein hath been very Scandalous & Lascivious and pernitious, thereby interrupting the peace and tending to corrupt the manners of his Maj^ties^ Subjects, the members of this Corporation. In reference to Thomas Burnham's Accusation, the Court Judge him guilty thereof, And doe Adjudge him to be comitted to ye Custody of ye Prisonkeeper, there to be secured during the pleasure of ye Court. And further this Court doth disfranchise the said Burnham of ye privilidge of his freedom in this Corporation. And like wise doe prohibit him for future for pleeding any causes or cases in this Civil Court except his owne. And that when he shall be remitted out of Prison he shall give in Security to ye Court or Secretary for his good behavior til the Quarter Court in June next.

Extracted out of ye Records,
pr Danll Clark, Secy."

Thomas Burnham Appeals

Thomas Burnham appeales from ye sentence of this Court to ye hearing and determination of ye Generall Court tomorrow."

"March ye 12, 1662. Thomas Burnham appeared before the General Court to prosecute Appeal against the sentence of the Court of Magistrates.

1.We humbly conceive yt we had not exact Justice In that we were put to ans: before we had an accuser yt was legally stated.

2.We doe also conceave there was noe p^e^sentment or accusation legally entered before we were called to answer.

3.We know of noe man that was bound to prosecute against us upon whom we might recovr damadges in case ye plea was not made good.

4. There was nothing which by law established was Mattr of fact yt was legally made good against us.

5. The penalty imposed doth not naturally arise from any established Law: which we are bound to observe. That which I propoundeth hath reference only to ye mattr of Betts."

Before the General Court.

The Accusation or complaint against Thomas Burnham in Bets his business.

His proceeding herein was pernitious to ye welfare of this Colony and obstructive in its owne nature to the current of Justice; the Evil effect thereof is obvious to ye Understanding of all men herein pursuing the wages and rewards of Iniquity.

2 ly. His carriage herein was illegal, contrary to ye foundations of Government in this Colony usurping and arrogating unto himself the Civil power established in the Civil Courts.

3 ly. His carriage was Lascivious, Vile and abominable below and beyond all moderation of manhood; utterly unsuteable for his Sect and one in his condition to undertaken promote or effect. To ye first: The test: of Ryder together with Burnham's test: Clearly Evince his undrtaking to save her neck, and his progress and indeavour therin Samll Boreman's test: doth likewise clear it.

2 ly. Out of ye covetious frame of his heart forsaking his Call: and lawfull occasions sole himself for a reward to doe wickedly.

To ye 2d. His own Testimony sufficeth wherein it appears he actually seperated Husband and wife contrary to ye Law of nature and rules of God's word, making himself the highest Judge in this oe Israell.

To ye 3d. His carriage was Lascivious et. his whole progress for the evidenceing the ground of this inhuman separation clothed with garments spotted with the filthy pollution of a loose, wanton, and unclean spirit.

On the back is endorsed.

"The Court have considered the nature of Thomas Burnham's offence from what hath been presented to their consideration, have come to this conclusion as is presented in ye Accusation, And therefore Grant Burnham for liberty to make any further plea for his clear: if not the Court will proceed to a Judgment."

Abigail Betts Sentenced

And respecting the expressions of Abigail Betts, This Court judgeing them a flagitious Crime of a holy offence in saying "Christ was a Bastard and she could prove it by scripture."

Doe adjudge the said Abigail to be comitted to ye Custody of ye prisonkeep til to morrow and then to be guarded as a Malefactor to ye place of execution, wearing a rope about her neck, and to ascend up ye ladder at ye Gallows to ye open view of spectators that all Israell may hear and feare."

Farther on in the Records.

It is ordered by ye magistrates upon consideration of an irreconcilable distance of spirit that is in John Betts and his wife in reference to Conjugal union. That John Elderkin, her father, shall take her under his tuition and Government until further order issue forth from ye Court or from ye Deputy Governour, Major Mason, with advice of Mr. Fitch and Mr. Buckley.

I find no punishment recorded, that was inflicted on Thomas Burnham, for defending Abigail Betts, excepting his being, deprived of his citizenship for a time, and prohibition from future pleading

[Note: Thirty years later (1692), 20 "witches" were tried at Salem, Mass. Nineteen were hanged and one was executed by "pressing". (See Fig. A-2—The Salem Witch Trials.)]

THE BURNHAM ESTATE

1694. Benjamin Burnham died in London, England, and left property, situated and valued, at that time, as follows, viz: real estate, (150 acres), including a part of Burnham Road, (now Regent street, London), Burnham Beach. Cottage, and Burnham Wood, valued at over $7,000,000, and

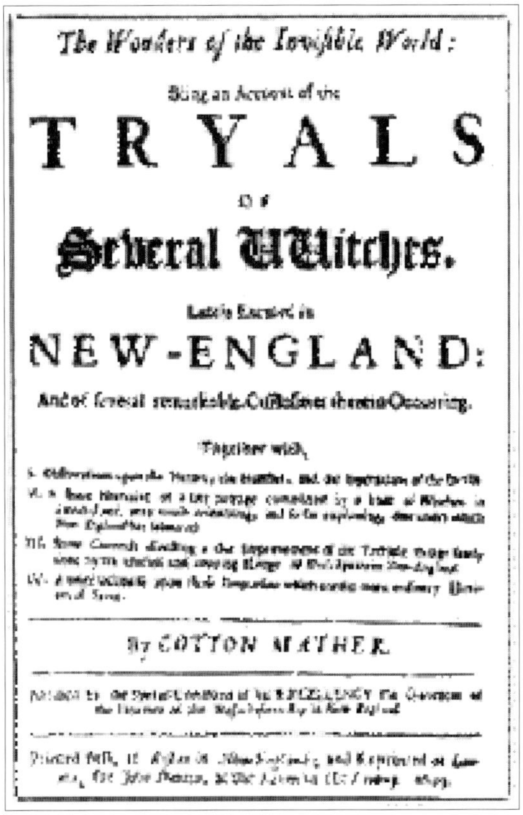
The Wonders of the Invisible World:

TRYALS

Several Witches.

NEW-ENGLAND:

By COTTON MATHER.

Fig. A-2. Cotton Mather advertises the Witch Trials.

rated at £4,500.

More recently, (1860), the property is described as follows, viz: real estate, situated in London, in and near Regent street Lambeth, Lambeth Walk, Carlton street, Dons street, etc. etc. etc., and is valued at about $22,000,000, yielding an annual rental of about $880,000; personal property invested in the East India Company.

Total value of real and personal property, $65,200,000, giving an annual income of $2,392,000.

This property awaits the heirs at law, supposed to be at present in this country. The heirs of Edward Burnham, Benjamin's elder brother, for more than sixty years, contested for possession on the ground that no heirs existed in America, and failed.

This statement of the situation and amount of the immense Burnham estate, is condensed from the information, from all sources, in the hands of the compiler. He does not hold himself responsible—for its accuracy, although he believes in the existence of the "estate" but has not the least faith that any one in this country will be in the slightest degree benefited by it.

The following letter, which explains itself, has been preserved in the family of Michael Burnham, Esq., of. New York, and was kindly furnished me for publication by his daughter, Mrs. Russ.

"State of Vermont, Rutland county, Middletown, Feb. 22, 1830.

To the Hon. OLIVER BURNHAM Of Cornwall, Ct.

Dear Sir—It has been rumoured in this section, among the people of the name of Burnham, for some time past, that there was in the National Bank of England, a sum of Money belonging to all the people of the name of Burnham, in North America. It is stated as high as thirty six millions of pounds sterling, about one hundred and sixty million of dollars. It is said that a man of the name of Burnham, went from Boston to South Wales, in England, about three years ago, and there saw in a London newspaper, an advertisement to that effect; and when he returned to Boston, he caused the same to be published in a Boston paper, and that the said Burnham was now gone to England for inquiry on the subject. I should be pleased to see such a publication, or information to that effect. I am directed by letter from Col. Wm. B. Sumner, of Middlebury, to write you on the subject of information. He writes, there is no doubt about there being a large property in England, belonging to the descendants of the Burnham family, and all that is wanting is to prove the lineage. I have taken the trouble of obtaining the information that a pedigree can be traced back to two of the ancestors which settled in Ipswich, Mass.

It is said that the Burnham family sprung from three brothers which landed at "Cape Ann," about 30 miles from Boston, not far from the commencement of the 17th Century. About this period the great political commotions in England began. My grandfather, John Burnham, who died in this town, in the year 1811, at the age of 96 years, was born in Ipswich, Mass., where two of the brothers settled; my father, John, died in this town, last August, age 87 years; was born in "Cape Ann". I have it from my grandfather, and father, the old stock of Burnhams, that when they left England for America, they left a large amount of property.

If you possess any information on this great subject, to us, please write me, and we will readily cooperate with you, or any of the name, to obtain this money.

Respectfully yours,
JOHN BURNHAM."

The above letter, in the original, is most perfectly written, on pink paper.

The following letter was handed me by Guy C. Burnham, Esq.

Johnson, April 9, 1828.

GEORGE BURNHAM, Esq.

Dear Sir—I received yours of the 5th inst. and in answer will inform you that I have lately heard from my brother, in Milford, N. H., that he has heard from his son, Capt. Asa Burnham, who is now (if not returned), in England. He informs that there is a large estate, but that there can be nothing obtained on it, but the interest, and that not without considerable trouble to show the lineage or heirship to it.

Yours, &c.

JONATHAN BURNHAM.

RODERICK'S SON HOWARD — KILLED AT CHICKAMAUGA

First Lieut. Howard Mather Burnham USA, (Eighth Generation), son of Roderick H. and Katharine L. Burnham, was killed at the battle of Chickamauga, Georgia, Sept. 19, 1863. The extracts below are from his letters, and from newspapers of that time.

[From a Boston, Mass. paper.]

LIEUT. HOWARD M. BURNHAM

Lieut. Howard Mather Burnham was born March 17, 1842, and died Sept. 19, 1863, on the battlefield of Chickamauga at the early age of twenty-one years.

When the first gun fired on Fort Sumter gave the signal of war, it did not take him unawares. Though excited, he was not startled by it. The fire had long been burning in his heart, and now it burst forth in all the glow of an enthusiasm which could not be gainsaid. He only waited for the consent of his parents, and on April 19, 1861, the memorable day when our Massachusetts soldiers were attacked in Baltimore, he joined the "City Guards" at Springfield. About a fortnight after, with a prospect of speedier service in active warfare, he united with the Tenth Regiment Massachusetts Volunteers, then forming on Hampden Park, in which he was chosen a lieutenant. A few weeks thereafter, received a commission as second lieutenant, Fifth Regular Artillery in the regular army. After several months' service as recruiting officer, and at Fort Hamilton, he was promoted to a first lieutenancy and ordered to join Battery H, Army of the Cumberland under Gen. Rosecrans.

As chief of artillery, and on the staff of Gen. Baird, he was assisting in the difficult task of conducting the artillery over Lookout Mountain when he fell. As was remarked at his funeral—He died at his post, serving his guns, surrounded by his brave men, in the very heat and ardor of the battle.

What pleasant memories have we all of that manly, open, handsome face, that laughing, eye that beamed so keen with honor and with friendship! We knew him as the obedient son as one who scorned from his deepest soul all meanness and untruth and deceit. We think of him as the type of gentlemanly bearing, and the model of courtesy.

He all along was unconsciously fitting himself for the career that was to distinguish his opening manhood. Full six feet high and finely proportioned, be became a proficient in manly sports and feats of strength; was a great walker, and felt perfectly at home in the saddle. He had grown rapidly; but the ability to "endure hardness" seemed to grow with his growth and strengthen with his strength. On the coldest winter day he disdained to wear an extra garment, and at night slept invariably with his window open, upon a hard bed, though born a child of luxury.

In his last letter, written amidst the haste and difficulty of getting the artillery through the mountain pass, he exclaims in all the overflow of his splendid health and spirits, "Oh this is a glorious life! How I should like to see you all, but not now. I cannot leave my post in a time like this." He had pined and longed in all the restlessness of his ardent soul for active service, and now it was his and he sniffed the battle from afar like the war-horse.

To one of the Sixteenth Regulars, who hurried to him as he fell, with the question, "Lieutenant, are you hurt?" his answer was, "Not much; but save the guns." He then asked for water. One of his lieutenants was soon after at his side, and said, "Burnham, do you know me?" Opening his eyes faintly, he murmured, "On with the Eighteenth!" and never spoke again.

CAMP DAWSON, NEAR STEVENSON, ALA., August 29, 1863.

Lieutenant Burnham's Last letter.

My Dear Mother:

The last letter I wrote told you that I took command of this Battery last Tuesday. I have since then been appointed Chief of Artillery for the First Division, Fourteenth Army Corps. I do not think we will leave our present camp for some time. The railroad bridge at Bridgeport will not be finished for sixty days, and though there are pontoons enough here to bridge the river, I am afraid they will not be used.

They are collecting large quantities of provisions at Stevenson, and the bulk of our army, some fifty thousand men, are encamped around and along the river in the direction of Chattanooga. Gen. Crittenden marched with his corps down the Sequatchie valley, and is now east of Chattanooga.

We have a new Division Commander, Gen. Baird, a major in the regular army. I think he will prove a fine officer. Being Chief of Artillery I am one of his staff, though I live with the Battery. I should love to see you all again, but would not like to leave this army at present,

I wish father would come down here. He would find my bed harder than that at Fort Hamilton. I have a rubber blanket, two soldier blankets, and an overcoat—the last I use as a pillow.

I have been so far in fine health, and like this outdoor life everything except waiting three or four days in camp. I suppose Longmeadow is looking very pleasant and our place more so, but I shall not probably see it this season.

Give my love to father, Ellie, and grandmother, and keep a good share for yourself.

Your affectionate son,

HOWARD.

Springfield Republican

From the Springfield Republican of the next morning, we quote the following brief notice of the funeral:

Funeral services were held Wednesday afternoon at his father's house in Longmeadow, over the remains of Lieut. Howard M. Burnham, who fell on the field of Chickamauga, last September.

The services were highly interesting and the attendance large. Appropriate remarks were made by Rev. Mr. Harding, of Longmeadow, bestowing worthy testimony to the noble character of young Burnham. The prayer was made by Rev. Mr. Buckingham, of this city, after which a beautiful dirge was sung. The casket containing the body was swathed in the national colors, and beautiful wreaths of flowers were placed upon it, while about the house were several relics of the young soldier's career, not the least touching of which was the head—board of his grave on the bloody field, with its rude and simple inscription. A large number of persons from this city were present.

HIRIAM BURNHAM[1]

My maternal great-grandfather **Hiram Matthew Burnham** was born in 1822 in Warwickshire England and died in 1895 in Rogers, Arkansas. My Great Grandmother **Madama Lafayette (Beatty) Burnham** was born in 1834 in Saline County, MO. and died in 1882 in Cooper County.

In 1826 Hiram M. Burnham immigrated to America at age 4 with his parents and younger sister Mary Morgan (age 2). The family originated in Warwickshire near Stratford-on-Avon. Fig. A-3-**next page** is a painting I bought at the Green Park Sunday art fair in London in 1985. I jokingly told Mom that it was the 'Burnham ancestral home'.

The Burnhams initially settled in upstate New York. Hiram's and Mary Morgan's father was a landholder there.

[1] From research by Marjorie (Babbitt) Brown and Jo Horner.

Fig. A-3. This is a painting I picked up at the Sunday Art show at Green Park, London. It hangs in our foyer. I told Mom that it was the Old Burnham Place in Warwickshire.

Fig. A-4. Mexican War. At Buena Vista, Gen. Zachary Taylor augmented his regular forces with Volunteer Divisions: Arkansas 1st, Illinois 7th, Kentucky 2d and Indiana 9th to rout Santa Ana. The Missouri 5th was activated but released after this unexpected victory. Feb 1847.

How Hiram came to be in Missouri in 1846 when he volunteered for the Mexican War (age 24), is a goal for further research. After his short military career he settled down to marry and farm some acreage 4-5 miles west of Boonville.

MEXICAN WAR

Hiram M. Burnham joins the 5th Division U.S. Army (Missouri Volunteers) at Boonville, MO

From the History of Cooper and Howard Counties Vol. 2 - W. F. Johnson, 1919 pages 167-168)

"Again the tocsin of war was sounded, in 1846. In the month of May of that year, the President of the United States called for volunteers to assist in the Mexican War. One company from Cooper County was called upon to join the troops in Mexico.

The alleged cause of the declaration of war by Mexico against the United States in April, 1846, was the annexation of Texas, but the more immediate cause was the occupation by the American army of the disputed territory lying between the Neuces and Rio Grande Rivers. On the 21st day of May of that year [1846] the Boonville Observer issued the following bulletin, or "Extra", which we give verbatim:

Volunteers.—A proper spirit seems to animate citizens of our country and especially the young men.

The call for one company from the fifth division has been promptly responded to. Forty-three volunteers were raised by General Ferry on Monday in Boonville, and on Tuesday, at Palestine, under the direction of Generals Ferry and Megguire, the number was increased to 61. They then elected their officers, and the following gentlemen were chosen: Joseph L. Stephens, captain, without opposition, who delivered to the volunteers on that occasion a spirited and handsome address; first lieutenant, Newton Williams; second lieutenant H.C. Levens; first sergeant, John D. Stephens; second sergeant, William T. Cole; third sergeant, Richard Norris; fourth sergeant James S. Hughes; first corporal, Tipton Prior; second corporal, A.B. Cele; third corporal, Wesley Amick; fourth corporal, A.G. Baber. The company thus organized, assembled in Boonville onWednesday, where they were exercised in military duty by their accomplished and gallant young captain.

The following is a list of the privates: Thomas Bacon, Samuel D. Burnett, Jacob Duvall, Charles Salsman, Ewing E. Woolery, Heli Cook, Joel Coffee, Joel Epperson, Jesse Epperson, Hiriam Epperson, John McDowell, J. R. P. Willcoxson, T.T. Bowler, William Sullans, Horatio Bruce, William J. Jeffreys, James M. Jeffreys, Hiram Burnam [sic], Edward S.D. Miller, John Whitley, Benjamin P. Ford, Philip Summers, George W. Campbell, Samuel R. Lemons, John R. Johnson, Thompson Seivers, Charles F. Kine, Jesse Nelson, John Colbert, Robert Thea, Edmond G. Cook, John B. Bruce, James P. Lewis, Benjamin C. Lampton, Oliver G. Ford, U.E. Rubey, W.B. Rubey, W.H. Stephens, John M. Kelly, George Mock, Samuel Elliott, Alpheus D. Hickerson, Edmond Eubank, Henderson C. Martin, Sprague White, William Woolsey, Martin Allison, Henry Francis, Robert H. Bowles, Justinian McFarland, Nathaniel T. Ford, James H. Jones, James C. Ross, Richard Hulett.

They departed today (Thursday) on the steamer L.F. Linn for St. Louis, where they will be armed and equipped, and immediately transported to the army of occupation on the Rio Grande. Our best wishes attend them.

When the steamer Louis F. Linn, Eaton, captain, Jewell, clerk, arrived in Boonville, on her downward trip, the company formed in line on the upper deck and many friends passed along the line, biding farewell and shaking each volunteer by the hand. The landing was crowded with people. The boat soon started, with cheers from the multitude, and waving of handkerchiefs by the ladies."

REPRIEVED

Fortunately for them, by the time the newly recruited volunteers arrived in St. Louis, positive war news had arrived from Texas and they were ordered to report to Jefferson City and stand in reserve. The Mexican defeats at Buena Vista (see Fig. A-4 above) and Chapultapec rendered the 5th Missouri redundant to the war effort.

When they got to Jefferson City, they were told to be in readiness and were then allowed to return home. Even though they never saw battle, the volunteers were welcomed home by large, cheering crowds.

YELLOW JACK

So Hiram returned home full of honor to a hero's welcome. He and his fellow volunteers got the free drinks and their pick of the girls.

Florence "Winky" Friedrich was kind enough to show me around her antebellum "Pleasant Green House." One of the many historical artifacts that Winky displays is a letter from her great great uncle (See sidebar at right.) who was a "real" veteran of the War with Mexico whom fate treated less kindly than my great grandfather. Conkright was in one of the regiments named in Fig. A-4.

[Author's note: In every war before mid-twentieth century, more men died of disease than from battle wounds. The Mexican War was certainly no exception.]

LETTER FROM PVT WM E. CONKRIGHT 1847

Source: Florence "Winky" Friedrich, Pleasant Green House. Conkright was her Great-great-uncle. The letter was originally published in Winchester, KY newspaper.

[Note by Winky's mother—"William E. Conkright served in Company L, 2d Regiment Kentucky Infantry, Mexican War. Mustered into service June 18, 1846 as a fifer of Captain Williams' company and was mustered out and honorably discharged as a private, May 27, 1847. He had been a volunteer under General Scott and served at the siege of Vera Cruz. He went to New Orleans to take a boat north to Kentucky, contracted yellow fever and died at the hospital in New Orleans.

His father, the Reverend John Conkright, made the trip by boat to New Orleans to bring his sons's body back to Kentucky for burial but failed in his mission. (Young

LETTER FROM WILLIAM E. CONKRIGHT

Dear Parents:—I feel that my time is nearly drawn to a close—my race almost run.

I know I have strayed from you. I feel you will forgive me, and God forgive my sins; and I am willing to go, and I want you to know it, although I am so weak I can scarcely hold my pen. I want to see you but cannot. I say to you and Cynthia, Margaret and Allen, do not grieve for me, but prepare to meet me in Heaven; and to Grand Father and Mother, and father Brock I know they have often prayed for me, and to them the same, I have to rest every few words. I wish I could see and tell you, for I cannot tell what I want. I would here exhort all my friends and connections to meet me. All I mind is the pangs of death. I suffer a great deal—I want to be out of my misery—I wish I could tell you what I want. Do not grieve for me, but think of meeting me where our troubles will be over, I hope to see uncle Isaac soon, and all my friends and relatives that have gone before. I expect to have a happy meeting when my soul quits this mortal frame. O I wish I was able to write sisters and brothers to meet me in Heaven. Obey your parents, for they know best what is good for you than you do. Farewell—no more on earth to meet. It makes me happy to thnk the day is coming that I hope of seeing all my friends where sickness never comes. All things will be peace and harmony. Shake hands with all my friends, and have a happy meeting at my funeral.

Your Son, W. E.
CONKWRIGHT

Fig. A-5. Hiram's brother was attracted by the California gold rush and he became a "49er".

Fig. A-6 Hiram Matthew Burnham 1822-1895, and his wife Madama Lafayette (Beatty) Burnham 1834-1882. Married in 1851. Hiram was born in Warwickshire, England and immigrated to New York with his family in 1826. Madama was born and grew up in Saline County, Missouri. 1870s photo.

W.E.C. had run away from home at the age of 17 to join the army as the infantry company fifer. Mrs. Friedrich displays the fife he carried through the war.)]

MADAMA LAFAYETTE BEATTY

On Saturday the 15th of April 1851 Madama Lafayette Beatty was given in marriage by her father Andrew Beatty of Saline County to Hiram Matthew Burnham, possibly at the Jones Chapel in whose cemetery she now lies buried. Hiram was 29 years old. She was 17.

The Burnhams (See Fig. A-6) owned and worked a farm 4-5 miles west of Boonville. When Jones Chapel Methodist Church was organized, the Burnhams donated the land for the chapel and adjacent cemetery.

Hiram and Madama had five children, the first of whom was my grandmother, Julia Ann.Their children were: Julia Ann 1854, Andrew J. 1855, Josephine 1857, Allen 1859 and Sarah Francis 1862.

Madama was 20 when Julia was born. She was 28 years

Fig. A-7. Pickaxe and Pan. This is how the '49ers' expected to get rich. Great-great-uncle Nelson Burnham knew better.

old when Sarah Francis, her fifth and last child, was born. So, by age 28 she had borne three daughters and two sons—roughly her quota for population replacement in those days.

In the 1850s infant mortality rates required 4-5 births to yield 2 survivors who would live to adulthood. As one old pioneer said, "You're lucky to get your seed back!"

JONES CHAPEL

Madama is buried in the small 'Jones Chapel' cemetery. This cemetery is about 3-4 miles north of I-70 just off the 'Santa Fe Trail' near Kuecklehan's Station and was contiguous to the Burnham farm.

Madama died of tuberculosis at age 48. Tuberculosis was a leading cause of death in the 19th century. Aunt Kate (Madama's grand-daughter, my mother's older sister) died of 'Galloping Consumption' in 1916.

Sadly, Madama was joined by her little granddaughter Bessie Lee Kendrick, Julia's third child, who died 8th of October 1885 just a month shy of her ninth birthday. No other member of the family seems to have been buried there and the cemetery was virtually abandoned for years after the chapel burned.

CALIFORNIA GOLD RUSH

After his aborted Mexican War adventure, Hiram returned to the family farm on the Santa Fe Trail near Boonville. He was not married when his half brother Nelson came out from New York in 1850 with the California gold strike on his mind. He wanted Hiram to go to California via the overland route.

Hiram demurred. Nelson "...continued on to California, opened a saloon and brothel. He made a bundle." Nelson knew where the money was and it was not in digging!

Brother Bob finally located this cemetery after we had searched for it for years. He drops by occasionally and puts flowers on Madama's grave after a century of our neglect.

One of the Vollrath boys of Fayette who has a grandfather buried there reclaimed it from its dilapidation in recent years and now it is pleasantly restored.

Fig. A-8 After a long search, Bob finally located the Jones Chapel Cemetery in 1995. The arrow indicates Madama's tombstone.

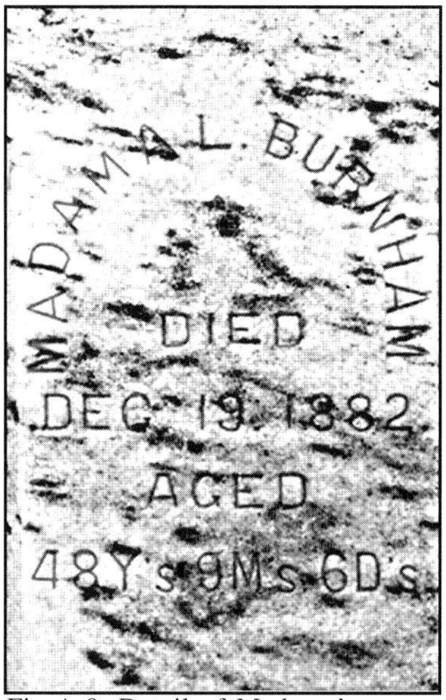

Fig A-9. Detail of Madama's gravestone inscription.

THE MARY MORGAN (BURNHAM) BABBITT LEGEND

I call the story a "legend" because it is an oral history that has been passed down over the generations (my information is from a copy of notes handwritten by Annabelle (Quint) Stretz, a great grandaughter of Mary Morgan Burnham and William Babbitt). As Annabelle concludes her notes: "This was told to me—Annabelle Quint by my grandmother Mrs. John Phillip Quint, many years ago daughter of Harry Quint." [Author's note. Some minor details may be in error. The main facts are true].

In 1843 Mary Morgan Burnham, Hiram's younger sister eloped to Missouri with William Babbitt, Marjorie (Babbitt) Brown's Great Grandfather, Babbitt was a young stable lad at the upstate New York Burnham farm. He met and fell in love with Mary Morgan. The Burnhams disapproved. The couple eloped to marry in Ohio then continue on to Missouri. Mary Morgan died at the birth of their ninth child—also named Mary Morgan—on December 31, 1861.

I tell the story in two letters as though written by Madama Lafayette (Beatty) Burnham, to Hiram her husband during days of crisis for the Babbitt and Burnham families as well as the entire nation. Hiriam had travelled to New York in early December 1861 to be with his dying father.

Boonville, Missouri
Sunday, December 15th, 1861

Dear Hiriam,

William has moved Mary Morgan to his folks' place and has asked me to sit with her when I can. She is in her 9th month now as you know and is not feeling very well. Even though I am in my eighth month, I can still read to her and keep her company. Mary and I no longer attend church services (we are both big as a house), so I sit with her while both families go to hear Rev. Pugh at the Pilot Grove church. Now please don't chide me. I know we are

charter members at Jones Chapel. You deeded the land and that is where our loyalties belong, but Rev. Pugh is an outstanding preacher and we meet the Babbitts there.

I must tell you that I am concerned about Mary's health. She has borne 8 children and knows full well how she should be feeling at each stage of her pregnancy and I think she senses something wrong. She is now 36 years old and not the strong young girl she was when she ran off with William. She never complains but I often see her in a pensive mood. Please don't mention it to her. William's folks are caring for her and the children just fine.

I must say that I am thankful to the Good Lord that the Burnhams, well at least you, had your reconciliation with Mary Morgan. In my estimate, it was long, long overdue. Twenty years of bad feelings over Mary Morgan's elopement with William is just silly. But, as they say, "The mills of the gods grind slow but exceeding fine."

When Nelson was here in '51 for our wedding, I noticed that he was greatly taken by Mary Morgan's little Harriet. I'm sure you saw it too. He spoke then of being Godfather to all his little sister's children. He still isn't married and, here, you and I have four children and a fifth due in February. How time flies.

Hiriam, I know there has been a lot of bad feelings between Mary and your parents. I didn't realize how much until she told me, "After William and I were married, my father forbade me to come home even for a visit."

She told me with tears in her eyes how you had sat all night with her during the passage from England in '26. I'm surprised you never told me this story. She said two weeks out of Bristol, the Lord Ligonier hit a furious storm with winds and 30 ft waves. She said she was so frightened she couldn't sleep and you sat with her all night and held her hand. And you were only 4! She was 2, but she told me that, since then, you had always seen yourself as your little sister's protector. I suppose this is the reason you sided with your father and "sent Mary Morgan to Coventry" when she eloped.

I know you were hurt when she let but try to understand their feelings. They're still family. I give thanks that Nelson defied your father and embraced William, Mary Morgan and their little ones when he was here. By the way, we got a letter from him. He is back in California and has a big orchard in the southern part of the state. The letter was mailed last summer.

I pray that you will be safe in your journey and not get involved in all this terrible strife. Please don't let your political opinions get you into trouble. William told me he had heard that you were talking with some gentlemen after church a few months back and stated your views rather forcefully. He reminded me that some of the southern sympathizers were bushwhackers and guerrillas. I told him that I had spoken to you on the matter and how you went to our bedroom and came out with that big pistol. I told him what you said, "If they come around here, this 6-shot Colt .44 Navy will even up the odds a little and I won't hesitate to use it."

Things are still unsettled around here. I often wake up at night and see strange, dark riders passing on the Santa Fe trail. I don't know if you knew this but I just hear that last summer, old Joe Sifers was murdered. Did you know him? He lived about two miles north of Pilot Grove and was a Union man. In the dark of the night a bunch of guerrillas surrounded his house and demanded he surrender his guns. He went out to see who it was. Too late, he realized it was no prank. He ran for the cornfield but they shot him dead and left him laying. Missouri is becoming a dark and bloody ground just like they say about Kansas.

I just pray every night that the outrages and lawlessness are brought under control. Gen'l Lyon began creating some "home guard" or "militia" groups to help police the area and your old Boonville friend Tom Brownfield is now a Captain of Militia. William is a member[2]. Maybe they can bring a halt to all the bushwhacking and robberies. No one feels safe any more.

I'm going to write to Nelson. I want to tell him about you getting trapped by the battle in Boonville. See if I have this right. On June 16th, you took a

[2] 52d Regiment of "Enrolled Missouri Militia". William was called to Federal Service in August of 1862 but his physical exam turned up his diabetes and he was rejected.

team to Boonville to get a roll of hog fencing. Col. Marmaduke had occupied the town and was trying to collect supplies for his 1500 rebels. Gen'l Lyons attacked from the east. Although Marmaduke had 3 times the men, they were untrained while Lyon's troops were regulars. In the meantime, you couldn't get home and stayed the night with the Tuttles.

Mary Morgan's children are all in fine fettle although Lydia and Agnes have had bouts with the grippe. I believe it is the unusual weather. The Babbitt's crops have been very good though it took a long time to get the corn in. The Vollrath boys usually help but they have gone off to the war.

I bring our children over to visit their cousins occasionally. Julie and Andy are ready and eager for school now but things are so disturbed, I don't know what to do. There are two subscriptions schools in Boonville. The cost is not so much but getting them the 5 miles to town would present a problem. I considered taking them to Babbitts and helping Mary Morgan pay for a tutor for the lot of them. What do you think?

Little Josie and Allen are still underfoot in the kitchen. They want so badly to help especially since their father is gone.

We wish you a Merry Christmas and we pray that your father is getting better and that the Good Lord will soon see you safely home.

Your loving wife,

Madama

PS. I have attached a clipping from the St. Louis paper on Gen'l Lyons death. It's old news from last August but this is the full account. I was surprised to find that Gen'l Lyon was only a captain when the war started.

General Lyon Killed

Springfield, Aug 13th 1861 Brig General Nathaniel Lyon was killed in a clash with Rebel forces under Genl Sterling Price at Wilson Creek near here last Friday. General Lyon was born in 1818 in Conn. He was a USMA graduate (1841) (11/52); Inf. He served in the Seminole War, on frontier duty, in the Mexican War (1 brevet, 1 wound), in Indian fighting, and in Kansas. The latter experience shaped the political views of the fiery little redhead, and he became a prolific writer, advocating Lincoln and the Republican party. Serving as a captain of the 2d US Inf. at the St. Louis arsenal in earlier this year, he and F. P. BLAIR, Jr. collaborated to safeguard Union property and interests from the siz able disloyal element in the state. Together they worked out and executed the strategy that saved the weapons in the arsenal, and captured the rebel force that was assembling at nearby CAMP JACKSON under Gen. D. M. Frost. Together they also succeeded in eliminating Lyon's pro-Southern superior, Gen. W. S. Harney, from the scene. With Blair's influence, Lyon was appointed Brig.Genl. of Mo. Vol. on 12 May '61, and he became Brig.Genl. USV five days later. He then undertook military operations in southwest Mo. that ended with his death at WILSON'S CREEK, 10 Aug.

[Author's note: In 1865, Gen. Wm. T. Sherman said, "Missouri suffered four years of needless torment and bloodshed because a courageous man died too soon. I refer to Genl Nathaniel Lyon."]

Boonville, Missouri
Friday, January 3d, 1862

Dear Hiram,

All here have agreed that I should write you with the terrible news. Mary Morgan was taken from us last Tuesday the 31st of December. She died quietly in her sleep sometime before the New Year. William made arrangements with Rev. Pugh for her funeral and she was buried yesterday at Sunset Hill in the Babbitt burial ground.

I don't know how to tell you of Mary Morgan's last hours. I have studied on it and prayed with the good Reverend Pugh who has been a rock in these dreadful times. The Reverend said, "You must give Hiriam a full account. He deserves plain talk."

At the time that I wrote you before Christmas, we were already concerned about Mary Morgan. I didn't dwell on it too much as I thought that with your own father in his last days, you could not come home and it would just make your life miserable to no purpose.

Mary began having her pains early Monday the 30th and Ira sent old Jim to fetch Mrs. Tavenner for the birthing. William brought us over and all the children went with him to town while Ira, Nancy and I stayed with Mary Morgan. She had been made comfortable in the main upstairs bedroom. Upon her arrival, Mrs. Tavenner went up to see her. Almost immediately, she came back downstairs and said, "I'm afraid there's going to be a problem and you'd better get Doctor Barnes over here as soon as possible. Young Doctor Hannibel Barnes recently finished Medical School in St. Louis and had set up his practice in Pilot Grove. Mrs. Tavenner said he was particularly good with difficult deliveries. Ira went with old Jim and returned with the doctor within the hour.

The young doctor went up the stairs two at a time. His examination didn't take long. "It's a "breach" and I'm going to need help!" I was frustratingly useless of course—I was almost as big as Mary. The doctor told me not to get involved for fear of my miscarrying. So Ira sent for black Thisby to help Nancy with the hot water and sheets. Thisby has a three month old baby herself which she left in charge of her older children. In looking back on Ira's decision, I see that he was already guarding against the worst.

The doctor and his helpers struggled for hours and poor Mary's cries were heart rending. Ira sent Jim to intercept William and the children on their way home from town so as to spare them. William took them to our home to await the outcome.

Dr. Barnes came down in late afternoon and I poured him a cup of tea. Although it was a cold and wintry day, he was sweating heavily. We gathered closely around him for a word. He just shook his head. "I'm afraid I'll have to make some incisions so I'll need lots of lint. There's going to be bleeding."

The weak winter sun had set and the dark shadows had already gathered when, finally, just after midnight, we heard the strong cry of a newborn. I said a silent prayer of thanksgiving. We tiptoed up to the birthing room and peeped in. The Doctor waved us in. "We've got a lot of bleeding and will need another roll of lint. Also, Mary's very weak. Some beef tea would be quite beneficial. Someone should stay with her tonight and make sure she doesn't get chilled. Give her a lot of fluids. I'm afraid the outcome is in the hands of the Lord. You should make other arrangements for nursing the baby."

All this was very frightening. But, her baby was strong, healthy and letting everyone know she was hungry. She's a lovely little girl with her mother's dark hair and the Babbitt's pixie features. You'll love her. She was taken down to Thisby who would move up to the big house to nurse her until Mary was stronger. Old Jim took me home to get a book to read to Mary. I brought the children home and we had supper.

I went up to Mary's room where Mrs. Tavenner was cleaning and straightening up. I made Mary as comfortable as possible with a featherbed to ward off the cold winter air. She tried to speak to me but was so weak I could not understand her. As she drifted back to sleep, I settled down in Ira's rocking chair as the hall clock struck nine. Later, she groaned softly and, remembering how you held her hand on that fearful ocean crossing, I took her hand. I gently squeezed it to let her know I was with her. She weakly squeezed mine.

The day had been stressful in the extreme and I must have dozed though I did not intend to. I awoke still holding her hand. It was cold and I drew the blanket over it while I gave her a reassuring squeeze. There was no response. As the hall clock mournfully struck midnight, an icy hand gripped my heart and I knew! Our hopes, shared over the past days, were fantasy and the cold dread we never mentioned was reality. Sometime during the darkness before midnight, her spirit had slipped away. Now she was with God.

But, my heart rejected what my mind knew full well. I thought, it was just that I was dreadfully tired and was not thinking aright. I would soon awakend to find it was all a terrible nightmare. I sat there praying.

Finally the feeble predawn light filtered through the curtains and I could see her wan, still face on the pillow, drained and with the light of the tallow candle guttering on her bedside table.

As I listened for life to stir below stairs, I walked to the window to look out on the desolate, wintry countryside and compose myself. The light was gathering now and I could make out the cold bare fields with just enough snow to make them ugly. The leafless trees behind the house held up their unsightly black branches to heaven.

Hiriam, I am only 27 years old and, God forbid, I may see worse times in my life—but that moment was the worst! I thought my heart would burst. "Just when the family rift was healing! Just when eight children need their mother so badly! Just when all the world seems to be going mad and we need all our strength and love!"

Fig. A-10. Mary Morgan "Jr" — Mary Morgan (Babbitt) Painter at 39 years. Photo taken in 1900. It appeared in the Boonville Daily News a few years ago.

The instant I heard movement below, I hurried down to find Ira poking up a fire in the cooking stove. As I poured out my heart, he looked like he had suddenly shouldered a heavy burden. He breathed a painful sigh and tried to comfort me. "There, there Madama—it's God's will." To him, it was not unexpected. I remembered how he had, at recent evening meals, returned thanks for the Blessings of Providence, and asked for Divine protection for Mary and all our loved ones but always ended, "...but, Thy will be done..." He had, all along, understood the ordeal that Mary Morgan was facing.

Ira said, "Jim will collect your children for breakfast."

"But," I objected, gesturing upstairs, "What about Mary Morgan?"

"She and her angels will wait. We'll compose ourselves to say goodbye properly."

We finished a silent breakfast. No one spoke and the older children had already guessed that something was terribly amiss. After a piece of bread and tea, William, his mother, his father and I led the children upstairs. I straightened the bed and sat numb with grief as, one by one, William escorted the children to the bed and they gently kissed their mother a final goodbye. Austin, Harriett, Lydia Ann and Agnes knew full well they were bidding their mother a final adieu. Will and Homer thought they were kissing her goodnight. We then descended and sent for Rev. Pugh.

In deepest sorrow, your loving wife—

Madama

Fig. A-11. Mary Morgan (Burnham) Babbitt tombstone, Sunset Hill Cemetery, Boonville.

THE OLD HOMEPLACE

At 110 East Fourth Street in Pilot Grove, Missouri stands an old wooden frame house (See Figs. A-12 thru A-14) which was last rehabbed with gray, faux stone siding in the 1970s. It has an old, faded and rusty green metal roof and is over one hundred years old.

The house is not only the birthplace of my mother, sister, brother and myself—its old walls hold memories of a century of other relatives—decades of laughter and lament.

The house dates from 1875, two years after the founding of Pilot Grove. In 1873 the Katy's John Scullins and his roughneck Irish track-laying gang were pushing rail east from Sedalia. The 'rail head' in that year, reached what Col. Stevens, Katy's General Manager, had laid out on Samuel Roe's land as the town of Pilot Grove.

Hiram Burnham, my maternal great-grandfather, bought a lot that year and built the house as a retirement home. He was then 53 years old and still years from quitting his farm just off the old Santa Fe Trail west of Boonville. But, he felt he should take advantage of the new development. Thus he and his wife Madama became founding citizens of Pilot Grove although they never lived there. Tuberculosis claimed Madama in 1882 (she was 48) and Hiram went to live with a son in Rogers, Arkansas where he passed away in 1895.

Hiram and Madama's first-born, Grandma Julia (Burnham) Kendrick and Grandpa Kendrick moved in when Grandma inherited the house. Aunt Kate was born there in 1893 as was my mother, Myrl Nadine Kendrick (1897).

Mom married Richard "Dick" Salmon in 1914 and when her mother had a stroke, she and Dad moved in to help care for her. Grandma Kendrick died in 1918— taken, it was said—by the great influenza pandemic of that year. After her death, Grandpa went to live with an older daughter in Rosedale, (now a part of Kansas City, Kansas) where he died in 1920.

Upon Grandpa's death, Mom and Dad bought the house from the other inheritors and lived there most of their lives. After our 1933 return from a short tour in Clifton City, Mom never lived anywhere else until she went to the Katy Manor nursing home on August 21st 1992 at age 95.

Fig. A-12. The "Ole Home Place" in summer 1890. L-R: John Maddox, Aunt Olive (Kendrick) Maddox 20, Aunt Allie Kendrick 10, Grandma Julia (Burnham) Kendrick 35, Aunt Pearl Kendrick 7, Great Aunt Josie Burnham 33, Aunt Clara Kendrick 5 and Grandpa Henry Kendrick 46.

Fig. A-13 .This was the"Ole Home Place" in 1900. Left to right: Grandpa John Henry Kendrick 56, Uncle Loyle Edwin Kendrick 11, Aunt Katherine (standing at top) 6, Grandma Julia Ann Kendrick 45, Mom (Myrl Nadine Kendrick) 3, Cousin Walter Veal 3, Aunt Allie (Kendrick) Veal 20, Aunt Mary (Kendrick) Berry 27.

Fig. A-14. The "Ole Home Place", Fourth Street, Pilot Grove - Spring of 1947, My new (1947) blue Harley Davidson '45' is in foreground.

UM "KEMPER NEWS"
·F JANUARY 31, 1916

14

y in

ıoma
ebru-
ıking
ersity
) and
n had
cadets
·n, so
is as-
l be

ıyed
Ken-
yan
ıtes
This
the

Captain A. D. Burnham, who e
pects to announce plans soon for a
other play. Captain Burnham h
been one of the English teachers he
for four years and each year presen
a play of much merit. He has al
taken an active interest in trainii

6

Fig. A-15. My Great-Uncle Captain Allen Burnham. He taught English and Drama at Kemper Military Academy Boonville, MO (See sketch below.) from 1912 to 1916.

Fig. A-16. Grandpa John Henry Kendrick at age 55 in 1890. The old veteran of Chickamauga is getting grey.

Fig. A-17. Kemper Military Academy Boonville, MO. "Winky" (Chestnutt) Friedrich's artistic sketch was selected by the United Missouri Bank for their 1998 calendar. (By permission - Florence Friedrich and Friends of Historical Boonville.)

"...trampling out the vintage where the grapes of wrath are stored." Julia Ward Howe - "Battle Hymn of the Republic."

JOHN HENRY KENDRICK

GRANDPA JOHN HENRY KENDRICK WAS BORN in Schuyler County, Illinois December 1, 1844. Schuyler County is in northwestern Illinois one county away from the Mississippi River. In August of 1861 he went off to Quincy, lied about his age—he was only 16—and joined the 50th Illinois Infantry Regiment volunteers then being organized, as a drummer boy [1].

Fig. B-2. John Henry Kendrick, 1844 - 1920. This tintype taken at the time of his joining Co. F, 50th Illinois Infantry - September 1861.

Fig. B-1. Action April 6-7, 1862 at Shiloh Church north of Corinth, Mississippi. Adapted from a 1995 Civil War commemorative stamp set.

JOURNAL OF THE 50TH ILLINOIS

At my request, the Illinois State Bureau of Archives sent me a day by day journal of Grandpa's regiment spanning the Civil War period. This official history records a clash with the notorious Confederate cavalry leader, Nathan Bedford Forrest[2] on 27th April 1863 at "Town Creek, Alabama"

To augment this official account of the regiment, I include (next page) a panoramic map summarizing the actions of the regiment, a detailed account and map of the action at Allatoona, Georgia in which Gramps was severely wounded and a "Soldier's Letter Home" from his convalescence in Chattanooga.

The tintype (Fig B-2) was probably taken at the time of his enlistment, by a photographer who specialized in recruits. The photographer probably added the scarf for a little martial flare. Actually, only cavalrymen wore scarves.

The 50th Illinois fought at Shiloh (Fig. B-1), Corinth, Chickamauga and Atlanta. In May 1862, after Shiloh, the 50th began the siege of Corinth, Mississippi. Following a decisive battle October 4th 1862, they occupied the town and used it as a base to suppress marauding Rebels in the region.

RE-ENLISTMENT PANIC 1863

Lincoln's Secretary of War, Mr. Staunton began getting very nervous in late 1863. Hundreds of thousands of enlistments would run out in the spring. Since it was evident that the war would be far from finished at that time, a re-enlistment drive was initiated offering a big bonus. (Military conscription—the draft—did not begin until March 1863.) To the utmost relief of the president, and to the surprise of all, most of the veterans re-enlisted. The 50th Illinois reported 75% re-enlistments.

John Henry Kendrick was among them. He 're-enlisted as a veteran' on 31st December 1863 at Lynnville, Tennessee. He got $402 and a 30 day veterans' furlough with transportation back to Quincy. His discharge from his first enlistment states that he was '5 ft 7 in tall, had a light complexion, blue eyes and his occupation when enrolled was —'farmer'.

It is signed by William Hanna, Major, Commanding Officer of the Regiment.

[1] In the 19th century U.S. Army, infantry companies were authorized two 'muscians'; a drummer and a fifer.

[2] Nathan Bedford Forrest, b. July 13, 1821, d. Oct. 29, 1877, was a Civil War Confederate general especially known for his brilliant cavalry tactics. He joined the Confederate Army in 1861 and became commander of a cavalry battalion raised and equipped at his own expense. He won fame for his daring and successful raids and for his repeated victories over opponents that outnumbered him. To his discredit, in the 1870s he was instrumental in coalescing, then leading, several political organizations into the Ku Klux Klan.

ACTIONS AND MOVEMENTS OF THE 50th ILLINOIS INFANTRY 1861 - 1865

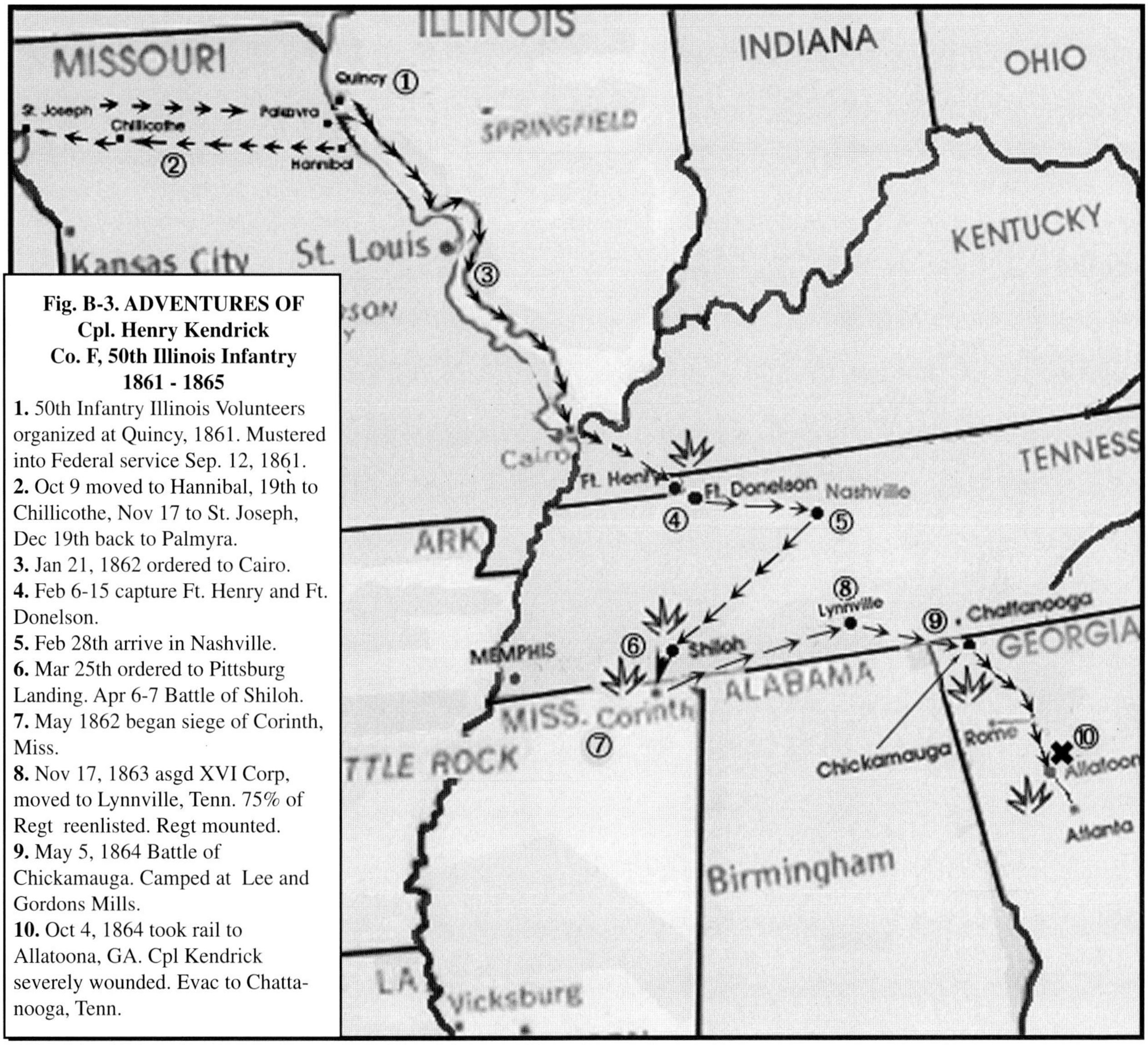

Fig. B-3. ADVENTURES OF Cpl. Henry Kendrick Co. F, 50th Illinois Infantry 1861 - 1865

1. 50th Infantry Illinois Volunteers organized at Quincy, 1861. Mustered into Federal service Sep. 12, 1861.
2. Oct 9 moved to Hannibal, 19th to Chillicothe, Nov 17 to St. Joseph, Dec 19th back to Palmyra.
3. Jan 21, 1862 ordered to Cairo.
4. Feb 6-15 capture Ft. Henry and Ft. Donelson.
5. Feb 28th arrive in Nashville.
6. Mar 25th ordered to Pittsburg Landing. Apr 6-7 Battle of Shiloh.
7. May 1862 began siege of Corinth, Miss.
8. Nov 17, 1863 asgd XVI Corp, moved to Lynnville, Tenn. 75% of Regt reenlisted. Regt mounted.
9. May 5, 1864 Battle of Chickamauga. Camped at Lee and Gordons Mills.
10. Oct 4, 1864 took rail to Allatoona, GA. Cpl Kendrick severely wounded. Evac to Chattanooga, Tenn.

SHILOH

Skimming lightly, then wheeling away
Henry watched the swallows fly low
Over the field on the cloudy spring day
Over the bloody field of Shiloh —

Over the field where the April rain
Through the quiet of the night
Had wet parched lips stretched in pain
That followed the Sunday fight
Around the church of Shiloh —

The Minié balls slashed like a heavy hail
Around that little church in the wood
A little drummer boy lived to tell the tale
Minié ball, bayonet and grape withstood
But all is now hushed at Shiloh.

Capt. Fee's company had held their ground
But it was no time for cheers just now.
There were missing comrades to be found
Kendrick's boys must do it somehow.
Around the church of Shiloh —

Bury those who would not again rise.
Dying comrades and foemen mingled there
The agony of that day would memorialize
Fame or country least their care.
Thus endeth that day at Shiloh.

In memory of Cpl. John Henry Kendrick, Co. F, 50th Illinois Volunteers. At Shiloh he was a drummer boy whose battle duty was litter bearer for the wounded and recovering and burying the dead. After Shiloh he was a corporal and had traded his drum for a .55 Cal. Sharps musket.

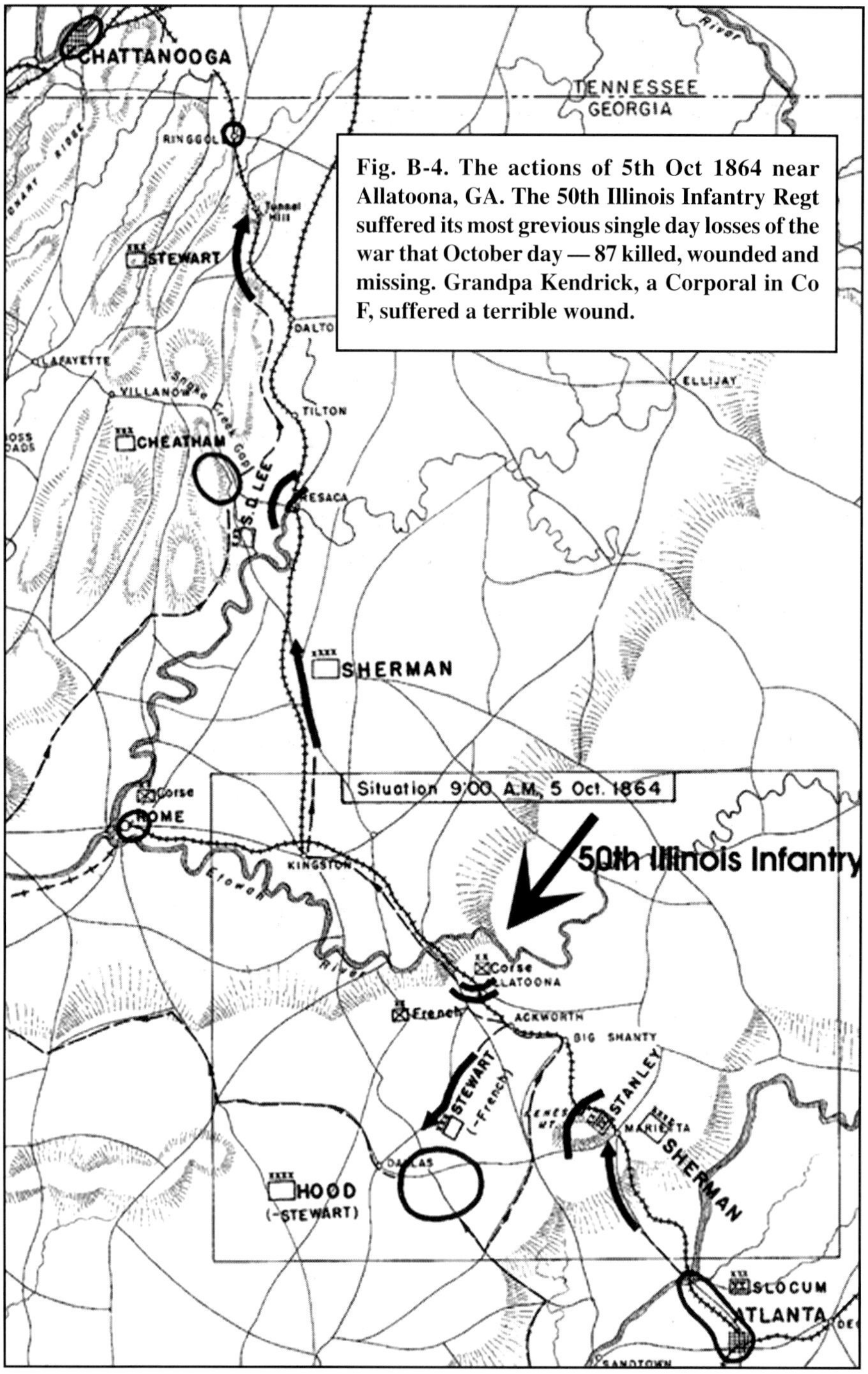

Fig. B-4. The actions of 5th Oct 1864 near Allatoona, GA. The 50th Illinois Infantry Regt suffered its most grevious single day losses of the war that October day — 87 killed, wounded and missing. Grandpa Kendrick, a Corporal in Co F, suffered a terrible wound.

ALLATOONA

Allatoona, Georgia—see map above—was a small village in 1864. It is even smaller today. But it was a giant Federal supply dump in 1864 and figured in the engagements called collectively the Battle of Atlanta. Allatoona was also where the war ended for Grandpa Kendrick.

The following is excerpted from "West Point Atlas of American Wars" Volume I, Map 149.

Hood, late on 3 October 1864, had split his forces, sending Stewart to the railroad and the rest of his command to Dallas (inset sketch), Stewart laid waste to the railroad between Big Shanty and Ackworth, while French moved on Allatoona. On the morning of the 5th, Stewart rejoined Hood near Dallas, while French attacked Corse. By 8 am, Corse was surrounded, but refused French's demand for his surrender. At 9 am, the attack began; Sherman watched anxiously from Kenesaw Mountain. Corse made a gallant defense and stopped the repeated Confederate charges.

At 4 pm the Confederates gave up and marched away to rejoin Hood, having seen Union reinforcements hurrying forward. [The 50th Illinois Infantry Regt., now a part of Corse's Division, suffered it's most grievous casualties of the war—87 killed, wounded and missing. Grandpa Kendrick, a Corporal in Company F, was one of those. Struck in the right breast by a Minié ball, he miraculously survived and was evacuated—along with hundreds more—via rail to a major evacuation hospital in Chattanooga for treatment and recuperation.]

The following is excerpted from "The Civil War Dictionary" Mark M. Boatner III, LTC United States Army, Pages 8-9.

ALLATOONA, Ga., 5 Oct. 1864.

This important Federal supply depot, containing a million rations of bread for Sherman's army in Atlanta, was successfully defended against French's division. Although there was severe fighting, the action is best known for a number of dramatic incidents associated with it. The garrison was composed of 860 men under the command of Lt. Col. John F. Tourtelotte, 4th Minn. When it looked as if the place might be raided, Sherman sent a signal to Corse (4, XIV) in Rome to reinforce Allatoona. French made a night march from Ackworth and made contact with Federal pickets around the town at 3 A.M. He did not know that two hours previously Corse had arrived with Rowett's (3d) brigade.

By 8:30 A.M. the Confederates had cut the main routes by which the place could be reinforced. There followed an interchange of notes in which French called on the Federals to surrender "to avoid a needless effusion of blood," and Corse answered "we are prepared for the 'needless effusion of blood' whenever it is agreeable to you." (See B.&L., IV, 323.)

Sherman, meanwhile, had reached Kenesaw Mountain and could see that Allatoona (13 miles northwest) was surrounded. He could also see the campfires of Hood's main body to the west near Dallas.

Since the telegraph wires north of Marietta had been cut, and his order to Corse in Rome had been sent by signal flag "over the heads of the enemy," Sherman did not know whether Corse had actually reinforced Allatoona. Messages had been signaled the afternoon of the 4th by Vandever on Kenesaw Mountain to the "Commanding Officer, Allatoona." At 2 P.M. this message was sent: "Sherman is coming. Hold out. At 6:30 P.M. this additional one went out:"General Sherman says hold fast. We are coming." (OR. Series 1, Vol. XXXIX, Part 111, p. 78.) Additional messages were sent the morning of the 5th, but there had been no answer. Finally, while Sherman was with him, the signal officer "caught a faint glimpse of the telltale flag through an embrasure, and, after much time he made out these letters: "C," "R," "S," "E," "H," "E," "R," and translated this message, "Corse is here." (Sherman's *Memoirs, 11,* 147.) This interchange of messages was "freely translated by current journalism into: 'Hold the fort; I am coming.' The episode inspired the revival hymn *Hold the Fort* —and so the pages of history were embellished with another indelible myth." (Horn, *The Army of Tennessee,* 377.)

Meanwhile, there had been heavy fighting. Sears' brigade and W. H. Young's Texans made repeated attacks against the key ridge. For two and a half hours the 7th and 93d Ill. and the 39th Iowa, under the command of Col. R. Rowett, fought off attacks from three sides. When they were finally driven back at about 11 A.M., Redfield's detachment of the 39th Iowa delayed the enemy long enough for the main body to reach and secure the main fort on the northwest shoulder of Allatoona Pass. Redfield fell dead of four wounds, and Rowett was wounded; but this delaying action proved decisive. Although there was no Federal infantry within supporting distance until the morning of 6 Oct. (Sherman's official report notwithstanding; see Horn, 377), French broke off the engagement early in the afternoon and withdrew.

Corse had been creased by a Minié bullet at about 1 P.M. and was unconscious for over 30 minutes. The next day at 2 P.M. he signaled Sherman's aide this much-publicized message: "I am short a cheek-bone and an ear, but am able to whip all h-l yet."

The Federals lost 707 out of 1,944 present for duty. French reported a loss of 799 out of "a little over 2,000" engaged in the assaulting force. W. H. Young was wounded and captured.

A SOLDIER'S LETTER HOME

In 1901 the Illinois Adjutant General made a report on the state's Civil War volunteers. This report included Grandpa's regiment. The narrative is terse with archaic punctuation thus difficult to follow. This reflects its origins—notes written in the field under battle conditions.

With this in mind I have attempted to put the flow of historical events into perspective. To make this less like a history lesson, I have used the form of a hypothetical letter from Grandpa Kendrick in a hospital bed in Chattanooga to his mother.

Though the trivial details are imaginary, the events are historically accurate. The everyday life of Cpl. Henry Kendrick as a typical Union soldier in the Civil War and his sense of the times is based on historical fact.

Chattanooga, Tennessee
December 5th 1864

Dear Mom,

I hope you are not mad at me for not writing the past few weeks. I've been in the hospital here in Chattanooga for about two months now. I still don't feel good enough to be writing no letter but I was afraid one of the other boys from Schuyler County would come by and tell you what happened to me. I want to tell you first so's you won't worry too much. what happened is—I got myself shot in early October.

It was serious enough that they don't think I'll be going back to my regiment, leastwise anytime soon. But don't worry. I'm patched up pretty good and I may get to come home when I heal up better and get my strength back.

I don't remember much afterwards but at the time, it felt like a mule kicked me right in the chest. That was Tuesday morning October 5th at Allatoona, Georgia. I'm just now beginning to get my head straight on exactly what happened. Some other boys from the 50th are in here and they filled me in:

On Monday afternoon, October 4th our Colonel Hanna comes charging back from the Second Division HQs (General Corse's Division) in an all fired hurry.

There were a lot of officers and serjeants running around shouting orders. Things were very confused around there for a while. Captain Fee comes down and tells us to draw 2 days cooked rations and 200 rounds of ammunition (beans and bullets, we call it). We got our horses down to the rail yard there in Rome for loading. I learned from some of the other Schuyler boys that Hood had sent Stewart's Corps against the rail-road south of Big Shanty. They tore up about 5 miles of track and was coming up the track right at us.

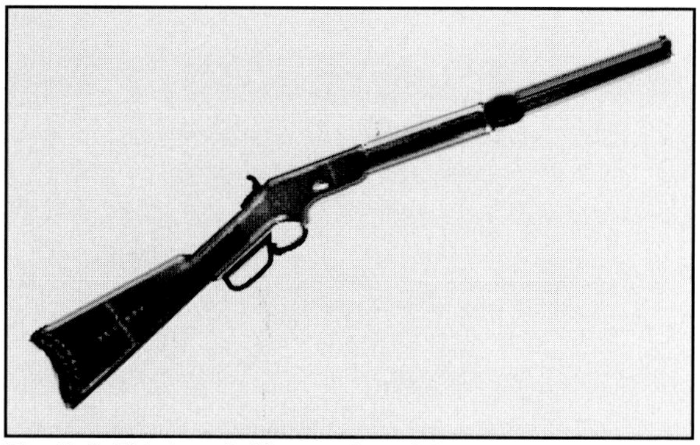

Fig. B-5. This is a civilian version of the Henry, 15 shot, .44 cal, rimfire, repeating rifle issued to Dragoons in 1864.

You've already read in the papers that old Sherman ran the Rebs out of Atlanta and burned the town down in the doing. Well, Hood and his army was whupped good in Atlanta but I guess they wasn't ready to quit. In early October they began making these raids on our supply lines. They knew that every bullet, bean and biscuit that Sherman's boys in Atlanta used was coming down the track from Chattanooga.

Anyway, we finally got everything loaded up about midnight and rode the train down to Allatoona. It ain't too far but they was being real careful and went so slow it was near daylight when we got there. Right off we heard that the Rebs was coming up the track, we got our horses off the train in a hurry.

Now, I never told you about them horses. About this time last year General Dodge ordered the 50th to be mounted. We got our horses but, we never was real cavalry. We didn't get none of them long sabers like the cavalry has. Some of my boys was kinda hoping we would, they look real soldierly. For myself, I'm glad we don't have to pack them things around.

Actually, we was a kind of "mounted infantry[3]". We just rode them horses to the battlefield then dismounted to fight afoot. The horses was a lot of work feeding and all, but I must say we were all very glad we didn't have to hike so much and, more important than that we got issued the new Henry repeating rifle[4]. It holds 15 cartridges that are already made up in brass jackets. Shoots as fast as you can lever the cartridges in. Beats that old 'Brown Betty' musket hands down. It don't have no bayonet though, so we have to use something else for tent stakes.

[3] Early 19th century armies called these units "Dragoons".

[4] Benjamin Tyler Henry, plant superintendent of Oliver Winchester's New Haven Arms Co., perfected this .44 short, rim-fire, 15 shot, repeating rifle in 1860. The U.S. Army wanted no part of it, "...there are already 100 different kinds of ammunition to worry about." The clerks won until 1863 when the men of the 6th Illinois Cavalry began buying their own. Finally the rifle was issued to cavalry and dragoon units such as Grandpa's. Winchester manufactured about 10,000 for the Union Army. It was the model for and forerunner of the famous Winchester Model 76 "the gun that won the West."

At first light in Allatoona we could hear skirmishers in our front and by 10 o'clock them Rebs came swarming at us like stampeding cattle. I never seen so many at one time since Shiloh. Captain Fee told us we was to reinforce the line and to hurry on up there. Actually, there really wasn't no line, but we went galloping forward anyway. We was about 100 yards away from them and getting ready to dismount when I got shot. It felt like a mule kicked me in my chest and knocked me clean off my horse. I landed kinda on my head and don't remember much after that. They tell me that as soon as Hood's boys was drove off (late afternoon) some of my boys picked me up and carried me back to a field dressing station at Allatoona.

Now that I know I'm going to be OK, I can tell you that there was a long time there that I thought I was a goner. That ball passed through my chest, broke some ribs, went through the top of my right lung and came out just under my shoulder blade. I reckon it was two things that saved me – since the ball passed all the way through, the surgeon didn't have to probe for it with his filthy fingers (I saw one do that at Shiloh and it near made me sick. I had carried this boy back to the dressing station and helped hold the poor fellow down on the table. The doctor stuck his fingers right into the hole in this boy's belly. He died and I think it was the surgeon probing for the ball that killed him.)

The other thing that saved me was the railroad. The trains moved us wounded boys right straight up the track to Chattanooga that very night. I wasn't conscious for much of this trip but I do fancy that it was a much easier ride than the wagon beds we used at Shiloh to get the wounded down to the boats at Pittsburg Landing.

I don't like telling you all this knowing how upset you have been at this whole war, but I think it is all over for me. I know you and Pa worried a lot. By the way, tell him that he was right, this war ain't neart the fun that I thought it was going to be back when I ran off to Quincy to enlist in '61.

You can write to me here in Chattanooga. When I get to feeling better, they'll probably send me home but they will forward my letters. I reckon I'm going to need a few more weeks to get my right arm working okay. I guess you can tell that by my terrible handwriting.

I didn't tell you yet why we was in Rome, Georgia in the first place. It was like this—after Sherman came down the railroad track from Chattanooga—that was early last May after all the fighting around Chickamauga and Missionary Ridge—all his supplies were shipped down that railroad. It was dangerous for him. The long railroad supply line could be cut any time by Hood's army. So thousands of troops had to guard the track. Our Regt was assigned to Corse's Division in Rome to patrol against Hood.

As I told you a couple of months ago, the summers down there in Georgia are pretty awful, hot and sticky. But the billets and the rations in Rome were pretty good. Me and my squad lived in an old livery stable bedding down on hay and out of the weather.

The food was good, and there was lots of it. Mostly, I reckon, that's because of the railroad. Lots of the boys still complain about the salt pork and hardtack but I'll tell you this—compared with the Secesh boys, we got it pretty good. Why, when we fought off a Reb attack on the railroad at Resaca I saw one of the dead Rebels. He looked younger than me, couldn't have been more than 15 years old. Some of the boys began going through his pockets, looking for souvenirs they said. I don't think that's right and I told them so but, they didn't pay me no mind. They only found an old pocketknife with a busted blade but the sad thing was—they found about a dozen goober peas[5] in his pocket. I reckon that was that Johnny Reb's daily ration.

Thanks be to the Good Lord, I just heard that Sherman cut loose from his supply lines on the 14th of November and is marching to the sea at Savannah. [He arrived there December 22d. The city, remembering Atlanta, surrendered.] There is this boy from my regiment that just came in here with real bad runnin' off the bowels, "dysentery" the doctors call it. In between trips to the privy he has been telling me what happened after I got shot.

He says Sherman took the larger part of the army and struck off for Savannah. They are just living off the land. They call them "Sherman's bummers" [foragers, authorized to seize materials for the army] and they have left a swath 60 miles wide that looks like its been picked clean by one of them plague of locusts right out of the Bible! They give them Secesh people a piece of paper and take what ever they want. Maybe the government will pay them some day. They even took up the railroad tracks, burnt the ties and after heating up the rails, twisting them into what the boys called "Sherman hairpins". He says it's just like a big combination Halloween night and 4th of July. He's back laying on his bed now and looks awful weak. I hope he makes it OK.

We have lost more boys from sickness than from Johnny Reb's minié balls. There is a lot of the boys in

[Author's note: When I was 6-7 years old we had an old windup Victrola and 5-6 ancient 78 rpm records. Steel needles were 10¢ a box (100 needles) so we often played them until they were blunt then sharpened them with a file.

One of those old records — "Marching Through Georgia" commemorated Sherman's march and may have belonged to Grandpa Kendrick. It was popular north of the Mason-Dixon line into the 1930s. Play it in the south and you'd get dirty looks. Play it in Georgia and you'd get lynched! But, I'm going to take a chance.]

Bring the good old bugle boys
We'll sing another song.
Sing it as we used to sing it
50,000 strong!
While marching through Georgia.

[5] Goober peas - unroasted peanuts.

this hospital that ain't going to make it. There was this boy across the aisle from me. They brought him in last week with gangrene in his leg. I could smell him clear across the room. Last night I heard him say to his friend "Fix me". I didn't know what he meant by that until his friend lays him out and pins his socks together just like laying out a corpse. He knew what he was doing because the next morning he was dead. The orderlies carried him out before daybreak.

When old Colonel Bane organized our Regiment— mostly to get on the good side of the governor—he never got more than three or four hundred boys. That's about average for the volunteer regiments. We never got any replacements, so after Chickamauga the whole regiment was down to less than 200 men and officers. Allatoona got half of them.

Colonel Bane got promoted to commander of the Brigade but resigned last summer and went back to Illinois. I think he was asked to go. He wasn't much of an officer, not half the man that our Lt. Col. Hanna is. Hanna was out there in the thick of it with us at Allatoona and was also wounded though I don't think he was bad hurt.

I hope you are doing well on the farm. I see the price of pigs is up quite a bit. When I was home last January I gave Pa $200 of my bonus money. I felt guilty all along about leaving you and him like I did. Last year when old Abe got so worried about all them enlistments running out in '64 they offered us $402 and a 30 day veteran's furlough. I said to myself then, "Here's how I can make it up to Pa for going off and leaving him." I would have give him more but when we was coming up the Mississippi on the Morning Star we got to talking about sleeping in a real bed, taking a real bath and eating a real home cooked meal so some of us got a hotel room and spent one night in Quincy on the way home. I spent more money than I had really planned on.

Fig. B-6. Shiloh after the battle. Shiloh was Grampa's first real battle. Union losses (killed, wounded and missing) were 13,700. Confederate losses were about 10,700.

Laying here in this hospital gives me time to think–after my close call down there at Allatoona I'd better make my peace with the Lord and with you and pa also. I feel bad about a lot of lies I told down there in Quincy when I enlisted. You see, I was told that you had to be 20 years old to enlist and of course, I wasn't even 17 yet. At the time the sarjeant looked at me kind of queer when I put down my age as 20. But he went on and signed me up and told me to go draw my crooked shoes[6]. It was like a circus down there and I guess he didn't want to disappoint any of the boys.

Well, it turns out that after I perjured myself and signed all them official papers the company commander, Captain Fee, comes in and looks me over. He called the sarjeant in and they talked. Then, he came out and looked me right in the eye, "You ain't really 20 years old are you?"

I couldn't just lie right in his face so I told him I was 16. He looked at the stack of paperwork and says, "Look here, Kendrick, you only have to be 18 years old to enlist. We might have believed you if you'd said that. But...if you're so all-fired eager to join up I tell you what we'll do. Each infantry company is supposed to have two musicians, one drummer and one fifer and we can enlist musicians under 18. Can you play the fife or the drum?"

I don't know exactly what a fife is so I thought I'd better not lay no claim to being able to play one. "I can drum a little", I lied. I figgered I could learn real quick and so I signed up as a 'musician' in company F.

The thing that bothers me is that I got lies all over my official state record – me saying I was 20. I

[6] Crooked shoes - until the time of the Civil War most shoes were made on one last. That is the left and right shoe were identical. The green country recruits thought these shoes were odd and called them "crooked shoes"

Fig. B-7. Drummer boy Henry 1862.

remember my teacher reciting this poem from that feller Scott[7]: "Oh, what tangled webs we weave when first we practice to deceive!"

Drummers have fairly easy duty but, I paid for it at Shiloh. You see, the musicians, cooks and such have got to carry the litters after the battle and recover the wounded and the dead. we carried wounded back to the field dressing stations.

At Shiloh I had some horrible experiences that I will not grieve you with. I just couldn't take it no more so I went to Captain Fee and told him, "I will be 18 my next birthday and I don't want to be no drummer boy no more. Just give me one of them Brown Bettys (that's what we called them old Sharps muskets) and let me go on the line."

He surprised me. He took me off that drummer job, and he gave me the two stripes of a Corporal. Best of all I didn't have to help the surgeons hold them poor boys down while they sawed their arms and legs off.

Oh, one other thing, they have started up a new outfit: the "Invalid Corps". They get boys out of the hospitals who are recovered from wounds but are still not fit for full duty and assign them to guard duty and such like. I'd rather come on home but with my luck I'll get throwed into such an outfit. Imagine that. Not yet 20 years old but declared a member of the 'Invalid Corps[8]'.

Your loving son,

Henry

[7] from "Marmion" by Sir Walter Scott

[8] And that is what happened. Cpl. Kendrick was enrolled in the 'Invalid Corps' and assigned duty guarding the railroad at Boonville, Missouri in the spring of 1865. He was discharged there in July 1865 and went to work for Hiram Burnham on his farm 5 miles west of Boonville just off the old Santa Fe Trail.

Fig. B-8. In this sketch, Winslow Homer captures the sense of the meager relief that could be offered Civil War wounded — often, only a drink of water.

RIGHT Fig. B-9. Union Volunteer 1861 - Bettmann Archives

Fig. B-10. General Grant never lost a battle. In 1864 he turned his army over to Sherman and went to Washington to take command of the Army of the Potomac.

Fig. B-11. While Grandpa languished in the hospital in Chattanooga, General Sherman marched, "50,000 strong", from Atlanta to the sea (at Savannah) and cut the Confederacy in two.

Names Index

NOTES—Names are listed last name first then first and middle names. Nicknames are in quotes, for example "Sonny". Maiden names are given in parentheses, for example Brown, Marjorie Ellen "Margie" (Babbitt). Many, but not all, ladies are also listed under their *maiden* names. That is, they appear in the index twice though the references are the same. Here, their *married* names are given in brackets [ ]. Example Burger, Marjorie "Margie" [Schmidt]. I've found that my software has bugs and some of the page numbers are off slightly. Generating Indices and Tables of Contents is monkey work—but it would take a regiment of trained monkeys a year to get this right. The page number puts you close, so I'll leave it at that.

A

B

E

F

G

N

O

P

T

V

W

Y

Z

Photo Index

B

C

Note: Look for photo references under *both* married and maiden names.

D

E

F

G

H

I

J

K

L

Q

R

S

T

ILLUSTRATIONS

BOOK ONE - TALES FROM THE VILLAGE

CHAPTER 1. INTRODUCTION

CHAPTER 2. HIZZONER DA MAYOR AND OTHER TOWN NOTABLES

CHAPTER 3. VILLAGE FOLKS

ILLUSTRATIONS

CHAPTER 4. VILLAGE LIFE

CHAPTER 5. VILLAGE PASTIMES

CHAPTER 6. SCHOOL DAYS

CHAPTER 7. MERCHANT PRINCES

CHAPTER 8. THE KATY YEARS

CHAPTER 9. THE WORLD TURNED UPSIDE DOWN

BOOK TWO —GONE FER A SOJER

CHAPTER 10. RECRUIT

CHAPTER 11. PACIFIC ISLANDS

CHAPTER 12. KANSAS PLAINS

CHAPTER 13. FORT BRAGG

CHAPTER 14. CADETS

CHAPTER 15. OKINAWA

CHAPTER 16. KOREA

CHAPTER 17. GOIN' HOME

CHAPTER 18. CAMP CARSON

CHAPTER 19. EL PASO, CHICAGO AND ENDGAME

APPENDIX A. THE BURNHAMS

APPENDIX B. CPL HENRY KENDRICK